WRATH OF LIONS

The Breaking World

WRATH OF LIONS

The Breaking World

David Dalglish

Robert J. Duperre

Text copyright © 2014 by David Dalglish and Robert J. Duperre
All rights reserved.

Published by 47North, Seattle

www.apub.com

Amazon, the Amazon logo, and 47North are trademarks of Amazon.com, Inc., or its affiliates.

ISBN-13: 9781477817957
ISBN-10: 1477817956

Cover Illustrated by Mark Winters
Map Illustrated by Paula Robbins & The Mapping Specialists

Library of Congress Catalog Number: 2013916731

Printed in the United States of America

To Morgan, Katherine, Connor, Tristen, and Legacy,
because your fathers are weird and you love us anyway.

ASHHUR'S PARADISE

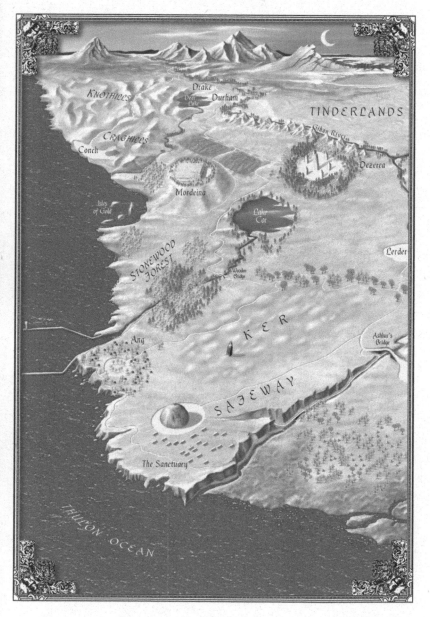

NELDAR

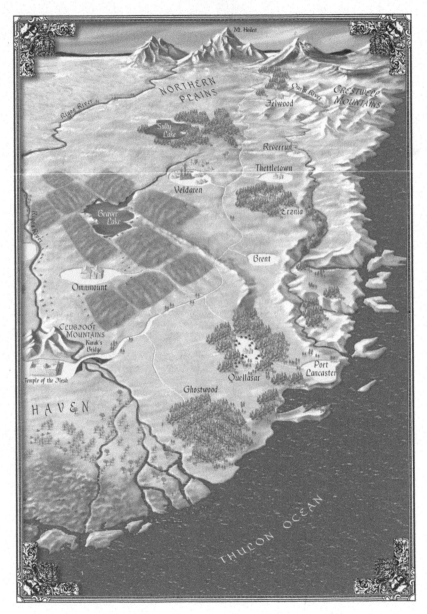

CAST OF CHARACTERS

ASHHUR'S PARADISE

ASHHUR, God of Justice, creator of ASHHUR'S PARADISE

—AHAESARUS, Master Warden of the west

—GERIS FELHORN, a boy 14 years old

—JUDARIUS, a Warden of the west

—CLEGMAN TREADWELL, master steward of ASHHUR

—AZARIAH, a Warden of the west, brother of JUDARIUS

—ROLAND NORSMAN, his confidant, 21 years old

—JUDAH, a Warden of the west

—EZEKAI, a Warden of the west

—GRENDEL, a Warden of the west

MORDEINA

BENJAMIN MARYLL, first king of ASHHUR'S PARADISE, 15 years old

HOUSE DuTAUREAU

ISABEL DuTAUREAU, first child of ASHHUR

—RICHARD, her created husband

—ABIGAIL ESCHETON, their first daughter, 71 years old

—TUROCK ESCHETON, her husband, 39 years old

—their children:

LAURIA DAGEESH, daughter, 24 years old, wife of UULON

CETHLYNN, daughter, 22 years old

DOREK, son, 19 years old

BYRON, son, 18 years old

JARAK, son, 16 years old

PENDET, son, 8 years old

—PATRICK, their only son, 66 years old

—BRIGID FRONIN, their second daughter, 63 years old, wife of BAYEN

—CARA, their third daughter, 62 years old

—KEELA NEFRAM, their fourth daughter, 59 years old,
   wife of DANIEL

—NESSA (deceased), their fifth daughter

—HOWARD PHILIP BAEDAN, master steward of the house

THE KARAK DESERTERS

—PRESTON ENDER, brother of CORTON, leader of the deserters

—EDWARD, his son, 17 years old

—RAGNAR, his son, 16 years old

—BRICK MULLIN, a boy from NELDAR, 19 years old

—TRISTAN VALESON, a boy from NELDAR, 14 years old

—JOFFREY GOLDENROD, a boy from NELDAR, 13 years old

—RYANN MATHESON, a boy from NELDAR, 16 years old

—BIG FLICK, a boy from NELDAR, 17 years old

—LITTLE FLICK, a boy from NELDAR, 15 years old

KER

HOUSE GORGOROS

BESSUS GORGOROS, second child of ASHHUR

—DAMASPIA, his created wife

—BARDIYA, their only son, 87 years old

—KI-NAN RENALD, his friend and confidante

—GORDO HEMPSMAN, a man of KER

—TULANI, his wife

—KEISHA, their daughter, 7 years old

—ONNA LENSBROUGH, a man of KER

NELDAR

KARAK, God of Order, Divinity of the East, creator of NELDAR

VELIXAR (formerly JACOB EVENINGSTAR), First Man of DEZREL,
High Prophet of KARAK

—OSCAR WELLINGTON, captain in THE ARMY OF KARAK

—MALCOLM GREGORIAN, captain in THE ARMY OF KARAK

HOUSE CRESTWELL

CLOVIS CRESTWELL, first child of KARAK

—LANIKE, his created wife

—LORD COMMANDER AVILA, their first daughter, 73 years old

—JOSEPH (deceased), their first son

—THESSALY (deceased), their second daughter,

—MOIRA ELREN, their exiled third daughter, 53 years old

—UTHER (deceased), their second son

—CRIAN (deceased), their third son

HOUSE MORI

SOLEH MORI (deceased), second child of KARAK

    —IBIS (deceased), her created husband

    —VULFRAM (deceased), their first son

      —YENGE, his wife, 34 years old

        —their children:

          ALEXANDER, son, 19 years old

          LYANA, daughter, 17 years old

          CALEIGH, daughter, 13 years old

    —ORIS, their second son, 67 years old

      —EBBE, his wife, 27 years old

        —their children:

          CONATA, daughter, 10 years old

          ZEPPA, daughter, 8 years old

    —ADELINE PALING (deceased), their first daughter

    —ULRIC (deceased), their third son

      —DIMONA, his wife, 42 years old

        —their children:

          TITON, son, 21 years old

          APHREDES, son, 20 years old

          JULIAN, son, 17 years old

    —RACHIDA GEMCROFT, wife of PEYTR, 52 years old

VELDAREN

KING ELDRICH VAELOR THE FIRST, second king of NELDAR, 38 years old

    —KARL DOGON, the king's bodyguard

    —PULO JENATT, captain of the palace guard

      —JONN TREMMEN, palace guard

      —RODDALIN HARLAN, palace guard

  —JOBEN TUSTLEWHITE, priest of KARAK

    —LAUREL LAWRENCE, councilwoman, 22 years old

    —GUSTER HALFHORN, elder councilman, 78 years old

    —ZEBEDIAH ZANE, councilman

—DIRK COLDMINE, councilman

—WALTER OLLERAY, councilman

—MARIUS TRUFONT, elder councilman

—LENROY MOTT, councilman

THE MERCHANTS

—ROMEO CONNINGTON, high merchant of RIVERRUN

—CLEO CONNINGTON, high merchant of RIVERRUN

—QUESTER BILLINGS, Crimson Sword of RIVERRUN

—MATTHEW BRENNAN, high merchant of PORT LANCASTER

—CATHERINE, his wife

—their children:

MARGERY, daughter, 14 years old

ELLA, daughter, 12 years old

RHODA, daughter, 9 years old

CATTIA, daughter, 4 years old

RYAN, son, 2 years old

—BREN TORRANT, his bodyguard

—URSULA, house maid

—PENETTA, house maid

—LORI, house maid

—PEYTR GEMCROFT, high merchant of HAVEN, husband of RACHIDA

—TRENTON BLACKBARD, high merchant of BRENT

—TOD GARLAND, high merchant of THETTLETOWN

—TOMAS MUDRAKER, high merchant of GRONSWIK

THE ELVES

THE DEZREN

STONEWOOD

—CLEOTIS MELN (deceased), former Lord of STONEWOOD

—AUDRIANNA, his wife

—their children:

CARSKEL, son, 182 years old

AUBRIENNA (deceased), daughter

AULLIENNA, daughter, 13 years old, betrothed to KINDREN
THYNE

—AAROMAR KULN, protector of LADY AUDRIANNA

—NONI CLANSHAW, nursemaid of AULLIENNA

—DETRICK MELN, brother of CLEOTIS, acting lord of STONEWOOD

—ETHIR AYERS, confidante of DETRICK

—DAVISHON HINSBREW, confidante of DETRICK

DEZEREA

—ORDEN THYNE, Lord of DEZEREA

—PHYRRA, his wife

—KINDREN, son, 17 years old, betrothed to AULLIENNA MELN

THE QUELLAN

—RUVEN SINISTEL, Neyvar (King) of QUELLASAR

—JEADRA, his wife

—CEREDON, their son, 96 years old

—IOLAS SINISTEL, cousin of RUVEN, member of the TRIAD

—CONALL SINISTEL, cousin of RUVEN, member of the TRIAD

—AESON SINISTEL, cousin of RUVEN, member of the TRIAD

—AERLAND SHEN, chief of the EKREISSAR

WRATH OF LIONS

LIONS

The Breaking World

PROLOGUE

Oris Mori stood at the edge of a pond deep within the forest behind Mori Manor and watched the water ripple as he threw small stones into it.

"I miss him still," said Alexander from beside him.

Oris turned to gaze at the boy, a near perfect mix of his parents. He had Yenge's thin nose and kinky-curly black hair and Vulfram's broad shoulders, rigid jaw, and soulful hazel eyes. Alexander's hands were also like his father's, thick fingers meant for gripping a sword's handle. Oris stared down at his own hand as he bounced a stone in his palm. The flesh was scarred and rippled, forever misshapen by the fire that had charred his body, leaving him in constant pain. Once those hands had been perfect. Once they had been just as strong as Vulfram's had been, which was quite strong indeed.

He let out a sigh.

"I know," he told his nephew. "I miss him as well."

"Will they send his body soon?" Alexander asked. "It has been six months. Mother promised they would send his body. *All* of their bodies."

"In time, son. I'm sure they will send them in time."

It was a lie, of course. Months ago he had learned of his family's horrible fate in Veldaren, the capital city to the northwest. His brother Vulfram, accused of murder, had been killed by the Final Judges; and then his other siblings, Ulric and Adeline, and his parents, Soleh and Ibis, had been executed for treason and blasphemy. As proof, the courier had presented Oris with a swathed package along with his letter. Inside was Vulfram's sturdy hand, severed at the wrist and blackened with rot. Still affixed to the pale index finger was a ring adorned with the image of the leaping doe, the sigil of House Mori. Oh, how Yenge had wailed. She'd held the severed hand to her chest, her tanned cheeks streaked with tears, pleading with the courier, "This isn't true—tell me this isn't true!"

But it was.

That had happened in autumn, before the worst winter in recent memory had flung its chill across northern Neldar. Oris should have gone to the capital then, he knew, to try and convince the king, Highest Crestwell, or even the Divinity himself to let him bring the corpses of his loved ones home for burial. Instead he had stayed in Erznia, doing his best to comfort his sister-in-law, no small feat considering she'd already lost her daughter Lyana to the Sisters of the Cloth. His lips drooped into a frown, his scarred flesh crumpling almost audibly. Winter had come and gone, and by now it was too late to hope for a burial. The sight of rot and bone would only make their losses worse.

"Why didn't Karak come to see us?" asked Caleigh.

Oris glanced at Vulfram's youngest child, who was squatting beside the pond. The bottom ridge of her heavy woolen smock was smeared with mud. She was only twelve, yet she'd experienced as much pain and loss as Oris had in his sixty-six years of life.

"He will come," replied Oris.

"Does he still love us?" the child asked.

"Don't ask that," snapped Alexander. "You'll end up like Lyana."

Oris silenced his nephew with a look. "Of course he still loves us," he told Caleigh. "We are Karak's children. He will *always* love us."

Her eyes gazed up at him, full of grief and skepticism.

"But Father was Karak's child too. And Grandmeem and Papa and Uncle Ulric…"

"Yes, Caleigh, but what happened was…complicated."

"How?"

"Stop asking questions!" her brother shouted, suddenly losing his temper.

Oris whirled, his misshapen hand grabbing the boy by the lapel of his surcoat. He pulled him in close, and though Alexander was nineteen and strong as an ox, he was helpless in Oris's clutches.

"Mind your tongue," he growled into his nephew's ear, "or I will mind it for you."

Alexander sniffled, then dropped his head in submission.

Releasing the boy, Oris stepped toward Caleigh and lifted her from the muddy ground, wrapping her up in his arms. She pressed her face into his shoulder but didn't shudder, didn't cry. She simply allowed him to hold her, like one of the dolls his wife, Ebbe, had made for his daughters when they were born. He wished he could remind the child how much wonder there was in the world, how their lives were gifts from Karak. The Moris were one of Karak's First Families. Their god would never bring undue hurt to them, he knew that.

At least, he had once known that. So much had changed over the last few months: the treasons for which his beloveds had been executed, the ever-growing army, the destructive attack on Haven, and the bloody clash between the brother gods. All of it had powered the tongues of merchants, bandits, and smallfolk alike. Keeping his surviving family calm and united had proved a near impossible task. The events had cast a pall of sadness over what had once been a sparkling outpost of Neldar.

"I wish Julian was still here," whispered Caleigh.

Oris nodded. Julian had been Ulric's youngest, a merry lad with an odd preference for dolls over swords and shields. He had been close to the girls—Oris's as well as Vulfram's—but Ulric's widow had taken her three boys in a fit of grief, leaving Erznia during a raging winter storm. Oris feared the worst for them. Yet another loving soul gone, yet another beloved family member taken away, making a place that had once seemed safe feel anything but.

"We will see them again," he said, keeping his voice low. He heard Alexander grunt behind him—the youth's failed attempt at hiding his sobs—and Caleigh leaned back in Oris's arms.

"In Afram?" she asked, her young eyes sparkling with hope.

Oris chuckled. "Hopefully sooner than that, sweet pie," he replied. "But yes, if we never again see them in this life, we will most certainly greet them in Afram."

If we can find our way through, he thought, but did not say.

Seeming to accept that, she once more rested her head on his shoulder.

A thick layer of clouds passed over the sun, and Oris released his niece, stretching to his full height. A strange feeling came over him, like an invisible phantasm whispering into his ear, and he shuddered. He turned to look at Alexander, and he could tell his nephew felt it too. The young man stared around wildly, his fingers playing across the hilt of the shortsword hanging from his belt. A wolf bayed, and the sound was far nearer than should have been possible. A fifteen-foot wall of pine and steel encircled Erznia. The only way a wolf could get inside was if someone let it in.

Then the beast howled again, and Oris realized it was no wolf.

Another sound emerged beneath the howling, a muted *bang* and *clank* that reminded him of the time he'd taken a tour of the Mount Hailen Armory in the far north.

Swords.

A queer sort of panic surged through him. Grabbing Caleigh's hand, Oris ran toward the Manor through the cover of the trees.

Alexander fell in step behind him. Oris's lungs, scarred after inhaling copious amounts of smoke while foolishly rescuing three whores from a burning brothel in Veldaren, no longer worked as well as they should. After a few paces he was breathing heavily, his pulse pounding in his ears, his heart about ready to give up on him. The sound of clattering steel grew louder in his ears.

But his heart did not give up, and he was very much alive when they neared the end of the wood and the rear courtyard of Mori Manor. It was empty, nothing but a flattened, pale green lawn populated by a few scattered goats. At the end of the courtyard rose the manor itself, a boxy construction of elm, pine, and oak that stretched a hundred feet in either direction. Despite its size, it was a simple construction, all earthy browns and deep burgundy, its great slanted roof spackled with tar and clay, seeming to mist beneath the overcast sky. Alexander began to push toward the manor, shoving aside vegetation, but Oris stilled him, pressing his palm against the young man's chest. Alexander's eyes were wide with the same terror Oris felt—a terror that grew as strange voices emerged from the other side of the manor.

"Stay hidden," he told the children. Caleigh, her hand still firmly gripped in his, nodded her understanding.

They progressed along the forest's boundary, using the copious overgrowth and piles of fallen limbs to keep out of sight. It felt strange to Oris that he should feel the need to take such precautions. Not very long ago, the sound of strangers within Erznia's walls would have been cause for excitement. But all that had changed when Vulfram returned to the township to punish his own daughter. That horrid turn of events, coupled with the courier's haunting message some months later, had caused the mood to shift. Now the presence of uninvited guests was a reason for fear.

Oris led his niece and nephew around the side of the manor, and the horror before him confirmed every misgiving. A legion of men in boiled black leather, decked out with pikes and swords, formed a row on either side of the beaten dirt road leading through the center of the settlement. Four flags of Karak fluttered on the bannermen's poles at the front line. The surviving members of Oris's family stood on the lawn of the manor, in the shadow of the peach tree to the left of the cobbled walk. Yenge stood front and center, her dark, curly hair cascading over shoulders that were thrown back in pride. Oris's wife, Ebbe, was beside her, her normally tan skin a pale russet after long months of sparse sunlight, and their children, Conata and Zeppa, were huddled in her skirts, tears running down their cheeks. Oris's heart went out to them. He wanted to run from his veil of twigs and leaves and gather them in his arms.

It was the sight of a man on horseback that stilled him. Naked and hairless, his skin looked as though it had been polished to a crystalline sheen. Yet muscles bulged and stretched beneath, as if they were too large and powerful for the shell that concealed them. A warhorn, the source of the baying Oris had heard, was cradled in his large hands. His eyes glowed an unnatural red, burning like the fires of the underworld, and the sight brought a lump to Oris's throat. He then took in the naked man's face—smooth and long, with a pointed chin and an upturned nose—and realized with horrible certainty who he was.

The former Highest, Clovis Crestwell. He looked inhuman; he was much larger than before, and he no longer had his long, silver hair. The Highest grinned, and it seemed as though he had grown extra teeth. Magister Muren Wentner, the decrepit old man responsible for upholding Karak's law within the settlement, stepped out from the crowd that had gathered behind the row of soldiers. His billowing gray robe flowed around him, making him appear to be a skeleton swathed in a mound of moldy fabric. From the look on the old man's face, Oris could tell Wentner too was shocked by Clovis's strange appearance and unabashed nakedness.

"We are...grateful for your arrival, Master Crestwell," Wentner said, falling to his knees before Clovis's horse. "I wish I had known

of your visit sooner, however, for I would have prepared a more…
appropriate greeting."

Clovis didn't respond. He simply smiled that horrible, toothy
smile.

Wentner shuffled on his knees, clearly uncomfortable.

"Er…what is the nature of your visit? Please tell me, so I can be
of service."

Without responding, Clovis dropped the warhorn and grabbed
his horse's reins. The horse stepped to the side of the road, appearing
slightly agitated, as if frightened by its rider. A heavy cart approached
between the two rows of soldiers, drawn by a pair of huge chargers.
The townsfolk behind the soldiers gasped, but the contents of the
cart were hidden from Oris's view. Magister Wentner rose from the
ground, hastily stepping out of the way. Once it reached the end of
the line, the cart pulled to a stop, exposing its ghastly contents to all.

While Oris's wife shrieked, lifting their children and backing
away, Yenge seemed to be frozen in shock, the tight line of her lips
and the twitch of her jaw the only signs of her distress. Oris was
helpless to avert his eyes from the four bodies hanging from the
slatted side of the cart—a woman and three young men. Even from
a distance he could tell the corpses were in a terrible state, the decaying remnants covered with gashes and splashed with old blood. He
recognized the tattered and bloody dress hanging from the carcass
of the lone woman and the ruby-encrusted necklace Ulric had given
Dimona on their wedding day.

The ball of terror that had built up in Oris's gut broke apart,
its fragments spreading waves of vigor through his limbs. His body
shook and his mind raced, but still he did not move. Instead, he
clamped his hand over Caleigh's lips before a shriek could leave her
throat, giving them away. He hoped Alexander had the good sense
to still his tongue as well.

Out on the lawn, Clovis proudly marched his horse to the front
of the cart.

"The traitors have been found and punished," Clovis said. Oris cringed at the sound of his voice, which was so unlike Clovis's. His tone still held the same gravelly quality, but there was something *more* there—it almost sounded as if two voices were speaking at once. "They have gone to the underworld to burn for eternity because of their sins against Karak's glory."

Caleigh began struggling, biting into Oris's palm, but he refused to let go.

"Why have you done this?" pleaded Yenge, her voice cracking.

"Yes, why?" asked Magister Wentner. His pale gray eyes stared in disbelief, his usually cocksure manner rapidly deflating. "The wife and children of Ulric Mori did nothing to deserve this fate."

The bald, naked man laughed, the sound assaulting the air like a wave of roaring flame.

"Did nothing, you say? The lady and her sons were heirs to a traitor and blasphemer, and they were set to follow in the footsteps of the one they called *husband* and *father*. They proved it when they attempted to flee west, into the arms of the bastard god who rules there."

"But what of us?" asked Yenge, bravely stepping forward to meet Clovis's burning red gaze. "Is our entire family considered as such? We have not fled. We have remained loyal to Karak despite our losses."

Clovis's sickening grin grew ever wider. "You have remained loyal, have you? Loyalty requires sacrifice, and you have sacrificed *nothing*. When your god asked for every able-bodied man to join the ranks of his army in preparation for the coming war, did you offer your son to the cause?" He turned in his saddle, addressing the townsfolk who had huddled in fear behind the soldiers. "Did any of you? Of all of Neldar's provinces, Erznia stood alone in her defiance. Not a single young man has joined the holy ranks, not a single woman has offered her services as a seamstress or nursemaid. You all huddled in your guarded forest, living apart from the god who created you. You dare call this loyalty?" Clovis spat on the ground. Magister Wentner tried to argue but was quickly shouted down. "I think not. The Mori family has disgraced our Lord, as has every other soul within these walls. Karak is the God of Order, and his ways are fair. You have turned your backs on your god, and so he has turned his back on you. May you all find forgiveness in the afterlife…if forgiveness is to be had for such cowardly scum."

At the Highest's command, a row of archers stepped forward, leveled their bows, and fired on those standing on the manor's lawn. Oris could only watch as pointed shafts buried themselves in his wife, Magister Wentner, and Yenge. Ebbe attempted to shield Conata and Zeppa with her own body, but arrow after arrow embedded in her back until she collapsed. Their daughters suffered the same fate; Zeppa, all of seven, received a bolt in the neck, and nine-year-old Conata was pierced through the back of the head as she attempted to flee. An agonized roar forced its way through Oris's clenched lips, but it was drowned out by the bloodcurdling shrieks of the gathered crowd.

Still, Oris did not advance. Releasing Caleigh, he whirled around and grabbed Alexander by the shoulders. The young man's eyes were rimmed with tears, and his body was quaking uncontrollably.

"Listen to me!" Oris shouted at him. "Leave now! Take your sister and go. Climb the wall and head east, across the river. Few live there, and there is a chance you might make it to the coast unharmed. Ask for favors—beg if you must—but stay alive. Do you understand?"

Alexander stared dumbly ahead.

"*Do you understand?*" he screamed, shaking the young man by the shoulders.

Slowly Alexander's eyes came to focus on his, and he nodded his understanding. Oris pulled his nephew into a tight embrace, then removed the shortsword from Alexander's belt.

"You won't be needing this," he said, handing over his own dagger in its stead. "It will only slow you down. The smaller the blade, the better. Now go."

Alexander took the dagger in one hand, snatched Caleigh's wrist with the other, and sprinted away. Oris watched them go, ignoring the clang of steel from the area beyond the wood as he waited until the two youngsters had distanced themselves before revealing himself.

He counted to twenty, grief and wrath causing him to bounce on his heels as he gripped the shortsword with both scarred hands. Then he turned sharply and barreled through the overgrowth. Twigs snapped and brittle branches slapped his disfigured face as he leapt out of cover and into the open.

It was a massacre. The soldiers had turned on the populace, murdering everyone in sight. Swords and pikes thrust again and again, the blood they spilled creating a pinkish fog. Oris saw Bracken Renson, a man he had known since childhood, have his head split down the middle by an ax. Carlotta Littleton, the woman who had been nursemaid to his children, was gutted by a spear, her body viciously kicked off the shaft once she ceased moving. A sparse few fought back, only to be overwhelmed by the soldiers who had superior training and weapons.

Bellowing like a wild beast, Oris forced his sore legs to carry him forward. Something sharp pierced his side, but he ignored the pain and kept running, his sword held high, his sights fixed on one man and one man only: Clovis Crestwell. The man's gaze shifted to him, and those blazing red eyes widened with what looked to be excitement.

Clovis leapt off his horse, his naked body bulging with muscle, his evil grin growing larger and larger. His mouth seemed to open wider than was humanly possible. It looked hungry enough to swallow the whole world. But Oris didn't care. *A wider opening to plunge my sword through* was all he thought as he lunged forward, the tip of his blade aiming for Clovis's gaping maw. It was then that he saw the man's teeth extending, growing outward, becoming sharp daggers.

He thrust with all his might, the shortsword plunging into the gaping maw with both hands. Clovis's inhuman red eyes widened as the blade exited the back of his skull. His expression shifted, and his dagger-filled mouth snapped shut on Oris's arms, tearing through flesh, tendon, and bone. Oris teetered backward, his arms severed just below the elbow, the stumps spurting blood. Clovis ripped the sword from his mouth as if it were naught but a splinter, then rushed forward, ramming its cutting edge into Oris's gut and twisting until his insides spilled all over the ground. Oris lost feeling in his lower half and collapsed, the rest of him awash with white-hot pain. He knew the end was near, but he forced himself to roll over nonetheless, staring back toward the forest, hoping beyond hope that Alexander and Caleigh had escaped. These thoughts persisted even as claws ripped into his back, even as teeth tore into his neck, even as his own blood washed over his eyes, even as the screams of those dying all around him faded away, leaving him with nothing but the agony he felt in his every nerve as he was slowly devoured.

CHAPTER

1

The bodies hung from the top of the castle walls, their eyeless faces staring accusingly at any who passed below. There were six in all, swaying side by side in the frigid early spring breeze. Four had been gutted, and what remained of their innards was blackened with rot, a putrid substance that streamed down their bare legs and dripped from their toes. The area of the walk under them had long since been stained with the sap of their deaths.

The day's light was fading fast, and Laurel Lawrence stood at the edge of the cobbled road in front of the Castle of the Lion, staring up at the corpses as she had been wont to do since the day they were hung. Though she had experienced much loss over her twenty-two years, she felt most hopeless when lingering in this spot. The bodies had lost their bloat long ago, and their most tender areas had become food for crows and parasites, but the long and bitterly cold winter had somewhat preserved them. Their flesh was gray and taut, stretched thinly over the bones beneath. Laurel could recognize the ghosts of the men and women they had once been: Ulric Mori, Veldaren's Master-at-Arms; Vulfram, Ulric's brother and former

Lord Commander of the Army of Karak, found unworthy by the Final Judges; Ibis Mori, father of Ulric and Vulfram, the sculptor whose hands had crafted the statues of Karak that decorated the city; and finally, Ibis's creator and wife, Soleh Mori, former Minister of Justice in Veldaren and matriarch of House Mori, the second family of Karak. At the end of the macabre line, someone had hung two additional bodies: Nessa DuTaureau, a child of the bastard western god, Ashhur, who had switched her loyalty to Karak, and her lover Crian, the son of Highest Crestwell. Their bodies had appeared a month previously, and Laurel was flabbergasted by their addition, for the doomed lovers had been publicly forgiven and accepted by Karak himself the night before their murder.

Despite their odd continued presence, it was the cracked and peeling face of Minister Mori, eerily lit by the torches below, that drew Laurel's gaze. She had known the Minister in life, Soleh often taking the time to stop her in the great hall and share a few kind words. As one of three women of power within the castle, they'd shared a unique bond. "Men hold tight to the power they think they wield, but it is those who linger behind the curtain who hold the true power," Soleh had told her once, a roguish gleam in her eye. "It is our duty to silently nurture that power, especially when men try to strip it from us or force us to play their game."

It was a relationship Laurel had cherished.

Laurel shook her head. It had all gone wrong so quickly. She'd been there at Nessa DuTaureau's baptism; she'd watched as the red-haired sprite kneeled before Karak in the great fountain, accepting his blessing. And the next evening she had witnessed Soleh's horrified response when Highest Crestwell presented the butchered bodies of Nessa and Crian, accusing Vulfram of killing them. It was the last time she'd seen any of the Moris alive.

"Councilwoman," a voice spoke from beside her.

She turned to see a guard standing there, his coiled black mop falling below his half helm, his hazel eyes shining through the gap in the visor, brimmed with moisture. Despite the horror of the wall and the strangeness of her visit to the castle, a rush of warmth filled Laurel's belly.

"Captain Jenatt," she whispered. Pulo Jenatt had been a member of Soleh Mori's personal entourage before being named captain of the Palace Guard after the former captain, Malcolm Gregorian, was given his own vanguard in Karak's new army. Each time Laurel visited the castle, Pulo joined her in offering his respects to the dead minister. They never spoke of their reverence publicly—it would be considered sacrilege to do so—but their silent bond brought them both a macabre sort of comfort.

"Your audience awaits," Pulo said, stepping back. "Please follow me."

They crossed beneath the portcullis, past a row of guards who stood sentry in the shadows of the twin onyx statues of leaping lions, and entered the courtyard. The three castle towers loomed above the grass, rising into the twilight gloom. The platform on which Minister Mori used to hold her daily sermons stood empty at a bend in the walkway, the boards soft and rotting.

Everywhere she looked there were women. Women selling other women fruit from a ramshackle stand, women juggling for coin, women shuffling snot-laden children out of Tower Servitude, women guiding horses to the stables, women begging for an audience with the king. It was an echo of what she saw each day as she made her way through the cold gray streets of the city. The only men to be seen were members of the City Watch or Palace Guard, the lowborn criminals whose torment of the city heightened with each passing day, those too old to be conscripted into Karak's Army or rich enough to buy themselves out of service.

The great door to Tower Honor was held open, and Pulo led her down the long corridor. The air was warm, and Laurel's boots sunk into the plush carpet as she walked. She wished she could strip off her hardened leather waders and curl her toes in the carpet's fibers.

Comfort and warmth had become fleeting concepts over the last six months. They'd been replaced by the monotony of her daily treks to the castle to fulfill her duties as a member of the Council of Twelve, a collection of individuals from the various districts and townships within Neldar whose purpose was to advise King Eldrich. Laurel was the only female member of the Council, and by far the youngest. Her mother had given birth to fourteen children, seven of whom—all boys—had died before reaching the end of their first year. The only male child who grew to adulthood had perished two years earlier, when starving peasants fell on her family's granaries with torches and pitchforks, demanding to be fed during an extended drought. Because she was the oldest surviving child and her father, Cornwall Lawrence, was suffering from the final stages of the Wasting, Laurel had been chosen to act as the court representative for her father's sprawling settlement of Omnmount.

It wasn't an easy task, truth be told. Even when she had the confidence to speak, her voice was rarely heard. Most of the men of the Council, when they weren't ignoring her, levied her with disapproving glances. She tried to tell herself it was because she was young, but she knew better. Soleh Mori's words often seeped into her thoughts: *"Men hold tight to the power they think they wield, but it is those who linger behind the curtain who hold the true power."* The strongest reaction she had ever received was when she'd attended court in a firming corset and low-slung satin chemise. How their eyes had bulged then, and when she offered advice to the Council that day, saying that an extra tax should be levied against the farms in the southern agricultural belt, those owned by her own family, in light of the grain shortages caused by the brutal winter in the north, the motion had actually been put to a vote. It hadn't passed, losing seven to five, but at least she'd been heard.

Since then, she had taken to flaunting seductive outfits whenever she entered court. It shamed her more than a little, but Laurel was nothing if not practical. Should she need to use her youthful beauty to accomplish her duties, so be it.

The doors to the throne room were opened by the guards, and Pulo led her inside. The walls of the cavernous chamber were polished stone the color of rust. Enormous tapestries and banners hung from them, with the sigil of the royal Vaelor house—two swords crossed over a shield adorned with the image of Karak's roaring lion—dominating all others.

Two men she knew well stood before the dais supporting the ivory throne rimmed with curved grayhorn tusks. One was the man who had sent for her, Guster Halfhorn. The senior member of the Council of Twelve, Guster was a withered old man approaching eighty, with a wattled neck and brown eyes whitened by cataracts. The other man was Dirk Coldmine, representative of the lower Neldar townships. He was burly, with a thick black beard, and he wore his natty woolen doublet as if it were a suit rimmed with gold. Both raised a hand in greeting, and Guster's pale lips lifted into a smile. Uncertainty and nerves sent dark thoughts spiking through Laurel's mind. She didn't know why court had been canceled earlier that day, nor did she understand why Guster had been so adamant that she arrive just as the rest of the castle was emptying out. *They know of my sympathy for the minister's plight....Perhaps they think me a harlot and betrayer?* She wrapped her arms over her breasts self-consciously and cast a fleeting glance behind her, fearing she would see a representative of the Sisters of the Cloth.

Captain Jenatt presented her to the two Council members, knelt to kiss her hand, and then left the throne room. The *clank* of his armor sounded impossibly loud to Laurel as she stood before Guster and Dirk, her arms still wrapped around herself protectively. She tried to say something, but worry formed a lump in the back of her throat that made it impossible to form words.

"I'm sure you are wondering why I called you here at this hour," Guster said, his tone deep, throaty, and heavy with knowledge, befitting one who had lived so long.

Laurel cleared her throat, found her voice. "I am quite curious," she replied.

The old man patted her on the shoulder, his gaze never leaving hers, even as her arms dropped to her sides. The same could not be said for Dirk Coldmine, whose eyes lingered on the swell of her breasts over her emerald-green bodice.

"There will be answers soon, my dear," Guster said. "But first, I wish to set your mind at ease. You are safe here and always will be. Please, let us go to the Council chamber."

With those words, Dirk offered Guster his shoulder and helped the older man scale the four broad steps onto the dais. Laurel trailed them, taking the familiar path around the massive throne, toward the door leading to the Council chamber. The vestibule was cold as ever, a stark contrast to the warmth of the rest of the tower.

They entered a room of rough gray stone to find Karl Dogon, the king's bodyguard, awaiting them. He lingered off to the side of the large table at which the council held their debates, the twelve wooden chairs—now empty—dwarfed by the king's tall mahogany one. Dogon's deep-set eyes stared blankly from his rectangular head at the visitors. He nodded to them, inviting them to sit, which they did, taking the chairs closest to the king's. Dogon then disappeared through the side entrance.

The three sat in uncomfortable silence for what felt like an hour, before footfalls pounded down the stairs on the other side of the door. Dogon re-entered, and then King Eldrich Vaelor appeared behind him. Laurel hastily rose from her seat in respect, as did Guster and Dirk. She held her breath as she took in the fact that the king was dressed in a modest, white, cotton tunic and breeches, not his usual lavish royal garb. She had always known him to be a gaunt man, but without the added layers of clothing, he seemed almost sickly. He wore his thirty-eight years as if they had been a burden, his eyes rimmed with black circles above sallow cheeks. He had never been an attractive man, yet there had been something about his offbeat demeanor that Laurel had found appealing. That seemed to have disappeared, leaving a wan, despondent creature in its wake.

The king motioned for his guests to sit. Laurel's heart beat so fast and loud, she feared the others would hear it in the insufferable silence.

King Eldrich sighed, and then leaned back in his chair, propping his elbow on the armrest so he could cup his bony chin in his palm. "First, the lesser business," he said. The thin man's eyes darted to his bodyguard, who stood sentry at the side of the table, and Dogon produced a folded piece of parchment from the sack hanging on his hip.

"What is this about, your Grace?" Guster asked when Dogon handed him the paper.

"Just read the letter," replied King Eldrich. "Out loud, if you'd please."

Laurel sank back into herself, feeling just as lost as ever. Here she was, privy to some sort of strange, private meeting, and she had yet to be acknowledged by the king. And it was so damn *cold*. She wished she were home in bed, her blankets piled high atop her.

Guster's eyes scanned the words on the page, and once he reached the bottom, he glanced across the table at Dirk.

"I'm sorry," the old man said. "Dirk, your brother, Deacon, has passed away."

Dirk grunted, his expression unchanging. "Figured as much, though it took them long enough to tell me. How did he die?"

The old man scanned the letter again, then shrugged. "It doesn't say."

"No matter," replied Dirk.

"Do you wish to retrieve the body?" asked the king wearily.

Dirk shook his head.

"Deacon made his own bed when he took a secret family. I've made sure his true wife and children are cared for. Honestly, Deacon's been dead to me for some time."

"You shouldn't be so harsh," said Guster. "Your brother paid his penance to Karak with his life."

"He did? And how did he do that?"

Guster shrugged. "The letter doesn't say, but we have both heard Clovis Crestwell say those words."

"Nevertheless, his actions allowed countless innocents to die," Dirk muttered under his breath. He glanced up at King Eldrich and asked, "Any word on his whore and bastards?"

The king frowned. "No. It seems they have...disappeared, along with most everyone else in the delta. According to Lord Commander Avila, his body was found in front of the destroyed temple. The citizens of Haven seemed to have left it behind when they fled their home." He held his arms out wide, his voice dripping with derision. "But then again, I am but a puppet king. We're lucky I received word of Deacon's demise at all, even if it was six months late."

Laurel scratched at her temple, utterly baffled by the conversation. She cleared her throat to gather her courage, and all eyes turned to her.

"I apologize for being rude, your Grace," she said sheepishly, "but I don't understand. Why am I here?"

The king smiled at her, a spark of life returning to his eyes. "Ah, Councilwoman Lawrence. You are here at my behest."

"Why?"

King Eldrich peered at each person in the room, then back at her. "Because you are young. Because you are nice to look at. And because Halfhorn has told me you're a bright young woman, and I often find myself surrounded by cravens and fools." He chuckled. "By that bastard Karak, some have called *me* both on more than one occasion."

"You aren't either, your Grace," she replied, trying to ignore his blasphemy.

He waved his hand at her. "We shall find out soon enough."

Laurel frowned. Guster's wrinkled hand fell atop hers, and the old man leaned forward, speaking kindly.

"These are trying times, Laurel, and there are few to be trusted. I have vouched that you are one of those few."

"I...I'm honored."

"And now that Crestwell has been replaced by the First Man as the Highest, the need for secrecy is paramount, which is why I cancelled court today and asked you to come here in secret," the king said. He lowered his head and shook it. "Clovis was an uppity fuck to be sure, but I trust the one who now whispers in Karak's ear even less."

Laurel swallowed hard. Clovis had become a rarity around the castle over the last few months, and the last time she'd seen him, he had looked...wrong. His head of platinum hair had been shaved clean off, his body had been hunched at odd angles, and his eyes had developed an unhealthy red hue. She thought of her father, dying in his bed back in Omnmount, and wondered if perhaps the Highest were succumbing to the Wasting as well. The thought of one of Karak's first creations, a supposed immortal developing such a sickness, gave her the shivers. The First Families were all but dying out. What would become of Neldar if none were left to guide them?

"What bothers you, girl?" asked the king.

"Nothing," she replied. She knew she must be strong before these men. It was a great honor to have been asked to this meeting, and she would not ruin it by exposing her weakness. Lifting her shoulders back, she took a deep breath and said, "However, I do not understand the need for secrecy, even if Clovis Crestwell is no longer the Highest. This is still Karak's kingdom, is it not? Does our Divinity not walk among us? What do we have to fear?"

All four men—Dogon included—burst into laughter. Laurel forced herself not to blush.

"There is much you do not know," said Dirk when the laughing died down. "For example, what do you know of Haven?"

She shrugged. "The truth. The delta was filled with thieves, murderers, and godless heathens who built a blasphemous temple. Karak and the Highest ordered them to tear it down, and when they refused, they were bathed in fire."

"True enough," said King Vaelor. "And then Ashhur appeared, and the brother gods came to blows. A formerly peaceful union was broken, paving the path to war."

Laurel nodded.

"And that, my dear girl, is the problem," said Guster. "Karak neglects his city. He locks himself in the temple beyond the walls, preparing for war with his brother, when he should be here, helping keep the peace. Our children receive no blessings; our frightened populace is granted no assurances. Instead, Jacob Eveningstar has appeared and grasped Clovis's mantle, taking a new name and foreswearing his loyalty to Ashhur." He offered a disgusted gesture. "Our men march in armies now, leaving our streets teeming with cowards and thieves. And that doesn't take into account those damn corpses hanging on the wall. The blasphemers I could perhaps understand, but Crian and the western deserter? It makes no sense. If Karak cared about his people in the slightest, he wouldn't have allowed the First Man to create such a display."

Laurel shivered. The First Man had long black hair and a haunting stare, and he carried himself with such confidence that the mere sight of him was intimidating. However, besides his command to hang the bodies of the treasonous outside the castle, the man who now called himself Highest Velixar had done nothing but linger in the background during Council meetings. Sightings of him were rare.

"I know little of the new Highest," she said. "But beyond a grisly reminder to the disloyal, what has he done that warrants such secrecy and blasphemous talk? And as for the coming war, it was Ashhur who broke his promise by interfering with Karak's punishment of his own creations. What would you have our Divinity do? Paradise must be taught a lesson, just like those in Haven."

"There is a time for war, and there is a time for diplomacy," said Guster softly. "I fear the latter would be more appropriate now."

"Are you doubting our god?" asked Laurel, aghast.

"We are," replied King Vaelor. The king leaned forward, his stubble-covered cheeks flushing red. "After all, we are free men, are we not? That was supposed to be Karak's promise—every man was to live freely so long as he pledged his loyalty to his creator. Let us ignore the paradox of that statement and deal with the facts as we know them. Karak's law says we are to honor him, but does it say anywhere that we are never to question his decisions?"

"Not explicitly," said Laurel.

"Exactly. Yet I fear that, should I march to his temple and pose these questions to him, you would wake up tomorrow with your old king hanging from a chain alongside the bodies of the First Families while a new king sat on the throne. Would you like that, girl?"

Laurel averted her eyes from the king's angry gaze. She felt like a minnow circled by sharks.

It was Dirk's turn to comfort her.

"Don't feel ashamed, Laurel," he said. "I love Karak as much as anyone. You know this. And I understand how shocking it can be to realize that life is not as simple as it once seemed. Even I can see the flaw in what is happening to our realm. The purpose of this meeting is not to decry our creator, but to come up with a plan."

"A plan for what?" she muttered.

Karl Dogon spoke for the first time that evening.

"For what will happen if Karak loses this war."

Everyone seemed shocked to hear his voice—all but the king, who looked relaxed as he reclined in his chair.

"Exactly," said King Eldrich. "The men who have trained all their lives to become blacksmiths, farmers, apothecaries, healers, horsemen, potters, craftsmen, stonemasons, shoemakers, and bakers have been taken from us. The women of the realm have been forced to take their place, and though you and I might argue about the merits of the fairer sex, you cannot argue with the fact that they have spent their lives as mothers, knitters, and nursemaids. Most have not been trained in the art of firing a kiln or fashioning iron, yet these skills are necessary for the success of our society. Our city is overrun by thieves and vagrants that our meager Watch is helpless to stop. Production of goods has come to a standstill, and those who are not in the military are slowly starving. After such a brutal winter, food is in short supply, and it would take all of Neldar working together to replenish our dwindling resources. But the men who march in our fields now wield swords instead of plowshares. Pleas for food come from every corner of our land…pleas I have no choice but to ignore since we have none to give."

Laurel thought of the battalions of armored soldiers she'd watched march down the streets of the city one month before. There had been hundreds of them, all Veldaren natives, their armor, swords, axes, and maces clattering as they worked their way through the crowds of women who cheered and shouted prayers for their safe return. *They* had appeared well fed, and the combined skills of Neldar had been showcased in every finely made piece of armor and sharpened blade.

"This war strains us greatly, but it will not last long," she said. "My mother told me of the people of Paradise. They are lazy and ignorant, and they expect their god Ashhur to grant them their desires so they may live in childish servitude. Weak and defenseless, what will they do when our soldiers march against them? When Karak leads our brothers into Paradise, the people there will have no choice but to bow before him."

Or else their bodies will be hung from a wall like Minister Mori's, she thought.

"I dream of such an easy war," said King Vaelor. "Ashhur has had six months to prepare. Do you think he has spent that time idly? Do you think he will allow his creations to be slaughtered without a fight? Yes, I have heard stories about Haven and the great fire from the sky that destroyed the blasphemers....But I have also heard of how the very ground shook when the brother gods battled, of how in his rage Ashhur cut down our soldiers with his sword as if they were stalks of wheat. No, I fear Karak will cross the river to find that a once frightened sheep has become a braying wolf. Six months is not time enough to train an entire populace in the art of war—an art that *we* have not yet mastered, mind you—but they will fight for the lives they've been given. And none of this takes into account the crisis of numbers we're facing."

"What do you mean?"

The king motioned toward Guster. The old man straightened in his chair and looked Laurel's way.

"Our society is strong, Laurel, and hearty, but compared to Paradise we are woefully outnumbered. Our years of incessant breeding have granted us a population of more than eighty thousand. However, of that eighty thousand, the force our god has gathered amounts to barely a quarter of that number. The rest of our society is comprised of women, children, and the elderly. Here in the east at least one in three children do not reach adulthood, but in Paradise there is no sickness; no mothers die on the birthing bed and no children perish. Health is in such abundance that we hear tales that a hundred from the *first generation* still endure, albeit old as sin. And believe me when I say that those in Paradise have bred just as feverishly as we have. Their people outnumber ours three to one, and that is a conservative estimate."

Laurel leaned back in her chair, stunned. She had never thought of that; the sheer numbers were staggering. It made her head spin.

"I didn't realize," she said, head bowed. She felt lost and afraid, her entire reality crashing down before her. It only made matters worse that she did not know what was expected of her.

"Do you understand now why we must prepare for the worst?" asked the king.

"I do," she said, her voice weak. "But why me? Why am I trustworthy when others are not? What do I have to offer?"

At those words, Dirk sat back in his seat and cupped his hands just below his chest. A charge of anger rushed through Laurel, making her dig her fingernails into her palms below the table, but she held her tongue.

"As crass as Councilman Coldmine might be, he has the truth of it," said Guster. His tone warbled, his wattle flopped. "But that is only part of it. The whole truth is that besides being a young and attractive woman, you are also highborn and quite clever. You are relatively new to the Council, whereas the rest of us have been advising King Eldrich since the crown was passed to him."

"Which means," said the king, "that you are relatively unknown outside these walls."

Laurel glanced at each of her companions in turn, taking in Vaelor's creased brow, Dirk's knowing smirk, and the concerned droop of Guster's jowls. Karl Dogon appeared disgusted by the proceedings, though it was hard to tell—that look of contempt never seemed to leave his face.

"I don't understand," she finally said.

The king began to tap restlessly on the tabletop. "In order to ensure our survival should the worst occur," he said, his tone that of a teacher berating an inattentive student, "we need the high merchants on our side. The Garlands, the Mudrakers, the Conningtons, the Blackbards, the Brennans—even the Gemcrofts, if Peytr still lives. Before the gods' clash in Haven, all but Peytr were dutiful citizens, paying far beyond their levies and supplying whatever goods we requested. Since the rumblings of war, however, they've become invisible. The house leaders have retreated to their estates and are either too fearful—or too smart—to emerge. We need their coin and resources if we are to protect ourselves from the possibility of an extended conflict."

"Why don't you make them give it to you?" Laurel asked, cringing as the question left her mouth.

The king frowned, his arms extending outward. "We have a powerful enemy west of the rivers. We do not need to make more here in our own land. No, what I need is a messenger, an individual who will not attract the wrong type of attention, someone these men will listen to and trust. And who is a powerful man more likely to trust than a beautiful young woman?"

"I can think of many examples, actually," said Dirk with a laugh.

Vaelor silenced him with a look, then turned his gaze back to Laurel.

"Do you accept my offer, girl? Will you be my messenger?"

"Do I have a choice?" she asked.

Dogon tapped the hilt of his sword, answering her question without words. Again she heard Soleh Mori's voice in her head. *It is our duty to silently nurture that power, especially when the men try to strip it from us, or force us to play their game.*

"Very well then," she said with a sigh, tightening the threads on the front of her bodice. The room seemed to grow even colder, making her shiver. "Tell me what you want me to do."

CHAPTER

Velixar bent over his desk in the forgotten throne room inside the Tower Keep, still dressed in his nightclothes despite the fact that it was past noon. He scribbled feverishly in his journal, a feeling of elation pulsing in his veins. It had been many months since he'd swallowed the essence of the demon whose name he had adopted, since he'd destroyed the last vestiges of his previous life. Jacob Eveningstar, the immortal First Man of Dezrel, now existed solely in the memories of his former friends, and when their bodies were rotting in the dirt, the only ones who would know of his prior existence would be his god and himself.

Each passing day was an adventure for him as he traversed the locked caverns within his mind. The knowledge of the demon Velixar, the Beast of a Thousand Faces, was immense. It seemed as though every hidden mental doorway he unlocked, however small, hid some long-lost secret. The secrets of ancient magics were spread out before him like a blanket of shimmering entrails. Biology, necromancy, otherworldly travels, the snaring of souls lost in the afterlife, the history of the universe itself—they all lay at his fingertips, his present understanding a mere hint at the possibilities that simmered beneath the surface.

His fingers cramped and he placed down his quill, shaking the ache from his hand. With the onset of that cramp, his frustration grew. Even with the strength he'd gained during the ritual, he was still trapped by the limitations of his physical form. Glancing to the side, he saw his reflection in the dragonglass mirror that had once belonged to Crian Crestwell. Despite the cataclysmic change that had occurred within him, he looked much as he always had: the same black hair, the same strong jaw, the same perfect posture. The only true difference was that his eyes were now rimmed with pale red, a color that flashed brightly whenever he accessed the magics trapped within him. In some ways he thought Clovis Crestwell lucky. Clovis, pathetic and egocentric fool that he was, had not possessed the strength to sever the ties that bound the creature's consciousness from its essence. Darakken had infused every fiber of Clovis's being, shoving aside the personality that had once resided there, altering his body's form to make room for its much larger presence. The Clovis that existed now only retained passing similarities to the man he had been. In that way, and that way only, he envied the former Highest.

He had knowledge in abundance. He understood more secrets of the universe than Karak and Ashhur combined. But *power*…power was the one thing he lacked, and it shamed him. There were constant limitations to his abilities. He'd assumed that by absorbing the demon's core he'd be able to transcend those limitations, transcend his *humanity*, but that hadn't happened. *There are no limits to how strong you will become in time,* he told himself. He hoped it would happen sooner rather than later, for the march into Paradise was rapidly approaching. Dropping his head, clenching and unclenching his fists, he once more begged for patience.

Soft footfalls sounded, and Velixar glanced up. The cavernous room he had taken as his own was the one he'd designed many years before as the throne room for the castle of Veldaren. It was four stories high and a hundred feet in either direction, empty but for his desk, which stood against the eastern wall, and his featherbed and small breakfront, which were positioned beneath the painting of the gods coming forth into Dezrel that graced the raised dais on the northern wall. There were no other furnishings or decorations, Velixar having removed all remnants of the statues carved by Ibis Mori, finished or unfinished, and interspersed them throughout the city.

A lithe form appeared in the doorway, taking a few cautious steps forward. Lanike, the wife Clovis Crestwell had created for himself, entered the light of the torches burning on the drab, gray walls. She was the keep's only other occupant, brought here as an insult to her husband, who was a prisoner in his own body. Lanike took care of the wash and cooking in Velixar's home like a lowly household servant. Small and fragile looking, her hair was slightly disheveled and her eyes wary. She was ageless, just as her creator had been, and not horrible to look at despite her mousiness. The draping cobalt robe she wore was satin, and it caught the womanly figure beneath with every other step she took. Velixar thought of the dead elf Brienna Meln, who had loved the First Man with all her heart and whose pendant he had long ago smashed to demonstrate the cleansing of his past. *She* had owned a robe like that; she would traipse through the cabin in Safeway wearing it, before he stripped her and ravaged her perfect form. For a moment he felt arousal, thinking perhaps Lanike would be a viable replacement. She was of the First Families, ageless just as he, and if he could make her love him…

"Enough!" he commanded, and the thought disappeared.

Lanike stopped in her tracks, staring at him with fearful eyes. She took a step back, tugging nervously on the sleeves of her robe.

"I apologize," she said, her voice soft.

"Not you," Velixar said. He groaned and stepped toward her. "Why have you interrupted my studies, Lanike? I told you I am not to be disturbed when I am at work."

The mousy woman refused to look him in the eye. "I understand, and I mean no disrespect, Ja—Highest Velixar. But there is a man here to see you. A man in armor. Captain Handrick, he said his name was."

Velixar nodded. "I see. Tell him I'll be with him momentarily."

"Very well."

Lanike hastily curtseyed and then left the room. She nearly tripped over her robe, crashing into the archway before she exited. In sharp contrast to his earlier feelings of desire—a weakness, he thought—Velixar felt a rush of loathing. He should have ended the pathetic woman's life long ago, and would have if he didn't need her to keep Darakken in line.

He changed out of his nightclothes, putting on a clean tunic, black leather breeches, and a surcoat edged with expertly stitched lions. He couldn't greet Captain Handrick looking slovenly. Harlan Handrick was a rough sort, headstrong and stubborn, in charge of the two hundred soldiers stationed just outside Karak's private temple on the outskirts of Veldaren. Having been a member of the Palace Guard for nearly twenty years, Handrick was one of the few in the city who had known Jacob Eveningstar before the First Man had pledged himself to Ashhur. They'd often come to disagreements about the proper use of armed force, but Handrick was a capable man, and Velixar hadn't thought twice before ordering him and his unit to march to Erznia three weeks ago, after Dimona Mori's attempt to flee the realm. Though he'd sent them to the hidden forest stronghold in Erznia under the pretense of a demand for fealty, what he truly wanted was for Oris Mori and his nephew Alexander to be rounded up and brought to the capital. The fire-scarred Oris was a beast with a sword, and Vulfram's son was a true child of Karak. They were respected throughout the kingdom, just as Vulfram had been. Having them pledge their fealty to him would only heighten his influence.

He found Captain Handrick standing in the foyer, looking dignified in his mailed suit over boiled leather. Almost immediately Velixar knew something was wrong. The captain's greaves were coated with deep burgundy stains, as was his longsword's scabbard. The gruff, older man eyed him with distaste as he approached, but Velixar saw something hidden beneath the veneer of loathing.

Fear. Guilt. *Failure.*

"Captain," he said, stopping a few feet in front of the man.

Handrick's heels snapped together. He offered a slight bow but neither spoke nor offered any show of reverence.

Velixar frowned and said, "How went the journey? I assume the men I asked you to retrieve are in the garrison readying to greet me?"

The captain's nose twitched.

"As a matter of fact, they are not," he replied.

Velixar's blood began to rush faster through his veins.

"And why not?"

"They are dead."

"Who are? Oris and Alexander?"

"All of them. The entirety of Erznia."

Velixar's eyes widened, and he took a step back. All of Erznia… dead? But why? His anger began to churn once more, but he held it in check. He thought he knew who was responsible, but he had to go through the charade, had to find out for sure.

"They fought back?" he asked, knowing that not to be the case.

The captain shook his head. "They didn't. We fell on them before they had the chance."

"Before *who* had a chance to react?"

"Every man, woman, and child."

His fury boiled over, but he refused to release it. Yet. This captain who was so brazen in his defiance would be made to understand who had the power. Velixar stepped forward and grabbed Handrick by the front of his mail, pulling him close. The armor's rings cut into his fingers the tighter he gripped, but he felt no pain.

"*Why* did you kill them?" he asked. "I gave orders that none were to be hurt, and yet your men slaughtered the entire settlement? Does that sound acceptable to you?"

"The orders were changed," replied the captain.

Velixar laughed, though the sound was without a hint of humor. "Changed by who?"

"Highest Crestwell," said the man proudly. "Or whatever our Highest has become. He joined us on the road and took command over our unit."

Velixar's eyes narrowed. "You know *exactly* what Clovis has become, Captain. I told you *explicitly* that the beast is neither to be trusted nor heeded. You follow *my* commands, not the demon's."

"I guide my men the way I see fit," replied Handrick "The demon may have altered our Highest's form, but Clovis still lives...."

"He is not the Highest—*I* am!" Velixar roared. Admirably, Handrick managed not to tremble before such an outburst, though it seemed to take him a moment to gather himself.

"Perhaps," he said. "But Clovis declared the citizens of Erznia blasphemers, and I agreed. They were to be punished, no different from how we punished those in Haven."

Amazingly, the captain's fear seemed to be diminishing, replaced by stubbornness and pride. Velixar could never let such defiance go unanswered.

"You did this even though your god ordered you otherwise," he said.

"Karak gave me no orders."

"*I* gave you the orders. I speak for Karak in our Divinity's absence."

"Like you spoke for Ashhur? Will you betray Karak as well?"

A deep throaty noise rose in Velixar's throat.

"Watch your words, mortal," he said.

Captain Handrick shoved him backward with one mailed fist, moving his other hand to the hilt of his sword. "You are no god, *Jacob*. And you could never take the place of the Highest. You are a delusional turncoat, and you can perish just as easily I can."

The man went to pull out his weapon, but Velixar was quicker. One violent swing batted Handrick's sword arm aside, shattering bone. A shriek left the captain's throat as he stared at his flopping appendage. Velixar grabbed him around the back of the neck with his left hand, then latched onto his lower jaw with his right, his fingers beneath the captain's chin, his thumb pressed against the inset of his lower teeth. Handrick struggled, but his strength was no match for his opponent's.

"You sealed your fate," Velixar whispered in his ear. "You shall never utter that accursed name again."

With one mighty tug, he tore Captain Handrick's lower jaw free from his face, ripping tendons and crushing bone and cartilage. The tongue severed from the lower palette and flopped against the captain's chest in a great spray of blood. Handrick tottered backward, eyes bulging as he desperately swiped at the empty space where his jaw had been, gripping his flopping tongue like it was a slithering worm. He collapsed onto the floor, his whole body quaking, a red stain spreading from his chest all the way down to his belt. A wheezing gurgle was the only form of protest he could offer.

Velixar tossed the mess that had been the man's lower jaw aside, closed his eyes, and spoke a few words of magic. The spurting blood vessels sealed themselves as the gaping wounds were gradually covered by a layer of new flesh, creating a wrinkled divot in the middle of which was the black cave of his throat. The teeth of his upper jaw hung over the cave like yellowed stalactites. In a matter of moments the captain stilled, his breath coming in short rasps as his dangling tongue still waggled in his hand. Velixar knelt before him and placed a hand on his shoulder. Handrick's eyes lifted to him, overflowing with soundless terror.

"As I said, you will never speak that name again," Velixar said. "Nor any other for that matter. You have disgraced your god, your kingdom, and your title, and so I leave you as the helpless, ugly bastard you have proved yourself to be. You have two choices, Captain: you can either learn to live like this or you can take your own life. It is your decision. If I were you, I'd choose the latter."

He stood up and turned away as Handrick began to sob. Lanike appeared on the stairwell, drawn out of her quarters by the sounds of conflict. Her hand rose to her mouth when she saw the horror below her. Velixar looked up at her and smiled.

"Lanike, my dear, please assist the good captain with anything he might need. And as you can see, there is some blood on the floor. Please clean it before I return. I feel it is time to pay our god a visit."

✚

Traversing the miles to Karak's private temple took the rest of the afternoon. Velixar walked the entire way, his heavy black cloak draped over his head, his face hidden by the darkness inside his cowl. No one accosted him on his journey; those he saw in the streets gave him a wide berth, often crossing to the other side of the road when he came within sight. Even the thieves and other unsavory individuals let him be. His legend had grown since he'd return as the dark-cloaked confidant of Karak. He was the undying punisher of the blasphemous, the tamer of demons.

He spent his walk in a sour mood, reflecting on the beast sharing Clovis Crestwell's body and its apparent disregard for Velixar's plans. Darakken had been more burden than help in the months since its awakening. It was a base creature, bred for violence, and its colossal appetite required constant nourishment. Ironically, this was perhaps its most useful aspect, as its voracious appetite had helped clear out the dungeons. Several times the demon had dropped to its knees before him, begging to be released of the chains of a shared body, pleading to be made whole once more so its true form could roam free. Velixar always denied it that wish. "When the war begins," he would tell the beast, "when Celestia descends from the heavens to assist her lover, Ashhur, in battle, only then will I free you. Only then will your true purpose be needed."

The city proper disappeared behind him, replaced by fields of turned and muddy soil. There were still patches of snow and ice, sparkling beneath the glare of the descending sun. Few resided here, but he could see the progress that had been made in expanding the city, before preparations for war had taken away all the craftsmen. Incomplete stone foundations dotted the road, and a few rough shanties had been erected. He saw a group of five women huddling inside an open-faced tent, warming their hands over a quaint fire while their children wailed behind them. Their faces were dirty, their teeth rotting from their jaws. These were the downtrodden, the lazy, who accepted their lives of squalor and filth without pursuing something more, something better. When the war was over and the soldiers returned to their civilian lives, construction would continue, and these creatures would be pushed out even farther, until they were forced to leave Veldaren's boundaries altogether.

They were agents of chaos, and Velixar felt no pity for them.

He finally arrived at Karak's black-bricked temple and scaled the steps, passing between the twin statues of onyx lions, mirrors of the ones guarding the gates to Veldaren's castle. He rapped on the heavy, oaken door, noting that the three dots that had always adorned it, representing the three gods, had been sanded away. The door was now smooth and black, ominous in its emptiness. When none answered his knock, he shoved the door open and stepped inside.

Just like the unused throne room of the Tower Keep, Karak's monastery had been cleaned out. The plants that used to line the walls now resided in the courtyard behind the temple. The pews that had filled the center of the room had been disassembled and used as timber for ax handles, bows, wagons, and other such items the army required. In their place a giant map of Dezrel had been painted on the floor by the god himself, a painstakingly detailed atlas showing every hill, valley, township, and holdfast both east and west of the Rigon River.

It was there he found his towering god, bent at the waist and hovering over the map, his giant feet following a path north along the great river that split the land in two, his glowing yellow eyes narrowed in concentration. Velixar said nothing as he approached. He stood in the god's shadow while torchlight flickered all around them. Karak was twice Velixar's height, and his hands were large and powerful enough to crush his head by simply making a fist. Most men were awed by his mere presence, forced to their knees by the Divinity's might. Velixar was not most men. When he bowed, he did so because he wanted to.

"My Lord," he said, dropping to a single knee before the deity.

"Velixar, my son," replied Karak in his booming voice. Rather than looking up, the god continued to trace lines over the huge map with his eyes. "I am glad you have come."

"Is that so, my Lord?" he replied. He rose to his feet once more and stood by Karak's side, where he should have been standing since his creation. Though he had been made by both brother gods, Velixar was convinced that Karak's path of order and discipline was the better.

"It is. I have put much thought into our last discussion and have come to a decision."

"Which is?"

The god's finger, as big as Velixar's forearm, pointed down at his feet. "I have near twenty thousand fighting men in my service, and my brother's Paradise is expansive. Our men are to be divided into four separate factions. One faction will head south, pass through the delta, and fall on my brother's Sanctuary." His finger moved north along the river. "One will cross the river here, across from the west's largest eastern settlement." Again the giant finger moved north. "The third will join with our allies in Dezerea." This time the finger traced a line to the northwest. "And the fourth shall sail along the Gihon, uniting with those Uther left behind in the northern deadlands, and face the spellcasters who live there. The three southern factions will slowly maneuver across the land, burning the areas where they find resistance, gathering as many converts as they can, and they will finally merge in Mordeina, which I am sure my brother will have fortified."

Velixar nodded. "And you will heed my advice and leave Ashhur's dark children alone?"

"I shall. Ker will fall after my brother has perished and his surviving creations have joined our cause, swelling our numbers. I fear you are correct about the risk they pose should their current desire for neutrality be broken. Once we have victory over Ashhur, I will leave them no choice but to bend the knee."

"Will you spare them if they do?"

Karak nodded. "Most, yes, but there are few who are too dangerous, their thinking too stubborn. The giant Bardiya, for example. Let those who would cling to Ashhur's simple-minded weakness find order in the life beyond instead."

"A wise choice, my Lord."

Karak stood to his full height, his majestic black platemail shimmering in the torchlight. He truly was an imposing figure. Velixar couldn't understand how any man, even Bardiya Gorgoros, Ashhur's greatest pupil, could deny him.

When the god looked down on him, his expression shifted to bemusement. "Why have you come, my son?" he asked. "I see something troubles you."

"I bear ill news," said Velixar. "Erznia is no more."

"Is that so?"

"It is. The demon Darakken took control of the detachment I sent there. Instead of bringing back the Moris as I requested, it ordered the slaughter of every living being."

Karak's expression darkened. "All of them?"

"Every man, woman, and child, according to Captain Handrick."

"And the captain let it happen?"

"Not only that, he *relished* it. He arrived at the keep this very afternoon, gloating. I taught the man the lesson he deserved, but even that will not bring back the lives lost, lives that would have been valuable to our cause."

The air seemed to grow hot, and Karak's arm shot out. He smashed his fist into the floor, disintegrating the painted depiction of one of Neldar's southern townships. An angry roar left his lips, and the vibration knocked Velixar back a step.

"This *will not do*!" the god shouted, gazing at him with eyes that seemed capable of burning out his soul.

"I understand, my Lord," replied Velixar, breathing deep to stay calm in face of the deity's wrath. He dropped to both knees. "I like it no better than you, but please understand that all is not lost. As much as you love your children in Erznia, the fact remains that they have ignored your edicts for months. I sent Handrick there to force their complicity. Darakken is a simple beast, one that understands only death, destruction, and loyalty to you. It simply doled out punishment in the only way it knows how."

Karak scowled at him, and for a moment Velixar thought the deity would strike him dead.

"You said you could control the beast," Karak said. "This is not the first time it has acted on its own. I do not want my people killed without reason. Chaos lies that way."

"I can control it, and I have. The spirit of Clovis Crestwell still lives and still elicits a small amount of influence on Darakken's actions."

"Yet it went against my decree."

Velixar shook his head. "It did not. It was the *soldiers* who disobeyed, not the beast. They all knew what was expected of them, but they succumbed to their bloodlust. The demon had no part in the plan, had no *knowledge* of the plan. It is *they* who should be held accountable, not Darakken."

Karak's visage softened ever so slightly. "We cannot have disorder in the ranks of our fighting men."

"I agree, my Lord, but that is the way of humanity. They are weak creatures, guided by instinct and emotion. That is the reason I chose you over your brother. He wishes to nurture their deficiencies, whereas you wish to mold them into something more, for only then will their freedom mean anything."

"You speak of them as if they are separate from yourself. You too are human."

"Not any longer, my Lord. Now I am something greater."

Karak chuckled at those words that caused anger to rise up in him once more. So even his chosen deity wished to mock him as Handrick had....

Velixar cleared his throat, trying to swallow down his frustration.

"My Lord," he said evenly, "I understand all of this, and I will work with the leaders of our army to instill a greater level of order and respect among the fighting men. I am Highest now, and they will learn to respect that. However, I must first confront the demon. Although I understand its actions, I agree that it cannot be allowed to operate in such a way, and will show it the error of its ways."

"Do you know where it is?" the god asked, his giant head tilting to the side.

"I do. A scrying spell revealed that the demon remains in Erznia." He swallowed hard, dreading his next words. "I wish to confront it immediately but lack the power to do so on my own."

"You are weakened."

It was a statement, not a question, and unfortunately it was true. Velixar had no dragonglass mirror to step through in Erznia, a tactic that had in the past allowed him to move from one point to another in an instant. And though the essence of the Beast of a Thousand Faces had strengthened his innate abilities, and he could ride the shadows, using them as portals just as Karak did, his ability to do so was weaker now than ever, presumably because that power was being exhausted by his newer talents. It would take him hours to cross the hundred miles between Veldaren and the Erzn Forest, and by the time he reached his destination, he would not have the strength to return.

"I am," he said.

Karak flicked his wrist at the torches on the far wall, extinguishing them, creating a deep pool of darkness between cascades of light. He then looked Velixar in the eye, his mouth firm, his glowing gaze as serious as a blade to the throat.

"My power is yours to use, my Highest," he said. His booming voice grew softer, but it still possessed a threatening undertone. "You are my greatest ally, the best of all my children. I trust you with the fate of my kingdom. Do not prove that trust unwise."

Velixar bowed his head. "I will not, my Lord. That is my solemn promise to you."

The god held out his hand, and Velixar took it. Energy surged through him, prickling his fingertips, making every hair on his body stand on end. It felt as if his chest had swelled to twice its size by the time he released the deity's hand and stepped into the darkness between the torches. He closed his eyes, concentrated on his destination, and was overwhelmed by the sensation of his body being broken down atom by atom.

An instant later he opened his eyes to find himself in complete darkness. When his senses returned to him, he muttered a few words. Flames licked from his fingers, revealing his surroundings to be a small room. Faint streaks of daylight shone through the gaps above and below the door in front of him, intruding only a few scant centimeters before being swallowed up by blackness. When he pushed open the door and stepped outside, the sun was beginning to dip behind the treetops.

The room was an empty shed on the edge of Mori Manor. The pillars on which the house banners once flew had been toppled.

There was blood everywhere, smeared on the sides of the houses, the grass, and the dirt path leading through the center of the settlement. Hundreds of corpses hung upside down from the rooftops on ropes that creaked as they swayed. The stink of death was virtually unbearable.

Velixar moved among them. Men and women, boys and girls, young and old, even infants; none had been spared. Their bellies had been ripped open and their insides devoured, leaving them nothing but empty shells. Judging from the amount of decay, he guessed they had been dead for at least five days, perhaps as much as a week. *The beast has been busy,* he thought. In a way he admired Darakken's fastidiousness. There was an exacting nature to the way the corpses had been hung—by height, ascending and descending and ascending again, as if the creature were trying to perfect its own sort of morbid symmetry.

Hearing the sound of tearing flesh, he stepped away from the dangling cadavers. He strolled down the center of the dirt road, the grooves from the carts brought by Handrick's men still etched into the soft ground. Glancing to the left, he spotted a massive creature sitting cross-legged in front of a small log home. The glimmering pate of the thing reflected the rays of the dying sun as its head moved up and down, up and down, ripping tubes of intestines from the body of the young boy that rested across his lap.

Velixar approached the beast. Clovis was completely naked, and his flesh had been stretched almost beyond recognition, to the point where it was virtually transparent. Hearing his approach, the beast's head shot up. Its eyes glowed brilliant red from the center of Clovis's bloated face, meaning the demon was in full control.

"You seem to have eaten more than your fill," Velixar said.

"My brother-made-master, did you come for me?" the demon asked, chunks of meat and strings of viscera dangling from its swollen lips. It was still strange to hear its odd inflection—the voices of two entities speaking simultaneously.

"I have," he said, stopping before the beast and folding his arms over his chest. "And I am not happy."

"Why is Velixar not happy?"

"Look around you. These people were my god's children, just like myself, just like you. And yet you destroyed them."

"They were blasphemers against the mighty Karak. I promised to sheer the flesh from thy enemies. Have I not done so?"

Velixar sighed. Darakken was indeed a simple beast.

"I do not wish to speak with you, Darakken. I wish to speak with Clovis. Bring him forth."

The beast grinned, showing its sharp, red-stained teeth.

"The little man is sleeping," it said.

"Wake him up."

"I do not wish to."

The creature plunged its claws into the gaping chest of the corpse in his lap, pulling out another sloppy pile of entrails and stuffing them in its mouth. Velixar calmly lowered his head, muttered a few words, and lifted his hands. Karak's borrowed power still flowed through him, and his fingertips crackled with black lightning and swirls of shadow. He pictured the demon's soul dangling by a slender thread, and he snipped at it, severing tiny strand after tiny strand. Darakken winced in pain, spitting out a mouthful of meat and gagging.

"I submit, I submit!" it shrieked.

The thing pitched forward, the body in the beast's lap rolling away as it collapsed face-first into the mud. It lay still for a moment, its rippling, distended form falling still, and then its head lifted and a pained gasp left its lips. Velixar could see the beast's eyes alight with panic, and they were no longer glowing. He stood over the thing-turned-man and laughed.

"Clovis, you fool, get up."

He did so, awkwardly, obviously uncomfortable with his stuffed, swollen bulk. He looked down at himself, at the bulbous forearms and sagging breasts, at the penis that vanished beneath a rolling gut.

Recognition slowly shone through in his stare, and Clovis Crestwell gazed on Velixar with fear and hate.

"Look what you've done to me," he choked out.

"Whatever happened to you, you did it to yourself," Velixar replied.

"I'm a monster."

"You were *always* a monster, Clovis, only not a very good one. You are much more efficient now."

The naked monstrosity turned away from him.

"Leave me alone, Jacob," he said. "Go away. You don't understand how horrible it is to exist like this."

Velixar lurched forward, grabbing Clovis by the shoulder. It sickened him to feel the clammy, sodden flesh beneath his fingers, and he had to restrain a wince.

"You will *not* turn away from me, Crestwell. *I* am Highest; *I* am your master now. You will do as I say."

Clovis swiveled toward him. His form was already starting to lose its extra weight as Darakken's essence swallowed the nutrients.

"What would you have me do?"

"I left you alive for a reason. I could have allowed the demon to devour your soul as it devours everything else, but I need you. You are what keeps the beast in line. And yet you shirked that duty by allowing it to slaughter this entire settlement."

"I had no choice. He is too strong!" Clovis pleaded.

"And were the Quellan too strong as well?"

Clovis tilted his head, confused.

"Another example of your failure, you weak fool," seethed Velixar.

"But…but the Quellan elves are loyal to our cause. Dezerea is ours now that they've taken it! Just as you asked…just as the *Whisperer* asked…"

"You were also told to protect the Meln family from harm. Yet the Lord of Stonewood and many of his underlings are dead, and his wife and younger daughter have fled and are in hiding."

"They acted on their own!" he shouted. "My son…my poor dead son…he told them the terms, and they ignored him!"

Velixar shook his head as if disappointed with his answer. "The betrayal of the Quellan only goes to prove that you never had any *true* power." He grinned and said, "Tell me, do you love your wife, Clovis?"

The swollen man stared back dumbly, then nodded.

"Would you like to see any harm come to her?"

Clovis dropped to his knees and clawed at Velixar's breeches. "No, Jacob, please no! Lanike is my creation and all that I have. Please don't harm her!"

He shoved the pleading half-man away. "I won't lay a finger on her," he said, disdain dripping from every word. "But *you* will. Should you not learn to keep this creature under control, should you allow him to disobey my decrees again, I shall cut the thread that connects you to your body. But I will not kill you. No, I will allow you to look through your own eyes as I set the demon on your wife, letting him use her in whatever way he pleases. What do you think will happen then, you miserable wretch? Will you enjoy watching Lanike flayed alive by your own hands, perhaps from the inside out?"

Tears streamed down Clovis's face. "I will try! I will do it! I will try! I will do it!" he shouted.

Velixar turned his back on the blubbering half-man and sauntered away from him, all smiles.

"Oh, and Clovis, one more thing," he called out over his shoulder as he approached the rapidly darkening forest. "If you call me Jacob one more time, you'll suffer that same fate. Remember that the next time I free you from your cage."

CHAPTER

The sores covering Patrick DuTaureau's thighs stung to high heaven as they rubbed back and forth against his saddle. He cursed softly and pulled back on his horse's reins, slowing to a mild canter so he could adjust himself. Reaching into his saddlebag, he pulled out a vial of greasy salve a man in Lerder had given him, uncorked it with his teeth, gathered a dollop on his finger, and shoved his hand down the front of his breeches. He closed his eyes in relief as the elixir worked its magic. His head lolled back until it rested against the hump in his misshapen spine. *Ecstasy,* he thought. *Pure fucking ecstasy.*

"What *are* you doing?" someone asked.

Patrick turned his head. Barclay Noonan, a youngster from the southern village of Nor, was trotting along beside him atop a scrawny mule. Barclay was all of fourteen, yet his chin was already covered with rugged stubble that put the sporadic growth on Patrick's cheeks to shame. The boy was quite strapping—tall and handsome, with a lean build—and Patrick was sure he had captured the heart of near every girl in his village, living a life of which he, with his twisted, uneven body and grotesquely malformed features, could only dream.

"Tending my aches," he told the boy.

"People are staring," said Barclay.

"Why should they?"

"Well, you moaned quite loudly. And your hands were down your pants."

Patrick shrugged. "Eh, I've never been big on modesty."

"You could have asked Father to heal you."

"I could have, yes. But your father's touched me enough already. Frankly, it makes me a bit uncomfortable."

Barclay gave him a queer look. He opened his mouth, then shut it.

"Just pretend that didn't sound near as terrible as it did," Patrick told him with a wink.

The boy furrowed his brow and backed his mule away without another word. Patrick swiveled in his saddle to watch as Barclay rejoined the massive swarm of humanity—some on horses, most on foot—which swallowed the Gods' Road behind him.

Turning back around, he adjusted his crotch and settled in for the long haul ahead. The sun shone brightly in the center of a pearly white sky, the type of clear spring day that promised warmth even though a chill wind still blew. The landscape was awash with contrasts of color—the vibrant purples of crocuses, the cheery yellow splashes of daffodils, and the brilliant dotted whites of bloodroot on the northern edge of the road seemed to wage a war of attrition with the jade green grasses that grew to the south. Even the landscape was in conflict. While rolling hills packed with wildflowers and thatches of trees lined one side; a sprawling flatland lay on the other. This part of the Gods' Road had always been Patrick's favorite. It was a conjoining of separate worlds that created a singular, complementary canvas.

It didn't seem so inspiring now, however—not after six months of traveling north and south, east and west, sleeping atop his bedroll at night and sitting in his saddle each day. Much of that time had been spent negotiating terrain that had never seen a single hoof of traffic as they visited one settlement after another. *At least we're on the actual road again,* he thought.

Yet as irritating as the travel had been, the duties he'd performed in each of the villages had been unnerving. In Lockstead, Po, Foldenville, Henkel, and countless other locales, both named and not, Patrick would climb down from his horse and join Ashhur's side as the god warned his children of the terrors that would soon befall them. Most often they were greeted with expressions just as queer as the one Barclay had given him. Even when Ashhur spoke of the destruction that had befallen Haven, the township of pariahs that had been nestled in the unclaimed lands of the Rigon Delta before it was blown to bits, or warned of Karak's gathering army, the people tended to just stare in confusion. Patrick wished there were more Wardens with them. The tall, elegant creatures who'd helped raise most of Ashhur's children would have been able to get the point across much better than Patrick, but nearly ten score of them, half of those from Safeway, had been left behind in Lerder to help prepare the most advanced township in all of Paradise for what lay ahead. Many other Wardens had been asked to stay in other townships to similarly prepare, greatly reducing their numbers.

Then again, even Ashhur was having trouble getting through to his people, so perhaps more Wardens would only have muddied the message. The people of Paradise simply did not understand what was coming. They had been sheltered for the entirety of humanity's existence on Dezrel. Theirs were lives of simplicity, of worship and play, of farming and breeding. None had experienced sickness, hunger, or terror. When someone grew ill, a healer mended him or her. When the crops refused to grow on their own, runes were carved in the dirt, and roots took hold. Lives free of hardship had left the people of Paradise with no knowledge of nightmares, and there could be no concern for life in a place where none feared an early death. When confronted with the possibility of war, a concept for which they had no frame of reference, they were helpless. In the end, Ashhur had decided he had no choice but to teach his children to defend themselves as much as he could in the short time they spent in each village, inviting those who were too afraid to remain in their homes to accompany them on the journey west to Mordeina. Few stayed behind. Patrick had once been as innocent as they were.

He was now hardened, an ageless, oddly shaped warrior, both a taker and a protector of life. When Karak's forces had fallen on Haven, he'd been on the front lines of the battle, hacking and slashing with his massive sword Winterbone, putting his life on the line to defend a society of outcasts. Fueling him onward had been his feelings for Rachida Gemcroft, the most gorgeous woman he had ever met, who had accepted him without judgment and was now carrying his child within her...a child he would never know. He had recognized the cynical blasphemers of the delta as his true brothers and sisters, closer to his heart than his *true* family ever had been.

Except for Nessa.

Upon thinking of his youngest sister, his shoulders slumped. Nessa had joined him on his journey to Haven when Jacob Eveningstar—the eventual betrayer of Ashhur—first sent him to the delta. It seemed like so long ago. He hadn't seen her in the months since she'd disappeared with her lover, Crian. Rumors claimed that the impulsive nymph had fled west into Paradise, but there had been no confirmation of the reports. In each village they entered, he described Nessa in painstaking detail, but his search had borne no fruit. When they visited villages that had trained birds—which were few and far between—he penned letters to his mother, asking after Nessa. So far he had yet to receive a response, but then again, the rapidly growing procession of humanity was never in the same place for long. How would the message even reach him?

As they continued their trek west, the Gods' Road curved around a massive hunk of red rock and then opened up, becoming wide enough for five horses to march abreast. Patrick remained at the head of the procession, guiding the countless masses onward. The wavering grassland to his left grew less pronounced, and the hills to his right flattened out. They were now on the border of Ker, a sprawling area of Paradise consisting of wide prairies and long stretches of brutal desert. Perhaps two hours farther west, they would come upon what his childhood friend Bardiya had dubbed the *soul tree*, an expansive cypress that had somehow taken root in the middle of harsh, arid terrain. Patrick felt another of those heart-wrenching pangs. He wished he could see his friend again, could give Bardiya his condolences after the deaths of the giant's parents, Bessus and Damaspia of the First Family Gorgoros. A part of him also wished he could run headlong into the Stonewood Forest and lay waste to the bastard elves who had murdered them. Yet he would not. Bardiya knew of the coming hostilities, yet he stood steadfast against any show of violence.

"Let him be," Ashhur had told Patrick. "I will no longer coerce my children into acquiescence. The choice is theirs whether to fight or surrender."

Patrick thought that was silly, but he stayed his tongue. *Ashhur knows what's best,* he'd told himself. *But I still wish you would reconsider, old friend.*

The road veered in the opposite direction, and the silhouette of the God of Justice, who had moved ahead of the convoy, appeared on the horizon. Ashhur was a magnificent sight to behold, twelve feet tall and wide as a grayhorn, his white robe fluttering in the breeze. The god gazed toward the south, his giant hand shielding his eyes from the sun. Patrick kicked his horse, galloping away from the thousands who followed him.

"Your Grace," he said as he approached the deity.

"Patrick," Ashhur replied, his lips spreading into a grin.

"Something interesting out there?"

The god nodded. "Another settlement."

"Another?" Patrick said with a sigh. He followed his deity's stare, cupping his palm against his distended brow. A hundred feet or so from the road was a ridge of red clay, and below it he could see a thin plume of smoke. There looked to be a single wooden construction surrounded by a great many tents arranged in a circle. "What's this one called?"

"Grassmere."

"Funny name for a hamlet, considering there's nothing but dirt and twine down there."

"Places are often named for that which the residents desire to have, but do not."

Patrick looked to the side of his saddle, where Winterbone was fastened.

"If you say so," he said.

Ashhur looked down on him and smirked. "Must you always debase my wisdom?"

Patrick slapped his knee. "Only when I realize we actually have to *talk* to these people, and I'm going to be forced to use these pathetic legs to climb down a slope covered in rocks."

Ashhur laughed, which warmed Patrick's insides. The deity had a laugh that could make flowers bloom in wintertime, coupled with a smile that could light up the darkest night. It was disheartening that both were in such short supply of late.

A family of antelope passed through the grasslands to the east as they traversed the rough terrain leading to the earthy settlement of Grassmere. As had become their custom, Patrick and Ashhur were the first to make the trek. The remaining thousands lingered on the road, using the reprieve to rest their legs, drink from their waterskins, or tend to the tired horses and other assorted livestock that accompanied them on their journey. It was only when Patrick had some distance from the procession that he realized just how *loud* they were. Myriad voices murmuring at once, hundreds of babes wailing, the constant clamor of shuffling feet. In that moment, he realized the *hugeness* of what they were doing. Ashhur had gathered a traveling city with a population as big as—if not bigger—than that of Mordeina. He was glad he'd never stayed behind to see what the land looked like after they vacated an area. With so many people and animals eating, pissing, and defecating, it could not be a very pretty sight. Or smell.

A massive throng of people greeted them once they reached the base of the plateau. Patrick looked all around him and realized there were no Wardens among the populace. He also noticed that as simple as Grassmere had appeared from far above, it was rather complex up close. There were more animal-hide tents than he'd first assumed, a hundred of them evenly spaced in an ever-widening spiral, all tilted to face the central fire pit. After the last tent in the spiral—the largest, as tall as two men; its canvas still covered with the speckled brown and white fur of the creature whose flesh had created it—there was that single wooden building. The granary, he assumed. Arranged in front of it were abundant gardens shaped in interlocking Ts, forming a geometric pattern that stretched out into the horizon. The gardens took nourishment from a series of narrow ditches that zigzagged between them, which were fed from a fresh spring that formed a shallow pool beside the granary.

Ashhur approached the throng, and they dropped to their knees, bending so low their lips touched the dusty ground. He lifted a small child, the six-month-old infant no larger than an apple in his godly hand, and kissed the babe on the forehead. Ashhur appeared solemn as he watched his creations.

"Rise, my children," the god said. "Stand, and greet me well."

The people did as their god told them, their expressions awash with wonder and bewilderment. Just as in every other settlement, the people of this town possessed distinct characteristics—in this instance, deeply tanned flesh, lean builds, and curly, brown- and black-tinged hair. If not for their eyes, which were different shades of deep blue and emerald green, they could have been mistaken for Kerrians, Bardiya's people and Ashhur's darker-skinned children.

Then again, almost every person who lived east of the Corinth was of mixed heritage. Gazing upon the beauty of nearly every face he set eyes on, Patrick had to admit that the results were spectacular.

A short, slender man, whose beard held patches of white, approached them. He bent his knee before Ashhur, taking hold of the god's hand and kissing his fingers one by one. He then rose and smiled. He was missing half his teeth, but those that remained were white as the winter snow.

"My Grace," the man said, "your arrival is a great surprise, and a joy beyond joy. We are honored that you grace our home with your sacred presence."

"And it is my honor to have come, Felton Freeman. Consider yourselves blessed."

The elder looked up, wonder making his face shine. "You remembered," he whispered. "I have not visited the Sanctuary in thirty years, yet you remembered."

"Of course, my child," replied the deity. "I always remember."

Patrick chuckled. It hadn't surprised him that Ashhur knew the names of the elders of every settlement they came across. He was a god, after all, and these were his creations. Yet none ever expected it, and it amused him greatly to see the looks of pride and awe whenever Ashhur greeted his children by name.

Ashhur helped Felton Freeman to his feet before addressing the entirety of Grassmere's residents. "I love you all, my children, but unfortunately the message I am here to give you is not one of spirituality. There are great terrors approaching to devastate our paradise. My arrival is a forewarning of the hardships to come."

"Wait for it," Patrick whispered out the corner of his mouth. Ashhur glanced down at him, frowning, but a second later it happened. Confused murmurs erupted in the crowd, faces looking on with slack-jawed puzzlement. Felton Freeman furrowed his brow and turned to look at his people before facing his god once more. Then his eyes moved upward, to the ridge of the plateau above Ashhur's head, taking in the sight of the massive gathering on the Gods' Road. The man appeared downright stupefied...just like every other man and woman who had heard this speech over the last several months. Patrick at first couldn't understand why his god would tantalize his people with such vague warnings, but over time he had come to understand. One could not confront a naïve people with grave specifics without first preparing them for the telling.

"I fear I don't understand, My Grace," said the elder.

Ashhur spoke once more, his voice rising, booming across the countryside. "My brother has declared war on Paradise. The pact between us has been broken. Whereas once Paradise and Neldar existed peacefully, that peace is no more. He has formed a great army in the east, and he has pledged to cross our borders and bring pain and suffering to all who do not submit. I do not know when he plans to march, nor do I know the size of the force he has built, but I can tell you beyond a shadow of a doubt that he *will come*. My brother is not one to make idle threats, and I have already witnessed the devastation he is capable of wreaking when he fell upon the delta."

More confused murmurs from the crowd, only this time a few voices were raised in panic. Felton frowned, looking small as a mouse before his towering god.

"I still don't understand, My Grace," he said.

Ashhur sighed, running a godly hand through his golden hair. "We must prepare for the coming war. The village must be fortified, and you must ready yourselves for horrors you have never before experienced. I am here to assist you in this endeavor. I will teach you all you need to know, though our time here will be short." The god pointed back toward the ridge of the plateau. "Those who doubt their strength are free to accompany me on my journey west to Mordeina."

A young woman dressed in a sarong of antelope hide stepped away from the mob. She had a suckling babe at her breast, the same child Ashhur had kissed when he first entered the settlement. Her azure eyes flicked to Patrick, and he saw her shudder for a moment before her gaze returned to her deity.

"My Grace," she said, her voice innocent and pure. "Why would Karak wish us harm? What have we done wrong? Is my little Quentin not innocent?"

"He is, and you have done nothing wrong," replied Ashhur. "My brother's motivations are beyond understanding, and I have no control or influence over him. All I can hope to do is protect you as best I can, my wonderful creations whom I love more than my own being."

"Is this a parable?" shouted someone from within the throng.

"A test?" shouted another.

"No," replied Ashhur.

The girl's lips twisted into a half frown and she rejoined the gathering of her villagers. Felton did the same, looking as lost and confused as a wayward pup. They stood as a writhing mass of humanity, talking among themselves, words drowning out words drowning out the occasional laugh or tentative plea. Patrick looked up at Ashhur, and the god leaned over.

"That went well," Patrick said sarcastically.

"As well as it could," said Ashhur, sounding dejected. "They do not understand. Not a one of them. I created them. Their naïveté is my doing."

Patrick shrugged. "No harm in that, My Grace. You wanted to create paradise, and you did. It was wonderful while it lasted. How could you know Karak would turn out to be such a bastard?"

Ashhur turned away without answering, his glowing golden stare settling on the eastern expanse. His expression was blank. Patrick didn't like that look. Not one bit.

The residents of Grassmere split into two groups—those who wished to stay behind and those who would accompany the god on the journey to Mordeina. Two thirds of the populace chose the latter, and they wandered up the slope of the plateau, carrying their meager possessions. Patrick spent the rest of the day lecturing those who remained, mostly young families, on how to protect themselves. They disassembled some of the tents of those who had departed, using flat-edged stones to whittle the tips of the poles to points for spears. As with most every settlement outside of Lerder, there was little to no iron available—even the large granary had been built with interlocking logs tied off with twine—so they would have to defend themselves with what they had. He instructed a group of men to dig into the soil and gather as many large rocks as they could to hurl at the enemy, and he made man and woman alike form a line and showed them how to thrust with the pointy end of a spear, describing the sensitive areas on the human body.

"Just like with animals," he told them. "Look for the soft spot, and strike for it." A few from those gathered on the Gods' Road, including four Wardens, came down to assist him in his duties. Stoke Harrow, a man who had accompanied Ashhur on his trek into the delta, helped him put on his mismatched suit of armor, so he could show his students the weak points.

All the while Ashhur sat in the center of the spiraling tents, chanting silently, using his godly magic to bring pillars of brightly colored stone and trees from the earth to form a jagged wall around the settlement. It was an amazing spectacle to see, and the pillars and trees caused quite a ruckus when they emerged from the crust, which made Patrick's teaching efforts all the more difficult.

Not that it mattered. The people took to their lesson as though it were a game, acting as if Ashhur's dire news were nothing to worry about. Frustrating as it was, he couldn't necessarily blame them. *You'll learn soon enough,* he thought solemnly.

They were back on the Gods' Road several hours later when the sun set below the western horizon. Tents sprang up all across the road, stretching outward for miles, lit by dozens of cookfires. Patrick spread his bedroll out on the packed dirt, far away from the noisy mass of humanity. Pigs squealed and horses whinnied. The scent of cooking meats reached his nose, and his stomach cramped. He was famished, having eaten only some salted beef that morning, but his body was too sore from the day's labor to move. Instead, he took a swig from his waterskin, wishing it were wine, then pulled a pile of blankets atop him to stave off the night's cold. At least he wasn't staying behind in Grassmere, as the four Wardens who'd assisted in the citizens' training had been asked to do. Four less guides to help lead this motley lot.

Ashhur sat nearby, legs crossed, gaze fixed on Celestia's star, the brightest in the heavens. He had spent much of the evening among his people, blessing them, joining them in laughter and prayer. He now appeared tired and worn to the nub, the light of the half-moon forming deep lines of worry on an otherwise perfect visage. Patrick shifted beneath his blankets, rising up on his elbow.

"You look troubled," he said.

Ashhur glanced back at him, his eyes glowing faintly.

"I am. It is an unusual sensation for one such as me to experience."

"What's the reason for the worry? Same as usual, or something new?"

The deity shook his head and glanced down at the settlement at the base of the plateau, with its new multicolored wall.

"I fear this may all be for naught. Those I leave behind do not understand what is coming for them. They will perish, and they will perish horribly. I should bring the whole throng of them with me."

"We go through this every time," Patrick insisted. "Yes, it's awful. But as you said, you can't coddle your children any longer. It's time for us to grow up and make our own decisions, and from what I saw in Haven, growing up is almost always painful. Take solace in the fact that those who come with us will be protected once we reach Mordeina. That is all we can ask for, is it not? And besides, those who stay behind will fulfill their purpose…"

"That is my hope," the deity said with a nod. He looked odd in that moment, more guilty than a deity should ever appear to be.

"Sometimes hope is all we have," Patrick said. "For example, I hope my mother's making progress on that wall you wanted, and I hope the king they crowned is up to the task of leading these people once we arrive, since I assume your attentions will be focused… elsewhere."

That seemed to snap Ashhur back to his old self. "Yes, it is my hope as well. Your mother is strong. Perhaps not strong in the same way Bessus was, but she has her talents. She is the only survivor of my first creations, and she's more than capable. I believe she will teach Ben Maryll well, just as she taught you."

Patrick scoffed inwardly at the notion. He had come to realize that his mother and father had very little to do with the man he'd become. He didn't correct his god, however, for Ashhur knew far more than he did. If Isabel DuTaureau's harsh and distant parenting could make this new King Benjamin anywhere near as strong as Patrick was now, there was a chance Paradise might be saved.

Patrick lifted his waterskin to his lips in a toast.

"To Paradise, to your ever loving grace, and to pounding Karak's ass when he finally arrives," he said.

"As good a toast as any," Ashhur replied, a somber smile lifting his lips.

CHAPTER

"Heave! You, stop that dawdling. There will be time for water when we set this stone. Stop worrying about slicing your hand open. I'll heal it if you do. You— the man with the torn breeches—don't stand there! If that rope snaps, you will be crushed. Is that what you desire? No, no, *no*! Stop jumping on those boulders. Do you think this a game, you fool?"

Ahaesarus took a step backward, throwing his hands up in frustration. Those who should have been working were laughing and cajoling instead. At the rate the stones were being put in place, they would never have the wall built before Ashhur's arrival.

After taking a deep breath to calm his nerves and tugging on his scarred ear, he allowed himself a moment to put things into perspective. It was early morning, the sun barely up long enough to take the haze from the sky, and there were already two hundred people working. The citizens of Mordeina stood among acres of mud, lifting granite blocks—each as wide as a small hut—from the nearby mountains with pulleys made from ropes and felled tree, attempting to swing them into place atop the uncompleted wall. Others stood atop the completed portions, pouring mortar into the gaps before the blocks were nestled into place. The progress they'd made over many months of labor was extensive, yet laughable considering how much still remained to be done. The main entrance was finished, a stone arch that had taken a full week to perfect. The wall in general was fifty feet high and went on in a semicircle for a span of six miles. It would take more than fifteen miles of wall to completely encircle the settlement.

We will never finish in time.

They had received Ashhur's letter describing the events in Haven in painstaking detail just as autumn took hold of the land. Along with that message came a warning of Karak's planned assault on Paradise. The final instructions were to begin construction of the protective wall around Mordeina, the planning of which had fallen to the Wardens. None of the humans knew anything of woodwork or masonry, never mind architecture. Each of the great structures that had been erected in Paradise—Manse DuTaureau, the Wooden Bridge, and the seven buildings in Lerder—had been conceived of and built by Ahaesarus's brethren. Even considering that fact, the designer of these edifices had been a single Warden, Boral, who still resided and worked his craft in Lerder, on the banks of the Rigon, hundreds of miles away. Most of the Wardens had been minor tradesmen in their past lives on their obliterated, faraway world. Ahaesarus, in fact, had been a farmer and a priest. He had risen in stature after his people were brought to Dezrel to become nursemaids, and he'd learned to appreciate his second chance. He had become a strict adherent of Ashhur's laws of love and forgiveness, a teacher whose loud voice served him well in gaining the attention of the juvenile beings under his care. His size and integrity had made him the most prominent of all the Wardens, climbing so high in the eyes of Ashhur that he had been named Master Warden and given the responsibility of tutoring one of the three youngsters who had been tabbed as potential kings of Paradise. He took pride in his duties and excelled at them.

But building a gigantic, fifteen-mile-long wall? He felt out of his league. He and his fellow Warden, Karitas, had painstakingly mapped out the giant oval that would surround the settlement, reconciling which areas of the surrounding forest would need to be cleared, how many massive stones they would require, and from where the stones would be harvested. He was often still anxious when he fell into bed at night, and sleep had become a rarity. The proposition was simply so *huge*. If not for the fact that they had Mordeina's thirty thousand residents at their disposal, they would have been lucky to raise even one section of wall.

Eveningstar would have been better suited for this work, he thought, and then shook his head in disgust. Jacob Eveningstar was a traitor who had turned on them all. It appalled him that he had not seen that betrayal coming. Ahaesarus had always considered himself a stickler for detail, yet he'd ignored all the signs. The fact that Benjamin Maryll, the boy who now was king, had been a chronic underachiever under Jacob's tutelage, only to flourish under the Warden Judarius's watchful eye, should have been sign enough that something was amiss.

He shrugged aside his guilt and threw back his shoulders.

"Get moving, you idle ingrates!" he shouted. "This wall is not going to build itself!"

He received countless groans and complaints in reply.

"What seems to be the problem, Master Warden?"

Ahaesarus looked to his right. Isabel, the matriarch of House DuTaureau and Ashhur's second creation, stood beside him. She had appeared from out of nowhere, and her intense green eyes were observing all the commotion before her. She was a tiny creature, but the confidence with which she carried herself made her seem larger. Her clothes were a study of contrasts: her tight-fitting, emerald-green gown, colored to match her eyes, made her look like a goddess of the sea, whereas the bundle of furs draped over her shoulders were more reminiscent of a barbarian. Some commonfolk whispered that her cold stare could turn men to stone, and others said that the bright red of her hair was a sign that the fires of the underworld burned in her veins. She was aloof and unflinching, a woman who guided the simple people of Mordeina with a heavy hand. Though she had never been nice to him, Ahaesarus admired her greatly.

"I apologize, Isabel. I did not hear you approach," he said.

"You should pay better attention," she said coldly.

"Perhaps you are correct."

"You didn't answer my question, Master Warden. What is the problem here?"

Ahaesarus cleared his throat. "I am simply trying to motivate the workers. They are easily distracted."

"They are. As well you would be too if you had only known a life of comfort."

"I have been in this world as long as you, Isabel."

As the woman gazed up at him, her steely gaze narrowed.

"Yet you also lived through war and hardship none here could imagine," she said to him. Her tone wasn't necessarily cruel, but there was an accusation there that made him feel like a child, even though he had outlived her by nearly a hundred years. "You cannot treat these people like they are your fellow Wardens. They are naïve, simple folk. They cannot wrap their heads around the concept of losing the safety they've always known. They don't understand it, and I fear they won't until Karak's Army stands before them."

"You have lived just as they have. How can *you* understand it?" he asked

Isabel offered him the chilliest smile he had ever seen.

"I may not have lived through the genocide of my people as you Wardens have done, but I have experienced my own hardships. I have never claimed to understand yours, so do not belittle mine."

He bowed his head. "Many apologies, Isabel. I meant no disrespect."

"Yet disrespect you did."

Ahaesarus had no retort for that.

The tiny woman cleared her throat. "Be that as it may, you are forgiven. Your presence in our settlement has been a blessing during trying times, and for that I am thankful."

He grabbed her hand, brought it to his lips, and kissed it.

"It is my honor, Isabel," he said.

She pulled her hand away as if he were diseased and frowned at him.

"I am sure it is. However, my purpose for stepping out of my home at this ungodly hour was not to exchange pleasantries. Judarius has returned from the north with guests. They arrived before dawn, and are now bathing. They will join you shortly."

A sigh of relief pierced his lips. "Thank Ashhur. Why did you feel the need to inform me yourself, Isabel? You could have sent another."

The woman dismissed his question with a wave. "I required air. The homestead grows more crowded by the day. Now, if you'll excuse me, I have a young king to instruct."

With that, she turned from him and walked across the muddy ground, heading toward the road that led through the center of the commune, accompanied by five of her personal escorts. Ahaesarus brought his attention back to the men working on the wall, who were now fully entrenched in their labor. Though Isabel had reprimanded him, he was sorry to see her go. She hadn't said so much as a word to them, but her mere presence had inspired the workers to new productivity.

He joined the men, helping brace loads and hoist stones. The workers were diligent at first, putting their every strength into the project and singing songs to keep their spirits high, but their exuberance faded as time passed. The complaints soon began, and Ahaesarus was once again reduced to shouting as he tried to keep his distracted subordinates on course.

Judarius arrived during a particularly venomous tirade. Ahaesarus was laying into a man for positioning one of the squared stones so that it jutted a good three feet from the wall instead of falling flush. It was yet another setback. They would have to remove the stone, reapply the mortar, and set it again—an onerous task.

He descended the ladder when he saw his fellow Warden approach. There were four men with him, rough-and-tumble sorts wearing animal hides and heavy leather boots. Each had a beard so thick it looked as though his eyes were peering out from a mountain of fur.

"My friend," Judarius called out. "Look what I brought with me."

Ahaesarus nodded, considering the newcomers standing before him. They didn't look like anything special, simply mountain men with broad shoulders. He had sent Judarius north, to the village of Drake, at Isabel's behest. She had told him of the troubles experienced in the secluded community on the banks of the Gihon River, and of the brilliance of the people who lived there, led by her son-in-law, Turock Escheton. Supposedly they had built four lofty towers to defend themselves against a renegade faction of Karak's Army that had gathered in the Tinderlands. Ahaesarus was skeptical—it seemed dubious at best that anyone could erect so many towering edifices in a scant twelve weeks—but he had sent Judarius to seek them out regardless. If even a portion of what Isabel had crowed about these people were true, they would certainly be a help to the cause, though by the look of them, he had his doubts.

"And your names are?" he asked, trying to hide his disappointment.

Judarius answered for them. "I give you Potrel and Limmen Longshanks, Martin Cleppett, and Marsh Gingo. They're part of the newly formed Colony of Casters from Drake."

"Well met," Ahaesarus said, bowing ever so slightly.

The one named Potrel smiled—he could tell because the man's massive mustache and beard arched upward—and moved past him without a word. The rest of his troupe followed. "Alright fellows, let's show these lugs how to build a wall!" the front man exclaimed, his voice rough and throaty.

Ahaesarus stood back, bemused, and watched as the four men ordered the other workers away from the construction site. Once the others had cleared away, they clasped hands and, staring at the giant stone that had been wrongly set, began murmuring as one in a language he couldn't understand. He looked on in amazement as the offset stone lifted slightly from its place, freeing sticky threads of mortar in the process, and then angled backward and nestled softly in the proper position. The workers who stood off to the side, two hundred strong, broke out into a round of hoots and applause. The four casters turned as one, faced their audience, and bowed.

"Oh…" said Ahaesarus.

Judarius squeezed his shoulder. "I experienced the same reaction when they demonstrated their skills on the Gihon's banks. I wish you could see the towers they've built. They are truly majestic and strong."

The four casters began organizing the other workers, positioning them at intervals along the wall. A few climbed to the top and applied mortar to the next section while the newcomers prepared to lift another giant stone from the mountain…this time without the assistance of the ropes and pulleys.

"How did they learn this?" Ahaesarus asked, astonished.

"They had a capable teacher," said Judarius. "Turock has spent his entire life learning the ways of magic. He had an elf for a teacher, or so he says. He began instructing others a few years back, and I think you can see how effective his methods are."

"Why have we not heard of this before?"

The green-eyed Warden shrugged. "Why would we have? Has there been a need for such talents before now? Turock's quest for knowledge was a curiosity, nothing more. It held no practical use in a land where people possessed all they needed and desired. Until now, Ashhur's magic has always been enough."

"True, I suppose. But the Warden of Drake still should have told us of these happenings."

"There is no Warden of Drake."

Ahaesarus glanced sidelong at his friend. "Why not?"

"The village is but ten years old, created by one man. They never requested the presence of one of our kind, so none of our kind went."

"I see."

"And also, you must take into account that—wait, you up there! Come down here this instant!"

Judarius stormed away from him, his attention now on a laggard who was reclining atop one of the massive square stones. The young man sat up sheepishly and slid down the side of the rock. Judarius loomed over him, then leaned down, speaking words Ahaesarus couldn't hear over the creaking of taut ropes and the grinding of stone against stone as work continued on the wall. Judarius did not look angry, and the youngster responded to his reprimand by leaping into action, grabbing a rope, and helping to drag another piece of thick stone across the muddy earth. Judarius then continued along the line of workers, murmuring words of encouragement that inspired them to dive into their duties with greater zeal.

"Take a break, my friend," his fellow Warden shouted to him. "I will oversee things for now. Get cleaned up and eat. You look pale as a ghost."

Ahaesarus hung his head and walked away from the work site, feeling annoyed and embarrassed. He and Judarius had long held a competitive relationship. They had been together ever since Ashhur and Celestia spirited them from their dying world. Their competence was the reason Ashhur had listened when they'd suggested forming the Lordship. Yet whereas Ahaesarus had come to be known for his terseness, loyalty, and attention to detail, Judarius had gained notoriety for being a great leader and educator. His friend was just as concise and no-nonsense in matters of faith and dignity as he was, but he showed a greater capacity for clemency and understanding. Judarius never raised his voice, and yet he seemed to get his point across with a look and a few pointed words.

Ahaesarus felt himself growing envious of his friend. Judarius had spent humanity's first fifty years in Mordeina, so he already had the confidence of the populace. Ahaesarus remained somewhat of an outsider. It didn't help matters that Ben Maryll, Judarius's adopted student after the death of kingling Martin Harrow, had been named king, while Ahaesarus's student, Geris, was an attempted murderer and raving lunatic who now spent his days bound in darkness.

Thoughts of Geris caused him to touch his scarred ear once more and steer himself toward the road. He was thankful once his feet hit the packed dirt, no longer sinking into the muck with every other step. It was approaching noon, and there were people everywhere. Men and women dressed for warmth strolled blithely along the road, laughing as they watched their children play. Others gathered in large groups, hands clasped, praying to Ashhur to continue their good fortune. To each side of him was a landscape of sprawling, hilly terrain covered with the tents and huts that had been erected by the citizens. The smell of meat and vegetables roasting over cookfires filled the air. It was just another day in Paradise. No one seemed concerned that an enemy force was on its way to reduce all they knew and loved to rubble and ash.

He moved toward the looming Manse DuTaureau, a rambling one-story construction of stone, brick, and elm, elegantly painted with gold, greens, and oranges. The vast courtyard atop the hill on which it sat was teeming with as many people as were gathered below. A cart path split from the main throughway, and he pivoted onto it. The mansion disappeared from view

On either side of the cart path were tall, shoddily constructed storehouses. They had been hastily slapped together with the trunks of fallen trees and hemp rope. The people who'd built them hadn't even bothered to strip the trunks of bark, so a thick layer of moss climbed up the sides of each edifice. It was in these structures that the fruits of summer labor were stored in anticipation of the rough northern winters. At this time of year, they were all virtually empty, ready to be filled again once harvest season was upon them.

Ahaesarus cared nothing for the barns or what was inside them. His goal was the covered stone hollow at the far end of the cart path. The hollow had been the access point of the settlement's original well, but the spring that once fed it had gone dry several years before. Over the past six months it had been modified to serve a different purpose, one that filled Ahaesarus with shame.

He grabbed the edge of the tied-together logs that served to shield the hollow's entrance and lifted it from the hole. He descended a set of rickety stairs between walls made of stacked stone—gray, black, red, and brown. The chamber the staircase ended in was rather large, twenty feet across and just as wide, though the ceiling was short enough that Ahaesarus needed to stoop so he wouldn't strike his head on the dirt-hewn ceiling.

Seven dying torches filled the chamber with faint light. Ahaesarus heard soft breathing and gazed toward the far corner, where the light didn't reach. He saw a pair of slender feet sprawled out on the dirt floor, the rest of the boy's body hidden in darkness. The room stank, as the wooden pisspot had been knocked over, its rancid contents leaking all over the ground. A bowl of half-eaten soup had been tipped over as well.

Grabbing one of the torches off the wall, Ahaesarus slowly approached the chamber's lone, unmoving occupant. The light spread across the floor, revealing the face of Geris Felhorn.

The boy who had tried to murder Ben Maryll scooted backward like a cornered beast, soft-slippered feet kicking until he was pressed tight against the uneven stone wall. The boy yanked on his restraints, which were made of the same tightly woven ropes that were being used to hoist the stones for the great wall. Geris was fourteen now, his birthday come and gone without celebration while he remained locked away in this chamber that never saw the sun. Ahaesarus knelt down before him, frowning as tiny whimpering sounds left the boy's throat.

It wasn't supposed to be like this. Geris had been a strong and capable boy, and Ahaesarus had been certain he would be the first king of Paradise. Yet sanity had fled him when the Wasting struck him; the tumor that had grown in the boy's spine had poisoned his mind to such an extent that he'd become a danger to all around him, even after the removal of the tumor itself. Geris had nearly killed young Ben, ranting and raving nonsense about demons, witches, and imposters. That single act had sealed both of their fates: Ben became king; Geris, a prisoner.

Not that the boy's imprisonment was supposed to have lasted this long. He should have been freed after a few short days, once Ben had been crowned. The greatest healers in all the north arrived at Ahaesarus's behest, laying hands on the ranting child, trying to cleanse him of whatever monster lurked within the dark recesses of his poisoned mind, but he had continued to rage day and night, shouting his delusions for all to hear. Once he had even attempted to bite off Ahaesarus's ear, resulting in the scar the Warden habitually touched. All who examined Geris were convinced that only Ashhur could cure him of his madness, and it was decided by Isabel that he would remain locked in the chamber above the old well until the god arrived.

Though he hadn't told anyone, Ahaesarus was doubtful that even Ashhur could save the boy. Geris's delusions were fierce, his belief in them absolute. Whenever he launched into one of his rants, Ahaesarus would stay until it passed, listening to every word that spat from his lips. The boy did not lie; in fact, Ahaesarus, blessed with Ashhur's talent for detecting truth from falsehood, had never sensed more truthful proclamations in all his life than those that issued from Geris's mouth. He could only conclude that the boy's mind was broken, so broken that not even a god could fix him.

His eyes welled up with tears as he reached forward, running one of his long fingers down Geris's cheek. The boy turned away from him, filthy blond locks slapping against his wrist, leaving a layer of grime on his white flesh. Ahaesarus retracted his arm and wiped the soot on his breeches, his eyes never leaving the boy. Geris's disdain was the final proof he required. Ahaesarus was unworthy of his title, his responsibilities, and of the second chance he'd been given at life. Finally the tears ran down his cheeks.

"I am so sorry," he said while Geris continued to push himself against the stone wall as if he were trying to force his way through it. "Please, Geris," he whispered, placing a hand on his leg. "Please, I just wish to be forgiven."

The moment his fingers touched the grimy material, Geris ceased his thrashing. The boy drew his knees to his chest, gazing at him with blue eyes that seemed clear for the first time since they'd left Safeway.

"It's not your fault," Geris said.

Ahaesarus drew back, astonished, and lost his balance. He collapsed on his side, striking his elbow hard on the packed dirt. He hardly felt the pain.

"What did you say?" he whispered.

"I said it's not your fault."

"You're speaking without screaming. Geris, how do you feel? Do you see the creatures that haunt you?"

"What creatures?"

"The shadow lion, the demon, the witch, the imposter—you have ranted about all of these. Are you saying you no longer see them?"

"No...I don't think so." He looked sane but confused, the yellowish tint of the torchlight attesting to his innocence.

"Please, tell me, boy, what do you remember?"

"I remember everything," he said, his eyes wide as a doe's. "I remember slicing Ben's throat....I remember screaming and being placed in this well, then a pain in my head, and after that…It was horrible, sir….I saw…"

He said something Ahaesarus couldn't hear.

"What was that? What did you say?"

"I saw myself, screaming, falling down a dark hole."

"What hole? What were you screaming at?"

Tears rolled down the boy's cheeks. "I don't know, sir," he said, almost pleading. *"Dreams are portentious."*

Ahaesarus took a chance and inched forward until he was close enough for Geris to lean into him, sobbing against his chest. He held the boy's head, his greasy hair slipping between his fingers. This was the most cogent he had ever seen Geris, and it gave him hope. Perhaps the boy could be saved after all.

They held that position for quite some time, until Geris's breathing slowed down and his cries ceased. At last the Warden pulled back, gazing on the youthful face with its watery eyes and quivering lips.

"Sir?" the boy asked.

"Yes, Geris?"

"I want to go home."

"I know, son. I know."

"Please, sir. Please let me out. You can accompany me on the journey back, and you can keep me tied up if you wish. But I want to see my family again. I want to be *home*." He looked like me might start crying again.

Ahaesarus slid backward, clenching and unclenching his hands.

"I cannot," he said.

"But *why*?"

He thought of Isabel's decree, of how stern she had been. He then tilted his head, showing the boy his ear.

"You see this wound, Geris? You nearly bit my ear clean off. And I am not the only one you have attacked in your madness. We cannot let you out until we are certain you no longer pose a threat to yourself or anyone else, and only Ashhur can decide that."

"But sir, no! Please! I'll do anything! I'm better, I promise!"

"I am truly sorry, but…but…I cannot."

Ahaesarus slowly grabbed the torch off the ground, stood as much as he could in the cramped space, and returned the torch back to its resting spot. Geris continued his protests in between gnawing on the heavy rope binding his wrists to the wall. Ahaesarus gazed at his student, and guilt ripped through his insides once again.

"I am sorry, I truly am," he told the crying boy, "but our god will be here soon."

"I know," said a small voice. "Thank you sir. I…I love you."

Ahaesarus bit back his tears and walked up the steps and out of the chamber. Once outside, he replaced the covering over the stairwell, sealing Geris in darkness once more. Less than twenty paces down the road, he leaned against the side of one of the carelessly constructed barns to catch his breath. This time he could not stop the tears from coming. He couldn't help doubting whether he'd made the correct choice, and when he closed his eyes, he saw Geris's innocent stare, the loving gaze of the child who cherished and respected him. Ahaesarus swore to himself that he would be strong for the boy, for Paradise, for his god. If Geris were indeed cured, he would be released, but only after Ashhur made that determination. In the meantime, he would work better, harder, and longer. The world might have gone insane, but he hadn't, and it was past time for him to put aside his uncertainty and help set things right.

CHAPTER

"Good-bye , my love, you will be missed," said Rachida Gemcroft, the most beautiful woman that Matthew Brennan, the richest man in Port Lancaster, had ever laid eyes on.

"As will you," Moira, the exiled daughter of House Crestwell, said softly. "I will carry you in my heart always."

The very pregnant Rachida eased aside a stray filament of Moira's silver hair and then leaned forward. The women's lips met and lingered for a long moment. Their arms were wrapped around each other's waists, locking them in a lover's embrace. When their lips finally did part, Moira was crying. Matthew stared at them dumbly, aroused by the display.

The night was cool as they stood atop the bobbing pier in Port Lancaster. Beside them was the dinghy set to carry Rachida and her husband to Matthew's galley, the *Free Catherine*, which waited out in the harbor, her sails withdrawn, her forty oars raised. Peytr Gemcroft stood by on the dinghy, tapping his foot impatiently while the women said their good-byes.

"Let's go, Rachida," said Peytr. "It's getting cold, and I don't wish to linger."

Rachida glared at her husband, her lips drawn down in a frown, and then brought her eyes back to Moira.

"Take care of yourself," she said.

Moira touched the pregnant woman's stomach. "I will. Don't worry about me. Our child will not grow up without his second mother."

"Enough," said Peytr. "The galley awaits."

Rachida placed one final kiss on Moira's forehead, paused to give Matthew a curtsey, and then Peytr helped her climb down from the pier and into the awaiting boat. Her back was to them as the high merchant rowed out into the gradually undulating water of Port Lancaster's inlet.

Matthew stepped to the edge of the pier, and Moira sidled in close as the dinghy became small and then smaller in the distance.

"Will they be all right?" she asked, her voice quiet, the question asked as if no answer were truly wanted.

"They'll be fine," said Matthew. "So far as I know—and I know much—the *Free Catherine* is the only fighting ship in all Dezrel. The deck is equipped with nine spitfires, and I assigned twenty of my most loyal men to the crew. They're all experts with a sword as well. Should they find trouble once they make landfall on the Isles of Gold, your friends will be in good hands."

"It's not trouble on land that worries me...."

"Pshaw," said Matthew, throwing out his arm as if presenting the sea to her as a gift. "I *own* these waters. The *Free Catherine* is the finest ship you'll ever lay eyes on. My father laid waste to any brigands who looted our clippers, and I've carried on that legacy. If there's a sailor on this sea who's worth his salt, it's because I trained him. Karak has no army on these waters. Rachida and Peytr will be safe, I promise you. Only the Quellan elves possess ships that come close to ours, and the pointy-ears have no horse in this race."

Moira stared after the fading ship, a frown on her face.

"I wouldn't be so sure about that."

Matthew laughed.

"By Karak, you are pessimistic."

She passed him a spiteful glance.

"Fuck Karak," she said.

Mist rolled in over the water, swallowing dinghy and galley alike. Moonlight turned the mist into a solid wall of glowing white.

"Well, show's over," Matthew said, ignoring Moira's blasphemous words as he steered her away from the ocean and led her down the pier to join his entourage. Six hard men escorted them through the quayside and into the heart of Port Lancaster proper.

Port Lancaster was the third-oldest settlement in all of Neldar, founded in the fourteenth year of man by Matthew's great-grandfather, Lancaster Brennan. It had begun as a quaint township, a mere thirty men and women Lancaster's age who had scoffed at the authority of the Wardens and struck out on their own. Leaving Erznia, they had settled far south along the shores of the Thulon Ocean. It was said that Lancaster had only felt comfortable when he could hear the crash of waves or feel the sting of the salty breeze on his cheeks.

Though the settlement had humble beginnings, a short eighty years later, it had become a bustling city, the most advanced in all of Neldar. Matthew; his father, Elbert; his grandfather Ansel—and, of course, Lancaster before him—had used the great wealth and resources they'd collected over the decades to create a shipping empire. The ocean and rivers of Neldar were Matthew's domain, and no consignment could be sent across the waters without using his ships. He was the highest of merchants, and the king came to beg favors of *him*, not the other way around.

He glanced sidelong at Moira as they strolled along the streets of the city, the soles of their boots clicking on the slate that lined the walk. Superb buildings crafted of stone, clay, and wood rose up around them—shops, lodges, and warehouses that reflected the light of the moon and cast a pale bluish glow over her features. Though not as exquisite as Rachida, Moira was still quite beautiful in the statuesque Crestwell way, her flowing silver-white hair complementing the soft tone of her flesh. She was more than half a century old, but she looked only slightly older than Matthew, a byproduct of the First Families blood that ran in her veins. Feminine and thin, yet exuding quiet strength, she was strangely resplendent in her mannish tight black leather blouse and leggings. Her crystalline blue gaze was intoxicating. The only blemish on her otherwise perfect skin was a thin scar that ran behind her right ear and circled around the back of her head. She told him the injury had been given to her by her sister Avila, without explaining the particulars.

Not that Matthew required the details. He knew of her exile from her family, knew she'd taken up residence in Haven prior to its destruction at the hand of Karak. It was his business to know these things, especially as it had been Matthew's boats that had ferried Karak's weapons from the stoves of Felwood to the Omnmount staging grounds.

That fact had made for an uncomfortable irony when the surviving citizens of Haven came to him for help. They'd arrived by sea, on rafts and ferries owned by Peytr Gemcroft. The quest had been Peytr's idea, the merchant being one of the few residents of Haven who had left Neldar by his own choice, seeking to mine the valuable jewels and minerals that hid beneath the delta's marshy soil. The two merchants had grown close over the last decade, and Matthew respected much about the other man, his eccentricities and sexual appetites notwithstanding. So when Peytr had shown up at his doorstep, pleading to use the walls surrounding Port Lancaster to hide his reviled, exhausted people, Matthew had surprised himself by agreeing.

He'd sheltered them for as long as he could, until the tides of war began to flow too close to his doorstep. Then it was time to send the survivors west to the Isles of Gold aboard his clippers *Twilight* and *Karak's Wind*, while Peytr and Rachida had taken their closest confidants aboard the *Free Catherine*. The Isles was an uninhabited archipelago off the coast of Ashhur's Paradise that he'd discovered during his teen years. Ashhur's children had not claimed the various islands, which hopefully meant that Karak would not think to search there when he stormed through the west.

They approached his estate, a four-story mansion that was the tallest building in Port Lancaster, with a turret that climbed high enough to overlook the wall surrounding the city. His six escorts ushered him up the front walk and into the foyer, where his maids, Ursula, Penetta, and Lori, awaited. The young women gestured for Moira to join them. One held a bottle of saffron and a wineskin; another, a small crate filled with squid dyes.

"Your transformation begins now," Matthew told Moira. She nodded her head to him and accompanied his maids down the corridor, heading for the opposite end of the estate.

"What're they doing, boss?" asked Bren, the head of his household guard. Bren was a rough and fiercely loyal man, his huge biceps and skill with a sword more than making up for what he lacked upstairs. He leaned against the foyer's bookcase, tapping his fingers on the wood.

"Making her look like anything but a Crestwell," he said.

"Why go through the trouble? Why not send her off with the queer and his wife?"

Matthew grinned. "Collateral."

Bren tilted his head, confused.

"Peytr's well has run dry," Matthew continued. "He could not offer me payment, so he gave me her instead. When all of this is over, and Peytr makes good on the land he promised, she'll be sent back to them."

"You took *her* as collateral? You got a wife; you got whores. Why's that tiny tart worth risking so much? Karak finds out you harbored them, and he'll rub you out. He might rub the whole *city* out."

"You worry too much," said Matthew, shaking his head and slapping Bren's shoulder. "Karak won't know. We transport our Divinity's goods up and down the Rigon at the expense of our other trade. He has no reason to doubt us." He displayed his most confident grin. "And trust me, sooner or later you will find out just how much Moira is worth."

"Like at the meeting tonight?"

Matthew nodded.

"If you say so, boss."

"I do."

Bren accepted his words, just as he always did. It was a good thing the man had no talent for reading body language, because Matthew was unable to stop the nervous clenching and unclenching of his fists. It wasn't that he was being untruthful. He truly believed that Karak would never discover his role in helping the Haven survivors flee to safety. His heart was hammering in his chest for a different reason. What worried him was the meeting Bren had referenced, which was to take place later that evening, after the taverns had emptied and the city slept.

He bade his men goodnight and slipped up the stairwell, stopping to peer into his bedchambers on the third story. His wife, Catherine, was fast asleep in their giant bed, a single torch filling the room with faint light. His five children slept with her, sprawled out on the feather mattress, pictures of innocence in their slumber. His eyes lingered for a long moment on Ryan, his youngest and only male child. The two-year-old was tucked into his mother's arms, lips puckered just below Catherine's exposed nipple. The boy was his crowning achievement, the eventual heir to his fortune. Satisfied, Matthew shut the door and proceeded to his solarium on the top floor.

A fire was already burning when he stepped inside. Though Port Lancaster was far south and the true cold of winter never reached them, the night air held a distinct chill nonetheless. He poured himself two fingers of strong brandy and took a seat in his cushioned straight-backed chair, resting his legs on a footstool. The heat from the fire before him illuminated the giant sword that hung above the hearth. He sat quietly, sipping the bitter brew and soaking in the warmth of the fire. Matthew had been born of summer. Sun and warmth made him feel alive the same way the cold made him lethargic and uninspired. It was one reason he loathed his frequent visits to Veldaren, with its gray skies and cool clime.

The greater reason, though, was the Conningtons, the brothers with whom he was set to meet in two hours.

Two hours. He closed his eyes and leaned back, listening to the beat of his heart in his ears. His fingers crept into his pocket, touching the note hidden within. *They asked for this,* he told himself. *And you need it. Your people are starving, and they've promised you food. If the brothers meant you harm, they would have just sent someone to assassinate you.*

True, his inner contrarian stated. *Yet they have tried before and failed. What if this is a new plan for them to be rid of you?*

Matthew chuckled. *Well, Moira can help with that, can't she?*

The brandy did its work, and he fell into an uneasy sleep, only to be awakened from an ill-omened dream by the creak of the solarium door. He jerked with a start and instinctually grabbed the dagger off the table beside him. The fire in the hearth had barely died down, which meant he couldn't have been out for more than an hour. He peered across the room, past the shelves of historical tomes given to his father by the best minds in Neldar and the Quellan elves, past his display cases of stuffed oddities found at sea, until his eyes came to rest on the noblewoman standing in the light of the doorway. Her purple gown was long-sleeved and high-necked, and her bodice had been pulled tight, making her small breasts swell, bringing attention to the moonstone pendant between them. Her hair was deep brown and had been cut short, exposing the scar on the back of her neck, and her face had been painted rosy at the cheeks and light blue above her sea-glass eyes. Her thin lips were twisted into a despairing frown.

"It's time," Moira said.

"Is it? I should've known, considering how pretty my girls have made you."

"Don't mock me. This is horrendous."

Matthew laughed. "You look wonderful, my dear. Much more a lady now than before."

She glanced down at herself in contempt. "It is not me."

"Get used to it, because if you are to hide in plain sight, this is who you'll have to be." He rose from his chair, tucked the dagger in his belt, and approached. "Is everything ready?"

"I saw the dimwit downstairs. He was pacing and muttering."

"Good."

He took hold of her hand. She flinched at first, averting her eyes from his as she brought her free arm up to cover her cleavage.

"Don't worry, Moira," he whispered. "You're here to protect me, not be my concubine."

"I know, it is just…" she began.

"You are uncomfortable. I know. Trust me, so am I."

They exited the solarium and descended the stairs, where they found Bren pacing in front of the estate's front entrance. The bodyguard glanced up at them and frowned.

"We shouldn't do this," Bren said. "Not like this, anyway. It's not smart. We need more people."

Matthew shook his head. "No, it has to be like this. *Three and no more, lest our agreement be broken.*' Those were the terms. I signed off on them."

"Your funeral."

"Don't look so distraught, Bren. If they kill me, you can sell yourself to the highest bidder. Just think, this might be your chance to see just how much you're worth on the open market."

Bren muttered a reply under his breath that Matthew couldn't hear. Moira sighed and rolled her eyes.

As they traversed through the darkened city with but a single lantern to light their way, Matthew couldn't help but wish that he actually felt as flippant about this meeting as he was acting. Beneath his self-assured exterior lingered the feelings of doubt he couldn't quite extinguish. He wrapped his fingers around his dagger's grip and held it tight, wishing the curved and wickedly sharp steel would infuse him with its cold assurance. With each twist and turn they made, his fear grew. By the time they entered a pitch-black alley cutting between two warehouses in Port Lancaster's fish-packing district, it was near suffocating.

And then a voice called out from above.

"Hey, Brennan, shouldn't you be sleeping?"

Before they could react, dark shapes fell from the rooftops on all sides.

"Those bastards," Matthew muttered. "They can't play fair, can they?"

Moira's slender fingers wrapped around his, pulling him out of the alley. Five men stepped into the moonlight, clothed in tattered deerhide, each holding a dirk. They smiled as they approached, and Matthew could see mostly toothless grins emerge from beneath unkempt beards. Bren drew his longsword and waved it before him, shouting for the men to desist.

Without so much as pausing, two of them leapt forward, swinging wildly with their dirks. Bren caught their attack head on, his steel clanking with theirs, the noise of the colliding swords deafening in the night's dead quiet.

The two attackers pressed onward, forcing Bren farther down the street. Beneath the frightened chatter of his own teeth, Matthew heard his bodyguard yowl in pain. The other three men continued to advance on him and Moira from the opposite side. Matthew took a deep breath, trying to steel his nerves. His hand slipped out of Moira's, and he moved to charge with his dagger.

Moira grabbed his shirt from behind with more strength than she looked to have, yanking him back until he struck the wall, knocking the breath out of him. The dagger fell from his hand, clinking off the slate walk. Moira fell to her knees, blocking their way.

"Please, sirs," she said, her voice high pitched and fearful, like a child's. "Please leave my love alone. I'll do anything, anything, but please don't hurt him."

The men halted, looking from one to the other. Finally one stepped forward, fixing Matthew with a mocking stare.

"What, Brennan, got yerself a whore to beg for you? That what you're into now?"

The men fell into a fit of laughter. Matthew wanted to scream at them, but his voice was trapped in his throat.

Moira shuffled forward on her knees while Bren continued his fight somewhere off to the side.

"Please, sirs, I'll do anything," she said. She was close to the one in front, and her hands reached out, clawing for the drawstrings on his ragged breeches. The man gazed down at her, his expression uncertain. He glanced from one of his partners to the other, and an expectant look crossed his filthy mug. "Anything," she said again, giving the string a tug.

"Lookit this," he said, laughing to his partners as his breeches came loose and slid down his hips. The arm holding his dirk slackened, and he lifted his gaze to Matthew. "The whore's eager."

Moira yanked the man's undershorts halfway down his thighs, then whipped aside her dress. Matthew caught a glint of steel as she shot upward, her hands moving so quick they were blurs in the moonlight. A wicked shortsword appeared from beneath the folds of fabric and lace, and she drove the blade into the man's groin. The screech that left his mouth was so loud that it could have shattered glass. Moira bounced to her feet and kicked him, yanking the sword from his nethers with a wet *plop*. Blood streamed into the air as he fell.

The remaining two gawked at their fallen companion, their jaws slack with disbelief. Moira turned on one, slicing upward with her blade. The man reacted too late, failing to parry with his dirk. The tip caught him under the chin, and he stumbled as he tried with his free hand to staunch the blood pouring from his throat. The other attacker leapt at Moira from behind as she bore down on her injured foe. Matthew tried to shout for her to look out, but his voice was faint. His heart raced out of control as he snatched the dagger from the ground and rushed forward, hoping to reach the unseen assailant before he buried his dirk in Moira's back.

His efforts proved needless. Moira plunged her sword in the chest of the fallen man, lifted her dress with both hands, and spun away in a blur of whirling cloth. Her would-be attacker passed through the space where she'd been standing only a moment before, tripping over his own feet and falling face first to the street, his dirk scattering across the stone cobbles. A *crunch* followed as his remaining teeth struck stone, and the man wailed in pain. Moira stopped twirling and looked down at the man before turning to Matthew with cold eyes.

"Finish him," she said, and then she was off again, pulling another sword from beneath her flowing dress and sprinting down the road, where Bren continued his clash with the two remaining attackers.

Matthew slowly approached the prone man, who moaned and flailed as he searched for his weapon. Matthew kicked the dirk, and it clattered away. He planted a boot in the man's side and rolled him onto his back. The face that stared up at him had been destroyed, the teeth nothing but bloody stumps beneath a nose that lay flat against the man's left cheek. Matthew straddled him and sat down hard on his chest, pinning his arms down with his knees. He heard a cry in the distance, followed by another, and he knew neither belonged to his companions.

He finally found his voice.

"Who sent you?" he asked. "Was it Romeo? Cleo?"

The man issued a pained laugh. "Fuck…off," he said.

"I'll make you a deal," Matthew said, leaning in close enough to smell the man's rank, liquor-infused breath. "Tell me now, and your death will be quick."

The man leered up at him.

"It will, huh?" he asked.

The man's leg shot up, catching Matthew in the ass. He pitched forward, freeing his opponent's right hand. The man reached for his side and the knife sheathed there. Panicking, Matthew stabbed without thought or hesitation. His dagger plunged into the assassin's throat, all the way up to the hilt. The man's body began to shake as he stared up at Matthew with bulging eyes. Blood spurted from the gaping second mouth created by the dagger, and then he fell still.

Moira and Bren were by his side in moments. Moira's dress was splashed with blood, but she looked otherwise unhurt, but Bren's left arm was bleeding. Matthew watched silently as Moira tore her other sword from the chest of the man she'd killed and searched all of the attackers' pockets, finding nothing but a small sack filled with silver coins embossed with the fish and hook of Matthew's own house. She handed the sack to him. Matthew sat there for a long while, surveying the five corpses spread out before him, and bounced the clinking pouch in his palm.

The bastards had been paid with his own coin.

"Who were they, boss?" asked Bren, panting.

Rather than answering, Matthew hurled the pouch as hard as he could. It opened, spilling the silvers down the street.

"Waste of good coin," Bren muttered.

"Shut *up*," Moira whispered.

"Yes, ma'am," replied Bren. "Boss, what's the next move?"

Lurching to his feet, Matthew flattened out his blood-streaked clothes, took a deep breath, and then began marching down the road. Bren and Moira fell in behind him. He walked with purpose now that they were so close to their destination. He kept the bloody dagger firmly in hand as he went, constantly on the lookout for more who might wish to do them harm.

He took the path preordained by the letter in his pocket, moving through the fish-packing district, until he reached Rat Harbor, the poorest area of Port Lancaster. Whereas the streets were empty in the more civilized part of town, a few roustabouts still lingered in the streets of the Harbor. Drunk women staggered down alleys—haggard prostitutes who were useless now that nearly all the men had left the city. Matthew grinned viciously. All who saw their small, bloody crew gave them a wide berth. The only ones who didn't were the young ladies who were already sprawled out on the ground, unconscious.

His destination came into view, an abandoned theater at the far end of Rat Harbor. Hard men, strangers to his city, guarded the entrance. They stood and drew their weapons when Matthew, Bren, and Moira approached, but then let them pass without a word of protest.

Matthew didn't knock, instead shoving the door open with all his might. The heavy oak panel swung inward, crashing against the wall. Matthew hurried through, his protectors on his heels, walking into a wide room packed with tables and chairs. A sill filled with alcohol rested against the far wall, and casks of mead and wine were everywhere. The clamor of conversation ceased, as those inside, armed men just like those who guarded the door, turned their attention to the newcomers. They rose from their seats, every hand reaching for a weapon.

"Sit down, everyone," a familiar singsong voice called out. "Don't be rude. These are our guests."

The men grumbled to one another and then retook their seats. Matthew stepped between them, head swiveling, seeking out the ones who'd requested his presence.

"Connington!" he shouted, fingers gripping his dagger so tightly his knuckles turned white. "Get the fuck out here and face me."

"There's no need for rudeness, Matthew," that singsong voice said once more.

Moira grabbed his elbow, and Matthew turned toward the sound of the voice. From behind the curtain hanging along the rear wall of the tavern emerged two plump, bald men, the powder on their skin rendering them pale beyond death. Cleo and Romeo Connington wore draping frocks of crimson and gold, and their chubby fingers were adorned with expensive rings, each set with a differently colored gem. They were outlandish and horrific at the same time, and their high-pitched and melodic voices only heightened the impression. Matthew breathed deeply through his nose, trying to keep his wits against the assault of too much lilac perfume.

Romeo, the elder brother, tilted his head in a curious manner. "Why are your weapons drawn, Matthew? Do you wish to murder us?"

"Perhaps."

"And to aid you in this endeavor," said Cleo, the younger, "you bring a man with a wounded arm and a pretty lass with a sword. Forgive me if I am not impressed with your…um, army."

"We only brought what you told us to," Matthew shot back.

Romeo stepped forward, holding his hands out in supplication.

"Come now, Matthew," he said. "Let us not be rash. You were summoned here in good faith."

"Good faith," Matthew growled. "Promises of food for a city in dire need of it. And you use that to try to kill me on the road."

The brothers exchanged a look.

"That explains the blood," Cleo said, shrugging.

Romeo approached him. "May I?" he said, lifting his frock to show he was unarmed. "Matthew, please think on what you say. If we wished to kill you, why wouldn't we make the attempt *now*, when you are surrounded by dozens of our armed men? Honestly, if you believe we are behind the attempt on your life, I'm stunned that you would come here. Of course," he snickered, "you did bring protection."

"If not you, then who?" asked Moira, joining Matthew at his side.

Cleo's smile grew all the wider—and more sickening.

"Could it be?" he asked. "Is this the lost Crestwell? We thought you had perished back in the delta. My dear Moira, you look absolutely ravishing. That hair color is quite fetching on you."

"Yes," added Romeo. "The Crestwell silver is…unsavory. Too shiny, too straight, too unseemly for a person of dignity." He ran a hand over his own waxed and powdered head. "Hence our own decision to remain bald."

"Dignity?" scoffed Moira. "What would *you* know of that word?"

"Not much, it is true," said Cleo. "But you cannot censure us for trying."

Matthew threw his hands up. "*Enough* of this!" he said. "Answer the question. If you did not try to kill me, then who did?"

Romeo's expression darkened. "I don't know, and frankly I don't care. Affairs in this city are your business, Matthew. Perhaps you should tighten security and keep a more zealous eye on those closest to you. To cast blame on us is an insult."

"Don't feign indignation, Romeo. You've attempted to kill and discredit me before."

"That is true," said Cleo with a sigh. "We certainly have had our differences, but the world has changed."

Matthew gritted his teeth. "How so?"

The brothers exchanged a glance, then Romeo stepped back, pushing aside the curtain from which they'd appeared. "I think some things are best discussed in private. If you would…"

Cleo stepped through the curtain. Matthew hesitated for a moment, then looked at his companions. His bodyguard shrugged, mouth dipping into a frown, while Moira scowled. All Matthew felt was confusion.

"Very well," he said, and waved his two protectors onward.

Romeo held out a hand, halting him. "I said *private*. You and you alone."

"Whatever you have to say, you can say in front of them."

"Is that so?" He peered at Bren. "Our long-lost Crestwell I can trust, but what of the brute? Is he faithful?"

"He pays me well to be," answered Bren.

"It's none of your business, but he is," Matthew said.

"It *is* my business, Matthew." Romeo sighed. "However, it seems you are intent on being stubborn, and I don't wish for this to go on all night. The three of you can come in."

The room behind the curtain had sagging ceilings and stunk of mold. In the past mummers had used this very room to practice their lines, perfecting the illusion they would then present to the theater crowd. The brothers gestured to the round table at the center of the room, and everyone sat down. Matthew was a mess; his blood still pumped from the failed assassination, and he could not come to grips with the fact that the Conningtons had yet to play their hand. At any moment he expected one of them to pull out a crossbow and drive a dart into his chest.

Romeo and Cleo sat across from them, reapplying powder to their faces as the newcomers watched. Matthew waited, counting his breaths, while Moira spun the handle of her shortsword and Bren nervously rapped his fingers on the table. Blood from the bodyguard's injured arm dripped to the floor.

Finally, Romeo put down his compact and lifted his eyes to his guests.

"I hope you are satisfied with this show of good faith," he said. "We are in this room unarmed, whereas each of you carries a weapon. If you wished, you could cut us down in seconds…though our men would run you through when they found out. Do you believe now that we did not try to kill you tonight?"

"We'll see," Matthew grumbled. "Talk."

"You asked for an explanation, so here it is," he said. "These are trying times, Matthew. As I said, the world has changed."

"Things change all the time," Matthew said. "Like when you took over your family business."

"Such harsh words," said Cleo with a grimace. "True, but harsh. However, our ascension to power brought about a decade of expansion and profit for both our families, no matter the...er, disagreements between us. This new change, on the other hand, has not been lucrative for those of our ilk. In fact, it could very well mean the end of everything we've worked for."

Matthew leaned forward, resting his elbow on the table. Moira mirrored him.

"I have a question for you, Matthew," said Romeo. "In the six months since the attack on Haven, have your profits increased or decreased?"

"Why?"

"Humor us."

"Of course they've lessened," he replied, rubbing his forehead. "The realm prepares for war. It is to be expected."

Cleo smirked. "Ah, Matthew, how very partisan of you. The sacrifices you make in the name of your god are truly admirable."

It was impossible to ignore his sarcasm.

"Yet answer me this," added Romeo. "Did these 'sacrifices' begin after the attack or before our beloved deity returned from his extended sojourn?"

Matthew thought on it a moment. His frayed nerves began to knit back together, a sense of looming dread taking its place.

"Before," he answered. "The conscription has been going on for more than a year."

"Oh, yes," said Cleo, clapping his hands together. "He is beginning to see, Brother! Now tell me this, Matthew; do you love Karak?"

"Well, yes," he said, hesitant. "Without him, we would not have all we do."

Moira laughed from beside him.

"Have you ever *met* Karak?" asked Romeo.

Matthew shook his head and rolled his eyes. "Of course not. He left Neldar before I was born."

"Yet he has since returned, has he not? Has he not come calling on you in this city, which is perhaps the greatest in the realm? When it came time for the war against his brother, did he ever formally request your services?"

"Of course not. He is a god, and my duty to him is preordained."

The brothers glanced at each other and sighed.

Cleo switched his focus to the lithe woman with the sword. "Tell me, dearest Moira, what does Karak preach to his children? What is the greatest wisdom our loving god bestowed on his flock? You were a member of the First Families. Though your dislike for Karak is plain and you are obviously no longer ageless, surely that wisdom hasn't left you."

"All mankind is free to live their lives as they choose, but they must make their own way, build their own wealth, and claim responsibility for their own actions," Moira spoke.

Matthew's frustration grew with each additional sentence of vague innuendo. He lifted his hand, drawing all eyes to him.

"What does this have to do with anything?" he asked. "Did you really ask me to come here secretly, to make myself vulnerable without my full guard, to discuss religion? I thought this was about business."

"Directness!" shouted Cleo with glee. "Our lovely Matthew is learning!"

"Very well," said Romeo. He took a deep breath and continued: "Despite this talk of Karak and war, my first question to you was the most important. I will give you the honor of peeking inside the thing that matters most to us—our coffers. Since this whole sordid affair began, our well has run dry. The three armories we operate are being overseen by Karak's young acolytes, and every ounce of steel is being molded into whatever our lovely deity's army needs. Whereas once the kingdom—not to mention my fellow merchants—paid handsomely for our products, our smiths are now working day and night without pay. Yet we, the captains of industry, must *surely* receive compensation for all the resources we offer, correct?"

"Wrong!" said Cleo, picking up where his brother left off. "We who have kept the kingdom running for the last fifty years are left to suffer as our laborers and products are taken from us in the name of war. Our pockets have been emptied, yet our people have needs. Homes are in need of repair, levees are in need of advancement, ships require patching, and many of the people under our care require medicine. These goods are running low."

"Are you telling me you have no hidden reserves?" said Matthew with a laugh. "You two don't strike me as the sort who go unprepared."

Romeo nodded. "Our people in Riverrun and Felwood are hardly starving, but with each passing day, the reserves we *do* have become ever sparser, and since most of our current laborers are womenfolk who have little experience tilling fields or raising the side of a barn, we will not be able to keep up with demand for long." He grinned. "You know this as well as I, Matthew, for we walked through Port Lancaster on our way here. Your people, your *women*, are starving in the streets."

Matthew grimaced.

"And it won't get better, dear Matthew," said Cleo. "This war has yet to even *begin*, and look how much it has cost us. Once the fighting starts, who knows how long it will last? One year? Five? Ten? And we, the most capable of all Neldar, will bear the brunt of keeping the people fed and clothed and *alive*. Karak will take and take until we have no more to give, and then what? When the war is over, and it is time to rebuild our nation, we will be decimated. There will be others who wish to take what we once had, and we will be in no position to stop them. If you think that unrealistic, consider the brigands who are even now running about the country. They already take what they want outside our townships. What happens when they realize we are too weak to defend ourselves?"

Matthew wrung his hands together. "What you say might be true, *is* true, but what are we to do about it?"

A sly grin came over Cleo's face, but it was Romeo who answered.

"We must ensure that Karak doesn't win," he said.

Moira laughed aloud as Matthew pushed himself away from the table in shock.

"What?" he exclaimed.

"We are resourceful people," Cleo said with a shrug. "In this time of strife we must set aside our differences and bond together to face a common enemy…who unfortunately happens to be our god. If we do, we just might retain the lives we have built for ourselves when all has been said and done."

"Karak will kill us for this blasphemy," Matthew muttered.

"Blasphemy? I think not," said Romeo. "What we propose is directly in line with what Karak preaches. His laws are clear as day. *Do not kill without reason. Do not murder the unborn. Do not take what is not yours. Do not defile the temple of worship. Do not turn away from Karak.* What we will be doing is *adhering* to those principles, not breaking them. Yes, he would kill us if he discovered our plans, but it is certainly not blasphemy."

"And if anyone has broken those decrees," Cleo added, "it is Karak himself. He has turned away from his own teachings by stripping us of the freedom he promised. If his temple is his law, then he has defiled it. *He* is in the wrong, not us."

Matthew dropped his head, took a deep breath. "So this is why we meet at night. You two might not have tried to kill me on the way here, but what you ask is little different. To do this, to work against our deity, would mean signing my own death warrant."

Romeo shrugged. "Could be. But then, we would be doing the same, would we not? The fewer who know, the better."

It seemed so surreal. Matthew couldn't get over the fear that he was being played, that somewhere in the room was a mystical object sending his every word and action back to his deity. But even though he knew not to trust the Conningtons, their every word made sense. Had he been younger and more devout, he would have left the moment they began their profane tirade, but as a high merchant and unquestioned ruler of Port Lancaster, he owed it to his people see if there were an opportunity here.

"What is your plan?" he asked.

"Weapons," said Romeo.

"Weapons?"

Cleo slapped the table. "Yes, weapons. Our cache is empty in that regard. The acolytes load *your* boats with the steel *we* forge."

"What does that have to do with me?"

"Two seasons ago you purchased a large reserve of weaponry from us to outfit your sellswords," said Romeo. "Two thousand swords, battle-axes, lances, mauls—you name it."

"And?"

"And I assume you still have them. We need them."

This time it was Matthew's turn to laugh. "You cannot be serious? You want me to arm your populace with weapons you could very well use against me? And free of charge? Ha!"

"Silly, silly Matthew," scolded Cleo. "We told you in our letter what our compensation would be. Right at this moment there are sixty carriages filled with grain, vegetables, and salted meats from Omnmount sitting a mile from your city gates, just waiting to hear that the deal is done. And we do not want the steel for *us*."

Sixty carriages of grain, vegetables, and salted meats. That amount of food could support the remaining citizens of Port Lancaster for months. Matthew's eyes widened.

"Ah, the deal is looking better, is it not?" asked Romeo.

He felt lightheaded. "Perhaps. But if the weapons aren't for you, who are they for?" he asked.

"We have birdies in our god's army," Romeo said. "And those birdies have told us that the one who now holds Karak's ear is wary of Ashhur's dark-skinned children in Ker. They are physically superior to the rest, perhaps smarter, and certainly more capable. They have been independent of Paradise for some time now, and word has it that our Lord is bent on invading their lands last. The steel is for *them*."

The deal was becoming more and more tempting for Matthew. Part of him tried to steer away from acceptance, but the logical part of him, the part that believed in the words of the god more than the god himself, began to sway.

"And you are willing to take this chance?" he asked. "What if Karak discovers us?"

"The way things are going, we are dead men already," said Romeo with a shrug. "If our time is about to end, we might as well go out trying to do something to stop it."

Matthew sat back, chin cupped in his hand. He was so deep in thought that he barely felt the tug on his blood-stained tunic. He turned to see Moira staring at him, concern in her icy blue eyes.

"A word?" she asked.

"Ah, dear Moira wishes to advise her brave Matthew!" exclaimed Cleo.

Bren rolled his eyes. "Shut it," the burly man said. "I'm in pain, and I don't need to listen to your squealing voice."

"Calm yourself, Bren," said Matthew. He stood from his chair, looked at Moira, and then gestured toward the corner. The slender woman rose to join him.

"What is it?" he asked in a whisper when they were far enough away from the table.

"I am not sure this is such a good idea," she replied. "You brought me here to protect you, and right now, this is the best protection I can offer. Turn them down. Walk away from here."

"I'm surprised at you, Moira."

"Why?"

"You hate Karak more than anybody. I would think you'd be all for their plan."

"I hate Karak, but I am not stupid," she said. "Are you sure you can trust these two?"

He shook his head. "Of course not."

"And yet you're seriously considering working with them."

"Strife makes for strange bedfellows. And besides, everything they've said makes sense. It's not as if I haven't had these very thoughts before tonight, and while I can't trust them, I can trust their *goods*. Who am I to turn them away if they can feed this city? What is a cache of weapons worth when your people are dying in the streets from starvation?"

"You intend to accept."

"I do."

"Then I hope you're not being an imbecile."

He went to grab her shoulder, but she eluded his grasp.

"You don't know me," he said, anger churning in his gut. "Remember, you're my property from now until Peytr pays me back. Disrespect me again, and I'll have you cleaning the privy nightly."

With that he swiveled on his heels and marched back toward the brothers. He bit his lip, half expecting a shortsword to plunge through his back and out his sternum. Peering over his shoulder, he met Moira's cold stare and thanked the gods his harsh words hadn't been met with a harsh reaction.

Stupid, Matthew. Stupid.

Romeo and Cleo both rose from their seats as he approached. Bren just stared at him, looking pale from blood loss. Romeo stepped around the table.

"Do we have a deal?" he asked. Amazingly enough, the fat man seemed nervous.

"We have a deal," he answered, and stuck out his hand.

Cleo began clapping in that queer fashion of his while they shook.

"My only question," said Matthew, "is how I am supposed to get the goods to the people they're meant for?"

"Fear not," Romeo said. "We have that covered. On the last night of spring, we shall send a boat to retrieve them. Until then, enjoy the goods we have given you, which is another great show of trust on our part." He jutted his chin at Bren. "But do not betray us, Matthew, for I'm certain your brute will do little to defend you should we send our master of arms, Quester the Crimson Sword, to collect on your debt."

"You will get what we discussed," said Matthew. "When I make a deal, it is final."

"I know," Romeo said with a grin. "Which is why we came to you first."

They released each other's hands and stepped away. Cleo came up and patted his brother on the shoulder while Bren struggled to rise from his chair. Moira appeared by his side and helped him stand. Matthew hoped his bodyguard hadn't lost too much blood to recover. Though an oaf, Bren really was the best protection money could buy. He nodded to both of them, and they started for the curtain.

"Oh, dear Matthew, one more thing," Cleo sang out before they left the room.

"What is it?" he asked.

"Do you still have the monstrosity your great-grandfather crafted for Karak when the Mount Hailen armory first opened?"

"The sword? Yes, I have it still. Why do you ask?"

"We wish to include that huge blade in our deal. If it would please you, of course. You can pack it in the crates with the others."

Matthew shrugged.

"Fine. It's an eyesore anyway. But why?"

Romeo laughed. "Let us say we intend it as a gift for a giant."

CHAPTER

All had been calm for hours on end. The birds in the trees tweeted; the insects chirped; the water in the stream flowed in a steady, calming rush. Bardiya's felt connected to those birds, those insects, the fish that darted through that water. In this isolated patch of forest outside of his village of Ang, he felt completely at peace while making his morning prayers.

It was true he missed the soul tree, the oddity of nature that sprouted in the plains bordering the Gods' Road, but the journey there and back took at least half a day. As the new spiritual leader of his people, in the wake of his parents' death, he could not afford to be away for so long. Ang and the whole unofficial province of Ker needed him.

A tickling sensation overcame him, interrupting his prayers. He opened his eyes, his body tingling all over, and looked down at his giant hands. They were open in his lap, resting atop his bulbous knees. A brightly colored caterpillar inched across his left palm. On his right perched a butterfly, its gentle wings splayed out, displaying blocks of vibrant orange and yellow.

"Why, hello there," he whispered. He lifted his hands to get a closer look at the two creatures. The insects were illustrations of perfection—each part of them had a design, a purpose. They were the embodiment of the life cycle, childhood on the left, adulthood on the right. All Bardiya had to do to bring the circle to a close was curl his fingers into fists.

Instead, he blew gently across his right palm, sending the butterfly's wings flapping as it rose into the air. The caterpillar he urged to crawl onto the bark of the spruce tree behind him. He then leaned forward, dipped his fingers into the bubbling stream, and splashed cold, refreshing water on his face.

Raised voices pulled him away from his meditations. He lifted his head, water dripping from his chin, and spotted two dark figures swiftly maneuvering down the vine-covered cliff face on the other side of the stream. The interlopers' flesh was dark like his, and one of them held a thick walking stick to offset a pronounced limp. He knew them immediately—Gordo Hempsmen and Tuan Littlefoot. He could tell by the way they carried themselves. Bardiya prided himself on his attention to detail. There was not a man or woman among his people whom he could not identify simply by gazing at his or her feet.

Gordo and Tuan reached the bottom of the cliff face, stopping on the rocks that formed the opposite bank of the stream. Gordo leaned against a tree, his mouth set in a grimace. His hip had been badly injured in the mangold grove the day Bardiya's parents were slaughtered by the elf, Ethir Ayers, and his henchmen. Though Bardiya had mended the man's wound as best he could, it remained painful. "You will limp the rest of your days," he'd told him, "but at least you will not need a cane."

Bardiya craned his neck, staring at the shoulder wound he had incurred that same day. He touched the spot, an eight-inch lump of scar tissue, and offered a silent prayer to Ashhur.

The two men stared at him from across the stream. Bardiya braced his right hand on the ground and rose to his feet. His body was wracked with another spasm of pain as he moved. It was the ache of growth, a sensation he'd come to both honor and deride over the many, many years of his life. Just like his faith, his form never ceased to expand. His height had reached eleven feet, dwarfing each and every one of his people and making him nearly as tall as Ashhur himself.

"How are Tulani and Keisha?" he asked Gordo as he cracked his sore back.

"They are fine," the man replied. "Just as they were when you asked yesterday."

"Each day carries its own burdens and joys," said Bardiya.

Gordo shifted his weight from one foot to the other. "I'm sorry. I do appreciate the concern, my friend."

"There is no need to apologize."

Tuan stepped forward, kneeling before the stream.

"Bardiya, your presence is required in the village square," he said.

"Very well. What is this about?"

"A few things, actually," said Gordo. "A group of men returned from a hunting trip two days ago, telling wild tales. Then two girls who wandered close to the Rigon came running home with reports of soldiers marching on the other side of the river. We would have ignored both reports if Onna Lensbrough had not run up to the rocks this morning, after fishing, with a similar tale. Tuan decided we should call an assembly, if only to quell the peoples' fears, so I did."

"A smart decision," Bardiya said.

"Thank you, Bardiya," Tuan said, bowing low.

"Please, do not bow," Bardiya said. "Save any reverence you would show me for Ashhur himself. I am only a servant among you all."

Tuan looked embarrassed as he rose to his feet and said, "I'm sorry."

Bardiya laughed heartily. "Think nothing of it, Tuan. Now let us go so I may speak with our people."

He stepped across the stream in a single stride and followed Gordo and Tuan back up the steep cliff. Once they reached the top, they exited the thin line of trees. A seemingly endless sea of sway-ing prairie grasses opened up before them, concealing the way back home.

For a normal human, the trek from Ang to the secluded forest would take forty minutes. On his own, given the immense length of his legs, Bardiya could make it in half that. In this instance he took it slow, shortening his strides so he could stay with Gordo and Tuan. He would not show them disrespect by leaving them behind.

When they finally arrived at the village, hundreds of people awaited in the center square. Ang was a quaint village, dotted with simple yet durable wooden shelters sealed with a thick mixture of pine sap and clay. The few tents were used to shield the village's reservoirs of food from insects and other predators. Bessus and Damaspia had quickly learned that any shelter they built would have to be constructed of solid wood to endure the unpredictable weather on Dezrel's lower west coast, especially the massive storms of the late summer months.

The layout of the village followed no particular pattern; there were homes built wherever there was space for them. The whole of the village was now an immensely wide clearing given the fact that most of the trees had been felled to build those many homes. The only true property people had were the shelters in which they lived. All the other land, including the many gardens dotting the land-scape, was communal. There was no trade or commerce or coin; every man and woman was a healer, a craftsman, a hunter, a fisher-man, a farmer.

The center square—an ample, grassy field near the thin layer of forest bordering the coast—was the only place where construc-tion was prohibited. That square was where the people gathered during times of celebration or mass prayer, when game or large fish were roasted over the great cookfire in the center. It was also where the populace gathered during dire times, of which there had only been three in all of Bardiya's life. The first was when the decision had been made to respectfully ask the Wardens to leave Ker fifty years before, the second in the aftermath of the deaths of Bessus, Damaspia, and the five others who had perished in the mangold grove, the third to announce the arrival—and acceptance as equals—of a band of refugee Dezren Elves from the Stonewood Forest. It saddened Bardiya to think of the disagreements during that last meeting.

A great many people milled about their homes as he walked through the village, and he spied the Dezren elves lingering around their huts at the far edge of the settlement. When he came to the center square, he found a large gathering of villagers murmuring loudly. They formed a massive semicircle around the firepit, gazing at the newcomers with expectant eyes. Gordo and Tuan stepped aside, allowing Bardiya to walk between them. He found his close friend Ki-Nan Renald, a tall, athletic man of thirty with skin as black as night, standing among the ranks. Bardiya regarded him with a nod. Ki-Nan was good with crowds. If things became unruly, he would help keep everyone calm.

When he reached the center, the mass of humanity shuffled to their feet, closing the circle. They looked so small to him, countless children pleading with him to quell their nightmares. In that moment a feeling of superiority came over him, a sensation he quickly quashed by falling to one knee and hunching over so he could converse with them at eye level. It was a painful position, but that was a small sacrifice to make in the name of equality.

He spoke the words of assembly—"With Ashhur in our hearts, our troubles are met"—and the meeting began.

A pair of identical young men, barely out of their teens, pressed two fingers to their lips, the Kerrian symbol of truthfulness.

"I am Allay Loros," said one of them.

"And I am Yorn, his brother," said the other.

"I know you well," Bardiya told them, gesturing for them to proceed.

Allay cleared his throat. "Five days ago my brother and I were hunting an antelope through the grasslands," he said, his tone confident yet respectful. "We were near the Gods' Road, very close to another settlement. The antelope was acting as if it were spooked. We had lanced it with a spear earlier in the day, but still the creature ran without tiring, as if no injury had befallen it."

"We hid behind an outcropping of stone," Yorn the twin continued, "and watched it gallop across the road and disappear into the hills. We were about to make pursuit when a great shape walked toward us, dust billowing all around him."

"It was Ashhur," said Allay.

"Are you certain?" Bardiya asked.

"As certain as if it were our own father," Yorn insisted.

"What did he do?"

Yorn said, "He stopped in the middle of the road, where the antelope had disappeared into the forest. He snapped his fingers and it emerged, walking right up to him. Ashhur touched the beast on the nose, and it collapsed dead, right then and there."

"Then others emerged from the east, so many that the land was swallowed by their ranks. Thousands of them. Perhaps hundreds of thousands—we couldn't tell. The noise was unbearable. Ashhur handed a group of men the antelope, then called out. A whole school of the beasts appeared from behind us, undaunted by the crowd. All of them were slain by spears, then taken for feasting. After that, Ashhur and a strange-looking man on horseback set off again."

"Strange looking? How so?" asked Bardiya.

"Strangely shaped," said Yorn. "Red hair, hunched back, but his arms might have been as big as yours."

Bardiya nodded. So it had started. Ashhur was gathering his children, and Patrick was with him.

"Did you reveal yourselves?" he asked.

Allay shook his head. "We remained hidden until nightfall, then ran back home."

"Yet," said Yorn, "I believe our god saw us. His eyes glanced toward our rock at one point, and I felt all numb inside. Allay said he felt it too."

To be expected, thought Bardiya. He looked to the two young girls who had stepped forward with the others.

"Sasha, Marna, please tell me your tale."

The youngsters, both of them eight years old, exchanged a look and smiled. Little Sasha raised her chin with pride. Her skin was much lighter than most who resided in Ang, like cream sprinkled with cinnamon.

"Marna don't talk," she said in her angelic voice. "She don't know how."

Bardiya ruffled her short, curly hair. "That is fine. You can tell it."

"Well, me and Mar were out with Father getting pretty flowers. By the skinny river near Ashhur's big house. Red ones, yellow ones, purple ones—all the pretty ones. We had three baskets full. It was *great*, but no one was there."

"Safeway was empty?"

The girl nodded, then her cheeks flushed. She looked to her friend, who shifted from foot to foot with downcast eyes.

"Go on, Sasha," Bardiya said.

"I can't," she said quietly. "I'm scared."

The crowd around them murmured.

He touched the side of her face, his hand larger than her head. "Go on. There is nothing to fear. I will not hurt you."

The little girl nodded. "The village was empty, but I heard people yelling," she said, her voice shaking. "Lots of them. Mar screamed and fell. I was in the big fat trees, and when I ran to her, I saw scary men on the other side of the skinny river. They had shiny clothes and spears."

"What were they doing?"

Sasha shrugged. "Walking. They had horses. And carts. And... and..."

"And what, my dear?"

She leaned in close to him and, her tiny voice trembling with terror, said, "Heads on sticks."

Bardiya pulled back and smiled at her, humming a soft, sweet tune. He then beckoned the silent Marna forward and wrapped both of them in a hug. By the time he released the girls, they had regained their composure, and Marna grinned at him from behind tears. Their parents came to retrieve them, their whispered thanks barely audible above the crowd's murmurs, and then Onna Lensbrough took center stage.

"My Lord, I need to tell you my tale," he said hurriedly.

Onna was a man fast approaching agedness, with a long white beard and deep crow's feet around his eyes. He was rarely seen in Ang, preferring to sail his *Kind Lady* across the Thulon Ocean's open waters. To find him freely on dry land, before such a crowd, was a bad omen.

Bardiya ran a hand through his own close-cropped hair. "How many times have I told you not to call me 'Lord,' Onna? Ashhur is the only lord of this land. Now tell your story."

"Okay. So I was…well, I was out trawling…you know, the blue-gills are migrating north this time o' year. Then I see these two ships—largest ones I ever seen. Three sails each, tall as the biggest pine tree in Stonewood. They float right on by me like I warn't even there…almost hit the *Kind Lady*. Would've tore her in two."

Bardiya frowned.

"It's not rare for ships to sail through our waters," he said.

"Yes, but…this was different. I was out by the Canyon Crags, near the islands. Never seen a boat try and get through that sui-cide run. And they was going too fast—almost hit one o' the crags, matter o' fact. Too close to shore."

"What were they after?"

"Don't know…but they flew the Lion's flags."

A chorus of gasps sounded. Bardiya looked for Ki-Nan's face, but his friend had blended into the crowd.

Onna continued. "Most ships from Neldar that come our way have different banners like…the hook and fish one. Never seen one with the Lion on it."

"What's it mean? Who were they?" the man asked.

It means Neldar moves at last, Bardiya thought. *Karak sails to Mordeina, and war.* He didn't speak his guess, however; though he had heard of the brother gods' clash in the delta, he could not know for certain if it had happened. Yet these tales, not worrisome when taken by themselves, drew a frightening portrait when put together. Ashhur had turned against his declaration of nonviolence, and now all of Paradise would suffer.

We will not take part, he told himself. *No matter what occurs, we will remain as our god decreed for us to be. It is the only pure way, the only* right *way.*

The throng pressed in on him, working itself into a panicked state. He heard Ki-Nan's voice rise above the others, pleading for patience and silence. Bardiya lifted himself from the ground and towered above them, holding out his arms and humming, beckoning wordlessly for them to calm themselves. They eventually did, dropping back into a hushed state. He lowered his arms to his sides and spoke loudly and clearly, hoping that even those who had not joined the assembly would listen.

"My people," he cried, "I love you, and Ashhur loves you. These events may indeed indicate troubling times ahead, but there is no reason for you to panic. You are safe here. Our land is remote and sprawling, and it is our own. Our laws govern it, laws passed down by Ashhur himself."

"But what of the rumors?" someone shouted. "What if Karak wants to kill us all?"

"Then so be it," he said, earning gasps from the crowd. "Should the brother god march on us, we shall lay down our arms and praise our Lord. We shall praise him as he was and honor his teachings. But it *will not come to that.* The desert is too wide, the terrain too formidable, for an army to risk traversing it. And our shores are protected by high cliffs and a rocky coastline. I believe that if we remain true to ourselves, we shall be safe. If Karak comes for Ashhur, it is because Ashhur has turned his back on his own teachings. We will not. We will remain perfect as we have always been, and no one shall trouble us."

The murmurs grew louder by the time he finished, and he gestured for the people to disperse. Rather than quelling their fears, his words seemed to have cast them into a deeper state of despair and worry. Not that he could blame them. Deep down, Bardiya feared he was wrong.

Ki-Nan lingered after the others had left. He gazed at Bardiya with compassion in his soulful brown eyes. In the months since his parents' death, it had been Ki-Nan who'd helped assuage his sour moods and the feelings of doubt. The man always seemed to know what to say and was as reliable as the sunrise, a fact that Bardiya appreciated more than he could express.

"What would you have me do, brother?" his friend asked. "I know you hid the harshest of the truths from them."

"You know me too well," Bardiya replied, shaking his head. "Honestly, the threats on land don't frighten me. We'll order our people to keep their hunting and foraging journeys to the desert and lower grasslands. No one will step within five miles of the Gods' Road or Safeway. We'll reign in our boundaries and stay out of sight."

"But the dangers by sea *do* worry you."

He nodded. "Our land pushes against the sea. Should any decide to make landfall…"

"The unknowing is the worst part, isn't it?"

"Yes."

Ki-Nan grinned. "If you'll allow it, I will take one of the smaller skiffs and search the Canyon Crags for Onna's lion ships. Would that help ease your worry?"

"It would, Ki-Nan," said Bardiya, feeling greatly relieved. "You would be willing to do this?"

"Of course. Anything for you, my friend. And when I return many days from now, I will have your answers."

He laid a hand on his friend's shoulder, and then they embraced, Bardiya dwarfing even Ki-Nan's ample height.

"Let us pray," Bardiya said, "that those answers are not the ones we fear."

✛

Aullienna Meln watched the gathering from afar. There was a mob of people down there, a sea of simple clothing and dark skin that almost swallowed the gentle giant Bardiya. She hadn't seen that many assembled since the day after she and her ilk had arrived in Ang, begging for sanctuary.

The last six months had not been easy, but life in the quaint fishing village was far superior than it had been in the dungeon beneath Palace Thyne. Here she did not starve, filthy and afraid, waiting for captors to come and take away another of her countrymen. Here she had a roof over her head and was surrounded by people she loved. But still it was difficult. Each day brought with it the fear that Neyvar Ruven's spies would find her and her companions. She was all too aware of the distrustful looks some of the Kerrians gave her, and she found their judgment unfair. She hadn't been among those who had murdered the seven innocents, after all. Yet as Bardiya had told her, no one had died before their time in Ker prior to that day. Her fellow Dezren elves had shattered that.

This discourse between self-pity and empathy constantly warred in her head, threatening to drive her mad.

The only thing that made life bearable was Kindren Thyne, her intended. Although they were required to remain far from the boundary of Stonewood to the west and the Gods' Road to the north, they still enjoyed walks in the empty plains, picnics in the forest, and hikes through the desert cliffs. They spent time alone on a small raft while the waves of the Thulon crashed against the rocks, and even practiced magic together, levitating sticks and lighting tiny fires with the tips of their fingers. They did *everything* together, and with each passing day, their bond became more powerful. During their stay, Aully had turned thirteen and Kindren, seventeen, and he had promised her that as soon as they found a permanent place to live, they would be married.

Married to her love. That was the shining beacon in the distance that kept her hopeful, even though she didn't know if they would ever find a home to call their own. And now, months later, those precious moments they enjoyed alone were becoming few and far between.

Kindren's arm slinked around her waist, and Aully grabbed his hand, allowing him to pull her close. Surprise made her smile. *Just when I'm at my lowest,* she thought. She caught a whiff of his scent, salt and fish and smoke, and she realized she had come to appreciate those smells because of him. His lips kissed the pointed tip of her right ear, and she felt a quivering feeling in the pit of her stomach. She fought the urge to whirl around and kiss him fully, given that so many of her people were milling about.

"What are they doing?" asked Kindren, pointing a finger at the assembly that was just now dispersing.

Aully shrugged. "Don't know. Some talk about gods and soldiers and boats."

"Should we be worried? And why were we not invited?"

Aullienna shrugged.

"Those are their concerns, and this is their village. We're just visitors."

Kindren frowned. "What if this ends up being our home permanently?"

"It won't," she replied in defiance. "It *never* will be. We're going home."

"But Aully…"

She spun around on him. "Don't *'but Aully'* me. We've talked about this. We belong in Stonewood or Dezerea, with our own people. Not here." She huffed from her nose. "And besides, they'll never accept us. We've been here for months, and we're still outsiders. That will never change."

"Aully," Kindren said, "I know you want to go home. I do too. I want to see my parents again; I still love them in spite of their betrayal. I want to walk through the palace and marvel at the paintings of Lords past. I want to explore the crypts and be amazed by history. But that might never happen, and it'd be foolish of me to refuse to accept that possibility."

"So you're giving up?"

"No, not giving up, just being realistic."

Aully pulled away from him, crossing her arms over her chest. "I'll die if I never go back. I'd rather rot in the ground than spend the rest of my life here."

"You don't mean that," Kindren said. "Please, say you don't mean that."

"What if I *do*?"

He dropped his arms, letting them dangle there. He looked so sad in that moment, more a little boy than an elf on the verge of manhood. He stuffed his hands in the pockets of his drab, dirt-smeared breeches.

"If that's the case," he said, "then I don't know you like I thought I did."

With that he walked away, his bare feet kicking up sod as he scuffed them against the grass.

"Kindren, don't go," she called out after him. "I'm sorry—I was being silly. Please come back."

"I think you need some time to think about what's important," he said without turning around.

She heard snickers from beside her and glanced at the six elves sitting on a log beside the cookfire, roasting cubed pork and shallots at the end of a skewer. They pointedly turned their gazes away from her, focusing instead on their mid-morning meal.

Her mother's cabin stood behind the cookfire. Ki-Nan, Bardiya's friend and one of the few in Ang other than the kindhearted giant who treated them as peers, had assisted in building the dwelling, along with the eight other houses for the thirty-two elves who had fled Dezerea after the occupation by Neyvar Ruven and the Quellan elves from the east. *If not for Ceredon, we would all be dead,* she thought. The Neyvar's son had assisted in their escape, a sure death sentence should his father discover his betrayal. Closing her eyes, she uttered a silent prayer to Celestia for his safety.

When done, she looked around her. There was no sign of Lady Audrianna among her people. Hardly surprising. Her mother rarely left the bunker she and her daughter shared; not for the past month, not since she'd heard the horrible news…

Aully crept up the steps and into the cabin, guilt eating away at her. The interior of the cabin was sweltering, and it reeked. She wished the butterflies she'd felt only moments before would return, but Kindren had walked away from her and it was all her fault. She and her stubbornness had struck again.

Her mother lay atop her hay-filled mattress, curled into a ball beneath a thin sheet. Aully sat beside her and shook her gently, but she only groaned in reply. Tears formed in Aully's eyes and poured down her cheeks.

"I'm sorry, Mother," she moaned, trying to wedge her head into the crook of her mother's arm. Lady Audrianna smelled like she hadn't bathed for days, which she most likely had not.

Guilt compounded guilt. Audrianna's condition was all because of her. For a long time she'd kept the death of her sister, Brienna, a secret, thinking her mother needed at least the illusion of comfort, the image of Brienna safe in the arms of her lover, Jacob Eveningstar. But finally Aully could not stand the weight of it anymore, and she'd blurted out the truth about the vision she'd seen as she and her mother sat around a fire one night.

After that night, Audrianna Meln, a woman who'd helped lead an entire realm, had become nothing but a shell. She had even taken to uttering a name in yearning that Aully had rarely heard on her lips—Carskel, the brother she had never met. She had heard stories about how he'd disgraced the family years before and been banished from Stonewood, but no one had told her why. Even Brienna had never mentioned him, and Brienna talked about *everybody*.

Audrianna must truly feel lost to reach toward that name for comfort.

Aully climbed into the bed, ignoring her mother's stench, and scooted beneath the covers. The heat coming off Lady Audrianna was intense, as if she had been running from demons in her sleep. It made sweat bead up all over Aully's body, but she didn't care. All she wanted was comfort, even if she didn't deserve it.

It was then Audrianna's arm swept around her shoulder, pulling her in. Aully's tears came even harder.

"Shush, child," her mother's groggy voice whispered in her ear. "All is good now. Just be still."

Aully did as she was told, and a few minutes later, she heard her mother snoring once more.

Restlessness overtook her. When she was sure her mother was sleeping soundly, Aully slipped out from under her arm and walked to the door of the cabin. She dutifully wiped the tears from her eyes with her drab, loose-fitting muslin blouse. She needed to look presentable when she reentered the world.

She opened the door to find Kindren standing there, his arm propped against the side of the cabin. He stared at her, eyes squinting.

"I didn't mean to..."

She collapsed into his arms before he could finish, her tears running anew. He held her, patting her back, running his fingers through her hair, but still the tears came.

"I'm sorry, I'm sorry," she whimpered.

"I know. I'm sorry, too."

Aully sniffled and said, "I miss them all, Kindren, and they're never coming back. I'm just scared, and want to go home."

"I know, my love, I know," he said, forehead pressed against hers. "One day we'll go home, I promise you. I don't care how many years it takes, or what we have to do. But we'll go home. We'll do it together."

CHAPTER

W ind blew past Ceredon's ears as he sprinted through the forest on the northern boundary of Dezerea. His keen vision allowed him to see in the near darkness brought on by the waning moon, to recognize the maze of trees standing in his way. He easily raced around them, creating a looping trail through the woods. He held the grip of his khandar tightly, the sword virtually weightless as adrenaline took over, propelling his legs forward even faster.

Voices shouted in alarm up ahead, and he steered his path toward them. He heard steel clash against steel and the *whoosh* of arrows cutting through the leafy canopy. One nearly clipped his shoulder when he took a sharp turn, the shaft embedding into a nearby tree.

A dense thatch of tangled underbrush appeared before him, and he leapt over the protruding branches and barbs just as another pair of arrows flew overhead. He kept his eyes on the trees while he flipped his khandar into his opposite hand and searched the ground blindly. His fingertips found a group of jagged rocks the size of his palm, and he began hurling them into the canopy, one by one, with all his might. Someone yelped in surprise, and the barrage of arrows stopped for a blessed moment. He took his opening, pursuing the sounds of conflict once more.

The sounds grew louder, and then he saw them—six elves dancing through the forest, three pressing, three retreating. Those in retreat were Dezren, members of the rebellion that had formed in the shadows to resist the occupation of their city and the capture of Lord and Lady Thyne. Ceredon could tell they were quickly tiring. Their parries were languid, their steps stumbling. Soon they would succumb to the greater strength and skill of their assailants.

It was all very frustrating—never mind frightening—for Ceredon. His family had been guests of Lord Thyne, but they'd betrayed their hosts during the celebration of their son's betrothal.

"Dark times are upon us," had been his father's only explanation. "And we must choose sides wisely."

It was a justification Ceredon did not accept.

One of the defenders tripped, and when he slowed to regain his balance, his pursuer caught him from behind. The elf howled in pain as a wicked blade pierced his chest. The stabber was a ranger of the Quellan Ekreissar—his hair was knotted atop his head in the Ekreissarian tradition, and he was wearing the green- and brown-dyed attire of that order. The bloody khandar withdrew with a wet *slop*, and when the elf fell, the ranger stomped on his head, bringing an end to his pleas by crushing his skull. The ranger's head came up as he scanned the forest in the direction where the others had escaped.

Ceredon snuck toward him, nearly soundless as his feet skated over the bed of nettles and fallen leaves that coated the forest floor. The ranger, whose ears were as highly attuned as his own, spun around upon hearing his approach, khandar held high. The elf's eyes narrowed when he saw who approached, and he visibly relaxed.

"Master Ceredon, I thought you were ahead of us," he said. He bowed his head in respect.

In one swift motion Ceredon snatched the ranger by the front of his leather tunic and drove upward with his own sword. The blade pierced the elf's belly, and Ceredon shoved it in beneath his ribcage. The ranger's eyes bulged from his sockets as Ceredon pushed up, up, up, until the hilt touched his flesh and blood spilled over his lips. Ceredon spun him around, avoiding the cutting edge of the khandar that protruded from his back, and clamped his hand over his mouth. He then guided the convulsing elf to the ground. In a matter of moments, the ranger stopped moving altogether.

Tearing his sword from the dead elf's flesh, Ceredon ran after the remaining four combatants. The *clang* of swordplay echoed throughout the darkened forest.

The two pairs battled it out on either side of a wide maple tree. The one on the left seemed to be faltering faster, so Ceredon ran in that direction. The ranger hacked down with his khandar, driving the rebel to his knees and shattering his sword. Just as the ranger lifted his sword to land the finishing blow, Ceredon took a deep breath and swung. An audible *swish* sounded just before his khandar pierced the back of the ranger's neck. The blade sunk in until it hit the elf's spine. The vibration shook Ceredon's hand from the hilt. He splayed out his fingers as he pitched forward, leaping over the prone rebel.

The ranger gurgled blood, his body going limp. The rebel scooted out of the way, and then his eyes turned to Ceredon. They shimmered, even in the sparse moonlight. Before he could say a word, Ceredon put a finger to his lips and shushed him. Grabbing the dead ranger's khandar, Ceredon slipped around the maple to where the final two elves battled.

The last rebel was in horrible shape, bleeding all over, half of his left forearm dangling by a thread. Yet he fought on, parrying each block he could, going so far as to slam his attacker on the side of the head with his flopping, half-severed arm. The blood loss had obviously made him weak, and one solid strike sent the khandar tumbling from his hand. The final ranger, Teradon, the biggest of the three and the only one Ceredon knew by name, grunted in anger and reared back, preparing to drive his sword into the haggard elf's belly.

"Stop!" Ceredon shouted.

Teradon, taken off guard by the sudden cry, stumbled as he thrust forward. He collided with the maimed elf, and they both careened to the ground and rolled around, arms flailing. Ceredon ran up to them and tried to grab the ranger by his tunic and pull him off, but at the last moment Teradon flipped onto his back and threw out his sword arm. He missed slicing Ceredon's throat by mere inches.

The bloody ranger rose slowly to his feet, twirling his khandar to keep Ceredon at bay.

"Traitor," he spat through blood-dripping lips. The rebel elf lay dead on the ground, the hilt of a dagger protruding from his mouth. Ceredon grimaced and bounced on his feet, ready for the much bigger Teradon to make the first move. He remembered his fight with the human Joseph Crestwell at the Tournament of Betrothal, which felt like ages ago. If not for the human purposefully throwing the match, Ceredon would have been bested. He'd taken Joseph lightly, allowing carelessness and impatience to override his speed and skill.

He would not make that mistake again.

Dancing to the side, he jabbed with short, quick thrusts, pushing Teradon into a constant defense. The ranger grunted, his breathing labored, as his huge khandar struggled to match Ceredon's much faster strikes. Ceredon was a blur in the forest's near darkness, landing tiny cut after tiny cut on his opponent's wrists, forearms, and sides. If he kept this up, Teradon would eventually bleed out.

The ranger had a different idea. He made a massive head swipe with his sword, forcing Ceredon to duck beneath the swing, and then rushed headlong into him, accepting Ceredon's khandar as it pierced his side. They plunged to the ground, the larger elf on top, landing blow after blow with his meaty fists. Ceredon, the wind knocked from his lungs, did all he could to avoid being struck with the full brunt of the blows. Yet even glancing strikes took their toll, and his vision began to spin. Teradon's bloody spittle bathed his face, the raging elf muttering curses beneath his breath.

Teradon leaned back, straddling Ceredon's chest, his hands clasped together over his head to deliver the final deathblow. It was then that his left eye exploded, splattering clear liquid all over Ceredon. The shaft that had obliterated his eye protruded from the socket like a post in a lake of red, the arrowhead dripping gore. Teradon's expression was one of dumb shock as his fingers clutched the shaft, and then he collapsed.

Ceredon helped his descent, shoving the large elf off him. He lay there panting for a moment, relieved to be free of the oppressive weight on his chest. When he finally gathered the strength to sit up, he found the lone surviving rebel kneeling by the base of a maple tree, an arrow nocked and pointed at him.

"I won't hurt you," Ceredon said, struggling to his feet.

"Of course you won't," said the rebel. "I could pierce your heart in a second if I so wished. Now stay still."

There was confidence in the elf's voice, but Ceredon also heard fear there. He ignored the rebel and bent over, picking up his sword.

"Nice shot," he said, kicking Teradon's corpse. "You saved my life, and for that I thank you." He turned to the rebel and glared. "Should you not be saying the same to me?"

The rebel's mouth opened, then closed. His steady aim wavered ever so slightly.

Ceredon shook his head, sheathed his khandar, and walked toward the rebel that had been killed by Teradon. He knew without looking that the survivor watched his every movement, but he didn't acknowledge him. Instead, he knelt beside the body, ripped the dagger from its mouth with a spray of red spittle, and proceeded to saw away at the dead rebel's neck.

"What are you doing?" asked the elf, keeping his voice a harsh whisper. "Leave him alone."

"Shut your mouth," Ceredon retorted, casting a glance over his shoulder, the gravity of which stopped the rebel cold. "I do what I must."

"But—"

"But nothing. Had I not stumbled upon you, you would have shared your friend's fate." The dagger finally did its job, and the head of the dead elf tore away from its body. When Ceredon gripped it by the hair and lifted it, a small bit of spine dangled from the severed flesh of the neck.

Ceredon showed it to the rebel.

"This could have been you," he said. "I hope you appreciate the gift I gave you."

"But…why?" the elf asked.

"Because I wanted to," he answered. "Now not another word—just listen. Tell your people you have a friend within the Quellan. Tell them I will protect as many as I can so long as I am able, but never say my name, if you know it. Should that happen, your only ally will be lost. Do you understand?"

The rebel nodded.

"Good. Now leave."

The elf, wide eyed, finally lowered his bow. He twirled around and darted between the trees, disappearing into the dark recesses of the forest. Ceredon watched until he could no longer see the rebel's outline, then stood, rolled his shoulders, and licked blood from his lips. His face and neck were sore from the beating Teradon had laid on him, but he was otherwise in one piece. He lifted the severed head, stared at the empty eyes for a moment, and then broke into a light jog.

It wasn't long before he ran across the scene of a massacre, stepping into a small clearing to find a battalion of ten rangers of the Ekreissar surrounding a heap of headless corpses. The heads were stacked in their own pile a few feet away. Aerland Shen, the chief ranger, stood in the center of the carnage. His tight-fitting armor, made from the black scales of swamp lizards and waxed to a sheen, glistened in the meager blue light. He held his two great swords, Salvation and Condemnation, out wide. Both blades dripped blood by the cupful.

Aerland's head was huge and nearly square, and his wide set eyes flicked in Ceredon's direction when he emerged from the thicket around the clearing.

"Master Ceredon," the chief ranger said, his speech slow and deliberate, his tone deep like a grunting bullfrog. "Where have you been? You were supposed to be with us."

Ceredon reared back and tossed the head he'd hacked from the rebel's corpse. It bounced twice and rolled, coming to a stop at Shen's feet.

"I heard fighting," he said, "so I followed it. The advance party fell under attack by a group of insurgents. I arrived too late to save your rangers, but I was able to kill two of the traitorous bastards before they fled."

"Rebels succeeded in killing my men?"

"Yes. They were taken unawares."

"Yet you live."

Ceredon shrugged.

"Both were wounded, and this time I was the one doing the ambushing."

The chief ranger grunted, cocked his head, and deliberately sheathed one of his two frightening swords.

"Do not run off again, Master Ceredon. You are under my protection while we patrol. Should you fall prey to the insurgents, the Neyvar will make sure it's *my* head on that pile."

Crossing his arms over his chest, Ceredon said, "I am under your protection, but not your orders, Chief Shen. Should you have a problem with that, you can take it up with my father."

Shen pointed the other sword at him and then slid it into the scabbard on his back beside its twin.

"Watch the way you speak, young prince," he said.

The Ekreissar went about clearing the area. A group of twelve Dezren was summoned with six flat carts, onto which they slung the corpses of their renegade brothers. Ceredon tried to appear untroubled though he raged on the inside. These elves were cousins to his kind, two races created by the hands of the same goddess. Yet now the Quellan were considered the Dezren's betters. Any Dezren elf who refused to bow before the Neyvar was thrown into the dungeons beneath Palace Thyne. The populace lived in fear, knowing that the slightest word might be taken as an offense worthy of execution.

He had argued vehemently with his father when he first caught wind of the plot to occupy the city. The Neyvar had chastised him and then locked him in his chambers for days without food. In the end, Ceredon had yielded. If he were to save these people, he would do it from the inside, with the support of an entire nation at his back.

His first act had been to free the Dezren of Stonewood from their cages, allowing them to flee the emerald city, and it was Aullienna Meln's face he saw on the body of each dead elven girl that was carted past the palace gates. He wondered how she was, whether she were safe. He dreamed almost every night of the precocious young princess who had become like a sister to him.

For you, Aullienna, he thought. *I do this for you.*

As well as for yourself, his conscience corrected. He could not justify the cruelty he'd witnessed. His father was wrong if he thought he could belittle the populace into submission. The rebellion was proof of that.

The Dezren threw the last body on the carts and then collected the severed heads. With a crack of whips, they rolled down the path back toward the city. The Ekreissar followed, forming two equal lines, with Chief Shen in the lead. Ceredon lagged behind, looking at the darkened treetops one last time. He swore he saw the twinkling of eyes among the branches. He lifted his hand and made a fist, his thumb and pinky finger outstretched to either side in the Dezren gesture of unity. If there were indeed any rebels hiding up there, he hoped they saw him. And understood.

✦

Palace Thyne was an immense structure of pure emerald, its spire rising two hundred feet into the air. Ceredon tramped up the steps leading inside, gladly leaving the gloomy afternoon behind. His head pounded from lack of sleep, and his jaw still ached from his clash with Teradon. The spiced tea and wickroot he'd taken to alleviate the pain had not yet performed its magic.

He passed by the Chamber of Assembly, a massive space that functioned as a throne room in a land without a king. Pausing, he glanced inside to see Lord Orden and Lady Phyrra Thyne kneeling before the giant statue of Celestia that dominated the rear pulpit. Their backs were to him, their heads bowed in prayer. He felt conflicted just looking at them. The Thynes had betrayed their own people by allowing his father to tramp over the populace and imprison whomever he wished.

Stop it, Ceredon thought. *You cannot be too harsh on them.* It was true. It wasn't their fault they had been taken off-guard by a gesture of friendship veiling a darker purpose.

Lord Orden cleared his throat, and when his head swiveled around, Ceredon hurried out of view. He continued down the hall, made of solid gemstone, until he reached the entrance to the main stairwell. Deckland, a member of his father's personal guard, bowed and stepped aside so he could enter.

It was a long climb up the fifteen flights of steps to the palace solarium. The sun-filled space was a tall and slender room, its walls smooth and shimmering green, filled with furniture crafted by centuries of talented Dezren hands. His father had once told him that all that remained of the history and glory of Kal'droth, the former home of the Quellan and Dezren before Celestia split the land in preparation for the coming of man, resided in this very place.

Neyvar Ruven Sinistel sat in a high-backed ivory chair positioned before the southwest-facing window, allowing the Neyvar a view of both the immense clearing in which the palace and supporting buildings were situated and the forest city beyond. His father's long white hair was loose over his shoulders, so long it reached his waist. His flesh was as smooth and flawless as Ceredon's own.

"Son, I'm glad you have come," said the Neyvar, his eyes still gazing out the window.

Ceredon approached the chair and knelt beside it. "Why did you call, Father?" he asked.

The Neyvar tilted his head to the side, gazing on him with forceful gray-green eyes.

"I was told you broke etiquette early this morning. You left those meant to protect you."

"I did," Ceredon answered. He spoke cautiously, measuring every word. "I knew the scouts had been sent ahead, and then I spotted a group of insurgents leaping through the treetops. I tried to save the scouts, but I arrived too late."

"I told you not to leave Aerland's side," his father said harshly. "You are my only heir, and you placed yourself in unspeakable danger."

"I am a man grown, Father," he replied, touching the smooth flesh on the back of the Neyvar's hand. "I have lived for ninety-six years. I am more than capable of surviving without a platoon of men looking over my shoulder." He paused, then said, "And I'm more than capable of besting an enemy."

Neyvar Ruven nodded. "Yes, I heard you put an end to two rebels."

"I did."

"How did it make you feel?"

Ceredon shrugged, trying to seem nonchalant. "These creatures are beneath us. Those who betray our doctrines and strike at us with swords and arrows will receive the fate they deserve."

His father withdrew his hand and patted him on the arm. He nestled back into his chair, a strange expression on his face, almost as if he were disappointed. "A hard doctrine. I suppose I should be proud."

"So," Ceredon said, trying to bridge the subject casually, "have you received any word from the rangers you sent out in search of the Melns?"

"No," said his father. "I recalled those rangers months ago and sent them back to Quellassar. Lady Audrianna and her family are irrelevant now that outside parties have 'forgiven' our transgressions. If they live, they are without home or sanctuary. Let them suffer in the wilds. They pose no threat to us."

The Neyvar shrugged his shoulders and closed his eyes. Ceredon glanced around with uncertainty, then stood up and grabbed a second chair—this one simply wooden, though gracefully etched with vines and roses and lacquered to a shine—and placed it beside his father's. He then sat down, staring out at the sparkling emerald city.

"This is ugly business," Neyvar Ruven said after a short silence. "But some find it necessary."

His father's tone was delicate, and every word that came from his mouth sounded heavy with regret. It was a moment of weakness that took Ceredon off guard. He had not spent much time with his father over his near century of life. His mother, Jeadra, had raised him, teaching him his lessons and showing him how to love, and his servant Breetan had accompanied him on hunting excursions, demonstrating how to string a bow and swing a khandar. Neyvar Ruven had always been a lingering presence, one that offered harsh criticisms and pointed words, but not much else. There were times when he wished his mother had remained in Dezerea instead of returning to Quellasar to maintain the city, for Ceredon had come to look on his father as one who existed solely to inform him of his unworthiness.

There was none of that attitude now, and the suddenness of the change frightened him.

"What are you saying, Father?" he asked. It was near impossible to keep his voice from shaking.

The Neyvar turned to him once more, those gray-green eyes holding none of their usual force. He reached over and squeezed his son's arm, though his grip seemed weak, as if all energy had been drained from him in the last few seconds.

"Look upon this place," he said. "Gaze upon the beauty it has to offer. Dezerea is the crown jewel of our people, Ceredon. It says much that Celestia chose to descend from the heavens to help build it. You must appreciate it for that."

"I'm not sure I understand," he said. He felt his eyebrow twitch involuntarily, a nervous tic he hadn't felt since the first time he'd spoken with Aullienna Meln.

His father shifted in his seat, leaned toward the window. He sounded almost whimsical when he spoke.

"You were not yet born when we turned down Celestia's offer to foster the humans, and you were only two when the land was divided to make way for the brother gods and their new children. How much do you remember of leaving the ruins of Kal'droth?"

"Some," Ceredon replied. "I remember Mother gathering our things, and I remember sailing south on the river and the hike that followed, but mostly I simply remember Quellassar being… home."

"Yes," his father said with a nod. "As well you should. After the destruction of our homeland, we were given the Quellan Forest to call our own. Previously there had been naught but a small fishing village there, but we went to work directly, creating a city among the trees."

"Yes."

"We are a capable people, driven and hardened by time and trial. But the Dezren…they have always been the more sensitive of Celestia's children. Lord Orden refused to relocate to the Stonewood Forest, where Cleotis and his small faction of the Dezren had taken up residence long before. He blamed me for our race's refusal to assist in the upbringing of the new humans—and he was right on that account. Because of his innocence, he wished to remain as close to his former homeland as he could. He pleaded with the goddess, and his pleas must have been hearty, for she appeared before his people in this very clearing and, with a touch of her glorious hand to the ground, she allowed their spellcasters to raise the structures you see before you from the very earth.

"Fittingly, the Dezren created a paradise within Paradise. And our people…our people were not amused. It seemed as though our creator were choosing them over us.…We Quellans were being punished again, just as we had been a thousand years earlier, when the last of our winged horses were destroyed during the Demon War. We were being punished for our *strength*. Why should the weak be rewarded with the goddess's assistance, our people said, when we had worked our fingers to the bone to create our city?"

There was no derision in the Neyvar's tone as he told this tale, which struck Ceredon as odd.

"Do you not agree with this?" he asked.

"No," Neyvar Ruven replied. "I do not."

Ceredon shook his head but remained silent, allowing his father to continue.

"To be honest," he said finally, "I felt for our poor cousins. Our way of life is vastly different from theirs. While we Quellan have always taken pride in our strength, hard work, and physical prowess, the Dezren followed a different path. We are hunters and warriors, whereas they are poets, musicians, and mystics. While we built architectural marvels and learned to manipulate the land with our hands, they honed their connection to the magic that is woven throughout this land. We once balanced each other out; we taught them to build with their hands, and they instructed the few spell-casters among our own people. When our singers sing, it is the songs of the Dezren that flow from their mouths." He sighed. "The coming of the brother gods changed that. They…disrupted things somehow. The connection our Dezren brethren had to the weave was weakened. Where once they could conjure great orbs of fire, command the lightning in the sky, and cause barren fields to suddenly take to seed, now it is all they can do to light a torch with their fingers or nurture a few plants to adulthood. I assume Celestia helped them erect this city out of pity."

Ceredon looked at his father in wonder. "But why did this occur? What happened to their magic?"

"The gods took it. Think of it, son. We now have two deities walking on this land. The power it required to create their physical forms must have been massive. They are weakened in their current states, which has made them sieves for magical energy. They draw it into themselves, slowly rebuilding their strength so they might one day regain their lost might. There is not an unlimited supply of anything in the universe, including magic. Balance, my son, every-thing must have balance. The arrival of the two gods destroyed the balance in the land of Dezrel."

"I see," Ceredon said, nodding.

"However, I am in the minority of those who feel this way. Most of our people look down on the Dezren. They feel we have been disowned by our goddess and creator. They gape at this sparkling city and wonder why we were left to fend for ourselves by the sea. Then the anger runs deeper, and they wonder why we were forced to abandon our homes at all for that lesser race of humans. They question the fairness of it."

"And you do not?"

The Neyvar smiled a sad smile. "I have. I have questioned every-thing. It is in my nature to do so. However, I came to peace with our status in this land long ago. I know Celestia loves us, even if she does not show it. I choose to think the goddess is challenging us because of our strength, not punishing us for it. But many think differently. We are the apex, they say, so we should take what we want rather than bending to the whims of a goddess that does not love us anymore. Then, a full four seasons ago, the opportunity to do just that came calling.

"That was when Karak's Highest, Clovis Crestwell, visited Quellassar with a proposal for the Triad, a proposal that was finalized by his son and the Triad soon after the betrothal. His plan was to crush the western god and the Paradise he had created. If we assisted him and his people, Karak would grant us whatever land we desired, upon his victory. We came here under the pretense of friendship, becoming conquerors instead." His voice dropped to a whisper, and Ceredon had to lean close to his father's lips just to hear him. "If not for the brother gods' damage of the weave, the Dezren would have crushed us with their magic the moment we attempted to usurp them. But instead they have *become* the weaker race that many have always assumed they were." His eyes lifted to the ceiling. "Sometimes I wonder if this was Celestia's design all along. A final test we have failed."

Ceredon sat back, shaking his head. "I am truly lost, Father," he said. "Why tell me all this now? Why enslave this city and its people when you don't believe it is right...or righteous?"

When the Neyvar looked at him then, his eyes had regained their hardness.

"I am the leader of my people. It is my duty to carry out the wishes of the best and brightest among us, even if I do not agree. And I tell you now because you are to one day replace me. I am nearly five hundred years old, son. I will not live forever. You must know how to lead, how to sacrifice your personal beliefs for the good of the Quellan Empire. If you do not, our cousins will destroy you."

"I thought you said the Dezren were helpless?"

"Not the Dezren. *My* cousins, your second cousins. The Triad, Ceredon."

Ceredon gaped at his father. The Triad consisted of Conall, Aeson, and Iolas Sinistel. They had held the Neyvar's ear for two hundred years, offering him counsel during times of strife. But the way he spoke of them in that moment...there was fear hidden beneath the Neyvar's outward confidence.

"Are you saying the Triad forced you to do this?"

"I said nothing of the sort. Though there are times, far too many now, when their power overshadows mine."

"So if you had your choice, you would not have overtaken this city?"

Neyvar Ruven did not reply. He simply grunted and turned his back to his son.

"Our time here is done," he said, gazing once more at the bright city beyond the solarium's windowpane. "Leave me."

"Very well, Father," he replied.

"One last thing," said the Neyvar as Ceredon was about to get up and leave.

"What is it?"

"There will be other raids, ones that have nothing to do with the rebellion. Conall is steadfast in his desire to show his strength for... what comes later. Do not interfere with those like you have others. They will involve humans, not elves. And the affairs of elves should always retain primacy in our hearts."

Ceredon bowed, replaced his chair, and left the solarium. He thought he heard his father, the great and powerful Neyvar of the Quellan Empire, moaning quietly as he walked away. A rush of embarrassment flooded him, followed by disappointment. This was what his father truly was? Not some immovable beacon of strength, but a tired, broken old elf? Who was he to bemoan his fate?

Aullienna had remained hopeful and defiant despite her imprisonment and the murder of her people. Then it struck him.

"Do not interfere with those like you have others...."

So his father knew. Of Ceredon's role in the Dezren's escaping
the dungeons, his slaying of the Ekreissar ranger...he knew it all. Ice
formed across Ceredon's spine as he stood unmoving in the stairwell, trying to understand what it meant. He viewed the lengthy
speech in a new light, and one part in particular stood out above
all else.

*"There are times, far too many now, when their power overshad-
ows mine."*

Conall, Aeson, Iolas. The Triad, his father's cousins. They were
the ones who pulled the great leader's strings; they were the ones
who'd ordered the torture and murder of so many innocent Dezren.
His father didn't want Ceredon to offer him absolution or pity. No,
he wanted to refocus Ceredon's rage, to give him a target worthy of
such a risk. The Triad would pay, and pay with pain. All Ceredon
needed was the opportunity...and a wickedly sharp knife.

CHAPTER

Velixar ignored those around him as he stared at his own reflection. He was pleased with what he saw. He looked like the leader of men he'd always known he was meant to be, his long black hair greased and tied back from his scalp, his face dashed with fine powder that lightened his usually tanned complexion. His clothes—horsehide breeches sun-splashed to a golden brown and a pale blouse bearing Karak's sigil beneath a heavy black doublet woven with metal rings—had been specially made for the occasion by the Castle of the Lion's most talented seamstress. The sword hanging from his hip was also custom made—the steel strong but nearly weightless, the pommel carved from moonstone in the shape of a yawning lion, fashioned so that his fingers were engulfed in the lion's mouth when he clutched it. He'd dubbed the blade *Lionsbane*, a fitting name for a sword that would help bring about the victory of his god.

Velixar stepped back from the mirror. He was in Tower Honor's rectory, where each day servants prepared the Highest's garments, stirred the ceremonial wine, and copied onto parchment the articles of Karak's law that were to be read before the royal court.

Large tomes of law were stacked on an oaken slab engraved with claw marks and red roses. The space was large and lavish, each countertop holding jar upon jar of incense, and the walls hung with portraits of Karak. The cupboards were filled with spices, carafes of wine, and clay ewers packed with ryegrass and fennel. The windows were stained glass, each depicting a scene of the gods' arrival in Dezrel. The floor was solid marble, the swirls of dark brown, black, and crimson playing across the expanse like dust in a high wind.

The rectory teemed with activity, the servants bustling to and fro, lighting candles, creating bouquets of flowers, fixing the hair of the young girls who would be carrying bouquets. It was like they were gearing up for an extravagant wedding, but in truth, the preparations were for the ceremony to present the new Highest to the people. Though many in the ruling class knew of Velixar's position, it had never been announced publicly. His time in the sun was about to begin.

The door to the rectory swung open, and the servants stopped what they were doing, bowing low when Oscar Wellington stepped inside. The soldier's mail rattled with every step he took. Oscar was young and eager, and each time Velixar looked into his eyes, he saw only loyalty. He had been second in command of the Palace Guard when Velixar handpicked him to take command of Harlan Handrick's unit. The jawless man had hung himself in a back alley. *A lowly death for a lowly cretin,* he'd thought. *No loss.* Velixar had randomly selected fifteen other men who had taken part in the decimation of Erznia and gutted them in front of the castle. Now their bodies hung beside those of the other traitors. It was a hard lesson, but one the rest of the fighting men needed to learn. According to what Oscar had told him in the weeks since he'd assumed command, they had. Velixar's orders were to be followed, always and forever.

Oscar dragged Lanike Crestwell into the room behind him. The noblewoman appeared flushed and frantic, her cobalt, sapphire-encrusted dress askew. Curls from the mop atop her head drooped into her eyes. He could tell she wanted to brush them away, but Captain Wellington held both her wrists.

"Here she is, Highest, as you requested," Oscar said with a bow, shoving Lanike toward him.

Velixar caught her by the shoulders, keeping her upright. The woman's teeth rattled as she stared up at him. Tears streamed down her cheeks, and he noticed a few of those loose curls were sticking to a small gash on her forehead.

"You hurt her?" he asked, leveling his gaze at Oscar.

The young captain appeared unflustered.

"We did not, sir. She tried to get away when we took her from the keep. She slipped on the cobblestones and struck her head. Not a hand was laid on her other than to pick her up and haul her here, I promise."

He sensed no lie in the man, although it was hard to tell for certain. His ability to read the truth, a gift from Ashhur, had been slowly fading ever since he turned his back on the god in the delta. In its place, his ability to traverse the shadows was growing in potency, though it was nowhere near as strong as he would have liked it to be.

He forcibly moved Lanike to the side. "Very well, Captain Wellington. Shall I see you at the rite?"

"Of course you will, sir. The whole of Veldaren will be there, and my unit will be front and center, marching you through the city and cheering you on."

"They will not be your unit for much longer," he replied.

Oscar appeared confused. "Is that so, sir?"

"Yes. The unit will remain in Neldar, under command of the acolytes, to scour the kingdom for those who have not yet volunteered for service."

"Am I not to stay with them?"

"No, Oscar, for I have need of you. You are a man deserving of the title and privilege of the Highest's Right Hand."

The young soldier froze for a moment, then beamed.

"Thank you, Highest. Thank you!"

The servants hurriedly climbed to their feet and continued with their preparations as Captain Wellington stood, offered a sturdy bow, and then swept out of the rectory. Velixar felt a swell of pride as he watched the young man go. Deep down he knew he'd made the correct choice.

He heard whimpering beneath the clamor of hustling feet and clanking pottery. Turning to the side, he saw that Lanike Crestwell was slowly moving toward the rectory's side exit, her hands held before her, her head down. Her wild auburn curls blocked her face. She looked like a woman who thought the whole world would disappear if only she could blind herself to it. It was pathetic.

"Come over here, Lanike," he said. She froze, her body shaking, and then shuffled forward, the soles of her feet never truly leaving the ground. Velixar reached out and swept the hair from her eyes. Taking a handkerchief from the inside pocket of his armored doublet, he spat on it and proceeded to wipe away the tears from her cheeks and the dried blood from her forehead.

"All of you, leave," he said, raising his voice, and the servants scurried away. He returned his attention to Lanike. "Why did you run?" he asked.

Lanike opened her mouth, but nothing came out. Her sprite's face caved in on itself in despair, and she broke down completely.

He clutched her chin firmly in his fingers and lifted her gaze to his. "There is no need for dramatics, Lanike. Tell me why you tried to run."

"I…I…I didn't want to come," she said, her voice cracking.

"And why not? Do you not want to see my coronation?"

She shook her head wildly. "No, Velixar. I don't wish to see… *him.*"

He knew of whom she spoke. A soft chuckle rattled his throat.

"But he is your husband, Lanike. Do you not love him?"

"No," she said, her words gaining strength. "No, he is *not* my husband."

"Oh, but he is. He is still the one who created you, the one who loves you with all his heart. And he always will be."

She brought her trembling hands to her mouth, covering her face with them.

Velixar sighed. Here was a member of the vaunted First Families, set upon Dezrel to guide the children of her god with strength and honor, yet she cowered with fear. She was as useless as the rest of them. Yet despite that fact, he couldn't help but feel for her. With her nymphlike features and agelessness, she still looked like a child, innocent and frail. His fingers gently touched her neck, feeling the softness of her flesh, and those urges he tried so hard to repress resurfaced. A painful face, a damned name he'd sworn never to think of again, entered his mind.

Brienna…

His pity turned to anger, and he quickly drew back his comforting hand and slapped her face. Lanike's head snapped to the side, snot and spittle flying from her nose and mouth.

"Stop your sniveling," he told the weeping woman. "You will attend the ceremony, and you will stand at your husband's side as our Lord presents me to the populace. You will do it, and you will not complain."

Lanike shrank from him. "Yes…yes, Velixar," she murmured into her fists.

He swept her hands away, and she gawped at him, wide eyed. "Cease your muttering," he ordered. "What is it? Do you wish to be free of this? Do you wish to do no more than sit in your room and mourn the loss of your former life like a broken child?"

She nodded while sniveling.

"You will *not*." He grabbed her by the front of her dress, ripping the bodice as he pulled her close. "There is so much you don't know, woman," he told her. "You don't realize how important you are to the realm. Your husband is key to everything, and you are the only one who can still reach that shredded sliver of humanity lingering within the beast. Whatever happens, you will live, you will endure, and you will stay by my side when we leave tomorrow to crush the people of Paradise."

He released her, and Lanike stumbled backward. She ran into one of the countertops, spilling a jar of incense, which tumbled to the marble floor and smashed to bits. She kept herself from falling, hands braced on the counter, knuckles whitening, staring at Velixar in horror.

"Does this surprise you?" he asked. "In a way, it's almost romantic. Every day, Clovis looks on as the demon inside him warps his body, works his limbs, fills his stomach with raw meat. His hands butcher anyone we place within them, and their flesh is shoved into his maw, feeding the beast. It takes tremendous control for him to sway Darakken's desires. Even when given his own daughter, he was unable to deny its hunger."

He rubbed Lanike's face with the side of his hand.

"That he can control it for *you* shows just great his love is for his little wife. Like I said...romantic."

"My poor Thessaly..." Lanike whispered, trembling. "Tell me you lie."

"I never lie," said Velixar with a sigh. He stepped closer to her, grabbing her arm and yanking her off the countertop. "Your husband understands what will happen should he fail. Too much rides on the power of the demon. Too much, and therefore I have done everything I can to ensure its obedience. And if it doesn't obey, well... I will sever all ties that bind him to the beast. The first one to fall prey to it will be *you*, Lanike. It's that twisted fate that gives your husband the power to resist. Imagine what would happen if the worst came about. Imagine what it would be like for him to helplessly inhabit the body of a monstrous creature fucking his beloved wife with its twisted cock, tearing her body apart with its jagged teeth...."

The woman slipped from his grasp, mouth ajar but unable to speak. Without another word to her, Velixar called one of his handmaidens back into the room.

"Get her cleaned up," he said. "I want her ready for the rite in half an hour."

The handmaiden led a still horrified Lanike from the rectory. The woman leaned on her as if the muscles in her legs had turned to jelly. Velixar turned away in disgust, then caught a glimpse of himself in the mirror. Some of the powder had rubbed off his cheeks. He reapplied it, took a deep breath, steadied his nerves, and marched out of the room toward his destiny.

✛

The streets of Veldaren were packed with onlookers beneath an overcast sky. The people stared—women, children, and the elderly—their faces drawn and pale, their expressions blank, much like those of the corpses Velixar had ordered hung from the castle walls. Captain Wellington led a small brigade of troops, fifty in all, down the center of the road. The bannermen in front held their flags high, the lions emblazoned upon them roaring down at the populace. None of the onlookers seemed to notice the banners at all; instead, their gazes were fixed on Velixar, who marched at the rear of the procession, feet landing in time to the beat of the war drum. He was disappointed by their reaction to him. They had no love for him, and no fear either, just simple uncertainty. None of them understood his motives; none realized what he had done to help them realize their potential.

Let them be skeptical, he thought. *Karak knows, and that is all that matters. When Paradise burns, they will understand, and they will bow in appreciation.*

Lanike walked in front of him. The handmaidens had done an admirable job of making her presentable; her hair was styled in an elegant sidelong swoop, her ripped cobalt dress replaced with a flowing white gown that made her look like a spirit of the wind. She walked with her shoulders held back, a prideful posture, but Velixar knew it was a façade. He saw it in the way her right leg shuddered beneath her weight, the way her left shoulder sagged ever so slightly. It seemed the only thing holding the woman together was the hand of the young soldier who marched beside her.

The most important being in all of Neldar. What a twisted joke.

The procession turned, and Veldaren's central hub came into view. Smallfolk were replaced with countless soldiers, their armor unblemished, their spears held high in one hand, their swords crossed over their hearts with the other. The great fountain loomed at the end of the column, the waypoint of traffic moving in all four directions throughout the city, its gray likeness of Karak standing rigid in the center, rising ten feet tall. Behind the fountain stood the god himself, standing on a dais that had been raised for just this event, resplendent in his sacred black platemail. His glowing golden eyes met Velixar's, and the god smiled.

Captain Wellington segmented his charges to either side once they reached the end of the line. Finally the whole of the dais could be seen. A throng of people stood atop it, clearly intimidated by the size and presence of their god. There was King Eldrich, his bodyguard, every member of the Council of Twelve, six Sisters of the Cloth, twenty red-cloaked young acolytes, and Joben Tustlewhite, the castle cleric whom those around the castle called "the mumbling priest." Also standing there, fully dressed this time in a draping gray robe, was Darakken in its Clovis Crestwell disguise. When Velixar squinted, he noted that the eyes of the beast were only slightly tinged with red, which meant Crestwell had assumed at least a semblance of control. *Good for you, Clovis,* he thought.

He almost laughed aloud when he saw Lanike pause at the bottom of the stairs, staring up with her mouth hanging open at the bald thing that used to be her husband. Her hand trembled as she grabbed hold of Joben, who had offered his assistance. Her feet were unsteady, even when they reached the top of the platform. Joben led her to her husband's side, but she refused to look at him. Even when Clovis's bulging arm draped over her shoulder, she did nothing but stand and shudder.

Shaking his head, Velixar climbed the dais. Once he reached the top and stopped, awaiting the signal to kneel, he heard the crowd below, smallfolk and soldiers alike, pressing in toward him. He knew that if he were to turn around, he would no longer see the road, just a never-ending sea of watchful eyes. The thought filled him with pride, and it took great effort to keep from swiveling his head for the tiniest of glimpses. Instead, he kept his stare fixed on his chosen god, ignoring the white noise of the crowd.

Joben stepped away from Lanike, nodding to his acolytes before taking his place by Karak's side. He spoke a few words that Velixar couldn't hear. Karak then held out his hand, and the cleric took whatever was in it. Clenching his fingers around the object, he cleared his throat. When he spoke, his voice easily rose over the noise of the crowd.

"Citizens of Veldaren," he said, his usual mutter suddenly magnified tenfold. "We come here today on the brink of war. Our very way of life is threatened by the cretins of the west, by the brother god who heinously tossed aside his pact with our Divinity. So many of our good men perished that day to Ashhur's rage, men who were sons and fathers, men who died well before their time. It is past due that we avenge their deaths."

The murmur of the crowd rose slightly in volume.

"But today is also a wondrous day. With dark times ahead, let us bask in the light of new leadership that will help lead us to heights we have never dared dream possible."

With that, Joben nodded to Velixar, then bowed and backed away. Velixar's heart raced as he dropped to a knee before his deity.

The glow of Karak's eyes was like the explosion of twin stars. The god stepped forward, raising his hands to his creations.

"My children, I come to you today as the father you have always wished me to be," Karak said, his voice many times louder than Joben's. "I have been apart from you for too long, but my forty years in seclusion were spent wisely. While I was away, you blossomed from the infants you were into the capable men and women you are now. You have built a great society that will be written about in the tomes of legend. *You* are the mighty, *you* are the worthy, and it is for you that I lead our brave fighting men to war. For a poison has infiltrated our kingdom, a poison spread by my brother himself. He thinks you are still children! He lords over his Paradise, refusing to allow his people the simple freedoms a human life warrants. However, those poor souls *are not your enemy*! They are like you, people of flesh and blood and a desire for liberty, who have been denied that freedom by the very god who created them."

The crowd grew deathly silent. To Velixar, it sounded as if no one even breathed.

"We embark on this great conflict," Karak continued, "not as invaders, but as *liberators*. We will free this supposed Paradise of my brother's tyrannical reign, and we shall spread our virtues of order, responsibility, and honor throughout Dezrel. By the time we are through, all of humanity will be united, a true brotherhood of man in which no further war is ever needed."

A single female voice shouted, "Praise Karak!" It stood alone for a brief moment, but a buzz slowly gathered as more joined the first. In a matter of moments the whole of the hub was awash in the united voices of the populace chanting, "Karak! Karak! Karak!" Once more, Velixar wished for a momentary glimpse of the spectacle.

The deity held his arms out wide, and the throng abruptly silenced.

"This will be no easy venture," he said, his words rumbling throughout the street, echoing off the gray stone buildings. "There will be sacrifice, there will be horrors, and many of our brave men will perish. For though we seek to liberate those in Paradise, many will not freely toss aside the shackles they wear. Those shackles are all they have ever known, and it will take force to break them."

It was then Karak's eyes fell to Velixar. "In any great conflict, even greater leaders are required, both in spirituality and in the ways of war." He held out his massive hand. "It is now that I present you, my people, with the First Man created in all of Dezrel, by the hands of both my betraying brother and myself. He who kneels before you is my greatest servant, Velixar. He speaks my truth, and he lives it."

The deity reached beneath his black plate and drew out a shining metal disk attached to a silver chain. It was a pendant, and it swung from side to side in front of Velixar's eyes. Sculpted upon it in bas-relief was the image of a lion standing atop the crest of a mountaintop. Velixar knew that adornment well. It was the very same pendant Ashhur had worn over his heart since the first day he could remember.

"The greatest servant in all of Neldar has served as Highest of Karak for months now, and he has served me well." The god's eyes flicked to the side. His holy lips rose in a grin. "However, I have come to the realization that he should no longer wear such a title."

What? Velixar's heart leapt in his chest. He tried to keep the sudden anger he felt from flushing his cheeks and making his eyes burn red, but heat crept up from beneath his collar. He clenched his fists tightly, fingernails digging into his palms.

Noticing his reaction, Karak's smile grew all the wider, almost playful.

"For Highest is a human designation," he said, as if the pause in his speech had never taken place, "and Velixar has advanced beyond humanity. He is the embodiment of an ideal, the embodiment of all I stand for. He is now a brother to me, much more so than my *true* brother ever was. Unlike Ashhur, Velixar shares my vision of a world without chaos."

A sharp exhalation left Velixar's lungs, and all his previous anger disappeared. He was too shocked to speak, to rise, to even breathe.

"It is because of this newfound brotherhood that I present to you, Velixar, the pendant Ashhur and I once shared. You shall wear it around your neck with pride, as it is now yours, and with new ownership comes new meaning. Where once the symbol carved upon this pendant was meant to portray a pact of peace between my brother and I, it now represents the shape of the world to come; that of my children winning victory over the blasphemous ideals of the west, that of the lion climbing to the top of the mountain and claiming it as his own." He bent down—quite far, given his immense size—and draped the pendant over the still kneeling Velixar's head. "This is the most tremendous gift I could give a man. Now rise to your feet, Velixar, and face your people. Rise to your feet, High Prophet of Karak!"

The deity touched his cheek, and a sudden surge of power rushed through Velixar. His mind in a numb daze, he stood. Karak grabbed both his shoulders, stooped over, and kissed him atop the head. The crowd behind them roared, a thunderous applause that swallowed him in a warm, pulsating embrace. Karak nodded to him, and he finally turned to face the people.

Countless common faces stared up at him, awash with hope and exhilaration. A litany of arms pumped into the air, thrusting forward in a single repetitive motion. All the while the throng chanted, "Velixar, Velixar, Velixar," just as they had shouted Karak's name only moments before. He glanced down the dais, where the king and the Council of Twelve were clapping. Darakken was gazing at him, its eyes an unnatural red, and Lanike had her head bowed next to it, her hair dangling in front of her face. He turned away from them and faced his congregation once more.

"I serve you!" shouted Velixar. "Forever, for Order, for Karak!"

High Prophet. His *High Prophet.*

Then and there, nothing could have kept Velixar from smiling.

CHAPTER

As Lord Commander Avila Crestwell marched her regiment south, she fondly recalled the moment three weeks ago when the raven had arrived under the cover of darkness, its wings flapping like the charred cloak of an old ghost. She had known what the letter strapped to the bird's leg would say before her fingers ever brushed the wax seal that bound it.

She was as restless as she'd been since setting camp in what was left of the township of Haven. The ruins of the Temple of the Flesh, which Karak had decimated with a fireball from the sky, marked their northern boundary, whereas what remained of the township itself lay to the south. In between were erected hundreds of simple tents, inside of which the five thousand men (and a few women) who had been placed under her command rested their weary bones.

Avila had hated every moment of their stay in the delta. The marshy land, the humid air, the fluctuating temperature, the aggressive insects that pecked away at her perfect skin, raising inflamed welts that she constantly scratched without realizing what she was doing—all these made life near impossible to endure. It was difficult to train men for battle under such conditions. The weight of their armor caused them to sink in the mud during exercises, the heat of the day inflicting dehydration and heatstroke. She ended up allowing the soldiers to train wearing only their smallclothes, using wooden practice swords instead of the genuine article.

Not that these men required much training. Other than a few green boys, they were the best of the best, those she and her traitor brother had instructed back at the Omnmount staging grounds. Yet no matter how skilled they were, a stagnant soldier was one step closer to falling on the wrong end of a blade, so she kept hounding them. The morning horns were always blown at the first hint of sunrise. Such practice was needed to keep them limber, for daily tramps through the southern portions of the delta did not do the job. Whereas Avila had expected pockets of well-trained and devoted opponents like those who had defended Haven the day the brother gods had come to blows, her search parties had discovered that the remainder of the delta was a deserted wasteland. There were few stragglers, just old hermits or some of the more unsavory bandits who dwelled deep within the swamp. These castoffs were easily dispatched once discovered, and their heads ended up gracing pikes when the squads returned from their searches. It seemed as though the rest of the populace had lifted their banners and fled.

Avila found the situation more than frustrating. She was a general without an opponent, which made her useless. The coming of the raven had given her purpose.

Yet as she trotted her mare south along the humid, packed-dirt road, leading her fighting men beneath a burning sun, part of her wished to be back in the encampment. The gurgling sound of one of the Rigon's tributaries flowed to her left, just off the beaten path, taunting her with its ease of movement. She had grown used to the immobility, to the lack of action. Her legs were developing sores and her back ached from sleeping the previous night on the hard ground. And that didn't take into account the ache of her loins...

"Something troubles you?"

A hand brushed the silver hair from the left side of her face, an almost tender gesture, and Avila jerked in her saddle. She stared incredulously at Malcolm Gregorian, the former Captain of the Palace Guard who had been chosen to serve as her new lieutenant. Malcolm's arm retreated swiftly, and his sudden movement caused his charger to take an unexpected step away. He grabbed tight to the reins and squeezed his thighs against the horse's side to keep from falling.

"Never touch me that way again," she spoke imperiously, keeping her voice low so the troops marching behind her would not hear.

Malcolm, stunning in his silver mail overlaid with deep blue plate, gained control of his steed. His lone good eye glimmered in the afternoon haze, light brown and soulful, matching the hair atop his head, which flowed in loose curls down to his pauldron. His left eye was milky white, forever encased between the four wicked scars that ran diagonally across his formerly handsome face.

Self-consciously, Avila tugged her silver locks back into place and turned away, hiding the gash of reddened tissue that slanted across the left side of her head—Crian's gift. She greatly disliked looking at Lieutenant Gregorian's scars. They reminded her too much of her own.

"Why do you cover yourself so?" asked Malcolm. "I wish to see your beauty in full."

She scowled at him, grabbing her sword and pulling it slightly from its scabbard.

"Do *not* speak to me of beauty. We are warriors in the Army of Karak, and I am your Lord Commander. You will address me as such, not treat me the way you would some tavern wench."

He bowed low. "Yes, Lord Commander," he replied gravely, though his scarred lips smiled. "Once more, you have my apologies. I will leave you in peace."

With that, Malcolm pulled back on the reins, circling his charger around. Darkfall, the broadsword that had been the property of the deceased Lord Commander Vulfram, bounced on his back. She heard him shout a phrase to the soldiers, who replied in unison, filling the moist air with their dedicated voices.

Avila glanced over her shoulder as he rode away, catching a glimpse of the seemingly endless procession of soldiers and supply carts that packed practically every inch of the southern pass. She could barely see their faces, for the gleam off Malcolm's silver armor had blinded her. She turned back around, closed her eyes, and offered a silent prayer to her deity. Once more her loins felt a twinge, and she inhaled sharply in frustration.

It was entirely her fault Malcolm acted the way he did. She had been so energized after the raven's arrival, a sort of nervous vigor with only one cure. In the past her brother Joseph had satisfied such cravings for her, though on a few occasions her father the Highest would fill the void. But Joseph was dead now, slain on the battlefield of Haven by the twisted beast DuTaureau, and her father remained in Veldaren, no longer his own man after giving his deity the greatest sacrifice possible—the use of his body as host to the demon Darakken.

With no other outlet, she had turned to Malcolm, who'd surprised her by being a more than willing participant. A man who had always been stoic and methodical, whose devotion to Karak was surpassed by none in all of Neldar, he'd taken her on her bedroll with a verve that bordered on violence, performing each thrust like he was driving a sword into an enemy. The aggression had at first enthralled her, and she'd accepted his cock as she would a divine tool, in worship and adoration, as she bit down hard on her lower lip, hard enough to make it bleed. But the man's passion had turned to frightful aggression, his grunts and shouts those of some feral beast wishing for nothing more than to spread its seed. At last she'd shoved him away with all her might before he could finish. At first she'd thought he would strike at her or scream, but when her chest began to hitch, his gaze had softened. He'd sidled up to her, trying to wrap a comforting arm around her shoulders. She'd ordered him from her tent immediately.

Afterward, she'd drawn her legs to her breast and cried. It was the first time Avila could remember breaking down, and it frightened her more than anything she had ever experienced. *I am an immortal Crestwell, Lord Commander of Karak's Army,* she chided herself. *Not some weak peasant girl.* But still the sorrow had come, and she'd longed for not only Joseph and her father, but for her mother and Thessaly, who had disappeared the night the Moris were executed for treason. She even missed Crian and Moira. In that moment of weakness she *had* become a weak peasant girl, one who wanted nothing but her family.

She clenched her fists, squeezing the reins as tightly as she could. *Stop this. Stop being a weakling.* She grabbed hold of her sword's hilt and drew it. The sword was Integrity, which had been Crian's before he'd turned his back on their family, and Avila had taken it as her own when she'd been named Lord Commander by the newly dubbed Velixar. She had allowed Malcolm to keep Darkfall, as the heft of the weapon proved far too great for her narrow frame.

She held the slender sword before her face, looking at her reflection in its smooth polished steel. She flipped her hair, exposing the ruined left side of her face. She looked hard, determined, her jaw rigid and her eyes intense. Immediately she began to feel better about herself. Her womanly weakness fluttered away like bubbles from a drowning man's nose. *I am Lord Commander,* she thought. *Karak's emissary, the bearer of Karak's law, the wielder of Karak's sword.*

She had barely slid Integrity back into the scabbard when she spotted shadowy figures by the side of the road, in the fields of swaying wheat. The figures halted in a small clearing between the rows of wheat, staring at the massive army with their hands cupped over their eyes to block out the sun. Avila squinted, trying to see them more clearly. It was hard to know for sure, but they appeared to be holding staffs. Or perhaps spears.

Malcolm appeared beside her once more. He was businesslike this time, which pleased her.

"The first of the flock," he said flatly. "Do you wish for me to take care of them?"

She tied her hair back in a knot, exposing her entire face, scars and all. "I think not," she said. "If any are to draw first blood, it will be your Commander. Captain, prepare the torches. This field will burn once we pass it."

"Yes, Lord Commander," Malcolm replied.

Avila kicked her mare and the horse turned off the road, bounding across the field. The heavy heads of wheat slapped at her knees, but she paid no mind. She relished the wind beating her face, even the insects that caused welts to rise on her arms when they slammed into her as she rode. The ache in her abdomen became but an echo of what she had felt before, and by the time she redrew Integrity, the sensation had all but disappeared.

The figures didn't move as she approached, as if they were scarecrows instead of people, and when she drew closer she saw that they were but children; one boy and one girl dressed in roughspun, both holding irrigation rods meant to poke holes in the hard soil. Their faces were dirty, but their teeth shone white when they smiled and began to wave. It took Avila a moment to register the sight in her mind. They were *smiling*. A rapid wave of confusion made her slow the gallop of her mare and drop Integrity to her side.

She sidled up to them, staring down, allowing the tip of the blade to hover and bounce a foot from their faces. The children, their locks golden and curled and their eyes a deep shade of blue, didn't pay the sword any mind. They did not even seem to see it. Their smiling gazes were locked on her.

"Hello," said the boy cheerily.

Avila felt at a loss for words. She swiped the sword back and forth before them, trying to elicit a fearful response, but the children simply bobbed their heads away as if avoiding a pesky fly. It made no sense that they would show no fear.

"Who are you?" she asked finally, lifting Integrity and resting the blade against her shoulder.

"Will," said the boy. He puffed out his chest and held his staff out to the side. "I'm eight."

"Well, Will," she said, "where are you from? Are your parents close?"

"We're from Nor," Will replied. He then snickered, jabbing his thumb over his shoulder. "Back thataway, past the tall grass. That's where Mother and Father are." His face grew suddenly serious. "You won't tell them you saw us, will you? Mother told us to stay put, but we ran off."

"Why did they say that?"

The little boy shrugged. "Everyone's acting strange."

"How so?"

"They built a wall, and now everyone's playing hide-and-find-me."

"That so?"

Will nodded.

Avila took a deep breath. She'd never related well to children, but if there were one thing she *did* know about young ones, it was that they were honest.

"So tell me Will," she said, "whom do you worship?"

He gave her a queer look.

"Whom do you worship?" she repeated. "Who created you?"

"Ashhur," the boy said, matter-of-factly.

"And would you die for your god?"

He looked like he didn't understand the question. "Um…yes?" he replied.

"And what of Karak?" she said. "What do you feel for the God of Order?" At the mention of that name, the little girl backed up a step, but Will remained right where he was.

"Karak's stupid," the boy said.

"He is?"

"Yeah. He's stupid and Ashhur's gonna send him back to the heavens."

"Fateful words, boy."

That was when Will squinted, gazing up at her as if truly *seeing* her for the first time. Avila held her arms back, revealing the painted symbol of the roaring lion that adorned her black breastplate. His smile slowly faded, his eyes widened, and his opposite hand began to move toward his staff.

Avila slashed Integrity in a tight circle. The sword passed through the staff, severing it in half, then crossed Will's neck effortlessly. A contrail of red followed the tip as it looped back up. The boy tottered where he stood, blood oozing down the front of his roughspun, and then fell over, landing flat on his face. The *crunch* of his nose breaking echoed in Avila's ears. She looked on solemnly as the boy's blood mixed with the red clay of the earth, deepening its color. Her heart grew heavy, a weakness she knew she had to quash if she were to fulfill her duty. *They are not children,* she told herself. *If they do not bend knee to Karak, they are merely wild dogs.*

The little girl stared down at the unmoving boy, then up at Avila. Her eyes filled with tears, but she did not openly cry. She appeared more confused than anything, nudging Will with her foot, watching as his body rocked and then fell still once more. She gaped up at Avila.

"Why won't he move?" she said. "What did you do to my brother?"

Avila lowered Integrity, and this time the girl reacted to its presence, her eyes focusing on its still dripping blade as she backed away.

"He insulted the one true god," Avila said.

"Will he get up?"

"No. He will lie there forever, rotting until he becomes one with the soil." She cleared her throat. "What is your name, girl?"

"Willa," the girl replied, sniffling now.

"How old are you?"

"Seven."

Avila took in the sight of the girl's blond curls and supple, dirt-streaked flesh. She had not been this girl's age in sixty-seven years, even though she still looked the same as she had on her eighteenth birthday. She wondered how she would have reacted if her brother had been killed before her eyes. And then she realized it *had* happened just seven months earlier, on that damned soggy soil of Haven.

Stop it, she thought. *Do your duty. Forget the rest.*

"I will ask you the same thing I asked your brother," she told Willa. "Do you love Ashhur? What do you feel for Karak?"

Willa shuffled on her feet, still staring at her brother's corpse. Tears cascaded down her plump red cheeks. She looked ready to run, yet too terrified to do so.

"I await your answer."

"I don't know," said Willa, her voice small. "Ashhur's our god. That's what Mother and Father say."

"But what do *you* feel? What has Ashhur done for you?"

The little girl's perplexed eyes rose to meet hers. "Gave me life?" It was said with uncertainty.

"No," replied Avila. "Ashhur might have created your ancestors, but your parents gave you life. Now tell me, what has Ashhur done for you?"

The girl shrugged. "Told us stories?"

"Is that all?"

Willa nodded.

The little girl looked so lost. Avila sheathed Integrity and swung her leg over the saddle, leaping to the ground. Little Willa winced but did not retreat. The girl was an ignorant simpleton to be sure, unable to comprehend death, the most basic of life's tenets. Even so, Avila felt a shard of pity. This girl was remaining remarkably strong given what she'd just witnessed.

Kneeling before the girl, Avila placed a hand on her shoulder and said, "Ashhur is a false god, child. He has raised his people in chains. And he broke his oath with his brother when he tried to destroy holy Karak on a battlefield where he had no place. Our Divinity then swore to cross the great river to free Ashhur's people from the chains with which they've been shackled. And what does Ashhur do? He leaves you, a mere child, alone to face the coming army. *My* army. Is this the kind of god to whom you wish to dedicate yourself? A god who would allow your brother to perish in his name?"

"Um...no?" replied Willa.

Avila ruffled her hair. "That is a better answer." She then grabbed the child's head and forced her to look down at her brother's body. She shoved the corpse over, exposing the gaping second mouth that still leaked blood below his chin. "Karak will give you the freedom to live your life as you wish. So long as you stay true to Karak's law, your life will be yours to live. Does that sound appealing to you?"

Willa stared at her dumbly and shrugged.

"Idiot," Avila muttered, and then, "Child, would you like to join me and see what befalls those who insult the true god of Dezrel?"

"I don't know..."

Avila grabbed dead Will by his ratty shirt collar and lifted him. Torrents of red poured over her hand, dripping on Willa's feet. The child shrieked and leaped backward.

"Or you could end up like your brother," Avila said.

The girl nodded her head up and down as she sobbed.

"Good," said Avila. "Now tell me where your village is. Just point girl, point!"

She did so, her sobs growing louder with each moment. When she outstretched her arm to the southwest, Avila nodded in approval. She rode to the supply carts and deposited the girl on the back of one of them before rejoining her company. The fighting men fidgeted, sweat drenching their smallclothes and leaking through the heavy leather and mail they wore. Malcolm frowned at her, but she ignored him. She knew what he was thinking, had known since he'd treated her like some craven weakling earlier. But Avila knew better, she knew *herself*. Malcolm might be stringent in his loyalty to Karak, but so was she. The girl would prove useful down the road, and when her usefulness ended, she would either bow before the deity or perish.

The convoy followed Willa's occasional directions, marching down a slender pathway cut through the fields of grain. Far behind, at the rear of the five thousand men, soldiers used buckets to spread a sticky concoction across the fields. Torches were touched to ground, and the fire spread rapidly, swallowing the land and the vegetation that grew on it. When the first crackle reached her ears, Avila glanced behind her, and all she saw was a thick wall of billowing black smoke that blotted out the sky.

The village of Nor came into view after an hour of riding. A makeshift wall surrounded it, constructed from jagged stone and twisted, unnatural-looking trees. It was almost as if the wall had sprouted from the very land beneath them. Avila held out her hands, halting the progress of her troops. Best she could tell, the wall was only ten to fifteen feet high. It was a laughable defense against the might she had at her disposal.

"Archers, forward," she said loudly, and sixty men stepped to the front of the procession, fanning out wide, thirty on either side of her.

"Did they think that shoddy wall would protect them?" asked Malcolm.

"I don't care," Avila snapped back. "They kneel, or they die."

Heads began appearing over the wall. She counted seventeen.

"With me, archers," she said. "March."

Gently snapping the reins, she walked her mare toward the walled village. Malcolm remained beside her, and the archers kept in stride with the horse, their feet moving in unison, a perfectly tuned machine of her creation. Pride filled her belly with warmth. *Father taught me well,* she thought. A slight pang of sorrow followed when she thought of him. The man's gorgeous platinum hair was gone now, his body warped by the presence of the otherworldly demon inside him.

Think. Concentrate. Lead.

When she was a mere fifty yards from the village, she shouted the order to stop. All came to a silent halt. She could hear the archers breathing heavily, and she knew it had little to do with the day's warmth.

Malcolm glanced at her and nodded.

"The moment is yours, Lord Commander," he said. An expectant gleam shone in his milky eye.

She lifted her chin to the sky and spoke.

"People of Nor, hear my voice! Open your gate and let us enter. None shall perish if you bend your knee to Karak, the rightful god of all Dezrel. We come here to release you from the bonds imposed by your hateful deity. Do not turn us away. Refusal to kneel is tantamount to blasphemy, and we shall not hesitate to batter down your weak wall and run you through."

Behind her legions, the raging inferno of the crops sputtered and hissed. A light rain of ash had begun to fall all around them.

Pausing, she edged her mare a few steps forward. She heard voices raised in panic on the other side of the wall. The front gate creaked open, catching on the dirt, and someone cursed in a familiar yet foreign tongue. Grunts came next, and the gate swung outward as far as it could go.

The gate was only six feet tall at most, and beneath it ducked two Wardens to join the third who had shoved open the substandard entryway. She was unsurprised to find she knew all three. They were Benedictus, Azrial, and Gabriel, Wardens from the east who had relocated to Ashhur's Paradise after Karak sent them away from Neldar. They stood tall and proud, their silken auburn hair hanging down to their waists. The simple hemp-spun clothing they wore made them look like absurdly giant elves, and the staffs they held in their hands, sharpened to points, made them resemble elegant barbarians.

All three stepped toward her, Benedictus taking the point, his two brothers falling to his flank. From the top of the short wall appeared human heads holding improvised bows, the stone tips of arrows aimed at Avila and her archers. It was a truly pathetic sight, and Avila couldn't help but laugh.

"Avila, turn around and go back home," said Benedictus. He stood before her, tall and proud, the porcelain sheen of his flesh so much like hers.

"You have heard my words, Warden," she replied. "Your people shall kneel, or they shall die."

The Warden shook his head, an action copied by the other two. "You have no place here, my dear," he said. "I have known you since birth, and while I realize your heart is cold, you must see that these people have no way to defend themselves save the shanty wall raised by their creator."

Ah, so it was Ashhur who raised the wall, she mused.

"It shall be as I said," she replied. "They kneel or they perish."

Benedictus took a step forward, and Avila's archers tensed.

"These people are innocent," he said in an angry whisper, leaning close to her. "You would kill them without cause?"

"There are no such things as innocents," replied Malcolm. "The only virtue that exists lies in the glory of Karak."

It was Gabriel who came forward this time, waggling his spear at Malcolm. "This is not Karak's land," the Warden growled, not attempting to hush his voice as Benedictus had. "You have no right to be here, let alone threaten the lives of seventy innocents!"

There are only seventy. This should be simple.

"We are well within our rights," said Avila. "Our authority was given by Karak himself, who claimed this land after your beloved

Ashhur broke his oath." She trotted her mare before them, pulling out Integrity and wielding it above her head. "All three of you know me, so you know how I love my creator....And you know that I am a woman of my word. If I promise them death should they not kneel, then nothing less will suffice."

The Wardens glanced at one another, then huddled together. Avila waited patiently, letting the heat from the sun prickle her flesh while a light breeze played her hair. She felt preternaturally calm, just as she always did before an attack.

Benedictus separated from his brothers. "If we kneel, we live?" he asked her. "Is that a promise?"

Avila chuckled. "If *they* kneel, *they* live. That is what Karak decreed, that is what shall be done."

"They?" said Azrial, blinking. "What of us?"

"The Wardens have no place in the Dezrel to come," she replied. "Your time is passed, and you will now rejoin your brothers and sisters who perished so long ago."

She turned her head slightly, lips locked tight, and nodded to Malcolm.

"Now!" shouted Malcolm.

Benedictus, Azrial, and Gabriel had no time to do anything but turn back toward the walled village, screams on their tongues, before sixty archers released at once, peppering them with arrows. The Wardens fell to the earth, wooden shafts still assaulting them, and their blood saturated the ground.

Avila sat tall in her saddle once their bodies had stilled. She lifted her chin high.

"People of Nor," she called out, "I will say this only once more. You are no longer the slaves of your Wardens and Ashhur. Step out from behind your wall, kneel before your liberators, and dedicate your lives to the true god of Dezrel. Do this, and none will perish!"

There was no surrender. From inside the wall people shouted, and the archers of Nor loosed their own arrows from their crude bows. Most fluttered harmlessly to the ground, and only one flew true over the heads of Avila and her men. It clanked off Malcolm's pauldron, barely missing his ear.

"They wish to fight!" Avila shouted, scooting her mare backward and summoning the horsemen from the flank. "Batter the walls, flood the gate, and kill them all!"

The horsemen sped past her, all galloping hooves and frenzied shrieks. Malcolm summoned the vanguard, which ran screaming toward the walls, those in front lugging a heavy oaken log with a curved tip. The villagers desperately tried to close the swinging gate, but it had been hung at an angle and the corner was wedged in the clay soil.

The men of Nor retreated inside, followed by those at the front of the vanguard, who'd tossed aside their ram once they realized the gate needed no cracking. Avila leapt from her mare when she reached the gate, arcing and slashing with Integrity as she ducked inside, finding purchase with each swing. Through her veins pulsed a sudden terror and excitement—with her words, her soldiers, the war against Paradise had begun. As her armored force streamed through the narrow gap in the wall surrounding the puny village, swords were drawn and pikes were thrust, her soldiers killing all they came across. The blood of Ashhur's children leaked in streams from the wedged-open gate, ash sprinkling atop it from the burning fields.

It was a glorious moment, but through the deafening clamor of it all, Avila could swear she heard young Willa's screams.

CHAPTER

10

Her name was Kaya Highrose, and she was the most splendid being Roland Norsman had met in all his life.

The girl nuzzled into him underneath a pile of fur blankets, the stars twinkling in the sky overhead. They were reclining against the hard and unforgiving roof of the inn, but he felt no discomfort. All he *did* feel was the smooth contour of Kaya's bare flesh, and all he could smell was her curly black hair, teased with lemon. The only other sensation he was aware of was the stickiness that covered his rapidly retreating manhood.

He had a hard time catching his breath, and when Kaya flipped toward him, her breasts pressing into his chest while her lips lightly brushed his neck, he felt his insides begin to stir once more. It was the most wondrous sensation in the world, even if the rapid *thump-thump-thump* of his heart frightened him. He hadn't experienced such a feeling for months, and the last time his heart had beat this way it had not been pleasurable....It had happened as he'd watched Jacob Eveningstar, the man he'd admired his entire life, turn traitor on the battlefield of Haven.

Those memories caused his excitement to wane, only to be stoked once more when Kaya's lips met his, her breath sweet with nectarines and cherry wine, her tongue gently caressing the inside of his mouth.

She pulled back from him then, smiling as she grasped for his manhood. Her fingers found it, danced across it, and played it back into stiffness.

Roland moaned. Feeling suddenly sore, he gently moved her hand away.

"I don't think I can again," he said, hissing between his teeth at the rawness he felt down there. "I'm sorry."

"You sure?" she asked playfully. "Why not?"

"It's just…it hurts a bit," he replied.

"It does?" She sucked on her lip. "Well, Mantrel Burgess once said I have a gift for healing. Let me see if I can heal *you*."

"What are you—"

Kaya disappeared beneath the blankets before he could finish his question. Her healing kisses began and chased away all other thoughts.

They made love again after that. Roland lasted more than a few short thrusts this time, immersing himself in the feel of their lower halves colliding while he squeezed the girl's ample breasts. And when he finished, it was so intense that he bit down on her shoulder a little too fiercely, hard enough to make her yelp.

When the act was done, Roland collapsed on his back, the soreness returning. The rest of him felt numb, euphoric, as if he weighed less than nothing and could soar into the sky, floating all the way up until he reached Celestia's star. Kaya rolled over, resting her head on his chest while she caressed the fine hairs below his bellybutton.

"Happy birthday," she said, smirking.

He gazed at her, dumbstruck.

"So, how was it?" she asked. "Second time as good as the first?"

"Um," he replied, feeling at a loss for words.

Kaya giggled. "What, did I steal your tongue?"

"Well, no," he said hoarsely. "It's just...it was all...well...you know?"

"Fun?"

He chuckled. "Well...yes, I guess that's as good a word as any."

She slid atop him, placing a single kiss on his lips as she squeezed his sides with her thighs.

"I still find it amazing that you haven't done this before," she said, her hazel eyes glinting in the moonlight. "I mean, by Ashhur, I lost my flower when I was fourteen, and you're no younger than I am."

Roland shivered, wiggled out from beneath her.

"Wait, you're done this before?" He'd believed he was her first, just as she was his.

"Of course," said Kaya. She cocked her head to the side and stared at him through squinting lids.

"Where are your children?"

A solemn look overcame the pretty girl's round features.

"I have none. Ashhur has yet to bless me with child." She looked so sad then, defeated. "Not for lack of trying."

She looked away, and in the moonlight he saw the shimmering start of tears. Roland's empathy overwhelmed his disbelief, and he pulled her close, suddenly feeling guilty even though he wasn't sure he'd done anything wrong.

"Why are you sad?" he asked.

Kaya sniffled. "I am one of eleven, Roland," she said. "All nine of my older sisters have been blessed with children. Me? I've been with five men since that first time, and none has been able to plant his seed. It is a mark of dishonor. Healers have touched my belly, but it hasn't helped. My mother jests that I'm cursed. No man will take me if I cannot provide him with children."

"You're not cursed," he said, grabbing her by the shoulder and pulling her to him. The blankets slid off them, piling up around his waist and revealing her fully. He drew back and was once again overtaken by how beautiful she was, with her wide hips and firm breasts. He had always thought his future was with Mary Ulmer, Master Steward Clegman's daughter. But Mary was gone now, having joined Ashhur's march toward Mordeina. And besides, as he stared at the woman before him, he couldn't imagine himself being with anyone else. Visions entered his mind of giving Kaya the children she so desired, of building a small hut in the hilly lands on the outskirts of Ker and living there until old age claimed them both. He had only known her for a few short months, but already that felt like forever.

"How do you know?" she asked, almost shyly.

"Because someone so wonderful could *never* be cursed."

She smiled, soft and sweet. "That's very nice of you to say."

"I'm not just saying it. I *mean* it. I would live the rest of my life with you, whether you bore my children or not."

"You would?"

"Of course."

A shooting star flashed overhead, making the night even brighter, and for a moment Kaya put him in mind of Brienna. When the mirage faded, he tilted his head forward, memories of the beautiful, lost elf washing over him.

"Though I must say, I don't know why you would need a child to make you feel worth. You are perfect as you are, Kaya. *That* is what should define you."

"But women are created to make children. It is our reason for being, our grand purpose, as my mother always says."

At one time Roland might have agreed with her. After all, until Haven, life in Paradise had always been about farming and breeding and praying. But he had seen too much, *experienced* too much, for him to feel that wonderful naïveté any longer. He was a different man, and though the world itself might not be better for it, he believed *he* was.

"That's not true," he told her. "Everyone has a purpose, a journey all their own. It's up to us to decide which path to take, which adventure to embark on. The only shame in life is if you do not find happiness with being *yourself*."

Those had been Patrick DuTaureau's words to him in the aftermath of the battle between the brother gods—sage advice from such a twisted and ugly being, obviously springing from personal experience.

Kaya leaned into him once more, a smile on her face. "You make me feel good, Roland. You really do." She pressed her cheek against his breast. "In more ways than one."

They reclined on the roof and gazed up at the midnight sky, Roland pointing out the stars, naming those Azariah had told him about, and together they mused on what the other worlds out there might be like. Roland's dark thoughts floated away as they laughed and kissed. He knew it was a feeling to cherish, even if it only lasted a night. Tomorrow they would be back at work, slaving away beside the Wardens as they prepared the town of Lerder—the only true town in all of Paradise—for the inevitable coming of Karak and his followers.

Stop thinking of it, he told himself. *Go with the moment.*

"What's wrong?" asked Kaya.

"Nothing," replied Roland. He quickly changed the subject. "So, Highrose, huh? Interesting surname. How did you come about it?"

Kaya shrugged. "The first of my family lived on the hills north of the Stonewood Forest. My grandmother said the Wardens had planted a plot of roses on the highest hill any could see, and it was the most beautiful thing for miles. So when the first couple chose a name, they picked Highrose." She looked at him queerly. "I don't know why you would think it interesting, though. It's not so odd as Norsman."

"That's true," Roland replied, laughing. "But my forbearers were odd, I think. They took our name from one of Warden Loen's poems, 'The Barbarians of the Beltway.'"

"I don't know that one."

"Not surprised you don't. Your family is from the other side of the Corinth; mine's from Safeway. Loen lives here, though. You should ask him to recite it to you when you get a chance."

"Which one's Loen?"

"You know: tall, gray eyes, straight golden hair?"

She scrunched up her face. "That describes half the Wardens in town. Like I said, which one is Loen?"

Roland laughed, a hearty snort that caused his whole body to quake. Kaya joined in his laughter, falling into his chest and writhing, planting tender kisses all over him. He thought he might be up for another tumble, but then came the cries of Morgan Eastwick, the proprietor of the inn atop which they lay, screaming that there best not be anyone on her roof. Laughing helplessly, they gathered up their discarded clothing and hurried to the to the slender rope ladder that had been hung at the side of the three-story building. When they climbed down and reached the ground, Kaya placed a kiss on his lips and ran off into the night, returning to the home she shared with her family, while Roland laced up his breeches and wandered toward the front of the inn, where he hoped to enter his room without waking Azariah.

✛

For Roland, morning came much too quickly. He felt sluggish as he moved along the outer edge of Lerder with a six-foot log propped on his shoulder. There was a pounding behind his eyes, and he felt out of breath. He tried to force his way through the discomfort, keeping his thoughts on his encounter with Kaya, but if there was one thing he hated more than the cold, it was being wet. And that morning, just like most mornings lately, was depressingly soggy.

The clear skies of the night before had given way to swollen gray and black clouds as spring rain pummeled the Rigon River's middle banks. He cursed the weather, even though both Kaya and Morgan had assured him the rains were a blessing for the harvest to come. He couldn't agree with them, not when his foot plunged into a cold puddle with every other step, and his clothes clung to his body.

He made his way down the causeway, his soft-soled boots sloshing on the wet slate. There were workers to his right, on the side facing the river, stacking logs and sacks of sand up as high as they could. Wardens and humans alike hefted and pulled, grunting as they labored in the early morning downpour. The Wardens took their places at the top of the makeshift wall, grabbing whatever the humans below handed up to them.

The wall stretched as far as he could see, thickest and tallest by the river, shorter and thinner where it circled around into land. Ezekai, the Warden in charge of the wall's construction, was convinced that when Karak decided to strike, he would target this spot. "The Rigon is more than a mile wide, sometimes two," he had said. "This town was built where it is thinnest. If Karak chooses to cross at multiple points other than Ashhur's Bridge, this will be one of those points."

It seemed reasonable enough, but even so, Roland questioned the logic of building the wall in the first place. He'd been there in the delta. He'd seen the might commanded by Karak. Although the eastern god's forces had swords, axes, and shields, Lerder had little more than sharpened sticks and heavy stones. The true weapons they possessed were few, just those given as gifts in the past by visiting elves. These, combined with a twenty-foot stack of sandbags and felled trees, would do little to stop an actual army, never mind a giant fireball brought down from the sky like the one that had decimated the Temple of the Flesh.

Just as he did every day, he began to doubt his choice to stay behind and assist with the reinforcements. He had wanted to leave with Ashhur, Patrick, and the majority of the townspeople, not to mention his family from home, but he'd stayed because of Azariah.

The Warden, who'd kept him from crossing the battlefield to join Jacob after the First Man's betrayal of their god, was his only true friend in the world, and Roland was hesitant to leave him. Or he had been before Roland met Kaya. Again his thoughts were filled with images of the life he could have with the frisky girl who'd given him his first taste of love. His spirits lifted ever so slightly.

They plummeted again when he reached his destination, a section of the wall that had toppled in the night. A few men came over to retrieve the log he carried, wedging it against the sandbags and rocks they'd used to brace the collapsed area. "We need more," one of the men told him. Roland moaned, hung his head, and headed back the way he'd come, where a cluster of Wardens were chopping down a thatch of evergreens that grew just inside the town's border.

More men carrying logs passed him on his trek, their expressions blank, their eyes weary. One of them stumbled, and Roland rushed over to support the heavy log before the man collapsed beneath its weight. The man thanked him cheerfully and headed on his way, whistling as he went. Roland's blood started to boil. Despite their efforts to fortify the town, none of those who lived here truly understood what was coming. Oh, they understood in *theory* that there was danger, but just like Kaya, they hadn't experienced what Roland had....They hadn't stared death in the face and lived to tell the tale. He blew a gust of air between his teeth, realizing that they would only understand when it was too late. If the Wardens hadn't been here to help build the wall...

Damn the wall, Roland thought. *Ashhur should have raised one himself, like he did in Nor.*

Azariah had been the one to squash that notion. The walls Ashhur had raised from the earth in the settlements along the Rigon tributaries on the way to Safeway were small. Lerder was huge by comparison, stretching four miles in either direction. There were actual buildings here, seven large ones in fact, including Morgan's Second Breath Inn and Ashhur's Temple by the Ford. The rest were small domiciles for the people. And there were roads that led from one structure to the others, which were lined with countless hovels and cabins. Unlike any of the other settlements he had visited, everyone in Lerder had a real roof over his or her head. There were no tents or lean-tos save those erected specifically to dry fish or hang grain. Elves, and even some merchants from Neldar, had oft frequented the town in the past, staying in the Second Breath Inn and drinking mulled ale in Barker's Tavern, which made the town a commercial hub of sorts. It was the only place in Paradise where trade was practiced at all.

All of which meant the barrier had to protect each of the tall structures, extending nearly seven miles around. Azariah had been adamant that the amount of godly power it would take Ashhur to raise a blockade from the ground would leave the deity greatly weakened, and his power would go to better use in Mordeina. Seventy Wardens stayed behind to assist in the construction, joining the mere two hundred townspeople who had chosen to stay. The rest had left with their deity, marching west along the Gods' Road.

As he scaled a small hill, Roland listened to the grunts and *thwump* of axes of sharpened stone biting into trees. At the crest he saw Azariah, his short, russet hair standing on end, sticky with sweat and sopping with rain, as he hewed at an evergreen. One of the other Wardens shouted, "Make way!" as the tree teetered and began to fall. A loud *crack* filled the air before it struck the ground, bouncing slightly on the springing branches. When it stilled, the other Wardens stepped atop it, swinging axes of their own to cut the trunk into six-foot sections.

There was a stack of already segmented logs close by. Roland prepared to lift one of them, but he heard his name called from behind him. When he turned around, Azariah stood behind him, an ax slung over his shoulder. He was naked from the waist up, and rainwater beaded all over his slender torso. His green-gold eyes sparkled in the morning's relative darkness, and a smile curled his lips.

"Back so soon?" the Warden asked.

Roland looked up. Just like all the Wardens, Azariah towered over him. It was something he hadn't minded in his youth, but now that he was a man grown, it made him feel insignificant in comparison. They were creatures from a different world, and at times Roland couldn't help but think they were humanity's betters, no matter what assurance Ashhur gave to the contrary.

"Need more logs," he replied, stepping aside so another returning laborer could heft the one he'd been preparing to lift. "Part of the wall fell last night, and we need to brace it."

"I know," replied Azariah. He leaned down and offered him a slight jab on the shoulder. "Perchance your midnight madness blew it over?"

Roland's cheeks flushed and he turned away.

"I thought you were sleeping," he muttered.

"I awoke when you attempted to sneak into our room," Azariah said. "At first I thought you might be sleep wandering, but your sighs told a different story."

Roland shook his head and began to walk away empty-handed, too embarrassed to face his friend. He heard the sound of something heavy thumping against the sodden grass, and then Azariah was by his side, walking with him.

"What bothers you, Roland?" he asked.

"Nothing."

"Come now. We are friends, are we not? You can talk to me."

Roland paused and glanced behind him, making sure he was far enough away from the other Wardens. He then looked back at Azariah and frowned.

"We shouldn't be here," he said. "We should leave."

"You know we cannot do that. We must help reinforce the town."

Roland threw his arms out wide. "But *why*? What good will it do? We can't fight an army! What happens when Karak comes? Everyone here…everyone…is going to…"

Azariah grimaced. "The girl. Kaya. You care for her."

"Of course!" shouted Roland.

The Warden cast a quick glance behind him, then hurriedly threw an arm around Roland, leading him away from the others. They reached a distant section of the wall that was barely taller than Azariah and constructed from flimsily stacked stones, twigs, and branches. When he turned to face Roland, the Warden's expression was serious, very much unlike the way he usually carried himself.

"Tell me what you fear," he said.

Roland took a deep breath, trying to calm down. He owed his friend that much.

"I just don't understand," he said.

"Understand what?"

"Why we're here. Why we're building this wall. It won't stop Karak from burning this place to the ground. You're smart. You know that. Yet no one else seems to understand!" He shook his head and lowered his voice. "And neither do I. When we first came here, I was still in shock from what happened to Brienna, and then what we saw in Haven. But now I see two futures ahead of me: one where I'm happy and free, and another where everyone's dead, and that one seems far more likely." He looked up at his friend once more, and he knew from the tears he felt dripping down his cheeks what he must look like. "Please tell me, why are we here? Why are we choosing such a horrible fate?"

Azariah stooped down. He looked to the overcast sky for a moment, his lips moving as if in prayer, and then his eyes found Roland's once more.

"We are here to be a barrier," he said.

Roland brought up his hands. "What kind of a barrier can we be?"

"A weak one, true enough," Azariah admitted. "But one that is necessary. Ashhur knows he cannot allow Karak to march into this land unimpeded. There must be obstacles in his way. There must be people left behind to fight the initial fight, to slow down his forces and allow the rest to reach safety."

"That's the reason?" Roland asked, not wishing to believe it. "But...he never told anyone that! All he said was that those who wished to stay could, and the rest could join him. Why didn't he tell everyone the risks? Why didn't he tell them their *purpose?*"

"But he did, Roland. Did he not warn them of what was to come? However, the people of Paradise are too inexperienced to truly understand. After Karak's Army starts to attack townships, word will spread. Perhaps it will finally awake our people to the danger that comes like a lion in the night. Ashhur would have taken everyone if he could, but forcing them would have slowed him down, making Karak's mission all the easier. Those who choose to stay might die, but they could be saving thousands of others' lives. Ashhur let them make that decision, but trust me, he did so with a heavy heart."

Roland shook his head.

"So the purpose...*our* purpose, is to die here?"

Azariah solemnly nodded. "In a way, yes. Unfortunately."

Roland collapsed against the slipshod wall. Pointed branches dug into his back as he slid down until his rump hit the wet ground, but he cared not. He felt lost and betrayed. Perhaps the First Man had had it right. Perhaps Karak was the more righteous deity....

"I want to live," he whispered. "I want to live."

"Roland," the Warden said, taking a seat beside him, "you *can* live. It is not the death warrant you think it. We here in Lerder must fight as hard as we can, but do not think we are fools. When the walls are breached, the Wardens will spirit away as many as we can. Horses are tethered in the forest not far from here. Only we will remain to occupy the troops. Only we shall stay until the bitter end." He sighed and glanced skyward again. "In many ways, it is a desire. I have lived a long time, my friend, much longer than I should have. My family died long ago, and on another world no less. It might be time for me to join them; it might be time for *all of us* to join them."

Roland stared at the faraway look in Azariah's green-gold eyes.

"You're giving up," he said.

"No," said the Warden, a smile spreading on his face. "I am simply accepting my fate."

They sat for a time in silence, and then Azariah asked Roland to help him chop a few trees. Roland did just that, although his friend's revelation had torn him up inside. A part of him wanted nothing more than to grab Kaya, take a couple of those hidden steeds, and run far, far away. *I still have time,* he tried to convince himself.

They worked straight through midday, pausing only to eat a lunch of salted trout and almond-encrusted oatcakes, until at last dusk began to cast an ominous pallor over the land. They had felled nine more trees, leaving only five standing. It was after the ninth tree fell, when the Wardens were about to section it, that a scream arose from behind them.

"What was that?" shouted one of the Wardens.

Roland spun around to see that the Wardens were racing down the hill, heading for the side of the wall that faced west. Azariah grabbed his arm, urging him along. Roland saw a flurry of movement in front of the shortest section of wall, where people had been loading grains and meats into Lerder's giant stone granary. It looked as if a fight had broken out, and shouting filled the air.

The closer Roland got, the clearer his view. There were eight—no, nine—men wearing all black, brandishing blades similar to the ones Karak's soldiers had used in Haven. They had hopped the short wall and were attacking a pack of Lerder natives, hacking and slashing with their swords. A man fell, his chest split open. A woman was speared through the eye with a sword. A young boy stared up at the attackers, not moving, and was cut down where he stood. A roar filled Roland's throat as he pushed his feet faster.

The Wardens, much more fleet of foot with their long legs, arrived at the scene first. Most still held the stone axes they'd used to chop down the pines, and they swung them in looping arcs. A few of the ax heads found purchase in flesh, mashing bone and splitting flesh, while others clanked off the heavily oiled chain armor worn by the attackers. It was chaos, all blood-curdling screams and blood-leaking wounds, a flurry of bodies and movement that sickened Roland.

Azariah entered the fray, swinging his ax with reckless abandon, and Roland followed suit. He had no weapon—he had dropped his ax when he first heard the screams—and it struck him too late that he had nothing with which to defend himself. An armored man came at him, blood running from beneath his half helm, his eyes wild with murderous rage. His blood-coated sword lifted above his head, and when he swung it, Roland dropped to the ground and rolled. Mud splattered his face, momentarily blinding him, and the tip of the blade struck inches from his ear. In a blind panic he scooted to his feet, driving his shoulder into the first dark shape that appeared before him. He pumped his powerful legs, forcing his opponent to the ground. A gust of breath caught him square in the face, scented with mint and brandy.

"Get *off* me, you fool!" came a shout from beneath him.

Roland wiped the muck from his brow and looked down into the furious face of the Warden Wendel, one of those who had been chopping trees on the hill. Roland's heart pounded in his ears, blotting out the sound of his apology as he slid off the Warden. Wendel glared at him before lifting himself up and rejoining the battle.

Soon all was silent but for a chorus of sobs and whimpers. Roland took to his feet, glancing this way and that. There were eighteen bodies bleeding out on the already drenched grass, nine invaders and nine commoners. All twelve Wardens who had rushed down the hill had survived, and he stumbled over to where Azariah stood panting, a wicked-looking gash running down his right side.

His friend held his ax up high, his body shaking as he peered at the wall.

It was then that a horn sounded, shaking the very air. Even the ever-present raindrops seemed to quake as they fell. Roland looked at Azariah, then at Wendel and Mularch and the others, not understanding the significance. Then the horn sounded again, holding its ominous note for longer this time.

"Oh, no," said Wendel, and then he and the Wardens were off again, leaving the distraught and horrified citizens of Lerder to deal with the corpses.

Once more Roland followed them, trying to stay fast on Azariah's heels. As they rushed by the huts and cabins bordering the road, the citizens who'd remained in the city gradually began to emerge, their faces masks of confusion. Roland scanned them as he ran, eventually finding Kaya, who was standing beside her parents. She looked just as bewildered as everyone else. Roland dashed up to her and took her hand.

"Come with me," he said, and took off running before she could answer. He could hear her parents shouting after them, but he was too far away to make out what they were saying.

They ran through the center of the town, past the Second Breath Inn, where old Morgan stood on the front stoop, her hands on her hips, gazing east. Next they rushed by the Tower of the Arts, the tallest structure in the town, where Roland had watched a few elderly ladies stage an impromptu play.

Finally they reached the wall. A thick mass of bodies stood before it, Wardens and humans alike. Some had scaled the supporting logs and were staring over the edge, their bodies frozen. Roland skittered this way and that, searching for Azariah, still holding Kaya's hand.

"Roland...Roland what's *happening*?" the girl shouted.

He swiveled to look at her, the blood rushing to his face. She was crying, which angered him all the more because he was too. He almost shoved her away, but Azariah appeared a split second before he could do anything rash, grabbing him by the soaked front of his shirt and spinning him around.

"Roland…" he said, his voice trailing out.

"What is it, Az? What's going on?"

Azariah turned to Kaya, giving her a sympathetic nod.

"My dear, you should stand aside for a moment. There is something I must show Roland."

She nodded and backed away without protest.

Azariah led him through the mob, to a pair of supporting logs. The Warden whistled, and the Wardens who were balanced atop the logs—Ezekai and Loen—glanced down before dropping from their position. Azariah shoved Roland from behind.

"Climb!" he shouted.

Roland did as he was told, gripping the wet, slippery sides of the log as he scooted his way up. Once he reached the apex, he wedged his feet beneath it and braced his arms on the sandbags on top. He peered across the expanse of running water that was the Rigon River, and his heart froze in his chest.

Ashhur save us all.

There were hundreds of soldiers, thousands even, gathering on the opposite bank of the river. As he watched, even more appeared over the gentle rise that led into Neldar. The rocky, jutting inlet, where the river was narrowest, was a few short yards from where they stood. There were men with pikes, swords, battleaxes, maces, and bows. Most carried shields. There were just so many of them, like a legion of raging black ants. Behind them appeared a caravan of wagons, thirty at least, sidling up to the edge of the river. As Roland watched, ten men who had braved the strong current of the river emerged on the Paradise side. On exiting the water, they dashed along the high bank, disappearing into the reeds.

There was little movement by those on the other side, however. Only the banners of the roaring lion seemed to be in motion, fluttering and snapping in the wet wind. A bead of water dripped into Roland's eye and he wiped it away, blinking rapidly.

"Look," he heard Azariah's voice say.

When he turned he saw that his friend was balancing on the log beside him. From below someone handed Azariah a long tube of wrapped leather with two small pieces of sea glass, one on each end. He peered through the looking glass, and then offered it to Roland. "Take this and look," the Warden said. "Please tell me my eyes are lying."

Roland did as he was asked, and when he pressed the looking glass to his eye, the army standing on the opposite bank came into sharp focus. He traced from one side to the other, gazing on every hateful face and scowling mouth, every mail-covered cowl and solid steel helm, until at last he saw *him*. His chest of platemail was massive, stark black but for the red lion at its center. Roland felt a lump form in his throat, and his knees begin to shake. The being who wore the platemail had a perfect face, his eyes a shining yellow, his hair dark, short, and wavy. That face was so similar to Ashhur's, yet at the same time there was a world of difference.

Roland lost his grip on the looking glass, and he almost tumbled from the log to catch it. But Ezekai, who was below him now, helped keep him steady.

"You saw him," said Azariah. "Didn't you?"

"Karak," Roland said. "The God of Order is here."

Azariah shook his head. "No, Roland, no. To the deity's right. Look again."

Confused, Roland peered through the looking glass once more, and into his vision came another man, much shorter than the towering god. This one wore a billowing black robe and his eyes burned red, as if the fires of the underworld raged within him. Roland gasped as he took in Jacob's all too familiar visage. The First Man seemed to be looking right at him, those burning eyes boring into his soul. There was such anger there, such hatred. Roland handed the looking glass back to Azariah. He could see no more.

"He has returned," Roland whispered.

Someone shouted something along the wall of sodden burlap sandbags, and Roland peered across the river again. He didn't need the looking glass to see what was happening. He watched as Karak and Jacob walked to the edge of the rushing water and lifted their arms. A great rumbling followed, and the massive boulders that formed Paradise's high bank began to shift. First one fell into the current, then another, creating a single column that rose out of the water. More rocks fell, rumbling and cracking and splashing as column after column rose into the air.

"They're building a bridge!" Azariah shouted, his cry echoed by all who stared over the wall.

Roland dropped his head into his arms as the commotion around him grew into an uproar. *Jacob, why?* his mind pleaded. *You were my hero, my master! Why?*

There was no answer but the sound of the grinding boulders.

Azariah grabbed him by the shoulder, giving him a shake. Tears rolling down his cheeks, Roland glanced at Azariah's face. The Warden tried to give him one of those reassuring smiles of his, but this time it rang false.

"The town is lost," Azariah told him. "Go down there and gather Kaya, her family, and as many others as you can. It will be some time before they are able to finish the bridge, but others will be crossing before they are through. Stay at the inn. Don't move until I come for you."

"Why, Az?" Roland gasped. "What are we going to do?"

The Warden glanced down at Ezekai, who nodded in reply, as if a silent message had passed between them.

"The time is now," his friend said. "I am getting you out of here before Karak rains death on us all."

CHAPTER

11

He had seen them. He had *seen them*. And he could not wait to get across.

The sun had fallen behind the western rise while men laid down long planks atop the newly formed scaffolding that crossed the Rigon River. It was tedious work for those building the bridge, but none fell into the water. The whole time Karak and Velixar continued their chanting, keeping the men balanced, raising stones and sludge from the riverbed to reinforce the structure. The river below rushed on unimpeded, the current oblivious to at all that was happening above it, while from the other side came the nearly inaudible sound of flapping wings.

Darkness had spread across the land by the time the bridge, a two-thousand-foot long, thirty-foot wide behemoth of stone, wood, and sediment, was complete. On the other side of the river, countless points of light shone from behind the makeshift wall around Lerder. It was a flimsy thing, their wall, haphazardly built and teetering in spots. *They did not have Ashhur's assistance to make it strong,* Velixar thought. *Nor did they have mine.*

He took his place beside Captain Wellington at the head of the vanguard and raised his right fist to the sky. His eyes, burning brightly, illuminated the bridge before him.

"For Karak!" he shouted. *"For a free Dezrel!"* The soldiers behind him—*his* soldiers—echoed his words before they charged, their captain in the lead. Velixar stepped onto the sturdy riverbank, allowing the vanguard to cross ahead of him. Their shouts became the bays of wolves, the sound of their booted feet clomping across the bridge an ever-present rumble of thunder. The first legion of horsemen cantered behind the vanguard, hooves clopping against the wooden planks, and Velixar followed them.

The bridge was wide enough for all to make it across without incident. The high bank on the other side was steep and muddy from the spring rains, and soldiers scampered over one another in an attempt to scale it. Men struggled to gain their footing, and a few careened into the Rigon's strong current, their plate and mail causing them to slip below the surface before the current could take them. The first few over the rise were battered by a rain of arrows, but few of the bolts found purchase. Their tips were either wood or stone, neither strong enough to punch through the armor and shields.

Where is the iron, the steel? Velixar wondered. He had not dared to hope it would be this easy.

Finally the first wave crossed the high bank. The shield bearers formed a protective barrier while behind them soldiers drove stakes into the ground, tied off ropes, and laid down planks of wood for those below. With actual solid ground beneath them, the rest climbed easily. The horsemen followed them up, their horses fanning out wide, once over the lip. The war cry began anew as Karak's soldiers rushed the makeshift wall.

When Velixar stepped foot on the bank, he saw that the wall encircling the town was even shorter than he'd originally assumed. It could not be more than fifteen feet tall, and his vanguard flung their grappling ropes over the side with ease. But as they began scaling it, the stacked wood and sacks of sand proved too unstable for their weight. The wall tumbled in spots, and more soldiers rushed through the debris, tramping atop the crushed bodies of their comrades. *Now there are gaps in the wall where the horsemen could ride through.*

Velixar's grin grew wider as he glanced behind him, where a towering Karak awaited with the bulk of their regiment. The deity stood at the foot of the bridge, arms crossed over his chest, his intense golden stare like a pair of nightbugs from this distance. Velixar nodded to his master, then faced forward and muttered a few words of magic. Air gathered beneath his body, lifting him off the ground. He sailed over the high bank, his feet touching ground just a few short yards from the wall.

A group of tall beings had emerged from the town to meet his vanguard head-on. He recognized each of them, even as they fell and died. The Wardens fought with swords and axes of stone, brave in the face of certain death, but they were not warriors and they wore no armor. Soon the humans' swords, battleaxes, and pikes ran red with blood.

Velixar walked past the various melees as if nothing could touch him, his sword bouncing on his hip as he fingered the pendant hanging around his neck. The night came alive with screams. One particular soldier caught his eye, a compact and powerful man with a teardrop scar beneath his left eye. The soldier fought expertly, his steel slashing into Warden after Warden while he led the vanguard.

As Velixar walked, the pockets of violence seemed to shrink away from him. Only once did a Warden approach him. It was Warden Croatin, who'd helped raise the Mori family in Erznia. Croatin's eyes widened when he saw him, and a mighty swing of his great stone ax dispatched the soldier with whom he'd been brawling. The Warden then charged, shoving aside other combatants, his ax held high above his head. Velixar calmly channeled the power of the demon whose essence he'd swallowed. When he brought up his hand, inky black shadows formed in his palm, solidifying into bolts. They shot out from his fingertips, striking the Warden square in the chest. Croatin fell to his knees, gasping as the shadows swirled around his body, constricting, cutting off his breath. Velixar searched his stolen knowledge.

How best to end this? he wondered. When it came to him, he grinned.

"Hemorrhage," he whispered, power flowing out of him. The air seemed to ripple as a bolt of something invisible and deadly traveled between the Warden's eyes. Instants later, blood violently erupted from his eyes, ears, and mouth. The elegant creature collapsed and fell still.

Velixar never drew Lionsbane. He never even stopped walking.

He entered through one of the gaps in the wall, stepping over spilled sacks of sand, shattered logs, crumbling stone, and horse dung. The town of Lerder opened up before him: the wide road, the seven widely spaced tall buildings with innumerable cottages nestled in between. There were Wardens everywhere, perhaps a hundred of them clashing with the foot soldiers and horsemen. The beings Celestia and the brother gods had rescued from a dying world fought valiantly, holding their ground. Their stand would not last long. Velixar moved aside, allowing a second phalanx to storm into the town. The air was alive with pounding footfalls, clattering mail, and raised voices. He lowered his head, the glow of his eyes intensifying. Holding his arms out to his sides, he watched electricity dance across his flesh. A few of the Wardens at the front of the battle went to rush him, but they never reached their target. The phalanx swallowed them in a swarm of armored bodies and sharpened steel.

The battle lasted for much of that dark, moonless night, and when it was over, Velixar toppled the rest of the wall with a word, using the power within him to help his men shove aside the detritus.

He felt strangely ill at ease as he walked the perimeter, looking on as his soldiers pried the surviving Wardens from their shelter within the Second Breath Inn. His next destination was the central town courtyard, where the bodies of the deceased were being carted and lined up on the grass. He went down the line, counting one hundred and seventy-seven dead Wardens.

All Wardens. No humans. And no weapons other than crude stone. This was far too simple.

He grunted, relieved yet slightly disappointed by the way the night had unfolded. He'd expected at least a few of Lerder's citizens to stay behind and make a stand, but other than his own men, there were no humans in the town. *They were here. I saw them.* It had been the sight of Azariah and Roland, two figures of importance in the life of Jacob Eveningstar, which had stoked his initial excitement. How he wished they were here now, kneeling with their hands bound behind their backs like the remaining Wardens.

It is no matter, he told himself. *They will not get far. And when I catch them…*

A shout brought his head around, and he glanced away from the sunrise to see Captain Wellington and two young soldiers marching toward him. All three dropped to their knees. One of the soldiers, he noted, was the wild beast with the teardrop scar.

"What news, Captain?" he asked.

Standing, Wellington went to speak but hesitated, leaning from one foot to another. His platemail creaked, in need of oil after days of marching in the rain. There was a gash on his temple and a stripe of dried blood streaking over his ear and down the side of his jaw, but otherwise he was unharmed. Even his armor had nary a dent or scratch.

"Out with it," Velixar demanded.

The captain cleared his throat. "We found corpses on the other side of the western wall, High Prophet."

Velixar raised an eyebrow. "How many, and what side?"

"Thirty. Twenty-three of ours, seven Wardens. And the wounds on ours are too clean and sharp."

"Swords and knives?" Velixar asked.

The captain nodded.

It made sense. The Wardens who'd defended the city had brandished spears, hand-fashioned bows and whittled arrows, and stone axes. The weapons that Lerder's master steward kept stowed beneath Ashhur's temple had never made an appearance.

"I gather," said Velixar, "that when our men search the town's armory chamber they will find it bare."

"We already have, and it is indeed empty."

Velixar looked to the west, imagining the frightened people in flight.

"The townsfolk took the weapons with them when they fled," he said.

"Does this worry you?"

Velixar laughed. "Not in the slightest. What they did was folly. By fleeing with the steel weaponry, they doomed the Wardens to a quicker death. We will still catch them."

Wellington seemed to accept that answer, but then he fidgeted again, his gaze dropping to the ground.

"What is it?" asked Velixar. "Spit it out."

"I searched the rookery, High Prophet," the captain said. "It is empty."

Velixar let out a sigh.

"Of course it's empty," said the young soldier with the scar below his eye. "Did you not hear the birds take flight when we first arrived? Did you think no one would bother to alert the rest of Ashhur's kingdom of what happened?"

Wellington glowered at the soldier, who hastily kneeled before him.

Many apologies, Captain," he said. "I spoke out of turn. I must still be on edge from the battle."

The captain raised his hand to strike the young soldier, anger burning in his eyes, but he seemed to think twice when he noticed that Velixar was staring at him. Wellington slowly lowered his hand.

Velixar couldn't help but chuckle.

"Ashhur has known of our plans for months now. The news will not surprise him in the least."

"And he will have prepared his defenses, am I right, High Prophet?" the young soldier asked.

"What is your name, soldier?" Velixar asked, more and more intrigued by this youth with each passing moment.

Straightening up, the soldier jutted out his chin. "Boris Marchant."

"Well, young Boris, look around you." Velixar gestured toward the destroyed rubble of the wall. "What defenses? The God of Justice *knew* this town was one of two places we might cross, given the narrow width of the river here, and yet he left his children to die. Those same children abandoned the Wardens, refusing to even leave them with true weaponry to fight us. Ashhur's children are frightened and confused—little more than beasts pissing themselves as they cower before an angered master. Of course Ashhur has prepared defenses, but we'll tear them down, every brick, every stone."

Boris and Captain Wellington both bowed; then the captain excused the trio to oversee the scout parties that were combing through the town in search of provisions they might take. He struck Boris in the side of the head as they walked away. It was a just punishment for publicly scolding his superior, but Velixar understood Boris's response. Combined with the soldier's actions on the battlefield, it made the young man rather interesting. He promised himself to seek the soldier out later.

Disappointment struck Velixar again. The town had fallen in six hours. *Six hours.* Lerder was the hub of trade in the west, the only town in all of Paradise that had even the slightest chance of protecting its borders. The cache of steel weapons from the elves, combined with the huge population, should have been sufficient

enough to provide a fight. With a properly built wall, a little training, and a decent harvest, the citizens could have held out for a
month, perhaps longer. Instead, less than a hundred of Karak's soldiers had perished while taking the town.

"Do you even care?" Velixar wondered, thinking of Ashhur's
face from his distant past. "Or have you foreseen your defeat and
chosen not to fight it?"

As the sun climbed the sky over the next few hours, Velixar
ordered his soldiers to set down sturdier ramps on the Rigon's
high western bank, to allow the rest of their ranks passage onto flat
land. The slow procession began in earnest as two hundred horses,
five hundred archers, four thousand soldiers, and sixty supply wagons crossed the newly constructed bridge. Once across, they maneuvered up the ramps and over the dismantled remnants of the wall,
trundling through the heart of the crumbling town. Not a board
or even a pebble came loose from the bridge during the march, the
result of a god's magic combined with well-trained craftsmanship.
It remained so until Karak himself crossed just past midday. When
the god stepped onto the moist bank, he turned and lifted his hand.
The bridge immediately shuddered and collapsed, countless tons of
rock and wood falling into the river. The boulders sunk while the
current quickly carried the planks downstream.

Velixar glanced up at his deity in curiosity.

"Should we not have left it intact for our return?" he asked.

Karak swiveled, taking in the sight of the sacked town. "We can
raise another bridge if necessary, my Prophet," he finally said. "For now,
I find it best to eliminate an easy route of escape into our own lands."

"I understand, my Lord," Velixar replied with a bow.

✦

The soldiers began stacking timber over the corpses, pouring from
clay jugs a sticky, flammable concoction over the various hovels and

buildings. The last of the supply wagons rumbled away, heading toward the main column, which awaited a mile or so down the western spine of the Gods' Road. Velixar remained behind with his god and a small regiment of men to take care of one final piece of business.

The surviving Wardens were bound hand and foot to the front stoop of the inn. Eighteen in total. Velixar ambled past them, studying each face, remembering each name: Loen, Crenton, Gabbrion, and Mordecai, among others. None of them spoke or so much as glanced his way, keeping their eyes fixed instead on the blood-splattered grass before them. Bareatus was there too, the Warden who had greeted him when he'd returned to Safeway from his journey to the Temple of the Flesh with the corpse of Martin Harrow strapped to the back of a donkey. *So long ago,* thought Velixar. Much had transpired since that day, and he was a completely different man now…if he could be called a man at all. More and more he understood himself as something greater, something transcendent.

He reached the end of the line, where the broadest of the Wardens knelt, his arms tied behind him at such an extreme angle that his back was arched. Yet this specimen showed no visible signs of discomfort and, unlike the rest, he did not bow. His head was thrown back, exposing his thick neck and broad chest. With his platinum hair, crystal blue eyes, and porcelain skin, he could have been a very, very tall member of House Crestwell.

"Ezekai," Velixar said. "You look well."

Ezekai had been the Master Warden of House Gorgoros before Bessus, Ashhur's first child, had sent the Wardens away from Ker. He was towering and headstrong, a natural leader. And unlike most of his brethren, Ezekai had received training as a soldier before fleeing his home world. It was fortuitous—and imbecilic on Ashhur's part—that he had been wasted on such a feeble defense.

"Any final words, Warden?" came a booming voice from behind Velixar. As Ezekai looked up at Karak, who stood with his hands on his hips, his godly head blocking out the sun, his eyes grew somber.

"Why?" the Warden whispered.

Karak ignored the question. Instead, he stepped in front of his High Prophet, grasped Ezekai by his hair, and wrenched back his head. Ezekai made not a whimper, simply staring up at Karak, tears running silently down his cheeks.

The god released him.

"You have outlived your welcome," Karak said. "Your presence is no longer required in my kingdom."

"Your kingdom?" the Warden spat. "You lord over a kingdom of rats and leeches. You are no true god. You are a disease. Ashhur created peace and harmony, yet all you bring is strife and death."

Karak laughed, and the sound echoed as if there were a hundred of him. "You know nothing, Warden, and never have."

Ezekai smiled sadly.

"I have eyes to see, ears to hear. You're creating everything you swore to avoid, Karak. You are a disgrace, a travesty."

Karak struck the Warden with the back of his hand. He did it slowly, as if it meant nothing to him, yet the power of it knocked Ezekai into the wall of the inn. His head struck hard enough to crack the wood, and when he opened his mouth to speak, he instead let out a soft moan as blood dribbled down his chin.

"You speak with a creature of the heavens," Karak said. "For one as lowly as you to question a god insults us both. You should learn from the examples of your brothers, who have accepted their fate with dignity. Come, my Prophet: put an end to this folly, so we may leave this place."

Karak stepped back, crossing his arms. He was waiting, watching. Velixar swore not to let his deity down. With a snap of his fingers, men came forward, dousing all eighteen Wardens with oil.

"What happened to you, Jacob?" Ezekai asked as the flammable liquid ran over his forehead and into his eyes. "You were once the best, and now..."

"I still am," Velixar said, cutting him off. He snapped his fingers, and fire spread about his hand, burning without consuming any flesh. Velixar felt the power rise up in him and reveled in it. Before him was life, and he was the deliverer of death. The power of it was intoxicating. The Wardens began to plead for mercy, some crying for Ashhur, others shouting the name of the long-dead god from their long-dead world. All but Ezekai.

"I should have butchered you in the delta, Jacob," he said coldly. Velixar matched his coldness.

"Neither man nor Warden can kill me, Ezekai. Only a god."

As Karak looked on in approval, Velixar brought his fingers to his lips and blew. Blue flame soared into the sky, accompanied by the sound of the great roar of a lion. The homes, the hovels, the grass. The Wardens. They all caught. They all burned.

CHAPTER

12

The rains had stopped and the air had grown warm, but the weather did little to brighten Laurel Lawrence's mood. *They're all selfish imbeciles,* she thought. *Every last one.* She cursed aloud and tossed a spent apple core into a thatch of wildflowers.

The cart she sat in bounced along on its way to Veldaren, the wooden bench in the back thumping her spine. The thin white canvas over her head shone purple and pink, promising that dusk would soon stretch its menacing fingers over the land. She glanced at the young boy beside her, no more than ten, who was staring at his dirt-caked fingernails. Swiveling in her seat, she pulled aside the curtain at her back.

"Moren, we need to go faster," she said.

The old man steering the wagon glanced over his shoulder. He snapped the reins, and the pair of exhausted horses that pulled the carriage leapt forward. The wagon pulled taut for a moment, jostling Laurel from her seat. She offered a small cry, but the carriage slowed down again almost immediately.

"'Fraid that's fast as I can make 'em go, Miss Lawrence," Moren told her, spit flying from between his wooden front teeth. "These beasts're old. Ain't been pullin' no wagon for years now."

Laurel sighed.

"Then why did we take them?" she asked, exasperated.

The old man shrugged and slapped the reins once more. "Because these are all I had, Miss Lawrence. My good horses got recruited just like my boys…'cept for Mo back there."

"Oh," she said, letting the curtain drop back into place. It was petty for her to blame Moren for their situation. The old farmer had been kind enough to offer his services when she needed them. Of course, it hadn't hurt that she'd given him two gold pieces from the stash King Vaelor had provided for her mission.

With each day, the task placed on her by Guster Halfhorn, Dirk Coldmine, and the king seemed to grow more daunting. She had spent weeks charting which high merchants to visit and when, going so far as to pick the brains of the other members of the Council of Twelve about the personalities of the merchants and choosing her wardrobe accordingly. After the assembly at the Great Fountain, where Velixar was named High Prophet of Karak and the army left the city in its quest to conquer Paradise, she put all that planning in motion. At the time she'd been confident it would be quick work. She was a young, pretty, and very persuasive woman.

Yet now, three long weeks after her assignment had begun, she was no closer to reaching her goal. She had walked the length of the Merchants' Road, visiting each of the manses that rested atop Estate Hill and the representatives of the great families of commerce who lived in Veldaren. Their representatives greeted her respectfully, dining her on succulently sweetened meats and aged cheeses, sharing with her cups of the finest vintage wines that were available nowhere else in the city. With each meal, she carefully passed along the king's requests, and each time she was rejected, sometimes politely, sometimes not.

What Laurel quickly realized was that most of the high merchants weren't in Veldaren anymore. They'd fled to other cities, leaving sycophants and distant relatives to watch over their belongings and attend pretty little dinners with pretty little women like her. It was enough to drive Laurel mad, and at last she gathered her things, found a wagon to carry her—not an easy task, given that most who remained in the city were women who were saddled with money-making responsibilities as well as child care—and headed out into greater Neldar. If the merchants had fled the city, she would seek them out in the townships where they now hid.

She was now heading back to Veldaren from Brent, her third stop after visits to Thettletown and Gronswik. She had chosen each sojourn based on both the location and the openness of the merchant, starting with the most amiable, Judd Garland, and working her way south for miles along the Gods' Road. Again her efforts had been fruitless. Judd had merely smiled, and with a hundred polite phrases told her to go fuck herself if she thought he would willingly give up food and coin to support the realm.

Three down, three to go.

Laurel's frustration grew. If she couldn't convince someone like Garland to help, how would she recruit swindlers such as the Connington brothers? The king's demands for fealty, provisions, and manpower were simply too steep, given that all he was offering in return was the promise of further lands, influence, and lesser taxes at the end of the war. *Perhaps I should always wear what I am wearing now,* she thought. Laurel glanced down at her leather bodice, polished to a shine and laced low to allow her breasts to swell over the top. She groaned in disgust. By Karak, she looked a common whore, like the ones who used to hang from the balconies of the many brothels lining Veldaren's roads. *You're no different,* she thought. *You're selling yourself just as they do.* Gripping the shawl draped over her shoulders with both hands, she pulled it over her chest and looked at young Mo. The boy was still studying his filthy fingers, for which she was grateful.

She recalled the gleam in Trenton Blackbard's eyes as he'd stared at her during their meeting three days prior. Skin was the man's trade; Blackbard owned practically every brothel in Neldar, near a hundred of them, and his lust for whores was legendary. Hoping to appeal to the merchant's baser instincts, Laurel had acted flirtatious throughout the encounter, making sure to squeeze her upper arms together as much as possible to draw his eye. *Capture a man's eye, and you've captured his thoughts,* Dirk Coldmine had said. Only the thoughts she'd captured had no connection to her offer. The pox-covered, greasy-haired merchant had offered her his bed for the night, and his company beneath the sheets. After her refusal, he'd casually asked her to leave his manse and return only when she felt in a more "accommodating" mood.

Laurel didn't expect to see him and his town again, and in truth, it was no severe loss. Sections of the Brent were beautiful, with its rolling landscape and elegant gardens, but just like Veldaren—and Thettletown, and Gronswik—there was an air of desolation about it. The lavishness of the manse and gardens were in stark contrast to the run-down collection of hovels and cottages along the mud-splattered throughways. The majority of the smallfolk, those not under Blackbard's thumb, were mostly women, and they appeared thin and sickly, their hair filthy and matted, their clothes threadbare, their expressions empty of hope. It was a contradiction she could not stomach, all that beauty interspersed with such bleakness, a thin camouflage that failed to disguise the hardships that the war on Paradise had wrought. *How quickly it all falls apart....Or was it already falling, and I never noticed?*

The cart struck another rut in the road, and the light coming through the canopy seemed to darken by half. She poked her head out through the curtain once more.

"How much longer?" she asked Moren, her tone more respectful this time.

The old man chewed on his wooden teeth and replied, "An hour, p'haps a bit more."

Laurel dipped back inside the carriage. "Not good," she whispered. Those softly spoken words finally broke young Mo from his inspection of his fingertips. The youth grimaced and began nervously tapping his foot against the wagon's wooden slats.

Being out after dark had grown increasingly dangerous. Most of the fighting men the realm had to offer were traveling with the army, and bandits and cutthroats ruled the roost. Laurel had known that going into this journey, and she'd taken precautions to ensure that come nightfall, she, Moren, and Mo would always have a safe place to rest their heads. Yet this time she seemed to have underestimated the shoddiness of the road and the strength of the weary horses that pulled their wagon.

Laurel swore under her breath. They should have arrived at least an hour ago, when the sun still cast its protective light over the streets, but the wagon had gotten stuck in a sinkhole not three miles outside the village of Crastin, and with no one traveling the Gods' Road, it was up to the three of them to wedge the wheel free. They'd lost a good portion of light, and they should have headed back to the village and stayed another night. But so desirous was Laurel of returning to her own bed that she'd asked Moren to press on regardless.

She prayed to Karak to keep them safe; yet as she did so, niggling doubt reared its head as it always did lately.

How could you leave us so? she silently asked her deity. *How could you abandon the children you've created to the violence of man?*

Man. The word stuck in her head, defiant in the face of blasphemy. *Karak has given us life and freedom, and allowed us to choose our own path. It is not the Divinity's fault that man has turned his back on his teachings.*

Yet Karak had taken away the realm's protectors, all to conquer a land few cared about. She began to wonder if perhaps Ashhur were the nobler of the two brothers, even given his sheltering ways. *He may simply love his children too much,* she thought, and a frightening question came next. *What does Karak love? Us or his ideals?*

She tossed the blasphemous thought aside as soon as she thought it. Trying to focus on anything else, she glanced at the darkening canvas around her, searching for the lightning bolt that would surely kill her where she sat.

When none came, she took a deep breath and offered a silent prayer of thanks to her deity, whom she refused to doubt. She crawled over her bench and beneath the curtain behind her, taking a seat beside Moren. As she flattened out her dress, the old man acknowledged her presence with a nod. She looked straight ahead at the rutted Gods' Road, which was filled with stagnant puddles bordered by forests grown treacherously muddy with the harsh spring rains. The sky was like a bruise, deep black above her head and pink and vulnerable on the horizon.

"It'll be completely dark soon," the old man finally said. For the first time in their trip, he seemed nervous.

Laurel placed her hand on his back. It was the only comfort she could offer.

They exited the Gods' Road a few minutes later, as the sky began its rapid descent into blackness. The southern path into the Veldaren was risky, as it was a narrow trail through a thick forest that closed in on either side, but it was the quicker way. Moren steered the horses expertly through the murk; nary a limb so much as scratched the side of the wagon as it rolled along. The carriage emerged from the line of trees a few minutes later, the wheels thudding as they passed from dirt path to cobbled road. The Watchtower, the headquarters of the City Watch, appeared to the right, looming over the road. For the first time she could remember, no bonfire burned in its spire.

It was a moonless night, which cast a sinister gloom over every building, stone and wood alike. A strange feeling came over Laurel, like she was missing something, and she stood on the carriage, cocking her head and listening for signs of life. She heard none. Not even the rats seemed to be squeaking. Only the clopping of the horse's hooves reached her ears. The smell, as usual, was horrendous—a combination of festering fecal matter, decomposing flesh, and raw fish—but she felt somewhat comforted by it. The stench would only grow stronger as they made their way north, toward the cluster of homes on the offshoot path leading to Brennan Gardens. *Brennan.* He was to be her next stop, way down in Port Lancaster. She would have gone there directly after leaving Brent if Blackbard had not confiscated the last of the gold King Vaelor had given her and refused to return it, forcing her to ride back north.

The thought drew her attention from the road ahead, but when she heard Moren utter a quiet curse, she dropped back down into her seat.

"What is it?" she asked.

The old man's eyes, barely visible, flicked back and forth.

"Shadows," he whispered. "Never a good thing when traveling."

She glanced about once more, and understood right then why she'd felt so strange earlier. All it took were a few short glances at the various street corners as they passed. There were no Watchmen to be seen…none at all. And all she felt was eyes watching her from the darkened windows of the shops and depots and the black alleys between them.

"Shadows," she muttered in reply to her driver. She did not trust them either.

Little Mo emerged from the back of the wagon, as if he'd sensed the adults' apprehension, and wedged himself between Laurel and Moren. The old man's left hand released the reins, and he draped an arm over his son. His wrinkled fingers brushed against Laurel's cheek on their way past, making her shiver. It was like being touched by a ghost. A cackle sounded from somewhere deep in one of the alleys, turning that shiver into a quake.

"Don't panic," Moren said. "Don't look around. And Miss Lawrence, don't go standin' on the carriage again, neither. Perhaps if we keep ours to ours, we won't be bothered none."

Laurel didn't think that was likely, but she did as the old man asked. The horses were moving at a decent clip—steady, not hurried—and they would reach the portcullis to the Castle of the Lion in minutes. Once that happened, she would bang on the gate and demand entry.

The outlines of the three great towers appeared in the star-spackled sky. The castle was only a few hundred yards away. Laurel took a deep breath and held it. *Almost there, almost there.* Again that strange cackling sounded, this time on the other side of the road. She flinched but kept her lips sealed.

That was when a dancing pinprick of flame appeared before them, bouncing along the side of a building ahead of them. It danced out into the center of the South Road, and was soon joined by another, and then another, until there were six flickering torches standing abreast in the street.

Moren pulled back on the reins, halting his exhausted horses. Little Mo whimpered, sliding his slender frame behind the bench and ducking beneath it. Laurel sat frozen, staring as the flames illuminated the six men before her. They were hardened types, all dressed in frayed burlap rags with thick beards, broad shoulders, and powerful arms. A shortsword dangled from each man's belt, the steel glinting in the firelight.

"Would appreciate yer steppin' aside so we may pass," said Moren after clearing his throat. Amazingly, the old man's voice didn't quaver.

"What, no help for hungry brothers?" one of the men said. His tone was gruff and tinged with the sort of sick humor Laurel had often heard in back rooms at court. "All we ask for is something to quench our thirst."

"No drinks on me but water," Moren said. "Best run along and see if a tavern somewhere's still open."

"Who says we're lookin' for ale, old man?" said another of the men. He stepped forward and drew his sword from his belt, pointing it at them. The whisper of the drawn steel cut into Laurel. "We could be convinced to let you go," the man continued, "if you let us look at what you got in back…or maybe what you got up front." The ruffian winked, his eyes twinkling.

Laurel's bladder felt ready to release.

"Got nothin' out back," said Moren, remaining calm. "Nor anythin' up front here but my daughter and son."

"Those'll do," another replied.

"You'll get none," Moren said. "In the name of Karak, I say you clear the road and let us pass."

"Karak's isn't here no more, old man. Looks like he left you to us."

Moren grunted and spoke sharply. "If I was you, I'd step aside lest I run you all down."

The men began laughing, nudging each other with their elbows. Without another word Moren threw one arm over Laurel's shoulder and cracked the reins hard with his opposite hand. Startled, the horses reared up and charged. Laurel was jerked back in her seat and would have fallen into the rear of the wagon without the safety of Moren's arm. The wind buffeted her face as the cart wrenched onward, slowly picking up speed. The men blocking the road shouted and scattered.

They did not stay gone, however. Laurel heard grunts and creaking boards beneath the louder sounds of stomping hooves and rolling wheels. The wagon seemed to buckle momentarily as extra weight was added to the back. She scooted forward on the bench, ducking away from the curtain just as a hand shot through the slit. Grimy fingers danced in the air above her, grasping and finding nothing until they fell on Moren's ragged tunic. The fist closed, and the old man's eyes bulged as he was violently yanked into the rear. He still held tight to the reins in his right hand, and his momentum jerked the bits in the horses' mouths, causing them to rear up once more. The wagon kept careening forward, crashing into the horses' hindquarters. Laurel fell toward the edge, barely holding onto the corner of the cart while a small shadow sailed over her head. Mo. The cart's rigging snapped, the old wood unable to stand the sudden pressure. The two horses squealed and galloped off, still connected to each other, the bridle dragging on the ground behind them.

Laurel heard shouts behind her, both of sadistic glee and sudden pain. In a panic she threw her legs over the front of the carriage. Her soft shoes hit the gravelly road and she fell, scraping her elbow. She barely felt the pain. Kicking as hard as she could, she pushed her legs to carry her far, far away, yet it was still not fast enough. She felt something slip between her feet, and then a fist struck her back, and she was rolling along the ground. When she came to a stop, her body was scraped and bloodied.

"Not so fast," a sinister voice said.

Then there were hands on her, strong hands lifting her off the ground. The flickering light of torches reemerged. She was half carried, half dragged to the side of the street and then thrown against the side of a building. Her head slammed against the stone wall, making her vision swim and a spike of pain shoot all the way down her spine. She collapsed, her arms and legs limp, and could do no more than stare up at the approaching men, wide-eyed and terrified. The one in front tucked his torch beneath his left arm while his hands untied the laces of his breeches. Behind him approached the other five, one with his sword out and dripping blood, another dragging the unconscious body of little Mo.

The man closest to her finished loosening his pants, and they fell to his ankles. He stepped out of them clumsily, now wearing only his smallclothes. A grin spread across his lips as he lifted the torch. His smile grew wider the closer he drew. "Nice," he said.

Laurel glanced down and saw that her bodice had come undone in the turmoil of the bucking cart. Her arms wrapped around her torso, hiding her breasts, while she brought her knees to her chest. She couldn't breathe, she couldn't speak, she couldn't even move. As her attacker began to yank down his smallclothes, Laurel prayed to Karak for strength.

And strength she found, though not from her deity. She thought of Minister Mori, her lack of fear, her stubborn resilience.

I am a Lawrence, Laurel thought. *I am my father's daughter, and I am no victim.*

When the man reached her, manhood dangling, he squatted down before her and fumbled for her breasts. Laurel remained still, waiting for him to get close, and then grabbed the bottom of the torch he held with his opposite hand and shoved it upward. The flaming top buried itself flush in his face, catching his greasy beard afire. Her attacker screamed and dropped the torch as he tumbled to his knees, batting at his flaming beard, embers swirling all around him. Laurel hesitated for the briefest moment, and then she was off, stumbling through the darkness.

Her dress was cumbersome, and despite vain attempts to rip it as she ran, she could not move fast enough. The angry shouts closed in on her, her chasers more like a pack of rabid dogs than actual men. Fists slammed into her shoulders, her spine, and the back of her head, knocking her to the ground and blasting the wind out of her. Multiple forms closed in from above, hands slapping and groping, tugging at her bodice and dress, trying to force her knees apart. Laurel shrieked, refusing to give in. She lashed out at them, thrashing with her arms and legs. Her knee found purchase, then her fingernails. One man grunted, another yelped, and then a hand lifted her by the hair, slamming her head down. Fog enveloped her world, and for a moment she thought she might black out. In that daze, she heard the roar of a lion.

The men ceased their attack and slowly turned. A low, rumbling sound, like a distant herd of cattle racing across the grazing fields in Omnmount, flowed over them all, accompanied by the gentle crunch of loose stones being crushed underfoot. Then came a deep voice, snarling and full of fury.

"Sinners."

"What the flying fuck?" one of the men asked.

Laurel felt their fear, could smell it in the air like a fragrant spice. She kicked her feet backward until she sat upright. When her dizziness faded, the stars leaving her vision, she saw that the six men were standing in a half circle, their torches thrust out before them as they waved their swords, searching for the speaker.

"Sinners," came that growl again, only this one was different, higher in pitch. The men turned again, and Laurel saw panic and doubt in their eyes that matched her own.

Spying Little Mo on the ground a few feet away, seemingly unconscious, Laurel risked moving. She crept along, keeping a constant eye on her attackers. Gathering Mo into her lap, she stroked his head. The boy's eyes were closed and blood dripped down his forehead, but he was still breathing.

The low rumble returned, and now Laurel recognized it for what it was—the throaty purr of a large feline. When she'd helped her father tend the farmland around Beaver Lake, the mountain cats had crept down occasionally to steal away with livestock—pigs, goats, even a few of the weaker cattle—and it had been up to Laurel to chase them off with her bow. Although this sound was instantly identifiable, something was very much different about it. In order for one of the mountain cats to make a noise that loud, it would have to be *huge*.

Massive shadows leaped from out of the darkness, yellow fur flashing, and Laurel's eyes went wide as blood began to explode around her. Torches flailed about as her attackers screamed, and she heard steel hit the ground, rattling against the stone. Within the chaos of torn flesh and claws, she saw yellow gleams, like fireflies. And then the smell of blood and rotting meat breathed over her, hot and sticky. She realized that at some point she'd closed her eyes, unable to watch.

Then came the roar.

It washed over her, so close, so powerful. She felt her bladder let go, and she clutched little Mo tightly against her breast as she let out a cry. All around her she felt the presence of death and fury, and whatever fate she would have suffered at the hands of those men seemed so meager, so worldly, compared to what she was witnessing. More than anything, she wanted to get away. She tried to stand, to lift Little Mo to his feet, but one second her hands were wedged in his armpits, and the next he was gone. Before she could open her eyes, something grabbed hold of her, lifting her off her feet. She struggled against whatever it was, but it was too agile, too strong. Laurel found herself flying up, up, up, while she floundered, and then there were no hands on her at all. She flew through the air for what seemed like forever, until she crashed down on a hard surface. Her shoulder took the brunt of the impact, and the pain was so intense, she feared it might be broken.

Down below, the last of the men screamed.

"Girl," said a kind voice from above. "Girl, would you be Laurel Lawrence?"

"What?" she asked, not truly understanding the question in her daze. She began to shake.

"Come now," said the voice. "You have nothing to fear from me."

Hands pressed at her back, helping her sit. The nozzle of a wine-skin was pressed to her lips, and she drank greedily from the sweetness within as it dribbled into her mouth.

"There, that's better," the kind voice said. "Drink deep."

The skin pulled away, and Laurel shook her head, trying to regain her senses. She glanced around and saw that she was on a rooftop. Three figures stood over her, mere shadows in the sparse light. The screaming down below had ended, now replaced with a revolting crunching sound. In the darkness she saw little Mo lying at her feet, and she was thankful that he appeared unharmed.

"Who are you?" she asked them. Despite her efforts, she could not keep the tremble from her voice.

The middle shadow snapped its fingers, and to either side of her, clay buckets of pitch burst into flame, filling the rooftop with light. Two of the figures were Sisters of the Cloth, one quite short and the other tall, both wrapped from head to toe in the bindings of the order. Only their eyes were visible. Two bundles of rope were coiled on the ground at their feet. A man stood between them—a youngish sort, handsome with a head of slicked-back blond hair with dyed red streaks; piercing blue eyes; a clean-shaven upper lip; and a yellow beard tapered into a pair of horns that fell down to the base of his neck. He wore a red doublet studded with ivory buttons and rimmed with gold trim. The hilt of the shortsword hanging from his hip was adorned with rubies.

The oddly beautiful man crossed his legs and bowed to her. When he did, the bells dangling from the cuffs of his doublet chimed.

"I am Quester Billings, milady," he said. "The Crimson Sword of Riverrun, at your service. Though you never did answer my question: Would you be Laurel Lawrence?"

This Quester had a smile that was just as strangely beautiful as the rest of him.

Laurel nodded. "I am." She took a moment to adjust her bodice and tie it, then stood. Her piss-soaked dress reminded her of her shame, and she felt her neck grow hot as she blushed. So far none of them seemed to have noticed, and if they had, they'd kept their mouths shut. Offering the man a quick bow, she said, "I wish to thank you for helping me, though I must ask: How did you know who I am?"

The Sisters said nothing, as the members of their order were required to keep silent for all their lives, but Quester seemed chatty enough for the all of them.

"Oh, you know how it is," he said as he strutted across the rooftop. "Just a lad with his nursemaids, wandering around in the darkness, looking for the famous Laurel Lawrence while trying to avoid the Judges' claws."

"The judges?" Laurel shook her head. "What judges? What are you speaking of?"

"The Final Judges, who sniff out sinners like yesterday's spoiled meat."

"Wait…you mean the Moris' lions? They're out of the castle?"

Quester jutted his chin toward the edge of the roof.

"I take it you weren't in a proper state to watch while you were up close?" he said. "Here. Come look and see for yourself, milady."

She knew she shouldn't trust this strange man, yet she did just as he'd asked, stepping around an unconscious Little Mo to lean over the short wall. Quester was by her side a moment later, holding one of the flaming clay buckets. Before she could protest, he tossed it over the side. The bucket shattered when it struck the ground, spraying burning pitch in every direction.

Laurel gasped. By the light of the pitch, she could see a pair of lions down below. They were the largest beasts she had ever encountered, easily the size of two men, perhaps three. They sat devouring the remains of the six brigands. If startled or annoyed by the shattering clay and sudden light, they did not show it. No, they were too intent on their meal, ripping out intestines, cracking bones between their enormous teeth, and lapping blood off the gravel-strewn ground.

"You've been gone for a while," Quester said quietly beside her, "so you weren't here when the priest Joben decided the Watch wasn't doing its job well enough. Can't blame them, really, given how few they number. So Joben let the beasts out of their cages and loosed them on the city." He nodded down at them. "They do their jobs well…*too* well. If not for the ruffians, Kayne and Lilah might have attacked you instead, and they'd be sucking the marrow out of your bones. The Judges don't discriminate intention, only sin. I know of thirty they've killed before tonight, and now you can add six more."

"They're so…big," Laurel whispered.

"They are," said Quester.

She shook her head. "I must have been dreaming. I thought
I heard them talk."

"What did they say?"

"'*Sinners,*' I think."

The man laughed, his bells jingling, his horned beard flapping.

"I wouldn't be surprised. Even those of us in Riverrun have long
known they hold a piece of Karak in them. Our beloved Divinity
gave them a portion of the gift he gave us humans. That's why
they're so big and smart. And now, apparently, they also talk."

He turned away, as if the two giant lions were of no more interest
to him. He pointed to the shorter of the two Sisters, who stooped
down and lifted Little Mo from where he lay on the roof. A second
later she disappeared over the side of the building. The rope nearest
her rapidly unfurled until it was pulled taut.

"Wait!" Laurel shouted. She went to rush toward the rope, but
the taller Sister stepped in her way, staring her down with those
cold, expressionless eyes. Laurel turned toward the Crimson Sword.
"Where did she go? Where is she taking him?"

Quester dismissed her with a wave. "Don't worry about the
boy. Mite is bringing him to his mother, since she's obviously all
he has now."

"And what do *we* do?"

"We wait here until Mite returns. You're in no shape to travel,
so we'll wait until morning, when the Judges go back to the castle
to sleep."

Laurel spun, looked below, where the lions were finishing their
meal, and then at the strange man with the bells and horned beard.

"Who *are* you?" she asked, totally bewildered. "What do you
want with me? And how could you possibly know who that boy is?"

Quester pulled a coin from his pocket and began flipping it
between his fingers.

"As I said, I'm the Crimson Sword, sworn protector of House
Connington." He bowed low to her. "My employers require your

audience, and I was instructed to bring you to Riverrun to meet them. It took a bit of bribery and alcohol to find out where you'd gone and when you'd be returning, but we've found you at last." He smirked, and even that sidelong look was stunning. "Milady, when it's safe to travel, I'd like you to accompany me and my pets to Riverrun, where Romeo and Cleo are waiting. It seems the three of you have oh so very much to talk about."

CHAPTER

13

Patrick's legs ached, but still he put one foot in front of the other. He followed at his god's heels as Ashhur marched north, leading their wandering nation into an unnamed settlement, the last before they rounded back south. Their destination was a hamlet that resided just outside the border of the Forest of Dezerea, nestled in the surrounding hills. There were grazing deer everywhere, and the trees were the tallest Patrick had ever seen. The place was idyllic, especially given that spring now had a firm grip on the land. The air had warmed and the flowers awakened, as had the leaves of the coniferous trees. Summer was still a few weeks away, but its scents filled the air.

They set up camp in a vast gulley, countless people pounding stakes into the ground and erecting their temporary shelters. They had been traveling for weeks since leaving Grassmere, moving away from the Gods' Road, and Patrick was nearing the end of his rope. The going was rough and painfully slow, and the procession of lost souls that followed him and Ashhur had started swelling immensely now that the deity had stopped leaving anyone behind. The entirety of the many villages and settlements they came across were added to the growing mass of human flesh. Patrick had to guess there were at least a thousand score traversing the land, maybe twice that, flattening the grasses of eastern Paradise and devouring all the sustenance they could find as they went. The mere sound of all these people performing the duties to keep themselves alive and comfortable was deafening. Patrick's head was throbbing. All he wanted was to lie down and rest his weary bones, but a giant hand grabbed his shoulder as he drove a tent stake into the ground, and he knew his desire would go unmet.

He turned around and saw Ashhur standing there, towering over him. There was a strange look on the god's face.

"Come, Patrick," he said.

"Where?"

"To the settlement."

"Now? How far is it?"

Ashhur pointed toward a steep, moss-covered hill. "Over that rise."

"Great," he said with a sigh.

Ashhur and Patrick left the rest of the flock, climbing the nearby hill atop which the deity assured him more of his children lived. When they arrived, they found a land that had come under recent strife. The trees were scorched, and the tents and crude huts that had served as shelters were trampled and torn. The commune was small, less than a mile wide, but there were no living souls to be seen. The only sign of human presence was a plume of smoke rising from behind a copse of giant evergreens.

They pushed into the forest and discovered a clearing. Patrick's heart beat more quickly in anticipation. The brightness seemed to fade as they moved forward, partly due to the vast amount of lingering smoke. In the center of the clearing was a huge, smoldering structure. The walls and roof were still standing, though blackened and flaking, and the iron nails that held the building together were hot to the touch. Something inside still burned, sizzling and popping.

Against his better judgment, Patrick kicked the barn's barred door while Ashhur lingered behind him. The boards were so thoroughly burned that the door seemed to disintegrate, filling the air with dust and ash. He covered his mouth and stepped through the portal, the hiss and sputter much louder now that the barrier had been broken.

What he saw inside made him fall to his knees.

There were at least two hundred corpses in there, most charred, some still cooking. Flesh was melted, bodies fused together, tangles of blackened arms and legs that looked like some hideous demon from the underworld desperately clawing for freedom. Some were piled over each other by the door, others in a scorched mass toward the center. There were floating embers all around, a few glowing, most gray, everything devoid of life. Brittle clumps of blackened debris crunched underfoot with each uneven step he took. His nostrils itched with the scent of burnt flesh.

He fell to his knees, billowing ash all around him. His hand slipped down and his fingertips found a charred rope, and when he glanced around him, trying to keep his eyes from absorbing the countless twisted and screaming faces, he found many more bits of burnt rope. The picture grew clearer.

The people had been herded into this barn against their will. Then the barn had been barred and set aflame from the outside. The inside had been stocked with bales of hay, which had caught fire easily once the flames climbed over and under the barn walls. The barn had been constructed solely for this purpose. *They were burned alive,* he thought. *Some rushed the door, trying to get out, while others huddled in the center, probably praying for their god to save them. They were men, women, and children, and they died screaming, they died screaming, they died...*

Patrick heard a screech and turned around to see Barclay, the youth who had taken to spending long, annoying moments with him on the road, squatting in the doorway. Patrick rushed out, gathered the boy in his arms, and gently held him. Ashhur, who had kept a slight distance, considered him with a tilt of his head. Patrick opened his mouth, but nothing would come out. His god's glowing golden eyes brightened, and the deity lumbered forward, ducking down to peer into the smoking barn.

Suddenly a thought took root. *Iron nails.* There was very little production of iron in Paradise, certainly not in a crude settlement such as this, yet the doors had been secured with iron nails. Karak's Army was still in pursuit of them, which left but one possibility. The nearby forest, and the kingdom within, was filled with elves who had so far remained out of the war. Or had they? Patrick thought of the deceased Bessus and Damaspia Gorgoros, slain while they knelt for morning prayers. Perhaps Neldar wasn't the only kingdom that wanted to see Paradise burn.

A moment later Ashhur retracted his head from the door. His expression had gone blank, and his chiseled jaw hung low. He didn't scream; he didn't fly into a fit of rage as he had in Haven; he didn't run toward the trees to punish the elves who bore responsibility. Instead, what he did was worse. He collapsed to his knees, still facing the barn.

And the god wept.

It was a disconcerting experience, hearing a deity cry. The sound was like the pounding of rain on stone mixed with the trumpeting of a hundred thousand grayhorns. Ashhur's sobs were the ebb and flow of the tide, the rumble of thunder in a rainstorm, the pull and crack of a great earthquake. His body shook as tears clear as water from a mountain spring cascaded down his godly cheeks. The sound summoned others from the sprawling camp below, and soon the clearing was ringed with a multitude of confused and sickened people, all watching the god who had made their existence possible. His hopelessness was echoed in the uneasy murmurs of the crowd.

Barclay continued to blubber, smearing snot all over the front of Patrick's tunic, but Patrick didn't notice. The sight and sound of his god wailing was the only thing that mattered. For the first time in a long while, Patrick felt truly afraid.

✚

"Fire is an inimitable beast," the great Isabel DuTaureau had once said. "It is the essence of the heavens, personifying the giver and the taker at once. It can be tamed, but with care, for it is greedy. Just like its brother, snow, a little is wondrous—too much and life ends."

Patrick had received that bit of wisdom after burning his hand over a cookfire while trying to roast gooey bits of a reduced sugar concoction. The reply was typical of his mother. He had been around nine years old at the time, and he'd run to her in hopes of a soft touch and some soothing words. Instead, she'd delivered a lecture on the philosophic components of fire, before sending him to the temple for the healers to mend his blistered fingers.

Even so, her words were all he could think of as he watched flames lick out of the small circle of stones before him two nights after the discovery of the barn. The paradox was palpable. Fire had made it possible to cook, to keep warm, to make tough wood pliant. Fire made up the sun that rose each morning, allowing plants to grow and forming the unmistakable distinction between day and night. Fire allowed them to send the souls of their deceased to the Golden Forever.

Yet fire was also used to forge steel, which was then crafted into knives, daggers, and swords. It was used to destroy fields of grain in order to starve frightened people, and then to end the lives of those very same individuals. This was a recent usage unique to gods and men...and elves.

Patrick grunted, shifted on his rump, and tossed another log onto the fire. Winterbone was beside him, the dragonglass crystal on its hilt reflecting the flickering flames. He shuddered, the image of the barn once again before him.

"Patrick?" asked Barclay.

He glanced across the flames, to where the youth was reclined on the other side of the pit. Barclay had rarely left his side since the discovery of the barn, which was still hidden in the trees atop the hill just beyond their camp. What had once been an amiable fourteen-year-old on the cusp of manhood had become a quivering child. He hadn't asked a silly question for two days. Instead he walked with a sulking gait, his lower lip constantly quivering. Not that Patrick minded much. At least he had silence.

On second thought, perhaps silence wasn't at all what he needed, for silence seemed to invite doubt.

"What is it?" Patrick asked.

"I can't sleep," said Barclay, twisting in his bedroll. "I'm scared."

"We're all scared," replied Patrick.

"Not you. You're not scared of anything. You weren't even scared of…of…*that*."

Patrick shook his head. He wanted to tell the boy that *of course* he'd been scared, that all he could think about was running back to Mordeina and curling into a ball while his sisters comforted him.

"Just close your eyes," he said instead. "What's the dumbest animal you can think of?"

"Uh…a sheep?"

"Well, picture a huge herd of sheep, and start counting them all. Don't stop counting either—got it?"

"Really?" said Barclay, his expression blank.

"Just do it," Patrick said. "Trust me. I've done this plenty."

"Do you use sheep too?"

Patrick cleared his throat.

"Sort of. I more use articles of clothing. Now go to sleep."

Barclay placed his head back down on his folded surcoat and closed his eyes. The boy's lips gradually parted and closed as he counted. By the time he hit thirty-nine, he was fast asleep.

"Sweet dreams, boy," Patrick said softly. "Someone has to have some."

There would be none for him tonight; that much he knew. Not after the last two days.

He shook his head, trying to force the lingering image of all those burned and screaming corpses from his mind, but it was no use.

"Shit," Patrick muttered. A chill overtook him as a light breeze caught him unawares. The fire had died down to embers, casting an eerie red pallor over the stones that formed the pit. He picked up Winterbone and used its tip to turn a log, one side of which remained untouched by the greedy flames. As soon as the bark touched the glowing cinders, it began to catch, fingers of red and yellow flame licking along the underbelly until the log was fully aflame, exuding warmth once more.

Fire giveth; fire taketh away.

He cocked his head, listening for the despairing resonance of Ashhur's weeping. It was still there, though less intense now, a moaning from the far-off clearing at the top of the rise. *Maybe he'll be done soon. Maybe he'll wash all his sorrow away.* A wave of hopelessness passed through him. The people of Paradise meant nothing to those who wanted it destroyed. Be it Karak or the elves, it was only a matter of time before bloodshed found this massive traveling enclave and reduced it to stinking piles of rotting meat just like those inside the barn. He grunted, knowing he should find peace in the fact that when the end came, his god would be by his side, but he couldn't. No amount of preaching about love and forgiveness would spare him the pain of what was to come, and he could in no way bring himself to accept his fate without a fight. Poor lost Nessa had instilled this combative spirit in him. Unyielding faith in an ideal was Bardiya's realm, not his.

Thoughts of his old giant friend made him curse and jab Winterbone's tip into the coals with more vigor. It was folly for the great Bardiya Gorgoros to deny his own god, to ignore his brothers and sisters in creation and isolate the wards of House Gorgoros from the approaching hostilities. The Kerrians were able hunters and gatherers, strong and athletic and *independent*. They were proficient with bows and spears, and regularly held competitions of physical strength—competitions Patrick had joyfully participated in when he was younger. Like Nelder, they had ousted the Wardens from Ker, opting instead to make their own way, using Ashhur's teachings as their guide. It was a sovereignty their god had only accepted after a lengthy summit with Bessus and Damaspia. *If only the people of Ker would join our fight,* thought Patrick. Their numbers, their skills, might swing the odds back to their favor.

Then again, perhaps they would simply roll over and die at Bardiya's orders. Scoffing, Patrick tipped back his skin, drinking down a massive gulp of potent corn whisky. The liquid burned going down, and he immediately felt dizzy. His anger at his friend only grew.

"Bite me, Bardiya," he whispered, emptying the skin. He wished he were with his friends from Haven, who had taught him to think and fight on his own. His stomach turned in knots, and as the world began to spin around him, he collapsed onto his side, holding his gut to keep from retching. He felt sick and dizzy, but he finally faded into a dreamless sleep, his heart beating in tune with his god's sobs.

When he awoke, his neck was sore from lying in an awkward position. The hump in his back throbbed, a headache pounded behind his eyes, and his mouth was dry. He spotted the skin lying to his right and knocked it away, cursing himself for taking to liquor to quell his depression. *I should have found a nubile young thing instead,* he thought groggily. *The aftereffects, come morning, are far less painful.*

Patrick lifted his head, experiencing more than a tiny bit of pain. The firepit was dusty and dry, and Barclay was nowhere to be seen. The sun was high in the sky, shining down on him from a hole in the canopy above. Trees rustled in a warm breeze that wafted the smell of roasting bacon.

He sat up and forced himself to his feet. Winterbone lay in the grass, its tip black with soot, and it took all his effort to lift the damn thing up, slide it into its scabbard, and sling it over his shoulder. The leather bit into his flesh, and the added weight seemed to multiply the ache in his head. Grunting, he stumbled forward, using the closest tree for support, and began descending the hill.

More than once he slipped, nearly tumbling down the tree-dotted rise. By the grace of Ashhur, he kept his balance, and eventually he caught sight of cookfires interspersed between the trees on either side of a babbling brook, where the rest of Ashhur's many, many children had set up camp.

He made his way through the maze of tents and people. Most paid him no mind, but others gave him curious glances as he wove his way through them, moaning. He was searching for Denton Noonan: Barclay's father, a healer and master of herbal remedies. If anyone could fix his aching head, it was him.

"Where are the Noonans?" he asked a pretty, black-haired youth. The girl reminded him of Bethany—or was it Brittany?—the young woman who'd used him for his useless sperm in what felt like a different life. Patrick felt his cheeks flush as the girl's wide, olive-shaped eyes widened as if he'd spoken elfish. He felt embarrassed, but at least his headache seemed to have lost some potency.

"Barclay Noonan," he said, speaking more slowly this time. "Where's the boy's father?"

The girl pointed behind him but remained silent. Patrick followed her finger. She was gesturing toward Ashhur's pavilion, which had been raised in the center of six widely spaced birch trees. He grumbled his thanks and lurched toward it.

The pavilion stood fifteen feet high and was so large that Barnabus, the Warden in charge of its care, usually did not bother to erect it. *Looks like Barney thought we might be staying awhile.* He thought of Ashhur's ceaseless sobbing, and he spun around, listening for it. He was shocked to realize it had stopped.

He came to the pavilion's entrance, where a pair of felled tree limbs held up the flap like a canopy. When he entered, he stopped short, nearly toppling over in the process.

Ashhur was sitting on a great oaken chair, one giant leg thrown over the other. The god's golden eyes were intent on a small piece of parchment that stretched between his pinched thumb and forefinger. A great hawk perched on his shoulder.

"My Grace," Patrick said, almost tripping over his words.

Ashhur glanced up, his eyes focused and intense. There were no tears, there was no flush in his cheeks; there was nothing to indicate that the deity had spent the better part of two days sobbing over the brutal murder of his children.

"Patrick, why are you staring at me so? What is the matter?"

Patrick shrugged. "Nothing's the matter. Got good and drunk last night is all. My head's pounding."

"And what do you want from me?"

"Well…actually, I was looking for Denton to cure my aches, but you always heal much better than he does."

Ashhur squinted, shook his head, and returned his attention to the parchment in his lap.

Patrick let out a moan. *Stupid, stupid, stupid.* Shuffling from foot to foot, he cleared his throat and said, "I'm glad you are feeling better, my Grace."

To that the deity nodded slightly. "I am."

"And who is your friend?"

Ashhur's posture seemed to grow more relaxed now that Patrick had assumed a more practiced tone. "A messenger bird. It arrived early this morning while I was still weeping in front of the scorched barn."

"What does the message say?" Patrick asked, though deep down he already knew.

"It has begun," the deity replied. "Karak is here."

"How far along is he?"

"I have no way of knowing, but it is as I feared. Warden Ezekai sent the hawk from Lerder, saying that Karak created a bridge and crossed into Paradise. No doubt another force of his crossed the bridges erected by us, which means we have at least two separate factions of to deal with. And others may have crossed still elsewhere."

Patrick felt a lump form in his throat. "They might not be very far behind us," he said. "What are we going to do?"

"We need to leave," answered his god. "Now. As it is, the elves who burned this settlement are still lingering. I can feel them in the trees, though they probably hesitate to quarrel with a god."

"So above and behind, we have enemies. The Wooden Bridge is only a two-day hike from here. If we depart now and march through the night, we can get there before sunset tomorrow—"

"No," said Ashhur.

"What, my Grace?"

"No. That will not do. We travel with thirty thousand of my children. It would be impossible to march with such haste without leaving many behind, and that is something I will not do. I fear my sacrifices have been for naught. My children must be made safe, no matter what the risk."

"So what are we going to do?"

"We will delay my brother. We will fight him."

Patrick threw his hands up. "We can't fight him, my Grace. He has trained soldiers, and we have…you, a few dozen Wardens, and me, I guess. We'd be slaughtered."

At that Ashhur grinned, and his smile was full of cold cunning. "Who says we must do the fighting?"

Without further explanation, Ashhur rose from his oaken chair and walked to the entryway. The hawk on his shoulder took flight, darting upward through the thick canopy. The god then began to walk away, gesturing for Patrick to follow. They curled around the camp and started up the rise. Headache all but forgotten, Patrick felt ill at ease, and it had nothing to do with the odd glances they garnered from those they passed. He did not like the look in Ashhur's glowing yellow eyes.

They reached the top of the hill where Patrick had slept the previous night, and kept on climbing. Three hundred yards farther up was the tattered settlement, and farther still was the clearing where the horror-filled barn stood. Patrick exited the copse of trees behind his god, and Ashhur marched right up to the blackened structure.

"What are you doing, my Grace?" Patrick asked.

Ashhur sighed and bowed his head. "They are gone now," he said. "They have found their way to the afterlife. What resides here are but their shells, pale reminders of the people they were. I have no more reason to grieve."

With those words, the deity placed his palm against the side of the barn. The wall began to glow, black being replaced by a brilliant orange, and then the whole structure was alight with blinding white flame. The weakened boards creaked and snapped, and the roof began to crumple. With a mighty groan, the barn caved in on itself, the wood crackling and dissolving, becoming wisps of ash that spiraled up in a funnel. A dome of bluish light formed over the crumbling ruins, pulsing, spreading, and then all sound seemed to be swallowed. A single *whoosh* followed, and what remained of the barn became a pile of blackened flakes that the wind picked up and carried into the sky.

When it was over, the only sign that there had been a structure there at all was a darkened rectangular depression. Ashhur walked to the center of the depression and stopped there. Patrick stayed by his side, afraid to do anything else. Ashhur closed his godly eyes, then lifted his chin. His lips parted ever so slightly, and his throat began to vibrate. Patrick couldn't hear a sound, but a moment later the whole of the forest erupted with a cacophony of animalistic howls. They came from every direction, from near and far, from the high ground and the low ground, and their approach was so loud that he was sure it could be heard for miles. Beneath the howling he noticed frightened shouts from their people far below. They must have been terrified. Patrick sure as shit was.

The forest came alive around them. Undergrowth rustled, trees swayed, and small saplings were trampled as countless forms approached, emerging into the clearing. The creatures were hunched on four legs, their backs arched, their fangs bared, snarling and snapping.

Wolves. A whole pack of them, if not multiple packs combined into one. Patrick tried counting them to ease his fraying nerves, but he stopped when he reached a hundred sets of rheumy yellow eyes. Some had black fur, some gray, and others were differing shades of brown or even patchwork. They were all mangy, and the heat of their combined breath seemed to close in on him.

Their growls became louder until Ashhur held out his hand, and then the beasts stopped their rumbling and sat on their haunches. Some offered whimpers and some lay down in submission, whereas others simply stared straight ahead with frostily primitive eyes that spoke only of hunger. Many of them had globules of red clinging to the fur around their jaws, bespeaking recent hunts. Patrick sidled up closer to Ashhur. Craning his neck as far as his hunched back would allow, he stared up at his deity's face.

"My Grace," he said, keeping his tone a faint whisper, "what are you doing?"

"My children are in need of protectors," Ashhur said, "and so I will create them."

With that he lifted his arms. Ashhur's glowing eyes became twice as bright, as words of magic flew from his lips. The atmosphere shivered, and the gathered throng of wolves began to writhe. They thrashed and mewled, offering braying protests to the heavens. Patrick covered his ears once more, his eyes wide as he watched the beasts flay and twist. A repetitious *crack* filled the air, rhythmic like the beating of a thousand drums at once.

"From the flesh you gain sustenance!" shouted Ashhur. "And like the plants, from the soil you grow!"

The foliage that lined the clearing liquefied, becoming a multitude of thin silver streams that flowed toward the thrashing beasts. The rippling fur of each wolf seemed to drink in the liquid, and then they began to *grow*. Their limbs stretched, their chests widened, and the cracking noise became all the more pronounced. Patrick looked on as paws flattened and then extended, furry fingers sprouting from the creatures' paws. Each of the beings wailed in pain as they thrashed, their newly formed arms and legs smacking at the silver liquid that flowed into them.

Then the moaning began. To Patrick, it sounded like a chorus of sadness, of wounded creatures lamenting the loss of their natural innocence. Ashhur ceased his chanting, and very slowly the wolves began to cease their struggles. The strange cracking sound died away, as did the bellowing. Soon all that could be heard was the combined rasps of hundreds of gasping lungs.

One by one, the wolves rose off the ground. Patrick looked on, not believing his eyes. The creatures were now twice the size they had been, and they stood upright on two legs. Patrick stopped breathing. They were a perfect combination of man and wolf, every single one of them, though they stared ahead with eyes that appeared just as icy and unfeeling as ever—the single-minded gaze of an animal.

Patrick happened to glance down, where the streams of silvery liquid had appeared, and he saw that the grass beneath the wolfmen's clawed feet, grass that had only moments before been the bright green of spring growth, was now light brown and dead. Looking up, he saw that the first row of trees behind the beasts was just as lifeless, their leaves crinkled and sagging, the bark breaking away in chunks.

He heard a thud beside him. Ashhur had fallen to a knee, the glow in his eyes faded. He panted, the knuckles of his right hand digging into the scorched earth beneath him. Patrick held out his hand, and the god took it. He instantly felt silly for the gesture, for Ashhur's hand swallowed his own like an infant's, but his act seemed to steady the god. Ashhur closed his eyes, rolled his neck, and then stood to his full height. When he did, every single wolf-man fell to his knees. They were clumsy even then, some falling over and rolling on the ground in panic.

"My Grace," Patrick began, but he could not finish the sentence. He didn't need to.

"We needed soldiers," said his god.

"But how?"

"The knowledge of form and function resides right in here," Ashhur said, tapping his temple. He was winded, but his voice hadn't lost any of its potency. "You can alter any form if you know the proper ways."

"Yes, but you made them grow as well."

"The universe is all about balance; other than the gods, nothing can be created from nothing. I gathered nutrients from the plants around us and minerals from the ground beneath us, and added them to their bodies, allowing them to grow. Everything in this world, from the stones beneath your feet to the whales living in the deepest reaches of the ocean, contains similarities I fear you would not understand. Just know that, for me, what I did was akin to piling sand upon sand to build a larger mound."

Patrick squinted. Ashhur looked a hundred times more exhausted than he ever had after bringing up the walls around the settlements. "But you're panting, my Grace," he said.

"Did I ever say it was simple?" asked Ashhur. "The power required was tremendous, and I fear I have overtaxed myself."

"Will they fight for us?" He looked around at the creatures. They seemed hungry, wanton. "They might stand upright, but they still seem like...well, wolves."

"As they are. They still have the minds they've always had and are driven by the same instincts. But they know my desires, and they will fulfill them as best they can. It will take them a few hours to adjust to their new forms, but nature is adaptable." Ashhur gave a sad smile. "Our armies may not have swords or armor, but these wolves will require neither. They hold their weapons in their mouths and at the tips of their new fingers."

Patrick looked at the curled, sharp claws protruding from each of their digits, both on their arms and legs. He shook his head.

"Why didn't you make them smarter?" he asked. "That might have been helpful."

"I cannot," the god said. "Not without great cost. This is not the same as when my brother and I brought man from the ether. We infused our power into the ewers, giving a small piece of ourselves that now resides in each man, woman, and child in Dezrel. We were weakened to mere shells of the beings we once were. Should I give these creatures a bit of my essence, my intelligence…Karak marches against us, Patrick, and I will surely face him again. When I do, it cannot be as his inferior."

"Oh."

Ashhur gestured toward his monstrous creations.

"They will fight for us, Patrick, for even as wolves they can understand my desire, for it is one they are very good at fulfilling. I want them to hunt…to kill."

The wolf-men howled as one, and a moment later they were rumbling into the forest on all fours, hand over foot, heading south. The god had it right; they seemed ungainly with their new, larger forms, but the speed at which they moved was uncanny. Patrick could see their muscular shoulders working as they galloped through the trees. In a matter of minutes, he and his deity were alone in the clearing once more.

"How much time do you think they'll give us?" he asked.

"Two days, perhaps three," Ashhur replied. "They are few compared to what approaches, but we have surprise on our side. If there is one thing I am certain of, it is that Karak will not expect this."

Frowning, Patrick said, "Karak is akin to you in many ways. Are you certain?"

Ashhur grinned. "Yes. No matter what occurred in Haven, my brother will still assume I'm playing by the rules."

It was an ominous statement, and one Patrick didn't press any further. Without consciously thinking about it, his mind drifted to Bardiya. His friend would hate the idea of Ashhur creating wolf-men to fight his battles for him. Bardiya believed in the sanctity of *all* life, not just humanity's. He would find it unsavory that the wolves of the forest were being sacrificed in such a way.

A memory of the barn and the destroyed bodies again entered his mind. He turned to Ashhur, threw back his oversized shoulders, and stared up into the deity's eyes.

"My Grace," he said. "I apologize, but I must ride south. I'll catch up with you at the Wooden Bridge, and if not there, in Mordeina."

Ashhur stared at him, and Patrick knew the god already understood his intentions.

"It will do no good," he told him.

"I wouldn't be so sure about that, my Grace. If you don't have to play by the rules any longer, why should Bardiya?" Patrick grinned. "And besides, if anyone can convince someone to break a few silly rules, it's me. I am his oldest friend, after all."

CHAPTER

14

Manse DuTaureau was an expansive structure. Its main hall stretched for nearly a quarter mile, and at its center, crossroads split off into four separate wings. There were fifty rooms—bedrooms, common rooms, dining halls, meeting rooms, vast closets, and two libraries—all built by Ashhur himself at the request of his second child, Isabel. The east and west wings were where the family DuTaureau kept their residence, their chambers small yet stylishly furnished. The main entrance and the atrium, where the family had once spent quiet evenings, were on the southern end. That space was now used to greet the many citizens who came to pay their respects to King Benjamin, the first ruler of Paradise. The northern wing ended in what had once been a dining hall and had now been transformed into the throne room—Paradise's seat of human power.

Ahaesarus marched through the atrium, following fast on the heels of Erstwell Karn, the man Isabel had placed in charge of repairing the hangars lining the township's eastern road in preparation for what was to come. Crops were being pushed hard, the people using the magics Ashhur had taught them to bring corn, grain, carrots, turnips, and other assorted vegetables to seed early and often. After only a few weeks, the barns were already a third full, and the last thing anyone needed was for the structures to topple, destroying food that would be necessary for survival once Karak fell upon the area.

Erstwell had caught up with Ahaesarus outside the manse while the Warden was heading inside for a conference with King Benjamin. The man had pled with Ahaesarus to see to a rule-breaker who was stowed away inside, accused of sneaking in to visit the still-imprisoned Geris Felhorn.

"She's down here," Erstwell said.

They progressed down the main hall, passing two privies and the southern kitchen. Daylight filtered in through the narrow gaps between rooms, making the brilliant reds stitched into the carpets pop. The man finally stopped when they reached the central junction. He pushed open a door to his left, the wooden hinges creaking as they swiveled inward.

The room had been used for meetings; he could tell as much by the large table of polished mahogany in the center surrounded by eight chairs, and the stand showcasing a loosely rendered map of Paradise. The walls were stone, sanded down and lacquered with a yellowish gloss. It was an ugly color, one that made Ahaesarus's legs twitch. He noticed he was not alone in that sentiment, as the girl who sat at the table seemed to be vibrating her own legs fast enough to take flight. She stared up at him with frightened blue eyes. Her hair, a satiny shade of strawberry blonde, flowed over the roughspun, brown smock she wore. She was young and quite beautiful, even with her simple attire.

Erstwell spat on the floor. "There she is," he said. "Penelope Travers. Little harlot has a lot of nerve."

The girl, Penelope, cast her eyes downward, ogling her own hands as they fiddled on the table.

"Leave us," Ahaesarus said.

"What? Me?" said Erstwell.

"Yes, you. I wish to speak with the girl alone."

"Hold on here. When I found her I was told—"

Ahaesarus glared at him, stilling his tongue.

"Yes, Master Warden," the man said, his cheeks turning red as he backed out of the room and eased the door shut.

Taking a deep breath, Ahaesarus moved around the table, pulled out a chair, and sat down beside Penelope. He placed his hands on his legs, sitting up straight as an arrow as he faced her. Her eyes flicked shyly in his direction.

"So, Penelope is it?" he asked.

The girl nodded.

"You have been accused by Erstwell Karn of disobeying the King's decree and placing all of Mordeina in danger, not to mention yourself, by secretly holding court with young Felhorn. What say you to these charges?" It felt so strange for him to accuse the girl of something of which he himself was guilty, and to say things like *King's decree*.

Penelope shrugged. "What is there to say?" she said. She spoke timidly, barely above a whisper. "I didn't even know there were king's laws. I always thought we were supposed to obey Ashhur."

"King Benjamin is Ashhur's voice when he is absent," Ahaesarus replied. "His decrees, and those passed down by his council, are spoken in our god's name."

She looked at him, eyes brimming with tears. "I'm sorry. I didn't realize I was breaking any rules. I was walking by the old well when I heard him crying."

"So you decided to enter the well and give Geris Felhorn food?"

"I…well…am I in trouble?"

Be gentle. You would wish for the same. "No, Penelope. The only punishment you will be given is the knowledge that you disobeyed the will of your god."

Those words seemed to make her relax. "Yes, I gave him food. I had just finished husking the corn for hanging when I heard him."

"You do realize he attempted to murder our king, do you not? His mind is broken, and he is dangerous."

"He seemed fine to me," she said with a shrug. "Dirty and hungry and sad, but he didn't try to hurt me."

"Looks can be deceiving," he said, though in truth he had noticed a change in Geris over the three months since his first visit to the old well. Ahaesarus had taken to visiting the boy almost obsessively over that time, and he did appear to be much better. However, he was Master Warden. He could not allow common citizens to take unnecessary risks. He turned his head and pulled back his golden hair, revealing the thin scar that traced his ear from lobe to tip. "If you get too close, bad things can happen."

"He didn't do that to *me*," she replied. "I've hugged him every time I've gone down there."

"Wait…you have seen him more than once?"

She nodded and blushed. "Yes, Master Warden. I have been going down there for…it has to be three weeks now. I even told Little Jon that I'd take over his duties, and I have." Her blush grew deeper. "I think Geris likes me."

Ahaesarus sat back, shocked. Jon Appleton had been assigned by Isabel to be Geris's keeper. He had not said anything about this young thing relieving him. Then again, Jon was a devotee of spiced wine, both the making and consuming of it. It was possible he might have seen this as an opportunity to devote more time to both practices.

He slipped one leg over the other, leaned back, and rubbed his chin.

"How old are you, child?" he asked.

"Fifteen," Penelope replied.

"Do you have children?"

"No," she said, shaking her head vehemently. "Father says it's past time I found a mate, and he wants me to wed Lancel Pitts. But Lancel's stupid and ugly, and he treats me mean."

"You find the would-be kingslayer more to your liking?" Penelope didn't confirm his query, but she didn't deny it. "I see."

"Master Warden, please hear me. Geris is better now. It took a few days for him to calm himself, but now he likes speaking with me, and his touch is gentle. He's told me stories of what it was like growing up in Safeway, in the shadow of our god's Sanctuary. About the lordship too, and the dreams that drove him mad. It was a madness that my…Master Warden, may I speak freely?"

"Of course, child."

"He says speaking with me helped cure him of that madness. Just like your visits help him."

Ahaesarus had no reply as he gulped down his shame. It seemed like something out of a story one of the Wardens might tell to pass the time around late night campfires.

"Now that his mind is free," Penelope continued, "he wishes for his body to be. If you allow it, he will go far, far away from here and never come back."

"Why has he not told me the same?" he asked.

"He's afraid of you, Master Warden. He loves you, but he fears you. You put him in the well."

Ahaesarus cringed, guilt building up inside him. The boy had certainly *seemed* like the old Geris as of late, and Penelope sounded so full of youthful optimism. Ahaesarus knew he should punish her, forbidding her from leaving her family's tent for the span of a week, but how could he punish her? He then felt his insides go soft at the prospect of Geris's progress being real. Penelope sensed it, and she placed her velvety fingers over his, looking him directly in the eye and doing everything she could to show her earnestness. *Yes, she is captivated by him,* he thought. *Just as all of Paradise would have been had he not lost his mind.*

He rapped his fingers on the table.

"Penelope," he said, "I feel the need to think on this. I bid you to return to your family, but do not tell others of what we've discussed. I will return to you when I have an answer."

"An answer to what, sir?"

He chuckled. "That, among other things, is what I must discern."

Erstwell entered the room when called and escorted Penelope from the manse. He did not look very happy about it. Ahaesarus lingered in the room for a moment, running his fingers through his hair, and then forced himself to move. He had his meeting with young King Benjamin to think of now, and he had the distinct feeling he was going to be distracted the whole while.

He found the king sitting on his throne in the old dining hall. It was the very same room where Geris had attempted to take the boy's life, the stain on the stone floor covered over by a patterned rug. A family of nine was kneeling before his throne, cobbled together of wicker and grayhorn ivory, the three young daughters handing him baskets of fruit and a horn of bread. Howard Baedan, the master steward of Mordeina, stood behind them, hands clasped behind his back.

Isabel DuTaureau was there as always, sitting in a chair to the right of the king, her frosty stare devoid of emotion as she watched the proceedings. Her husband, Richard, the matriarch's near twin, hovered by her shoulder, his fingers lingering on the nape of her neck. The man's eyes kept flicking toward King Benjamin, and there seemed to be something spiteful about his stare. Ahaesarus felt a moment of disgust. If there were one individual in all of Paradise that he didn't care for, it was Richard DuTaureau, who was just as icy as his wife, but without her occasional charms and gift for leadership. It didn't help that Richard had once tried to murder his own son before he was born. If any god other than Ashhur had lorded over the land...

The matriarch of House DuTaureau glanced up, saw him standing there, and then leaned forward and whispered into the ear of the young king. Benjamin offered a pointed nod at Baedan, who quickly said, "Our king has other duties to attend to, my good people. Let us leave him to it." The family said their good-byes and headed for the exit. They were all laughs and smiles, their teeth pearly white and their simple clothing clean. They passed within a few feet of Ahaesarus, and he could smell rosemary and sage coming off them, as well as a hint of saffron. Each member of the family, from a child of four to the father, who was in his mid-thirties, met his gaze, their innocent smiles widening. It both warmed Ahaesarus's heart and troubled him.

Once the doors to the makeshift throne room were closed, King Benjamin rose from his throne.

"Master Warden Ahaesarus," he said, "it is splendid that you have chosen to greet us this fine day."

"My presence was requested, my liege," Ahaesarus replied, squinting in confusion.

"Of course it was," the king said, giving a questioning glance to Isabel, who was as still as stone, her hands folded over her lap. She nodded to the boy king, and Ben Maryll shifted uncomfortably before returning to his throne. He tugged at the scarf wrapped around his neck, revealing, for the briefest of moments, the jagged white bolt of scar tissue that stretched across his throat. Though Ahaesarus, Daniel Nefram, and a team of Mordeina's greatest healers had succeeded in mending the wound Geris had given the boy, they had barely saved his life. The new king would forever be marked by that fateful night.

Ahaesarus approached the raised platform and knelt before it, but he did not incline his head. That would have been akin to worship, and the only being in all of Dezrel who deserved worship was Ashhur.

It had been a long while since Ahaesarus had seen King Benjamin, for most of his time was spent working on the wall. He took a few moments to examine the boy, and it was an odd sight. Ben was clean, his skin well powdered. Rouge had been applied to his cheeks, which gave him a more childlike appearance than he should have possessed at fifteen years of age. His clothing was draped velvet, both smooth and crushed, in varying shades of maroon, emerald, and lavender, the dominant colors of House DuTaureau. His hair was chopped short and shining with oil, and a plain wooden crown rested evenly atop his head. Ben was growing pudgy around the middle and starting to develop a second and perhaps even third chin.

In most every way, this Benjamin Maryll resembled the child that the traitor Jacob Eveningstar had tutored during the majority of the lordship. Although Judarius had whipped the boy into shape, Ben seemed to be reverting to his old ways. He had a lax demeanor, very unlike the hardened youth his fellow Warden had helped mold. It was amazing how much could change in less than a year's time. Ahaesarus wondered if Isabel was spoiling her pet king into complacency or if this was simply Ben's natural state.

"So, Master Warden," said the young king while he rubbed his hands over his throne's ivory armrests, "tell me: How does the wall progress?"

Ahaesarus cleared his throat. "It progresses well, my liege. There is but a small section yet to complete, and we still have a sally port to cut, but all being equal, I would say our progress is back on schedule."

"You have led your workers well, Master Warden," said Isabel in her remote, emotionless tone. "I see a change has come over you, and one for the better. It was only a few weeks past when you could not reach those who would be your wards." A smile finally came across her lips, and Ahaesarus had to admit it made her even more beautiful. "Now they work themselves day and night, and success is within our reach."

"They work not for me, but themselves," he retorted. "They are beginning to understand the gravity of what will befall them."

"And you had much to do with that. The progress you have made is admirable."

Having four talented spellcasters has helped.

"My Liege and Lady Isabel, it is the people of Mordeina whom you should be lavishing with praise, not me," Ahaesarus said. "I am merely a teacher, a Warden. If what I have taught has taken seed, if the men and women I care for have come to realize the preciousness of the gift of existence that has been bestowed on them, then it is they who deserve to be rewarded."

"You truly mean that, don't you?" sneered Richard DuTaureau, who still hovered behind his wife.

"I do," Ahaesarus replied. He glowered at the petty little man and took the opportunity to rise from his kneel. Ahaesarus towered over everyone in the room, and Richard fell back a step, his expression uncertain, and then retreated. The man's reaction made Ahaesarus want to laugh aloud, especially when he heard Richard's footfalls disappear into the alcove to the rear of the hall. It might have been petty, but he *so* did not like that man.

"I agree with you, though the time for honoring my people shall come later," said Isabel, seemingly unconscious of her husband's departure. She leaned forward in her seat, her fathomless green eyes narrowing in on him. She had a sudden aura of seriousness that made him shudder. "Right now, I only wish to ask you a few questions."

"Yes, my lady?"

"Do you love the people you call wards?"

"With all my heart."

"Why? Is it true love, or a debt you feel you owe to Ashhur? Tell me, Master Warden. I will know if you lie."

He felt confused, unsure. This was not the line of questioning he'd expected.

"It began as duty, my lady," he said. "For many years, I have watched humanity grow, and I have guided them with all my ability. From the moment Ashhur's first thousand were created, their tiny clay vessels shaping themselves into fully formed youths, I have stood by their side, nurturing, attending, entertaining, educating. I showed them how to farm, fish, speak; I taught them their letters, their numbers, how to raise their children. My brothers showed

them how to build with stone and wood, how to sew using a por-
cupine quill for a needle. We told stories borrowed from our dead
world, creating parables that would instill a sense of responsibility
in the young race, and we taught them practical magics, drawing on
the enchantments Celestia had buried deep within the soil to help
crops grow quickly, paving the way for Paradise to prosper.

"And, of course, I taught my wards Ashhur's laws, preaching
about forgiveness and love and service to their fellow man." The
momentum built up inside him, and it was impossible to stop. "But
if I am being honest, I never truly *understood* my wards. I was what
I still am—a creature from a different world, very much like the
humans I teach, yet completely dissimilar. On our own world, our
race had lived for near thirteen thousand years when the demons
severed the fabric of our universe and fell upon us. Our society was
old, our ways settled. We were, in a phrase, bound to our station,
sprouting from the womb seemingly already molded, the course of
our lives set before we took our first breaths. My father was a farmer,
and so I was to be a farmer too, until it was all ripped away in the
cruelest way possible.

"When we were saved by Ashhur and Celestia, their rescue came
at a price. Once more I found myself predefined: I was a Warden,
one who would guide humanity through its infancy and into a pros-
perous adulthood. There were no other paths for me—for any of us.
And though I was grateful for the second chance at life, a twinge of
resentment grew nonetheless. I looked on mankind, at all the gifts
and advantages they were handed, and felt…jealous."

"Jealous?" asked Isabel, her voice animated by curiosity.

"Yes," he replied. "Look at us, those you call Wardens. We are
physically superior and far more advanced in almost every way.
Each gift humanity was handed—aside from those bestowed by
Ashhur—came from us. Language, arts, mathematics, agriculture—
they were all gifts from we who could have been conquerors instead
of nursemaids. Especially in those earliest days, humans appeared

so feeble compared to us, so weak and useless. Coddled, treated as if all they had was their *right* rather than their privilege. When my brothers were thrown out of Neldar and the lands of House Gorgoros, they should have been free, and yet they were called back into service, once more coddling these lesser beings who had so unfairly been lifted on high.

"That was why I suggested the formation of the lordship." He inclined his head toward the king. "It was not wholly noble, I must say. A few of us wished to embarrass Ashhur, to show him that his children were frail and undeserving. It shames me to say that I was one of them. One of my confidants stated privately that we should instruct them halfheartedly, that we should allow those chosen to fail. Yet I am a flawed creature. I am too proud, too headstrong, not to give all I do my greatest effort. So when I became young Geris Felhorn's mentor, I pushed him toward success, and slowly my desire to see humans fail fell by the wayside.

"Still, old emotions die hard, and after my student lost his sanity, I fell back into resentment. It did not help that one of the few humans I had looked on as my equal, Jacob Eveningstar, was the grand purveyor of a nefarious scheme to overthrow our beloved deity. Suddenly I was placed in the position of taking these innocent children I had privately begrudged and trying to help them save themselves. Only this time I saw myself as a disappointment, not those under my wing. Their failures were my failures, for it was my leadership, my pride, my patience that were lacking. Once more, it was Geris who saved me." He swallowed deeply, wondering whether he should reveal his actions. Finally, he went on. "I have been visiting the broken boy in the well, and he *forgives me*. He loves me. He lifted the veil from my eyes, and now, for the first time ever, I see things clearly."

"What do you see?" asked King Benjamin.

"I see innocence. I have lived a long time, my Liege. And yet... yet I had never seen the true face of virtue in a mortal creature."

He swept his arms wide. "It is reflected in the joyous expressions worn by each man, woman, and child in Paradise. Their futures are not preordained, as I always felt mine was. They live their short lives for the moment; they love, they laugh, they comfort....They could have been molded any way the gods chose, and Ashhur chose innocence. That was the folly of my ways....It took me this long to understand what our Grace was trying to accomplish. He wanted to give birth to an *ideal*. Since the day of my awakening, I have become the teacher and mentor humanity has deserved all along. So to answer your question, my lady...yes, I have come to love my wards, and that love is very sincere."

"Would you die for them?" she asked.

"Without hesitation," he replied, and it did not surprise him that he truly meant it. "If any were to lash out at Ashhur's children, I would strike them down or perish trying. And when Karak arrives on our doorstep, he will discover just how much I mean those words."

"You will not have long to wait," said Isabel.

Ahaesarus tilted his head forward. "What do you mean?"

The fire-haired lady lifted a sheet of parchment from the table behind her. "My daughter sent word from Drake," she said. "Enemy forces have been attempting to cross the Gihon for some time now. Turock and his casters have held them back, and the villagers have as well, but the enemy is numerous and we are few. It is Abigail's fear that Karak's soldiers will overwhelm her husband's defenses. Should that occur, the forces of our enemy will arrive south before the wall is complete."

"I understand, my lady," Ahaesarus said softly.

King Benjamin stood up. The folds in his neck flapped ever so slightly when he spoke. "You are to take a company of fifty of your fellow Wardens to help defend the line."

"I will do as you command, my Liege," replied Ahaesarus. "But may I ask why?"

"You have been visiting with Geris Felhorn," the boy king said. "You have broken my direct decree that my competitor for the throne of Paradise, who tried to slit my throat, be left in isolation until Ashhur's arrival. You have proven that you cannot be trusted."

The young king turned, grinning, and mouthed to Isabel, "Was that okay?" The matriarch nodded, patted his cheek lovingly, and guided him back to his seat. The lady of the house then said, "Consider this another lesson, Master Warden. You are not the only Warden who can oversee the raising of our wall. Judarius will do just as well. And when you return, you will remember your place. Am I understood?"

Ahaesarus thought on what he'd just told them and swallowed his pride. "I understand," he said. *Though I do not like it.* Thinking on the duty he had just been given, Potrel, Limmen, Martin, and Marsh then entered his mind, and he cleared his throat. "What of the four spellcasters?" he asked. "Should I return them to their home, to aid in its defense?"

Isabel looked annoyed by the question. "Of course not," she said. "They must stay here and continue work on the wall."

"I see. The wall is why we are being sent and they aren't."

She nodded. "Four talented spellcasters mean more to me here than fifty Wardens." Those words she spoke with nary an emotion. "You will leave on the morrow. Good day to you, Master Warden."

In the past Ahaesarus would have taken offense to both her tone and message, but he realized that she was correct, and he had nothing but respect for the fact she'd come right out and just said it. He bowed and took his leave, marching through the hall with dignity while the young king whispered behind him.

Howard Baedan, the master steward of the house, greeted him in the corridor, and Ahaesarus asked him to fetch Judarius. He needed to inform the other Warden of his impending departure, for Judarius would be in charge until he returned.

Alone once more, he realized that he might *never* return. He was running headlong into the heart of a war, if the letter Lady

DuTaureau had received was accurate, and if there was one thing the invasion of his home world had demonstrated, it was that war had many casualties. Given that possibility, he had no choice but to settle a certain matter on his own, and in his own way, no matter what Lady Isabel or King Benjamin had decreed.

✠

He could see the uncertainty in the girl's eyes as they reflected the torchlight. She fiddled before him, two sacks of clothing sitting by her feet. Her gaze flicked from him to the Wardens standing to his rear and back to him again.

"This should not be happening," said Olympus, one of his fellow Wardens.

"Yet it is," replied Ahaesarus.

"Isabel demanded that he be kept bound," another of his group chimed in, an unusually stunted and broad Warden named Judah.

"I know what was decreed," Ahaesarus said calmly. "This decision I make on my own. Any repercussions, I will bear. You need not let it vex you."

"Still…"

They stood before the old well, Geris Felhorn's prison for nearly nine months. It was past the witching hour, and the half-moon shone down on them disinterestedly. The barns and warehouses to their rear lingered like large midnight sentinels, the structures groaning in a chill breeze.

Penelope looked down at her hands, then at the tethered logs that hid the stairs beneath. Ahaesarus had visited her in the pavilion her family called home after leaving King Benjamin and Lady Isabel. He asked her what she most desired in regards to his former pupil. "To be with him always," had been her response.

Now she was hesitating when her desire was on the verge of becoming reality. Ahaesarus understood her fear. She had been sheltered all her life, and if she acted, she would be faced with spending untold months, perhaps years, in the wilderness with no one but a potentially insane boy for company.

"You may turn back if you wish," he told her.

The girl bit her lip, then shook her head. "No. I want this."

He offered her a knife of sharpened stone and gestured toward the covering. Two of his Wardens lifted it, allowing the girl to descend the hidden staircase, torch in one hand, knife in the other. He stood still and listened once her head disappearing from sight. Faint, joyous sounds filtered through the opening, followed by hushed sobs and urgent whispers. He heard sloshing, and then something snapped, a sharp *crack* that brought goose pimples to his flesh, but Penelope giggled, and his nerves calmed ever so slightly.

It seemed to take forever, but finally the two youths appeared. Penelope had tears in her eyes as she led Geris forward. The boy's gait was hunched—all those months spent tied up in a cramped space had weakened his muscles and wreaked hell on his posture. Geris's face was clean, the curls in his blond hair nearly bouncing. He wore a fresh tunic and breeches, though Penelope had not brought clean clothing down into the well. He cocked his head at her.

"I told you," she said, chin jutting out with pride. "I've taken good care of him."

"I suppose you have," he replied with a chuckle.

At the sound of his voice, Geris stumbled. Ahaesarus reached down to help him stay steady, but the youth pulled away as he tried to keep his own footing. Penelope wrapped her arms around him, steadying him with a bear hug.

The boy's blue eyes flicked up then, staring right into his own. The combined moon and torchlight gave them an even deeper resonance than usual. The corners narrowed, and Geris slowly lifted himself fully upright, with Penelope's assistance. Ahaesarus cringed when he heard the *pop* of vertebrae slipping back into place.

For a long while they remained silent, boy staring at former master and vice versa. Expressions shifted, and those not involved in the staring match began to shuffle back and forth and murmur restlessly. Judah muttered that the boy was obviously not well and ought be returned to the pit, a statement Ahaesarus decried with a fierce look.

A pained cry escaped Geris's throat, and he careened toward Ahaesarus at breakneck pace. His fellow Wardens rushed forward, but Ahaesarus shouted for them to back away. Geris collided with him, arms squeezing around his torso. The Warden tousled the boy's hair as Geris pressed his cheek against his doublet and sobbed. His hands worked the fabric around Ahaesarus's back, kneading and stretching. "I'm so sorry, I'm so sorry," he said over and over. Eventually, the Warden gripped him tight by both shoulders and gently pulled him away. He knelt down before Geris, who, despite his gauntness and pale skin, looked just like the child he'd thought would one day be king.

"I know you are sorry," he said. "You have told me every time I have visited for the past three months."

Geris nodded.

"And I am sorry too," said Ahaesarus. "For what you suffered, for placing you in that well...for everything."

The boy chewed on his bottom lip, his cheeks glistening in the moonlight.

"Son, how do you feel?" he asked.

Geris shook his head. "Better. Not perfect," he said with a sniffle. His lips twitched between a smile and a sorrowful frown. "Please tell...please let Ben know I never wanted to hurt him."

Ahaesarus pulled him in close once more and rubbed the back of his head. "I will. That is all in the past, son. Tonight you begin anew."

"But what if I'm not better?" the boy asked.

"If you were not better," said Ahaesarus, glancing at Penelope and trying to sound confident, "you would not be leaving with her."

He stood up then, and Penelope came forth, twining her hand with his former student's. She handed him one of the sacks and slung the other over her own shoulder. They stood there in silence, two youths looking to the Warden for guidance.

"What will we do?" the girl asked.

Ahaesarus pointed off in the distance. "You will head away from here, away from Mordeina and humanity. Find a way to cross the river just west of here. Go to the shore, or maybe the Craghills. It is a wild land, unvisited by humans. The nearest settlement is Conch, many miles north, but you are not to go there unless as a last resort. There will be war in Paradise soon, and only after that war has ended should you consider letting your presence be known." He cleared his throat. "Remember, distrust everyone you encounter until you learn the outcome of the war."

"What's that mean?" asked Geris. He sounded younger than fourteen in that moment.

"It means we do not know who will win," Ahaesarus said gravely. "Should you emerge from the wilds, the flag of the lion may fly over the place you once called home."

There were teary good-byes as student left teacher, wandering into the pitch-black forest through the gap in the wall and disappearing as if he'd been swallowed by nothingness. Ahaesarus shivered. He was frightened for the two youths, but he knew in his heart that he had made the right choice. All of humanity deserved its chance to thrive. Geris deserved it most of all.

"What if he is not cured?" asked Olympus. "How can you be sure?"

"I trust my own eyes," Ahaesarus said with a shrug. "For the last eleven weeks he has shown marked signs of improvement. But even if he is still ill, that girl will guide him through it." He slapped his hands on his knees and turned to his brothers. "But let us not think of things outside our control any longer. We have a war to fight and quite a ride to get there before we can fight it."

"And what of the boy?" Judah asked. "Isabel will not be happy when she discovers you set him free."

Ahaesarus shrugged. "And? This journey is already my punishment, and by the time she discovers he is missing, we will all be long gone."

CHAPTER

15

Matthew stood at the base of a jetty, feet balanced on the slippery rocks, while he watched waves ripple across the bay. The night was overcast, the air muggy and filled with the scents of salt and decay. In the darkness, the gently undulating water became a shimmering black cloak, the surface hinting at peace and harmony while concealing a torrent of activity that raged beneath. Right now there were small fish being fed on by larger fish, which were then being devoured by larger fish still, a sharply climbing scale of predator and prey, all of which were eventually rendered helpless by the nets and harpoons of men.

Just as the might of the gods renders man helpless, he thought with a shiver.

He wrapped his cloak tight around himself and fidgeted. The sight before him was depressing. The docks of Port Lancaster had teemed with activity for all of Matthew's thirty-six years, yet now they were virtually empty. A scant nine boats bobbed in the harbor, and only one was of the Brennan fleet, a mid-sized clipper named *Harmony Rose.* The rest of his ships were away—some with the survivors from Haven in the Isles of Gold to the west, some ferrying goods up and down the northeast coast—and his free river barges had been conscripted by Karak for purposes left unsaid. A small envoy from Veldaren, led by a few red-cloaked acolytes, had arrived in the city to demand use of them, and Matthew, needing to preserve his perceived loyalty to his deity, had no choice but to give them over. At least the visitors and their battalion of armed soldiers didn't seem to have noticed the dearth of vessels in the bay.

"Any sign yet?" asked a familiar female voice.

Matthew pivoted on his heels to see Moira approaching, lantern in hand. Her attire, a pair of velour slacks, a shawl, and strappy sandals, was suitable for negotiating the tricky footing of the coast, yet still regal. He appreciated that she was maintaining her disguise as a noblewoman. Knowing how much she despised what she referred to as "monkey garments," it was a great sacrifice—though it was a worthwhile one, for the acolytes had not recognized her. And though her hair had grown out some, now falling just above her shoulders, she had kept on dyeing it dark, even though the dyes had the unfortunate side effect of making each strand brittle.

"Not yet," Matthew told her.

"Are you sure tonight is the night?"

"Yes. The last evening of spring, just as Romeo said."

"Perhaps they were held up."

"Perhaps. Or perhaps they won't come at all."

He returned his eyes to the sea as Moira fell in beside him. Her lantern added a needed touch of brightness to the black, making him feel less alone. He could hear her breathing: short, pointed bursts of air that left her lips as if she were preparing to give birth. Having been around Moira for some time now, he knew it meant she was preparing for the worst, readying herself to snatch the two swords hidden beneath her overcoat and leap into action.

"Are you not frightened to be out here alone?" she asked.

"Not alone," he said, jabbing his thumb behind him at the great wooden structure that loomed over the rocky shore a few hundred yards back. "Twenty crossbowmen are on top of the warehouse, and Bren has another twenty swordsmen with the merchandise." His hand swooped from beneath his cloak, clutching a glossy black tube of sulfur and a metal striker. "Should something go wrong, all I need do is light the warning flare. We'll be fine."

"What if they arrive with a hundred men bent on doing you harm?"

He shrugged. "Then we run and pray we're faster. No use dwelling on it, though. I put my trust in the Connington brothers. I must believe they will not betray me."

"Faith ill placed, I think," she said with a chuckle.

"Shush, you. I'm trying to ignore that detail."

Moira laughed. It felt good to hear it.

"Poke fun all you want," he said with a smirk. "Truth is, if anything *should* go wrong, who do you think will face death sooner, you or I?"

She laughed again. "You, of course. I'm not in one of those horrid dresses this night. Any hope you have of outrunning me is long gone."

Matthew chuckled, but the sound was hollow. He stared off into the ocean, letting his mind wander.

"Why so quiet?" asked Moira. Her velvety fingers brushed his cheek.

He glanced her way and blushed, his insides rumbling. Spending so much time with Moira had caused his feelings toward her to shift. She was no longer simply collateral; she was a beautiful woman who proved her loyalty and aptitude each day she spent at his side. If he thought, for even a moment, that she felt the same way...

"Just thinking," he said. "It's been months, and we still have no further information on who made that attack against us. There's no record of those men entering the city, and no one was willing to admit to knowing them. It's as if they were ghosts paid by shadows, neither one leaving a damn clue."

Moira took a step back and joined him in staring out across the water.

"Is there someone who wishes you ill?"

He laughed.

"Many someones: Tod Garland, the Mudrakers, the Blackbards, the Conningtons even. They all hate me equally, though I'd cross Romeo and Cleo from the list because of our deal. Still, those sneaky bastards are far too loathsome and clever for me to make even that assumption."

Matthew shoved his hands in his pockets and once more watched the undulating waves as they lapped the rocks.

"Tell me," Moira said, breaking the silence. "Why the distrust between you and the Conningtons? I would think that the services you both render would make you…allies. Working together would make more sense than squabbling. It would be more profitable."

"There is no profit to be made now," he said. "There is no trade, no industry to speak of. Not until the war ends." He thought of two gods locked in combat, two equal halves that might never gain an advantage over each other. "If it ever does."

She shook her head. "No. I'm speaking of before. This discord isn't new. You told me so yourself."

"True," he said with a sigh. "I guess we're all ambitious men, and ambitious men don't tend to be willing to share. It doesn't help that I believe them responsible for the rumors claiming I was using Karak's long absence to usurp power from the king."

"Were you?" Moira asked.

"Ambition is not treachery," Matthew said. "I do still love my god in my own way—don't give me that look, Moira, I know how you feel—and the throne has been nothing but good to my family since the crowning of the Vaelor line. These rumors were spread to discredit me and lessen my family's hold on the realm's markets. The Conningtons were supposedly grooming a man to take over Port Lancaster in the event of my death, and building boats in an attempt to wrest away my loyal customers. They might have succeeded, had I not a supporter in Veldaren to put these rumors to rest three years ago."

"Minister Mori?"

"Yes," he said, feeling a pang of sadness. "Gods rest her soul. Soleh did not deserve the fate she received. The minister loved her god more than any other. I will never believe her a blasphemer."

"There are many of Karak's judgments that aren't to be believed," Moira said. She seemed to be enjoying his discomfort. "He is more wed to his need for order than his love for his own."

He silenced her with a wave of his hand. "I can see that. But do you understand my dilemma? This is the god that created us. Coming to the conclusion that he does not hold our best interests in mind has been…difficult."

She grunted, shaking her head. "Be that as it may, the minister is gone now. And you have made a *new* pact with the Conningtons, one that directly opposes the Divinity. Do you not see the contradiction?"

"Oh, I do," said Matthew. "But these sorts of things are complicated. You heard what the brothers said in the theater. This very well may be a long war, longer than the entire world could realistically handle. We must look out for ourselves."

"By giving weapons to Ashhur's children?" asked Moira, gazing toward the storehouse on the pier off to her left. She grinned. "I applaud the sentiment, obviously, given my dislike for Karak. But still…inner conflict is never good for the soul. Are you sure you're doing the right thing?"

"I need to believe I am," Matthew whispered.

"Even if the loss of those weapons leaves you open for the Conningtons to attack you?"

"Even so. This is not a decision I came to lightly. We are human, after all, and as I said, the only ones we can rely on…are ourselves. I needed to feed my people. I have not put my trust in the brothers lightly."

Silence fell between them after that. Matthew paced across the slippery rocks. It was all he could do to keep from tearing out his hair. He knew Moira was right, knew that all of this—his pact with the Conningtons and the aid he'd given the survivors from Haven—was threatening to undo everything his family had worked so hard to build. *I have no choice,* he told himself. Neldar was on the verge of starvation and violence. If the gifts he had to offer could help protect the future of his family, he had to at least try.

Moira pointed into the distance, snapping him out of his thoughts.

"It's here," she said.

A ship appeared in the bay, blacker than black atop the waves as it passed between the walls and cliffs of Port Lancaster. It came forward slowly, sails unfurled, quiet as the grave. Matthew shuddered, thinking of the ghost ships from his father's stories, shadow vessels that never reached shore, their decomposing crews hanging from the decks, the bones of their fingers clanking against ethereal hulls. Deep down he knew they existed only in stories, but it was impossible for his waking mind to dismiss the image.

As the ship neared, he saw that it was only made of wood and not some unearthly protoplasm. It was a handsome longboat, narrow and low to the water, built for speed and secrecy. There were two masts and six portals for oars on either side, though no oars slapped the undulating water. He saw no crew, though a single lantern burned in the aft shanty, the shadows behind it hinting at a human silhouette. A white flag fluttered on the bow.

"It's time," Matthew said, an uneasy feeling in his gut.

"Are you sure?" asked Moira. "There could be men with swords below deck."

"The Conningtons gave me sixty wagons of food, Moira. Not exactly something they can take back. I trust it as a sign of honest business."

"Yet you prepared for the worst."

"Of course. I'm cautious like that."

He turned toward the pier, pulled out a second sulfur stick, this one laced with copper, and struck it with flint. The green flames shot out from the end, and he held the stick up high as he marched over the slick rocks with Moira at his side.

When he reached the pier, Bren and the sellswords were already hard at work, lugging three enormous crates out of the storage shack at the base of the pier. Moira went to help them with the labor, while Matthew strolled farther down the dock, watching the mystery boat as it approached.

A rope flew from the deck of the vessel, thrown by unseen hands. Matthew caught it and tied it to the post bolted to the floor of the pier. A few of his sellswords came to his aid, catching even more ropes as they were cast from the boat. Soon it was tethered tightly to the docks, rocking and swaying, nary a sound nor a movement to be seen. Matthew felt the fear of the unknown once more, of ghosts and demons and otherworldly things bent on doing him harm.

It was then a trio of lanterns hanging from the masts of the mystery ship came to life. Three figures appeared on deck. Matthew's heart rate quickened. They were tall beings, not quite so lofty as Wardens, but still imposing. They wore heavy cloaks, cowls sheathing their faces in darkness. They slid a gangplank over the side of the ship, fastening it to the hull with steel brackets, before descending to the pier. When they walked, they held their hands in front of them, hidden in bulky sleeves.

"Welcome," Matthew said. His men had hauled the three crates down the dock, and he stood before his inventory like a carnival mystic preparing to reveal the secrets of the world to his audience. "I'm sure you'd like to examine the contents. If you give me a few moments, I will have one of my men open the first so you can see for yourse—"

"No," the middle figure said. His voice was gravelly and low, more like the growl of a wild animal than the voice of a man. "We've

been assured of your cooperation." The one who had spoken looked
to the stars. The cowl moved with him, keeping his face cloaked in
shadow. "The night progresses. We must be at sea by sunrise."

"Well, all right then," said Matthew. He stepped aside and gestured to the crates. "They're all yours. Will you need help loading
them onto your vessel?"

"Place them in the aft," another of them said. They were the last
words any of them spoke before disappearing into the darkness-
shrouded ship.

"Men with so much to hide are not to be trusted," Moira whispered into his ear. "They hide even the skin of their hands with
those robes."

Matthew glared at her.

"We plot behind the backs of gods. Their precautions do not
surprise me. Besides, the price the Conningtons paid is well worth
the risk." He turned his attention to his men. "All right, boys, you
heard him. Let's get the cargo on board, and be quick about it."

"We're all going to be getting a raise, right?" asked Bren with a
grin.

"Shut up and move your ass."

Grunts of exertion followed, and by the time all three crates
had been loaded onto the longboat, the eastern horizon, mostly
blocked by the wall and the bay's concealing cliffs, was beginning to
brighten. The ship pushed off the dock, and long pikes plunged into
the water, turning the nose around. The sails lifted, and a brisk wind
kicked up as if summoned from the heavens, propelling the boat
across the bay toward open ocean. Matthew stood on the pier and
watched it go, hoping beyond hope that the Conningtons' plan was
viable. The livelihood of all of Port Lancaster—of Neldar itself—
could very well depend on it.

CHAPTER

16

Despite the blazing sun overhead, the sand felt cool between Aully's toes as she walked barefoot through the desert. Those who had lived their whole lives in Ker assured her that in a few weeks that sand would become hot enough to raise blisters on the feet of anyone foolish enough to venture into the arid region without the proper attire. She loathed the thought, for exploring the wilds of the desert was her favorite pastime. She and Kindren went hiking near every morning, visiting the small settlements that popped up sporadically throughout the vast wasteland of dunes and red cliffs. They would sit with the locals, chat with them, and display small feats of magic in return for conversation and a taste of the local fare—fried cactus stuffed with oat and wildflower mash, roasted ferret, sweet leek soup containing chunks of lizard meat, usually finished off with pomegranate wine. Given the giant Bardiya's strict decree that none were to venture near the borders, these expeditions were the last bastion of entertainment in all of Ker.

Right now, she wished she and Kindren were wandering as they usually did, instead of sneaking after Bardiya, who had left earlier that afternoon with an admonition that none were to join him on the day's quest. It was an odd command for him, both because he always took company with him on his prayer missions and because it was rare for the inhumanly tall man to make such iron commands.

Bardiya was nothing but a shimmering black dot in the distance, and Aullienna allowed herself to set aside her fears and focus on her surroundings. She found beauty in the desert; the rippling sand and high dunes were like waves in a white ocean that moved so slowly that not even an elf's keen eyes could decipher the movement. The cliffs they came across were tall and majestic, like stone fingers offering salutations to Celestia, and every so often they would come upon a small thatch of trees, in the middle of which was a patch of crystal blue water. Lizards often congregated in those magical little spots, along with the occasional desert hare. No land, no matter how harsh, was completely uninhabitable.

Her heel sank into the sand and she stumbled. She yelped in surprise, teetering to the side, but Kindren was there in an instant, his hands slipping beneath her armpits. His fingers brushed her right breast, barely covered by the sheer lambskin linen she wore that day, and her insides fluttered.

"Watch it," her love said, chuckling. "Don't want to break a leg way out here."

"Sorry," she said, blushing.

He wrapped an arm around her waist. "Here, lean on me for a while."

And so she did, just as she had come to do in so many ways. Her eyes lifted to the bright blue sky, toward the star of her goddess, concealed by the brightness of the day. *Thank you for him, Celestia,* she prayed silently. *I don't know what I'd do without him.*

Looking up at Kindren, Aully felt her mouth stretching wide. "Forever," she whispered, the only word she could think to say. Her love glanced down at her with a smile.

For ten paces they held each other's gaze, and when Kindren finally lifted his eyes to their surroundings, he paused, his grip tightening on her side.

"What is *that*?" he asked.

They had unwittingly made their way to a ledge of sorts. Behind and off to the side was a triple-peaked rock face, the lower ledge packed with desert flowers and wavering brown grasses, a natural bridge of stone spanning between the second and third peaks. In front of them was a slightly pitched cliff, the stone worn smooth from decades of wind blasting sand against its side. To the left of the cliff was what looked to be a gritty path packed with hardened sand, leading down the gentle slope. The formation was the same yellowish-white color as the sand, making it virtually invisible to the naked eye until they were right on top of it.

But the rock face and cliff were not what had captured Kindren's attention. Aully followed his gaze, which was fixed on a strange black finger of obsidian down below them. Bardiya was standing beside it, and the thing was three times as tall as the giant.

"Wow," she whispered.

"Stay low," Kindren said, gently pushing her down until both of them lay on their bellies in the shifting sands. A gust of wind blew, assaulting her face and eyes. She buried her head in her arm, waiting for it to stop.

When it did, she glanced over to see Kindren spitting and wiping splotches of dirt from his mouth. He smiled awkwardly at her, his pale cheeks flushing red.

"Stupid wind," he said.

"Missed some." She reached over, wiped a few stray granules from the corner of his lip with her thumb.

"Where would I be without you, Aully?"

"Probably locked in your room back at your parents' palace."

She had meant it as a joke, but Kindren grimaced just the same, averting his eyes and staring down at the jutting black rock. Aully sighed, muttered a curse to herself, and did the same, shielding her eyes when another squall hit them.

"Who else is down there?" Kindren asked. His voice was soft.

Aully squinted. "Don't know. Hard to see through the wind and all."

"Looks like a guy on a horse. Or *with* a horse. He's all shiny too." She looked at Kindren, who was straining to see, as if he could create a looking glass by squeezing his eyelids together tightly enough. "He looks…funny."

"Funny how? I can't see anything. It's all blurry."

Kindren shrugged. "Shaped funny. Don't know. Probably just a trick of light or something."

"Maybe."

He rolled over then, peering at her with frowning lips. "Aully, that wasn't fair."

"What?" she asked. "I just said 'maybe.'"

Kindren shook his head. "No, not that. What you said about me being locked in my room. You know I risked everything to get you out of Dezerea, but what I did…I didn't do it just because of you."

She stared at him, uncertain of what to say.

Kindren closed his eyes, took a deep breath. "I helped Ceredon free you because it was *right*. Because it was horrible what the Neyvar and my parents did to your family. I would have done it under any circumstances. Please know that."

Shame filled her.

"It was just a joke," she whispered. "I'm sorry."

He threw his arm around her and smiled. "I know. And it's okay, I'm not mad. I'm really not. I just…I just need you to understand the kind of man I am. It's not always about just you and me. If we're ever going to get home, we have to think about what's right for everyone else too. That is something you want, right?"

She nodded.

Kindren kissed her, then slapped at the sand. "You know what? Let's head back. There's nothing to see here, and it makes me feel dirty spying on the one human who considers us his equals."

"All right."

They stood up while the giant and the mystery man continued their summit down below. Turning back, they began the journey home. The sudden winds had erased their tracks in the sand, giving Aully a moment of fright, but Kindren seemed confident. Her spirits rose ever so slightly, and she leaned into him, pressing her ear to his chest so that she could hear the beat of his heart.

"Thank you," she said, smiling.

"For what?"

"For dealing with me."

She gazed up at his beautiful face as he guided her along, and her heart nearly stopped when his expression darkened and he brought them both to a halt. *What did I say now?* she thought, but then she heard a low, guttural rumble.

They were standing before the rock face. A shape appeared on the pure sandblasted surface of stone, a creature that matched the white and taupe colors of the desert, slinking on four legs through the arch between two of the peaks, tramping over the bronzed grasses at the base of the formation. A blood-red tongue licked over a pair of wicked incisors as the sandcat stalked closer.

"Get behind me, Aully," Kindren whispered from the side of his mouth. "Go slow, no sudden movements."

He gently nudged her, and she slipped around his back, holding onto his thin cotton tunic with both hands. Kindren backed up one step, then another, hunkering down and holding his arms out as if preparing to grapple. The sandcat came closer still, its paws sinking into the sand with every stride, its emerald-green eyes desperate with hunger. The thing was barely as big as Aully herself, but when it yawned out a sound like a bag of rocks shaking together, she realized just how huge its jaws were. She squeezed her eyes shut, trying to remember what Bardiya had told them about the beasts. All she could recall was some nonsense about sandcats being just as sacred as elves and humans, and they should feel honored if and when they came face to face with one. "Until it rips out your throat and eats you alive," Kindren had quipped afterward.

It didn't seem so funny now.

"They're afraid of fire," she whispered, remembering the one lesson she had taken from Bardiya's lecture.

Kindren made a steeple with his fingers, holding them in front of his face.

"Then let's give it a show."

He muttered a few words of magic, and a small flame rose from his fingertips. The sandcat paused, and when Kindren swung his arm in an arc, making the fire trail in a circle, the beast backed away.

"That's right, go back where you came from," said Kindren. It sounded like he was laughing.

That laugh did not last long. The sandcat lunged forward, its paws a blur as it raced toward them, its maw opened wide, baring its deadly teeth. Aully screeched, and Kindren shoved her away. The fire from his fingertips fizzled in his panic as he brought up his arm to shield his face from the sandcat. Aully watched, frozen with terror, as the creature's jaws bit down on his forearm, causing her love to scream in pain. Blood flowed down his elbow as he fell to the ground. The sandcat's paws raked frantically against Kindren's sides, ripping through tunic and flesh, painting the desert sand red.

Watching her love be mauled by the sandcat enraged Aully. She scampered to her feet in the shifting sand and raced toward the beast, her ears filled with the sounds of Kindren's pained shrieks and the sandcat's snarls and growls. She leapt atop the beast, pounding her clenched fists into the back of its neck. It was like punching a stone wall covered in moss. Her fists having had no effect, she grabbed the thing by its ears and pulled with all her might. The sandcat reared up on its hind legs, shaking itself free from her grip. The force of it flung her back, and she landed hard, the wind knocked out of her. When her vision stopped spinning, she saw the sandcat staring at her, green eyes glaring with hunger.

Aully stumbled to her feet once more, trying to run from it, but she was too slow. She felt searing pain in her spine as its claws tore through fabric. It was worse than when she'd broken her arm falling from one of the trees back in Stonewood, when she was eight. In a last-ditch effort, she dove to the side, jarring her chin and swallowing a mouthful of sand when she fell. The sandcat raced past her, sliding on its side when it tried to veer too sharply.

Aully reached around to touch her torn back, and when she brought her hand in front of her face, it dripped with blood. The sight of it somehow cooled the pit of fear and panic in her stomach. Everything she'd experienced, every bit of suffering since the Ekreissar's march into Dezerea, came flooding back. Her father's death, their time in the dungeons, the systematic execution of her people…her poor sister Brienna's death at the hands of faceless attackers in some barren land. All the unfairness, all the injustice flared deep within her, flooding her with an anger she could hardly believe was her own.

Lightning sparked at her fingertips.

The sandcat whirled around, gaining its footing for another charge. Aully uttered no words of magic when she thrust out her hands. Blue lightning leapt from her palms, striking the sandcat in the side. The beast yelped and skittered, falling to the sand. A thunderous boom echoed inside Aully's head, and all the colors in her vision momentarily reversed. She fell to her knees, completely drained.

Despite her exhaustion, she felt a new sense of control over the world's chaos and the dark things that sought to harm her. The sandcat rose up, unable to lift its left rear leg, its side charred and blackened above its front hip. The beast licked at the wound and glanced at her, and she saw fear in its emerald-green gaze. Then the beast limped away, heading back for the three-tiered rock face where it likely lived.

"Did you see that?" Aully panted. "Kindren, did you see what I did?"

There was no answer.

She turned, groggy, and her eyes fell on Kindren. Her breath quickened and she scooted across the sand, her panic returning tenfold as she took in the blood surrounding his prone body. She reached her prone love and lifted his head into her lap. He was a mess, with deep gouges all over his torso and puncture wounds in his neck. His cheek dangled in a flap, exposing the musculature of his jaw and his rear teeth.

"Kindren," Aully whispered.

Her hand touched his chest. She could not feel his heart beating. She leaned over him, crying, kissing his maimed face, her lips lingering just below his nose. No breath came from his nostrils. Agony filled her, and whatever rage she'd known while fighting the sandcat suddenly seemed pitifully small compared to her sorrow.

"Kindren!" she screamed.

✛

"But what about the barn?" the deformed man said. "Does such rampant evil not need to be stopped?"

Bardiya gazed down at his old friend Patrick, who was standing next to his horse, his intense blue eyes filled with disappointment. Bardiya swore he could see contempt there as well, and it wounded him deeply. But he would not change his mind, no matter how much he was disappointing his friend. He would stay forever strong, just like the timeless Black Spire, which loomed beside them.

"I am sorry, Patrick," he said. "I made a promise to my people, and it is a promise I intend to keep."

Patrick shook his head, the half helm atop it shifting and clanking. "Dumb. Just fucking dumb."

"Save your harsh words. Surely Ashhur told you what my answer would be before you came here."

"He did." The misshapen man looked up at him in scorn. "But I thought maybe the story of what our people suffered would change your mind. I thought you'd be smarter."

"Intelligence has nothing to do with it."

"Oh, that's right. We're talking about the great Bardiya, he of the grand ideals. Those ideals are going to get you and everyone else you love killed!"

"If that is what comes, that is what comes."

Patrick pulled off his helmet and flung it to the ground.

"Oh come *on*! You cannot be that stupid. You can't! Too many people are depending on you."

Bardiya jabbed his fists into his hips. Feeling anger rising in his gut, he took a deep breath, slowing his heart rate.

"Ashhur preached peace, love, forgiveness, and nonviolence. He created Paradise. I will not taint that by becoming all I disdain." He swallowed hard. "I have seen the price of brutality, Patrick. I have lost control before. It will not happen again."

"You think *you've* seen the price?" Patrick exclaimed. "You didn't see Karak kill thousands of innocent people with flames from the sky! You didn't see those people burned to a crisp while they were trapped and screaming!"

"I am not so free of the world as you'd think," Bardiya said, gritting his teeth, "but I am determined to practice the words of our god. I met those who killed my parents, and I put Ashhur's sermons to use. I forgave them. And because of that forgiveness, we have been left alone."

Patrick kicked the helmet, but it was halfhearted, and the metal barely moved.

"You really think that's the reason, don't you? What about when Karak comes storming southwest, ready to burn and kill everything you hold dear? You think your forgiveness is going to help then?"

Bardiya frowned.

"You said Karak's forces approach the Wooden Bridge. They've already skirted our borders; yet instead of invading, they turn north. If what you say is true, why has the Eastern Divinity not descended on us? He has had every opportunity."

Patrick screamed an incomprehensible curse at the sky.

"I have no idea. Maybe he's waiting. Maybe it's because you're ten fucking feet tall. Who knows? All I *do* know is that he is closing in on Ashhur, and the god you spent your whole life dedicated to might *die* if you don't get off your ass and help!"

Bardiya extended his arms to the sky in supplication. "Do you not see, Patrick? Karak pursues Ashhur because Ashhur violated his own edicts. He succumbed to violence, he assailed when he should have stood idle. It is our god's fault that his Paradise is threatened."

"Wait! Hold on," said Patrick, his jaw dropping open. "You're mad that Ashhur refused to keep his vow of nonviolence, yet you won't condemn Karak for bringing a whole fucking army into our nation to slaughter thousands of those innocent people?" The man took a step back, looking thoroughly defeated. "My god, Bardiya... you've lost it. Truly lost it."

Bardiya's pride felt wounded, and he hated the look he saw on his friend's face.

"Karak's beliefs have nothing to do with me," he said quietly. "And when a child wanders into the forest only to be attacked by a wolf, you do not blame the wolf. For myself, I choose to remain impartial, just as our beliefs have always dictated."

"Beliefs change. *Circumstances* change. Even Ashhur can see that."

"Mine do not."

Patrick's horse whinnied, and he placed his hand on its cheek, stilling the beast. The mismatched armor he wore was dull and scratched, and he seemed weighted down by the massive sword strapped to his back, a weapon whose presence in Paradise Bardiya had long loathed. His old friend looked like a sad imitation of the noble warriors from the Wardens' stories, and Bardiya felt pity for him. Perhaps Patrick DuTaureau was the one who was truly lost.

"There is still time," Bardiya said, picking up the helmet and handing it to him. "Decry violence. Turn your back on this war, and convince Ashhur to do the same. Even if you perish, you shall do so nobly. The gates of the golden eternity will swing open wide for you, and you will be greeted as a hero."

"There you go again," Patrick said with a sigh. "Sometimes I think you'd rather be up in the heavens than here in the flesh."

"I wish to have both, my friend. One cannot enter the heavens if the flesh is not pure."

That elicited a chuckle. "Then I have no chance either way. My flesh hasn't been pure for a long, long time." His smile faltered, and he bent down, brushing the sand with his fingertips. "All of Ker buries their dead under these sands, correct?" he asked.

"Yes, we do."

"How many now? How many have you buried?"

"Four hundred and eighty-seven."

"And your parents are under here as well?"

"Yes."

Patrick stood to his full height, looking somehow both noble and ridiculous at the same time.

"I'd prepare, if I were you," he said. "You'll soon to have a lot more dead to bury."

Patrick took two steps away and then froze as thunder echoed in their ears. A blood-curdling scream ripped through the afternoon sky a moment later. Bardiya felt his heart leap into his throat.

"What the fuck?" his misshapen friend said.

Bardiya whirled around. The Black Spire rested in one of the more desolate areas of the Kerrian desert, the landscape a white wilderness as far as the eye could see. The only exception was the majestic rock formations along the path leading from Ang, which were the same shade as the sand and virtually invisible. That was where he looked now. He swore he saw movement there, the juxtaposition of dark beige against light, like a tiny cape flapping in the breeze. Then came another scream, and a chill flowed through his veins.

"Up there!" he shouted to Patrick as he began sprinting. His strides were longer, his progress faster. He heard Patrick's mare huffing as its four hooves stomped along the sandy terrain. Bardiya surged ahead like a man possessed, every fiber of his being in a panic. He wanted nothing more than to put an end to whatever torment the poor creature was experiencing at the top of the rise.

Though the wind blew past his ears with the force of a hurricane, he could still make out the sounds of tormented crying as he drew nearer. Images of broken bodies painted his vision, memories of his parents in the grove, their bodies bleeding from a dozen wounds. And then he crested the rise, and all his fears proved true.

The elf girl Aullienna leaned over the body of Kindren, the young prince of Dezerea. Deep gouges crisscrossed the pale skin on her back, and the elf boy's body was mangled, his flesh slashed in repetitious four-pronged patterns. Punctures dotted his body too, large half circles, and the flesh of his right forearm had been shorn away, leaving behind a glistening mess of muscle and sinew. The elf girl did not look up as Bardiya approached, but kept her forehead pressed against Kindren's chest, bathing his body in her tears.

"What in the bloody underworld…?" he heard Patrick gasp from behind him. Sand kicked up as the horse he was riding skittered to a stop.

Bardiya slid to the ground, his massive knees digging into the desert floor. Only when he placed his giant hand on the unmoving chest of the elf prince did Aullienna acknowledge his presence. Her gaze lifted to him, eyes bloodshot, tears forming thick rivulets down her face. She opened her mouth to speak, a pleading look coming over her beautifully innocent features, but only a shrill moan came out.

Reaching out, Bardiya placed a finger to her lips, quieting her. He then leaned over Kindren, placed both hands on his chest, and closed his eyes.

"Please help him," he heard the girl say, her voice a whisper.

The young elf was perilously close to the end. Bardiya prayed and prayed, knowing his lips were moving, though he could not feel them. At first there was nothing, and it took all his carefully trained willpower to tamp down his panic. His mind was full of questions and doubt, but he had to push all of it away. Taking in a deep breath, Bardiya continued to pray, forgetting his role as a leader of men, forgetting the power he wielded, the decisions that lay on his shoulders, the future shrouded in danger. He was here, now, with a life in peril…and through him, that life could be saved. That was what mattered. That was *all* that mattered.

Ashhur, grant me strength, his mind whispered.

The damage to the elf's body became clear to him: the severed muscle, the torn fibers in the boy's flesh, the gouged stomach, the snapped bones. Each wound struck him as if it were his own, and the burning sensation in his hands was as if he'd plunged them into the heart of a star. Much like when he'd healed Davishon— his would-be elven assassin—the pain lessened as Kindren's body mended itself, fractured bones binding with their broken halves, burst blood vessels closing, skin knitting itself shut. A final burst of energy flowed from his palms into the elf's chest, shocking his stilled heart back to beating. A gasp reached Bardiya's ears, and his mind returned to the physical realm.

He fell back, his energy drained. It took great effort just to lift his hand and wipe sweat from his brow. He opened his tired eyes and looked on as Aullienna cradled her mate's head in her lap, her tears of sorrow replaced by ones of relief. Kindren's eyes were open, but he looked like he did not understand what was happening.

"You are hurt, child," Bardiya told Aullienna wearily. "Come, let me heal you."

"Rest a moment," he heard Patrick say as Aullienna continued to hold Kindren. Bardiya twisted his head around. His friend was sitting atop his horse, staring at him and shaking his head.

"Her back is bleeding," Bardiya said.

Patrick shrugged.

"Let the nymph have her moment. The boy almost died."

"He should have," Bardiya whispered, and he heard wonder in his own voice.

"Yet you brought him back," said Patrick. "Good job, big guy. I just hope you learn your lesson."

"And what might that be?"

The redhead pointed to the couple on the ground.

"What you just did there? It was all because of Ashhur. Your god gave you the power to heal. You prayed to him, and he lent you his own strength so you could bring someone back from the brink of death. Amazing, if you think about it. And you'll never, ever be able to do that again once Karak has destroyed the god you love. The next time you try to save a life, you'll have to watch someone die instead."

Bardiya stood on weary legs, and as much as he wanted to deny his friend, he did not possess the strength to argue. Patrick's face hardened.

"Your place is coming to the aid of others," he said. "And your earlier example is shit. You may not blame the wolf for attacking a boy who wanders into the forest—I get that. But only a coward would stay outside the forest after discovering a child was missing."

Patrick turned his horse, glaring over his shoulder as he rode away.

"And the gods help the man who would watch that child die instead of *defending him from the wolf.*"

CHAPTER

17

The figurine was a foot tall, illuminated by ambient light reflecting off the chamber walls. Ceredon knelt to study it, his elbows pressed into the round oaken table. It was of a naked woman, wide at the hips and bosom, her hair flowing about her in unruly spirals. Though the statuette had been carved from plain sandstone, he still thought he could see the peach hue of her flesh. Her eyes were black, bottomless pits where mere mortals such as he lost themselves.

The figure's stance was odd: arms stretched up above her head, fingers fanned out, waist slightly bent, legs bowed and crossed at the ankles, head thrown back, mouth opened wide. The placement and pose invited wildly divergent interpretations: The upheld arms could represent a gesture of freedom or the stance of a bound woman; the arrangement of the bowed legs was common in both dance and swordplay; the opened mouth could be screaming in either pleasure or pain. Her every feature seemed to be wholly human, yet the curvature of her body was unmistakably elven. Ceredon shook his head. There was no contradiction here, no duplicity. This was the goddess, and for her, there was only balance.

"Celestia," he whispered, placing his hands on either side of the icon and closing his eyes. "Please, tell me what I do is right."

He sat listening to the rumble and creak of the massive crystal structure above him, waiting for some sign from his creator. But none came, not even a subtle shudder that might have suggested she was listening. Perhaps Father was right; perhaps Celestia no longer cared for her people.

"So be it," he said. His eyes snapped open, and he leaned forward to place a kiss on Celestia's bosom. "We may not be worthy of your love, but I have never stopped loving *you*. If you're watching, please know that what I do now is out of love—love for the people you created, love for the wisdom you taught us."

He stood up, took off his belt, from which his khandar still hung, and placed it on the table. He then removed a short dagger from his boot and examined it. The blade was sharp enough to slice down the length of a piece of thread. "I serve you always," he whispered. "Even in the darkest of moments."

Sheathing the dagger in a leather wrap and tucking it back into his boot, he lifted his eyes to his surroundings.

It is time, he thought.

He was in a chamber far underneath Palace Thyne, accessible via a passage in the crypts hidden beneath the sarcophagus of Ra'an Dultha, the first Lord of the Dezren. Tantric Thane, leader of the rebels fighting his father's regime, had revealed the passage's existence to him. "From the tunnels you can access any section of the palace unnoticed," he'd said. "We have tried to use them before, but to no avail. The palace is too large, the tunnels too narrow, the rooms too numerous. It took us three full evenings just to examine eight chambers, and all we found inside were servants and underlings...and your quarters. However, if you could tell us exactly where to look..."

"No," Ceredon had replied. "I must be the one to do the deed."

He had first he met Tantric in his bedchamber in Palace Thyne on the evening when his room was discovered. It had happened after yet another patrol during which Ceredon had protected the very rebels he'd been assigned to exterminate. They'd talked for only a short time before Tantric handed him the dagger that was now stowed in his boot, marked with the Thane family crest, which would help steer suspicion away from Ceredon when he used it. After that, the old elf had told him of the secret door behind the emerald fireplace that connected to a series of narrow, interlocking tunnels, one of which led to Lord Orden Thyne's secluded shrine, where Ceredon now prayed.

The time for prayers was over, though, and the elf breezed past the table, fingers sliding over the chamber's glimmering green walls as he disappeared inside a geometrical trick: one wall was positioned slightly forward from the other, creating a nearly invisible gap wide enough to slip through.

Although the exterior of Palace Thyne was of shimmering emerald, the foundation and what lay between the walls was pure granite, hard and compacted and bleak. When Ceredon exited the breach, leaving behind the twinkling green chamber, he was thrown into near darkness. He waited for his eyes to adjust and then placed his foot on the first step of a constricted staircase. The well was a steeply angled upward climb, the walls so close on either side that he had to move sideways so as to not scrape his shoulders against the rough stone. Every thirteen steps, a level ended, and four narrow openings in the floor led to small, circular tunnels containing access points to concealed entrances in dozens of rooms in the palace.

He climbed floor after floor, keeping count of how many times the stairwell rotated, until he reached the ninth story. After another quick prayer to Celestia, he dropped on his belly and pulled himself forward on his elbows, entering the north tunnel and a darkness so bleak that even his elven eyes could not adjust to it.

Panic tickled at the hairs on the back of his neck. The blackness was a living thing, squeezing in on him, trying to crush him. He had never experienced its like before, not even in the deep caves or the catacombs beneath the city. An urge to retreat to his room filled him, and he had to fight it. He felt ashamed of his cowardice. It was only darkness, and he would navigate the tunnel as he must, his claustrophobia and fears be damned.

He inched himself along, shooing a few squeaking rats away, sounding like a rat himself as his cured elk-skin breeches scratched against the rough stone. His hand fell on one portal to the right, one to the left, one to the right, one to the left, each emitting a soft, whispery puff of fresh air. He counted seven openings before stopping, swiveling on his stomach, and steeling himself for the task at hand.

Reaching above, his fingers found a thin stone shaft. He latched onto it with both hands and pulled himself upward, sliding from the tunnel like a snake. The world brightened, the air growing pleasantly warm. There was a second shaft above him and he ascended that as well. The heat grew with each passing moment, and when he drew himself up, he met a haze of smoke.

Just like all the portals, this one opened up behind a wide hearth. Ceredon carefully placed his feet on the sooty stone ledge and inched his way to the side. He had to hold his breath to keep from coughing, and every so often one of the dying embers would pop and leap, threatening to scorch him. Luckily none did. Perhaps Celestia was looking out for him after all.

There was a latch on the far side of the interior of the hearth, and when he pulled it, the corner bent away with a quiet rumbling, opening space for him to exit. He crawled out, not bothering to slide the corner back into place. He'd need it ready for his escape. Brushing himself off, he pulled the dagger from his boot and stepped into Conall's bedchamber.

The room's emerald walls lightly twinkled with the fading glow from the coals. The room's eastern-facing windows were covered with heavy drapes, blocking out light from outside. Still, Kindren could make out a pair of dressers arranged on one side of the room, a wardrobe positioned along another. Straight ahead was a four-poster bed, finely crafted from lacquered mahogany. The sheets on the feather mattress were silken and glossy, bulging in the center where a sleeping form lay.

Creeping across the room, Ceredon made sure his soft-booted feet made no sound. One wrong move and Conall would awake, summoning the Ekreissar to protect him.

When he reached the bed, he stopped, hovering over it for a moment. His father's cousin rolled onto his back, eyes firmly shut, chest rising and falling at steady intervals. Ceredon slowly knelt, even the faint creak and crumple of his clothing sounding much too loud to his ears. With one hand he grabbed a pillow. With the other he pressed the dagger against the side of Conall's neck.

In a single smooth motion he ripped it across the jugular. As blood erupted across the bed, Ceredon shifted, slamming the pillow against the older elf's mouth to hold in the sudden surprised shriek he emitted when he woke from his dream. Conall thrashed, clutching at his gushing throat, and from beneath the pillow came a subdued gurgle. Ceredon pressed harder, keeping the pillow positioned so that no blood splashed on his own clothes. The crimson fluid soaked the satin sheets, forming macabre patterns.

When Conall finally fell still, Ceredon pulled back the pillow, and he shuddered involuntarily at the sight of the ghost-white look of horror on the dead elf's face. Swallowing down bile, he moved to the window, careful not to step in the puddle of blood that had dribbled down to the floor. Pulling aside the curtain, he gave the pane of stained glass a quick strike with his gloved hand. The glass shattered, the shards tinkling when they struck the shimmering emerald floor.

The deed done, he hurried back to the hearth, sparing only a single look back at the mess he'd created, at the corpse of one of the three powerful members of the Triad in his fine satin sheets.

"And then there were two," Ceredon whispered before crawling back through the raised corner of the hearth.

✚

The occupied forest city of Dezerea was thrown into chaos in the aftermath of Conall's death. Countless Dezren men were taken from their treetop homes and brought to the palace courtyard. They were forced to bow, near two thousands of them crowding the grass, while the Ekreissar stalked up and down the lines, prodding them, taunting them, trying to force a confession. Aerland Shen paraded Lord Orden and Lady Phyrra before the stooped masses. The former rulers of the city had been beaten so badly, they were barely recognizable, and the plain white robes hanging off their backs were torn and speckled with dried blood.

"One of our own has been murdered!" screamed Neyvar Ruven, standing on the dais in front of the emerald palace's gate. "Who was it? Who leads the rebellion? Come forward, speak, and spare yourselves pain and suffering."

None did, though a murmur began to rise from the sea of bowed heads.

Ceredon felt his stomach clench as he watched the spectacle from his position at his father's side. A part of him did not understand the Dezren's lack of action. They numbered greater than eight thousand, their ranks more than adequate to overwhelm the scant forces the Neyvar had brought with him. It seemed absurd that the only ones standing against them were Tantric's rough and battered group of brave souls. Yet then he remembered his conversation with his father. Many of the Dezren were farmers, teachers, philosophers, musicians, and spellcasters. They were not warriors. The Quellan Ekreissar, on the other hand, were trained in the art of battle and had been since the Demon War a thousand years before.

"If the brother gods were not draining the power of the weave, the Dezren would have crushed us," his father had said. Now their spells were but a sad echo of the deadly force they had once wielded. The Dezren had been lessened by measures not of their own choosing, and Ceredon promised himself not to forget that.

His father, the Neyvar, continued to pace back and forth on the dais, shouting at the cowering male populace. Ceredon could see through his façade now. The anger in his voice was too righteous, his gestures overly exaggerated. Ruven was acting a part, and it seemed as though others were beginning to notice as well, for Aerland Shen scowled when he looked at the Neyvar, his hideous, wide-set face crumpling into an animal expression. Neyvar Ruven scowled in return and then turned in a huff and left the dais.

Aeson took the Neyvar's place, continuing the verbal assault on the kneelers. It was *he* who ordered Shen to lash Lord and Lady Thyne's backs with five-pronged whips while they were strapped to the feet of Celestia's grand monument. The lord and lady wailed, their eyes locked onto the goddess's likeness as their clothes and skin were flayed from their backs. Ceredon had to fight his urge to end their torment. Killing Conall would help them in time, he knew, but it was a shallow comfort. Ceredon's deed had brought them suffering. He had to remind himself that this was only further proof of the necessity of his nighttime assassinations.

They won't be killed, he thought as Lord and Lady Thyne slumped before the statue, the beating finally over. *They're being used to keep the people in line.* Once the last two members of the Triad were dead, once his father had regained full influence over the Ekreissar, the Thynes' suffering would end.

Aeson ushered the anguished and limping royal family away, then ordered the masses to rise. They did, hesitantly, and Ceredon could see the hatred painting each and every face. His father's cousin offered closing remarks to the Dezren men, and his words worried Ceredon.

"You are free to go," Aeson said, his lips twisted downward with anger. "But think twice if you consider turning against us. Come the morrow, you will know the full scope of the power we have at our disposal."

The next morning, Ceredon discovered the elf's meaning.

Warhorns blared as the swarm descended over the hills bordering the Gihon River, using the same route Shen and the Ekreissar had traveled a lifetime ago, then poured into the heart of Dezerea. The humans were wearing black and silver armor, and the banners of the eastern god, Karak, flew high above them, the wrathful lion roaring down on all who witnessed its fluttering countenance. Ceredon watched the endless procession from the dais, where he stood beside his father. He tried to count the troops as they formed into brigades before the palace steps, but he could come to no solid number. There had to be near a thousand men on horseback, bearing long spears, heavy axes, and sharp swords. There were at least four times that number on foot, with a hundred horse-drawn wagons trailing behind. The entirety of the human force overwhelmed the forest city like an invading colony of deadly ants. The Ekreissar, who lingered around the humans, seemed nervous and resentful in the same instant. Of those on the dais, including the entire consulate that had originally traveled to Dezerea for the betrothal, only Aeson and Iolas appeared content.

The horseman in front approached the dais. He was a hefty, bald man, his black leather overlaid with bronze chain, and he rode a majestic white charger. Everything about him seemed wrong: his face was too broad, his posture too hunched, and his eyes emitted a reddish glow. His flesh was also abnormal, for it seemed stretched to the point of translucency. Ceredon could see a web of red and green veins running beneath it. Every so often part of the man's body would throb, as if there were things lurking beneath his skin that might burst through the surface.

Then the man spoke, and the strangeness doubled.

"In the name of the mighty Karak," he said, his voice quite odd, almost as if two beings were speaking as one, "we come to your fair city in the trees. We seek food and shelter, as was our agreement. This shall be our base of operations in the west: our ferries shall remain untouched in the river, and you will give us all we require."

Ceredon opened his mouth to protest the strange bald man's demands, but his father squeezed his arm, silencing him. The Neyvar stepped forward and offered the odd horseman a slight bow.

"It is our pleasure to assist Karak and his soldiers, Highest Crestwell," he said in the human's tongue. "You will have all that was promised. We Quellan do not break our vows."

The leering, bald man offered a queer half grin, then bowed in the saddle.

"I was assured that would be the case," he said. "But I am Highest no longer, great Neyvar. Clovis will suffice."

"As you will," Neyvar Ruven replied.

Iolas stepped forward. "Will you come inside the palace, so we can discuss further terms?" the ancient elf asked. "Our rangers will assist your soldiers in situating themselves while we are detained, if that is acceptable to you?"

Clovis nodded, dismounted his charger, and wobbled up the steps. He seemed uncomfortable in his own skin, a strange trait for one with so much authority. Ceredon lingered behind as the man passed him, and he noticed a strange odor, like sulfur. Aerland Shen began barking orders, as did a second human on horseback, and the soldiers broke rank. All was deafening chaos as Ceredon followed his father into the palace, and he could hear grumbled complaints from many of his brethren. Being forced to assist humans was anathema to them.

The group settled into the Chamber of Assembly. Aeson and Iolas covered the statue of Celestia with a large tapestry at the request of the odd-looking human, and then they all took their places at the great table, Neyvar Ruven at one end, Clovis Crestwell at the other. Ceredon found it hard to hide the affront he felt when Celestia's likeness was concealed. Why should they do so for this human who came into an elven city under another god's banners? It was blasphemous.

Clovis sat board-straight, and it looked like it took his every effort to retain that posture.

"You wished to speak of terms," he said. His voice sounded even stranger when it echoed in the cavernous chamber.

The Neyvar nodded. "We risk much by giving you access to our city. You know our goddess demands neutrality in the affairs of humanity. I understand our cooperation was already agreed on, but if we are to break that pact—at great risk, I may remind you—we require further compensation."

"What do you have in mind?"

Neyvar Ruven gestured to Aeson, who spoke next.

"We seem to have encountered some resistance during our occupation. We would like your men to assist us in seeking out these rebels and eliminating them."

"How great are their numbers?" asked Clovis.

"A hundred, perhaps a score more."

The human laughed, and it sounded like the utterance of a hideous creature from the ocean depths.

"I bring with me five thousand troops," he said when his laughter died down. "And you would require their aid to defeat a mere hundred mutineers? We had always thought the Quellan to be great warriors. Perhaps we were wrong."

"They have proved...resourceful," countered Iolas.

"Then perhaps you should be even more so," snapped Clovis.

Neyvar Ruven lifted his hand. "It is not only that," he said, sounding weary. "We have a precarious hold on this city. The Dezren outnumber us greatly. Should they decide to join their rebel brethren, we would be overwhelmed. If that were to happen, there would be no safe haven for your soldiers to return to, no fields of turnips and grain for you to refill your supplies once they are exhausted. Given how your own armies are razing Ashhur's lands, our aid will be paramount to your success."

Clovis held up his hand. For a moment, Ceredon swore he could see a worm wriggling beneath the flesh of his palm.

"We understand this," the man said gravely. "The razing is occurring strictly south of the Gods' Road, to seal in those who might wish to aid their countrymen. Yet we will still help you. I can spare five hundred men, but not a soul more."

Neyvar Ruven nodded. "Yes, that would work."

"However, we must also balance the scales. If we are to keep these men behind, a show of good faith is required."

"We *have* shown good faith," insisted Aeson. "We let you march unimpeded through our lands and into our city. We attacked a pair of human settlements to the south to clear your way, and their loss of life was total. No man or elf should have reason to question our loyalty to the pact."

The man laughed. "That is appreciated, yes, much appreciated. Yet I must ask, how many of your best fighters are in this city?"

"About as many as you are giving us," said Iolas, looking despondent.

Clovis grinned. "We require a hundred of them."

"What?" Iolas gasped. "Why?"

"Our reasons are our own."

"We could ne—"

"Consider it done," said the Neyvar, cutting his old cousin off. "Are there any other claims you wish to stake?"

"As a matter of fact, there are." Clovis brought up his hand, rubbing it over his bald pate. Then he frowned, as if he'd expected to find hair. "For every show of good faith, there must be another in return. We shall place your best warrior in control of Karak's forces, and we will remain here to assist you in regaining control of the city."

Ceredon looked on as every elven face scrunched up in confusion at the human's odd wording.

"Excuse us," asked the Neyvar, "but who would 'we' be?"

The human cleared his throat. "Many apologies. Me. I. Clovis Crestwell, the captain of this quarter of our god's army. I will remain behind."

The table broke out in bickering between the two remaining members of the Triad, the Neyvar, and the four other advisors who had joined them. Ceredon remained silent, keeping an eye on his father the entire time. He noticed that Clovis was doing the same. When the argument eventually ended, it was the Neyvar who won.

"That is acceptable as well," he said. "You shall have Aerland Shen, the greatest of our Ekreissar, to lead your god's forces."

Crestwell smiled wickedly. The others who were present grumbled.

"You choose wisely, Neyvar."

"Just promise us one thing," Ruven said.

"What is that?"

"This bargain comes with another price. Upon Karak's victory, our lands must be increased tenfold, not fivefold as was discussed. Our sacrifices deserve that much."

The frightening human's grin became all the wider and more off-putting.

"You will have all that and more."

The summit ended, and the Quellan consulate retreated deeper into the palace, with the exception of Aeson, who huddled close to the human, talking with him in a lowered voice. Eventually, they too broke company, and Clovis left for another meeting, this one with Chief Shen. Ceredon didn't like the odd man's expression. Clovis had sneered at the departing elves, and Ceredon was sure he'd seen hatred in his red-tinged eyes. Upon his exit, Ceredon was at last alone in the Chamber of Assembly with his father's cousin.

"Why are you still here?" asked Aeson.

"I wish to uncover our goddess and pray for a while. I do not like this," he whispered to Aeson in the elven tongue.

The elder elf grinned.

"There is much not to like, but we must take what benefits present themselves. Clovis wishes the dungeons below the palace to be filled to their limits with Dezren prisoners. Once they're rounded up, we may begin exterminations as we see fit. Why rely on the cooperation of the Dezren when we can thin their numbers until they are no longer a threat? With more men at our disposal, even if they are humans, we may be able to accomplish that goal. Once Karak's Army marches, I'll discuss it with your father."

Aeson winked at him and took his leave of the chamber. Ceredon watched him go, anger boiling in his veins. His job might have just gotten harder, but at least he knew whom to target next.

"Sweet dreams," Ceredon whispered in the empty chamber.

CHAPTER

18

The horse faltered, almost pitching Roland and Kaya to the ground.

"Whoa, girl," Roland said, trying his best to keep them both firmly in the saddle. The poor horse straightened out, took a few firm steps, and then its leg crumpled once more. Roland cursed and pulled back on the reins, halting the animal. If it had pitched any lower, they would have been thrown to the rocky, root-infested ground. He and Kaya dismounted, Kaya caressing the horse's side, while he circled around to face her head on, watching her shake her head and blow her nose as if in frustration. Roland tugged on his belt, trying to swing the uncomfortable sword that hung there into a less dangerous position.

Azariah trotted up beside him, his gold-green eyes focused on the horse. Tall trees rose up behind him like swaying sentries.

"Check the hoof," the Warden said.

His friend sounded sullen, depressed, and fully unlike himself, a change that had come upon him since their last day in Lerder. Roland grimaced up at the Warden, then bent down and coaxed the horse into lifting her leg. The poor creature whinnied, blood dripping from her hoof. Roland immediately spotted a jagged piece of stone wedged into the soft tissue on the inside of the hoof.

"What is it?" asked Kaya from over his shoulder.

"Rock got stuck," he said. "Comfort her as you can. I'm going to pull it out."

He glanced at Azariah, who nodded.

Kaya did as he'd asked, her tone soothing as she spoke to the horse in words he was sure the animal couldn't understand. Yet the horse seemed to relax nonetheless, her leg muscles going slightly limp, allowing Roland to cram his fingers beneath the stone and give it a solid tug. It came free with a *thwop*, the blood from the sensitive tissue running a deeper red. Azariah handed him a swath of yellow fabric, and Roland stuffed the cloth into the horse's hoof to soak up the blood.

"It's best we find a place to rest for a time," the Warden said. "I will need to heal her."

Roland shook his head. He looked behind them, at the procession of panting horses in the forest, each holding two or more frightened individuals. A hundred more walked behind them.

"You don't mean here, do you?" Roland asked, looking around at the tall trees that circled all around them. "Shouldn't we find someplace more suitable, where the horses can graze on something that isn't poison berries?"

Azariah peered at the canopy above their heads. "It is almost dusk, Roland. Travel will only grow more dangerous."

"I still think we should find a different resting place," Roland said. "We shouldn't be too far from some settlement or another, right?"

"And what will we find when we get there?" the Warden asked with a frown.

Roland hung his head, dejected. Even Kaya rubbing his back wasn't doing much to soothe him.

They had kept off the Gods' Road in their travels, steering through the northern hill country in hopes of throwing off any potential pursuers. At first every village or hamlet they passed was deserted, but for a handful of humans and Wardens, but soon they discovered that the war had, in fact, crossed in front of them. Two settlements they'd encountered on their quest for the Wooden Bridge had been reduced to rubble and ash, the bodies of human and Warden alike strung up in trees. The areas surrounding each settlement had been trampled under countless feet and burned, leaving Azariah's group with little opportunity to restock their dwindling supply of food. In other places even the fruit trees had been decimated, each apple or pear snatched from the branches, nothing but rotting remains around the trunks. Fields had been stripped clear of all vegetation. And that didn't even take into account the problems they'd encountered with the horses. The poor beasts were constantly getting rocks or splinters lodged into their hooves, and at least three had broken limbs during the journey, costing them precious time while the Wardens healed their wounds.

"We'll find what we find," Roland replied softy. "And make do with that."

Azariah gave him a strange look.

"I cannot decide if you are stubborn, foolhardy, or wise, though I do find it amusing that you feel you know best. So let us continue, Roland, and discover which of the three it is."

The trek continued, the land rising and falling as they headed forever west. Just as the sun began to dip closer to the horizon, they came upon a small stream, and where they took a few moments to water the horses, who were exhausted to the point of collapsing. Roland refilled his waterskin and shared it with Kaya, who stayed latched onto his side like a growth. The water tasted off somehow, rotten and unseemly, but he drank it down just the same. He was parched beyond belief, and it hadn't rained since the day they'd left the riverside community. It amazed him that he actually wished for the rain to return. While building the wall, he'd hated it with a passion, but now he stared at the sky with desperate hope each time he saw a cloud.

But the stream meant there was probably another settlement nearby, which buoyed Roland's spirits slightly. When they finally began the journey once more, he had Kaya ride in the saddle with her younger sister while he walked beside the horse. The pair started singing, and he felt almost hopeful.

That hope died the moment they came upon civilization—or what was left of it. Jaquiel the Warden introduced the place as the village of Lockstead, yet no village remained. Ashhur had been here, that much Roland could tell; there were shattered chunks of stone and wood everywhere, the remnants of the wall the god had raised for the unfortunate few who'd stayed behind. Beyond the crumbled rubble were the burnt scraps of tents, a few toppled huts, their thatched roofs still smoldering, and a single demolished granary. The grass was scorched black, and when Roland squatted down to trace the outline of a large boot heel in the earth, he realized it was still warm.

"This happened recently," he said.

"So did the others," Azariah replied.

"But where are the bodies?"

The Warden shrugged.

Roland stood and circled, looking into the trees, but other than a few blackened lower branches, nothing had been disturbed. Strangely, the lack of bodies made him shudder. It was almost worse than seeing them all swaying in unison.

Kaya tugged on his shirt.

"Roland, I hear water," she said excitedly.

"The brook might be wider here. Perhaps it is even a stream," said Warden Jaquiel as he knotted his long auburn hair behind his head. "We might be able to snatch some fish."

Kaya's sister jumped in place.

"We could stay here for the night then?" she asked.

Roland exchanged a glance with Azariah.

"I think we should," Roland said. "It's dark now, and Karak's Army has already passed. There's no one to spot us. What do you think, Az?"

Azariah let out a sigh.

"Yes, we'll stay. Roland, come with me. I wish to check the nearby stream. Perhaps Jaquiel has the right of it, and there are fish to be had."

As the rest of the people flooded out of the forest, Roland and Azariah crossed the hill leading to the bubbling stream. As they neared the water, Roland felt his stomach twist into a knot. There would be no fish, not that night. The dead of Lockstead, perhaps seventy of them, bobbed there in the water. They had not drifted far, the stream too shallow and littered with twigs and felled branches to move them. The corpses had snagged and halted, colliding and piling on each other into a dam of sodden, rotting flesh. Roland dropped to his knees and vomited. The water…the peculiar taste of the water…

When finished, he popped the top of his waterskin and dumped the rest of it. Azariah watched, quiet, his face ashen.

"Not all is lost," the Warden said, his voice hoarse. "I know a spell to purify the water."

That night they slept in the open spaces of the desolate village. The horses hovered between nestled clumps of people, snorting and huffing. Roland lay on the bare ground beside a collapsed hut, with Kaya pressed against him, the supple feel of her body a small but necessary comfort. Her parents and siblings were beside them, most sleeping, some just pretending to. As he rested, his back sore and his hand aching from holding the reins too tightly, Roland swore he could hear a great rumble descend over the land. He chalked it up to the unified grumblings of two hundred hungry bellies.

He covered his ears with his hands, trying to block out the sound to get some sleep, but when he closed his eyes, he saw the glowing red stare of Jacob Eveningstar as his former master helped Karak raise the bridge across the Rigon. Frustrated and afraid, he lifted Kaya's arm from his chest and sat up. She stayed sleeping, tucking her hands beneath her chin. It amazed Roland how attached to her he was, how interwoven their lives had become. Yet that attachment had brought with it a deeper well of fear; now when he pictured the dead hanging from trees, they all had Kaya's face.

"I love you," he whispered, and kissed her cheek.

He stood and left the gathering, hoping a walk would calm his nerves. After taking a few steps, he realized he'd forgotten the sword Azariah had given him. As he bent to retrieve it, he was struck by how much his life had changed. For twenty-one years he had lived without so much as seeing such a weapon; now it felt as though his life depended on having one near.

Once he was away from the town, Roland felt horribly exposed. His footsteps led him into the forest, where he might find some sort of cover. The moonlight was faint through the thick canopy of maples and elms overhead, and he stumbled through the darkness, arms held out before him, fending off branches and vines that threatened to slap his cheeks or poke out his eyes. He walked for some time, the night deepening around him, and it was not until he reached a circular clearing, littered with rocks and knee-high grasses, that he allowed himself to rest. He sat on a stump in the middle of the clearing, its bark spongy and brittle to the touch. The tip of his sword's scabbard scraped against the rocks below.

"Roland?" someone asked.

Startled, he swung around on the stump and almost fell off. Behind him was a beautiful specter in a burlap nightshirt, playing with the kinky curls of her hair. The ghost rubbed the bridge of her nose, which she always did when she was uncertain, and the mirage broke.

"Kaya?" he asked. "What are you doing out here?"

"You left me," she answered. "You promised you'd never leave me."

He stood up and ran to her, wrapping his arms around her and holding her tightly. Though she was the same age as him, and more experienced in many ways, she seemed younger in that moment, like a frightened child wishing to be comforted after a nightmare. *But that's what we all are,* he thought. *Frightened children, hoping and praying for the best.*

"You were sleeping," he said, placing a light kiss on her forehead. "I just needed to take a walk. To think."

"I saw you leaving," she said softly. "I was worried."

"Kaya, there's nothing to worry about."

"Yes there is. You don't have to lie to me. Why else would you have brought the sword?"

He stroked her hair, refusing to answer. He thought of when he'd first used that sword, the night of the attack on Lerder. Moments after he and Azariah had scaled the makeshift wall around Lerder, a group of twenty assailants, those he'd watched swim across the river and scale the western bank, had come screaming around the bend. Though the townspeople had been given every armament stowed beneath Ashhur's temple, none brought their arms up in defense. Three Wardens were cut down immediately, the rest jumping to action and herding the people into a tight group at the edge of the forest. A handful of attackers had forced their way through the wall of defending Wardens, slaying four more, one of them leaping at Kaya as she sat crying atop his horse. As if on instinct, Roland had rushed forward, driving the tip of his sword through the man's gut. Blood gushed, screams echoed across the valley, and in a matter of moments it was all over.

"What is that?" Kaya said suddenly, jerking him from the recollection.

"What is what?"

"That light. That sound. Over there."

He turned his head, looking toward the edge of the forest. Very humanlike noises were issuing from that direction, a grunt or two, followed by a strange jangling, like a giant chime clanging in the wind. The foliage began to quake. Roland felt himself freeze in place, Kaya clutched in his arms.

A shadowy figure stepped into the clearing, looking just as much a phantom as Kaya had. It was a large man with long, dark hair hanging in front of his face. His armor marked him as one of Karak's soldiers. The man acted groggy, like he was recovering from a long night of wine and laughter. If he saw them, he did not react, instead turning to face a tree a few feet in front of them. There was a faint splashing as he urinated on the trunk.

Roland felt Kaya tremble, and he covered her mouth with his hand. The man finished his business and shook himself off, then ran his hands through his nappy hair and groaned. He started back the way he'd come, but then paused. Slowly he turned, as if in a dream, and gaped at Roland and Kaya.

"What the...?" the man muttered. He fumbled at his waist, grabbing the hilt of a short dagger wedged there, and then took a few staggering steps toward them, the dagger held out before him. Kaya yelped and struggled in Roland's grasp, which made the man halt for a moment. His face was a mask of confusion and panic.

"Who're you?" he asked, scratching his head with his off hand.

Roland stayed mum, squeezing Kaya to make her keep quiet as well.

"I said *who are you?*" the man repeated, his voice panicked now. He turned, gathering air into his lungs as if he were about to shout, but a blur flashed across the clearing before he could utter another word. A gleaming shaft of steel erupted from the place where his head met his neck, and Kaya let out a small shriek. The man offered a choked protest as his body shuddered, then went limp. The blade retracted, and the man teetered backward, falling to the stony soil with a *thump*.

Azariah hovered over the corpse. The shortsword looked comically small in his large hands, the blade dripping with the dead man's blood. He glanced up at Roland, his green-gold eyes narrowed, his mouth turned down in a grimace.

Roland couldn't stop his body from shaking. He gaped at his friend, finding it difficult to form words, as Kaya sobbed in his arms.

"I always know where you are," the Warden said, answering the unasked question. "It is my duty as your protector."

That was all Roland could take. He broke, tears streaming down his cheeks and soaking the top of Kaya's head as she continued to cry against his chest. Azariah stepped up to them, wrapping them both in his long arms.

"Hush now," he said with tenderness. "You have been strong this whole time, when you could have easily given up. Both of you. You must remain strong even now."

Roland swallowed a gulp of bile, trying to force his heart to beat slower. The feel of Kaya's breath against his neck was even more calming than Azariah's embrace. He imagined his first night with her on the roof, and the few times they'd explored each other's bodies in the dark of night while the rest of their troupe was sleeping. His frayed nerves unwound, and a seemingly unnatural relaxation came over him.

"Better?" asked Azariah.

"A little," Roland answered.

"And you, Kaya?"

"I…I think I'll be okay," she said timidly.

"Good." The Warden released them and walked toward the tree line from which the now dead man had emerged. "I am going to see where he came from," he said. "Stay here. I will be back soon."

"No," said Roland, shaking his head. "No, we're coming with you."

"We are?" asked Kaya.

Azariah fumbled through the pouch at his waist, pulling out a handful of something Roland couldn't see.

"If you insist on accompanying me," he said, "then this will ensure you don't do something to give us away." He tossed whatever was in his hand into the air. It tumbled down like bits of twinkling ash, and Azariah spoke a few incomprehensible words. The particles disappeared, and the air around the three of them stretched into a liquid sheen before retracting, as if snapping back into place. "There. We are hidden now, mostly. Only someone very close, and very attentive, will see us."

"What was that?" asked Roland.

Azariah shrugged. "A magical barrier. It makes those within it… dim. It does nothing for sound, though, so do not stomp through the forest like a mule."

"I didn't know you knew magic…well, other than healing and other practical stuff."

"A bit. Well, more than a bit, actually." The Warden frowned. "When one spends a great amount of time with Jacob Eveningstar, one tends to learn a few tricks."

Roland winced at the sound of Jacob's name but said nothing.

Silently they made their way through the trees. Azariah saw quite well in the dark, as Wardens' eyes were almost as discerning as elves'. They maneuvered over small hills and thick tangles of vines, and Roland prayed to Ashhur that the *snap* of branches under their feet would be drowned out by the cacophonic commotion of a million chirping insects.

Ahead was a red glow, which became more and more pronounced as they approached it. After a time, it seemed as if the forest were on fire. Azariah hushed them as the telltale noises of a military camp reached their ears. Roland obliged without question. From the idle chatter, to the crackle of fire, to the *clank* and *clink* of stone on metal, it sounded as if hundreds of people were somewhere out there.

Azariah led them to a coppice of thick undergrowth, then halted. Leaning up and over the twisted mesh of twigs and fallen limbs, he gestured for the other two to do the same. Roland and Kaya joined him, trying to rise up just high enough for the tops of their heads to clear the barrier.

Another glen lay before them, many times larger than the one with the stump. To the left, a few men wandered amid what seemed to be hundreds of horses, giving them water and changing the feed bags over their snouts. To the right was a massive pavilion, behind which stood even more horses. Between them, numbering far too many to count, were tents, most of them bordered by crackling cookfires. There were men everywhere, dressed much the same as the one Azariah had killed, along with, amazingly enough, the occasional elf. Roland could not guess at their numbers, but he knew there must be thousands.

For a moment, Roland felt as if he were reliving the time when Jacob, Azariah, Brienna, and himself had spied Uther Crestwell's ghastly ceremony in the Tinderlands. Even the Warden's expression was the same—dismayed and breathless. Azariah took a steadying breath and pulled them down into the cover of the thicket.

Kaya looked to the Warden with pleading eyes. "Can we go back now?" she whispered.

Azariah seemed like he couldn't hear her. He simply stared at the ground, shaking his head.

Roland sidled up to his friend. "What's wrong?" he asked. "Azariah, please talk to us."

The Warden lifted his gaze.

"They burned the ruined settlements we saw," he whispered. "Karak and Jacob did not circle around us like I first thought. This force must have come from the north, and there are *thousands* of them. Even worse, it looks like the elves have sided with them." Once more he shook his head. "There is no place for Celestia's children in this conflict. They were to remain neutral."

"What are you saying?" asked Roland.

There was a dire look in Azariah's eyes that scared Roland to his core. Even Kaya noticed, inching closer to him and clutching his hand so tightly, it felt as if she'd crush it.

"All of Dezrel is against us," Azariah said. "Enemies behind, enemies in front and above, possibly even below." He glanced at the glow above the thicket. "Let us return to camp. We must alert the others, and we must all hurry away."

"How much of a chance do we have?" asked Kaya, her voice cracking.

"A chance of what?"

"Of crossing the bridge. Of reaching Mordeina."

"Of not dying," added Roland.

"Slight," Azariah answered. He gave no other explanation. He simply took them both by the hand and led them out of the woods, away from the camping army, away from the death that awaited them all.

CHAPTER

19

It was a sprawling machine of organized chaos, and Avila was the architect.

She sat astride her mount at the forefront of the vanguard, Integrity held out before her like an extension of her arm. Her charges obeyed every word that leapt from her mouth, holding back from the left, pushing in on the right, fastening ropes to the spires atop the twelve-foot wall surrounding the village—the same ineffectual barrier they'd encountered at nearly every settlement during their long campaign first to the north and then the west, circling around the lands dubbed Ker, where she had been forbidden to venture.

The arrows that fell from the sky were also familiar, crude bolts of wobbling wood with frayed bits of vulture feathers for fletching. Most dropped harmlessly to the parched earth, and those that did find purchase in flesh rarely sank deep. One thudded off Avila's silver breastplate while she screamed commands to the right flank, reinforcing the notion that they were mere aggravations.

In this village, no one had emerged from behind the wall to drop to their knees in submission to Karak, as had happened at many of the other small villages. Another change was that there was no clumsily constructed gate for them to storm. Instead, a heavy boulder had been rolled in front of the lone gap in the barricade. Her cheeks flushing with annoyance, she directed the vanguard to part in the center, allowing a trio of sturdy chargers to come through. Her archers fired just above the wall, keeping those on the other side from cutting the thick ropes that were slung around the timber spires, while soldiers fastened the ropes to the harness binding the three horses. When it was done, she gave the order, and the horsemaster lashed at the chargers. Hooves pounded the dusty ground, and the muscular beasts grunted with exertion. The wall creaked slightly, causing the horsemaster to push his pets all the harder, until a section of the wall cracked beneath the pressure. Timber splintered and fell as the chargers began galloping away, dragging the downed section with them.

Shouts rang out from inside the village as Avila sounded the battle cry, then kicked the sides of her mount and galloped through the gap. It was a sufficient breach, the width of at least ten men, which allowed ample room for the rest of the vanguard to follow her through. On entering, she was greeted by eight Wardens. The tall and elegant creatures lined up shoulder to shoulder, holding rudimentary shields, while those behind them—humans all—brandished polearms. She tugged back on the reins, her horse rearing up on its hind legs, while her men charged past her into the wall of wood. The humans with the polearms thrust between their protectors' shields, impaling two soldiers through the shoulders and nicking the cheek of a third. Swords, maces, and axes began chopping with abandon, sending splinters into the air. An agonized bellow sounded as one of the Wardens had his hand severed above the wrist. Blood spewed from the stump, blinding one of her soldiers, giving a skinny, olive-skinned man the chance to spear him in the face with his pike.

More of her men streamed through the opening, only to be rushed from the right by a charging mob of at least thirty humans and Wardens, each wielding basic bludgeons and stone axes as they shouted the name of their god. The two sides met in a flurry of hacks, slashes, and bashes, the anger and will of the defenders making up for the steel and skill of the attackers. Avila glanced at the red cliff behind her. The remainder of her unit waited on the Gods' Road. She had assumed this tiny community would be as easy to defeat as the countless others they had obliterated on their journey, so she had only brought seventy men in the vanguard—ten horsemen, forty-five foot soldiers, and fifteen archers. Now it looked as if she might have to do the unthinkable: flee the village, scale the rise, and order more men to come to her aid.

She shook her head, anger boiling in her gut. That would be failure, and a Lord Commander could not fail.

Shrieking, she stormed ahead on her mount once more, entering the melee. She swung Integrity in measured arcs, bloodying her blade on the gathered mass of flesh. Something heavy thudded against her knee, drawing a sharp breath from her throat. The resulting throb rankled her all the more, and she hacked and slashed, her slender sword piercing flesh and chopping down to the bone.

The horsemen entered the village last, charging the town's defenders with deliberate thrusts and hews. From their advantageous positions atop their steeds they avoided major injury while dishing out the maximum punishment. The tide turned, the Wardens and townspeople dying by the handful, their meager weapons of stone and wood no match for those fired in the Mount Hailen kilns. The foot soldiers formed a circle around the survivors, cutting down any who still lived.

Avila continued her breathless assault, every fiber of her being alight with energy. Someone grabbed her from behind, and instinctually she swiveled, lashing out with Integrity in a sideways cleave, thinking she was about to behead a Warden. Instead, her strike was parried with a powerful *clang*, the vibration traveling up her arm and stinging her shoulder. It was Malcolm, Darkfall clutched tightly in both hands, his steel kissing hers. Avila glared as she pulled her sword back and flipped its hilt to her opposite hand, clenching and unclenching the fingers of her sword hand.

"The battle is done here, Lord Commander," her lieutenant said. He backed his large stallion away and sheathed Darkfall on his back. "Please allow me to finish off the miscreants."

"The battle is done when I *say* it is done, Captain," she snapped at him. With that, she jerked the reins to the side, spinning her mount around. She took in the scene around her, the dead humans and Wardens who were sprawled out on the ground, their blood painting the sand red. A few of her charges moved among them, thrusting daggers through the eyes of those who still moaned. Though she had felt fear when the townspeople fought back so bravely, she found that fear to have been completely misplaced. As far as she could tell, they had lost only seven soldiers during the raid—the most casualties in any conflict so far, but according to the books Karak had given her, tomes from far-off worlds translated into the common tongue by the god, such losses were acceptable. She kicked her mount and tramped farther into the village.

The place was more an encampment than a true village, and it had been set up strangely: there was a single giant firepit in the center, and countless tents spun outward from it in a spiral. At the far end of the spiral was a large building surrounded by a myriad of raised garden beds. The building was most likely the granary, and given its sturdy construction, it was the one shelter in the village that offered the illusion of safety.

The afternoon sun shone down on her as she rode through the spiral of tents, gazing at the unsophisticated bedding and clothing that spilled from each. The sounds of the battle—if it could still be called a battle—grew quieter behind her. She heard sobs as the few remaining humans fell to their knees, begging uselessly for mercy. Avila grunted and rode onward. They had lost their chance when they'd refused her call to surrender.

The granary was made from crisscrossing logs held together by sturdy twine. There was a single door tall enough for a Warden to step through without stooping. Avila dismounted and grabbed the door's handle, holding Integrity at the ready in case anyone inside meant to surprise her. It occurred to her for a moment that she should leave this task for her men, but she shrugged the notion aside. There was no challenge to be met here, at least not one she couldn't handle.

The door was heavy, its wooden hinges swollen from the heat, so it took a few tugs to open it. She stepped inside, smelled the musty odor of old vegetables mixed with the sharp scent of pickling herbs. There were portholes in the ceiling, allowing sunlight to filter inside. To her right was a mountain of sacks presumably filled with grain and perhaps corn kernels; to her left piles of potatoes, carrots, pomegranates, turnips, and onions.

A strange noise reached her ears, almost like one of the feral cats that roamed the forests of Brent. She approached the bags of grain, her each deliberate footstep causing the boards to creak, and then stopped. Reaching out, she grabbed one of the sacks and pulled it down violently, lifting Integrity in a defensive position as she leapt backward.

The heavy sacks tumbled in an avalanche, and when the dust cleared, a young woman came into sight. She was wearing a smock that seemed to be made from the same material as the grain sacks, and she held something in her hands. Her hair was dark and quite curly, tied in a knot at the top of her head, and her skin tone was tanned almost to brownness. She had wide, pretty azure eyes, and thick rosebud lips. The woman trembled, edging away from Avila until her backside struck the mountain of sacks behind her.

That odd mewling came again, and Avila glanced down. The thing in the woman's arms shifted, a grimy blanket falling away to reveal the unsullied pink flesh of a very young child. The baby clucked and cried, kicking its chubby legs. *Willa once looked like that,* Avila thought, then shook her head to banish the invading thought.

The woman held the child closer to her chest. There were tears in her eyes.

"Please," she said, her voice high and pleading. "Please, don't hurt my baby."

Avila paused, uncertainty washing over her. The whole of her body went numb, and prickles danced beneath her flesh. It was as if she had been wrapped in invisible chains.

The woman slid along the sacks behind her, heading toward the granary door.

"Stop," Avila said, the word coming out as barely a whisper. If the woman heard, she didn't show any sign of it. She continued moving along the wall of sacks, heading for the bright opening.

"Stop!" Avila shouted, finally regaining her voice, and the woman froze in her tracks.

The beautiful young mother trembled in fear. Avila still felt numb, even as she raised Integrity into the air. The woman dropped to her knees, tears cascading down her cheeks in torrents now. Her eyes lifted to the ceiling, her mouth working in a silent plea.

"Do you renounce Ashhur, the false god of this land?" asked Avila. She sounded shaky even to her own ears. "Will you dedicate yourself to Karak, the Divinity of Dezrel, with all your heart and eternal soul?"

The woman shook her head, not looking at her.

"Ashhur, I pray to you. Ashhur, keep me safe, and keep my baby safe—let no harm come to him." She then nodded, as if a voice had given her a reply. She lowered her eyes, and strangely, she smiled. It might have been the most frightening thing Avila had ever seen. "His name is Quentin," said the woman.

The mother stood and stepped away from the wall, holding the baby out for Avila to see. Avila retreated one step, then another. Her mind began playing tricks on her; she saw this child as Willa, herself as its mother, holding those puckered lips to her breast, waiting for the tiny thing to suckle, the sustenance produced within her body.

"Stop it," she whispered, waving Integrity as if to ward off an evil spirit. "Come no closer."

The woman did not seem to understand. She tilted her head as she continued her approach.

"Hold him," she said. "Go ahead. Ashhur's teachings say you can feel the innocence in children, and it fills the soul. Here, take him."

She extended her arms outward, the squirming child in her hands. For a moment Avila almost accepted. She found herself drawn to them, her heart rate quickening in a way it never did in times of conflict, whether on the battlefield or between the sheets. The sensation frightened her, and she skittered away from the woman. Integrity fell from her hand, clattering to the floor.

"Get away from me!" she screamed.

A shadow passed through the open doorway, and in rushed Malcolm. His lone good eye glanced first at Avila, then the woman. Hearing the *clunk* of his boots, the young mother turned in time to see Malcolm heft Darkfall from the sheath on his back. The smile left her face.

Malcolm hauled his massive sword back and swung it with all his might, his neck taut, his teeth grinding together in anger. The blade cut through the woman where neck met shoulder, snapping easily through bone and tendon. Before Avila could react, both mother and child had been sliced through. Blood spurted everywhere as Darkfall's tip smacked against the wood floor. The woman dropped both halves of her now silent child, her eyes wide and glossy as her upper torso and right arm slid away from the rest of her body and landed with a *thud*. The remainder of her collapsed shortly thereafter.

Malcolm looked up at Avila, his hoary left eye opened wider than the good right one.

"Karak hears no pleas for mercy," he said, panting. "There is order, or there is death."

Avila stood frozen, staring from her lieutenant to the butchered mother and child and the ever-widening lake of blood. Malcolm rose and wiped the gore from his sword with a rag from his belt. The sun from above lit him strangely, and for a moment it appeared to Avila as if his blade were glowing a deep purple.

He stuffed Darkfall back into its scabbard and the glow vanished. He approached her.

"Lord Commander, you do not seem well," he said, reaching for her. "Take my hand."

She batted his offer away, scooping Integrity up off the floor. She ran past him with clenched teeth, ran until she reached the wall, ignoring the queer looks she received from her men, who were lining up the village's dead for burning. All she could think about was getting out of this place, away from the prying eyes of those who would judge her, away from thoughts of how disappointed her deity would be in her. But she did not desire to be alone; more than anything, she longed to put a knife through the throat of the one who had made her this way, the one who had weakened her and turned her into a shell of the great warrior of Karak she had once been.

The Gods' Road was packed with the remainder of her division; nearly five thousand made camp in dirt that looked like it had already been packed down by a previous, even larger congregation. A few stood on the edge of the cliff watching the action down below. This was the fourteenth settlement they had liberated over the last few weeks, and their duties had become gradually more uninteresting with each stop. The men gained more enjoyment in their cups or sitting around cookfires telling lewd jokes than in combat. Many soldiers stood as she approached. Avila slowed to a brisk walk, but when the men caught sight of her face, their expressions grew quizzical, even perplexed. Avila did her best to scowl, hoping a derisive look might make them turn away. Of course she looked out of breath and odd. She'd just been in battle!

She passed a grouping of twenty crude, slanting tents. This was where the converts stayed, those from Paradise who had accepted Karak into their hearts instead of facing the executioner's sword. They were positioned at the center of the encampment to ensure they were surrounded by soldiers at all times. Standing up as she approached, each haggard soul looked on her with a mixture of hope and fear. *They are not converts,* she told herself. They had no love of Karak. They had simply pledged their loyalty to save their own skins.

The mere concept made her want to cry, which in turn made her angrier.

Two guards stood outside the pavilion of the Lord Commander. She stopped short of them, giving herself a moment to wipe her damp cheeks and take a deep breath. Marching forward, she demanded that none bother her until morning, when they were to continue their western trek. These were two of her best soldiers, and they simply nodded when she gave the command, neither looking directly at her, for which she was thankful. One held open the pavilion's entrance flap, and she ducked beneath it.

Though the walls of the pavilion were only canvas, thin enough for soft light to filter through, the material still seemed to make the noises of the outside world disappear. All was silent but for a single voice, soft and gentle and innocent, nearly angelic. The voice sang a somber tune. Avila undid her belt, letting it drop to the ground. She knelt before the travel chest at the foot of her bedroll to remove a sharp knife.

"Karak's will be done," she whispered.

A curtain hung on the opposite end of the pavilion from her sleeping area. She could clearly see the outline of a tiny figure there, the source of the singing. Avila crept across the space, crouching, holding the knife blade down. When she reached the curtain, she ripped it aside.

Willa sat cross-legged on the floor, bent over, her lips drawn tight in concentration. She did not look up, even as the curtain fell from its hook and fluttered to the ground like drifting smoke. The little girl hunched over a sheet of parchment, one hand holding the paper flat while the other held a slender piece of charcoal. Black covered the girl's clothes, arms, cheeks, and painted the ends of her curly golden locks. She drew feverishly, and when she was finished, she pushed the sheet aside, where it joined at least twenty others. The simple act of watching the child caused Avila's anger to wane.

"Willa," she asked, "what are you doing?"

"Drawing," the little girl said. She looked up from a new blank sheet of parchment and smiled. There was a twinkle in her eye, a blithe happiness that seemed to narrow the world to the two of them. Her blue eyes shifted to the knife Avila held above her, and she flinched.

Quick as a whip, Avila slid the weapon behind her back. With its disappearance, Willa seemed to forget it had ever been there. The smile returned to her face almost immediately.

"Sit with me, Avila," she said, virtue oozing from her mouth like poisonous sludge.

Ashhur's teachings say you can feel the innocence in children....

Avila joined the girl against her better judgment, folding her legs over each other as she nestled in beside her. Willa smelled sweet, like powder and strawberries, and Avila both hated that scent and longed for it to be with her always. She had hesitated in the granary. In the past she would *never* have hesitated, which meant she had changed. It was Willa who had changed her, who was *actively* changing her. She needed to end the deception this child embodied, and quickly.

Yet when she looked into blue eyes so similar to her own, she saw the mother and child who had been shorn in two by Malcolm's sword, and the horror of it made her insides twist and coil.

"Do you want to see one?" asked Willa. Without waiting for an answer, she grabbed a sheet and lifted it to her. Avila squinted, staring at a black blocky image surrounded by seemingly random black slashes.

"What is it?" she asked.

"My favorite place in all the world," Willa answered, bouncing enthusiastically on her little rump. Her finger jabbed at the picture, smearing her rough lines. "That's where you said Ashhur lived. In the grasses."

The Sanctuary. Safeway, Ashhur's home, had been the third stop on their journey before heading back to the north. They'd found it completely abandoned. They had camped there for four days, giving the men time to rest by the sea before the longest and hardest part of their quest commenced. The Sanctuary, a majestic, round building of smooth stone and impeccable architecture, had become Malcolm's obsession. Her captain had declared that he would return one day, and that Ashhur's Sanctuary would become Karak's seat of power in the west, a final posthumous insult to the false deity. Avila had brought Willa there, showing her the many etchings that depicted the false stories the God of Justice had told his creations.

Avila had been surprised by the beauty of the Sanctuary, which was filled with such light and joy and serenity. There was no place like it in all of Neldar, not even in the Castle of the Lion, which she had once thought the pinnacle of splendor and achievement.

Willa touched her leg, and she realized she was drifting.

"Karak can live there too," she said. "When he beats up Ashhur, he can go back there and live in the building. He can tell us stories and keep us safe. Is that right?"

"Yes, that is right."

It hit her all at once. Willa had not been poisoning her mind. No, the child was starting to understand and accept Karak's teachings. She was always excited when Avila visited her during the afternoon meal to give her lessons about the glory of the God of Order. If Avila was feeling doubt, *she* was the one at fault, not this innocent young thing. And was there anything wrong with doubt? Despite her misgivings, she still obeyed her god's commands, still worked to purge this heathen land of all the devotees of the weak, pathetic deity.

There is nothing wrong with allowing myself a small amount of joy, she thought, staring at Willa. *Mother did the same with us when we were young, and she never lost her faith.*

Avila spent the rest of the day within the confines of the Lord Commander's pavilion, drawing alongside her tiny companion. She told the child stories, played games with her, and instructed her as best she could on the proper way to live in an ordered society. The latter concepts were obviously beyond a seven-year-old's comprehension, but she admired how intently Willa listened, how her face scrunched up in the most adorable of ways when she was concentrating. For the first time, Avila answered the girl without hesitation when asked for the hundredth time what had caused her facial scars.

She felt happy, truly happy, and the memory of the slain mother and child started to lose its grip on her.

That night they took their dinner inside, and when Avila blew out the candles, Willa asked her to lie down beside her. Avila allowed the child to curl up in her arms, feeling the smoothness of her skin beneath her cotton nightclothes. Soon the girl was snoring, and Avila uttered a silent prayer of thanks to Karak before nodding off herself. Her sleep was black and dreamless.

Come morning, when the horns blew and the sounds of her division dismantling the camp invaded the thin canvas walls of her pavilion, Avila stretched her arms high above her head. Her back cracked and she felt a twinge of pain in her side. She was sore, unusual given the pure blood of the First Family that flowed in her veins. She glanced at the still sleeping Willa, rosebud lips puckered, tiny chest rising and falling with each breath she took. *I slept in an uncomfortable position is all,* she thought, and went about packing up her things as well, allowing the child to doze until she awoke on her own.

CHAPTER

20

"As you can see, milady," said Quester the Crimson Sword, "every amenity you could desire is right here. Bath houses, eateries, delicatessens, theaters, two wonderful brothels, a vineyard, a huge commons, arenas, and taverns. Here in Riverrun, we spare no expense. The founders have seen to that."

Laurel rode on her horse beside him, with the two Sisters of the Cloth—Mite and Giant were Quester's pet names for them—riding behind. She looked wherever the stunning young man pointed, hanging on his every word. He was right. Riverrun was indeed the most picturesque town she had ever visited. Veldaren was a cold, gray tomb by comparison.

All along the main thoroughfare leading away from the Gods' Road, there were cottages and chalets, finely crafted homes of interlocking logs atop sturdy stone foundations. In many ways it resembled the other merchant towns she had visited—Drake, Gronswik, and Thettletown, the latter of which they had passed through on their way here—but the *feel* was much different. The road was well maintained, the many gardens popped with color. Merry people streamed in and out of the seamstress shop, the apothecary, the taverns. The outdoor market they rode past teemed with women both young and old, and they did not seem battered down or sullied. Their men wore boiled leather and ringed armor, and each had his weapon of choice hanging from his belt. At first Laurel had feared they were bandits—the vast majority of the men she'd seen of late were just that—but they were clean and seemed to be in good spirits.

"The men," she asked, after passing a group of four chatting together before the entrance of a tavern. "Why are they so many? Have Karak's soldiers not come here to conscript like they have elsewhere?"

"They have, but merchants hold a particular...sway within the kingdom." Quester grinned while playfully flicking his forked beard. "My masters in particular have good standing with both god and king. Most of our common men were sent away with our deity's army. Yet Riverrun has kept the fires stoked at Mount Hailen and in Felwood, supplying Karak with all the steel he could desire. For that, we were allowed to keep our hired hands." His grin grew wider. "It just so happens that most of our hired hands also hold swords."

"Is that not...well, unfair?" asked Laurel.

The Crimson Sword shrugged.

"Fairness is a matter of perspective, milady. Is it fair to my masters that gold, silver, and bronze have lost much of their value because there are few left to earn it, never mind spend it? Is it fair that the trade they built their livelihoods on now teeters on collapse? It is not, but they know this war will not last forever, and when it does end, when trade returns to its full strength and gold retains its meaning, those who hold the reins will once more be the most powerful men in the land. If we were denied our protection, roving bands of brigands could easily conquer our town. No one, not the temple, not the king, not even Karak himself, wants to see that happen. Once the engine of commerce resumes, the transition back to normalcy needs to be as painless as possible." He swung his hand out wide. "And besides, that means my home gets to keep its inherent loveliness, which is never such a bad thing."

Laurel had no choice but to agree with him. There was something rather comforting about offering a nod of greeting to a passerby and receiving one in kind. In many ways, it seemed as though Riverrun existed in a bubble all its own, untouched by the strife and lawlessness brought about by Karak's war.

The throughway passed by a great stone amphitheater, a tall structure whose walls were made from a strange, smooth substance, and then a massive commons. There, several boys and girls were at play, tossing small rounded sacks and chasing each other with sticks. Mothers sat on blankets on the edge of the field, eating apples, pears, grapes, and other assorted fruits plucked from wicker baskets, while they watched their children play. More sellswords stood behind them, grinning while they watched the fun, but Laurel could tell their attention was elsewhere. Their eyes skittered nervously at the sound of the horses' hooves when Quester and Laurel approached with the Sisters of the Cloth in tow, their fingers dancing lightly on the hilts of their swords. It was a reminder, however subtle, of the dangers that lurked all around them.

Before long they reached the Queln River. The road veered sharply, following along the swiftly flowing waters. There were even more children playing in a sandy fjord, splashing and kicking and screeching in joy. Farther along, when the river widened, Laurel saw a fleet of rafts and barges tethered to a great dockhouse that jutted out over the water. There were men working the docked crafts, unloading baskets of fish onto the plank for others to dump into a giant crate and sort through. There were a great many Sisters of the Cloth present, a sight that made Laurel cringe. The wrapped women were like phantoms, lurking around, acknowledged by none. She glanced over her shoulder at Mite and Giant, and suppressed a shudder when she took in the blank look in their eyes.

The farther south they rode along the river, the more prevalent the Sisters became. Soon, they were all she could see, standing in front of gatehouses, guarding the entrance to a steaming smithy on the river's edge, escorting horses pulling wagons filled with hay, fish, meat, or billowing cotton. Quester noticed her guarded stares, steered his horse over, and took her hand. His grip was firm, his skin soft as silk, yet hardened by calluses at the fingertips. Combined with the man's inherent beauty, his touch lit something inside her that it was difficult to quell.

"Some of my masters' most inspired purchases," he said. "They've bought three hundred Sisters over the years. Quiet, hardworking, completely loyal, and many are quite capable in the art of defense, like my pets." He gestured at Mite and Giant.

"Three hundred?" said Laurel, aghast. "How can there be so many?"

"Oh, three hundred is a low number, milady. There are more than two thousand sisters spread throughout Neldar. When courts are controlled by theological law, these things tend to happen."

Laurel grunted in disgust. She had been told stories of the Sisters of the Cloth since she was a little girl. It was a warning to all of the fairer sex that a horrible life awaited them should they break Karak's laws. For men, it was either imprisonment or death. Laurel thought it unfair, though, of course, many men sentenced to death would probably argue otherwise.

The landscape began to change, growing rocky and unsuitable for growth. There were cliffs ahead, craggy outcroppings that fronted the lesser mountains bordering the western bank of the Queln. The road they traveled veered inland, following the base of a foothill. There were more Sisters here than anywhere—dozens of them sparred in the open area to Laurel's right, steel clanging as their daggers met again and again. A massive ring of stacked stone, taller than her horse, emerged ahead, built into the base of the foothills. Its thick door was guarded by a pair of Sisters.

"Welcome to the Connington Holdfast," the Crimson Sword declared.

He motioned for her to stop and dismount, which she did. The ground felt hard and unforgiving beneath her feet, very different from the yielding, almost spongy earth they'd camped on the evening before, outside of Thettletown. She stretched her legs for a moment, then approached the door. The two Sisters guarding it barred the path, crossing their daggers. She stepped back, staring into their dead eyes.

Quester walked past her, undoing the tie in his red-streaked golden hair and letting it fall to his shoulders. He leaned over and whispered into the two Sisters' covered ears, and they fell back to their original positions on either side of the door. He turned to Laurel and smiled.

"One cannot be too careful," he said with a chuckle. "There are enemies everywhere, perhaps even ones as lovely as you. Precautions must be made."

The handsome young sellsword knocked three times on the giant oak door, then backed away, tapping his foot on the packed ground. More than five minutes passed before the door finally swung outward, revealing a set of stairs that led down into a torch-lit stone hallway. A woman stepped out, her silvery gray hair falling past her waist. That hair, combined with the folds in her neck and her crooked fingers, suggested she was quite old, yet her face was strangely bereft of wrinkles. She wore a flowing gown of crimson and turquoise, studded with onyx beading. Her eyes were icy blue, as was common in those from the north.

"Councilwoman Laurel Lawrence," the woman said with a slight bow. "Please, follow me."

She glanced up at Quester, who nodded and then threw an arm each around Mite and Giant, who had positioned themselves at his sides.

"Are you coming?" she asked him.

"No," he said. "This meeting is for you and my masters alone. I am useless in these matters." He tapped the hilt of his shortsword. "Besides, I have other duties to attend. Don't worry, my masters mean you no harm. They simply wish to talk. I will be here when you are finished to escort you back home."

With that he turned away, gently nudging Mite and Giant as he approached his horse. In a single swift movement he was back in his saddle, and before she had time to absorb what was happening, he was riding away, his pets trotting behind. Laurel loitered there for a moment, watching him grow smaller and smaller, until the old woman tapped her on the shoulder.

"Please, Laurel, your audience awaits."

She took a deep breath, steeling herself against her nervousness, before following the strange old woman through the door and down the stairs. The Sisters closed the door behind her, the sound echoing throughout the hallway as loud as a thunderclap. She started, peering at the void of darkness behind her.

The old woman spun around to face her, the folds of her gown twirling.

"There is no reason to be nervous," she said coldly, looking her up and down. A brief flash of disappointment shone in her blue eyes. "As Quester said, my sons have no desire to harm you. It is an insult to assume otherwise, especially in their place of business."

My sons?

"I…my apologies, Lady Connington," Laurel said. Though she spoke softly, her voice still reverberated throughout the passage, making her shudder. *Stay strong,* she told herself. *You know what they want, what they expect. Your father is a powerful merchant, just like them.* Gathering her confidence, she threw back her shoulders and said, "You must understand, I have had some rather unpleasant experiences with many high merchants over the last few weeks. It is a rare merchant who has prospered because of his honesty. To walk into this meeting blind and trusting would make me a fool, and the daughter of Cornwall Lawrence is no fool."

Lady Connington smiled at that, her features softening noticeably. With her face more relaxed, the hints of crow's feet were readily noticeable around her eyes, and creases of age appeared at the corners of her mouth.

"Very well, Councilwoman," she said. "But you must understand how special it is for you to be here. Other than myself, women are not allowed inside the holdfast. Even my sons' wives are kept at the homestead in the heart of town. That you are here at all is a testament to how serious my sons are taking these unfolding events."

"I understand. It's an honor."

"It is indeed. Now follow me."

The hallway led to a central hub cut with six colored passages. Laurel was amazed by how much larger the holdfast was than it had appeared from the outside. The compound appeared to be relatively new, with smooth stucco- and plaster-lined walls. Much of the structure existed underground, and she shuddered to think of how many hours of labor—paid or forced—it had taken to construct it. The windowless walls closed in on her, seeming to constrict with each step she took.

She was led down a passage painted from floor to ceiling in crimson. The light of the torches gave it an ominous feel, as if it were some hellish compartment of the underworld. There was but a single door at the very end of the corridor, stark white and staring out like a giant eye. Lady Connington stopped before the door and turned to her.

"Act like the daughter of Cornwall Lawrence," she said, "and all will be fine."

She opened the door, and Laurel stepped into a massive circular room, painted red. There were no decorations save the Conningtons' golden hawk's head banner, which hung on the far wall, as large as life. In the center of the room sat a single table, stained a deep burgundy, on which there was a giant carafe of red wine. Three chairs circled the table, and Romeo and Cleo Connington, two plump men wearing draping frocks the same color as the room, sat in two of them. Numerous rings adorned their fingers, and their heads were shaved and powdered. Laurel smelled the distinct and bitter odors of lemon and menthol combined with rosewater. She remembered that scent from the many times they'd come to the Council begging for some favor, and it was overwhelming in such a confined space.

"Miss Lawrence," the brothers said in turn, taking her in with icy blue eyes that were near mimics of their mother's.

"Romeo, Cleo," she replied. "Or should I refer to you as the Masters Connington?"

Both giggled at that, an unseemly and disturbing sound.

"Our first names are fine, Miss Lawrence," said Cleo.

"Call me Laurel."

"Fine," Romeo said. "Take a seat, *Laurel*. Have some wine. Perhaps unlace your bodice. You appear to be...somewhat hindered."

She frowned and glanced down at herself. She was wearing the same revealing ensemble she had worn the night she'd met Quester, the one that had been meant to seduce Trenton Blackbard into listening to the king's pleas. She suddenly felt dirty, though she had done her best to bathe in a stream the previous day. She pulled her cloak tighter around herself, covering her breasts.

"Such a shame," said Cleo.

"Though it does seem odd to present yourself in such a way for a matter of business," added Romeo. "Tell us, Laurel, why did you dress like a whore? Was it for us?"

She rolled her eyes. "Certainly not. It was for Trenton Blackbard. I never had the opportunity to return to my home to change before your Crimson Sword whisked me away."

Cleo grinned, exposing his perfect, pearly white teeth. "Ah yes, Quester is a fine one indeed. Very talented in all we ask him to do, even the...unsavory matters."

"*Especially* the unsavory matters," Romeo added. "As for your outfit, Laurel, may I ask if that scandalous outfit served its purpose?"

"Unfortunately, no," she grumbled, wishing the conversation would move on.

Romeo nodded. "I thought not. A foolish act, dressing that way to sway a man like Blackbard. His business is flesh. Products are to be used, not bargained with. It would be the same as petitioning a farmer while dressed as a cabbage."

"Though I would give good coin to see that," said Cleo, leaning in toward his brother.

Laurel blushed. *Keep calm,* she told herself. They were just trying to unnerve her, tear down her confidence. It helped little, though, that she felt so stupid now, like nothing more than a damn foolish girl. Instead of defending herself halfheartedly, she sat down in the third chair and grabbed the carafe of wine. She poured an ample amount into the cup on the table before her, smiled sweetly at the brothers, and proceeded to swallow it down in one huge gulp. The mixed tartness and sweetness infused her throat and her sinuses, effectively diffusing the brothers' off-putting smells.

"A girl after my own heart," said Cleo. "A strong man accepts an insult with a swig and a smile that promises retribution later."

"I am no man," Laurel snapped, placing the cup back on the table.

"Obviously not," said Romeo.

"I much prefer you to anyone else our lovely king might have sent," added Cleo.

"I was not sent," she said. "You retrieved me, remember?"

Cleo clapped. "Oh, Brother, she plays the game so well!"

"We'll see about that," said Romeo, his usually shrill tone lowering an octave. "Yes, Laurel, we sent for you, but only after discovering *you* were about to seek *us* out."

"Is that so?" she asked. "How would you know? You haven't been seen in Veldaren for months."

"Ah, child, we have eyes and ears everywhere," said Cleo, almost singing. "There is much we see and know, even in places you would least expect."

"Such as where?"

Romeo waved his hand at her. "Forget that. The king wanted a meeting, and so he has one. Tell me Laurel, what does dear Eldrich want from us?"

She cleared her throat. This was it, the sales pitch, the same one she'd given all the others.

"The gods' war is upon us," she said. "Despite all promises to the contrary, our king does not think Karak will so easily defeat his brother. Should the war drag on, or in the horrible event that our Divinity loses, we must be equipped to provide for ourselves. In the event of that—"

"Stop."

Laurel's lips snapped shut, and she gazed from one brother to the other. Romeo was shaking his head, Cleo laughing silently to himself.

"Did I say something wrong?" she asked.

"Do you trust Karak with all your heart?" asked Romeo.

"I believe in him completely, yes."

To that, Romeo chortled.

"Of course you believe in him, girl. He is a god among men, just as real as my brother and myself. To not believe in him would be to deny reality."

"Yet if we are to speak of belief," Cleo chimed in, "tell me, do you believe in Karak's *actions*, his *laws*, his *love for you*?"

"Yes," Laurel said. "I thoroughly trust in the grace and wisdom of our beloved Karak. He is without error, without—"

Romeo slapped the table.

"I think we are done here. Cleo, fetch Mother to escort the councilwoman back to the village. Tell her to have Quester bring her back to Veldaren as soon—"

"Wait, stop," Laurel said, accidentally knocking over her empty cup in the process. "Don't send me away, please."

"Then give us the truth, Laurel," said Cleo. "Not practiced lies."

Both brothers stared at her, seemingly without breathing. Her hands shook and her words caught in her throat.

"I doubt," she said. "It hurts to say, but it is true. I doubt."

"What do you doubt?"

"Everything."

"Explain."

She wavered for a moment, trying to think of what to say. Finally she gave in and hung her head.

"I don't know how."

Romeo leaned back and smiled, and Cleo clapped his hands once more.

"Excellent answer," the older of the two said. "It is best to be honest about one's feelings, especially in matters such as these. Otherwise you will be taken for a craven or a fool. We don't think you're either."

Cleo took a sip from his cup, the wine staining his lips a sickish shade of purple.

"The truth is, Laurel, we understand how you feel. You might think otherwise, but it was difficult for us too when we discovered our god did not have our best interests in mind, as he has proven time and again."

"How so?"

"Karak created Neldar," said Romeo, "and all the people within its borders. He gave us all the knowledge we could ever wish to have, helped build our greatest city, spoon fed us his laws and decrees, and told us to name a king. And then he disappeared. Our young race was left alone with vast amounts of knowledge we could not truly understand or build on, expected to govern ourselves using contradictory notions and ideas we hadn't the experience to justly value."

"Karak either does not understand our plight," Cleo continued, "or he does and he is simply curious as to how we will react. That means he is either unqualified to rule us, for he does not understand us...or that he is like a youngster who's curious how an ant will walk if he tears off half its legs. Every bit of Karak's doctrine is a negation. He says our hearts are unbound, yet if he is not first in those hearts, we are blasphemers. He demands we exercise our freedom, yet every principle he preaches leads to servitude in his name. It is ludicrous."

"You don't just doubt the Divinity," Laurel whispered. "You *hate* him."

Romeo shook his head. "You have it wrong. I too love the deity that allowed me to have life and bread and gold and land. More than anything. But I stopped *trusting* him long ago."

"Such a sad time," said Cleo.

"It was. It is *always* difficult when you realize your creator is bound more to a principle than to the people he made. All Karak cares for is order. Look at Karak's law, Laurel. Take a look at the wording. His laws are presented without ardor, without room for interpretation. Order in all things is what Karak demands, his endgame. It is the *nature of his being*. And we firmly believe he will sacrifice anything to achieve it. Soleh Mori was the most cherished member of Karak's First Families, yet he allowed her to die, and for what?"

"I don't know," muttered Laurel.

"No one does for sure," Romeo said. "Though the rumors we hear claim her death paved the way for this war, a war to bring order to all of Dezrel. If Karak allowed his most beloved creation to perish, what assurance do the rest of us have?"

Cleo sighed, sounding almost wistful. "He is so unlike his brother. I have seen firsthand how much Ashhur loves his children. How he dotes on them, shields them from harm, and ensures that their lives are as perfect as can be. He created Paradise, and has done all he can to make sure it remains just that."

Laurel's heart began to race. "Are you saying you would rather Ashhur rule this land than Karak?"

"Not at all!" Cleo said with a hearty laugh. "Do you not see, Laurel? Both are entirely flawed. They are mirror images of each other, their people slaves to their different concepts of righteousness. One may treat his creations better than the other, but the final outcome of either philosophy is the enslavement of an entire race of beings."

"But they are gods, and that is to be expected of gods," Romeo said. "They exist forever. How could they possibly understand creatures that live a finite existence, that think and feel and desire and eventually die? Our souls might be immortal—at least, that is what they tell us—but our bodies will one day expire. What does a god know of that? We are destined to be instruments in their cosmic game and nothing more. I believe that fully."

"But what of Celestia? She doesn't control the lives of her elves. They are free to do as they choose."

"So it seems," said Romeo. "But the goddess also punished her people for not obeying her request—*request*, not order—by destroying their home of two thousand years, exiling them from the wasteland that became the Tinderlands. Celestia may not walk among the elves, but I assure you, they are just as much a slave to her whims as we humans are to our deities."

Cleo took another sip of wine. "Nothing good can come from a land where gods walk the earth. I would argue that no good can come from a world where gods exist at all."

"You can tell our lovely king that for us," said Romeo.

Everyone grew quiet, Laurel uncertain of what to do next. Though their sermon had been difficult to hear, she could not deny there was truth in it. Ever since Soleh's death, she'd been questioning Karak's love for his people. The hangings, the stricter laws, not to mention the horror of the Final Judges. The cruelty and hunger of those lions, coupled with the dead eyes of the Sisters of the

Cloth, bore witness to the extremes Karak was willing to go to in his quest for order. Everything within her rejected it, even though the very notion of rejecting Karak filled her with fear. What would she be left with? A belief in nothing? Or would she perforce turn to Ashhur, a god about whom she knew nothing?

The bald brothers looked down at their cups, twiddling their fingers, until Laurel finally broke the silence.

"Do you wish to hear the rest of the king's decree?" she asked.

"No. We reject Eldrich's request," he said simply.

"Wait…what?" she replied. "I haven't even spoken the terms…"

"We will not prepare for the worst to happen. The worst has already happened. What we must do now is defend ourselves. We must take the reins of this life we have been given, rather than sit and wait for this war to play itself out. No Laurel, we must make our own path."

"How?"

"Can we trust her?" asked Cleo, turning to his brother.

"Of course we can," Romeo answered. "She is Cornwall's daughter, and Cornwall is the most noble and trustworthy of us all."

"Is this true, Laurel? Are you as trustworthy as your father? Will you swear that the words we tell you will not leave this room?"

"Yes," she said, puffing out her chest. "Now please answer my question."

"Which was?"

"How will we make our own path?"

Cleo chuckled. "By making sure both gods lose."

She shook her head. "You make it sound so simple. We are human, and they are gods. They each have nations sworn in allegiance. What could we possibly do to influence them when they could so easily destroy us?

"They are few, and we are many," answered Romeo. "We are fluid, and they are stagnant. Our lives are irrelevant, while theirs have swayed nations. Think on it, Laurel. The termite works in the dark, building its nest in the wood, breeding there, expanding its family. We do not notice them in our homes because they are small and hidden. Yet those same termites can cave in a roof and tumble down walls. Just a termite, something you or I could crush underneath our heel, can wreak unimaginable destruction."

Cleo grinned, nodding vociferously.

"You've already begun planning," said Laurel, amazed. Her heart began to beat out of control.

"We have," said Romeo, "and that plan is underway. We have made our *own* pacts with the other merchant lords. Even Matthew Brennan has agreed to our terms. We have formed alliances even in Paradise, and our spies have infiltrated Karak's Army, working to weaken it from within like the lowly termites we are. The pieces are moving, the betrayals are coming, and soon important people will die…and it will all lead to our freedom from those annoying brother gods."

"How can you be so sure about that?" asked Laurel.

"Because when the people see how little their gods care, when we show them we can control our own destiny, they will turn their backs on Karak and Ashhur. Once that happens, whichever deity survives this war will have two choices: end it all, or set us free." He laughed heartily. "Either way, we will no longer be in chains."

Cleo perked up. "So listen closely, Councilwoman. We have a new message for you to bring back to King Eldrich. He might not like hearing it, but he is a puppet of Karak as well, and should understand what we say more than any other man in this realm. When our plan comes to fruition, we will be the ones in power, the ones who hold the materials of life at our fingertips, the ones who can sway the people. Remind him that if men can turn their backs on something so powerful as a god, what hope is there for a king?"

Laurel leaned back in her chair. "I would say no hope at all," she said. "Do you think this plan of yours will succeed?"

"Of course," said Romeo with a grin.

"Why?"

"Because we have the support of the most powerful men in all of Neldar behind us, including your father."

"*I* speak for my father."

Cleo laughed. "And you are still here, listening to our gravest secrets without running away. I would say that is a telling sign in and of itself."

Even with uncertainty swelling inside her, Laurel nodded. "It is."

"Are you with us?"

"I am."

"Then this is what I would like you to tell our dear king…"

CHAPTER

21

Boris Marchant entered Velixar's pavilion, dragging behind him a man older than sin. The man's hair was long and white, brittle as straw in the middle of a drought. His face was creased and wrinkled, his gait stooped and painful to watch. Velixar looked up from what he was doing and gestured for the soldier to deposit the man in the chair opposite his writing desk.

"What are your plans for him?" Boris asked, a queer sort of curiosity shining behind his deep brown eyes as they flicked toward the journal that lay open on the table. He rubbed at the teardrop scar on his cheek, as if impatient. Velixar took that to mean the young soldier was eager to learn. In fact, with his curly hair, thick build, and flawless skin, Boris reminded him of Roland. A wave of both revulsion and longing washed over him. He forced himself to veer toward the latter. Roland had been a good apprentice. Perhaps Boris could take his place.

"Do you have duties to tend to?" he asked the soldier.

Boris shook his head. "Too many men fell ill, so camp has been set for the afternoon. The practitioner thinks it may be heatstroke and scurvy. Captain said we are only a hundred miles from the

Wooden Bridge, and since the rejoining is not for another week or two, we'll remain here to tend to our sick. 'Let no one be left behind needlessly,' he said."

"Smart man," replied Velixar with a smile, though inside he was seething. He knew Captain Wellington's decision was logical, but Mordeina was close, so close. "Since you are free, I would like for you to stay with me. There is much for you to learn."

"Yes, High Prophet," said Boris. The soldier then snapped his heels together, moved to the pavilion's canvas wall, and stood there, still as a statue.

Velixar turned his attention to the old man seated before him.

"Your name?" he asked.

"Cotter Mildwood," the old man answered in a strained voice. He leaned forward in his seat, squinting his faded brown eyes to see more clearly. "I know you," he said. "I know that voice."

"I assure you, you do not," said Velixar. He grabbed a blank sheet of parchment, lifted his quill, and wrote down the man's name and description. "Now tell me, Cotter, why did you bow to Karak when we arrived in your village? Why not leave with Ashhur when he passed through?"

"I have no stomach for strife," old Cotter replied. "And a hurried march would end me. My body is breaking, and I near the end of my days. My hope was that Karak would forgive an old man and allow him to end his life in peace."

It made sense, of course, though Velixar's chest tightened at the thought of the man abandoning his allegiance to his deity so easily, so callously.

"Tell me, Cotter, how old are you?"

The old man smiled, revealing a mouth half-filled with pearly white teeth.

"Ninety-four," he said with pride.

Velixar hesitated. "Ninety-four, you say?"

"Yes. I've been alive for ninety-four years."

"That cannot be so."

"It is."

Cotter clumsily lifted the bottom of his ratty tunic, exposing his wrinkled midsection—a midsection that lacked a bellybutton. Then he dropped his shirt and leaned so far forward his elbow struck the desk. He winced a bit, but it did not break his concentration as his squinting eyes stared at Velixar's face.

"I knew it," he said, clapping his misshapen hands together. "I *do* know you. The First Man. Jacob Eveningstar. Still so handsome. You look not a day older than the last time I saw you... had to be at least fifty years ago...though your eyes seem strange." His expression dropped as a spark of memory flashed in his eyes. "I heard of your exploits in the delta. Ashhur spoke of it when he gathered up the willing and took them from my village."

Velixar remained silent. He glanced at Boris, but the soldier simply watched, stoic.

"So it's true," Cotter said. "But of course it is. Ashhur tells no lies."

"He does not," said Velixar.

Cotter nodded. "You were always such a nice man to us. My son was born in my second year, and you brought a bale of hay and twigs to help build his cradle. I don't remember what you told me that day, but I remember your voice plain as if it were my own."

"A shame I do not remember you," said Velixar. "I have met so many over the years. And age has not been kind to you."

"It is true, it is true." Cotter's frown grew deeper. "I have a question for you, Jacob. Why? Why have you turned your back on your god?"

"I am Jacob no longer," he said, keeping his voice level and his pulse steady. "I am Velixar now, High Prophet of Karak, and I would appreciate it if you would offer me the respect of addressing me as such." He sighed. "As for my actions, I never turned my back on my god, old man. I am a child of *two* gods, not one, and

I chose Karak. Choosing one god does not mean I turned my back on the other."

The old man looked confused. "But…that makes no sense. You were Ashhur's most trusted. Now you seek to destroy him. Though I am not one to talk given that I bended my sore knee to Karak, but it seems like a betrayal to me."

"My aim is not to destroy," Velixar said, "but to liberate. Ashhur's notions are grand, but he is *wrong*, Cotter, wrong about what is best for humanity. I would show Ashhur the error of his ways, but he is not prone to change. If that means killing him, if a god can even *be* killed, then so be it. What I'm doing, what we're all doing in this army, is fighting for humanity's future. It is mankind I serve, and what is best for mankind. Karak is the truer deity. He is the god of freedom and prosperity, not chains and sacraments."

"But Jacob—"

Velixar slammed his fist on the desk, silencing him. "Enough, old man," he said. "I am the one who asks questions here, not you. And do *not* call me Jacob again."

"I apologize…Velixar," the old man said, bowing his head. "I meant no disrespect."

Breathing deep, Velixar gathered his patience once more. He glanced at Boris and nodded to the soldier, who returned the gesture.

"Let us speak on other matters," he told Cotter. "You have sworn yourself to Karak, which means you are now a part in our god's ever growing congregation. And an important one at that."

"Important? How?"

"You will assist me in the quest for knowledge."

Cotter's thin lips twisted in confusion.

"Can you read, old man?" asked Velixar.

"I can."

Velixar turned to his journal, opened to a page he had inscribed just the night before, when another surge of the demon's ancient knowledge dripped into his brain like sweet nectar. He turned the journal to face Cotter and slid it across the desk to him.

"The way the human mind works is a mystery to me, to all of us," he told him. "There are certain words and images that mean something to one person and something completely different to another."

"I don't understand."

Velixar gestured at the journal. "Please, all I ask is that you read the words written on that page and then study the diagram drawn beneath. After you do so, tell me what it is you see."

Cotter leaned over the pages, cloudy eyes squinting even more as they traced letters and illustrations drawn in black ink.

"The words make no sense," he muttered.

"Sound them out best you can," Velixar said. "They'll feel natural in time."

Cotter's thin lips mouthed unintelligible words, his brow furrowing. Velixar leaned forward, watching with interest as the old man's mouth slowly sagged, his neck growing taut and his hands clenching and unclenching on the desk. It looked like the beginning of a seizure. Faster and faster he spoke the words, now an audible whisper. Then a moan escaped Cotter's lips, and his eyes rolled into the back of his head. The old man threw himself back in his chair. He forced out laughter between violent coughing fits, spittle and blood flying from his mouth.

Velixar stood, and though Boris looked frightened, the Highest only smiled.

"Fascinating," he whispered.

Cotter began to shout animalistic bellows and nonsensical phrases. His body rocked in his chair, and then he lurched to a standing position, arms held out to his sides. His ragged tunic was soaked with the blood that seeped from his mouth, nose, and ears. The old man's eyes bulged, his pupils the size of the tiniest pinprick. He gaped at everything and nothing, his stare as empty as the dead. His lips continued to move, spewing yet more blood. He stuck out his tongue and in a swift motion his mouth snapped shut, his remaining teeth gnashing the appendage in two. The severed portion flopped to the ground while the mouth in which it once resided continued to speak in soundless chants.

"So fascinating."

Cotter began slamming his blood-soaked face into one of the pavilion's heavy support struts. Velixar heard a *crunch* as the man's nose shattered, and he glanced at Boris. The young soldier was watching the scene with abject horror, his hand resting on the hilt of his sword, tiny rivulets of sweat beading on his neck.

Boris stepped forward wordlessly, drawing his sword. He grabbed Cotter by the shoulder and whirled him around. The old man's hand lashed out, striking the soldier across the cheek. Boris released him, stumbling backward in surprise, and Cotter lunged forward, mouth opened wide, baring his remaining teeth, his gnarled hands bent into claws.

The soldier thrust upward with his sword, the tip piercing the underside of the old man's chin, then exiting the back of his head with a *pop*. Cotter's arms went limp, and his body collapsed against Boris, who stepped back, letting him fall. The young soldier looked like he wanted to turn on Velixar, to scream and rant and perhaps drive a blade into him, but he shook it off as if physically shedding his anger. He then calmly reached down, wrenched his sword from Cotter's head, and wiped it clean before returning it to its sheath.

"You promised you wouldn't hurt him," Boris said when he was done. Despite the delay, his voice still quivered a bit.

"And I did not. He hurt himself, and then you ran him through."

The soldier gaped at him.

Velixar leaned forward, gazing with disappointment at the stilled body on the ground, before sitting down and grabbing the sheet of parchment on which he'd written Cotter's name and age, and then he started scribbling with his quill. "A shame," he said. "There is much I could have learned from this one."

"Learned?" asked Boris. The tiniest quaver in his voice betrayed the calm he was trying to portray. "What could you possibly learn from *that*? That was…that was…unnatural."

"No," Velixar said, lifting his head from his writings. "It might not have appeared so, but it was actually quite natural. It is fascinating the effects certain stimuli have on the human mind. Everything has a cause and consequence. The only failure was on my part, for I did not know what outcome this passage would bring. It could have made the man calmer, or more intelligent, or reduced his mind to that of a child." He shrugged. "Instead it drove him mad."

Boris strode up to the desk, grabbed the corner of the journal, and turned it toward himself.

"What kind of witchcraft is this?" he asked, his eyes dipping to the opened page.

Velixar's arm quickly shot out, slamming the massive tome closed.

"Do *not* read that!" he shouted at the soldier. "Do you wish to die? There are some things the human mind was not meant to comprehend. That passage is obviously one of them."

Boris slowly backed away.

"I was…I just wanted to see what it said, what it looked like," he said.

"Then you would have ended up like the man you just ran through," Velixar said, jutting his chin at Cotter's corpse.

"Oh. But did you not write it? Why can *you* look on it when others can't?"

Velixar withdrew his hand, sighing.

"Because I am beyond humanity now. I am the High Prophet of Karak, privy to knowledge that transcends mortality—that transcends the fabric of the universe itself. Do not insult me by insinuating that the sniveling old man's mind was of equal strength to mine."

Boris considered the now closed journal. "Is that book full of similar…things?"

Velixar smiled, amused by the soldier's almost reverence toward his personal writings.

"There are more than a few spells in here that might render a man mad, Boris. It is a chronicle of my life and all I have learned, from ten years before the gods created you until this very day. The history of the elves, the first baby steps of man, Karak helping to erect the city of Veldaren and the commune of Erznia, Ashhur forging the Sanctuary and adopting the cast-out Wardens, countless remedies and spells—all are within these pages." He patted the tome's leather cover. "I once wrote this as my gift to the race of man, a legacy of wisdom and knowledge in case of my death."

The soldier gave him a wry smile.

"Once?" he asked.

"Now I do not know who I write it for," Velixar said, surprised by how he was revealing himself to the soldier. "Not even the brother gods have seen what is written here. The spells are archaic, many of them dangerous.…Still, I find myself driven to record them, to test the limits of my newfound wisdom. I should destroy the book; part of me knows that, yet I cannot bear the thought. It will no longer be a gift for mankind, though, I do know that. There is danger in too much knowledge. After all, one might accidentally loose a demon on the world."

Boris frowned, looked at Cotter's body, and shifted awkwardly on his feet.

"I suppose I should clean up the mess," he said, bending over and hefting a stiff arm over his shoulder. "I will send a squire to wipe up what is left."

He began dragging the corpse along the ground, leaving a trail of blood behind him.

"Young man," Velixar said, halting the soldier in his tracks. Boris turned to him, expectant. Once more Velixar was reminded of

Roland. So much potential. So much desire to learn, consequences be damned.

"There is no need to send a squire," he told him. "I will handle this mess. And though you may never look within the journal, I would not deny you some of the wisdom inside. Prove yourself, Boris. Dedicate your service to Karak, and show our god the true cleverness of your mind. I have been without a capable steward for some time now. When our Divinity claims Paradise as his own, I may require another one."

"Yes, High Prophet," he said, grinning. And then he ducked beneath the flap.

When he was gone, Velixar snatched up an empty inkwell, stood, and circled his desk. He hovered over the trail of blood and raised his free hand. With a few chanted words of magic, the blood began to shimmer and rise up off the ground, the droplets shimmying and swaying like hovering puffs of cotton. The liquid rippled, drawing together the higher it floated, until it became a single massive bubble. Velixar held out the inkwell, and the blood formed into a narrow tube, gliding through the air and entering the open top of the bottle. When the tail of the crimson serpent disappeared inside, he placed a cap on it and set it down.

He slowly shook his head as he stared at the capped container. A shame Cotter had died. To have custody of one of the first humans crafted by Ashhur, his blood pure and unmixed with others, could have been useful. Still, he couldn't blame Boris for killing him. The boy was only human, prone to fear and doubt. Still, it bothered him, for there were many more pages of mystical transcriptions he longed to experiment with, all written within his journal over the last five days. He shrugged. No matter. They had collected a great many refugees from the towns they'd sacked, all of whom had bent their knee to Karak. There were plenty of other subjects for his experiments. Perhaps even Lanike Crestwell would do. The wife of Clovis was locked in her private wagon on the other end of camp, likely chomping on her fingernails and crying herself to sleep. All it would take was a word and she would be brought before him, eyes wide and pleading. It was tempting, if not for his need to keep Darakken in line....

A shrill scream rose in the distance, stealing away his daydream. He paused, thinking it might have been in his head. But then another scream sounded, followed by panicked shouts. Velixar snatched Lionsbane from the back of the chair on which it hung and swiftly ducked beneath the pavilion's entrance flap.

It was dusk, a gloomy mishmash of crimson and purple that hovered over the miles of flattened grassland where the army camped. Velixar's pavilion was positioned on a slight hill, close to a thick expanse of forest in the shadow of Karak's own dwelling. The soldiers' tents stretched out below him like folded bits of paper, from one distant line of trees to another, the entire area ridging the Gods' Road. A great many people gathered at the northern edge of the camp, those who'd decided not to join their mates around the bonfires for food and drink. There were a hundred of them dashing this way and that, many fumbling for their weapons, their faces masks of confusion and fright. Smelling something odd, Velixar cast a quick glance toward the southeast, and despite the darkening of the day, he could easily spot the billowing black clouds of smoke that filled the sky, evidence of Lord Commander Avila's continued onward march as she circled the province of Ker, sealing Ashhur's tall, dark children in behind a wall of scorched earth.

Yet what he smelled wasn't fire. It was meatier than that, more visceral. He took a step forward, fastening Lionsbane's scabbard to his belt, while he peered in the opposite direction. Karak stepped out of his pavilion, which was three times the size of Velixar's, and stood eerily still, his arms crossed, his glowing eyes glaring at the chaos around him.

He looked disappointed.

Someone collided with Velixar from behind; uttered a hasty, halfhearted apology; and then ran off toward a cluster of soldiers gathering at the northwestern ring of forest. Velixar studied the man's face, committing it to memory. The High Prophet of Karak was to be respected, and this soldier would receive a scolding once all was settled.

Velixar hurried across the empty space separating his dwelling from his god's. Karak's head slowly turned, those soul-crushing eyes making him feel small as he approached. The god's face was still as stone in that moment—forever unmoving, forever unmoved.

"I sense power here," Karak said. His booming voice made the din of bedlam seem tranquil by comparison.

"Power?" he asked. "What kind of power?"

"A god's power," Karak answered, remaining stoic. "My brother has brought the fight to us."

Velixar felt his heart leap.

"Ashhur is here?"

"No, Prophet. He sent pets to do his business for him."

Wheeling around, Velixar looked on as three soldiers came tramping out of the forest, dragging a screaming man behind them. The man's armor had been frayed, his legs a ghastly mess of shredded flesh and exposed bone, his teeth gnashed together, his face scrunched up in pain. His fellow soldiers thrust swords and spears into the thick copse of elms and evergreens, fighting unseen attackers.

What looked to be a huge black shadow darted across the murky forest, appearing and disappearing as it crossed behind the trees. Then he saw another and another and another. Soon the forest was filled with dark outlines, black on black, growing ever closer to the clearing. The soldiers retreated, stumbling over the first line of tents, collapsing several of them.

Eyes appeared next. One pair, two, twenty, fifty—slanted and bloodthirsty, reflecting the day's dying light. Velixar took a step forward, unsnapping the leather strap across Lionsbane's hilt. He drew the sword slightly, exposing steel, but remained on the hill with his god just behind him.

"What are they?" he asked.

"Monsters," Karak replied.

"Ashhur made them?"

"Yes. I feel his essence dripping from them even now."

One of the beasts lunged from the trees, crushing a fleeing soldier beneath its bulk. It was tall as a man, but it hunched as it ambled. Suddenly, Velixar knew what it was—a wolf that walked on two legs. The creature was covered in gray fur streaked with black, each hair rippling as its powerful muscles flexed and relaxed. Its jaws were open, saliva dripping from wicked incisors. The fur below its jaws glistened with red all the way down to its breast. Its stare was haunting and primitive, projecting hunger, wrath, and the most frighteningly basic form of intelligence. The soldiers froze before the thing, weapons extended in shaking hands. It seemed everyone had stopped breathing. The wolf-man paced back and forth before them, dropping down on all fours occasionally, as if to show off the powerful build of its long arms. When it raised its eyes, they seemed to stare right through Velixar, shining invisible beams of hatred at the god behind him.

The wolf-man turned toward the forest and let loose a mighty howl, throwing its head toward the crimson and purple sky. A second later a wall of fur, muscle, and angry eyes erupted from the shelter of the forest, driving into the frightened column of soldiers. The men did their best to hold the line, but soon the wolf-men overwhelmed them, claws slashing and jaws, filled with sharp teeth, snapping. Men screamed, armor crunched, and steel fell harmlessly to the ground.

The sound of escalating slaughter drew the sick and the early sleepers from their tents. They glanced about with surprise and apprehension, none understanding the scene of carnage before them. A few of the wolf-men spotted them, and they disengaged from their victims, claws and teeth dripping blood, and leapt over their already fallen prey to greet the newcomers. Always, it seemed, they remained aware of Karak and his larger than life presence.

And still more rushed from the forest, a seemingly endless wave. Velixar stood agape as he watched them approach. There had to be a hundred of them. Already they had butchered fifty or more soldiers and left many more on the ground, who screamed as they held stumps where their hands had been, cradling gaping wounds in their chests, long gashes on their faces.

"The ease of our path has made our men soft," said Karak, sounding disgusted. "These beasts have size and form, but they are no wiser than when they ran on four legs and howled at the moon. Our men have armor, weaponry, tactics. My brother sends a half measure, and we are not prepared."

The deity stepped forward then, his glowing eyes becoming twice as bright as usual. He extended his massive arms out to both sides of him, bolts of purplish electricity encircling his palms like bands.

"Wait, my Lord!" Velixar shouted.

Karak paused, glaring back at him. "Why do you stop me, Prophet? The slaughter continues."

He rushed forward. "It does, my Lord, but let the men fight. Let me fight with them. Our army has experienced nothing but the Wardens' token resistance. Please, Lord, let me guide them. Let me *help them win*."

Karak cocked his head and frowned in thought.

"Be swift and brutal," he said. "I do not enjoy losing more resources than necessary."

"Thank you, my Lord," Velixar said. He drew Lionsbane and charged down the hill toward the approaching horde. Many of those who had stumbled from their tents were now being slaughtered, but as the wolf-men pushed deeper into the camp, they'd begun to encounter groups of men who'd had time to throw on their armor and ready their weapons. At least ten wolf-man carcasses lay between the trampled tents, bleeding out on the grass.

Concentrating, Velixar focused his power.

"Come to me, men!" he shouted, his voice magnified a hundred times, echoing across the grassland as if he himself were a god. "Come to your Prophet! Come fight in the name of your god! To me! Let us defend our brothers!"

Velixar leapt into the air, narrowly avoiding a wolf-man's swiping claws. He spun once and hacked down with Lionsbane, cleaving through the beast's snout and leaving a gaping, leaking hole. The thing shrieked from its mutilated face, the sound like a buzzing nest of wasps, only to be silenced when Velixar plunged his blade through the bloody maw. It fell to the ground and stilled.

More came at him from behind, barreling on all fours. Spinning around, he held out his hand and shouted words of magic. The power flowing through him was robust, and bolts of shadow and black lightning leapt from his fingertips, scorching one of the beasts, its fur erupting with purple flame as it fell, thrashing and writhing in pain. More flames danced onto a second, but it extinguished them with its paw. The third carried on unabated, bearing down on him, leading with outstretched claws.

Velixar dove to the side, and the closest wolf-man stumbled past him. He pointed a finger at the second, muttering, "*Wither*," and the creature suddenly lost all form. The flesh beneath its fur undulated, its legs became like rubber, its body caved in on itself. The only form of protest it could offer was a pathetic whine before it fell.

Lost in the glory of his spell, Velixar almost failed to notice the third wolf-man had circled around back for him. Claws ripped through the air, shredding the back of his cloak but missing flesh. Velixar pitched himself into a forward roll, avoiding a second deadly swipe, before rising up on his knees and holding Lionsbane out before him. The wolf-man collided with the sword, the blade sinking deep into its chest. The beast's hungry eyes bulged in surprise. Velixar ducked beneath another of its strikes, then released the weapon so he could roll out and away. When he came to his feet, he felt a strong surge of power, and he recognized the weapon as the primitive thing it really was.

"I don't need steel," he said, walking toward the beast as it ripped the sword from its chest. "I don't need a blade. All I need, I have."

He lunged, grabbing the creature's face while it still struggled to remain standing. The power channeled through him, down his arm, out his palm, and into twisted flesh. It released a shockwave and a thunderous sound. The wolf-man howled as it died, the bones in its body shattering as the spell rolled through it. When Velixar released his hand, it dropped, an unrecognizable sack of meat and fur.

Velixar had no time to bask in the glory of his success, for still more wolf-men charged. Countless dead soldiers lay before him, their wounds feeding the soil with their blood. Many of the wolf-men stopped to feed. Others still were locked in combat with those soldiers who had not yet fallen, their claws and teeth easily besting armor and steel. Velixar ripped Lionsbane from the wolf-man's carcass and glanced behind him. More men ran up from the camp to join the fight, but their movements were slow and hesitant, their hearts not engaged. A great many glanced toward Karak's towering figure in the distance, as if waiting for him to come to their aid. The sight filled Velixar with fury, and he addressed them again.

"For glory!" he shouted, magnifying his voice once more. "For victory! For Karak!"

A group of nine joined his side, several of them bloodied from combat—a sign that they'd killed some of the wolf-men. He cried out a charge, and the ten of them raced toward the hill and the thick of the combat.

"Form ranks!" he cried. "Form ranks, shoulder to shoulder!"

The creatures were all around them, swarming and panting and growling. Velixar saw that one was about to descend on a lone man, and he pointed his finger at it, letting his rage fuel his power. An arrow of darkness shot forth, spearing the creature in the eye, before dissolving.

"I said *form ranks*!" Velixar roared, and the man scrambled to join the others. Turning, Velixar opened his palms as he speared several more of the creatures with lightning, targeting the ones that appeared the largest and most threatening. Two charged him head on, and Velixar was proud when soldiers at either side of him stepped forward, their swords and shields forming a protective wall. Velixar sent out several more arrows of concentrated darkness, the projectiles shimmering red and purple as they plunged into the beasts' thick flesh. The two wolf-men weakened and were then hacked to pieces by his guardians' swords.

Still the wolf-men crashed into the ever-growing lines of soldiers. They were single minded and deadly, stronger than mere humans, and their weapons were always in hand. Velixar felt himself beginning to tire, his magic only wounding the beasts upon whom he unleashed it, instead of killing them outright. One of the beasts crashed through the line, tossing aside a soldier to slash Velixar's chest. He fell back as another of the creatures ripped a gash across his right forearm. Landing in the blood-soaked earth, he lifted his arms as a hungry maw lowered for his throat.

The thought of falling before the war had even begun, and to such a creature, flooded him with terror.

"Not like this!" he screamed out in primal fury. The air around him rippled, driving the wolf-men back. The blood on the ground came to life, forming tentacles that lashed like whips, pinning several of them to the ground. Dark fire leapt from his hands, and the nearest beast crossed its arms as flames washed over it, burning away fur, then flesh, leaving only bone and ash to fall and scatter. Struggling to one knee, Velixar reached deep inside himself, tapping into a well of power that suddenly seemed endless. Light gathered in his palms, growing ever brighter.

Endless, he thought, focusing on that power, pulling to mind the words of spells that would break and destroy anything in his way. With sudden clarity, he knew he could kill every last one of the wolf-men—and not just them, but the fleeing nation of Ashhur, even the god himself. All he had to do was speak the words, use the power deep within him, and watch it all burn.

He never had that chance. The might he felt at his disposal, the seemingly endless well, disappeared as quickly as he had found it. His hands went dark, and the pendant around his neck, Ashhur's pendant and Karak's gift, burned into his flesh. Over his head soared a gigantic black shadow trailing purple fire, and then Karak landed in the midst of the remaining wolf-men, his ethereal sword glowing. In giant, swooping arcs, the god dismantled his foes, cleaving torsos, lopping off heads, reducing the once-powerful creatures to piles of discarded flesh and bone. Even Karak's own soldiers were not safe—those still locked in combat and unable to retreat suffered the same fate, Karak's mighty blade slicing through them as if their bodies were made of water.

And then it was over. One moment there was an army of mutated beasts approaching; the next, just a field strewn with blood, bones, and entrails. The remaining wolf-men, a third of the original number, darted into the forest, yelping and baying. Velixar stumbled to his feet, feeling weaker than he had in a hundred years, his body aching, his brain throbbing. Turning around, he saw that half the camp had gathered around the base of the hill to watch Karak dispatch the murderous invaders, their jaws hanging open in awe. One by one, they dropped to their knees before their deity. Karak turned to them, not even winded. The glowing sword in his hand slowly faded away until it blinked out of existence.

"Today, we failed!" the god bellowed, and his worshippers dove forward until their faces kissed the dirt. "Who are these things before me? Surely they are not my children, trained and blessed with the finest weaponry and strongest armor in all the land? What am I to do with you, you pathetic, frail lot? What have the fruits of all my labor delivered to me? One day I will lead an army against the west. One day I will drive the scourge of chaos from the land, and establish a blessed order in Dezrel. But it is not this day. It is not with this army of children and cowards and fools!"

Velixar struggled to his feet as Karak abruptly turned and stormed away. He had to run to keep pace, so great were his god's strides.

"My Lord, we had them," he said, winded. He clutched the pendant through his chain and smallclothes. "Please, you must give them another chance."

Karak said not a word. He simply stormed up the hill and violently batted aside the flaps to his giant pavilion. Velixar followed him in, his strength slowly returning, and with it, his anger.

The god faced away from him. A brisk wind blew outside, rippling the pavilion's walls and seeming to heighten the din of pain and tragedy from the outside world. The pavilion itself was virtually empty—the only adornment was a small ring of stones in its center, a waft of black smoke rising to the hole in the top of the tent from the dying embers within the ring. Velixar stopped, huffing while he stared at his god's back.

"You have failed me," Karak said. His voice was soft now, yet it retained its potency.

"We did not fail you, my Lord," Velixar insisted. He could not keep the edge out of his voice.

The god turned slightly, fixing him with a dissatisfied glare.

"No? Tell me, Velixar. Tell me how this was a great victory. Tell me how losing two hundred men to a small battalion of my brother's ill-conceived monstrosities is a triumph."

"I—"

"You cannot say, because it would not be true." Karak fully faced him, and never before had Velixar felt so small as he did in that moment. It was a bitter sensation, and it made his blood boil. "My creations may be inexperienced, but inexperience is no excuse for abject failure. We have been fortunate up until now. Ashhur has made us lazy by showing only token resistance as he slowly gathers strength. And when we battle against foes that are actually *eager* for a fight, I watch my trained men die like rats at the feet of lions."

Velixar gritted his teeth. "It is a learning experience, my Lord. The men shall not fail so mightily again."

"So you say. Yet how many more would have perished had I not intervened? I watched you lead the charge. You are powerful, and some of the men were willing to fight, but the beasts overran you still. I saw one of them towering above my own High Prophet, ready to feed. Yet now you glare at me as if I have done wrong. Tell me, Velixar, should I have let the monstrosities tear you apart, all so my soldiers might have *experience*?"

Velixar's pride was taking more wounds than he could endure.

"It never would have happened," he said. "I would have proven my might to you, if only you'd waited."

The god shook his head. "Such self-assurance. It will be the end of you."

"Perhaps. But children must always stumble before they walk. What you see as failure, I see as a presage of greater glory."

"We have neither the time nor the numbers for such failures," the god retorted. He gazed at the walls once more. "Until now, each victory has come with greater ease than the one before. It has made the men soft. That is unacceptable. Those beasts you faced…my brother erred by not giving them intelligence to match their might. Had he done so, those few that assailed us could have wiped out half our force without my intervention. Imagine that, Velixar. A scant hundred beasts slaughtering two thousand men. A feat such as that would have been well worth the cost." The god frowned. "Perhaps Ashhur has stumbled upon a wiser path than my own. I may need to start over, cast aside this sorry lot and make beasts more powerful, faithful, and driven."

Velixar reacted without thinking.

"Do it, and you have already lost," he said. When Karak brought his eyes to bear on him, he tensed, waiting for his god to end him then and there.

"And how is that?" Karak asked, arms crossing over his chest.

"Because then you cannot claim your way is superior. You cannot show the greatness of the nation your children have sired by casting those very children aside and fashioning beasts into mindless servants and warriors."

Karak stared him down, then let his hands fall to his sides.

"You are right," he said. "My brother's creations are not what I war against, but my brother himself. And though altering life forms takes power, imbuing them with intellect requires a sacrifice of self. Even the little I gave Kayne and Lilah weakened me slightly. Ashhur and I are precariously balanced. Should either of us fall too far below the other…"

Velixar bowed low.

"Then you must trust us, trust *me*, to do what is right. These men are capable, my Lord. They will not fail you again."

"Trust you," Karak said. "Indeed, I do trust you, but I fear that trust will turn against me in time. You are flawed, as are all men, but you refuse to see it."

Velixar felt his mouth turn dry. The pendant on his chest throbbed.

"Flawed," he said tonelessly. "Tell me my flaws, my god, so that I may fix them."

Karak shook his head.

"You claim to have the power of the demon, yet all you have done with it is scribble in your book and experiment on those who have bended their knee to me. You consider yourself wiser than humanity, yet your wisdom did not see Ashhur's gambit before it arrived. You think yourself aware of the world in a way mere humans are not, yet you do not realize that those who betrayed you are within striking distance even now."

"What are you saying?"

"As of this very moment your old apprentice Roland travels along the Gods' Road with a great many refugees from Lerder," said Karak. "They approach the Wooden Bridge, thinking to find safety in Mordeina. I believe the Warden Azariah is with them."

Velixar felt his pulse quicken.

"How can you know this?" he asked. "Is it a spell? An aspect of your divine nature? Tell me, I beg of you."

Karak smiled, but there was a hint of mockery in it, a touch of pity.

"A message came this morning by way of a raven. One of my rearguard patrols captured a deserter from the group and questioned him thoroughly."

Velixar shook his head, feeling humiliated.

"Why did you not tell me earlier?" he asked.

Karak placed a mighty hand on his shoulder. His tone lowered, becoming more compassionate.

"You must learn humility, Velixar. You have become absorbed with your perceived betterment. Though you are privy to the demon's ancient knowledge, and your body is a timeless perfection, you are still only a man. You will not reach the heights I know you are capable of until you understand and accept that."

Velixar wanted to shout at his deity that the demon's intellect had given him the knowledge that Karak too was fallible, but he kept his mouth shut. Instead, he quietly seethed, attempting to accept his lesson, no matter how painful, as a faithful servant should.

"Yes, my Lord," he said.

"Good," Karak said. "Now leave me be. Allow the men a short rest, but that is all. In two days we march—healthy, sick, and injured alike."

"Yes, my Lord. But before I go, might I ask…what will you do about the group crossing the Wooden Bridge?"

Karak shrugged as if it were no important thing.

"A few hungry refugees are no reason to upset our camp and rush the recovery of our wounded."

"As you say," Velixar said, bowing low. He turned on his heels and went to leave, only stopping when Karak called out to him one final time.

"Do as I say," the god commanded. "If you wish for these men to learn, you will learn along with them. At my side, or not at all."

Without another word, Velixar left the deity's pavilion.

The three-quarter moon rose when darkness descended on the land. Once the bodies of the deceased wolf-men and soldiers had been burned, Velixar reclined on his pile of blankets, staring at the heaving roof of his pavilion. More of the demon's experience flowed into his mind, making him anxious. He glanced at his journal resting on his desk. Suddenly writing in it seemed a worthless endeavor. If Karak saw him as no better than a mere mortal, what good was the wisdom within it? Who was it even for? Velixar tired of the god's impertinent treatment of him; he needed to *prove* to Karak his superiority to the rest of the men.

He sat up with a jolt, anger flowing in his veins once more. After retrieving Lionsbane, he stormed across the pavilion to the far end of the sleeping camp. There he found an exhausted Captain Wellington, his shoulders slumped as he guarded the temporary stables filled with hundreds of beasts that grazed on the sparse grasses beside the Gods' Road.

"Captain," Velixar said, and Wellington snapped upright.

"High Prophet," the man replied, his face awash with apprehension.

"Find someone else to watch them," Velixar said flatly. "And gather twenty of your best men. Bring them to me. You have fifteen minutes."

"Um…might I ask why, High Prophet?"

Velixar grinned, and it felt untamed on his lips.

"Because tonight we ride. There are blasphemers on the road ahead of us, and they will suffer the retaliation Ashhur's ambush deserves. Now go. There is no time to waste. And Captain, make sure the ones you gather are the most brutal you can find."

CHAPTER

22

Patrick could not go back the way he'd come. Where only days before there had been flowing fields of wheat and dense thatches of maple and birch trees, all that remained was a smoldering wasteland. Flames still crackled in some places, trees and underbrush licking red and yellow, and the air was thick with smoke. He had to cover his nose and mouth with the smallclothes beneath his armor to keep from hacking. There were hidden shallots like Grassmere dotted throughout the lands bordering the Gods' Road, and if what he saw now were any indication, they must have been razed along with the surrounding lands. He thought back to the burnt barn and the ghastly secret hidden inside. If he avoided the area, at least he would not have to see more corpses.

Hopefully.

He ended up backtracking, guiding his horse out of the destruction and entering the desert once more. The red clay cliffs were just ahead of him. He hoped the scorched earth didn't reach that far, but then realized it was a silly fear. Sand did not burn like vegetation did. To set fire to a desert would require a god's power.

He came to his own tracks, leading across the endless expanse of sand to the Black Spire. If he kept heading west instead of north, he would soon come on the prairie where antelope and hyena roamed. That path was fraught with danger, as the night's predators would surely smell his presence and stalk him, but if he reached the Corinth River, he could follow it back north and hopefully reunite with Ashhur at the Wooden Bridge. Then again, given how much time had passed, it was likely the god had already crossed. It had been eight days since he'd left the mass of refugees to have his ill-fated and aggravating reunion with Bardiya. They might already be far into the west. He thought of the scorched earth he had just left behind and shuddered. *Or they might all have been slaughtered.*

That night he made camp beneath a jutting stone that offered scant protection from the assault of flying sand kicked up by the winds. The temperature dropped, and his feeble fire flickered and died. His horse whinnied as it gnawed on the bits of cactus he had chopped for its meal. He had stripped the cactus in the dark, so he hoped he'd succeeded in removing all the spines. The last thing he needed was for a barb to get lodged in the beast's throat. Wandering across the desert with only his uneven legs to propel him would be a good way to get killed.

As he lay down in the sand, pulling his paltry lone blanket up to his chin to ward off the chill, his mind wandered to Bardiya once more. He cursed his friend's stubbornness and devotion. Bardiya was willing to allow his people to perish, and for what? Some woebegone notion of belief? It seemed downright idiotic. Why Ashhur didn't simply head down to Ker and force them to join was beyond his understanding.

It struck him how backward the whole scenario seemed. In Safeway and the far west of Paradise where Patrick had been raised, Ashhur had treated his children like, well, *children*. He'd done so ever since their creation, coddling them, giving them all they desired as he hovered like an overprotective parent. And yet ever since Bessus Gorgoros decided to give his vast corner of Paradise a name ninety years ago, Ashhur had treated the wards of House Gorgoros differently. He'd allowed them their sovereignty, letting them deal with their conflicts with the elves in their own way, without interference.

He grumbled and took a sip of cactus nectar, the question lingering in his head: Why had Ashhur treated Ker so differently?

"It's time for your children to grow up and make their own decisions, and from what I saw in Haven, growing up is almost always painful."

The realization struck him like a blow to the head. *He* had spoken those words, and to Ashhur no less. He hadn't received an argument either. Could it be that Ashhur *did* wish for his children to be independent? Perhaps it was why he had allowed Ker to remain neutral, why he did not interfere in their dealings. He must desire such independence for *all* of Paradise. Otherwise he would not have allowed Ker to exist at all, never mind the formation of the lordship or the crowning of the King Benjamin. It was the same reason Patrick had been allowed to take his journey south despite Ashhur's insistence that it would not succeed.

"All for the sake of each other," the god had once said. "With your creator residing in your hearts."

Patrick suddenly felt very, very small. And stupid.

The next morning came much too quickly, the rising sun baking away the night's chill and causing waves of heat to rise from the sand. Exhausted, Patrick continued on his western trek, crossing from the desert and into the plains by midday. A horde of antelope bounded in the distance, along with wild horses and a few grazing buffalo. At one point he caught sight of a group of tall, darkskinned men and women working their way through the grassland, spears and bows in hand. He raised his hand to them, a gesture they returned in kind. The city of Ang was two days south, and he was tempted to go there. Instead he ground his heels into his horse's flank and kept riding.

He passed a bubbling stream beneath a rocky outcropping and stopped to fill his waterskin and allow his horse a drink. Then it was back in the saddle again, heading toward the red and brown hills in the distance.

At the crest of a weathered hill, he stopped and gazed southwest at a line of great trees in the distance, the edge of the Stonewood Forest. He also saw the jagged gash of the Corinth stretching out in both directions, the flowing waters sparkling beneath the light of day. A smile came on his face, the first in some time. By this hour tomorrow, he would be at the bridge, hopefully following in the footsteps of his god's massive entourage.

Suddenly, Patrick's attention was drawn to the sound of gruff murmuring and the scrape of something heavy on stone. His head shot to the side, and he saw a thin stream of smoke rising from behind one of the hills to his right. There were people there, and they were not more than a quarter mile away. He almost let out a shout, calling to those hidden behind the rocky hill, but then stayed his voice. Bardiya had told him his people were forbidden from venturing this close to the river after what had happened to his parents. It might be a group of Stonewood Dezren sitting there, sharpening their khandars and stringing their bows.

Of course, if they *were* elves, he was close enough that their heightened senses would have picked up the sound of his horse's hooves clomping over the rocks as it crested the hill. So they were either friendly or they were humans…but on which side? Had Karak's Army moved so far west already? Having avoided the scorched lands closer to the Gods' Road, Patrick had no way of knowing.

He steered his horse toward the voices, edging it down the hill at a gentle trot. Hearing the sound of laughter, he stopped, cocking his head to listen. The path he was traveling was bordered by a pair of rocky ledges, apparently leading to the speakers. The laughter came again, this time from multiple sources. It sounded strained, almost nervous, but his ears could just be telling him something he wanted to hear. *Best to avoid them,* he thought. He could circle around one of the hills, get closer to the river, and be out of sight before any were the wiser.

"Fuck Karak."

The statement echoed through the vale, followed by desperate, hushed petitions for silence. Patrick chuckled, then looked back in the direction of the smoke.

"To the abyss with it," he muttered. He would likely get along well with anyone willing to shout such a statement. He placed his half helm atop his head and unsheathed Winterbone, propping the heavy blade against his armored shoulder. He then trotted toward the voices.

The group must have detected his approach, for all speaking ceased, and he heard feet shuffling over rocky soil. Patrick swallowed his doubt and pressed onward. Pursing his lips, he began to whistle, mimicking a lighthearted tune the Warden Lavictus used to sing to him when he was young and still wet the bed. He continued to whistle even as he rounded the corner. Strangely, his fear left him, and he became almost giddy with expectation.

What he found was a generous culvert that split the knoll in two. On either side of him were earthen walls, worn smooth by the passage of time. The alcove would be virtually invisible to any wayward eye. The ground was disturbed by tracks, and there were nine horses hovering on the other side of the culvert, but no people. The mounts were adorned with black draping that hung beneath the saddles on their backs, the roaring lion of Karak stitched on them in red. They snorted and kicked up dirt on his arrival, but made no move to flee. The remains of a fire smoldered in the center of the alcove, the source of the smoke.

He pulled on the reins, halting his mare, and continued to whistle while he glanced about him. The stitching on the horses suddenly made him wonder how badly he'd erred. There were a great many large stones dotting the culvert, most likely the remnants of the earthen walls collapsing, and he spotted something gray behind one of them. His lips squeezed together, cutting off his whistling, and the gray object dipped out of sight.

"Saw you," he said, clinging to his jovial attitude despite his rising fear. "Come out, come out, little rabbits."

He heard shuffling, but no one emerged.

Sighing, he said, "By all that is holy, I know you're there. Just show yourselves already."

"We want no trouble!" shouted a man's voice. "Leave us be!"

"Well," Patrick shouted back, "I want no trouble either. But unfortunately you're in Ashhur's land, with Karak's horses. So you're either from Neldar, or you stole those horses."

"How did you find us?" asked the voice.

"Smoke," he said. "From your fire."

"I *told* you lighting a fire was stupid!" someone said in an urgent whisper on the other side of him. Patrick turned in that direction.

"Shut up!" said another voice.

Patrick waited a few more seconds, and when no one emerged, he sighed and shook his head.

"I'm waiting," he said. "Get out here. *Now.*"

Again that metal-sheathed head popped up, only to swiftly disappear.

"We want no trouble," whoever it was repeated. "We have Karak's horses, but we hold no loyalty to him. And we're not thieves, honest. Please, sir, just let us be. We don't wish to fight."

"I don't want to fight either." Patrick grunted as he sheathed Winterbone. He was taking a chance, but it didn't seem like a very large one. "I simply want to see your faces. Come now, I know I'm ugly, but it's been a long journey and I'd love some company. Can you not give a wayward traveler that much?"

"You promise not to hurt us?"

"On Ashhur's immortal soul, I promise."

Grumbling followed, and soon men appeared from behind their rough stone barriers. There were nine of them, each dressed in silver mail over black boiled leather. The sigils on their chests had been scored over with scratches and crude white paint. Eight of the men were very young and strapping, with the look of the east about them, their locks varying from brilliant silver to russet. One was much older, with a head of full gray hair, though his body looked just as strong and durable as the rest. The elder was strangely familiar, his full beard framing a bent nose that must have been broken many times and a pair of steely gray eyes. The man stood strong and tall, while the others wilted behind him despite their greater numbers. The scene made Patrick laugh.

"Well, aren't you a sight," Patrick said, grinning.

"Who are you?" asked the older man.

"*What* are you?" asked one of the younger ones, obviously louder than he'd expected to since he blushed and moved behind one of his mates. The older man scowled at him.

Patrick squinted, appreciative of the elder's reaction but not showing it.

"My good man," he said, "I am from this land. Ashhur made me and my family. You are the trespassers here. If any has a right to demand a name and a story, it is me."

The older man removed his helm and inclined his head. Drawing his sword from the scabbard on his hip, he drove the tip into the dirt and dropped to one knee. The eight others scrambled to follow his lead. Chainmail jingled as they each tried to find enough space to mimic him. It was truly a comical scene, and in any other circumstance Patrick would have broken down laughing.

"My name is Preston Ender," the older man said with a tone of great respect. "I come from Felwood, a village in the northern part of Neldar. Until two weeks ago, I served as a soldier in Karak's Army under the leadership of Lord Commander Avila Crestwell."

"Ender?" asked Patrick. He snapped his meaty fingers. "I thought you looked familiar. Any relation to Corton?"

Preston smiled softly when he nodded, and the similarity was locked in stone.

"Corton was my older brother. I have not heard that name since he fled to the delta twelve years ago after being accused of bedding Tomas Mudraker's wife. How could you know his name?"

"I spent some time in the delta," Patrick replied, feeling dangerously at ease given the man's similarity to Corton. "Months, in fact. I helped defend Haven and that damn temple when Karak's forces made their attack." He patted the dragonglass crystal on Winterbone's handle. "Your brother taught me everything I know about swordplay. He was a great man. I called him friend."

"You speak of him in the past."

Patrick nodded, his smile faltering. "I'm sorry, Preston; he died in the battle at Haven."

"Did he die a good death?"

"Is there ever such a thing as a good death?"

Preston shrugged.

"Fighting for a cause you believe in? That's a good death. Protecting someone you love? That's a good death. Running like a coward to die hungry and alone? That's the farthest from."

Patrick chuckled.

"Then consider me privileged to tell you your brother did indeed die a good death, a very good death."

Preston looked pleased, but seemed at a loss as to what to say. Patrick pointed behind the older man, hoping to get things moving.

"Now enough about good deaths and old friends," he said. "It saddens me, and I just met *new* friends, so I don't wish to be sad any longer. Tell me about the rest of you. I'm guessing you all are—how should I put it…deserters?"

Preston stood and stepped to the side, allowing the younger soldiers to line up behind him. He worked his way down the line.

"Deserters indeed, all of us. These two are my sons, Edward and Ragnar; this meaty lad is Brick Mullin; the skinny whelp is Tristan Valeson; the white-haired nymphs are Joffrey Goldenrod and Ryann Matheson; and the two bald behemoths over there are twins, Big Flick and Little Flick."

"Big and Little, eh?" said Patrick. He was almost eye level with the both of them, even though he sat astride his mare. "How do you tell the difference?"

"It ain't obvious?" Big Flick asked.

Patrick blinked.

"Uh. No?"

The two laughed as if his comment were hysterical, leaving Patrick bewildered.

"And your name is, my good man?" asked Preston. "If you are indeed our new friend, I should have something to call you."

"Other than 'freak,'" Ragnar whispered from the corner of his mouth.

Preston silenced his son by setting the flat edge of his sword to his chin. The youth collapsed, cursing.

"Patrick DuTaureau," said Patrick, swinging his stunted leg over the horse and jumping from the saddle. "Only son of Isabel and Richard."

"DuTaureau," said Preston. The man paused, looking unsure of himself. The others seemed to feel the same way. "So that means you're from one of Ashhur's First Families."

He nodded. "And you know this how?"

Preston shrugged, still seeming uncertain. "We studied all the First Families when we were younger. It's a tradition that seems to have gone by the wayside over the last forty years or so, but I've tried to instill the same quest for knowledge in my own boys. It's healthy to learn our own history, even if it's a short one."

Edward rolled his eyes. "Short and boring," he muttered

"Quiet."

"Yes, Father."

"That's right," Patrick chortled. "Keep that boy in line." He wobbled across the short expanse separating him from the nine easterners. He extended his hand and Preston accepted it. Throughout their shake, the older man could not keep his eyes off Patrick's massive forearms.

"Those are mighty impressive," he said, a look of awe on his face.

"Your brother thought the same."

Patrick worked his way down the line, shaking each hand in turn. When he took the hand of the sandy-haired youth named Tristan, the youngster seemed to be on the verge of saying something, but he kept his lips sealed, his eyes averted. In fact, all but Preston and the two Flicks refused to truly look at him, which made Patrick moan inwardly. When he was finished, he stepped back, taking them all in. Part of him thought they looked like a group of guilty children lying to their parents about stealing a loaf of bread.

"You know, you said that until two weeks ago you served in Karak's Army, but I don't think you ever said why you stopped. The pay not very good? Perhaps the food was terrible?"

The group fell silent, and Preston cleared his throat before he continued.

"Every person standing here was conscripted into service months ago," he said. "None of us wished it. My sons and their friends here were guards for the Garland family in Gronswik, and I was second guard master. A convoy came to Tod Garland's estate, demanding men, and he offered them half his regiment. Not even the high merchants were exempt from paying their dues to the realm. Already having been trained as fighting men, we were shipped off to Haven to join the Lord Commander's battalion." The older man swallowed hard but kept his composure. "They made us help clean up the bodies. That's a hard duty, Patrick, especially when every blackened face might be your brother's. After that, they sent us south, into the swamps."

"To do what?" Patrick interrupted.

The others looked away, even Preston.

"We were ordered to leave no survivors," Big Flick offered. "And so we didn't."

The news sent Patrick back a step. He felt stupid for being surprised by it, for hadn't Peytr Gemcroft sailed to the Pebble Islands to avoid such a fate? Still, part of him had hoped Karak would focus on marching west instead of seeking petty vengeance. He gestured for Preston to continue.

"When word came from Veldaren, we crossed Ashhur's Bridge into Paradise," the older man said. "We went from village to village, and each time it was the same. Those who bent the knee lived. Those who didn't, plus the Wardens, well…" He shook his head, and when he looked up at Patrick, tears made his crow's feet glisten. "It was horrible. I was trained to fight, but it was always to protect the innocent from bandits, thieves, and the like. What they made us do? We were burning homes with people still in them. No one was safe. Not the elderly. Not the women."

"Children," Little Flick said, and the conversation halted once more.

"Yes," Preston said, wiping at his face. "Children. That bastard Gregorian was the worst of them. He beat Ragnar one day for not running through a child of four, then forced him to hack the young one apart with a sword at his back. I have never seen my boy so *defeated*." Preston grabbed his son's arm and yanked up his sleeve, showing Patrick a jagged slash across his wrist that was crusty with scabs and leaking pus. "He tried to kill himself that night. That's when I decided we would leave that fucking place and disappear into Paradise. These boys are young, Patrick. Edward's the oldest at eighteen. Even the Flicks are still teenagers, big as they are. They don't deserve this life. They aren't killers."

"And yet they've killed," Patrick whispered. "How many?"

"What?"

"How many? How many helpless souls have your lot put to the sword?"

Preston shook his head. "I don't know. I *couldn't* know. Too many."

"I...this...fuck..." Patrick rubbed his hand over his nose angrily, as if he were going to rip his face off. "I really don't know what to say."

"Just let us go on with our lives," Brick said. "We just want to get away from all that...butchery."

"No one has to know we're here," Preston added. "You can move on, pretend you saw nothing."

Patrick grumbled and shuffled from foot to foot, trying to channel Bardiya's penchant for forgiveness, if nothing else....

"You're in Ashhur's land, the part ruled by Bardiya Gorgoros. Clumsy and numerous as you are, you won't stay hidden forever, which means we need to figure this out here and now. Look, I've killed before, but those men were armed, and if I hadn't killed them, they would have killed me. What you're talking about is different. You're talking of the *murder of innocents*. Ashhur preaches tolerance, love, and forgiveness, but I also watched him storm onto the battlefield and tear Karak's soldiers to shreds when he saw innocents destroyed. Why do you deserve different?"

Tristan stepped forward and dropped to one knee. Patrick could see a *no* forming on Preston's lips as the youth opened his mouth to speak.

"Because we're sorry," he said, head bowed. "Because we want to make amends. We all do."

In his peripheral vision, Preston visibly exhaled in relief.

"Is that true?" asked Patrick.

Mumbles of confirmation followed, accompanied by nods and sniffling. Patrick felt his heart break at the sight of them. Young men, burdened with such acts, and there was still something they weren't telling him. What could it be? He couldn't imagine what could be worse than cutting down children with a sword. To do such things must make a man less than human....

"If you truly seek atonement, then I know of a far better way than hiding in the middle of nowhere," he told them. "And if you do as I propose, I promise you we will indeed be friends. Good friends. And together we just might find a way to have ourselves a good death."

"Ten good deaths," Big Flick said, and he clapped Patrick on the back. "A good number."

"Good indeed," Patrick said, allowing himself to smile.

CHAPTER

23

The first sounds of combat pulled Ahaesarus's mind back to Algrahar. He remembered his bright world growing dark, saw the sky tear open as if it were a thin sheet of black cloth ripped through by an invisible knife. He watched fire rain down from the sky, looked up in terror as great winged demons swooped down on his people. He heard thousands of innocents wail as they were put to blade and spear, heard the sickening *thud* as the demons dropped them from great heights, their bodies breaking when they struck the unforgiving ground. He felt the last breaths of his wife, Malodia, released in ragged gasps. He gaped at the wrecked bodies of his children as he was forcefully ushered away by the demons and rounded into a pen with his fellow survivors, where a vicious death surely awaited them.

He experienced the memories all at once, and tears welled in his eyes.

Fighting the dirge of sadness and terror, he squeezed the reins tighter and slapped them against his charger. The steed picked up speed, careening forward at a reckless pace. A litany of pounding hooves sounded from beside and behind as his brother Wardens, fifty of them, did the same, all in a desperate rush to arrive before it was too late.

The burning heat of early summer did not seem to reach the far north of Paradise. With the sun now set, a distinct chill hung in the air, and a breeze came from the east, gusting over the raging Gihon from the destitute Tinderlands beyond as if carrying the dead land's message of hopelessness. *Hopelessness.* Even the hope he had felt as he watched Geris and Penelope disappear into the forest fled him. With the memory of his own dead world fresh in his mind, Ahaesarus struggled to not let himself fall into that miserable pit.

The land around Drake was rocky and harsh. If not for the abundance of great pines that grew on the ever-rising mountains, it might have looked just as lifeless as the elves' old homeland. As it were, with the half-moon partially concealed by wayward clouds and the mountainside forests shrouded in darkness, it looked to be a land of ghosts. The fact that the town of Drake itself had been abandoned, as Isabel had warned them, only served to heighten that impression.

A pack of grayhorns grazed in a wide field of sparse grass as he and his brothers raced by. A bright flash of white lit the horizon, like lightning without thunder, and soon a faint red glow began to rise. The Wardens pushed their mounts all the harder, stampeding onto a path that led around a looming cliff face. The waters of the Gihon were close now, only twenty feet away, forcing the Wardens to form a line as they circled the cliff. Ahaesarus could feel the cold sting of mist from the rapids against his cheeks.

Once they rounded the bend, heading away from the river, the land opened up before them once more, revealing a sprawling camp of hundreds of white tents erected in a gravel-strewn meadow. There were many people visible by the light of the cookfires. They were nearly all women and children, and they glanced up as Ahaesarus and his fellow Wardens passed them, their expressions containing only the faintest touch of hope. They seemed resigned to their likely fate. Again the sky brightened, momentarily blinding him and forcing him to slow to a stop. When his vision returned, he was surprised to see that the people were still going about their business, pausing only for the occasional wary glance at the ridge.

Ahaesarus glanced to his side, where Olympus sat high in his saddle, his black eyes intense, his smooth raven hair falling to his waist. The Warden held a stone ax in one hand and his horse's reins in the other. He jutted his chin at the hill and the ever-growing red glow radiating from behind it. Ahaesarus wheeled around to gaze on their forty-eight brothers.

"We ride into battle!" he shouted, though the strange behavior of the women in the camp robbed his statement of a bit of its potency.

Toward the hill they rode, and as they went, Ahaesarus noticed something strange. A huge black lump blotted out the rising glow, a portentous obelisk that reminded him of the portal the demons had descended from in Algrahar. *They are not here,* he told himself. *These are only men. It is a trick of your eyes in the darkness—that is all.*

Only it wasn't. What he saw was a round tower, built close to the riverbank, rising seventy feet into the air. Ahaesarus and his brethren gaped up at the building, bringing their horses to a sudden halt. Isabel had informed him that her daughter's husband had overseen the construction of four towers, but he'd had trouble believing it, even though Judarius had seen one of them with his own eyes and described it in detail. Even if he had believed it, he never would have pictured *this.* Given that he had watched the spellcasters Potrel, Limmen, Martin, and Marsh for much of the last two months, he should have had more faith in the casters' abilities.

Windows lined the whole length of the tower, most of them facing northeast, and men hung from each of them, some firing arrows, some throwing spears, and others hurling small fireballs or bolts of lightning from the palms of their hands. Still others stood on the rocky riverbank, making the same assaults. The opposite side of the Gihon was too awash in flames for him to see the opponents. They were surely there, however, as he watched a volley of arrows rise high into the sky. The men on the banks hunkered down, some lifting their hands and chanting, while others held wooden shields above their heads. The arrows bounced off invisible walls and plunked into the heavy wood. Twelve men were struck, three multiple times, and the injured were dragged by their mates to be tended by men in white cloaks, who had gathered a hundred or so feet away. The white cloaks bent over the wounded, whispering familiar prayers to Ashhur. Their hands glowed blue, but the illumination was faint.

"I don't believe it," said Judah, trotting up beside him. "This is…unreal."

"Dismount," Ahaesarus said, raising his voice so the rest could hear. "Mennon, Florio, Grendel, Ludwig—assist their healers in tending to the injured. The rest of you—with me to the tower!"

They ran toward the lofty structure as another torrent of arrows fell from the sky. The shafts landed mere feet in front of them, forcing them to shift directions. They sprinted, their long legs allowing them a preternatural speed, until they reached the broad base of the tower. Once they reached the cover of the mountain of stone, they changed course again, heading straight for the huge western-facing doorway cut into the tower. They could clearly hear the voices of the men standing on the banks now, shouting insults and provocations at the unseen enemy. A few swiveled to watch the Wardens, and they raised their weapons in surprise. Ahaesarus lifted his palms to show he meant them no harm, and a few moments later the humans returned their attention to the other side of the river. Ahaesarus looked on in wonder as the line of them, at least a hundred in total, nocked their arrows like experts, launching them at their enemies. He spotted swords hanging from the belts of more than a few of the men. He blinked twice, thinking that it was an illusion, but it was not.

Before he could process everything, the tower door swung open. A heavily bearded man came stumbling out, with long red-brown hair and a tattered leather jerkin worn over beige cotton breeches. His expression was frantic as he met Ahaesarus's gaze.

"You came," he said, and from the skittish sound of his voice, Ahaesarus could tell the man was very young. "Turock wasn't sure if Abigail's letter had reached Mordeina. Getting her lady mother to respond has been…unreliable." The young man offered him a tired yet optimistic smile. "But she did, didn't she?"

"She did," Ahaesarus said. Another hail of arrows thumped the ground all around the tower, followed by more shrieks of men in pain. "What is going on here?"

An arrow clanked off a granite wall, showering bits of stone that made the young man duck. When he rose back up, he brushed the dust from his curly hair and gestured to the doorway, his eyes darting this way and that. "Come inside," he said. "It's not safe out here to talk."

"Wait, we came to help. What can we do?"

The man eyed the hill. "We left the rear of the camp undefended. Can the Wardens guard it for now?"

"You do not need us at the river?"

"Not at the moment, no. But if soldiers chose to cross farther down…"

Ahaesarus got the message. He instructed most of his fellow Wardens to head back up the hill and form a perimeter around the women and children. Olympus and Judah stayed behind and entered the tower with him. What they found inside was a huge round room, packed with crates and bulging burlap sacks. A wide spiral staircase wound up the full height of the structure. The men who were firing arrows or strange balls of magic flame from the windows lined the staircase.

"Turock's up top," said their young guide. "Oh, and my name is Bartholomew. Nice to meet you."

"Likewise," Ahaesarus said as the young man started up the stairs, not bothering to wait for the Wardens' names. The three of them followed him up. Given their larger size, it was a much greater effort for them to squeeze past the archers manning the windows. At one point, Olympus collided with a man holding a crossbow. The man would have tumbled from the window if Ahaesarus had not grabbed the back of his breeches. The crossbowman turned abruptly, looking ready to attack whoever had almost killed him, but after taking one look at Ahaesarus's intimidating form, he spun around and continued to fire on the enemy. Ahaesarus stared at the shortsword hanging from the man's hip, then at the other men who lined the stairwell. It was uncommon to see weapons in Paradise, yet every defender had steel at his disposal, presumably pilfered from those of Karak's soldiers who had been killed after crossing the river. The sheer abundance told him just how many had tried, just how dire the situation must be.

They were led to the very top of the tower, which ended at a hatch leading into another round room. The young man climbed up first, and the Wardens followed closely behind. Ahaesarus heard multiple people shouting and cursing, but one of the voices stood out from the rest. It sounded upbeat, almost *playful*. He hoisted himself through the hatchway, squeezing his shoulders together make it through, and looked around. Three men were present besides their young guide, and all were looking out of the three east-facing windows. The two on the outside wore long brown robes, while the robe of the one in the middle was a strange shade of violet. A thick mane of reddish-blond hair flowed from beneath the strange tilted cap on his head. His back heaved as he leaned out the window, and the air crackled with energy, raising the tiny hairs on Ahaesarus's arms.

The bearded youngster in the tattered doublet cleared his throat. "Master Turock?"

The garishly dressed spellcaster bent backward, glancing over his shoulder. He was an odd-looking man, with a carefully maintained mustache and pointed beard. His face was intense, his smile not humorous in the least, and his blue eyes did not seem to register the three Wardens.

"What is it?" he asked in that same playful tone. "Can't you see we're toasting Karak's hairy cocks out there at the moment?"

He turned around again and started uttering more words of magic.

"Um," Bartholomew said, "help arrived from Mordeina. I thought you might like to know."

The red-haired man whirled back around, and this time he *did* see Ahaesarus, Olympus, and Judah. His eyes widened, his smile grew broader, and he made a sweeping bow.

"Oh my, Wardens of Ashhur, come to assist us in our troubles." He stood up and slapped Bartholomew on the shoulder. "Can you believe it, lad? My wife's mother actually proved her worth for once." He turned to the Wardens. "So Olympus and Judah I know, but who are you, with those golden locks and that severe—oh yes, *severe*—stare?"

The man laughed, even as the continuing sounds of death came pouring in through the window. Ahaesarus felt completely at a loss.

"Ahaesarus, Master Warden of Paradise," he replied.

"Oh, I *have* met you! You visited when Martin was named kingling, yes?"

Ahaesarus nodded. "I did, though I do not remember you, and I feel that I would if I had been given the privilege of meeting you."

"I do tend to be memorable. It's a trait I like to encourage."

An arrow flew through the window just then, so close that it lifted Turock's hat from his head. Arrow and cap struck the stone wall, the arrow snapping in two. The redhead stared in horror at his now ruined hat, and for the first time since Ahaesarus's arrival, he actually seemed angry.

"Fuckers!" he screamed, heading back to the window. As he began barking his magical phrases, lightning leapt from his fingertips.

"Bartholomew, bring them back downstairs," he snapped over his shoulder. "We'll be done here soon. Now go!"

"We have some questions—" began Judah.

"Can't you see we're busy? Get out!"

Ahaesarus glanced at his fellow Wardens, who shrugged. He returned the gesture.

"We will aid your fight as best we can," he told Bartholomew on their way back down the stairwell. "Tell us where the need is greatest, and we will defend you with our lives."

The young man exhaled deeply. "I thank you for that." An explosion sounded, and Bartholomew flinched. There was sweat running down his brow despite the night's chill. "And I must apologize for Turock's…er, pointedness. He's under a bit of stress at the moment."

"Do not worry yourself over it," said Ahaesarus. "We will work this all out after the battle is over."

They reemerged into a night filled with fire, arrows, and pained cries. Bartholomew pointed the way, and the three Wardens spent the next two hours hefting sacks of freshly fletched arrows from inside the tower, bringing waterskins to the fighting men, and tending to wounded soldiers. Whenever he looked to the river, Ahaesarus could make out little beyond fire, billowing black smoke, and piles of corpses at the edge of the river, some dragged into the water by its harsh current. Ahaesarus could only hazard a guess as to their enemy's numbers. Whenever a soldier bearing the sigil of Karak on his armor rushed through the fire, he was either struck down or carried away by the river.

Ahaesarus felt utterly useless as he ran from menial task to menial task, constantly dodging incoming projectiles, no easy task given his large size. A part of him realized he was putting his life in danger for absolutely nothing. The citizens of Drake, led by Turock's spellcasters, had the situation fully under control.

Do not fall into that trap, he told himself as he handed a fresh waterskin to a short, blond, robed man. *You told Isabel you would do whatever it took. At the moment, this is what it takes.*

The cross-river skirmish lasted only another hour or so. Come sunrise, the barrage of arrows from the other side slowed to a trickle. When it finally stopped, Turock left the tower and joined his men on the shore. The flames were petering out, and the smoke on the Tinderlands side of the Gihon had cleared as well, revealing a mess of bodies splayed out on the rocky, uneven ground, some still bleeding out, others burnt beyond recognition. Ahaesarus guessed the enemy had lost at least fifty men, though it was difficult to tell given how many had been carried away by the current. Only three of Drake's defenders had perished. An eerie quiet came over the defenders, whose fatigue showed in the huge black circles that had formed under their eyes. Soon the men were wading in the shallow edges of the river, extracting snagged corpses and carting them north along the bank, dumping them in a massive, stone-rimmed firepit. As Ahaesarus helped remove the bodies, he noticed they were small, even for humans, as if they were underdeveloped. The fires were lit, the bodies burned, and the near constant chill that had pervaded the evening gave way to oppressive heat.

When they arrived back at the tower, Ahaesarus left Olympus and Judah and approached the Turock, whose jibes and carefree attitude seemed to have vanished. His entire demeanor had changed from when he was in the thick of battle. Turock squinted against the glare of the steadily rising sun and winced. More than anything, he looked exhausted, both mentally and physically. It was as if leaving his nest in the sky had caused the world to fall directly on his shoulders.

"You won the battle," Ahaesarus said, hefting his huge stone ax onto his shoulder, the weapon having gone unused the entire night. "Why such sullenness?"

Turock craned his neck to look up at him, his eyes glossy, but a rustling from behind drew his attention before he could answer Ahaesarus's question. The other Wardens were loping over the concealing hill, a group of thirty or so young men and women trailing behind.

Turock rose up on his toes and patted Ahaesarus on the shoulder. "I know you have questions, Master Warden, but right now I'm rather useless. I need sleep." He lazily rolled his head in the direction of the camp. "You could no doubt use some as well. Have Bartholomew show you where. Come back to the tower at noon, and I will answer any questions you have."

Bartholomew directed the Wardens to an ample thatch of empty land on the northwestern edge of the camp. Sleep did not come easily for Ahaesarus, even though the crude tent where he rested blocked out much of the daylight. His mind was awash with images of a burning night sky, the whistle of arrows soaring through the air, and the screams of the dead and dying, both seen and unseen. He felt shame burn in his chest when he realized just how frightened he'd been. For months he had been nothing but a glorified carpenter, organizing the people of Mordeina in the construction of the wall. Before that, he'd been a tutor to a princeling. Up until a few hours ago, the coming war had been just as much a fiction to him as it had been to the humans of Paradise. Once within the chaos of a battle, he'd almost reacted exactly as he had back on Algrahar: freezing up in terror and allowing the oncoming hordes to do their worst.

And the previous night had been relatively bloodless, battling a concealed opponent with little to no chance of a close encounter. The gods only knew how he would react when he experienced *true* combat.

Certain that sleep would not come, he rose and paced around the camp in an attempt to tamp down his worries. He stopped to visit some of the women who were roasting salted grayhorn meat and cabbage stew over their cookfires as their children milled about. The camp was indeed large; there were at least two thousand people residing here, and the conditions were crowded.

Come noon, Ahaesarus returned to the tower. His body ached and his mind swam from lack of sleep, and when he climbed the rounded staircase, it felt as though he were moving through water. He was winded by the time he reached the roost. Pushing the hatch open, he saw that two people awaited him—Turock and a familiar-looking petite woman with fiery red hair and fine freckled skin. She wore a modest cotton blouse and had flowers in her hair. For his part, Turock wore the same violet robes he'd had on previously, wrinkled as though he'd slept in them. Without his hat, his hair was a wild mess of reddish-blond curls. Even his beard seemed unruly. The pair was a study of mirror opposites. They sat on a bench in front of a rounded table that had not been there the previous night.

"Abigail DuTaureau, I presume," Ahaesarus said, bowing to the woman before taking the only other seat at the table.

"It's Escheton now. I haven't been a DuTaureau for twenty-three years."

"Twenty-three *long* years," said Turock, a bit of color in his cheeks and a gleam in his eyes.

"Many apologies, my lady, I meant no disrespect," said Ahaesarus. "I have seen your mother day in and day out for nearly a year, so the name and face are etched in my mind."

"No disrespect taken."

Turock scoffed. "By you, maybe."

"Shush, dear."

"Hush yourself."

Turock leaned over and placed a gentle kiss on Abigail's dainty, upturned nose. Ahaesarus was baffled by them both, Turock in particular. This was a man who had been fighting a battle against forces that hoped to obliterate him and everyone else in Drake mere hours ago.

Turock noticed him staring and raised an eyebrow.

"What?"

Ahaesarus allowed himself to smile. "Simply marveling at your fortitude, my friend. You look like you slept quite well, while I found I could not sleep at all."

With a wink, Turock pulled a small vial from one of his robe's many pockets.

"Tricks of the trade," he said. "A drop of this, and three hours of sleep feels like twelve." He handed the vial to Ahaesarus. "Go ahead, Master Warden. Smell it. I'm sure you'll recognize it."

He uncorked the top and sniffed the liquid inside, then gave the spellcaster a confused glance.

"Nightwing root?" he asked. His left hand fingered the pouch that hung from a slender rope around his neck, containing the last of the root he had brought from Algrahar, a portion of which he had administered to Geris Felhorn in the hours after the healers had removed the wasting tumor from his neck. "How in Ashhur's name did you come across this?"

Turock took the vial back from him.

"Easy answer: I didn't. What you smell is similar, but not genuine. The Warden Assissi introduced the wonder of the root to me when I was quite young, before I headed out to find Errdroth Plentos, the elf who trained me. Worked great as a sleep aid, but he had very little. He only gave me a pinch, and I saved that pinch for years. One of the first things I did after Plentos died was attempt to uncover its secret properties. I discovered that ginger root is very similar, and by combining it with an extract of crim oil, I was able to approximate the formula. It's not an exact copy, and gods forbid you take it if you feel any *real* pain, but the sleeping properties still work. Though you shouldn't get too reliant on it, because eventually you'll collapse and sleep for a good eighteen hours or so. Not that I, uh, know from experience."

"Amazing," said Ahaesarus.

"Not really," the spellcaster replied with a shrug. "Simple trial and error." He winked. "And a lot of luck. Some say I'm the luckiest man in all of Paradise, which is saying something."

"Is that how you have been fighting off those attempting to cross the river?" asked Ahaesarus. "With luck?"

He had meant the statement as a joke, but Turock's expression darkened.

"No, not luck. Lots of skill and hard work. And patience. Loads and loads of fucking patience."

Abigail frowned at her husband.

"I apologize," the Warden replied, bowing his head to the man. "I do not think before I speak at times."

Turock brushed the comment aside. "Nonsense. Pride is one of my faults, and I just fell victim to it yet again. The thing is, these past months have been hell on us. We're all exhausted and frightened, and we've been working ourselves to the bone, trying to defend what is ours."

"I am curious, how did it come about?"

"How did what come about?"

Ahaesarus lifted his hand toward the three eastern-facing windows. "The fighting, the soldiers on the other side. I will be honest....I know little of what has transpired here."

Turock opened his mouth, but Abigail answered for him.

"It began over a year ago, when we still resided in the town. People were being taken in the night—men, women, and children alike. More than twenty went missing over the span of three weeks. We set up patrols, but they did nothing. We had no idea who was taking our townspeople, if anyone, until one morning we found a trail of blood that ended at the narrow gap where this tower is now located.

"We set up camp on the spot and brought everyone with us, deciding that with such close and open quarters no more would be taken, or at least the culprits would not go unseen. Turock originally thought some wild beasts roaming in the Tinderlands might be at fault. But then strange things began to happen."

Ahaesarus frowned, trying to guess what might have been taking them, but unable to think of a plausible reason.

"Strange things such as what?" asked Ahaesarus.

"No one who went riding outside our borders returned," said Turock, his expression serious. "No birds from our rookeries every flew back. When the moon was high, we'd hear strange chanting from across the river, deep in the Tinderlands. To be honest, we felt under siege without having the slightest idea what was tormenting us. I began to build this tower so that sentries could keep watch at night, hoping it might grant us more sleep come nightfall."

"We were lucky Turock had already been training many of our fellow citizens in the lessons Plentos had taught him," Abigail said.

"More out of boredom than anything else," Turock admitted.

Abigail continued: "We in the far north are an eager lot, and we make fantastic students. Having a legion of spellcasters, even amateur ones, helped us build this structure much faster than we ever could have otherwise."

Ahaesarus could attest to that. He had seen firsthand how quickly the construction of Mordeina's wall had progressed with the help of the four Drake spellcasters.

"But we still didn't know what we were dealing with," Turock said. "That is, until Jacob Eveningstar arrived with his elf lover, a Warden, and a young man…Roland, I think was his name. They promised to discover what plagued our village, then disappeared into the Tinderlands for over a week. Then the elf and Warden returned one night, chased by soldiers bearing the sigil of the lion. The elf died before we could put an end to the invaders, as did sixty of our own people. The First Man arrived the next evening with his apprentice. He killed the one hostage we had taken—Uther Crestwell, you know of him, right?—and then he had me create a portal to Safeway for him and his remaining party." Turock chuckled. "It was the biggest portal I've ever made. Still don't know how I pulled *that* off."

Silence followed for a few moments, Abigail staring at her hands, Turock gazing through the western windows at the sprawling camp behind the hill.

"What then?" asked Ahaesarus.

"Then...nothing," replied Abigail. "All we knew was that if Karak's soldiers were willing to cross the river and attack our people, it was time to begin fortifying our homeland for the war that was sure to come. We scouted along the river, both north and south, seeking out where the crossing is narrowest, and then we built more of our towers."

"You've built four from what I was told, yes?" asked Ahaesarus.

"Five now," Turock said, and there was no hiding the pride in his voice. "Tower Green went up just last week."

"Five towers in six months?" Ahaesarus shook his head, stunned. "Are your students that talented in the art of magic?"

"They are, relatively speaking." The spellcaster frowned. "Magic in Dezrel is strange. Plentos told me stories of how powerful the Dezren once were, able to summon fireballs the size of houses and form bolts of lightning that could rip across an entire countryside. When drunk, he even claimed that the most powerful elven spellcasters could alter miles upon miles of land, bending the rock and stone to their whim. I've tried to calculate the power required to do such a thing, and it seems beyond possible." He stood and walked over to the central western window. "Here, come look."

The man chanted a few words, hands held out before him. A ball of fire formed from nothing, two feet wide and spinning inches from his open palms. Pushing his arms forward, the fireball whooshed across the sky, arcing down until it struck the soil on the other side of the river. A puff of smoke rose up in its wake, and the meager shrubbery began to burn. Turock's cheeks paled.

"That is the largest I can create," he said, sounding disappointed. "If I try to summon anything beyond that, the spell just…dissolves on me. It's like trying to lift a weight that's too heavy for your arms. Yet that's not quite right, because deep down I *know* I'm strong enough. It's like…lifting a small stone that's somehow been invisibly nailed to the ground. But even with these limitations, I still have hope we can accomplish something special. I have fifty-two novice spellcasters under my tutelage, including those we sent to Mordeina to help Abby's mother. If we can grow our power and work together, we can build enough towers to man the Gihon all the way down to the fork in no time at all!"

He sighed and shook his head.

It was almost too much for Ahaesarus to absorb. "Tell me more about the other towers," he said.

"Well, they each have names. This one we call Blood Tower because it was built over the very spot where our people bled. The others are color-coded. Tower Gold, Tower Red, Tower Silver, and Tower Green. Green is ten miles east of Durham, which is the closest settlement." He lifted his sleeve. "We're actually starting to run out of colors. I suggested the idea for Tower Violet, as I'm partial to the color, but my students decided it was too feminine. So the next tower we build will be named just that. Each tower is manned by five of my best students, along with twenty men of suitable fighting age. I'm aiming to expand our operation, but our resources are running low. Our little town was home to less than two thousand, and there is only so much labor I can demand of the people. These are common folk, not warriors…though defending your life can make anyone quite adept at doing just that."

"Very true. When did Karak's Army begin its attack?" Ahaesarus asked.

Abigail glanced up. "Two months ago. After the long winter ended and summer returned. Arrows began flying from the dark one night, and they haven't stopped since. Every few nights it begins again. They fire arrows; we fire back."

"Besides that first night," said Turock, "when eighteen of our men and women died, we have lost very few. But it's still harrowing. The attacks seem to happen at random, though always after the sun sets. Sometimes all five towers are assaulted at once; sometimes they are individually targeted. We kill any who try to cross the river. Yet those who cross are small, stunted…runts, I guess you could say. I feel like we're being toyed with, and I do *not* like being toyed with."

"From what I've heard, it sounds like your wall of towers is in no danger," said Ahaesarus, scratching at his temple and staring at Abigail. "Yet Lady DuTaureau told me you feared that the line would break and the soldiers would pour across the river. I see no evidence of this, so why request our presence if you have everything under control? How can we help defend the line if there is no real line to defend?"

Abigail looked to her husband.

"We don't need you to defend the line, and we certainly didn't need this many of you," Turock said. "We wanted a few of your kind for…other reasons."

"I spelled it out clearly in my letter," Abigail said, looking frustrated. "Leave it to Mother to get the message wrong."

Ahaesarus waved his hand at them. "Enough. Just tell me: What is it you wish us to do?"

"I want the Wardens to take a small group of our men into the Tinderlands," Turock said, rubbing his fingers together. Faint sparks of electricity danced between them. "The majority of the attacks have occurred here, at Blood Tower. Which means that wherever this army has gathered, it is nearby."

"You want us to *strike* at them?" asked Ahaesarus. "That is suicide!"

"No, not strike," replied the spellcaster, holding up his hands in a calming gesture. "I simply wish to discover the size of the force assembled there. That information would go a long way toward

planning our defense tactics, especially if the letter sent by my wonderful and perfect mother-in-law told the truth and Karak is invading from the east as well."

"She does not lie," Ahaesarus said. "Karak's Army has crossed
into Paradise, and even now they set the northern fields of Ker
aflame. We Wardens are needed in many places, so why summon us
for a simple scouting party?"

"Look at you," said Turock, holding his palms out as if what
he was about to say were plainly obvious. "You're bigger than us,
more agile, more *capable* in almost every way. You taught us nearly
everything we know, helped grow this civilization from infancy. The
entirety of what I know of the Tinderlands I could write onto the
back of a dung beetle. Whatever dangers are out there, I trust you
to handle them. More importantly, I trust you to safeguard the lives
of my men."

Turock reached out and squeezed Ahaesarus's shoulder.

"I cannot afford to lose many more men," he said. "Should
even a single tower fall, the village beyond will certainly fall next.
I can't stand the thought, so I must assess the strength of my enemy.
I am sending a party of four into the Tinderlands to do just that. If
the same number of Wardens accompanied them, it would greatly
reduce the risk. A full-out assault is building—I can feel it. I just
don't know when, and I don't know where."

"Only four?" asked Ahaesarus.

"More than that would be too noisy to go sneaking around in
the darkness. The rest will stay with me and help form the first line
of defense should another attack come."

Ahaesarus bowed his head. The odd man made sense. Just as
Isabel had implied, the Wardens were expendable. If their skills
could ensure the people of Drake endured, then so be it. It was a
risk he would gladly take. Besides, he couldn't stand the thought of
dodging arrows from an unseen foe for even one more night. Better
if he could at least be on the move.

"We are sworn to protect and guide you, and so we shall," he said, bowing his head. He swallowed hard, thinking about the night when Ashhur and Celestia had rescued him and his many brothers from Algrahar. There would be no such rescue should events turn sour this time. *Yet that is our lot,* he thought. *We were given a second chance at life for a reason.*

Abigail rose from her seat, taking her place beside her husband. Ahaesarus knelt before them.

"It would be a great honor for me to join your expedition, my friends," he said. "My brothers and I are at your beck and call."

"Oh, get up," said Turock. "We're not your masters." He started chuckling, then said, "How good are you with a sword? Those stone axes you brought are pretty cumbersome, and I don't think they'll last long against real steel should it come to that."

"My training with any weapon is modest at best, but why a sword?"

Abigail winked at her husband.

"Because we have swords to give you, Master Warden."

"Ah, yes. From pilfering the dead."

Turock laughed and smacked him on the back. "Not in the slightest."

Ahaesarus stared at him, confused.

"Not many who try to cross the river even carry weapons," Turock said. "I told you, I'm a driven, hardworking bastard with a brain as sharp as my looks are good. We began mining iron on the other side of the cliff a few months ago, and smelting it soon after." His smile grew wider. "Amazing what you can accomplish when an ancient elf decides you're a worthy student."

Ahaesarus shook his head. "I...I am speechless."

"I'm full of surprises, so get ready to feel that way a lot more often over the next few weeks," Turock said. "Assuming you don't die in the Tinderlands, of course. So! Let's get you a sword to try to keep that from happening, and maybe refresh whatever training you had. Step one: Shove the pointy end in the fleshy bits of your opponent."

"And step two?" Ahaesarus asked as he followed Turock to the staircase.

The spellcaster shrugged.

"That's all I got. For me, step two is to shove a fistful of lightning into their face until the smoke escapes their ears. I figured you Wardens would have a more elegant solution."

With that, he was gone, and Ahaesarus cast a baffled look to the man's wife.

"You do get used to him," she said, kissing the Warden on the cheek. "I promise, he's really not that strange."

"Could have fooled me," Ahaesarus said, following her down the steps to see what other surprises Turock might have in store for him.

CHAPTER

24

The guiding pyre burned brightly, casting a beam of rippling light over the dark ocean waters. Bardiya stood beside it as he did each night, watching the sea for any sign of Ki-Nan. His friend had been gone for so long now that many days he felt ready to give up hope of his return. He shook his head, banishing the thought. Ever since Bardiya's parents had been murdered, Ki-Nan had been a reliable friend and advisor. When in his more frustrated moods, Bardiya sometimes saw him as the only real friend he had; all the rest were like children in need of nurturing or aged parents in need of protection.

A ghostly form appeared at the base of the cliff. Bardiya knew from the exaggerated swing of the man's arms that it was Onna, the old seafarer who sometimes joined him during his vigils. Onna crested the rise, huffing as he rested his old bones on a weather-beaten stone bench beside the pyre.

"Still waiting, eh?" he asked.

"I will always wait," Bardiya replied. "For Ki-Nan, for anyone."

"You ask me, it's a freeman's farce for you to think that boy could survive out there for this long. Be more than a little bit of a miracle."

"He is fine. I'm sure of it."

Onna laughed. "Is that optimism or just plain stubbornness, big fella?" His eyes narrowed. "Even worse, maybe it's a lie. Not that it matters to me. Spent enough years on the ocean to know all the dangers that wait out there when the waves start a-rollin'. A man could get lost at sea quite easily, and then…"

Bardiya looked down at him.

"Stories," he said with a sigh. "When will you ever give me anything but stories, Onna? You, my friend, are the only man in all of Ker who would rather spend his days rocking on the waves than on solid ground, yet you love telling tales of how dangerous it is. It's a wonder you're alive at all, if even half of them are true."

The older man shrugged. "I might fancy my stories up a bit, but each one of them is more than half true. Your children may not take well to the sea, but beyond Ker there are others who are more willing to risk the dangers." He glanced up, the firelight dancing in his eyes. "Like the easterners whose corpses washed up on shore not far from here."

Bardiya grunted and shook his head. "Ki-Nan is cautious, and better equipped than foolish sailors from the east. He will return to us, and he will be well."

"Even if he found the lions?"

Bardiya's mouth snapped shut without saying a word. The argument was folly, for there was no guarantee Ki-Nan would return. It was just wishful thinking at this point, something he indulged in often as of late to offset his new pain. Bringing the elf boy back from the brink of death seemed to have affected him in unexpected ways.…Each day his soreness grew more unbearable, joints grinding together, muscles pulling and stretching. The spiking headaches behind his eyes were so severe at times that he needed to lie still in the dark to keep from vomiting. His heart raced at odd intervals, as if struggling to keep pumping blood through his massive form. He wondered if he had altered the natural order of things, if by thwarting the elf's death, he had been sentenced to a slow and painful demise. Or perhaps this was his punishment for turning aside Patrick when his friend needed him most. If that were the case, if everything he believed was wrong…

"Well, I'll be," Onna gasped beside him.

"What is it?" he asked, stepping in front of the pyre. He had been staring into the flames, and red and white blotches blotted his vision.

"There, coming closer," said Onna. "A boat. I'm sure of it."

Bardiya blinked rapidly, and slowly his eyes readjusted to the darkness. At first he saw nothing more than the reflection of the pyre and the undulating waves, but then a speck of black passed over the lighted ocean. He squinted and took another step, coming so close to the edge of the cliff that he heard pebbles *clunk* off the rocks below. His vision cleared, and then he saw it: a long, yet slender vessel glided atop the surface of the water. Excitement filled his gut, making him forget about his physical discomforts.

My friend is home, his mind cried. *Ki-Nan has finally returned.*

His exhilaration dulled as he slid down the edge of the cliff, drawing near the crude jetty to which Onna's *Kind Lady* was tethered. The approaching skiff was moving too quickly and advancing at the wrong angle. Though it was dark, he could swear the figure on the boat was slumped over, his hand weakly grasping the tiller of the lone sail.

"Ki-Nan!" he shouted, cupping his hands around his mouth. "Ki-Nan, is that you?"

The figure stirred, slowly straightening and taking a firmer hold on the sail's guiding tiller. Though he made no verbal reply, he raised a hand in greeting. The rudder was turned to the side and something dropped overboard, slowing the skiff's approach. Bardiya jumped into the water, waves lapping at his shins and sharp rocks beneath the surface scraping his giant feet. He waded forward while stooped, his arms held out to catch the skiff if it suddenly picked up speed once more.

It did not. The stone craft slowed, bobbing to a stop mere feet in front of him. The anchor—Ki-Nan had dropped the anchor. The bow was greatly damaged, split nearly down the middle and scored with scrapes and gouges. Several arrows protruded from the port side. Fear gripping his heart, Bardiya sloshed through the water and grabbed the moaning figure whose hand was still wrapped around the tiller. The hand fell limply away as he scooped the man up like he would a child.

"Is it him?" Onna asked, pacing back and forth on the jetty.

Bardiya looked down at his quarry. Ki-Nan's eyes were closed, one of them swollen, and there was a gash along his brow. Blood covered his threadbare clothes. Bardiya pressed his head to Ki-Nan's chest and could hear his heart beating. Tears flowed down his cheeks.

"He's here—wounded, but alive."

Onna tethered the damaged skiff while Bardiya loped away, climbing the rocky precipice with his friend tucked gently in his arms. He headed straight for his parents' cabin, which had gone unused since their murder. It had been built for men of a normal size, so Bardiya had to drop to his knees just to enter. Dust rose in a thick cloud when he placed Ki-Nan on the straw-filled bed. Bardiya lit a few candles, then pressed his hands against his friend's chest, pouring all the healing energy he could gather into him, praying that he had not used up Ashhur's good graces on the elf boy.

He worried for naught, for Ashhur's healing magic was just as strong within him as it had ever been. After a few minutes, the white glow faded from Bardiya's hands. Ki-Nan's face was clear of bruises and scratches, and the shoulder that had hung down near the bottom of his breast had been reset in its socket. He groaned and rolled over, his eyes still closed. Bardiya slumped to the ground, exhausted. His own eyes drifted shut a few moments later, and he lost consciousness.

When he awoke, it was nearly morning, the sky a purple bruise. The candles had melted down to nubs, dried wax forming frozen tears that were suspended from the table. Bardiya glanced at the bed, where his friend was sitting up, flexing his hand and feeling his forehead and cheeks, as if making sure they were still as they had always been. He did not look in Bardiya's direction.

"You healed me," Ki-Nan said suddenly, his voice quiet and sad.

"I did."

"Thank you."

"I would do it again in a heartbeat, my friend."

For a moment both were silent, then Ki-Nan groaned. Bardiya reached over and gave his friend a comforting squeeze, his massive hand nearly swallowing Ki-Nan's arm.

"Something bothers you, so tell me what it is. What happened during your voyage?"

Ki-Nan tugged on his thick growth of beard.

"I found the Lion's ships," he said. "Floating between the Isles of Gold beyond the Crags."

"Did they see you?" Bardiya asked. His heart began to race, a *thump-thump-thump* that felt nearly strong enough to rattle the world.

"I don't think so," Ki-Nan replied. "I beached the skiff on one of the archipelago's many small islands, one crowded with thick vegetation. From there I watched for two days as the Lion's ships were loaded with supplies and soldiers. The boats then departed the inlet, sailing northeast, toward the mainland. They must be planning to invade our home, Brother, and there were so many it took nearly a full day for them all to disappear over the horizon. Only when they were gone did I dare shove the skiff back into the water and begin the journey home.

"The sky filled with black clouds, and powerful gales pounded my sails. I had to pull them down, which left me with nothing but the oars to fight the waves. It was hard to breathe with all the water, and it all made my head pound like a drum. At night it was worse—trust me on that."

"I cannot imagine," Bardiya said, giving Ki-Nan's arm another squeeze.

"There is more," said Ki-Nan. "When the skies cleared, I tried to force my tired body to raise the sails. I was almost done when I saw it behind me, gaining on me. It was a midnight ship flying the Lion's banner, making nary a sound as it glided across the water. I tried to outrace it, but it was so fast, and it had closed half the distance by the time I caught my first sight of blessed shore. They started loosing arrows the nearer I came. Couldn't do much but duck and pray as the bolts flew over my head, striking the sides of my skiff and tearing little holes in my sails."

Ki-Nan paused for a moment, took a drink from the cup of water on the table beside the bed. Bardiya didn't press him.

"I panicked," he continued. "I rowed as fast as I could, even though another barrage of arrows came racing toward me. But the wind stayed strong, and I kept just ahead. Then I managed to steer my ship straight into the Canyon Crags."

Ki-Nan smiled, which seemed like a strange expression to have in such a moment. He almost began to laugh as he continued with his tale.

"Ashhur heard my prayers, Brother. The skiff never ran aground, and it didn't scrape along the jagged stones. That damned ship was far too large to follow me, another answered prayer. I floated there among the Crags for two days, right at the mouth of the Corinth, too frightened to make for land. I was certain the ship was waiting for me, you know? I boiled seawater to drink, using parts of my own skiff as firewood, and speared fish with a sharp, broken board. Wasn't good at it, mind you, but I caught at least one fish a day to ease my hunger. At last, when I could take it no longer, I inched my way out of the Crags."

"And the demon boat?" asked Bardiya, his heart beating fast.

"Nowhere to be found," Ki-Nan said. "So I began my way home, staying as close to land as I could, drifting in and out of consciousness. The last I remember, I was still many miles away. I don't even remember arriving here."

"Ashhur protected you indeed."

"He did, Brother. He did." Ki-Nan shimmied on the bed, looking uncomfortable. "But do you know what this means, Bardiya?"

The giant sat silent for a moment, thinking on the story he'd just heard. A niggling insect of doubt inched its way into his stomach, but he swatted it away.

"To us?" he said, determined to stay the course he had set. "It means nothing."

"Oh, but it does. It changes *everything*. The Lion is coming, and he is angry. By now the god's ships have already unloaded their soldiers onto the soils of Paradise. By now our brothers and sisters in creation and faith are dying. Ashhur may be the more noble deity, Bardiya, but in the ways of violence Karak is his better. He will crush our creator and the rest of Paradise, and then he will come for us."

Bardiya sighed. It was like speaking with Patrick all over again.

"You cannot know this, my friend."

"I can. The midnight ship…the demon riding it…any god willing to bring such treacherous beasts into his employ knows nothing of mercy. Believe me, Karak will surely march on our soil, and he will destroy us all."

To that, Bardiya nodded. "Perhaps, but it changes nothing."

"What?" asked Ki-Nan, looking baffled. "Why not?"

"We made a promise, Ki-Nan. We pledged ourselves to Ashhur's teachings. We pledged ourselves to peace. It would be wrong to turn our backs on that."

"Are you saying it would be a sin to defend ourselves?"

"I am."

Ki-Nan looked away.

"Remember when I was a boy," he asked, "and you took me into the lowlands to teach me lessons of the gods?"

"I do," Bardiya said, furrowing his brow. "You were eight or so at the time. Why do you ask?"

"Do you remember when we stumbled on an antelope that had been separated from its herd? It was being stalked by a pack of hyenas. For a long while afterward, I could hear their cackling in my dreams."

Bardiya nodded. "I remember."

"I cried for that beast," Ki-Nan continued. "I knew what would happen when the hyenas circled it. I saw the panic in its eyes when it realized it was trapped. That's when I tried to run after the hyenas, screaming at them to leave the poor creature be."

Bardiya felt himself slipping into the past. The memory was a warm one despite the harshness of the lesson.

"Yes, you looked ready to take on the whole herd by yourself, armed with but a stick. I couldn't decide whether it would teach you a better lesson if I stopped you or let you get nipped by the beasts."

"You stopped me in the end," he said, turning to face Bardiya, his eyes dark. "You grabbed me by the arm and told me to watch, not interfere. The hyenas tore into that poor antelope. I wailed at you to stop it, asking why the gods would allow their creations to suffer. You told me that it was the natural order of things, that nature is like a constant game of Man on the Hill. That for every creature born, there is another that perishes."

"It was natural," Bardiya said, remembering that conversation well.

"And I called it evil," Ki-Nan said, running a hand through the tight curls atop his head, which had grown wiry in his absence. "You said there is no evil in survival, that the antelope's life was a gift to the hyenas, that its sacrifice would allow their pups to live without hunger for another day. And you were right, Bardiya; I understand that now. Those hyenas were doing what they could to survive, and though I hated to see the antelope suffer, I had no right to call those cackling beasts evil."

Ki-Nan reached out and grabbed Bardiya's arm, his grip fierce. When he stared up into his eyes, they were bloodshot, their expression fierce.

"But you were so eager to forgive the hyenas that you forgot the plight of the antelope. It had a family of its own. And if the antelope had trampled and killed one of the hyenas to protect its life or the life of its cubs, would you have dared call it evil?"

Bardiya went to reply, but fell silent.

"Of course not," Ki-Nan said. "That's you, always willing to give others a chance. But Karak's Army is not made of hyenas, my brother. They're worse, far worse. They don't kill out of hunger or for survival. What they do, what they *will* do, is evil. You think you'll be the antelope, but you're wrong. I remember it, Bardiya, clear as day. When the hyena pack descended on that poor beast, it didn't lie down to die. It ran, it fought, no matter how outnumbered it was, no matter how hopeless its plight. It *fought*...which is more than what you would have us do."

Bardiya tried to think of a way to explain his reasoning. Humans were different from wild dogs and deer; humans aspired to something greater than the callous cruelty of nature.

"You must hear me," Bardiya insisted. "This principle we hold fast to...*that* is what needs to survive. What point is there in living if goodness cannot overcome all, if love, forgiveness, and honor are not respected and honored? This is *important*, my friend. The words Ashhur has taught us...they are all that matters in the world."

Ki-Nan slowly hefted his legs off the bed and put his weight on them. He grimaced as he straightened his back, but waved aside Bardiya's offer to help.

"No," Ki-Nan said. "It is all that matters to *you*. Tell me how, in Ashhur's name, things like goodness and love will endure when Karak has wiped our people from the face of Dezrel? We'll all be in our graves, you damn fool. Preach all you want about how we must stay true to Ashhur's words, but let us see how effective those words are when the Lion comes for us. Let us see how peaceful our people really are then."

"They will not fight. I will forbid it."

Ki-Nan shook his head.

"As you've said many times before, no man in Ker is better than any other. You are no god, Bardiya, no ruler—just a simple spiritual advisor. You haven't the right or the power to forbid anything."

With that, Ki-Nan left the cabin, the door slamming against the wall with a *crack* when it swung open. Bardiya stared at the empty space where his friend had stood, half wanting to call him back inside. Instead he folded his legs beneath him, steepled his fingers, closed his eyes, and prayed. For the second time since he'd confronted Ashhur in the shadow of the Black Spire, he began to doubt himself. So when he prayed, it was not to Ashhur or even the god of gods. Instead, he sent his prayers to the Golden Paradise, deep within Afram, seeking out his parents' presence, their lexis, their knowledge, their strength.

Tell me what to do, he pleaded. *Tell me the path I have chosen is righteous.*

He received no answer.

✦

Kindren and Aully walked hand in hand along the rocky shoreline. Clouds had passed over the moon, bathing the world in darkness, but to them it was no obstacle. Their keen eyes could still spot potential tripping hazards and puddles. But most importantly, they could see through the trees that bordered the shore and would be able to detect if any were watching them.

They had snuck away after the village settled down for the night, as had become their custom in the aftermath of the sandcat attack. The daylight hours were dedicated to sharing their lives with community and family, keeping spirits high, assisting with the daily chores, and making sure the small society of elves in Ang remained close-knit. Nighttime was a much more intimate affair. It was the only time Aully and Kindren could talk freely, the only time they could entwine their bodies in comfort, and the only time they could practice magic without fear of prying eyes. Their talents had grown by leaps and bounds.

Each evening they pressed a little bit farther toward the boundary of Ker, edging closer and closer to the mouth of the Corinth River and the Stonewood Forest. They stayed by the edge of the ocean at all times, where the brisk wind played with their hair and the cool sea mist beat their faces. That they drew closer and closer to Aully's childhood home remained unspoken between them, but it was not unintentional.

The tree line began to shift, the shorter trees along the shoreline becoming larger, more menacing. Great pines rose to dizzying heights above them, their tips so high they seemed to poke at the stars. Aully shivered, and Kindren released her hand and wrapped an arm around her, pulling her close.

"You're cold," he said.

"No, not cold."

"Then what is it?"

"I feel it," she said, leaning against him.

"You feel what?"

"Home. The closer we get to Stonewood, the more I feel this weird vibration. It's like the forest is trying to call me back where I belong."

Kindren laughed softly. "You talk like you're much older than you are."

"You always say that," she replied, nudging him. "Sometimes I can't tell if you're complimenting me or humoring me."

"You decide."

"Shut up."

She grinned and kissed the back of his hand, which dangled over her shoulder. An easy quiet passed between them, as if their feelings were being dispatched back and forth through the simple touch of flesh on flesh.

The peaceful feeling did not last long. Aullienna glanced northeast, to the darkness of distant smoke that blotted out the dimmer stars. Bardiya had offered no explanation for the fires or what they meant, but Aully didn't need him to spell it out for her. Whatever secret plan the Triad of the Quellan had hatched with the eastern realm was now in motion. The forces of Karak were on the move. She often thought about the strange deformed man with his mismatched armor and his enormous sword, and how he'd stared in disappointment at the giant. She was certain that soon Ang would not be safe for any of them.

"We have to go back," Aully whispered finally.

"We will," Kindren said. "Soon. Once the sky is blackest, we'll turn around."

"No," she said, shaking her head. "Not to the village. To the place where *we* belong. To Stonewood."

Kindren seemed to swallow a mouthful of spit. "We can't, Aully. You know that."

"Do I? Do *we*? We've been here for nearly nine months. Nine months, and no one has come searching for us. What if we were told lies? What if Stonewood is as it had always been, and it's safe to return?"

He shook his head. "We can't. Ceredon said he'd contact us when the time is right to return. We haven't heard from him yet. That means we stay."

She pushed away from him, throwing her hands up in frustration. "He hasn't contacted us? How in Celestia's name would he do that? *He doesn't even know where we are!* How do we know if he's even alive? Should his father discover how he betrayed him... Think of Zoe, Kindren. Think of her! If the Quellan could do that to a child, do you really think they would be merciful to Ceredon, whether he's the Neyvar's son or not?"

"Well—"

"They wouldn't!" She was screaming now, her voice carrying over the rumbling of the waves. Kindren looked back at her, his mouth dropping into a frown, his eyes filled with sadness. She took a deep breath, calming herself, and spoke more quietly. "I'm sorry, Kindren. I didn't mean to yell at you. But the world is breaking. Bardiya said that the afternoon we arrived here, and there is evidence of it every day. The distant fires, the fear on the faces of the Kerrians, the whispers of invasion...we are alone here. We're only thirty-two. Who will defend us should the worst happen?"

He shrugged. "Bardiya won't let anything bad happen to us."

"Won't he? The people here speak freely their gruff tongue, thinking we don't understand them. They say Bardiya won't lift a finger, even if Karak comes to destroy everything he loves. We'd be no different."

"Those are just words. They don't know what will happen anymore than we do."

"Maybe. But I don't want to take that chance."

"So what *do* you want to do? Take our people and march into Stonewood? You said if they'd kill Zoe, they'd kill Ceredon. You think the same doesn't apply to us?"

"I don't care," she said defiantly. "You might not trust my people, but I do." With that, she turned, gazing toward the west and the gigantic trees rimming the distant mouth of the river. "I just... I know staying here isn't what we're meant to do. We're meant for more. We're meant to go *home*, and set things right."

Kindren's hand found hers once more, and she looked up at him. The clouds moved away from the moon, and its light twinkled in his eyes. She felt suddenly disarmed, and she leaned against him, wishing that the warmth of his skin and steady beat of his heart would sooth her. They did, but only just.

"Let's go back," he whispered into her ear. "To Ang, I mean. We can talk about this again tomorrow night."

"All right."

The young couple turned and began the return trek to the fishing village. The tide began to roll in, forcing them to move closer to the rocky ledge. The fissures in the massive stones were larger here, sometimes three feet wide, and they had to jump from boulder to boulder. Aully made a game of it, counting her steps before each leap, trying to see if they could both make it across with their hands still locked together. It felt good to let go for a moment, to feel like the child she was.

Then, once the trees of Stonewood forest had all but disappeared behind them, she spotted something strange—a seaweed-covered obelisk jutting up from one of the gaps between the boulders, just to her left.

"What's that?" Aully asked, stopping in her tracks.

"Huh?"

She pointed. "Over there."

Kindren followed her finger and shrugged. "Don't know. Maybe a piece of ship or something? It's been stormy lately. Something probably washed up on shore."

"You want to see what it is?"

"Sure, but we should make it quick. It's late as it is, and I don't want your mother to wake up while we're gone."

"We'll be fast," she said. She took off toward the object, skipping over the rocks in a carefree manner, Kindren fast behind her.

When she reached the object, she saw that the gap it rested in was quite large, stretching down too far for moonlight to illuminate the sandy bottom. She also saw that the object she'd spotted was a wooden crate. There were three of them stacked up in the hollow, the top crate teetering to the side, resting against the rim of stone.

"What in the abyss?" whispered Kindren.

Aully shrugged. "Maybe you were right, and they washed ashore from the sea."

There was wonder in Kindren's eyes. "If so, it's a miracle the crates didn't break. And that they're heaped this way."

She squinted, staring at the boxes. "You think someone put them here?"

"Yes, I do."

"Want to find out what's inside?"

He hesitated, then shrugged.

"Of course I do," he said, his grin hiding his nervousness.

Aully balanced herself on the lip of the crevasse and removed the slimy seaweed from the top of the crate, then pressed her hands against its wooden sides.

"Be careful," Kindren said, a warning she brushed aside. She pushed as hard as she could, but still the crate wouldn't budge.

"It's heavy," she said.

"I'd imagine it would be," Kindren laughed back. "Look at it. Ten of you could fit inside."

"Very funny."

"You're right. It's more like twenty."

Kindren joined her at the edge of the fissure, tracing his hands over the corners of the crate.

"Here's the seam," he said. "Looks like it opens outward." He pried his fingers into the ridge and made funny grunting noises as he tried to pry off the front. It wouldn't budge. Aully joined him, her delicate fingers getting splinters as they slid back and forth along the wood. She cursed and withdrew her hand, sucking a dot of blood from her fingertip.

"It's sealed shut," Kindren said. "We need a wedge or something. We can come back tomorrow and try again."

"No," Aully insisted. "We can do this right now. Step back."

Kindren did, wisely choosing to keep his mouth shut. Aully extended her hands and whispered a few careful words of magic.

A thin bolt of energy burst forth from her palms and struck the corner of the crate. The force was more than she'd intended, and a loud *crack* filled the night as the wood exploded outward. She yelped and shimmied back along the rocks, losing her balance. She would have teetered over and smashed her skull had Kindren not been there to catch her.

The sound of clanking metal filled her ears. She stared wide-eyed at the crate, waiting for the smoke to dissipate. When it did, the two of them inched forward on all fours, peering over the lip of the crevasse into the now opened crate.

"Oh…"

The crate was filled with weapons. Lots and lots of weapons. Long swords, short swords, broad swords, lances, daggers, battle-axes, mauls, maces—all were tumbling one after another from the blasted-open enclosure. She couldn't know for sure, but it looked like that single wooden box held enough to arm at least two hundred men, if not more. Kindren whistled beside her. It was a sound filled with equal parts awe and fearful uncertainty.

Aully stared at one of the swords, hissing as it slowly slid down the pile, its polished steel glinting in the moonlight. She thought once more of Stonewood, of home, and a smile came to her lips.

"Kindren?" she said.

"Yes?"

"This is the answer to our prayers. Now when we walk into Stonewood, we won't be unarmed." She laughed aloud. "My love, we're going home."

CHAPTER

25

The door to Matthew's bedroom burst open, and he sat up with a start. His wife, Catherine, yelped, gathering the blankets about her neck. The torches had gone out, and in the light from the doorway he could see a hulking black shadow. Matthew snatched his dagger from the table beside his featherbed and got up on his knees. He was vulnerable in his nakedness, and he cursed himself for letting his guard down.

Those bastards, he thought. *I knew the Conningtons wouldn't stay true to their word.*

"Hey, boss," the shadow said. "You awake?"

Matthew sighed, his heart still rocking like a skiff in a violent windstorm. He placed a soothing hand on Catherine's shoulder. At least their children were in their own rooms this night and wouldn't be frightened.

"I am now," he grumbled. "What are you doing here, Bren?"

"It's happening."

"What's happening?"

"You know. That thing we weren't supposed to talk about."

Matthew groaned, rubbed his eyes.

"Now?" he asked.

The shadow nodded.

"Shit."

"Matthew, what is he talking about?" asked Catherine, her voice still husky from sleep.

"Nothing. Don't worry about it." He turned to his bodyguard. "And Moira? Is she awake?"

Bren lit a tinderstick and touched it to the torch on the wall. He shook his head.

"Hasn't come out of her room. Hopefully it stays that way."

Under different circumstances, Matthew might have found Bren's fear of the waifish Moira humorous. Now it just filled him with dread. The woman was a brilliant fighter and had been his willing captive for nearly three months now. Though they had grown close, he didn't know how she would react if she found out he'd been lying to her the entire time. The thought petrified him.

Matthew rose from bed, not bothering to hide his nakedness from his bodyguard as he threw on a clean tunic and breeches from the bureau on the far side of the room. A half-full carafe of brandy sat on the desk beside the bureau, and he took a long pull from it before he dressed. The liquid burned going down, swelling his tongue and making him cough, but at least it took the edge off his nerves.

"Well, let's not delay the inevitable," he said with a sigh. He turned to Catherine. "Dear, sleep in Ryan's bed for the night. I'll see you when you wake in the morning."

"Matthew, you're scaring me," Catherine said, letting the blankets fall, exposing her body from the waist up. Even after birthing five children, she was a resplendent woman. Her chestnut hair was wavy and as smooth as satin, her flesh almost flawless, her gray eyes hauntingly beautiful. The only parts of her that bore the signs of childbirth were her sagging breasts and long, slender nipples; five children sucking vehemently on them for sustenance had taken its inevitable toll. Matthew hummed quietly as he looked down at her.

"Worry not, my dear," he said, tying his belt tightly around his waist. "All will be well. I simply have business to attend to."

"You *always* have business to attend to."

Bren chuckled behind him.

"The price of marrying a merchant," Matthew said with a grin. He waved his hand at Bren, and the bodyguard left the chamber. Matthew followed closely behind him, his fingers dancing over the hilt of the dagger wedged into his belt. He knew the blade would be useless to him—his true talents resided in other areas—but the feel of its cold steel helped reassure him nonetheless.

The sound of wailing reached his ears the moment they began to descend the stairwell. By the time they reached the ground level of the estate, three floors down, the sound was akin to the shrieks of a feral cat defending its alley.

Bren led him around the corner and into the foyer. His six personal guards stood before the great bookcase on the northern wall, their faces awash with confusion. They kept peering at the bookcase cloaking the secret passage. Down here in the foyer, the wailing was so loud that it was as if the wailer were in the next room. He silently cursed himself for not packing cotton around the hidden entrance to the Brennan Estate's underground refuge.

"What's happening, sir?" asked one of the guards, a young, blond man named Curtis. "What's behind the bookcase?"

"None of your damn business," snapped Bren.

Matthew placed a hand on his bodyguard's shoulder.

"Calm down, Bren." He turned to face the other guards. "I cannot tell you," he said, "and you have not heard a sound. All went as usual, there were no disturbances, and you heard no pained cries. Understood?"

All six nodded, though they still appeared confused.

"Uh, boss?" said Bren.

"The foyer is to be the last stop each of you make. Do not return for an hour. I want the rookery thoroughly examined, and I want my bedchambers ransacked for potential threats. And please make sure to hang heavy drapes over all the windows to ensure that any possible sounds are dampened for those outside."

"*Boss!*"

Matthew turned on Bren.

"What?" he barked.

Bren gestured with his chin, and Matthew followed his gaze. He froze at the sight of a spent-looking Moira dressed in wrinkled nightclothes, her dyed hair matted on one side and sticking up on the other. Penetta, one of Matthew's maids, lingered behind her, looking just as sleepy-eyed as the former Lady Crestwell did. Penetta's sheer gown was crumpled and damp, her auburn hair disheveled. Matthew wondered what they were doing together at this time of night, but discarded the question nearly as soon as he thought it. That Moira was standing in the foyer while the screeching issued from behind the bookcase made any other consideration moot.

No one said a word, and Moira's eyes narrowed. Her gaze shifted from Matthew to Bren, to the guards, and then settled on the bookcase. She took a deep breath, puffing out her chest.

"Go upstairs," she whispered. Penetta shuffled from side to side as if she hadn't heard. Moira turned to her, grabbed her by the front of her threadbare nightclothes, and pulled her close.

"Go...upstairs."

"Yes, ma'am," the petite young woman replied. She curtseyed, though the pleasantry looked ridiculous given her outfit, and then disappeared around the corner. Her soft footfalls could barely be heard beneath the wails, which were now coming in shorter spurts.

Matthew held Moira's gaze.

"You all have your instructions," he told his guards. "Now get to it."

The guards hustled from the room, heading in opposite directions. Bren remained where he was. Matthew could hear the *clink* of the guards' chainmail, but he dared not take his eyes off Moira. When all fell silent save for the tormented cries, he finally blinked.

"What…is that?" asked Moira as yet another wail echoed off the thick stone walls.

Matthew swallowed hard, trying to remain strong. "It is nothing for you to concern yourself with, Moira. Go back to your room with Penetta. Do whatever it is you do with her."

"No." She breezed past him and Bren, heading straight for the bookcase. He made no move to stop her. The woman might be small and unarmed, but the way she carried herself made her seem deadlier than a lion's jaws. Even Bren, big and rough as he was, gave her a wide berth.

Moira stopped before the bookcase, running her fingers over the tomes stacked within. She then stepped to the side and rapped on the wall. A dull *thud* sounded each time her knuckles struck the wood.

"It's hollow," Moira said. The iciness in her voice made Matthew shiver. He had met her sister Avila on a couple of occasions—*Karak's bitch* as many called her. Right then Moira sounded very much like her.

"It is," said Matthew.

"What's behind it?"

"A staircase."

"*Who* is behind it?"

"I'd rather not say. You should go back to bed."

She glared at him, her dyed hair hanging in front of her blue eyes. "Open it."

Bren tried to protest, but Matthew simply shook his head and stepped forward. The secret was out, and there was nothing the two of them could do about it. He went to the side of the bookcase and wrapped his fingers around the back ridge. Finding the catch, he slid it down. A loud *clank* sounded, and then he pressed his shoulder into the massive wooden obstruction and shoved. It slid along the wall before coming to an abrupt halt, revealing a three-foot-wide black portal. The screams from down below heightened twofold.

Moira went to shove past him, but he gathered enough courage to stop her, placing a palm firmly against her chest. "I go first," he said.

She stared at him blankly, making no response. He turned away and descended the dark stairwell.

The estate refuge had been built by his father, Elbert, thirty-eight years ago in the aftermath of Karak's departure from Neldar, when corruption and thievery were on the rise. The refuge had been intended as a safe haven for his family should the rambling packs of wrongdoers band together and attempt to use violence and murder to purloin the family's wealth, a possibility which had thankfully never been realized. It was a single large room, as wide as the estate itself, with a hatch beneath it leading to an underground stream that dumped directly into the ocean. In theory, those who were holed up inside could use the stream as a last resort to flee from danger, but in practice it had been used for the opposite purpose. Over the years Matthew had used the underground stream as a way to have young maidens snuck *in*, so he could enjoy their carnal pleasures in private. He thought about how the screams from the refuge could be heard throughout the estate's first floor and cringed. Had Catherine been able to hear his trysts?

Fuck me sideways, he thought, leading Moira farther down the stairs.

The refuge's current resident had been snuck in three months ago. She had lived down there in relative luxury, while the rest of the world went on above her as if she didn't exist. How Matthew wished that that were still the case.

He came to the bottom of the stairwell, where a pair of torches bordered a thick oak door, and rapped five times. He felt Moira lingering behind him, her breath on his neck. It would have been easy for her to plunge a knife into his back if she had one on her. The screams came once more, bouncing off the narrow stone walls on either side of him, and he jumped.

A series of scratching sounds came from the other side of the door, like rats scurrying in the walls. In reply Matthew knocked twice more, then ran his fingernails across the wood, ending with two more knocks. The heavy *clunk* of a bolt being undone came next, and then the door to the refuge swung open.

He walked into an expansive and elegantly furnished space, well lit by a great many torches and candelabras. The floor was adorned with brightly colored rugs. To the left, there were a table and chairs, a washbasin, and a series of shelves displaying stylish glassware and plates. To the right, concealed by a curtain, was the privy, which dumped into the stream below. On the far side of the room, opposite the door, was a hearth with a lit fire, its smoke disappearing into the estate's main flue. In front of it was a line of five beds, a huge four-poster one in the center. There, atop the bed, lay the source of the incessant screaming.

Matthew heard Moira gasp behind him, but the three individuals surrounding the wailing woman did not turn toward the sound. They were too intent on the task at hand.

He took a few steps closer, studying the naked, sweating body of Rachida Gemcroft. Her breasts were huge and her midsection even more so. Rachida's eyes were closed, her face awash in agony. The young man propping her up brushed back the sodden clumps of her curly black hair, while the two in front of her, an older gray-haired woman and a girl who looked no older than fifteen, each braced one of her knees on her shoulder. The older woman was Gertrude Shrine, but Matthew knew the other two only by their first names: the young man was Raxler and the young woman, Shimmea. He had brought them in to care for Rachida months ago, and they'd lived in this refuge with her ever since.

"The baby is crowning, my dear," said Gertrude. She pressed harder against Rachida's leg, stretching her nethers as she forced it back. Rachida hollered in pain.

"You're hurting her!" cried a desperate voice.

Matthew didn't have time to turn around before something slammed him from behind, nearly knocking him to the floor. Moira darted past him, rushing to Rachida's side. She grabbed Shimmea by the hair and yanked her back, then drove Gertrude away with an open palm to the chest. Next she turned on Raxler, fist drawn back as taut as a bowstring.

"My love," Rachida said through clenched teeth. "Stop, now." If she was surprised to see Moira, she didn't show it.

"But—"

"But nothing, my love. It's coming. Our baby is coming. It's *comiiiiing*!" She threw back her head and screamed.

Gertrude shoved Moira out of the way, taking her place once more.

"Dear, we know what we're doing. Please stand aside."

She was joined by Shimmea, who hesitantly returned to her position.

"It will be soon, milady," Gertrude said. "Breathe deliberately, in and out, in and out, and wait for the next one to come." Rachida did as she was told, while the two women pushed against her legs. Soon the contraction came, and Rachida screamed louder than before, her every muscle tensing. Her face flushed red, the muscles in her neck and jaws so tight that Matthew feared she might somehow injure herself. When she calmed down, her eyes opened, and her gaze immediately found Moira. She reached out the hand that was not busy squeezing Raxler's fingers. When Moira cautiously approached, Rachida took her hand, brought it to her lips, and kissed it before another spasm began. Leaning against the bed, Moira fell to her knees, her expression one of surprised alarm.

"Disgusting," Bren said, staring with wide eyes at Rachida's crotch.

"Then don't watch," Matthew told him. "I never did for my five, and for good reason."

Bren grunted. "Just look at that bed," he said. "Blood all over it. Looks like the mattress will need replacing."

"Now you're disgusted by a bit of blood, eh, Bren? To think I hired you for your skill at spilling blood."

Bren waved him off.

"This is different and you know it. I'm going upstairs for a drink. Come get me when it's over."

An hour later, the room was filled with the gurgling of an infant. A baby boy with a thatch of curly red hair emerged into the world, screaming just as his mother had been. The birthing chord was cut, the afterbirth expelled, and afterward Gretchen, Raxler, and Shimmea set about cleaning the mess, dropping soiled blankets into a canvas bag, and mopping up the afterbirth. Rachida and Moira reclined together on the red-streaked bed while the new mother fed the infant from her swollen nipple. As he watched the scene unfold, in a moment of ill-timed humor Matthew thought the child might be the luckiest male in all of Neldar.

Matthew sat at the table, fidgeting. Feeling like an invader, he tried not to watch. The two women were so enamored with the babe, he thought he could leave without either noticing him.

Just then Moira glanced at him, and it seemed as though a whole new person took over her body. She rolled off the bed as if fleeing a fire and raced toward him, snatching a sharp and wicked-looking instrument from Gertrude's bag. Matthew lunged from his chair, but Moira was a raging ball of hate, her shoulders rising and falling, her eyes throwing invisible daggers of death as she stalked forward. Gertrude, Raxler, and Shimmea backed against the wall.

Moira stopped a few feet in front of him. "I trusted you," she said, her voice barbed. "She was here, and you didn't tell me."

"I couldn't," Matthew insisted, his heart pounding.

"Bullshit!"

"I'm not lying. Telling you would have meant risking everything I'm hoping to gain."

Moira's hands shook with her anger.

"Gain?" she asked. "What did you hope to gain by keeping me from her? Tell me, you bastard!"

"I'm not the right target for your anger," Matthew said, trying to keep calm. "These were Petyr's orders—*strict* orders, I might add. I'm sticking my neck out by hiding her here, and you as well. Try and remember that before you stab me."

Moira looked back and forth between him and Rachida. The other woman looked exhausted, only halfway aware of what was taking place.

"But why?" asked Moira. There were tears in her eyes, but her hardness never abandoned her. She hovered there before him, swaying.

Matthew glanced to Rachida, and she nodded to him. He took a careful step closer to Moira, his hands raised to show that he meant no harm.

"Do not think I enjoyed keeping you in the dark," he said softly. "You have talents, Moira, talents you proved your first night in Port Lancaster. Bren and I would have been slaughtered without your intercession." He laughed and shook his head. "Small as you are, you are better with a blade than any warrior I've ever seen. You make even Bren look like a clumsy oaf."

Moira cocked her head, giving Rachida a look. "That answers nothing. When did you return? *Why?*"

"We had it all planned," Rachida said, shifting the mewling baby from one breast to the other. She sounded tired, very tired. "I took a raft back to shore, and then Matthew's men brought me here. As for the reason....There are no settlements on the Isles of Gold. I couldn't help tame the land and build the township, not in my condition. And you *know* that our fellow renegades are not the brightest bunch, especially in the healing arts. Antar and Lommy both died in Karak's attack on Haven, leaving only a gaggle of farmers and brigands capable of no more than administering crim oil to livestock or putting down a dog. Given the nature of my pregnancy, given the magics required for Patrick's seed to find purchase, I feared something might go wrong. What would happen if there were no healers or midwives to assist me?"

At the mention of the name *Patrick*, Moira's fists clenched. Matthew had no idea who the man was, though he didn't find it shocking to learn that the child was not Peytr's. And the look on Rachida's face was one he easily recognized. The woman was stalling, trying to change the subject.

"And *they* are better?" asked Moira, jabbing her thumb at the three who cowered against the wall.

"They are," said Matthew. "Gertrude is the greatest physician in the realm, the fourth generation of her family to practice medicine."

"I am," Gertrude said, stepping away from the wall. "And I have been here with Rachida for almost three months. I've watched her progress, protected her, fed her the foods she needed to thrive, and offered her support. She has been in the best of hands, milady. Of that I can promise you."

"But what would have happened if anything *had* gone wrong?" pleaded Moira. "You would have perished right beneath me, and I would never have known!"

"That's not true," said Rachida, shaking her head sadly.

"Another part of the deal," added Matthew. "Should anything befall Rachida, should she die in childbirth or beforehand, you were to escort her body back to the Isles of Gold, with the child if possible."

Rachida looked at her gravely. "We play a dangerous game, my love. The Conningtons are no friends to Peytr, as you well know. No matter how much he has lost, Peytr still holds deeds to the most promising and productive lands in Neldar and beyond. Once the war ends, the value of those holdings will be tremendous. The brothers knew that I was pregnant with his heir. Should they have discovered my presence here, they would have sought me out and killed us both."

"And yet you trusted *Bren*?" Moira asked. "I was kept in the dark, but that idiot was allowed to know?"

"Bren may be a big dumb oaf, but he is as loyal as he is stupid, which he has proven time and again," Matthew said. "Besides, the decision was Peytr's, not mine. You're more than welcome to scream at *his* face until your voice is hoarse."

Moira began to pace, but her eyes kept finding their way back to Rachida and the baby.

"What I want to know," she said, "is where do we go from here? Since the child was born without issue, are we free to flee to the islands…together?" Her gaze grew pleading as she stared at her love.

"No," said Rachida. The sadness in her voice was palpable.

"Why not?"

Matthew gathered as much courage as he could and said, "Because Peytr's debt is still not paid. He has my boats, my arms, my captains. I like him, just as I like you and Rachida, but I risked too much by helping him to go unrewarded. *You* are that reward, Moira. Even disregarding your skills, it gives me a great advantage to have the daughter of Clovis Crestwell as a hostage, *especially* one who has so publicly railed against her creator. The amount of leverage I could gain by presenting you to Karak as a trophy is worth its weight in gold."

"You would never…"

"I wouldn't, but there are many who would," he shot back, trying to keep his voice strong. "It's all posturing and position, and it must be done to ensure that Petyr and I behave as the gentlemen we pretend to be."

Moira hardly looked convinced, but Rachida called her over.

"Come, my love, sit with us…sit with our son." Moira crept across the room, tears in her eyes, and curled up in a ball beside the sublimely gorgeous daughter of Soleh Mori. Just watching the two of them broke Matthew's heart, and he had to bite down on his tongue to keep from breaking down. It was truly unfair of him to make Moira say good-bye to the love of her life twice. He thought of his own past, of the way he'd railed against the authority and memory of his own father by marrying Catherine against his wishes. Had he been in Moira's shoes…

Best not think on it, he told himself.

The door opened, and down came Bren.

"The screaming stopped," he said, giving them all a weird look, as if confused by their tense expressions. "Figured that meant a good thing."

"The baby is well," Matthew said, slumping down at the table again. Bren joined him, and he nodded toward Moira, lowering his voice so he would not be overheard.

"How'd she take the news?" he asked.

"As well as expected. I almost died. Glad to have you at my side, you dumb ox."

Bren shrugged.

"Wouldn't have mattered. I'll protect you from assassins, thieves, and cutthroats. When it comes to Moira Elren, you're on your own."

Matthew chuckled despite his dour mood.

"This never should have happened," he said. "Our precautions were foolish and incomplete. We'll need to keep a closer eye on the help who worked tonight, along with the various soldiers in the vicinity. Any one of them could leak word to the Conningtons in Riverrun, and while they might not know who the child is, Romeo or Cleo are smart enough to put it together."

"Can't change what's been done," Bren said. "But I'll do what I can to make sure no loose lips are in this house. So what happens now, boss?"

Matthew sighed. "In two days, Rachida and her child will get on a ship and head to the islands."

Bren pointed his chin at Gertrude and her helpers. "What about them?"

"Oh, them," Matthew said, shaking his head. He leaned in and whispered into Bren's ear. "Should word get back to Veldaren that we were harboring fugitives from Haven, particularly with that emissary on her way…"

Bren leaned back and looked him in the eyes. "You saying what I think you're saying?"

He nodded. "Gertrude will accompany Rachida to the isles. As for the other two…well, Peytr was adamant that only one of them could join his wife. Something about having enough mouths to feed. And we can't afford to have potential loose lips with secrets to tell. Just make it quick, would you? Painless."

"I'll do what I can."

Matthew looked over at Gertrude, who was dictating to Shimmea on the other side of the room. The young girl jotted the words down on a piece of parchment, a smile on her face.

"And make sure no one finds the bodies," he said.

"I'm not an idiot, boss." Bren looked at the two supine women, who were doting on the now sleeping child. "I hope this is all worth it."

Matthew leaned back in his chair. Peytr Gemcroft had offered him half the gold on the isles to ensure his heir was born, quietly, safely, and without anyone knowing. His desire to keep Moira in the dark had stemmed from a fear that the lovers would flee after the baby's birth. Now that Moira knew, Matthew hoped they would not decide on such a foolish course of action. Because if Moira did decide she and Rachida were leaving the mansion, Matthew doubted all his house guards combined could prevent it from happening.

"Who knows if it will be in the end?" Matthew said, feeling far too tired to worry about it. "And don't you have work to do?"

"Yeah, yeah."

Matthew stood up, bowed to all present, and left the room, with Bren right behind him. His heart hung heavy in his chest. The last words he heard before the door closed behind him were Rachida's, answering a question posed by Raxler.

"His name is Patrick," the gorgeous woman said, "after his father. His *true* father."

CHAPTER

26

Ceredon watched at his father's side as Clovis Crestwell paced the courtyard of Palace Thyne. The odd human's hands were clenched behind his back, and his red-tinged eyes tightened as he stared at each corpse he passed. He ran a hand over his smooth, bald head, fingers undulating as they passed over the lumps on his cranium. The man looked angry beyond words, and with good reason.

Six of the corpses were his soldiers, and the other two were members of the Ekreissar. Each victim's throat had been slit, a parting gift from the rebels who were making life difficult for the seizing force. Crestwell turned his attention to the gathered Dezren. There were fifty of them, the strongest males the elven city had to offer. Members of the human army and the Ekreissar had forced them to their knees, and there they remained, their noses inches from the ground. A throng of women and children looked on, kept in place by the remainder of Clovis's soldiers.

Ceredon suppressed a shudder. The city had been rife with conflict since the humans' arrival, the Dezren rebels intensifying their efforts, striking from the shadows seemingly every night. Though they were rarely more than an annoyance to Clovis and Aeson, the latter of whom had taken the reins of the Ekreissar in Aerland Shen's absence, the previous evening they had landed a crucial blow by killing the eight who were now on display in the grass. One of the humans had been Clovis's second in command, and the two Ekreissar were among the oldest and most talented archers in the order. Argo Stillen, the captain of the Archer's Guild, was one of them. Ceredon knew such actions could not go unpunished, and he wished he had been more adamant in his attempts to convince Tantric, the rebel leader, to forego the ambush.

"I once thought all elves were the same, and that our arrival would signal a time of peace between our people," Clovis told those who were crouched on their knees. His voice had become loud and strong—*united*—much different from when he'd first arrived in Dezerea. The man continued: "However, I seem to have been mistaken. All elves are *not* the same. While the Quellan have accepted us with open arms, as brothers, you have done…this." He gestured to the corpses. "Six of my men and two of the Neyvar's. This is to say nothing of the other deaths, including the murder of one of the Quellan Triad. Why has it come to this? Because we've dared to ask for your hospitality in a time of strife?" The human turned and continued to pace. "This rebellion can go on no longer. This secrecy, these craven assassinations under the cover of night…are these the acts of a proud and dignified race? I think not. I understand that you have all been questioned about the location of the insurgents and that you have all pled ignorance." His mouth twisted in a sadistic smile. "I do not believe you. Some among you *do* know where these rebels are hiding, and I will reap that information from you even if I have to flay the very flesh from your bones."

Neyvar Ruven gasped and stepped forward.

"The rebels act of their own accord," the Neyvar insisted. "We have imprisoned those who would speak out or act against you.

You've seen our crowded dungeons, Clovis. The rest that remain are simple folk, not warriors. They know nothing."

"That is quite ignorant of you," said Clovis, scowling. "But you're an elf, and such delusions are only natural. Your kind has an overly idealistic view of your own race. We humans hold no such illusions. We are barely beyond animals, and we know it. We understand that we will lie, cheat, and steal, if not out of desperation, then out of joy. We know we are rats, and we cling to our god because of it. Your race might live longer, but a five-hundred-year-old rat is still just a rat."

The Neyvar went to protest again, but Iolas grabbed his elbow and pulled him back in line. Ruven shrugged off his cousin's grip, a look of disdain on his face.

Ceredon hated it, but he knew his father had no choice but to endure. Karak's Army was rumored to be but a few short miles from Dezerea's borders. Although the humans in the elven city could easily be dispatched, an entire *legion* of them was marching with their god—nearly twenty thousand, if the rumors were correct. Should they betray the God of Order before Ceredon eliminated them, bringing the Neyvar back into a position of power, the Quellan could very well become footnotes in the history of Dezrel.

Clovis turned to the kneelers. "Eight have died, so eight will be questioned," he said. "These men were our strongest, so we will take the strongest of you as well." His soldiers stalked behind the kneeling Dezren and jerked the eight most strapping to their feet, leading them to the center of the assembly, twenty feet in front of the dais on which Ceredon stood with the Quellan ruling class.

The eight Dezren puffed out their chests, held their arms straight by their sides, and jutted their chins to the sky. They were images of pure defiance, even as the soldiers stripped them of their shirts with knives, spitting on them and hurling insults as they did so. When all were naked from the waist up, Clovis held out his hand, and his squire handed him his sword. The human drew the thick blade from its scabbard and held it above his head. His muscles bulged and rippled beneath his black leather tunic, and Ceredon couldn't help but wonder how the man had become so hefty and muscular so quickly. He'd appeared slender just two days ago, scrawny about the neck and waist. Now his flesh seemed to have taken on a different sheen—instead of being waxen and translucent, it looked pink and healthy, and the odd bulging spots that had covered him had all but disappeared beneath his heft. It was a shocking change, and Ceredon wondered how it could have come about given that the man had spent the majority of his time in Dezrea in the now restricted dungeons below Palace Thyne. Clovis seemed to gain and lose weight by the hour. Something was certainly amiss....

Clovis approached the first in the line.

"What is your name?" he asked.

The elf remained silent.

"How old are you?"

Nothing.

"Have you ever consorted with the insurgent Tantric Thane?"

No response.

"Do you know where the rebels hide?"

The elf licked his lips but said nary a word.

"Your silence screams of guilt," Clovis said. He signaled to one of the Ekreissar, who rushed forward and kneed the Dezren in the groin, doubling him over. He fell to the grass on all fours. A soldier pinned the elf's knees down while two more held his shoulders. The ranger who had kneed him took a wooden block and shoved it beneath his head, then ground his foot into the elf's cheek, pinning him to the block. None of the Dezren made a move to save their doomed comrade.

Clovis stood to the side of the restrained elf and raised his sword up high.

"You are hereby sentenced to death for the crime of treason," he said.

"Celestia, open your arms for me!" the Dezren shouted in the elven tongue, though he did not struggle against his captors.

The sword came down, slicing easily through flesh and bone. The body fell, the stump of neck gushing blood, and the ranger picked up the head by its long, golden-brown hair, holding it up for the rest to see. When he garnered no reaction, he tossed the head aside.

Clovis moved on to the second in line, asking, "What is your name?"

When silence was his only answer, the questions stopped, and the ranger drove the man down to receive Clovis's sword.

Ceredon forced himself to watch as one by one the defiant elves were cut down. He was glad Lord and Lady Thyne were not present for the display, having been locked in their room in the palace. The couple had experienced far too many beatings as of late.

Soon, only one Dezren was left. The lone survivor's eyes twitched, and his jaw and neck were tense. As with the others, he remained silent as the questions were asked. The ranger stepped toward him holding the blood-soaked block, then bent to place it on the ground. Before he could knee the elf, the Dezren dropped to the ground, placing his head on the block. The other elf paused, seemingly confused.

Clovis chuckled. "Before you die, can we have the honor of your name?" he asked.

"Pomerri," was the answer.

"How old are you?"

Pomerri opened his mouth to reply, but then lunged to his feet, ramming his forehead into the crotch of the ranger in front of him. Reaching up, he grabbed the elf around the back of the neck, then slammed his nose against the block with all his might, shattering it, the Ekreissar's blood mixing with that of the seven slain elves before he rolled to the side, howling and clutching his face.

"No!" shouted Clovis. He hoisted the executioner's sword and stepped over a headless corpse, his powerful arms rippling as he swung the blade down with all his might.

Ceredon held his breath, thinking this to be the end of the brave elf, but Pomerri danced to the side, narrowly avoiding the violent chop. He ducked into a roll, and his feet collided with the head of the still bleeding ranger. The ranger's head snapped to the side, and his eyes rolled into the back of his head. That was all the opening the renegade needed. Pomerri snatched the handle of the khandar fastened to the ranger's belt and yanked it free with one mighty tug. Then, whirling around on one knee, he led with the sword's curved point.

All of the witnesses froze in shock, even the other Ekreissar who should have been trying to subdue the prisoner. Clovis howled at the top of his lungs, his massive executioner's sword lifted high above his head for another chop. His entire body lunged forward to give the hit power, but Pomerri's strike came faster than he'd anticipated. Clovis's eyes widened, his entire body freezing in place as all those gathered, from the soldiers to the Ekreissar to the Quellan royal family to the distant mob of terrified Dezren, gasped as one. The giant sword fell from his limp fingers, burying into the soft soil.

Pomerri released his khandar, buried to the hilt in Clovis's chest, and then lifted his hands, his fingers hooked in a symbol of peace and perseverance. A smile was on his face. Still none moved to subdue him.

Clovis fell to his knees, blood dribbling from his lips as he coughed.

"I do not fear you, *any* of you," Pomerri cried, turning to face his Quellan conquerors. "Kill me where I stand, but know that you will soon join me in the afterlife. And when Celestia judges you, may her judgment be harsh and brutal!"

In that silence came wet, vile laughter.

"No judgment is as harsh and brutal as that of Karak."

Spoken in elvish from the grinning mouth of Clovis Crestwell, the voice was deep and layered. Pomerri spun around, a look of disbelief washing over his face as he watched the kneeling Clovis grasp the khandar with both hands and slowly pull it from his midsection. With one final tug it came free, torrents of red flowing from it. He tossed the blade aside. Ceredon looked on in horror as the gash gradually knotted itself back together, blood slowing to a trickle, then stopping completely, flesh weaving over flesh until no damage was left. Clovis's eyes glowed an unnatural red as he grabbed the bottom of his leather tunic and lifted it, staring with grim satisfaction at the bare yet knobby flesh of his stomach. Not even a scar remained.

What sort of dark magic is this? Ceredon's mind screamed as the crowd gasped all around him.

The human stood up, appearing somehow thinner now than he had before. The sick sound of his laughter reached Ceredon's ears, making his stomach queasy. Pomerri stood frozen, and when he glanced at the khandar, Clovis lunged like an animal descending on its prey. His meaty hands wrapped around the elf's throat, lifting him off the ground. The renegade's face turned purple, then a ghostly shade of white as Clovis's hands squeezed all the tighter. Ceredon heard a wet *pop* as the elf's neck snapped. Bile leaked from the corners of his mouth, and his head lolled to the side. Clovis unclenched his hands and dropped the broken body to the ground. The gathered women and children, who were prevented from leaving by the human soldiers, wailed and protested. The humans looked just as horrified as everyone else.

"All of you, *on your feet!*" Clovis shouted to the remaining Dezren males, who were still on their knees. They did as they were told without help from the Ekreissar, gazing on Karak's representative with terror in their eyes. "My life for order, my life for Karak!" Clovis shouted as he stalked before their ranks. "Behold the power of Karak! My faith has made me pure, *strong!* Even death holds no sway over me!"

"Karak is mighty! Praise his name!" shouted Aeson from the dais, his hands clasped before him, as he looked on the human with reverence. Ceredon scowled but held his tongue. Thankfully, so did his father.

At Clovis's signal, one of his young soldiers approached.

"Bring them to the dungeons with the others," he told the soldier, pointing at the dead elves. "And get the onlookers out of my sight."

The soldier nodded and hurried away, and both the Quellan and the humans went about ushering the Dezren back to their forest dwellings, while a few soldiers dragged away the bodies. Ceredon wondered why Clovis wanted the bodies in the dungeon, but feared it related to whatever dark magic had kept the strange man alive.

Clovis turned his attention to the dais, looking to each of those standing there in turn.

"As for you," he said, pointing at Aeson, "your idiocy brought about the deaths of my men. You gleefully took the reins of your precious Ekreissar, yet you command them from afar, not wanting to dirty your own hands. You sent a patrol straight into an ambush, costing us valuable lives." The man shook his head, the glow in his eyes receding to a barely perceivable pinkish hue, before bending over and lifting the khandar that had impaled him off the ground. "I should offer you the same fate as the others. Or perhaps I should give you over to the Dezren to do with as they wish? I'm sure they would find ways to entertain themselves...."

"Please, Lord Clovis, have mercy," Aeson stammered, falling to his knees on the dais. Ceredon flinched at his use of that title.

"I should kill you right now, but I will not. However, your life does come at a price."

"Name it, Lord Clovis. Anything you wish."

Clovis dipped his head low, staring from beneath his wide brow. "Tonight, you will lead the rangers yourself, heading due northeast, toward the rocky hills by the edge of the river. It is where the rebels are hiding, and you will wipe them out."

"You know this?" asked Ceredon, unable to stop himself from speaking.

"Yes."

"Then why the spectacle? Why not tell us sooner?"

"A show of strength, a test of knowledge, a test of *obedience*. A test you all failed."

Aeson stepped forward. "You should have told us your information, Lord Clovis. The deaths of your men could have been avoided...."

"Enough!" the human shouted as he lifted the bloody khandar. Spittle flew from his lips. "You will do as I say, and do it now. None of your people will try to stop me if I choose to end you. Considering the way you betrayed our trust before, you are lucky I don't devour each and every one of you where you stand."

Ceredon glanced at the faces of all who still lingered on the dais. He was confused by the latter part of the man's statement, but he completely understood the desire to rip Aeson's and Iolas's heads from their shoulders.

"I...but I...Lord—" said Aeson.

"Do *not* call me 'lord' again. Karak is the only lord of this land. I am but a servant."

"I apologize. But please, I tell you, I am three hundred years old, and my best days are behind me. The Ekreissar are more than capable of defeating the rebels without my involvement. It would be a death sentence for me to be at the front of the vanguard."

"Fight with your men and die by the sword, or refuse me and die by the sword," said Clovis, taking a menacing step forward. "Those are your only choices."

"I..."

Ceredon stepped forward. "I will join Aeson in the field," he said before Aeson could dig himself a deeper hole. His father reached for his sleeve in protest, but Ceredon gracefully moved beyond his grasp. "I am young and capable, and I will keep him safe, if that is what he fears. I am confident that with my assistance, the rebellion will be snuffed out before this night is over, and our casualties will be few."

Clovis gazed at him with mild curiosity. "The son of the Neyvar, offering his services to the realm? Who is it you do this for? Whose name will you shout when every last one of the insurgents is dead?"

"Karak's," Ceredon answered. The name felt dirty on his tongue, and he almost gagged on it.

The human laughed.

"Is that so? You turn your prayers to my god now?"

"Karak has proven mighty, while Celestia has abandoned us. Tell me, Clovis, what reason would I have *not* to fall before him beyond tradition and stubborn pride?"

Clovis seemed to mull this over for a moment.

"Very well," he said finally. "At dusk you will depart. I want none to return until the deed is done."

With that, Clovis pivoted on his heels and stormed away, following the trail of blood that led toward the rear of the palace, where the dungeon entrance was located. He seemed to be limping, and his shoulders appeared narrower. It almost looked like he was deflating before their eyes, as if whatever magics had healed the wound in his chest were now sapping the rest of his body. Ceredon had to fight the urge to follow him, for he desperately wished to know what went on in that dungeon, but a regiment of humans guarded it day and night, and he knew he would never get close. Unfortunately—or *fortunately*, depending on what he might find— the dungeons were the one part of the palace that could not be reached through Lord Orden's tunnels.

When he turned around, his father was shaking his head at him. The Neyvar pursed his lips and stormed back into the palace, followed closely by Iolas. To the undiscerning eye, Neyvar Ruven might appear disappointed, but Ceredon had seen enough of his father over the past few months to know better. It was thinly veiled fear that the man was feeling.

Aeson grabbed his elbow, squeezing tightly. Ceredon slowly craned his neck to look at his father's cousin, member of the Triad, the mastermind of the torture of the Stonewood Dezren, and violently jerked his arm away.

"You insult me with your actions," Aeson said, brimming with false confidence now that Clovis was out of earshot. "Clovis is only human, and I do not require protection, especially not yours."

"You were the one who bowed before him," he said.

Aeson sneered. "It is part of the game. You are but a child. Your father should have paid more attention to you when you were younger. Perhaps then you would not be so useless."

Ceredon breathed deeply, shook his head, and marched away from the belligerent elf. His anger boiled over. If only Aeson knew how Ceredon had manipulated him, using whispers and carefully placed evidence to point the way toward the previous night's trap, he would not think him useless any longer. But he let the elf enjoy his false sense of superiority, for it was Aeson who would surely prove himself useful in the coming hours. Just like the Dezren who had been executed, he would prove how well he could bleed.

The moon was full, but a thick layer of clouds had rolled in, making the darkness nearly complete as a hundred Ekreissar rangers crept through the forest. The skilled rangers made nary a sound as they glided over the leaf-covered ground. The same could not be said for Aeson, who lacked the proper training. He had donned a green and brown outfit in place of his usual imperial robes and was forging a path at the head of the group, hacking away at the vines and branches that blocked his way instead of ducking beneath them or moving aside. Every so often he would grunt and swear, which Ceredon could tell drew the ire of the other rangers. Backward glances revealed a few rangers rolling their eyes, and some made gestures implying that they'd murder Aeson if he made another sound. It was a pleasing sight. The Quellan had long regarded the Triad as Celestia's voice, the few beyond reproach who held the Neyvar's ear. It was good to see that trend reverse itself.

"Ceredon, halt," Aeson said, and Ceredon felt the whole group wince at the noise. Ceredon did as he'd been asked. The other Ekreissar halted too, but Aeson motioned them onward. "Continue on to the rendezvous point. We will be there shortly."

"Why do we stay?" Ceredon asked after the last of the rangers disappeared farther into the forest. "Clovis insisted that we lead…"

"I don't care what that idiot insisted," Aeson said. "I told him I had information about Tantric's whereabouts, and he ignored me. Let the rest of the Ekreissar waste their time pursuing the rebel hideout. Tantric is close, and I will defeat him, taking the glory for my own and then shoving it right in Clovis's face. You are confident in your ability with a khandar, are you not?"

"I am. Why?"

"There are two of us and only one of him, and we are catching him unaware. He will be easy prey. Follow me."

Perfect, thought Ceredon.

They maneuvered through the brush, Aeson taking greater care this time to remain silent as they slid down the rocky descent on the other side. The roar of a waterfall soon reached their ears, and the air grew thick with moisture as they continued their downward trek. Finally, they stepped through the threshold of trees, and a lagoon of shimmering black water greeted them on the other side. The gulley was deep, far below sea level, and a nearly solid sheet of water thirty feet wide dumped runoff from the river into it. It was an entirely isolated refuge, invisible from the rest of the forest.

"Why are we here?" Ceredon whispered as he crept alongside Aeson.

"Tantric likes to bathe beneath a particular waterfall while his little nymphs treat him," Aeson said. "That waterfall resides right behind those trees, in the gulley...."

Aeson drew his sword as he approached the water's edge.

"There is a worn path over the stones," he said, having to raise his voice to be heard over the roaring waterfall. He seemed charged with enthusiasm. "We will take that."

"As you wish," Ceredon replied.

They stepped carefully over the moss-covered boulders as mist assaulted their faces. The path led behind the waterfall, which careened so far outward they were able to pass underneath it while remaining mostly dry. They found a wide mouth cut into the substratum of the rock face hidden by the falls, leading to a pitch-black tunnel. Aeson didn't so much as pause. He held his khandar out before him and stepped confidently into the mouth, scampering like a dancer in his excitement. Ceredon followed him in, keeping his own weapon sheathed.

The tunnel stretched steadily wider and taller. Sealed off from the outside world, there was no light to see, even with their capable eyes. Soon their steps began to echo, and they ran headlong into a solid wall.

"It is too dark," Aeson said.

Ceredon pulled a bag of tindersticks from his rucksack and struck one. When the flame blazed, he curled up a sheet of parchment and lit the top, forming a makeshift torch. Holding it out before him, he turned in every direction. They had entered a rounded cave, fifty feet in either direction, ending in jagged walls. The ceiling was too high for the light of the torch to reach.

"No one is here," Aeson said. He sounded disappointed.

"Perhaps the rumor was false," Ceredon said.

"Not this one."

"Are you so certain?"

Aeson gave him a glare.

"I heard of this place from the lips of Neretha, Tantric's estranged wife. He was to be here. That whore must have lied to me."

"Perhaps," Ceredon said. "But what if this is just the wrong waterfall, and there is another nearby? We should search the hills. There could be other gullies about."

Aeson shook his head, looking dejected. "No. This is the one. Neretha will feel my wrath when this is done. We must rejoin the Ekreissar before they get too far ahead."

"Very well. At your command."

Aeson turned to leave, but Ceredon remained still. His father's cousin offered him a queer, impatient look.

"I said we leave," he said.

Ceredon squinted, the light of the torch making the shadows around him dance. "I have one question I must ask," he said.

"So ask and let us get on with it."

"In the courtyard, Clovis mentioned something about betrayed trust. What was that about?"

Aeson shook his head and laughed.

"*That* is your question? Come—let us go. I have no time for this."

"I wish to know."

"It is none of your business."

"Humor me, Aeson. Humor the elf who will one day be your Neyvar. I would remember it fondly."

Aeson looked at him cockeyed. "Very well. Humans approached the Triad a year past, asking for a partnership. We were told the eastern deity would soon war with his brother and that we would be handed lands west of the Rigon if we assisted them. One of their conditions was that the delegation from Stonewood remain unharmed."

"Yet they *were* harmed," Ceredon said. "Cleotis Meln was killed, as were many others who had arrived for the betrothal."

"Yes. The Triad decided that while we would help the humans to rebuild the might of our people, we would not follow such specific demands, especially when they put the entire coup at risk. The Quellan are not slaves to a lesser race."

"Did my father know?"

Aeson laughed.

"You have much to learn if you are to be Neyvar one day, pup. Your father may be the face of our people, but we of the Triad pull the strings."

"So the executions…the random selection of prisoners to hang in the galleys outside the palace…that was the Triad's decision?"

Aeson offered him a wicked grin, raising his khandar in the process.

"No, that decision was mine. What better way to teach a lesson to dogs than by showing those dogs the price of disloyalty to their betters?"

"I can think of ways," Ceredon said, and that was when the cave filled with the light of many torches lit from above. Ropes descended to the ground and a multitude of forms slid down them. Aeson shrieked and backed away, whipping his khandar about, eyes wide with terror. Those who'd descended the ropes formed a circle around the two Quellan. They were tall, their flesh pale, their hair golden and light brown. One of the Dezren rebels stepped away from the others, a brusque sort, missing the pointed tip of one ear and with burn scars winding from the corner of his mouth down his neck. He held a maul in his hand.

Ceredon lifted his head in pride.

"Aeson, I introduce you to Tantric Thane, leader of the insurgency."

"You lit—" Aeson began.

Ceredon struck him across the cheek. Blood dribbled over Aeson's lips.

"No speaking," Ceredon said in a growl. "Did you know that Tantric's aunt lived in Stonewood, and that one of her daughters was serving as Audrianna Meln's handmaiden?"

Aeson stared at him, mouth agape, and said nothing.

Tantric swung downward with his maul, connecting with Aeson's hand. Bone shattered, the elf screamed, and the khandar he was holding clanked on the ground.

"Zoe Shendara was my niece," Tantric said, his voice dripping with hatred. "You remember her?"

"Get away from me!" screamed Aeson, gripping his pulverized hand with his good one.

"You had her murdered, you bastard. You ordered the death of a *child*. Celestia will never forgive you for that."

The circle of Dezren rebels closed, pinning Aeson down. One stretched out his left arm, holding it against the ground, and Tantric came down with the maul again. The *crunch* that followed echoed through the cave as Aeson's shrieks intensified in their urgency.

The rebel leader then tossed down his weapon, approached Ceredon, and threw his arm around him. He started leading him down the tunnel, away from Aeson's screams.

"Thank you for this," said Tantric. "We would not have survived this long without your assistance."

"Nor I without yours," Ceredon replied. He smiled, a bit sadly. "Neretha performed her part beautifully, but I fear what might happen to her should the humans discover her involvement."

Tantric laughed.

"I know," he said. "Don't worry about my wife. She is strong, and vicious as a wolf when cornered. She will keep our secrets safe, no matter who may attempt to pry them from her lips."

They paused in the middle of the tunnel, staring at the blue-black sheet of water that cascaded over the opening.

"Tell me, Tantric," said Ceredon, "what will happen to the Ekreissar?"

"A few will die, but not as many as I'd like. We've moved inland now, to a series of grottos near Lake Cor, but we set up a few traps beforehand. Spiked vines, swinging logs, that sort of thing. Though it is bothersome that the human knew about our old hideaway.... Perhaps I should press further to learn who has betrayed us."

Ceredon glanced into the darkness behind him. He could still hear Aeson screaming.

"And what about *him*?" he asked.

"The bastard will live through the night, perhaps even until tomorrow night. But the pain will be epic. He will *wish* he died much sooner, you can trust me on that."

"Good. However, you must do one thing for me now."

Tantric shrugged.

"Anything, just name it."

"You need to beat me."

Tantric narrowed his eyes. "Care to clarify?"

"You need to beat me. Do not hold back. Attack me mercilessly, as if I had just raped your daughter. Strike me until I lose consciousness. And then drag me out onto the path, beat me some more, and leave me there."

"Wait…why?" The battle-hardened elf looked visibly perplexed.

"We need this ruse to be believable," Ceredon replied. "I'll fall under suspicion, no matter what happens, but I was the last to be seen with Aeson before his disappearance. If I survive without harm…"

Tantric sighed. "Very well. I will do this, but I won't like it."

"I know. Consider this my payment for all the torment my people have inflicted on yours. Just make sure you do it well."

"I will. I happen to be an expert at this sort of thing."

Ceredon closed his eyes, and the beating began. Tantric proved his statement true, for the pain he doled out was indeed expert, and Ceredon lost consciousness before long.

CHAPTER

27

Roland felt elation for the first time since his tryst with Kaya on the rooftop of the Second Breath Inn. The survivors of Lerder had finally arrived at the Wooden Bridge, a structure as wide as ten men that stretched across the calmly flowing Corinth River. The planks lining the bottom were warped and darkened by age and weather, but when he dismounted his steed and took a few steps onto the bridge, he could feel its sturdiness beneath his feet. He smiled up at Kaya, who stood on the beaten dirt path of the Gods' Road with her younger sister. After many frightful days of weaving through the forest, carefully trailing Karak's forces and struggling to evade discovery—a difficult task for a group of two hundred frightened souls—they were finally on the verge of safety. Once they crossed the bridge, they could be in Mordeina in a week.

He stepped off the bridge, wrapped his arm around Kaya, and approached Azariah and Jaquiel, who stood to the side with the other nine Wardens, their elegant faces all exhausted. The humans from Lerder gathered behind them, impatiently milling about and casting furtive glances at the eastern expanse of road. At least

Azariah managed a smile. It was something Roland hadn't seen in far too long.

"We're here," Roland said.

"We are," replied Jaquiel.

"How safe is it?" asked Kaya.

Azariah seemed distracted, his eyes focused on the forest around them, but he still responded. "It will be quite safe," he said. "The bridge was Warden Boral's first handiwork, gods rest his soul. He designed it, and Ashhur helped him build it. It was across this very bridge that the first five hundred fair-skinned children of Ashhur crossed into the northwestern lands. Jaquiel was there that day."

Jaquiel nodded. "It has not been used often since…or at least, it *had* not been. It appears Ashhur has passed through here before us…and strengthened the bridge on his way."

"What makes you say that?" Roland asked.

"Look around you," said the Warden. "The Gods' Road is deeply rutted, and despite the recent rain you can still see the imprints in the dirt. There are new scuffs and scratches covering the bridge too, and it appears abnormally strong considering that it has not been maintained for ninety years. Also, sniff the air if you so desire. There is dung everywhere."

"There are also the remnants of many cookfires scattered about," added Azariah. "A large group of people clearly crossed this bridge not long ago. You can even see the remnants of carriage tracks on the other side."

"How can you be sure it was Ashhur?" Roland asked, feeling a bit of his elation slide way. "What if it was Karak's Army instead?"

Jaquiel knelt down and ran a finger along the looser dirt to the side of the Gods' Road, where there was a clear footprint.

"Most of the prints were made by bare feet, son. There were hundreds, if not thousands of people traipsing along the road wearing light moccasins. From what I saw of Karak's Army when I spied on them, they wore heavy boots."

"Then we're close to Ashhur," Kaya said, and there was no hiding the excitement in her voice. "We'll be safe soon!"

"I pray it is so," Azariah said, smiling at her. "Now we must get everyone across. We still have a few hours of sunlight left before nightfall. We might have steered away from Karak's forces, but we don't know when they will emerge from the forest. I want to be far away when they do."

They started to cross, a relatively slow process given the unevenness of the bridge. It creaked as they piled atop it, and the hemp rope trusses that held the planks together pulled taut from the weight. The thirty thick pillars beneath the bridge, rising from the river like wayward trees, groaned as well, but the bridge itself hardly swayed.

Roland stood off to the side, tapping the handle of the sword on his hip as he watched his fellow survivors cautiously step onto the bridge, one after the other. He would nod at each as they passed him, offering words of good tidings. The fatigued people offered him the same in return, their weary eyes brightening with hope. That same hope blossoming inside him, Roland leaned over and kissed Kaya on the cheek. She blushed and nuzzled up against him, and suddenly, with safety seemingly within reach, all Roland could think about was making love to her again.

Perhaps I can give her what she desires....Perhaps I will make her with child. We can be a family, safe with Ashhur....

That thought disappeared the moment a strange noise reached his ears, as if a brisk wind were kicking up. He heard a *thunk* by his feet and looked down to see the shaft of an arrow bobbing from the ground. His mind blanked at the sight of it. He turned his head toward the forest's distant border, and saw them....At least twenty riders were racing toward them, their bodies covered in black and silver armor, swords and axes held high above their heads. Roland gasped, and Kaya swiveled around, screaming when she caught sight of the advancing men.

"Go!" shouted Jaquiel. Only half the people had begun crossing, and the black-haired Warden ran around the rest, pushing them, shoving them, trying to get them all onto the bridge at once. Everyone began to shout in panic, and a logjam formed at the mouth of the bridge. A few fell, trampled underfoot while others pushed their way forward in desperation.

Roland stood frozen as he watched the rushing soldiers fan out, forming a straight line. While their steeds charged onward, four of them lifted bows, nocked arrows, pulled back the strings, and released. The arrows arced toward the survivors, their steel tips gleaming in the late afternoon sun.

Only one found purchase in flesh, driving into the back of a young woman at the rear of the bridge. She fell to her knees, wailing, her hand reaching around to try and grasp the shaft as she collapsed in a heap. Roland looked at her, his mouth hanging open, then glanced back at the approaching soldiers. It was then that he noticed the one riding at center, the one with flowing brown hair and glowing red eyes.

Jacob. Two hundred yards away and closing fast.

That broke Roland's paralysis. He rushed to the side of the bridge and tried to conduct traffic. Someone grabbed the girl with the arrow in her back and lugged her across. Kaya helped as best she could, but she was frightened and shaking.

"Go with them!" Roland shouted at her frantically.

She shook her head, crying.

He shoved her in the back. "Just go! I'll catch up with you on the other side!"

Kaya's father appeared and grabbed hold of her hand. He tugged his daughter away, shoving his shoulder into the mass of humanity. After they disappeared into the horde on the bridge, Roland turned, sword in hand, to face the soldiers who were fast approaching. He rushed over to Azariah, who stood with the rest of the Wardens along with ten brave yet terrified men, forming a wall of flesh in front of the bridge. More arrows sailed overhead, and more screams erupted from behind them, but Roland didn't turn and look. If Kaya had been struck...

"We must meet them head-on!" yelled Jaquiel.

The Warden ran forward, his long legs churning as he wielded a two-headed ax above his head. The Wardens followed his lead, and after a moment of hesitation, so did the men. Roland opened his mouth and bellowed, mimicking Jaquiel's posture with his sword. It felt so heavy, crushing down on his shoulders. Shit, he didn't even know how to use the thing—not really—but his heart was beating too rapidly, his lungs burning too painfully for him to worry about it much.

He ran as fast as he could, ignoring the line of soldiers and focusing instead on Jacob. His former master must have seen him as well, for he pushed his steed even faster. Karak's soldiers were close now, so close that the sound of hammering hooves was deafening, so close that Roland could almost smell the acrid breath of the horses as they panted. Jacob's image blocked out all else, and Roland watched as he swung his arm back, lifting a sword twice as long as Roland's and twice as shiny as well. The blade began to surge forward and Roland's heart nearly stopped. *He's going to kill me—he really is!* A part of him had not thought it possible; he'd only disobeyed Jacob once, in the aftermath of the First Man's betrayal of Ashhur. Could he really be blamed for that?

Roland dropped to his knees, holding his pitiable sword out defensively. Steel met steel with a raucous clank, the vibration jarring his molars and bringing roaring pain to his fingers. He fell to the side, clutching his hands and hollering, as the soldiers' horses galloped past him.

Screams and more clashing of steel rang out all around him. Roland lifted his head, watched as the brave Wardens who had stepped to the forefront were cut down. Ribbons of blood filled the air, accompanied by agonizing moans and whimpers. Jaquiel collapsed, bleeding, clutching at the stump of his left arm. The surviving Wardens and men turned to flee, but they too were struck down, blades tearing into their backs, hacking off limbs, severing heads. Still on his stomach, the world a dizzying array of death and horses, Roland bellowed Azariah's name.

But his friend had not been harmed. When Jacob's horse turned, facing him once more, Roland caught sight of Azariah, who had retreated to the bridge. The Warden knelt, hands clasped before him, head thrown back as he shouted words to the heavens. The soldiers on horseback bore down on him, but Roland could not watch, for Jacob's black steed came charging again. He rolled out of the way just as the blade swiped over where he'd been, swinging so low that it sliced through the muddy earth, flinging clumps of it on the upswing.

Roland scampered to his feet and tried to run toward the tall grass covering the southern barrier of the Gods' Road, but his clothes were so soaked with sweat and muck that they clung to his body, making his strides awkward. He stumbled, hearing the *ca-clomp* of Jacob's horse wheeling about once more. He was sure Jacob would kill him this time. In his mind it became a foregone conclusion. *I will never see Azariah again, never lie with Kaya, never have a family.* Resignation made his feet slow. *It will not be so bad…only a moment, and then it will be over….Perhaps Celestia will be kind, and I will get to see Brienna again on the other side….*

Roland fell to his knees, unable to run anymore. Head bowed, he clasped his hands, begging Ashhur for the end to be swift. But instead of experiencing pain and the flash of death, he heard the howling of wolves. Panicked shouts quickly followed. His curiosity overcoming his fear, he tilted his head back and peered over his shoulder. Terror gripped him as he laid eyes on the largest wolves he'd ever seen. They came leaping from the trees, only instead of running on all fours, they loped like the monkeys that he had seen when Jacob brought him to one of the many of the small islands that peppered the southern coast of Paradise. There were six of them, with massive, muscle-bound arms in the place of front legs. As Roland watched, one of the beasts used those powerful arms to knock a soldier from his horse as if the man weighed as little as a paper doll. He fell to the ground, his armor clinking, and the wolf-man tore into him without delay.

Roland's bewildered mind could hardly interpret what his eyes were seeing. Daring to feel hope, he looked over at Azariah, and his confusion only grew. Where once there had been plain earth, now a great wall of rock jutted out from the ground, at least six feet tall and fifteen feet across. The leading soldier's horse crashed into it as Roland watched, pitching its rider into the stone. As he lay there, another wolf-man leapt atop his body, teeth tearing into flesh, until another soldier rode past, skewering the creature with a sword through its chest.

The First Man sat high atop his horse, a furious expression on his face as he watched the battle between beast and man rage before him; Roland had become an afterthought. Seizing the opportunity to act on the fiery rage that flooded him, Roland turned. The First Man, Jacob Eveningstar, his longtime friend and master, was now willing to murder him without a word spoken first? He raced toward the man.

Roland didn't slow until he collided with the side of the black horse, shoving Jacob's dangling foot upward as hard as his strong arms would allow. The impact knocked Roland's breath out of him. He fell to his rump while the First Man careened sideways from his saddle, hitting the ground with a wet *thump* and a surprised shout. The steed, frightened, took off.

Quick as a cat, Jacob's head swung around to face him. His eyes still glowed, but they were dimmer now, more of a light pink than a burning red. He scurried to his feet and picked up his sword, which was skewered in the ground beside him. Having developed no real plan, Roland searched frantically for his own blade. Not remembering where he had dropped it, he scooted backward on his rump, feet kicking up mud as he slid.

"*You!*" Jacob roared, stalking toward him.

"Stop!" shouted Roland. He felt so foolish now, so stupid and reckless. "Please, Jacob, no!"

Jacob stopped mere feet in front of him. He dropped the sword and brought up his opposite hand, fingers bent into claws.

"*Hemorrhage,*" he said, his voice sounding like a snake's hiss. Roland kept scooting backward, feeling a sudden, intense tightening in his gut. Quick as it came, the sensation passed. Jacob stared at him, one eyebrow raised higher than the other, lips twisted into a tiny line in the center of his face. His hair, once dark and wavy, was slicked down with muck. He thrust his hand forward.

"*Crumple,*" he said, and this time Roland felt his head go dizzy, his arms and legs tingling as if they had fallen asleep and were now awakening. Again it passed in mere moments. Jacob drew back his hand, staring at his fingers as if they were broken. The confusion passed, and a disgusted look passed over his face as he lifted his sword above his head.

"You betrayed me," he said. He offered no other words before taking a step forward, preparing to strike.

Roland squeezed his eyes shut and screamed, finding it hard to channel his earlier acceptance of death. It was so much harder now that it was here before him, in the angry grip of a man he had once called friend. Yet the fatal blow did not come. Instead, over the din of the battle between soldier and beast, he heard the sound of thumping hooves and a startled cry of pain. He opened his eyes to see Jacob sprawled out on the ground, clutching at the side of his now bleeding head. His sword lay far away, almost sunken into the muddy earth.

A horse rode into view, and down jumped Azariah, a maul held tight in his grasp.

"And you betrayed Ashhur," he said, staring down at the prone First Man.

Jacob glared up at him, his eyes now back to their original soft blue tint.

"I betrayed no one," he growled. "My actions were noble, you bastard! There is only one true god in this land, only one who will bring your wards to greatness, and it is not Ashhur. I did what I thought was best, what I *know* is best. Search in me, Warden. See the truth in the words I speak."

Azariah hesitated, the maul in his hands lowering ever so slightly.

"I sense no lie in your words, Jacob, but you speak a truth shrouded in gray." The Warden looked deeply saddened, almost beyond repair. "You speak no truth at all," he whispered. "I wonder if you ever have."

"You're a fool, Azariah. Always have been. And my name is *Velixar.*"

With those words, Jacob lunged toward Azariah. Roland watched as Azariah sidestepped his former master's swipe, swinging the maul around and slamming the handle into the back of Jacob's skull. Jacob fell face-first into the muck, a muted gurgle leaking from his lips. The Warden then hefted the weapon high in the air, prepared to bring its spiked head down for the killing blow. He stood there for a long moment it seemed, frozen in time. He slowly lowered the maul, letting it dangle in his grasp as if it weighed more than the world itself.

The Warden hung his head, then looked at Roland in dismay.

"I cannot," he said. Tears ran down his cheeks.

Roland forced himself off the ground. Beyond them, on the other side of the Gods' Road, the soldiers and the remaining three wolf-men were still locked in combat. The soldiers were winning. Roland looked at his friend and opened his mouth, but no sound came out.

"Gifts from our god," Azariah whispered. "They will not last long. Come, we must hurry."

After one final glance at Jacob's unmoving body, Azariah mounted his patiently waiting horse and helped Roland climb onto the rear of the saddle. He then whipped the reins, and they moved away from the melee in a wide arc, circumventing the barricade of earth Azariah had magically summoned as they approached the Wooden Bridge. Roland eyed the nine dead Wardens and ten dead men from Lerder, and he offered a prayer to Ashhur that they would find their way safely through Afram to the Golden Forever. The horse's hooves thumped onto the bridge, and he thanked the gods that none of the corpses they passed had Kaya's curly black hair, even though the thought filled him with guilt.

They had almost reached the other side when Roland lurched forward, his chest feeling strangely tight. He tasted salty liquid in his mouth that he couldn't keep down. It dribbled over his lips and down his chin. He glanced at his own chest, saw the red liquid there, and then the thin brown shaft jutting from the torn section of his filthy tunic. Roland felt his whole being go numb.

"Az?" he said. "I think…I think I see…"

Azariah turned, saw the arrow jutting out of him, and paled. He started shouting something, but Roland couldn't hear it, couldn't hear anything as he felt the world growing dark, his body strangely foreign and no longer needing him anymore.

CHAPTER

28

Avila marched her horse back and forth in front of the sixteen prisoners. They were dressed in roughspun, their faces dirty, their eyes downcast. Their unnamed village burned behind them, its protective wall shattered.

Letting out a sigh, Avila examined each and every face before her. The sixteen were all old. It had been the same in the other settlements they'd recently liberated. No young men or Wardens had stayed behind to fight. Just the old and sick. Her nerves were frayed, and her men were growing lazy and foul tempered.

Feeling a tug on her hair, Avila glanced behind her. Willa, sitting firmly on the rear of the saddle with her arms wrapped around Avila's waist, gazed up at her with innocent blue eyes.

"Miss Avila, will they follow Karak too?" the girl asked.

"We shall see, young one."

Her soldiers, formed into ranks behind her, shuffled on restless feet. She spied Malcolm standing at the forefront, his helm resting in the crook of his arm as his one good eye stared at her with interest. His sword hand flexed. She knew what he wished her to do: *There is no mercy. There is order, or there is death.* Once more Avila looked at the little girl.

I give my own mercy, she thought, her heart welling with pride. *Karak has granted me that freedom.*

She nudged her mare toward the awaiting prisoners. One of them, a woman with thinning white hair, fell to her knees and wept. Avila nodded, drew Integrity, and pointed it toward the ground.

"You have been liberated!" she shouted at them. "Karak has shown his compassion by allowing you to live. All who relinquish belief in the false deity of Paradise, fall to your knees like your sister has done. You will be granted a life of liberty for the rest of your days."

The woman who had collapsed looked up at her with confusion and then raised her hands. At first Avila thought she was about to sing Karak's praises, but the elderly men beside her took hold of her arms, lifting her up. She stood there, swaying, head down, white hair dangling in front of her face. None moved to kneel.

Another woman stepped forward, stared at Avila with sadness in her eyes, and began to sing. The rest of the sixteen joined in, one after another, until the morning air was filled with joyous song. Avila recognized the tune and the words coming from their mouths; it was one of the songs of the Wardens, taught to her when she was still a child, just a year or so removed from her mother's breast.

The singing echoed throughout the valley. Avila gaped at the sixteen in disbelief. Not only had they turned aside the chance to live, they were actively denouncing Karak with their song. It was an audacious act, one she had not expected. Those who had been given this same offer in the previous three settlements had acquiesced immediately. Avila felt her soldiers tense behind her, felt Malcolm's hard stare on her back. Lifting Integrity, she pointed it at the sixteen, made a quick swiping motion. It did nothing to silence them; their song only grew louder.

"Enough!" she shouted, her voice cracking so that she sounded like a pubescent girl instead of the Lord Commander of Karak's

Army. The sixteen closed their eyes, lifted their chins to the sky, and kept right on singing. Avila spotted movement behind her, and she knew exactly who it was.

"These are *my* prisoners, Captain," she told Malcolm, halting his path with her sword. "Mine to do with as I choose."

Malcolm stared up at her, head tilted to the side. Strangely enough, he did not seem angered by Avila's show of authority; he appeared more intrigued than anything. He bowed his head and rejoined the soldiers to the rear.

Avila knew what she must do.

"You must get down now, little Willa," she said, turning to look at Willa. "Miss Avila has duties to attend to."

Willa glanced at her sword. Avila followed her gaze and saw the child's reflection in the blade. "You're going to cut them, aren't you?" the girl asked.

"I am," she replied.

"Why?"

"Remember your lessons? To worship Ashhur is to turn away from Karak, and to turn away from Karak is to invite chaos into your life. It is a mortal sin, and one that cannot go unpunished."

Willa sucked in her lips, looking to be deep in concentration. "But what if they don't know any better?" the girl finally asked. "What if they just want to sing pretty, and they need a good teacher, like you?"

"Well," Avila began, but no reply came to her.

"I'll talk to them, Miss Avila," Willa said. "Can I? Please?"

She stared at the girl, uncertainty washing over her. She knew hundreds of eyes watched her this very moment, knew that her men were judging her. But in that moment, she realized she didn't care. Sheathing Integrity, she threw her leg over the saddle and dismounted, then helped Willa down as well.

"I'll do good," the girl said. "I promise."

With that, Willa toddled toward the sixteen. Almost as soon as she reached the old woman in front, the one who had sung the first note, the song faltered. The woman gawked down at the young girl, who was insistently yanking on the front of her smock.

"What is it, child?"

Willa beckoned her forward with her finger, and the old woman bent her arthritic back so the girl could whisper in her ear. The old woman nodded once, twice, and then gave Willa a soft smile. By that time the others had stopped singing as well, staring at Willa and the old woman. They gathered around the two of them, and Avila could hear soft murmurs from the knot of wrinkled flesh.

When finally they ceased their talk, the elders nodded at the young girl with the bouncing golden curls as she skipped away from them. A few even had the audacity to smile. The old woman who had first spoken with Willa stepped forward. She bowed her head in Avila's direction while those behind her milled about.

Willa took her place at Avila's side, and Avila felt a tiny hand slip into hers. The little girl was beaming, all dimples and tiny teeth as she stared up at her. Avila's heart fluttered as she brought her attention to her captives.

"Do you renounce Ashhur?" she asked once more. "Do you reject chaos and allow Karak into your hearts?"

"No," they all replied, one after the other. Their voices sounded weary yet strong. Beside Avila, Willa let loose a high-pitched whimper filled with anguished surprise.

Avila frowned at the young girl. "You wish to seal your fate in the eyes of Karak?" she said to the sixteen.

The old woman who had begun the song lifted her eyes.

"Our god is our god," she said. "Ashhur is love and forgiveness, and we will not forget that, even though the sprite has begged us otherwise."

Avila turned toward her charges, summoning Malcolm and four underlings to come forward. She then addressed the sixteen once more.

"You have been found guilty of blasphemy," she proclaimed. "The penalty is death." She looked to Malcolm. "Be brutal in the face of our god, captain."

"As always, Lord Commander," said Malcolm, smiling.

The captain nodded to his underlings and began to slide Darkfall from its sheath on his back. Willa broke down in tears, causing the sixteen to frown and shake their heads. The old woman even mouthed *I'm sorry* to her. The girl started to tug violently on Avila's armor. She glanced down, saw those tiny, perfectly smooth cheeks stained with tears.

"Please no, Miss Avila," Willa said, her lower lip quivering. The girl's eyes kept darting toward Malcolm, who drew ever closer to the blasphemers.

"You know what must happen, Willa," Avila reminded her. "They have decided their fates."

"But they *sang*."

"Yes…the songs of Ashhur. They turned their backs on Karak."

Willa tugged harder on her armor. "But maybe they just don't know better, Miss Avila!" she cried. "Couldn't we just…capture them? You could teach them like you've taught me. Wouldn't Karak like that better than killing them?"

Avila stared down at her, uncertainty washing over her. When she tore her eyes away from the girl, she saw Malcolm grab the old woman at the front of the sixteen and toss her to the ground while the four underlings prepared a large stone to place beneath her head. She looked at Willa once more, saw the tears that were now flowing in torrents.

What would Karak want? Converts or destruction?

"Captain, *stop*!" she called out.

Malcolm slowly turned toward her, Darkfall held out by his side. His good eye narrowed. Willa squeezed her hand, the warmth of her flesh giving Avila strength.

"These sixteen are not to be harmed," she declared. "Bring them to the other converts. They will be shown the glory of the Divinity, whether or not they wish it."

The captain cocked his head, a look of disappointment on his scarred face, but he did not move.

"*Now*, Captain Gregorian," she said. "Get them out of my sight."

Malcolm stepped back and sheathed Darkfall while the underlings helped the old woman back to her feet, leading the sixteen to the massive tent where the converts of Paradise were kept. The soldiers gathered around, many of them shaking their heads in apparent disgust. But they did not concern Avila. Her focus was on the sixteen; she watched the expressions on their faces, the tiny waves the women gave Willa as they passed her. Avila then looked down at the girl, whose smile stretched wide across her rosebud lips as she returned their waves. She heard Malcolm shouting for the men to return to the camp on the other side of the Gods' Road. The repetitive clomping of their boots kicked up a massive cloud of dust, echoing the smoke that rose into the air from the smoldering village.

Only after her soldiers had disappeared over the ridge did she lift Willa into the saddle. The girl was still smiling, and she seemed reluctant to release Avila's hand. When she finally did, Avila removed her glove and petted the child's satiny golden locks.

"I'm sorry they didn't say yes to Karak," Willa said.

"I know, and so am I. But worry not, young one, they will. We will make sure of that."

The girl kicked her legs happily. "Good."

"I am curious, though. What did you tell them?"

Willa's head bounced from side to side.

"I told them they could learn to love Karak just like I had. That I really, really wished they would, because I didn't want to see them get cut."

Avila chuckled. "Very smart of you, Willa. Very smart indeed. I am proud of you."

"Thanks, Miss Avila."

She patted the girl's back. "I give praise where praise is due, little one. Now slide back onto the saddle and hold on tight. We are heading back to camp. I think Varshrom the cook is making mushroom stew this evening, and I, for one, am famished."

Willa's cherubic face scrunched up in a grimace. "I don't like mushrooms."

Avila leaned in and whispered in her ear. "I don't either, little one. But I hear they will have lemon cakes too."

The little girl's eyes widened with excitement. "Yes!" she said in an urgent whisper. "I *love* lemon cakes!"

Avila thought her heart could melt.

✦

She watched the girl sleep, her tiny chest rising and falling, her rosebud lips parting every so often to mutter dream-speak. Avila stroked her hair the whole time, unable to stop herself, even when Willa whimpered and rolled onto her side. There was no mistaking it; for as much as she might have once wished it weren't the case, Avila was smitten.

Not that it was such a bad thing. Having spent countless days with the little girl, Avila had begun to give her the same sort of doting attention she'd received from her own mother at that age. It felt as if she had discovered something missing from her life. She had always felt a sort of emptiness, a hole that she'd once thought could only be filled by Karak. Now that hole was slowly disappearing. She lifted Willa's limp hand and kissed her chubby little fingers one after another. With each kiss she promised the child that she would never leave her, that once Karak won the war she would build a homestead at the base of the mountain range that bore her family's name, and they would settle there. She would become a mother instead of a soldier. Perhaps she would even find a mate to fill her with seed, giving Willa a sister or brother, perhaps several, a whole lot of brats who would bicker and cry and fight and call her *Mother*. She would get old and die, and she would be happy for it.

She thought again of her own mother, whom she had not seen for nearly a year. She missed her so, just as she did her father, although she would never have admitted it in the past, for it would have meant admitting to weakness, and Lord Commander Avila Crestwell was not weak.

Sighing, she placed Willa's hands over her chest and rose from her lounging position. Fastening a curtain to shield the girl from the brightness, she lit the candles on her desk. The light danced off the canvas walls of the pavilion, creating shadows that became formless monsters, beasts bent on destroying the child behind the curtain. There was nothing out there, she knew, but she shivered nonetheless. That was another thing Avila had learned since she'd taken Willa in; while she felt no fear in the face of death, the thought of harm coming to the girl filled her with dread.

She sat down in her chair and moaned at the sudden onset of a backache. This was new as well; her bones constantly throbbed, her hands and feet felt hot all the time, and she was having trouble sleeping. She had often heard of the healing magic possessed by those most devout to Ashhur, and right about now she wished for a touch of it. Her hand came up to trace the scars Crian had given her.

Yes, I could use some healing magic indeed.

Something soft scraped past the entrance flap of the pavilion, making her jump. She instinctively reached for Integrity (*Crian's old sword*), but it was far away, hanging from a hook beside her bedroll. Tensing, she glanced behind her, listened for Willa's tiny breaths, and then turned toward the entrance once more. A hand snuck through the fold, pulled the flap aside. For a fleeting moment she thought it was a demon of living shadow, coiling and writhing and ready to suck the life from her little girl. But then Malcolm stepped into the pavilion, and that image faded.

"What are you doing here?" she asked harshly. Realizing she wore nothing but her smallclothes, she hastily grabbed the blanket from the back of her chair, draping it over her body. The impulse surprised her. She had never been one for modesty.

"I wish to talk," Malcolm said, respectfully bowing his head.

"It is late, Captain, and I require sleep. Return in the morning."

"This is important, Lord Commander."

"Important enough to deny my orders?"

Malcolm raised the eyebrow over his good eye. "As a matter of fact, yes."

She shook her head in resignation and kicked at the chair opposite her, knocking it back a foot. Malcolm took the hint and approached, sitting down beside her. His posture was rigid, professional, but then again, that was Malcolm. She had only seen him drop his soldier's discipline once, and that had been the night she'd kicked him out of her bed.

"So speak, Captain. I do not wish to be up all hours."

Malcolm leaned forward, his elbows jabbing into his knees. His fingers traced the knobby scars that crossed over his milky left eye.

"Did I ever tell you how I got these scars?"

"Everyone knows, Captain. They were given to you by the Final Judges, when you proved your loyalty to Karak and earned your life."

"Yes, but do you know why I was placed before the Judges in the first place?"

Avila drummed her fingers on the desk, waiting.

"I was a wild youth," he said with a grimace. "I loved my liquor, I loved to fight, and I loved the ladies. I entered the academy, expecting a high position in the City Watch. It was the same position my father had, so I was owed it, right? That's how I felt anyway. I was lazy, too self-confident for my own good, and I thought my future would be handed to me.

"I lagged in my training, and Vulfram Mori, who was Watch Captain at the time, sent me away. My father tossed me from the house, saying I had brought disrespect to the family, and my mother did nothing to stop him." He smiled then, though his expression brimmed with disappointment. "That evening I went to the tavern, spent countless hours drowning in my cups. A certain girl struck my fancy, and though I cannot remember her name, I remember her face clearly. Eyes like sapphires, hair like soft wheat, skin pale and supple. I advanced on her, but she wanted none of it. Just like my father, she turned me away. For the rest of the night I watched her laugh and dance with the other maidens, even steal a kiss or two from dullards who could not hold a candle to my strength or station."

His voice changed, growing cold, distant. Avila shivered, guessing at what came next.

"When the girl left, I followed her. I dragged her into an alley beside the tavern, and then I raped her, stabbed her, and left her to die. Afterward, I made my way to my parents' house and killed them both as they slept."

Avila swallowed hard, unsure of how to react. The deed was horrific, far worse than she'd anticipated, yet he spoke of it as though someone else had performed the vile crimes. She felt scared to speak, lest she break the spell and release the drunken, murderous beast from his tale.

"A member of the Watch caught me later," Malcolm continued. "I was drunk off my heels and covered in blood. Someone had found the girl's body by then, and it didn't take them long to put it all together. They found my parents soon after, and by then my fate was sealed. I was arrested and brought before the court, where the Minister sentenced me to death. I called on the Judges, as was my right."

Rocking forward in his chair, Malcolm met Avila's gaze.

"Have you ever been in the same room as those lions?" he asked.

"Of course."

Malcolm chuckled.

"Then you know the Judges are truly frightening creatures. I'm not one to scare easily, but the first time I saw them in that arena I knew true fear. I looked deep into their eyes as they stalked me, and I saw a world charred and broken, a world of death and desolation in which there was no law, no order. It was the underworld, of that I am certain—the embodiment of chaos. Then I saw my own reflection in their eyes. The chaos I saw in their eyes was the same chaos they saw in me. I'm not sure how I knew, but I did. I had become an agent of everything our god strives against. My life was one of slothfulness, pride, anger, drunkenness, and hate. Worthless. I felt more insignificant than the scum at the bottom of a festering wheat barrel. I fell to my knees, but I did not pray for forgiveness, for there is no such thing. Sin can only be absolved through sacrifice, as Karak has long taught. So I lifted my chin to the ceiling of that damned cold arena and offered my neck to the Judges so they could rip it out, releasing me from my sin."

He rocked again, and he swallowed as if he'd just chewed something.

"Yet they did not kill me. Instead the male, Kayne, held me down while Lilah raked my face, taking my left eye and scarring me for life, ensuring that all who look on me know of my past sins. They then ambled back to their cages, leaving me alive and breathing. After that, Highest Crestwell took me into employ in the Palace Guard. Not once, not in all my days and nights of servitude, have I ever forgotten my sins, nor that the servants of our Lord allowed me to live."

He stopped then, staring at her with his one good eye without moving.

"An interesting story," Avila said, careful to keep her tone neutral. "Though I fail to see why the telling of it was worth disobeying my orders and interrupting my rest in the middle of the night."

"I tell it so you may understand me when I say that though we bear similar scars, we are very different." He reached out to touch the side of her face. Avila batted his hand away, and he frowned at her. "You have lost your way, Lord Commander. You have forgotten that forgiveness is foreign to us. You have turned your back on our god."

Avila's mouth dropped open. "How *dare* you enter my chambers and speak so to me? Have you forgotten your place, *Captain*?"

"I have not," Malcolm said. "I am here to be your council, your advisor. And I advise you that the path you are taking is wrong."

"I am a free women, a child of the First Family of Neldar. I will take whatever path I choose."

"Even if that path leads away from Karak? You are being influenced by a demon in an angel's guise." He pointed toward the curtain hiding Willa. "You have fallen from Karak's grace. Sacrifice is the only way to make amends. Those whose lives you spared today were unworthy of such a gift. They should have been cut down where they stood."

"They are to be converted," Avila answered. Inside she was shaking. "Our purpose is to bring order to the people of the west, not death. Which would Karak rather have, an army of corpses, or an army of believers?"

Malcolm shrugged. "It matters not what I think, only what I know you must do. If you do not sacrifice them, then another is required. I know you love the girl…and now you must cut her down to prove to Karak you still love him most of all."

Avila stared him down, her two eyes to his one.

"Get…out," she seethed, then shot up from her chair to retrieve Integrity.

"You wake up each morning sore," Malcolm said. "You suffer from headaches, your muscles spasm, and your legs grow weaker each day. Where once your hands were smooth, now they are rough to the touch."

On hearing his words, she stopped in her tracks and turned to him. Malcolm approached her slowly, measuring each step, until he was close enough to touch her. He lifted his hand and traced the outline of her eye with his finger.

"There are grooves here now, the creases of age. They are small at the moment, but they will grow larger, more prevalent, as time goes on. You are no longer ageless, Avila. Karak is no longer first in your heart."

She closed her eyes as he sketched out the new lines in her flesh. He didn't lie. She had noticed the signs herself. His hand withdrew, and he held her close, palm resting on the small of her back.

"You have lived your whole life in servitude, Avila," he said softly. "I understand this. You have removed yourself from people, from the human pleasures all of Karak's children seek out every day. You want to feel like a woman. Let it be me who makes you feel that way. Use my body, decimate it if you wish, wring my throat if you must. That is my sacrifice to you, so that you may find your way back to our god. But you must turn away from this lie that has enraptured you. There can be no more forgiving those that do not deserve forgiveness. This child is slowly warping you, turning you into a creature I do not know. I want the old Avila back, the woman who was the most trusted child of the Highest himself, who judged the guilty with swiftness and brutality, who would never once think of turning her back on her god. That woman, the true Lord Commander, needs to return. Do you not want the same?"

Avila let out a short gasp of air, confused by his words, his touch.

"I do," she whispered, though there was no thought behind the words. All she felt was horror at the idea that Karak might be displeased with her.

"Then do what must be done," Malcolm whispered. "Lay her on the altar of order and become the lioness once more."

Her eyes snapped open. She saw Malcolm's face before her, the candlelight washing out his features into sickly yellows and reds. She glanced at the curtain, then back at his nodding head. In her mind's eye she saw Willa, broken and bloodied, laid out on the ground just like the girl Malcolm had raped and murdered in his life before. *Karak would never demand such atrocities!* she silently screamed. Rage filled her, and she shoved him away. Dashing to her bedroll, she yanked Integrity from its scabbard and pointed it at him. Despite her anger, the tip did not waver.

"Get out," she said, her voice low and seething. "Get out and do not return to my quarters."

Malcolm straightened himself, his soldier's resolve restored, and bowed.

"As you wish, Lord Commander. I only desired to help."

"To help? To *help*? Instructing me to slaughter an innocent child is not helping, you bastard."

He shook his head.

"Innocence is a false principle," he said quietly. "It saddens me you that have become so lost."

"Leave. *Now.*"

The captain turned and headed for the entrance, pausing once he shoved the flap aside. He turned to her one final time.

"We will reach the Wooden Bridge in two days' time," he said. "The other divisions will be there, Karak with them. Do not think that the changes in you will go unnoticed by the Divinity. I will tell him myself if I must. My loyalty is to him, Avila, not you. Best you remember that."

Malcolm slipped out the entrance, and the flap fell down behind him, fluttering like ocean waves. Panic hitting her full in the chest, Avila dashed across the pavilion, tore aside Willa's curtain, and dropped down beside the girl, gathering her in an embrace. The child's eyes flickered opened, and she offered a sleepy yawn.

"What's wrong?" she asked.

"Nothing, little one. Close your eyes. There is nothing to worry about. Nothing to fear."

For the rest of that night Avila didn't sleep, proving how little she believed her own words.

CHAPTER

T he back of his head throbbed, and when he touched the sore spot, he felt a massive knot beneath his sodden hair. It was a burning pain, very much unlike the gash on the side of his face, which stung like a hundred needles poking him at once. Velixar grunted and spit onto the wet ground. He peered over his shoulder, spied the Wooden Bridge sitting there vacant, surrounded by the corpses of Wardens, wolf-men, and humans, both his soldiers and those who had tried to defend the bridge. He would have cursed aloud at the sight of them, but a hacking fit overtook him and he doubled over.

"Here, take it."

Velixar saw a man holding a cloth down to him, and he took it, using it to wipe the phlegm from his lips, the blood from his cheeks.

"Thank you," he said, offering the cloth back. Captain Wellington stuffed it into a side pocket. The captain appeared nervous as he paced between Velixar and his remaining troops, the healthy tending to the injured. Velixar sighed and touched the knot on the back of his head once more. He fully understood the captain's edginess, for in the distance was the sound of thousands of marching feet.

This time he did curse, though it didn't make him feel better in the slightest.

They had been right there. Roland and Azariah, the closest remnants of his past had been standing right before him, ripe for the slaughter. They should have been defenseless against his might, yet the power he was so proud of had fled from him at the moment of his conquest. One moment he had been Velixar, master of demons; the next, he had been Jacob Eveningstar again—learned, ageless, superior in his own way, yet still merely a man. His insides ran hot with rage. He promised himself that the next time their paths crossed, the two would suffer long, torturous deaths.

The muted thump of marching feet grew ever louder.

If Karak doesn't end me first, he thought.

He reached beneath his surcoat and pulled out his pendant. It felt heavy in his hands, as great a weight as a lifetime of sin on a man's soul. He released the pendant, letting it dangle from its leather strap. For the briefest of moments he considered tearing it from his neck, tossing it to the ground and stomping on it before climbing onto his horse and galloping into the forest. If the gods were kind, he could make the Tinderlands in a week and disappear into the rocky, desolate wilderness for the rest of his endless days.

Foolish dreams, he thought. *The gods are not kind.*

"I'm sorry, my Lord," he whispered to himself. When Captain Wellington approached him once more, offering him a sip from his waterskin, Velixar turned him away. He would seek no comfort, not in the aftermath of abject failure. He would simply await his god's judgment.

It was an hour before the army came into view, looking like a serpent composed of thousands of bustling ants as the forces marched along the distant road. Another three hours after that, beneath the full heat of midday, they drew close enough for him to make out the roaring lion emblazoned on the banners held aloft at the lead of the procession. Velixar heard one of his soldiers shout. When he turned his head to the left, he saw that Captain Wellington had formed his troops into a defensive horseshoe, pointing arrows and swords at the forest from which the wolf-men had appeared. The foliage shook, the trees swayed, and then men emerged from the woods. Most wore the familiar silver mail over black leather of Karak's Army, but a few were dressed in russet pants and cured deerhide tunics dyed a deep shade of green. Their skin and hair was like dark satin, their ears pointed. *Elves.* They were Darakken's regiment from Dezerea, arriving at the bridge as had been planned. He did not yet sense the demon's presence. He prayed it had obeyed orders this time and remained in Dezerea. The last thing he wanted was to see that disgusting beast before he had a chance to speak with Karak.

Wellington and the rest of his men retreated to him as the soldiers marching from both directions began setting up camp. The field on the east side of the Wooden Bridge was huge, nearly a half-mile wide, but the combined force overflowed from it like fizz at the head of a mug of ale. They raised tents from the edge of the northern forest to the beginning of the southern grasses, and when Velixar craned his neck to watch the distant road, he saw countless more tents being erected. Only the Gods' Road itself remained bereft of obstruction, allowing room for the supply wagons to make their way up the line. Food was distributed among the fighting men, and those from Darakken's regiment, who had been traveling in rougher conditions, began singing boisterous and crude songs as they tore into the salted pork and pickled vegetables that were brought to them.

The whole while, men worked around Velixar and his crew, some offering words of greeting, most giving confused stares. One group of soldiers, their eyes bloodshot and tired, shouted at them to get off their asses and help.

"We should do as they say," Captain Wellington said, fidgeting on his feet. His men chimed in their agreement.

"No," Velixar replied. "We stand here, and we wait."

"For what?"

"For Karak to call on us."

"Why would he call on us?"

"He won't," Velixar admitted with a shake of his head. "He will call on *me*. But you joined me on this quest, and so our fates are tied together."

"As you command, High Prophet."

Wellington crossed his arms over his chest and began to gnaw on his bottom lip. Velixar turned away from him. A small part of him wanted to assure the captain that all would be fine, but he knew there was no such certainty.

Finally, when the sun burned low and red on the horizon, Karak's colossal carriage snaked its way along the Gods' Road. The carriage was three times the size of any of the other sixty they had brought with them on the long march west. Drawn by a team of eight massive chargers, it stood twenty feet tall and fifteen feet wide and rolled forward on twelve wheels. The weight was considerable, particularly when Karak was inside, so it moved slowly, a fact that only heightened Velixar's tension.

When the carriage stopped at last, a mere thirty feet from where Velixar and his men waited, the rest of the camp had been set up; soldiers were relaxing outside their tents, cookfires had been lit, and the horde of smiths that traveled with both parties was collecting weapons for sharpening and armor for oiling. Just as always, the recently erected encampment was deafening. All the noise—numerous voices speaking at once, the *clink* of the smiths' hammers, the crackle and pop of fires—mixed into a single, ear-numbing din. Still, Velixar and his company were ignored.

Beside him, Captain Wellington's stomach rumbled audibly.

When the sun began to set behind the subtle rise of the western mountains, the twenty soldiers who had come in behind Karak's carriage removed roll after roll of canvas from the storage space beneath the coach and started to assemble the god's pavilion. Other groups of soldiers tore down their own tents to make room. Only once the pavilion was finished, complete with Karak's banner fluttering from the pole at the top, did the door to the carriage open and the deity himself step out. All sound, save the snorting of horses and the crackle of flames, immediately ceased.

Velixar fell to his knees, and he heard Wellington and the rest of his personal charges do the same.

Karak cast an imposing shadow in the growing darkness. His dark hair flowed above his shoulders as if alive, while his glowing golden eyes observed everything around him. Unlike three nights ago when Velixar had left camp, the god seemed pleased by what he saw. He did not face his High Prophet, however, nor did he even acknowledge his presence. Instead, he turned north, toward an approaching brigade of thirty elves, who were led by a wide-shouldered beast of a creature dressed in oily black armor that looked like the skin of a reptile. Two swords, just as black as his armor, were crisscrossed over his back.

Karak greeted them with a nod, then began to converse with their leader in the elven tongue. The other captains approached to greet the elves as well. Captain Wellington inched forward on his knees

"What are they saying?" he whispered into Velixar's ear.

"Karak is thanking the elves for joining his righteous fight," Velixar whispered back. In truth he could only hear every third word that came from the god's mouth, but judging from what he *could* hear and the deity's body language, he supposed his assumption was correct.

When the conversation ended, the elves bowed as one and made their way back to their camp site. The congregation around Karak dispersed, leaving the deity alone in the center of the Gods' Road. Finally, Karak pivoted to face Velixar. The sudden silence seemed to stretch for miles. Karak's hands went to his hips, and he shook his head. Velixar could see no anger in his stare, only disappointment. In a way, that worried him more.

"High Prophet," said the deity, "you have failed me."

Velixar lowered his eyes to the ground. "I have, my Lord. We came on the enemy from behind, ready to strike them down, but they proved resilient. Wolf-men from the forest came to their assistance, and though we killed all the beasts, we were too badly wounded and beaten to make chase."

Karak crossed his arms, tilted his head.

"Are you not Velixar, my High Prophet, swallower of demons and betrayer of nations? You have told me your power was beyond measure. Yet a few pups and a fleeing band of Wardens managed to hold back you and your best?"

Karak was openly mocking him, drawing subdued snickers from the massive crowd of onlookers. Velixar refused to fall into the trap. Instead of reacting, he dropped even lower and stared at the ground.

"My power fled me, my Lord, and has not returned. For that, I was unprepared."

"Are you certain, Prophet? Can you not feel the power surging through you even now?"

"I…"

Velixar closed his eyes, and sure enough, there it was, the force of the demon he'd swallowed, bubbling up within him like magma deep in a volcano. Confusion filled him, numbing any elation he might have felt. Why had it not been there when he needed it? What weakness of his had allowed it to vanish in his time of need?

"What do you have to say?" asked Karak.

He lifted his eyes to his god, rose to his knees, and held his arms out in supplication.

"I beg you to allow me to atone for my sins, my Lord," he said, pleading, "I was weak and deserve to be punished."

"And what should that punishment be? Your life?"

"My life is already yours to do with as you choose, my Lord."

He closed his eyes and waited for Karak's deathblow, but it never came.

"Rise, Prophet," said the god. "Come to me."

Velixar stood on rubbery legs and crossed the short expanse between them. Strangely, he felt the might inside him growing stronger with each step he took toward Karak. The deity stared down at him, a frown stretching his face.

"Disobedience of my law is the first step toward chaos," Karak said. "I told you that if these men are to crush our opponents, they will do so at my side. That includes you, Prophet. And yet you disregarded my word and went out on your own."

"I am sorry, my Lord."

"Your admission of guilt means little, Prophet. You have sinned against me, and now must pay the price."

Velixar cringed. "I accept your judgment."

"Good." Karak raised his head, his voice booming across the entire camp. "Failure to abide by my law is blasphemy, and the penalty for such a sin is harsh and unyielding." He looked down at Velixar. "Prophet, your punishment is death."

Velixar felt his entire body freeze, his heart stop, and the air in his lungs come to a halt.

"My Lord..." he whispered.

"However," Karak said, "you may offer me a sacrifice in your stead. Turn to those who accompanied you in your betrayal, use your power, and destroy them."

Velixar's head shot up and he stared at his deity with confusion.

"What? But why?"

"This is not a time for questions, Velixar, but decisions. Kill those who joined you in disobedience. Let their deaths be a lesson to all."

Velixar hesitated a moment, then gradually turned to look at Captain Oscar Wellington, who was standing in line with the rest of the surviving men who had rode out with him. The captain's expression was filled with shock and betrayal. His hand lowered to the hilt of his sword, but he did not have time to yank it from its scabbard.

Other soldiers encircled them, weapons drawn. The injured were hefted from the ground and thrown to the front of the line, where they cringed, begging for mercy. One of the men tried to flee, only to have the tendon on the back of his ankle sliced from behind. He too was tossed, wailing, into the place of judgment.

"Bastard," Wellington muttered. He stepped forward, head held high. It saddened Velixar to see the strength the man portrayed, knowing what he had to do. It was either their lives or his.

In the end, it was no choice at all.

Without a word, Velixar brought his hands up. The power inside him flowed from his pores, shadows swirling around his hands as he lifted them, facing the thirteen who had survived his failed mission. The other soldiers backed away, shouting in fear at the display of dark magic. The tendrils of pulsing darkness then surged forward, pouring into the mouths, noses, and eyes of Captain Wellington and the rest of his men. Their mouths opened, but they could not scream; their eyes bulged, but they could not see. The shadows crushed them, both inside and out, snapping bones, liquefying organs. Soon their bodies were formless masses, empty shells of flesh encased in armor. Velixar dropped his hands, the shadows retreating back into him, and what remained of Captain Wellington and his men collapsed with the clank of steel and the thud of flesh on flesh.

"So be it," said Karak. He addressed the camp once more. "It is done. Order has been served. Burn the bodies and carry on. We are done here."

With that, the deity turned and disappeared inside his massive pavilion. Velixar stood horrified, watching as the soldiers built a large pile of wood, then stripped the armor from the corpses and tossed the remains atop it. The bonfire was lit, and the flames filled the burgeoning night sky. The soldiers stood around the fire for a few moments, their heads bowed in reverence, then went about their business. They gave Velixar a wide berth, glancing at him with fear in their eyes.

He took a deep breath, gathered his courage, and swept into Karak's pavilion. There he found the god sitting in the center of the huge space, legs crossed, hands on his knees. While sitting, the god's gaze was level with his own, and those divine eyes snapped open when Velixar cleared his throat.

"Leave me, Prophet. Your tent was erected by the hawk carriage. Go there and think on what you have done."

Velixar shook his head, willing himself to be strong. "Those were good men," he told his god. "They were the best of the lot, the most brutal and loyal. It was a useless loss of life."

Karak sighed.

"I expected more from you, Prophet. More knowledge, more *understanding*. Humans cling to their own lives above all else, and after that show of force, they will be more inclined to resist their chaotic impulses. None will betray me if they know it will mean their death."

"You did not have to kill them. There are other ways to teach a lesson."

"*I* did not kill them," said Karak, tilting his head. "*You* did."

"I…" Velixar began, but words failed him.

"You think you understand so much, Velixar, yet your pride will be the end of you. You have lived a little more than a hundred years, while I have existed for an eternity. Do not begin to think you know as much as I do."

What game is this, wondered Velixar. *What trick?*

"You told me to execute them," he said.

"I did, but the choice was yours. I am not blind to your selfishness, Prophet. I gave you a choice between killing the men who loyally followed your orders and sacrificing your own life. You chose to preserve your life, your *power*, and let others suffer the consequences of your failure. Consider that a lesson."

"A lesson of what?" he asked. "That I am worth more than a few pathetic soldiers whose bones will be dust before a single gray hair sprouts from my head?"

Karak's face seemed to darken.

"The lesson is that you fear death as much as any human. The lesson is that whenever you betray me or ignore my wisdom, people will die. With me you are powerful, Velixar. Without me, you are nothing."

"*I* am nothing?" he exclaimed. His anger grew, and with it his audacity, however misplaced. He began to shout without thinking. "I know things, *my Lord*. I have knowledge you wish to keep hidden, about you and Ashhur and your long, sordid history. You speak of failure? What of *your* failure, the one that led to the creation of humanity on this world? Yes, I know how you came to be, who you and Ashhur were before. I know of Kaurthulos's destruction of countless worlds—and he attempted to do the same here in Dezrel. Darakken, Velixar, Sluggoth, they were *your* creations, weren't they?"

"That was before we became who we are now," Karak said softly.

"Before you split into pieces," Velixar said. "Before you became Karak and Ashhur and countless others. I've seen your failures in the demon's memory; I've seen how your brother, Thulos, another aspect of your fragmented former self, slew the other gods and began his conquest. Celestia saved you from ruin and brought you and Ashhur here to redeem yourselves from your misdeeds. You two *fled* here from your own mirrored reflection, and yet you would call *me* nothing? I have seen it all, Karak."

Karak said not a word. Feeling emboldened, Velixar continued.

"Without you, I am nothing? Where would you be without my aid? You were hiding in the mountains when I set into motion the events that would lead to your reign. I poisoned Vulfram Mori into renouncing you. I manipulated Clovis into building the temple in the delta to incur your wrath. I served Ashhur for seventeen years—*seventeen years!*—biding my time, working my fingers into his subconscious, earning his trust and ultimately leading him to Haven. Your fight with that discarded piece of yourself you call a brother was *my* doing. *I* was the one who thought humanity could reach greatness, *I* paved the way for this war, and *I* am the one who first believed it was you who should rule all of Dezrel! And all I receive in retu—"

"*YOU...KNOW...NOTHING.*"

The god's words hit Velixar like a fist to the face, knocking him to his knees. He stared up at Karak, unable to breathe, as the deity rose to his full height above him.

"You think yourself greater than you are, Prophet," Karak said. His tone was chilling, and the invisible fist around Velixar's throat squeezed tighter. "Do you really think I am blind to what happens in my own kingdom, blind to the actions of my own creations? I knew your plans the moment you hatched them, and I allowed you the freedom to carry them out. I even allowed the death of Soleh Mori, the child who had proved her love and loyalty to me beyond all others."

The grip around his throat loosened.

"Why?" Velixar was able to gasp.

"Because I was disappointed with the immaturity of my children. Because I tired of watching Ashhur's degeneration into a weak, cowardly being. Because I knew in my heart that order would only thrive if all of Dezrel were mine to lord over as I chose. But mostly, I was curious to see if you, the First Man, could accomplish the grand schemes you had set in motion."

"You knew...and you said nothing....You let me believe..."

Karak nodded, his eyes burning into Velixar's soul.

"All you have done, all you think you are—it is because I have *given* you the power you required. Power that I can take away, power that I *have* taken away, the moment you disobeyed me, the moment you let your pride and arrogance place you above me in your heart and mind."

Velixar's eyes widened as he stared at his god in disbelief.

"Yes, Prophet, you understand *nothing*. You have spent more than a century chronicling the history of magic on this world, yet you never once knew that so long as my brother and I walk among you, the only *true* power you will ever possess must be channeled through us." The deity sighed. "I stripped you of your power last night so you would learn. So you would know, once and for all, that everything you have accomplished has been through my hand. Your power, your station, even your wisdom, has come through me or my creations. And that which I have given...I can take away."

The god reached down, tugged the pendant out from under Velixar's tunic. His finger traced the bas-relief of the peak on which the lion stood.

"I gave you this to show you my trust, but also to demonstrate the scope of my plan. A mountain is the highest place one can stand. Those with the strength to conquer it can forever clutch what is rightfully theirs, defeating any challengers. It is a symbol of might, of conquest, of *power*. I have watched humanity in all its forms for eons. I have watched your struggles and your unpredictability; I have seen how you clutch chaos to your breast as if it offers you sustenance, when all it ever gives you is pain. I have *always* known this...yet I dared hope my brother or myself might finally find a way. We began our grand experiment, but within a single generation the old ways began anew. It was either coddle humanity forever, as my brother would do, or let you all succumb to a life spent with your backs to your gods and your hearts filled with lust and greed and fear. I will not allow it. All of Dezrel will either bend the knee or know the peace of the grave. I am tired of this world, Velixar. I am tired of the way mankind scratches at my mind, every sinful act carving into me like a grain of sand carves away at a rock wall. Your race could achieve such great heights, but too many of your kind are sick. You are like a great oak held down by rotting branches. There is only one recourse; burn the sick branches with fire; otherwise, the whole tree will die."

Karak turned away from him, returning to a seated position in the center of the tent. He closed his eyes, an eerie calm washing over his godly form.

"You shall live, because I will it," he said calmly. "My brother and I created Jacob Eveningstar to be a guiding light for humanity, and that purpose has not changed simply because your name has. You will remain my prophet, and you will teach the people of my glory for the rest of your days. Be my greatest disciple. Be my wisest friend. The world is changing, the new future coming, and I would have you at my side. But if you are not at my side…then your ageless body will, for the first time in its life, know pain, know fire, know death. Now leave my quarters, Velixar. We are to cross the bridge in four days' time, and I need to gather my strength for what is to come."

Velixar needed no other invitation. He staggered to his feet and left the pavilion, collapsing the moment he was outside. His body was sore, the wounds on his head barked, and his mind spun a mile a minute. Everything he'd thought he knew suddenly seemed so limited and pathetic.

The moon was low on the horizon, and wisps of smoke and cloud passed over it like floating snakes. Most of the soldiers had turned to the safety of their bedrolls, and those few who remained out were well into their cups. Velixar began to walk toward the Gods' Road, avoiding the glowing rubble of snuffed out cookfires until he reached his destination. He then followed the beaten path east, passing row after row of tents. There were so many of them. As he looked toward the undulating horizon, he realized he could still see them dotting the landscape in the far distance. Now that the force from the north had arrived, Karak's Army was near ten thousand strong. Once Lord Commander Avila's regiment arrived, they would swell to fifteen thousand.

The numbers were staggering.

It took him nearly an hour to find his own pavilion, which had been assembled beside the cart that acted as the rookery, just as

Karak had told him it would be. He walked into the pavilion and lit a few candles. The place had been set up just the way it always was, complete with his desk, bedroll, and dresser. The three squires who tended to his belongings certainly knew how to perform their duties.

"What choice have I left?" Velixar asked as he hung Lionsbane on its hook in the center of the open space. All the confidence he had in himself, all the pride he had in his own wisdom, now seemed like a mockery. What wisdom was there in bragging to Karak about his knowledge of things Karak already knew? What wisdom in glorifying a power that came from Karak? He was a princeling bragging to his father about his great wealth. All that was his had been inherited.

So what did it mean?

"What choice," Velixar whispered again. He could rebel, denying Karak's power and wisdom. Or he could find a way to draw power without the need of his deity; he could seek to learn what even his god did not know.

Velixar closed his eyes, and he felt the power of the demon surge up within him. There was the other way. The more frightening way. He had always believed Karak's path was the wiser. He had always trusted his laws and desires to be superior to Ashhur's naïve, foolish hopes. But had he ever given himself over? Had he ever let his trust become faith? No, he'd always held back, relied on his own wisdom to confirm each decision. He followed Karak not because he believed in him, but because his mind *agreed* with him.

He fell to his knees, and as he prayed, he knew his god would hear.

"My life for you," he whispered. "Before my faith was hollow. Make it overflowing. Before my faith was weak. Make it strong. Whatever I have done, whatever I may do, it is now all for you. Let your words pass through my lips. I am your prophet, and may I forever speak your truth. Burn away my doubts with fire. The time for them has passed."

Bleary and weak, he rose to his feet. He felt a strange lightness. Part of him wondered if anything had changed, but deep in his heart he knew. He felt a vast power growing inside him.

The moment was already fleeing, and he felt an intense desire to record it. He rushed to his desk, and then paused, his brow furrowing. He knelt down, searching the shelf beneath it. When his fingers found nothing, he raced through the rest of his pavilion, tearing through his chest of books, his sacks of clothing, his dresser, the coffer where he would store his armor once he removed it, beneath his bedroll. Panic rushed through his veins, causing his wounded temple to throb.

"No, no, no," he repeated over and over again.

He hunted through the night, even going so far as to question his squires and the soldiers who were camped nearby, but all his searching was for naught. His precious journal was nowhere to be found.

CHAPTER

"This isn't good, is it?"

Patrick glanced beside him. The dim moonlight revealed that Preston was mimicking his posture: flat on his belly, his eye pressed to a looking glass as he cautiously peered over the lip of a rocky knoll. The old man shook his head.

"Not at all," he said.

"But is it really so bad? It's night. Most of them are probably sleeping. We could circle around, sticking close to the river, then slip onto the bridge when no one's paying attention."

"A fool's hope," Preston said. "There are forty men guarding the bridge." He gestured again to the expanse beyond. "And we would not make it very far in any case. There are eyes watching, and not all of them are human."

"What's that mean?"

"See for yourself. Over there, by the trees, to the right of the massive stable of horses."

He handed Patrick the looking glass, and the crooked man squinted through it. The encampment spread out before him, larger than life. Thousands upon thousands of individual tents of various sizes were perched on either side of the Gods' Road, interspersed with wagons and the occasional pavilion. Starting a few hundred feet in front of the Wooden Bridge and stretching all along the road's eastern path, the camp seemed almost as big as Mordeina itself. There appeared to be no end to it. He suppressed a shudder. *So many…*

Following Preston's instructions, he found the horses. There looked to be over two hundred of them, squeezed shoulder to shoulder, feed bags fastened around their snouts. He inched the looking glass slightly to the right and spotted six tents that stood out from the rest. These were tall and triangular, with thick poles supporting the leather sides and smoke trailing from the holes in the roofs. There were men pacing around the odd tents, patrolling with their heads held high. Patrick quickly realized what it meant.

He had met few elves in his life. The relationship between the two species was shaky at best, which he understood completely. His mother had told him how Celestia had destroyed their homeland to make way for the dawn of humanity. Yet this, combined with the torching of the innocents in the barn, signified something much stronger than mutual dislike. To have elves marching alongside their army…

"Shit," he muttered.

One of the pacing elves stopped abruptly, raising his eyes toward Patrick. *There's no way,* he thought. At least two miles separated them. There was no way the elf could have heard, could have seen…

Not wanting to take a chance, he slid down the rise a few feet, pulling Preston with him as he dropped out of view.

"What was that for?" the old man asked.

"Just a precaution," Patrick answered with a wink.

"One looked your way, didn't he?"

Patrick nodded. Preston patted him on the shoulder.

"Smart choice, then."

"Thanks."

They slid down the remainder of the hill, rejoining the young men who waited below. The only cover to be found in the red cliffs was in the hills themselves, which seemed to make them nervous. Tristan flicked small stones against the ground. Joffrey, Brick, and Ryann obsessively brushed their horses, and Preston's sons Edward and Ragnar worked on sharpening their swords. Only the Flicks seemed at ease; the massive twins were lying down with cloths over their eyes.

Tristan glanced up at their approach. He brushed aside his stringy brown hair and asked, "What's it look like out there?"

"Crowded," replied Preston.

"Ashhur or Karak?" Edward asked.

"What do you think, idiot?" snapped Ragnar. "You really think Father would be acting so cautious if it was Ashhur?"

"You have the right of it, son," Preston said. "Though you'd do well to keep your voices down. The elves have joined Karak's cause."

Joffrey moaned. "Elves?"

"Yes."

"Fuck."

The two Flicks took that moment to tear the cloths from their faces and sit up. Big looked at Little, then Little asked, "What's your plan?"

"Not a clue," Patrick said.

Ryann cleared his throat.

"Um, maybe we could swim?" he said. "Hike back a few miles so we're out of sight, and then just jump in the river?"

"Not unless we absolutely must," Preston said, and his tone brooked no argument. "The Corinth is at its highest point because of the rains. The current's too strong, the span too wide. One of us might get swept away, and I don't fancy losing any of you."

"And besides that," said Patrick, "I can't swim." He stepped back and held his arms out as if presenting himself to them. "This handsome body sinks like a rock in the water. Not built for floating, it seems...or much else, really."

"I could carry you," Big Flick said.

Patrick laughed.

"I'd like to see you try, but let's experiment in shallow water first, eh? Besides, we would have to discard our armor, our weapons, and our horses. That hardly sounds like a good idea."

"How about farther south?" It was Tristan again. "The river seemed to thin out by the tall trees."

"The river does grow thinner when it passes through Stonewood," Patrick said. "However, it is a place we'd do best to steer clear of."

"Why?"

"The elves, remember?" said Preston. "The bridge is guarded, and the countryside is swarming with soldiers. There's no sneaking across, no disguising ourselves. We might just have to lay low until they leave."

"That can't happen," Patrick said. "Beyond the bridge, the road is pressed by Stonewood on one side and Lake Cor on the other. Given the size of his army, if Karak were to pass before us, there would be no way to get around them until we were within sight of Mordeina. Tens of thousands of men would stand between us and our destination. No, if we do this, we must figure out a way to do it now."

Everyone groaned except the Flicks, who exchanged a glance and then stood up. Big stepped forward.

"Has the Lord Commander arrived yet?" he asked.

"I don't think so," Preston said. "There were still fresh fires in the distance today, so they're probably a good couple mile or two away. Why?"

"Well, perhaps we shouldn't be sneaking at all," Big said, tilting his head toward Patrick. "Perhaps we can just walk right through the camp?"

Patrick frowned. "Come again?"

Big bent over, picked up a rock, and began scraping it against his breastplate. The crude white paint gradually chipped away, revealing the roaring lion beneath. The image was scratched a bit, but it was difficult to tell in the moonlight.

"We're soldiers of Karak," Little said, joining his brother's side. "What better way to set the others at ease than if we come bearing a prisoner?"

Preston snapped his fingers. "Yes," he said, excitedly. "We have a DuTaureau here, after all. What a wondrous gift that would be. We march down, say we were separated from our regiment, and found this one wandering through the desert. And then, when they drop their guard…"

"Um, excuse me, I'm right here," Patrick said, his heartbeat quickening. "I don't think I like this plan very much. The part where I'm dragged into the middle of Karak's entire army as a prisoner is rubbing me the wrong way."

Preston turned to him, half grinning. "What, has our brave Patrick suddenly gone soft? You were the one who said we needed to cross now. Besides, sooner or later, the regiment we abandoned will arrive, which would make this even *more* dangerous. If you don't like our plan, you'd better think up an alternative fast. I don't think this collection of dolts is likely to come up with a better one."

"Fabulous."

"Oh, and one more thing. We must be quick. Patrick, do you remember the huge pavilion that sat toward the front of the camp?"

"Yes."

"Well, it's probably Karak's pavilion, which means we must hurry past it at all costs. So we had best present ourselves and then make a run for it before the god himself gets involved."

"What if someone decides to escort me away?"

"That won't happen."

"Are you absolutely certain?"

"Er, mostly. So long as we're quick about it."

Patrick moaned, dropping his head. "This keeps getting better and better."

Half an hour later, after the others had scraped the paint from their breastplates as well, the entire party marched over the hill. Dawn was fast approaching, the black of the night sky deepening in readiness for it. All were atop their horses, and Patrick rode between Preston and Edward, a rope binding his mare to theirs. Patrick's wrists were bound too, though the knot was loose enough for him to wiggle his hands free if need be. He still wore his half helm, pulled low to mostly cover his twisted nose. Winterbone bounced on Preston's lap, and Patrick gazed at the sword longingly. It was the first time it had been out of his reach in over a year, and it felt as if a part of him were missing.

The camp stirred as they made their approach, and seeing it up close, Patrick was more awed and terrified than ever. Preston had guessed that ten thousand soldiers were gathered here, and while the multitudes traveling with Ashhur was perhaps three times that many, the numbers Karak had amassed were imminently more dangerous. And they were so *organized*; the tents had been erected in even rows, a cookfire between every two of them, entirely different from the slapdash and jumbled camps set up by Ashhur's people. Weary soldiers marched outside the rows, guarding those inside from whatever dangers the night offered.

They passed a few sentries when they crossed the high grasses at the base of the hill and reached the edge of the camp. The guards allowed them passage without question—with Patrick hidden in the middle of the group, their torches only revealed breastplates that bore the roaring lion.

Farther on, past the guards, the space between tents was only wide enough for a single horse, so they split off into two columns as they trotted through. Preston took the lead, with Patrick directly behind him, the old man's rope now the only one tethered to the neck of Patrick's mare. He looked down at the cloth enclosures as he passed them, his eyes fixing on the stacks of swords, mauls, and axes that lay beside each tent, twinkling in the moonlight as if they'd been freshly sharpened and oiled. He could hear the snores and night mumblings of those who slept within the tents, and realized right then how vulnerable they were. All it would take would be one misstep, and thousands of soldiers would emerge and give chase. Patrick squeezed his eyes shut, trying to block out the image, but he saw the potential horror even more clearly in the darkness behind his eyelids.

When they finally reached the Gods' Road, passing a mere ten feet or so in front of Karak's massive pavilion, the two columns combined once more. Edward retied his rope to the neck of Patrick's horse, and father and son led the approach to the bridge. A few random soldiers appeared, dressed only in filthy smallclothes and stumbling drunk. None seemed to pay them any mind. One even collided with Ragnar's horse and then staggered in the other direction, muttering something about wolves in the night. Patrick gazed at the man with confusion, longing for a drink himself. He would do anything to get his heart to stop thumping so quickly.

His heart rate only increased when he glanced to the right. They seemed to have gained the attention of the elves pacing the tents close to the forest. Celestia's children gathered in a line, watching the procession with interest. They were still a good distance away, but that fact gave Patrick little relief. He had heard stories of their proficiency as archers, and he watched as two of the elves picked up their bows, slinging them over their shoulders. Only when the massive stable of horses obstructed his sight of them did he allow himself to even breathe.

He wasn't the only one. All it took was a single glance around him to see that the youngsters felt just as unsure as he did. Only Preston and the Flicks seemed to exude any confidence.

They had almost reached the Wooden Bridge when finally someone shouted for them to halt. Each horse stopped, one after the other, and the beasts sidled nervously in place, blowing air from their snouts. Patrick bowed his head and held his hands out in front of him, making sure his binds were prominently displayed.

"Remember," Preston said from the corner of his mouth, "I do the talking. The rest of you stay quiet."

"What?" Ryann asked from the back of the pack.

Brick jabbed him with an elbow. "Shut it!" he hissed.

"What's going on here?"

Patrick lifted his head ever so slightly to look at the three approaching soldiers. They wore no helms and their gaits were cautious. Their hands rested lightly on the hilts of their swords, ready for confrontation if one were required.

"Who am I speaking with?" asked Preston with a commanding tone.

"Nicholas Potter," said the one in the center. "Captain of Karak's Third Regiment." He stepped forward, and Patrick could see he was a handsome young man, with a slender jaw and piercing blue eyes that glowed in the moonlight. His hair was quite long, hanging to his breast, and wavy. *He would make a beautiful woman,* Patrick thought, and had to keep from chuckling.

Preston inclined his head. "Captain, be well met on this eve. But did you say Karak's *Third* Regiment?"

"I did," the man said. "I'm new to command because of the unfortunate loss of the late Captain Oscar Wellington."

"Such a shame," Preston said, talking as if in no great hurry. He dipped his head in respect. "Oscar was a good man, I have heard. Consider us well met, Captain Potter. I am Preston Ender, of Karak's Second, in service of the Lord Commander."

Nicholas's head tilted to the side. He seemed to be studying Preston's breastplate. His fingers inched down his side ever so slightly, and Patrick tensed.

"The Second, eh?" he said. "They aren't expected to arrive until two days from now. You're a long way from where you're supposed to be, soldier."

"I am," replied Preston with a nod. "We were sent ahead to scout after we toppled Nor, but we lost the path in a sudden sandstorm. Spent three days in the desert waiting for the rest of the regiment to arrive, but we'd moved too far west. When we saw fires burning to the north of us, we began to follow them, but we had to be careful. We were in Kerrian land, after all. I knew our orders were to leave the dark-skinned people alone, so we had to avoid their hunting parties whenever we came across them." He shook his head. "And there were many of them."

The words slipped out of Preston's lips like practiced vows.

"Praise Karak you stayed safe," said Nicholas. He walked up to Patrick, nudged his leg. "So what do we have here? Some sort of desert monster?"

"A prisoner," Preston said. "Found him traveling through the desert. An odd creature, this one."

"Odd, eh?" The soldier rose up on his toes and tilted back Patrick's helm, revealing his face. He backed up a step, his nose scrunching up as if he'd tasted something sour. The two soldiers who had joined him burst out laughing.

"What *is* that?" the captain asked Preston.

"Fuck off," Patrick muttered under his breath.

"What was that?" he snarled.

Preston cantered up to Nicholas, placed a hand on his shoulder.

"He's surly, so best be careful. This one claims to be the Ogre of Haven."

Potter's eyes widened. Patrick squinted at Preston, wondering why the man had altered his own plan; Patrick DuTaureau would have been a far greater prisoner than some twisted soul whose only claim was monstrosity.

"The Ogre of Haven?" Potter asked. "Are you certain?"

"Not certain, but hopeful."

"If that is true, his reputation does his ugliness no justice. How did you capture him? I've heard the Ogre killed over a hundred of the Divinity's best men."

"Stories exaggerate, Captain." Preston said, but he chuckled, allowing a bit of pride into his voice. "Truth be told, we ambushed him while he slept. Without that weapon of his, he's just a man like any other." Preston lifted Winterbone, wincing at the weight of it, and showed the sword to Nicholas.

The captain ran his fingers over the handle, closely inspected the dragonglass crystal affixed to the hilt. Preston pulled the sword slightly out of its scabbard, displaying its cutting edge.

"Handsome weapon," Nicholas said, glancing up at Patrick. "How did a freakish sheep from the delta come to own it?"

Patrick grinned, the thrill of defiance running hot in his veins.

"I fucked your mother and felt something sharp up there. Turns out it was hidden in her cunt."

The soldier's face ran red. He snatched Patrick by the upper crease of his armor and yanked him low, so he could slap him across the head. Patrick's helm dropped to the damp ground with a *splat*, and his ears set to ringing. The man then shoved him upright and drew his sword.

"Who are you to insult your better?" the man seethed. "I should cut off your head here and now."

Preston reacted in a flash, reaching down and grabbing Captain Potter's sword arm tightly.

"I would think twice about that," he said, as if talking to one of his boys. "Karak will want to see the prisoner alive. Our god would want to punish the Ogre of Haven himself, I think."

The captain stepped back and spat to the side in anger. With his neck flushed and his nose flaring, he didn't look so womanly any longer.

"Very well. Yerdo, Hollen, fetch seven of your brothers, then come with me to wake our Lord." He offered Patrick one final glare, and there was a sick sort of pride behind his eyes. "We'll see how painful a death the Divinity offers you, after disturbing him in the middle of the night."

Patrick didn't reply, but he wanted to.

"We will remain here and watch over the prisoner," Preston said. "You do that."

Once the two underlings returned with the rest, the ten men marched away from them, heading toward Karak's pavilion, which was thankfully a good distance away. Six other soldiers stepped forward to take their place, standing shoulder to shoulder across the Gods' Road. Preston sighed and leaned over.

"Did you have to insult him like that?" he whispered.

Patrick shrugged. "Best to have him angry. An angry man is a careless man. Your brother taught me that. But why did you not tell him who I truly am? Would that not have been more...appealing?"

"Perhaps, but that might have revealed..." The older man averted his eyes, then peered over his shoulder at the six who guarded the road and the thirty who stood watch at the bridge. Just when it seemed Preston was about to answer his question, he said, "Are you ready for this?" instead.

Patrick sighed and slipped one hand from his binds as the rest of the youths gathered in around them. The horses whinnied.

"What are you doing?" asked a strange, accented voice, right when they were preparing to charge.

Patrick leaned back, trying to see beyond Big Flick's massive body. An elf stood there, his bronze skin turned an odd shade of gray by the moonlight. The elf's eyes were narrowed, intense, and he held his strange curved sword by his side.

"What business is it of yours, elf?" asked Preston.

"I saw that one gazing over the hillock," the elf said, pointing at Patrick. "Do prisoners often serve as lookouts in Karak's Army?"

"Well, no," Preston said. Patrick could tell his confidence was shaken. He was accustomed to handling men of Karak, but the determined stare of the elf was another matter entirely. "Surely you are mistaken."

"I know what I saw." He took a menacing step forward, raising his sword. "That one there can be mistaken for no one else. Dismount, now. Whatever you have planned..."

"Oh, fuck this."

Patrick ground his knees into his mare, spinning her. In one swift motion he snatched Winterbone's handle, yanked the sword from the scabbard, and then urged the horse to turn in the opposite direction. The elf reacted quickly, hopping backward and raising his thin blade in defense, but he was not prepared for Patrick's immense strength. The elf's sword shattered against Winterbone's power, and the massive blade carried on, slicing through the elf's face like it was a block of soft cheese. The top half of his head slid off from the jaw on up, and his body teetered and dropped, blood pouring onto the Gods' Road.

The soldiers who had been standing before them panicked. They turned tail and ran toward the bridge, screaming for the rest of the men to stand up and fight. Patrick laughed as they ran, the fire of conflict overcoming him. He hadn't been in battle since Haven. It surprised him to find that he'd missed it.

"You're *enjoying* this?" Preston exclaimed when he heard Patrick's laugh.

"Of course! Aren't we soldiers? Now ride—ride, and run over any who bar your path!"

With that, Preston drew his sword, shouted *"Heeya!"* and drove his knees into his stallion. The beast took off at a gallop, Patrick at his heels. He heard a litany of hooves pounding behind him, and despite his exhilaration, he hoped it was the rest of their party and not a group of Karak's men running them down from the rear.

Preston felled the first of defender of the bridge with a single downward chop. The other soldiers closed in, screaming bloody murder as they flailed at them with swords, axes and mauls. Patrick feared for the rest of his party, but he knew he could not spare them attention. He looped Winterbone with a single arm, hacking through armor and flesh alike as his horse crashed into the soldiers' line. Blood splattered him each time he connected, coating his armor, soaking his smallclothes, staining his flesh. He didn't care. A primal roar vibrated up his throat and he simply kept on hewing, even as his horse slowed to maneuver around the living obstacles standing in its way.

He was hit hard from behind, but did not fall, and when he thrust back his elbow, it crunched against the face of a man holding a dagger. The man's jaw imploded, the severed tip of his tongue falling on Patrick's thigh. The attacker fell away, holding his face and screaming, and Patrick turned his attention forward once more. He was mere feet from the Wooden Bridge now, with only three soldiers blocking his way. Preston's stallion was already almost halfway across.

"With me!" Patrick shouted, baring his teeth and charging the three soldiers. He watched their eyes grow as large as saucers the closer he got, and they leaped out of the way before he reached them, allowing his mare to stampede onto the wooden slats unhindered.

"*Cowards!*" he shouted over his shoulder. The wind buffeted his face as he thundered across the bridge, and as the rush of battle began to wane, he glanced behind to see if the others had made it. He couldn't tell. The horses coming up on his rear all looked the same, as did their blood-smeared riders.

Once he reached the other side, riding into the northwestern half of Paradise, Patrick kept right on racing, keeping up with Preston's frantic pace. It wasn't until they were a good two miles away, when the Wooden Bridge was no longer in sight, and the sky had become like a wound leaking deep crimson, that they finally stopped.

They all sat there atop panting horses, they themselves equally exhausted. There were nine of them now, each with blood staining his armor. Preston had a wicked gash in his side, the top of Little Flick's head was a gaping maw, Edward's left arm hung limp by his side, and Ryann's ear had been hacked clean off. The rest had smaller wounds, and many were still bleeding. All but Brick Mullin, who was nowhere to be found.

"We lost one," Preston said, dejected.

"We did," answered Patrick. "But *only* one. And he died a good death. We'll mourn him later. For now, we must move. We just made a mockery of Karak's entire army, and I don't think he'll be too happy about it."

CHAPTER

31

Laurel made her way back to Veldaren in the daylight, just in case the mumbling priest Joben Tustlewhite hadn't come to his senses and reigned in the frightening Judges. The last thing she wanted was another run-in with the two huge lions, never mind one of the roving bands of low men who had murder on their minds.

She had been gone from Veldaren for eight days, and the Conningtons had given her a carriage for her journey, a mode of transportation that was finer than any she'd experienced in her short life of luxury, for while her father's wealth was indeed vast, Cornwall Lawrence was a modest, simple man. The same could not be said of the Conningtons. The sides of the coach were so expertly crafted that no seams could be felt on the glossy wood, and inside were twelve massive pillows stuffed with downy feathers. The fabric was silk, the handholds grayhorn ivory. Lady Connington had even provided her with new attire, a finely spun, ankle-length, turquoise dress bedecked with rubies. She was amazed by how comfortable it was, like wearing her nightclothes—so different from the restrictive and revealing ensembles she'd forced herself to wear over the course of her long and frustrating mission.

She had even been given servants, of all things. The Crimson Sword had given her possession of Mite and Giant, the two Sisters of the Cloth who had been his "pets." Though Laurel hated the very notion of the Sisters and refused to consider them her possessions, she couldn't deny how much safer the two wrapped ladies made her feel. Just looking at them as they hung close to the carriage's windows, their gazes intent on their surroundings, calmed her nerves. She had come to think of them as *her girls*. Though their long journey back from Riverrun had been uneventful, it was something she did not take for granted. Now all she had to worry about was how King Eldrich would receive the Conningtons' counteroffer. Although they had agreed to assist the realm with coin, commodities, and manpower, she was certain the king would not be very happy with what they'd demanded in return.

The carriage turned onto the eastern Road of Worship. Smooth cobbles replaced the bumpy packed earth of the Gods' Road. Laurel peeked out of the porthole. A hot breeze and Veldaren's unique stink struck her head-on. The driver steered the two horses onward, past the empty fields where one day even more abodes and places of commerce would be built, past the stacks of felled lumber, mossy from sitting unused in the elements for so long, past the Temple of Karak. The sight of the temple, a looming black obelisk that seemed to swell and retract in the day's heat, as if breathing, caused her to cringe. She cast down her eyes.

"I love you, my Lord," she whispered. She may have lost faith in her god's teachings, just as the Conningtons claimed they had, but unlike them she refused to relinquish her love, whether she was about to betray Karak or not.

Buildings began to appear by the side of the road, a sparse few at first, then more and more, until they were packed together like fish in a barrel. Laurel breathed out a wistful sigh. The drab gray stone and weepy brown wood of the city was actually a comfort. Veldaren had become more than her home over the last four years. It was where she had bloomed into womanhood, where she had earned her independence. Protecting it from the coming strife was the main reason she had agreed to the king's proposal in the first place.

Her eyes narrowed as she watched the city roll by her window, a stone of unease burying itself in her gut. It was closing in on noontime, yet there seemed to be fewer women on the road than usual. Those she saw had a faraway look about them; eyes glazed over, gaits hunched, as if each carried a heavy weight. There were virtually no unwatched children running through the streets, a sight that had grown common over the past months.

The cart neared the great fountain at the center of the city, where the daily market was held. The square was completely empty. There were no vendors hawking their fruits, vegetables, meats both salted and freshly butchered, textiles, trinkets, or shoes. The only soul within eyesight was a single woman sitting on the side of the road, holding her stomach. Her clothes were filthy, her body so thin she resembled a skeleton. Her head was down, her dirty hair concealing her face. Laurel sucked in a breath. She couldn't tell if the woman was alive, and when two other women hustled past without a glance at the slouched one, she realized that no one cared.

"What's going on here?" she asked aloud. Mite's blue eyes and Giant's brown ones turned toward her, but neither said a word. Not that they would. She had tried to engage them in conversation numerous times since they'd left Riverrun, but true to their order, they had remained silent. Attempting to make them speak was a fruitless task.

She returned her gaze to the road, searching for a member of the City Watch in the hopes of asking him to check on the poor, thin woman, but none were within eyesight. It was then, as they circled the roundabout and joined the South Road, that she realized she hadn't seen a single man in a Watch uniform since they'd entered the city limits. This struck her as odd. Odder yet, she hadn't noticed any men at all. Her stomach began to rumble with unease.

The streets remained sparsely populated as they drew closer and closer to the castle, where crowds were usually abundant. Laurel looked down at the letter she held in her hand, which had been delivered two days ago by a female courier with skittish eyes, a reply to a correspondence she had sent via bird just before leaving Riverrun. In it Guster, her kindly and elderly fellow Councilman with the neck wattle, gushed about how splendid it was that her task was nearing its close, saying that King Eldrich eagerly awaited to hear what the merchants had to say about his proposal. It also reported that a special Council session had been planned to begin on her return to Veldaren. She had scribbled her reply and handed it to the courier, who'd wheeled her horse around and rode off without another word.

The sight of the three castle towers made her breathe a little easier. Soon she would tell the king of the Conningtons' demands, and she would get answers about what had happened to her home. She closed her eyes, telling herself that she was acting like a frightened little girl. *There must be a logical explanation,* she thought. *Once you hear it, you'll realize how silly you're being. We're fighting a war now. Things are bound to change.* Yet, given how strange everything was in the city, it was difficult to keep her fear from ruling all other thoughts.

The carriage rocked to a stop in front of the portcullis of the Castle of the Lion a few minutes later. Mite opened the door closest to the street, and out stepped Giant, who then turned to assist her new mistress. Laurel's feet fell to the cobbled walk and she flexed her toes inside her thin, feminine shoes, appreciating the hardness after trudging on packed dirt for so long. The driver—a young woman whose family trained all the horses in the Conningtons' stables—nodded to her before cracking the horses' leads. The two steeds trotted off, pulling the empty carriage behind them. Unlike her new dress and Quester's two pets, apparently the carriage was not hers to keep.

The reek of decay reached her nose, causing her sneeze, and Laurel turned toward the castle. She cringed, gazing up at the twenty-one corpses dangling there. It felt strange to see them there, as she could have sworn Guster had told her that the Council had decided to take them down. Yet they hung there still. The heat of early summer had quickened the moldering that had been stymied by the cold of winter. Her eyes skimmed past the fifteen dead soldiers before landing on Minister Mori's sunken face. The flesh was gradually peeling off her cheeks, and Laurel felt her eyes water. She half expected Captain Jenatt to appear and join her in mourning as he always had in the past, but he was nowhere to be found. In fact, strangely enough, there was no one guarding the portcullis at all save the two onyx lions. But she was not alone in paying her respects to Soleh's memory. Mite stood beside her, and the Sister's formerly expressionless blue eyes brimmed with tears. Her tiny body seemed to tremble, and Laurel reached out a hand to comfort her. Giant swooped in before Laurel could make contact with Mite's bandage-swathed arm and, giving the smaller sister a stern look, she shoved her toward the gate. Laurel grimaced and followed them, not sure what to make of the display she'd just witnessed. *This day could not get any stranger,* she thought.

Much to Laurel's surprise, it did. When she passed through the unguarded portcullis and into the castle courtyard, her jaw dropped open. Among a scant few plainly dressed women were at least fifty Sisters of the Cloth, some pulling carts filled with fruit, others walking horses, and still others busily tearing down Minister Mori's dilapidated old podium. Laurel's head was on a swivel as she looked all about her. There weren't quite as many Sisters here as had been present in Riverrun, but it was shocking to see this many in the city. Still, it was entirely possible the other merchants had returned to Veldaren and brought their stables of Sisters with them.

Even more shocking was the lack of purple sashes. Nowhere in the courtyard could she spot a single member of the Palace Guard.

Suddenly two men appeared from the massive doorway of Tower Honor, the first males she had seen all day. They waved to her urgently as they took step after hasty step. Laurel recognized them as Walter Olleray and Zebediah Zane, two of her fellow Council members.

"Laurel...Laurel Lawrence," Walter said as he approached. He was a balding fat man who carried his girth much less gracefully than the Conningtons. His cheeks were ruddy by the time he reached her. He panted as well, and his breath reeked of eggs, which made Laurel swallow a grimace.

"Walter," she said. "Zebediah."

"Laurel, you must come quickly," Zebediah said. He beckoned her with both hands, stepping backward. He walked with a pronounced limp, the result of having a wooden left leg.

"What's going on here?" asked Laurel. "Where are the guards? Where is the Watch? Why are there so many Sisters here?"

"Guster will explain everything," rasped Walter.

"Yes, the Speaker will tell you all you need to know."

The two continued to lead her forward. Laurel opened her mouth to ask another question, but then shut it and shook her head. Walter and Zebediah were the lowest members of the Council of Twelve other than herself. They had no opinions of their own; whatever Marius Trufont said, they reaffirmed like obedient puppies. Marius was the Council's second senior member, from a rich family descended from the Mudrakers. If these two were present, Marius would not be far behind.

She nodded to Mite and Giant, and then fell in step behind the two men. Her Sisters stayed to each side of her, not seeming to register anything but her and the path ahead. They seemed blind even to the others of their order. Laurel wasn't sure if that was a good thing or not.

Tower Honor's tall doors were opened by another pair of Sisters. Laurel entered to find the foyer and the grand hall in complete disarray. There were scattered bits of parchment everywhere, tables which used to hold finely crafted pots and vases filled with flower arrangements had been knocked over, and the carpet underfoot, which used to be thick and soft, was matted and sodden with a pinkish liquid, squishing with each step she took. Even here, the Palace Guard was absent. Fear began to clench in Laurel's belly as she watched Walter and Zebediah proceed through the mess. She had the sudden desire to turn around, walk out of the tower, the courtyard, and then the city, never to return. Taking a deep breath, she balled her hands into fists, dug her fingernails into her palms, and forced herself to move onward.

Sure enough, Marius was waiting for them at the top of the steps leading to the double doors of the throne room. Marius was fifty and average in every way, from attractiveness to height, to style of dress. It was only his wealth and aggressive cockiness that made other members of the Council fear or respect him.

Those traits were not currently on display, for Marius was fidgety. He was chomping on his lip and whispering to Lenroy Mott, the councilman from Gronswik, who stood beside him. Neither man looked up until Zebediah cleared his throat. Laurel cocked her head; she heard a faint buzzing, as though water were trapped in her ears. She yawned, trying to release the pressure in her head, but the buzzing persisted.

"Ah, Laurel," Marius said. Normally, he was the first one to make a lewd comment about her appearance, but not today. His eyes didn't rake her figure, nor did he utter a word about her dress. His voice sounded as if he had recently been crying, though his cheeks were dry. "They are waiting," he said, grabbing the handle of one of the doors.

"Wait," Laurel said. Mite and Giant squirmed uneasily beside her, as if their wrappings had suddenly tightened uncomfortably. Perhaps they'd heard the noise as well. "Where is Guster?" she asked. "Guster is supposed to be here."

"He's inside, with the rest," said Lenroy as he fiddled with his long white hair. "Waiting for us."

"Is that so?"

"Well, yes," insisted Marius.

"Please, Laurel, don't be difficult," pleaded Walter. His jowls waggled when he spoke.

"Yes," added Zebediah. "Don't make this any harder than it has to be."

"Wait…what's going on here?" she asked. This time she did back away, only to be stopped by a monster of a Sister who made Giant look small by comparison. The enormous woman grabbed Laurel's arms so tightly she thought her bones might snap. Walter pulled a dagger from beneath his shawl, handling it nervously. Laurel's head spun as she frantically sought out her two protectors, but her girls had disappeared. Her heart thumped out of control.

The Sister began to shove her toward the steps leading to the throne room. Fat Walter paced alongside, the dagger still in hand, though she could tell by the anxious look in his eye that he did not want to use it. Marius turned and faced the doors again, his palms pressed flat against the solid wood.

"I have done nothing wrong!" Laurel screamed as she was forced up the steps. Her foot caught on the hem of her dress, tearing it down the side with an audible rip.

"Unfortunately, that is not for us to judge, Laurel," said Lenroy.

"But I am the king's trusted servant!"

Marius shook his head.

"The king is no more," he said gravely. "This city serves new masters now."

With those words, Marius pulled hard on the doors. They swung outward, creaking, and the buzz Laurel had believed to exist only in her head exploded into a din so loud the air itself vibrated. She was pushed up the last two steps, then flung headlong into the throne room. She hit the ground hard, and the buzzing grew even louder in her ears. The doors slammed shut behind her.

Laurel raised her head and almost instantly vomited. The buzzing came from the millions of flies that filled the chamber, forming living black clouds around the corpses that covered the floor. The bodies were naked yet sexless, ripped apart, parts of them black with rot, their spilled insides writhing with maggots. The stench was horrendous, all encompassing. Her head warbled, her vision wavered, and she vomited again. Suddenly, hands were lifting her up, smacking her awake. She stared into Marius's eyes, which were filled with a haunting emptiness.

"Keep yourself together," he whispered. "Face the end with pride."

He released her, letting her fall into the puddle of her own vomit. Laurel froze in place, trying to be brave in the face of such atrocities. Marius's heels clicked as he walked away from her. She took that opportunity to tear a strip from the top of her dress, pressing the cloth over her nose and mouth. That done, she looked around once more.

The throne room did not remotely resemble the place of dignity she remembered. The banners had been ripped from the walls, and in their place human remains clung to the stone. Everything was dark, and even the flickering torches offered only sparse light. She glanced at the throne, which had been ripped asunder. The grayhorn tusks that had once rimmed it were strewn around the shadowy dais. That was where Marius stood, just to the side of the steps, his head bowed and hands clasped before him as if in reverence.

A moan sounded to her left, and Laurel turned. A man was slouched on the ground only a few feet away from her, his back resting against the gore-splattered wall. He too was covered with blood, glistening in the torchlight, and when he coughed a red mist issued from his lips. She inched toward him, recognizing his slightly crooked nose, his wattled neck.

"Guster?" she asked softly.

The old man's eyes cataract-filled eyes opened, seeming to brighten as they gazed on her. He reached out with his right hand. It looked as if he wanted to say something, but he coughed once more and grasped his chest.

Laurel scurried toward him on all fours. At first she meant to throw her arms around him, but she recoiled in horror when she saw his injuries. Long slashes covered his chest, yawning wide whenever he breathed. His left arm was gone, in its place a stump that was blackened on the end as if it had been seared.

"Oh…" Laurel said numbly. Her mind went blank.

Guster feebly lifted his one remaining hand, beckoning her to come closer. Laurel could hear the rattle of his lungs through his chest whenever he took a rasping breath. Tears rolled down her cheeks as she shuffled closer to the mutilated, dying man. She tried to swat the flies away, but they were too many and too persistent.

He grasped at the front of her dress, pulled her toward him. "They…learned," he croaked. "They…*know*…"

His mouth kept moving after each word he spoke, as if there were other things he was intent on saying but could not verbalize. Laurel's tears fell all the harder. She was about to ask him *who* learned, *who* knew, but the answer was plainly obvious from the carnage that surrounded her.

Guster's eyes began to roll into the back of his head, and a long, phlegm-filled gargle bubbled in his throat. Laurel pulled him upright, her fingers slipping on the slick gore that coated his flesh. "Stay with me, please, stay with me," she pleaded. "Guster, where is the king? Where is Eldrich?"

On speaking the king's name, Laurel saw a hint of a smile appear on Guster's blood-streaked face. "The king…is safe," he said. "The guards…they gathered him up…brought him away…when they first rose up…when they first spoke…"

His voice trailed off, and another croaking moan left his lips. After that his hand loosened, falling limply to the floor. Laurel continued to shake him, repeating his name over and over. Guster's head flopped forward and back.

"He is gone, dear," a voice said.

Laurel released Guster's body, letting him drop to the floor, and spun about on her knees. She watched as a man dressed in a flowing red robe emerged from the shadows behind the throne. His hands were held together, an entreaty to the gods, and his beady eyes peered out between wisps of his thinning gray hair. Marius bowed to him as he backed away from the throne, edging toward the doors.

"He was judged a sinner," the cleric Joben Tustlewhite said, "and he was punished as such."

He spoke more confidently than Laurel had ever known him to. Joben was the mumbling priest no longer, it seemed.

"He was no sinner," she said, her voice sounding small and feeble to her own ears.

"The masters of Veldaren decided it was so," the cleric replied. "They are the vessels of Karak's law."

They are here, she thought, her body going numb. *I will be shredded like the rest.*

The man stepped aside, and sure enough, in the darkness behind the throne two sets of sparkling yellow eyes stared out at her. The two lions emerged side by side from the shadows, skulking slowly toward her. They had appeared large from the top of the roof the night Quester, Mite, and Giant had saved her, but now she understood just how huge they really were. Even on all fours they were nearly as tall as Marius, who was slinking in the corner.

The male lion opened his maw wide, running his tongue over his incisors, while the female simply lowered her head, considering Laurel with eyes that radiated intelligence. The two swung their heads toward each other, exchanged a glance, and then turned back to her ever so slowly. A deep rumble sounded in the male's throat, growing louder as he took another step toward her, then another. The female swiped at the buzzing flies with her tail, matching her mate's strides. They were testing her, she knew, mocking her with the certainty of what would happen next. Laurel drew her knees to her chest, closed her eyes, and prayed.

She refused to open her eyes, even when she felt their hot, stinking breath moisten her flesh. A wet nose, easily the size of her fist, nudged her shoulder, yet still she refused to look. She kept repeating her prayers over and over again, her voice growing louder in defiance.

"Karak has not abandoned me, Karak has not abandoned me, he is the light in the darkness, the champion of order, I love you my Lord."

"Unsure."

The word was spoken clearly, though in a voice that was not human. The sound of it broke her from her prayers, and her eyes finally snapped open. The Judges were standing above her, so close that their whiskers tickled her flesh. Laurel didn't dare move. She simply looked on as the female glanced at the male and opened her mouth.

"Sinner?" Lilah asked.

Kayne didn't reply. Instead he gazed down at Laurel, and then his mouth opened wide, and he roared. Massive incisors the size of an infant's arm dripped with pink saliva. Wind scented with rotting meat buffeted Laurel in the face, and she finally screamed, planting her fists onto the bloody floor and scooting backward, only stopping when she collided with Guster's slippery corpse.

"Sinner," the male lion said. It sounded like he was laughing.

Both lions lowered onto their haunches, looking like they were preparing to leap at her, but they straightened suddenly, their giant heads turning toward the throne room doors, their ears twitching. Laurel followed their gaze, trying to listen through her fear, but she couldn't hear anything over the sound of buzzing flies and the thrumming of her heart. Then the doors flew open and Lenroy Mott stumbled in, accompanied by three Sisters. Walter waddled in right behind them. The lions stayed frozen in place, staring at the newcomers with their mouths agape, saliva clinging to their jowls

"Masters, they are here!" Lenroy exclaimed. "The Watch have stormed the front gate!"

At once, both lions leapt into action, bolting across the gore-splattered floor and out the door. A moment later, Laurel could hear the *clang* of metal and men screaming. Her jaw trembled. She wanted to get up, to sneak into the chamber behind the throne and scurry up to King Eldrich's private quarters, but she was frozen in place.

Marius, who had been cowering in the corner throughout Laurel's ordeal, stepped out into the open. He was shaking, though he tried to hide it. When he went to exit, Joben stepped in front of him.

"You, take care of her," the former mumbling priest said as he shoved Marius back into the room. "Bring her to the dungeons, and then take out that useless sword of yours and join the fight."

"Do you think that wise? Should we not be hiding? I feel the Sisters—"

Joben lifted the front of his cloak, revealing flesh scarred in an interlacing pattern by the lions' claws.

"You will not question my words, Councilman. I have been marked by the Judges. I serve them, and by serving them, I serve Karak. You...are nothing. My acolytes are mere boys, and they are better than you. Should you find fault in my commands, you can face judgment as well."

Marius closed his mouth and vehemently shook his head.

"Good. Now go."

Joben left the throne room, and moments later Marius marched across the floor, grabbing Laurel by the arm. Her mind was reeling. None of what was happening made any sense in the slightest.

Her fellow Council member yanked her out of the horrific throne room and into the hallway beyond. Instead of heading toward the front entrance, where a battle raged, he hauled her down a side passage. Laurel had never been in this part of the tower before, and when Marius threw a door open, she understood why. A set of stairs led into total darkness. Her captor hauled her down them, into a torch-lit burrow whose ceiling was so low they had to squat, and then up an opposite stairwell. At the top was another door, and when Marius shoved it open, a double row of iron-barred gray cells was revealed.

The gates to the cages were open, and Marius threw her into one of them. She landed hard on the hay-covered ground, cracking her chin and biting her tongue in the process. Blood pooled in her mouth. She rolled over, saw that there was a corpse in there with her, and hastily crawled away from it. She kicked over the piss pot in her desperation, which spilled its contents, making the stink of the place all the more unbearable. As the gate to her cell swung shut, she drew her knees to her chin and rocked in place, her mind a whirl of terror and disbelief.

Marius lingered at the bars for a moment, staring at her, his plain features turned malevolent in the torchlight.

"I do pray the end for you is quick, Laurel," he said softly. "But perhaps I will ask Joben if I can spend some time with you first. You have always been nice to look at." Yet there was no power behind his words. When he left, he snuffed out the only torch brightening that level of the dungeon, leaving Laurel in complete blackness, and when her mind broke and she began to scream, she was very much conscious of how strange it was that such a primal sound could come from her little mouth.

CHAPTER

32

Rain fell in sheets, creating streams that flowed through gaps in the rocks where the group of humans and Wardens were hiding. Lightning flashed overhead, illuminating the camp in front of them in a brief moment of clarity. Hundreds of tents were perched on the harsh, dead earth. There were horses too, more than one could count, along with carelessly built wagons and one durable wooden structure. Soaked banners bearing the mark of Karak hung limp from their poles. It was a huge settlement, and those gathered were arguing quietly among themselves as to how many might be sleeping in the tents below. Ephraim Wendover suggested five hundred. Judah countered with ten thousand.

"Enough. They will hear us if you keep arguing."

Ahaesarus sighed and looked at the camp through the curtain of his sodden hair. He didn't care how many men were gathered in the valley. All that mattered was that they had found it, and quickly.

There were eight of them in the group: Ahaesarus led the Wardens Judah, Grendel, and Ludwig, while Ephraim had been placed in charge of three young men, Craxton, Enoch, and Uulon, Turock and Abigail's son-in-law. Each carried a sword that had been recently hammered out at Turock's secret new smithy. They had departed via raft from Blood Tower just as sunset stretched its crimson fingers across the sky, and after making landfall on the other side of the raging Gihon, they had proceeded to follow their enemies' embedded footprints deep into the lifeless hills and valleys of the Tinderlands.

The cold rains had started to fall after only an hour, the downpour washing away many of the tracks. When the footing turned treacherous, Ahaesarus started to think they should turn back. But luck seemed to be with them, for only a few moments later they stumbled on an overturned carriage whose wheel had become stuck in one of the many gaping cracks in the earth, snapping its axel. From there they climbed the uneven rise where they now stood, and found the sleeping encampment spread out beneath them.

Ephraim turned to him, squeezed water from his thick beard, and scrambled to get a better position on the perch. "I assume we're done here?" he whispered. "Turock wished to know what we were facing, and now we do."

"No," Ahaesarus said, shaking his head. "We already knew Karak's men were here. What we need to know is their true numbers and whether this is their only camp. The attacks have been spread out for miles. It's possible this is but a portion of their total force."

Enoch crept closer. Water dripped from the tip of the young man's large nose, drawing attention to the way one side of his mouth was twisted higher than the other in a frustrated grimace.

"We're only eight; what else could we possibly do?"

Ahaesarus closed his eyes, listening to the camp through the constant patter of the rain.

"They are overconfident," he said, a plan forming in his mind. Opening his eyes, he scurried along the edge of the gradient, trying to find a better vantage point.

"So?" asked Craxton. "How does that matter?"

"It means there are no guards," Judah replied, and Ahaesarus silently thanked him. The Warden's hair, black as night, appeared almost blue in the rain. Judah had been by his side when Ashhur and Celestia arrived in Algrahar. If any knew what he was thinking, it was he.

"Which tells us much about their camp and their defenses," he said. "They don't view this as a true war. It has never crossed their minds that the people of Drake might attack them or deploy scouts." He pointed toward the camp, and seven sets of eyes followed his finger. "There should be soldiers marching the perimeter, keeping an eye on the surrounding hills. Yet I hear nothing but snores and the occasional whimper of one who fell too far into his cups and regrets it."

"All I hear is rain," said Enoch.

"A Warden's ears are better," Ahaesarus said, though not unkindly.

Ephraim shrugged. "That is all well and good, Warden, but again, what are we to do?"

"We will take from them the information we seek," Ahaesarus said, as if it were obvious.

"How?"

He grabbed Ephraim by the front of his drenched leather surcoat and pulled him toward the edge of the gradient. "Do you see that tent down there?" he asked.

"Which one? Point all you want; there's dozens of tents down there."

"The largest, standing twice as high as the rest. The one with a banner on each corner post."

Ephraim squinted. "Yeah, I see it. What of it?"

"Whoever leads this army will have the most luxurious accommodations, a way of reaffirming his position and power to the others. Their leader sleeps in that tent...a tent guarded by nothing but sleeping men."

"You're insane," Ephraim said. "But by Ashhur, I think I like the craziness you're suggesting. Let's go grab the information we need!"

Not five minutes later, seven furtive intruders scampered down the other side of the rocky hill. Craxton stayed behind so he could flee back to Drake should they be captured. The pounding rain helped erase any noise they made, which was not inconsiderable. The hill was covered with water, and there were a slew of loose stones underfoot. Many members of the party bounced down the hill with each blind step, but no one in the sleeping camp was the wiser.

When they reached the camp, they took it slow, tiptoeing between the many tents. The four Wardens took the lead, their stronger eyesight allowing them to spot obstructions that might give them away, such as a stray cooking pot or an empty jug of wine resting against one of the tent's support ropes. The whole while the rain kept falling, the sound the drops made when they struck the canvas tents eerie in their fleshiness. Careful as they were, it took them nearly half an hour to weave through the obstacles and reach the largest tent. They drew to a halt before it, the awning providing a needed respite from the downpour, and listened for any noise from inside. There was none to be heard, not even snores. For a moment Ahaesarus feared he would enter the massive canvas enclosure and find it empty, but he shoved that thought away and signaled to Ephraim that it was time. The bearded man's eyes were alive with nervous energy when he nodded in reply.

The party slowly and carefully drew their swords, and Ludwig pulled back the tent's entrance flap. The humans entered first, as they were able to pass through the opening while standing fully upright, whereas the Wardens needed to stoop. Ahaesarus was the last to enter. He left Ludwig outside to keep watch, touching his lips with two fingers, telling his fellow Warden that if there were trouble, he should call out to them. The flap closed quietly behind him after he squatted through the opening.

The interior of the tent was like another world. Instead of hard stone and meager tufts of yellow grass, boards had been placed down to create an actual floor. Luckily, those boards were covered in many places by plush mats, which damped the sound of the water dripping from their hair and clothes. The place was furnished with a washbasin and chamber pot on one side, and two large cabinets on the other. In the center was a large table on which burned the candles that provided scant illumination.

But it was what rested opposite them that drew the six farther inside. A bed was raised off the ground on four thick legs. Beside it was yet another cabinet, and hanging from that was a suit of armor and a massive, curved sword. On the bed was a lump whose chest rose and fell lazily.

Ahaesarus handed Grendel his sword, and Ephraim gave his to Judah, and without a word spoken between them, they inched their way across the wooden slats, approaching the bed. As they steered around the table and chairs, they caught sight of a map that had been opened atop the table, the corners held down by the burning candles. Ephraim turned and pointed at it. Uulon and Enoch sheathed their blades and removed the candles, rolling up the map.

His heart hammering in his chest, Ahaesarus and Ephraim snuck even closer, until they stood on either side of the bed. Ahaesarus looked down. The sleeper was middle aged, perhaps in the midst of his fifth decade, with straight hair cut short, graying around the temples. The side of his face was marred by a scar that ran along the side of his chin, rounded his jaw, and stopped at the vacant hole where his left ear should have been. Ahaesarus glanced around the room once more. *You certainly paid for your rank,* he thought.

He withdrew a burlap sack and piece of cloth from the bag tied to his belt, while Ephraim uncoiled a length of rope. Ahaesarus then leaned over, holding his hand in front of the man's face, feeling the sleeper's breath on his fingertips.

Ready? mouthed Ephraim. Ahaesarus nodded. In an instant, Ephraim shoved the cloth across the man's mouth as Ahaesarus wrapped his arms around the naked man's neck. The man immediately began to thrash and tried to cry out, but Ephraim pressed all the harder. So too did Ahaesarus tighten his arms, choking the breath out of the man. Together they kept his cries muffled as he struggled, until at last his movements slowed, and his body went limp.

Their quarry down and out, Ephraim went about binding the man's wrists and feet while Ahaesarus stuffed the rag deeper into his mouth and threw the burlap sack over his head. Uulon and Enoch tried to lift him, but the man was too heavy for them to hold up without great effort, so Ahaesarus and Judah took over the duties of carrying his unconscious body. They left the large tent, eliciting a surprised grunt from Ludwig, and then worked their way back through the camp. The rain had slowed, making their movements noticeable this time. The fear was ever present that they might stir the sleeping soldiers to wakefulness, especially given the difficulty he and Judah had in lugging the man's dead weight between them. They even heard a few moans and groans from the smaller tents as they passed them. Ahaesarus felt as though he were holding his breath the whole time. Right then and there he decided that should the soldiers awaken, should they emerge to find the seven of them sneaking off with their leader, they would simply throw the man's body down and flee, their mission be damned.

It proved unnecessary, for they reached the rocky hill from whence they'd come without incident. A few moments later, after slipping and sliding and almost careening into one another, they made it over the top. Their tracks were still visible, and they followed them back through the decaying wasteland. The thought occurred to Ahaesarus that the soldiers would wake eventually to find their leader gone, and would follow their tracks. *It does not matter,* he thought. If luck were with them, they would be back at Blood Tower with their prize before any were the wiser.

"You did it," said Craxton when they rejoined him on the other side of the hill, before hustling over the stones and gullies of the Tinderlands. "I thought Turock was sending us to our deaths, but you did it."

"We did," Ahaesarus said, though as he looked at their prisoner's naked body as it hung between Judah and him, he had a hard time taking any pride in that fact.

CHAPTER

33

Matthew was restless. Each night he was haunted by the wan faces of Raxler and Shimmea, eyes sewn shut in the Brennan tradition, lips purple and swollen. He could even smell the rot coming off their corpses. The glow of the fire that rose from the dinghy where their bodies had been placed remained a phantom vision, assaulting his eyes each time he blinked.

He sighed, poured a finger of rum into his cup, and downed it in a single gulp. Bren had done just as he'd asked, killing Gertrude's assistants painlessly by poisoning their wine when they toasted the successful birth of Patrick Gemcroft the day after Rachida and Gertrude set sail for the Isles of Gold. Though silencing them had been a necessary evil, the guilt of it bore down on his soul. As underhanded as he could be in matters of business, he had never ordered someone's death before. He felt dirty, as low as the brothers he constantly fought.

They did this to me, he thought. *The fucking Conningtons made me a murderer.*

Shaking his head, he swallowed another finger of rum. His head was beginning to go fuzzy, but it wasn't banishing his shame. Lately he was discovering how impossible it was to drown his sorrows in liquor, for it seemed the liquor only deepened his sorrow.

The solarium was mostly dark, the shades drawn against the outside world. The chair that usually brought him comfort now dug into his back and elbows, and he shifted restlessly as he stared at the small flames dancing in his hearth. It was the middle of the night, and he knew he should be sleeping in preparation for the next day, but he also knew that sleep wouldn't come. A letter had arrived from Veldaren demanding that supplies such as grain, casks of water, and men be sent to the capital city. The most strident demand, however, was for weapons, and a delegation was on its way to make sure such supplies were dispatched without delay. The correspondence had been signed by the cleric Joben Tustlewhite, the letter sealed with the sigil of Karak's temple, rather than that of House Vaelor. Matthew groaned. Dealing with the king would have been far more preferable, for men of practicality were easily lied to, while the truly faithful required detailed explanations when their demands could not be met. How could he give away his sellswords when he had less than a hundred left? Would they wonder at his excessive amounts of wheat and cattle, payment from the Conningtons for the weapons? And worst of all, how could he get around explaining that those weapons, a matter of public record as they had been purchased in the king's court with Vaelor mediating between Romeo Connington and him, were now missing?

The questions caused a headache to spike behind his eyes, and he rubbed his temples. A muted whimper echoed throughout the solarium, and he sighed. Moira was at it again, moaning as she sometimes did. Ever since Rachida and baby Patrick had set sail for the Isles of Gold, she'd been in a terrible frame of mind. Yet another thing to improve his foul mood…

He snatched up his rum, took a long pull straight from the jug, wiped the excess with his sleeve, and then stood up. The thought of Moira tossing and turning on her bed…well, perhaps that was one thing he could resolve. His drunkenness lending him courage, he stormed down the stairwell, using the wall for support, and then stepped off at the next level down. He passed the door to his bedroom, and those of his daughters and son, until he reached the one at the end of the hall. He barged in clumsily and closed the door behind him, too far gone to care that the sound of it slamming would echo throughout the hall.

Candles burned on either side of the large featherbed. Matthew took a step forward and saw Moira balled up on the bed, a sheer nightgown all that shielded her cream-colored flesh from view. A scarf was wrapped around her hands, which she held to her face.

"What are you doing here?" she asked. Her eyes were red, as if she'd been crying. Matthew approached her, his thoughts askew. Actually seeing Moira as a vulnerable waif threw him off. He sat down on the edge of the bed, letting his hand wander across it until it fell on her shoulder. He thought she might push him away, but instead she pulled closer to him until her head was resting in his lap.

Matthew stroked her hair, stiff like hay from the constant dyeing. The scar that ran behind her ear and onto her lower jaw was raised and red, as if it too were sad.

"It's all right," he said softly. "I just wanted to…do what I could to make you happy."

"If you desired that, you would have sent me to the Gold Isles with her."

Matthew winced.

"You know my reasons, Moira."

He looked down at her, at the way her body quivered, at the side of her dainty breast, visible through a gap in her nightclothes. Her head resting in his lap was the final straw. The way it nuzzled, the look of her slightly parted lips, brought fire to his loins. He gently moved her head and, moving his hands to her shoulders, pushed her flat. Pinching her nipple, which poked against the thin fabric of her nightclothes, with his left hand, he slipped his right between her legs.

A fist struck him in the jaw, bringing stars to his vision. He felt a moment of weightlessness, his insides tightening from the combination of liquor and excitement, and then his body hit the floor. Pain shot through him and he let out a whimper, grabbing for his hip, which had struck the ground first. Before he knew what had hit him, he was being dragged across the floor.

When he was slammed into the wall, he opened his eyes, but surprise and drink had rendered his surroundings a blur. A weight pressed into his abdomen, and something struck his right cheek, causing the back of his head to hit the wall. A hand grabbed his hair, pulling at it, forcing his chin up.

"You don't touch me," a cold voice said, and he was slapped again.

Gradually, Matthew's vision returned to him. Moira's face was all he could see, her eyes narrowed, her lips pulled back, her nose scrunched. She had him straddled and helpless, and she slammed his head against the wall once more. He shouted in pain this time, but her hand stifled the sound. He noticed she held a dagger and gawked at her, confusion and terror running through him. Moira grabbed him under the chin with one hand, and pressed her cold steel against his jugular, the cutting edge feeling much too sharp.

"I am not yours to have," Moira told him, the order spoken as if he were a disobedient animal.

"I…I'm sorry," Matthew managed to say, his voice sounding weak to his own ears.

The dagger pressed harder against his flesh. Her voice was devoid of feeling.

"I tell you this now, Matthew, and you'd best remember. Everything I do, I do for Rachida's safety, and right now that involves staying here as your prisoner. But whatever good will I had for you died the moment I realized you had lied to me. You kept me from my beloved Rachida, even when she was *right here in this house*. And then you dare to come in here with the drunken hope of taking advantage of my pain? Fuck you. *Fuck you.* You will not touch me again. You will not offer a kind word. You will not so much as look at me in any way that suggests an impure thought." She drew back the dagger, eliciting a relieved gasp from him, and waved it in front of his face. "Should you disobey, I will open your throat and let you bleed out on your own carpet. Do I make myself clear?"

Sniffling, Matthew nodded.

"Good. Now leave my room."

She climbed off him then, jamming the tip of the dagger into the nightstand and flopping back onto the bed. She glared at him, not moving an inch, until he left her presence.

Matthew wandered down the hall, feeling close to tears. His brush with death seemed to have cured him of his drunkenness, and the clarity of mind that followed sunk him even lower than he'd been at the start of the evening. In desperate need of comfort, he slunk into the bedroom he shared with his wife. Catherine was awake, propped up in bed with countless pillows, her nose buried in a book. She offered him a solemn smile.

"Darling," Catherine said. "You look a mess. Come here."

He obeyed, stumbling with each step, until he was awkwardly perched on the edge of the bed. Catherine put down her book and inched toward him. She was naked, but he refused to look at her.

"You reek," she said. "How much did you drink tonight?"

"Too much," he replied.

Her fingers danced across his face, turning his head.

"Your cheek is swollen." She lifted his chin. "And there is a cut on your neck." She said these things plainly, as if they did not require an explanation. She helped him into a reclined position, and then took his handkerchief from his breast pocket and dabbed at the blood.

"You are a silly man," she said, shaking her head. She looked sad.

He closed his eyes, rested a hand on her thigh.

"Could very well be," he said.

"No, not could be. *Are.* In fact, one could say that you trying to bed Moira Crestwell goes beyond silliness and enters into the realm of complete stupidity."

His eyelids shot open and he stared at his wife in disbelief.

"Come now, you have no right to be offended by that," she said. "Any fool can see she has no desire for a man, *any* man." She chuckled and unbuttoned his coat, spreading it wide and stroking the hairs on his chest. "You should know better, darling. It is like trying to fuck a grayhorn. No good could come from it."

He pushed her hand away and sat bolt upright on the bed, staring at her.

"Catherine…you…"

She nodded in a sorrowful way. "Of course I know, Matthew. I know about all of it."

He felt his chest tighten, and his mind leapt to the worst possible conclusion.

"All of it?" he asked.

"Yes. You think me deaf, dumb, *and* blind? Come now. Your secret room is not so secret. And besides, a woman knows the smell of other women, especially when that smell is stuck to her husband."

Matthew was speechless. He shuffled away from her, glancing toward the nightstand in the sudden fear that she might have a weapon nearby.

Catherine shook her head.

"Matthew, I'm not going to hurt you. I have known of your affairs since the week after we were married. If I wanted to kill you for them, I would have done so long ago. Karak knows, I've had the opportunity."

"I…I don't understand," he managed to say.

"You wouldn't," she said with a sigh. "You are a man, a powerful and *important* man. You have certain…needs and desires that require nourishment. It is 'the price of marrying a merchant,' you are fond of saying to me. Only you've never realized how much of that statement I truly understand."

She pushed back the blankets and got off the bed, heading toward the hearth and the table beside it. She swung her hips in an exaggerated way as she walked, sweat from the muggy evening glistening on her skin. She poured herself a cup of wine and drank it, then sat down on the chair beside the fire, crossed her legs, and stared at him from across the room. Her arms folded beneath her slightly sagging breasts, propping them up.

"Why didn't you tell me to stop?" he asked, feeling comforted by the distance between them.

"What would that have accomplished?" she asked.

"I might have stopped."

She laughed. "See, even now you cannot bear the thought. Might have stopped? Might? No, you would not. I've known you since we were both children, Matthew. Perhaps you might have tried harder to hide it, feeling guiltier each time you strayed. At worst, you would have killed me like you did those two who helped deliver the Gemcroft woman's child."

"Wait," he said. "How do you know about that?"

"I know about everything, Matthew. I have eyes and ears, and I pay attention. It is a wife's *duty* to know what goes on in her husband's life. My existence, and that of your children, depends on you."

"Yes," he said. "But *how?*"

"I have my ways."

She stood up and strolled to the bed once again. Matthew swallowed hard, his mind awash with confusion. She stopped when she reached him, letting her arms fall to her sides, exposing all of herself to him.

"You are a good man, Matthew," she said. "I may not like all that you do, but I understand it. You must know that being a woman, while wonderful, comes with its drawbacks. We are smaller than menfolk, weaker. Though our minds are just as sharp and we are the ones who nourish life once it is created, we are still considered secondary. The men are the ones who make the decisions; the men are the ones who decide the laws of this land."

There was no hiding the bite to her voice.

"I thought Karak made our laws," he interjected, half in jest.

Catherine didn't seem to take it as a joke.

"That is exactly my point. Karak, though a god, is unquestionably male. As is his brother. If Karak and Ashhur truly made humanity in their image, then men are superior, for they more closely resemble their creators." She shook her head. "Women are an unfortunate necessity, that is all. We are…replaceable."

"Do you truly believe that?"

"I do, because there is no 'belief' required. What I say is a simple fact." She pointed to the book she had been reading. "It says so in all the tomes I read, those written by *men* who have documented the short history of *man*. If we were truly equal, then why does the royal decree state that only a king may rule, that on his death the title shall pass to his closest male kin, be it a son or brother? Why does the same hold true for those of wealth, such as yourself? Your father and grandfather long expressed their displeasure with your family's penchant for creating mostly girls. Think about it. Should you perish, who would gain fortune of your control?"

"Well, eventually it'd be Ryan's."

"That's right. Your precious heir, a two-year-old who still shits his pants. I'm but an afterthought."

Matthew rubbed his eyes. He didn't want to hear this, couldn't handle it. What did she even want from him?

"Why now?" he asked. "Why are you telling me this now?"

She slowly shook her head.

"Because you *need* me, Matthew, so you don't make another blunder like you made with Moira…like you are about to make in two days when the delegation from the capital arrives."

"So you know about that too," he said. Considering all else she had said, he wasn't surprised.

"Of course I do. As I said, I know *everything* you do. I know of the pact with the Conningtons, I know of the weapons you sent west. Did you think twenty tons of grain feeding our women would go unnoticed?"

He frowned. "No," he made himself say.

Catherine stretched out beside him and took his hand. "I thought not."

They remained that way for a short time, the room silent but for the crackle of the fire and their breathing. Matthew felt the full range of human emotions in those moments, not the least of which was awe. The docile Catherine he had known his whole life was a mirage. He didn't really know her at all. That fact alone filled him with unease.

"Where do we go from here?" he whispered.

She turned to him, tracing her fingers along the small cut on his neck.

"We do as we have always done, with one small change," she said. "You will continue to run your affairs while I care for our wonderful children. However, you will hide nothing from me, not even your whores. If there is a difficult decision you must make—such as executing two innocents—you will discuss it with me first. Perhaps if we make these decisions together, they will not weigh so heavily on your soul. I can share the burden. As for Moira, let me deal with her from now on."

"And what of two days from now? What of the delegation?"

"You will have me at your side," she said, a wry smile appearing on her face. "And you will promise to hand over everything they request in time. Karak is a thousand miles away. Who is to say he has not already received whatever the priests come begging for?"

His gaped at her, startled. "Who knew you could be so devious?"

Her eyelids fluttered demurely. "Why, my lord of freight, whatever do you mean? I am but your humble servant, your wife and the mother of your children, nothing more."

Matthew laughed at that, genuine, hearty laughter. "If only that were true."

"As far as anyone else knows, it is. Now come here, Matthew Brennan, and pleasure me. I think I deserve at least that much."

"Yes, I think you do."

He rolled atop her and worked his way down her womanly body, placing tiny kisses all over, even as he stripped off his own clothing. When he entered her, she howled and bucked, and Matthew understood just how lucky he truly was.

CHAPTER

T he body was laid out on a slab, dressed in an elegant gown of the deepest blue, its eyes and mouth stitched closed. The wavy chestnut hair was draped over the pillow in a way that made it look like the corpse's head rested on a bed of curls. The flesh was pallid, the woman's normally rosy cheeks off-white like dirty snow.

Lanike Crestwell was no more.

Avila brushed her fingers against her mother's skin, which was cold and rubbery to the touch. Despair welled in her heart as she bit back any tears that might come. Her mother, like her father, was supposed to be perpetually young. They were supposed to have lived forever, guiding Karak's children through the wilderness of life, helping them to reach the heights her god had promised them. Avila suffered from the realization that her family was no more. Lanike, Joseph, and Crian were dead; Thessaly was missing; and her father might as well be dead or missing, given that an ancient demon now resided in his skin. Moira, the sister who had shamed her family, was far away, perhaps dead herself. She touched the mess of scars that marred the left side of her face, the wound Crian had given her, and felt a pang of regret. She was alone in the world.

"When did it happen?" she asked, lifting her eyes.

She was in Karak's pavilion, the god towering over her on the other side of the slab. The First Man, he who now called himself Velixar, stood beside the deity. They were the only three in the tent. Velixar's gaze was fixed on her mother's corpse. He seemed almost as despondent as she was.

"Three days ago," Karak said, his voice low and soothing, like a gentle breeze on a summer day. "Her handlers discovered her dead in her carriage. I have kept her body here since then. As her only surviving child, you deserved to see her before I disposed of her shell."

"I see."

Avila leaned over the body. Lanike's arms had been crossed respectfully over her chest. Avila grabbed the one on top, lifted it, and examined the underside. On the wrist was a deep gash that ran almost the length of the forearm. The wound yawned wide as she attempted to swivel her mother's stiff, lifeless arm, the cut deep enough to expose bone.

"The other is the same," said Karak.

"And the weapon?" Avila asked. It took a great deal of effort to keep her voice as level and free of emotion as her position demanded.

Velixar extended his hand, and Avila took the proffered knife. It was slender, a simple serrated blade meant for slicing meat at dinner. She looked again at her mother's corpse and handed it back.

"I am sorry for your loss, Lord Commander," her god said.

"And yours as well," she said, glancing up at him.

"Yes. And mine as well."

Avila shook her head. "I do not understand, my Lord. Why would she take her own life? What tormented her so?"

"Only Lanike knew for certain, my child," said her god. "And that knowledge died with her."

She looked up at them, the two who had greeted her that morning when she guided her faction of the god's army into the camp. They had insisted she come with them immediately, ordering Captain Gregorian to get the soldiers situated. Avila had followed without question, thinking she was about to be briefed on any updates to the plan now that the three major regiments had been combined. She was excited by the opportunity to finally command the full force, as was her destiny. She'd never expected *this*.

"Why was she even here?" she asked softly.

"What do you mean?" asked Velixar.

"Why was my mother here? Why was she not at home in Veldaren, tending to the king? She had no purpose on a battlefield."

"She was with us so we could protect her," Velixar said, and there was something off-putting about the way he spoke his answer.

Avila's voice cracked when she spoke. "You seem to have done a piss-poor job of *that*."

"An oversight, Lord Commander," Karak said in a scolding tone. "There was a skirmish at the bridge. Something important was stolen from us."

"And your mother was forgotten in the confusion," added Velixar.

"When my father finds out about this, he will be furious," she said, pointing an accusing finger at the First Man. "We will see then what your—"

"Silence!" Karak boomed, and Avila recoiled. The god's eyes glowed brighter than before as he leaned forward, massive hands propped on her mother's slab.

"You have been granted information others have not," the god said harshly. "You know what Clovis is now, what he means to our cause. He will remain in the dark for so long as I see fit. The results could be disastrous otherwise. Darakken is not an entity to be taken lightly."

"But—"

"But *nothing*. Remember your place, child. I named you Lord Commander because you have proven time and again to be my most loyal and capable servant. Should that change, should your emotions override your common sense, I will strip you of that title."

"Yes, my Lord," Avila said, dropping to a knee before him. "I understand."

Velixar stepped around the deity and approached her. He held out his hand, which she accepted, and helped her stand. When she brushed the hair from her face, she noticed he was staring at her, head cocked to one side.

"You look...different," the First Man said.

She hesitated, chewing the inside of her cheek to keep from making a sound. Velixar's hand rose up, and he lightly touched the corner of her eye, where new crow's-feet were beginning to appear. The First Man shrugged, brushed back his long, dark hair, and returned to his god's side.

Avila breathed a sigh of relief, and when her heart slowed its pace, she approached her mother's body once more, placing a final kiss on her cold forehead. She then bowed to her Divinity.

"I am at your command, my Lord," she said. "I apologize for my weakness."

Karak nodded. "I will forget this oversight in light of your grief," he said. "You have served me well, Lord Commander. Your fires have sealed in the south, causing my brother's more capable children to retreat toward the sea. They will not be a part of this war until we bring it to them, and for that, you have my utmost respect."

"Thank you, my Lord."

"Now rejoin your men. My Prophet and I need to speak. I will call on you, and perhaps Captain Gregorian, this evening. Until then, find peace with your loss. We must be strong when we face whatever Ashhur has planned for us."

"Yes, my Lord," she said, and bowed one last time before leaving the pavilion.

It was a mile walk back to where her regiment had set up camp, and the entire distance was packed with tents, carriages, and makeshift stables. She was glad for the respite, even though the hearty laughter of the fighting men as they gathered around their late morning cookfires felt at odds with her deep misery. She did her best to fight off the feeling, to force the tears from her eyes, before any saw the weakness that was growing within her.

At one point she ducked into a temporary privy shack and bawled. She wept for her mother, for her poor trapped father, for all her lost siblings. The weight of her sorrow threatened to crush her, and though it was horrible to experience, she latched onto it, immersed herself in it, allowing her whole body to be infused with sadness.

It was an indulgent act, but at the same time it felt *right*. She had lived her whole life as a coldhearted servant to her god, denying herself the simple pleasures Karak had promised to his children.... And now that her family was gone, now that she had no one, she realized how little it all meant.

But I do have someone. I have Willa.

She straightened herself up, wiping her face clean of tears. She wanted to see the girl. *Needed* her to fill the emptiness she felt growing inside. Thinking of Willa, she understood why her mother had taken her own life. Lanike Crestwell was not a warrior. She had always been the caretaker, the doter, the silent strength that lurked in the shadows behind the husband who had created her. With her children gone, with Clovis a monster, she'd thought herself useless.

She left the privy and continued her march through camp. A few minutes later she saw that her men had been hard at work; her own pavilion stood tall on a slight hill to the right, bordering the southern grasslands that her soldiers would burn on the morrow after Karak's Army crossed the Wooden Bridge. She turned off the road, her feet plodding across the overturned dirt as she wove in and out of the many tents. The sun bore down on her, making her bake in her armor, and she began to sweat. Her heart thumped in her chest in anticipation of seeing Willa.

As she approached her pavilion she hesitated, looking to the right, at the beige marquee housing the converts from Ashhur. Whereas the rest of the camp was a din of chattering voices and the clanging weaponry of those practicing their swordsmanship, the massive canvas structure was eerily silent. She approached it cautiously, her soles squishing on the damp earth. When she glanced down, she realized the bottom ridges of the canvas were stained a deep red. She ran toward the huge tent and stopped short once she reached the cavernous entrance.

There were bodies everywhere, more than two hundred of them. The blood of the slain flowed from beneath the canvas walls, pooling on the sodden dirt like miniature lakes. A few still moaned. She took a couple of steps into the tent, watching in horror as spurts of red issued from the neck of a man who clawed weakly at his mortal wound. She knelt, her knee sloshing into a puddle of blood when it struck the ground. The dying man's eyes flitted toward her, his mouth making gurgling sounds as he tried to form words. An instant later, a violent spasm rocked his body, and he fell still.

Her head swiveling, she took in the grisly scene before her. All of them, every single convert they had taken from Ashhur's villages before they'd sacked them, had been murdered. She had only been gone for two hours at most, leaving Captain Gregorian in charge of raising their camp. What could have happened between then and now to make...

Malcolm's words to her during their encounter in her pavilion echoed in her head.

"Sacrifice is the only way to make amends. You love her...you must cut her down."

"No!" she screamed as she stumbled to her feet and burst into the sunlight. She emerged to find a great many soldiers gathered around the tent, their hands stained with blood, scowling at her as if she were a common criminal. Irman Freemantle, the young warrior with the kind face she had placed in charge of caring for Willa while she was gone, was one of them....

Cursing her stupidity, Avila turned on her heels, sprinting as fast as she could toward her pavilion. It was no more than two hundred feet away, yet it seemed like time slowed down, stretching the distance. Panic made it difficult to breathe. When she was close to the pavilion, she made a desperate leap, diving through the entrance flap, curling her body up in the air so that she rolled to a stop.

In a single motion, she rose up on one knee and yanked Integrity from its sheath. The curved saber rattled, pointing in the direction of two bodies locked in a struggle. Willa was on the ground, her face blue, and her tiny hands grasped at the thin bit of rope around her throat. Malcolm was behind her, mouth drawn back in a grimace as he pulled the rope taut, choking the little girl's life away. He glanced up at Avila but didn't stop his assault.

"I am...sorry, Lord Commander," he said between labored breaths. He pulled tighter, forcing Willa's head back. The little girl's eyes bulged from their sockets; saliva poured from her mouth. "I must help you...save yourself."

Avila didn't hesitate. She lunged forward, swiping at his neck with her sword. At the last moment Malcolm ducked out of the way, but he was a tad too slow. The very tip of the blade caught him just north of his collarbone, opening a cut. His hands lost their grip on the rope as he spun away, and Willa dropped onto her back, coughing and crying. Avila snatched the girl up, holding her tight against her breastplate, keeping Integrity pointed at Malcolm all the while.

"I'm trying to *save you!*" he shouted at her.

"You killed them all," Avila said, growling. "You will not kill my daughter."

Malcolm laughed. "Your daughter? Your *daughter?* This is one of Ashhur's bitches, Lord Commander, not the fruit of your loins."

She didn't hear his words. "Why, Captain? *Why?*" she screamed.

"I told you I would demonstrate to Karak how you had failed him," he replied with a shake of his head. "But I took compassion on you. I will tell Karak nothing, Avila. I intended to give you one last chance to take control of your emotions. Yet now you are proving to me again just how lost you have become."

"You think this is proof that my faith has wavered?" she shrieked. "You have proven *nothing!*"

"Why argue?" he asked, shrugging. "Let Karak be the judge."

"Miss Avila?" croaked Willa, who drooled across Avila's breastplate. Her eyes looked sleepy, confused.

"Hush, child," she said, bouncing a bit to calm her. "All is well."

"I'm scared."

"As well she should be," snapped Malcolm. "She is a lamb in a den of lions. She is not of our ilk, Avila. Cast her out now, restore order to your soul before it is too late."

Avila lashed out at Malcolm, striking the side of his head with the flat of her blade.

"Outside. Now." The captain's eyebrows rose, and then he walked around her and out of the pavilion. Avila followed close behind, keeping Integrity trained on him, her other arm still holding Willa. The crowd that had gathered around the slaughtered converts had moved, forming a semicircle around her pavilion. It also seemed to have at least doubled in number. A murmur worked its way through the throng, and hundreds of expectant eyes turned toward her.

She placed Willa on the ground. The little girl gingerly touched her neck, which flared an angry shade of red. Avila knelt beside her and forced herself to smile as she gently brushed aside a bobbing blond curl.

"All will be fine, little one," she said.

"What's happening, Miss Avila?"

"We are going to fight now."

"You and the bad man who hurt me?"

She nodded.

"Will you hurt him?"

"I will. For you, my love."

Willa stared back at her, tears in her eyes.

"What if he hurts *you*?"

She leaned in close. "Then you run, little one," she whispered. "You run as fast as your little legs will carry you and do not stop until I am nothing but a memory. Understand?"

Willa nodded yes.

Avila stood and turned away from the girl. The swarm of onlookers had created a fifty-foot circle, and Malcolm stood at the far end, his legs shoulder-width apart. One of the soldiers handed him his sword, and he snatched it firmly in both hands. He ripped off the scabbard and lifted Darkfall high into the air. "Karak!" he shouted, which drew cheers from the crowd.

So you have all turned against me.

"Mother, I love you," Avila heard a tiny voice say. She glanced behind her and saw Willa kneeling, holding tight to the pole that supported her pavilion's canopy. Tears streamed down her cheeks.

"I love you too," Avila said. "Do not fear for me." Then, after taking a deep breath, she stepped into the center of the ring. Malcolm did the same.

Malcolm had the advantage in both size and reach. Though not an overly large man, he was taller than her by half a head and outweighed her by nearly a hundred pounds. Also to her disadvantage was the fact that Darkfall, Vulfram Mori's old sword, was a massive blade that dwarfed Integrity. His arms were strong—they had to be to wield such a mighty weapon—and his fighting style was technically flawless, though robotic. Although Avila relied more on grace and fluidity to best her opponents, she knew deep down that she understood more about technique than the captain. She had the advantage of having been raised under Clovis Crestwell's wing while Gregorian had been busy indulging in drunkenness. She was also wearing her light chainmail and solid breastplate, whereas he had on only his boiled leather under armor. Another advantage.

The largest advantage she had, however, was the rage that surged in her veins. She closed her eyes for the briefest of moments and pictured Willa's face, eyes bulging, tongue lolling, as Malcolm choked the life from her. When she opened them again her entire body tingled. She raised Integrity so the hilt rested beside her ear, gripping it with both hands, wrists twisted so that the blade hovered in front of her. She hollered her mother's name, then kicked her back heel and ran forward.

Malcolm brought Darkfall up in front of him, breathing heavily. Avila leaped into the air at the last moment, driving downward with the tip of her blade as she soared past him instead of attacking head on. Malcolm was caught off-guard by the maneuver, and he had to stumble backward to avoid the piercing tip. The crowd gasped at the near miss.

Avila landed and spun around, dropping into a low crouch while Malcolm regained his footing. His good eye stared at her, but there seemed to be no hatred there, no wrath. There was no panic either. The sight only made her angrier.

"Fuck you!" she yelled, and hawked a wad of spit onto the ground.

"So lost," replied Malcolm sadly.

He came at her then, rushing forward with Darkfall held straight up in the air. Avila uncoiled her legs, springing herself upright and swinging Integrity in a sideways arc. Malcolm shifted his giant blade, and the two swords collided with a raucous *clang*. The impact jarred Avila's shoulders, almost forcing her to her knees. She spun Integrity around just in time to deflect a two-handed thrust, and Darkfall's silver blade soared past her, so close she could see her reflection in the steel.

Grabbing hold of Malcolm's sleeve, she used it as leverage to pull herself up, spinning at the same time. She swung her elbow mid-spin, catching him square on the side of his face. He grunted, spittle flying from his lips as he tottered to the side. Avila lashed downward once she completed her revolution, hoping to slice through his ankle, perhaps sever a tendon. Malcolm proved quicker than expected, however. He instinctively stepped to the side, and her blade found nothing but dirt.

He was on her again an instant later, charging with a vicious downward hew that Avila easily deflected. She danced away, hopping on the balls of her feet. Malcolm's nose was bleeding, and she could see that the good side of his face was starting to swell.

"Almost," she muttered, and then feigned a lunge. Malcolm reacted predictably, spinning Darkfall to the side to parry, and Avila took her opening. She skipped to the right, flipped her sword around so she was holding it backward, and then thrust the tip into his breast. Malcolm's eyes widened as the tip pierced his leathers, sliding into the flesh beneath. The captain fell to one knee, dropping his sword and clutching Integrity's blade with his bare hands, trying to keep Avila from shoving it in any deeper. His blood dripped from his clenched fists as Avila pushed harder, the cutting edge slicing his hand.

"You are *not* my better," she said with pride.

The smile left her face when Malcolm fell backward, bringing up one leg in the process. Integrity slid out of him and the pointed toe of his boot caught Avila in the groin, sending spikes of pain through her midsection. She stumbled away, gasping. The silent crowd roared back to life, cheering and jeering with equal aplomb. She whipped her head around, sending death stares at each of them.

The sound of boots sinking into wet earth brought her back around, and she saw Malcolm running at her, Darkfall in hand once more. His left arm hung useless by his side, and he hefted the colossal sword in one hand as if it weighed nothing. Avila gaped, then rolled out of the way as the blade passed through the space where her head had been. Her legs were still numb from the blow to the groin, but she tried to tell herself she had the advantage. Malcolm only had the use of one arm, for Karak's sake!

She managed to get to her feet again just as Malcolm swiveled on her, chopping down with his sword. Their blades met once more, only to separate again a moment later. He drew back and swung, and their swords met yet again with a sound like the dinner bell when it rang out over the fields of Omnmount.

He was relentless and seemingly tireless, shoving her backward with every thrust and swipe. She retreated, trying to circle the larger man, but he cut her off each time. Eventually, she found herself pressed against a wall of flesh, colliding with the soldiers who surrounded them. Greedy, intruding hands grasped at her, and she flung her free elbow back to clear some room. The men were mauling her, distracting her from the duel. Someone squeezed her thigh, and in surprise she ducked down to swipe the hand away. An instant later, blood fell in sheets, drenching her neck and shoulders. She dropped to her belly and rolled, and when she looked back, she saw a soldier with half a head teeter and fall while his friends screamed and stared in horror at the convulsing body. Malcolm, his sword bloodied, ignored the carnage and continued his assault.

His blows rained down with ever-increasing brutality, and Avila breathed heavily as she blocked them, the force weighing on her muscles, tiring her out. She was losing speed, and her sidesteps came a half second too late to allow her to spin around her foe. Integrity began to weigh her down, and after one particularly brutal strike, she had to grasp the sword with both hands lest she lose it.

Malcolm swung his upper body and his limp left arm flailed out, striking Avila on the shoulder and throwing her off balance. She stumbled and almost fell, shrieking as Malcolm swung Darkfall in a wide arc. The blade pierced below her breastplate, where the mail was thin. It easily sliced through the metal and dug deep into her flesh. She felt one of her ribs snap at the impact, and blood began to pour from the gaping maw. She staggered backward, staring down in horror. Joseph had died from a similar wound, given to him by that ogre Patrick DuTaureau.

She lifted her eyes to see Malcolm take an offensive position, holding Darkfall high so it crossed in front of his face. Her eyes grew wide in disbelief. The blood on the blade, *her* blood and that of the soldier, began to glow. Purple fire erupted from the steel. It was the same phenomenon she had seen in the village of Grassmere, after Malcolm had sliced the young mother and infant in two. She had thought it a mirage then, and it seemed no more real to her now. She wondered if it were a fever dream from loss of blood, but then an energized buzz came from the crowd of soldiers, proving that yes, it was real.

"Karak blesses *me*," Malcolm said, the purple flames dancing in his milky eye. "You were wrong, Avila. *I* was the faithful one."

He charged her one last time, flaming sword leading like a lance. Avila tried to bat aside the attack, but when Integrity met its counterpart, the trusty curved saber broke in two. The upper half flew through the air and fell harmlessly to the ground, and then Darkfall's fiery tip pierced Avila's breastplate as if it were made of paper. The flames scorched her as the blade entered her chest, burning her from the inside out, yet when they licked off Malcolm's flesh, they did not seem to make a mark. She gasped, smoke rising up her throat and billowing from her mouth as she fell to her back. The mass of onlookers, their bloodlust brought to a boil, began to hoot and holler like madmen. Beneath it all, she heard a young girl shriek in anguish.

Malcolm yanked Darkfall from her chest.

Avila's world grew hazy, her strength fading. Before her world went dark, she gathered enough strength to look to the side. She saw, for the briefest of moments, a flash of golden hair disappear behind a tangle of grubby legs. For the first time ever, she prayed to a different god from the one who had created her.

Keep her safe, Ashhur. Let this not be for nothing. And please let me find my mother and siblings in the afterworld.

"Karak's will be done," proclaimed Malcolm, standing over her in victory.

"Fuck Karak," she blurted out, blood spewing from her lips along with the words.

Avila allowed herself to smile as darkness took her.

CHAPTER

35

Where there had been one corpse, there were now two. Mother and daughter were laid out beside each other, both pale in death. Velixar leaned in closer to get a better look. Avila had been stripped of her armor, and he squinted as he examined the hole in her chest. The flesh around the wound was blackened and charred as if it had been touched by a great flame, while the meaty bits inside were a mass of blackish-pink soup. Whatever had run her through seemed to have melted her breastbone, three of her ribs, her left lung, and half her heart. It was as awe inspiring a display of mutilation as any he'd seen. He raised his eyes to Karak, who lingered silent in the corner, and took a deep breath.

"And to think," he said, "only a few hours ago she was right here in this tent, mourning the loss of her mother." He looked at the man who kneeled opposite him. "Tell me, do you mourn as well?"

Captain Gregorian kept his head bowed in reverence when he said, "I do, High Prophet, with all of my heart. The loss of the Lord Commander weighs heavily on my soul."

"Yet it was your blade that felled her."

530 ■■ DAVID DALGLISH • ROBERT J. DUPERRE

"It was."

"And you still feel remorse?"

"Not remorse. Only sadness…Avila was a mighty soul, perhaps our Divinity's most able warrior. I could not bear to see her fall so far from grace. I challenged her to save her from herself."

Velixar glanced once more at the body. "You said she was Karak's best warrior, and yet you bested her. Does that mean you are the best of us now?"

Malcolm shook his head. "No, High Prophet. I am but Karak's humble servant."

"I see."

The captain's sword, Darkfall, was displayed next to the bodies on a slab of its own. Velixar circled around to it and lifted the heavy weapon, which he himself had presented to Gregorian in the aftermath of Vulfram Mori's demise. The steel was polished and shining, not a scratch on its surface. When Gregorian had marched into Karak's pavilion, a few of his underlings carrying Avila's body behind him, he had immediately confessed to killing the Lord Commander and handed over the sword, which he claimed not to have cleaned since the clash took place. Yet it looked as new as the day it had first left the smithy, not a spot of blood on it.

"How did you defeat her?" he asked the man.

"I drove that very sword through her chest, High Prophet," the captain replied. "I thought that part was obvious."

"Yes, but *how*. Avila Crestwell was trained in the art of swordplay since she was still sucking her mother's tit. The only man in all of Neldar who even approached her skill was her younger brother." He looked at Gregorian once more. "You, Captain, are a meager swordsman by your own admission. So how did *you* manage to strike the killing blow?"

"Karak," he answered.

"Karak?"

"Yes. Karak." The captain lifted his lone good eye, which was ringed with a nasty-looking bruise, and stared at the silent deity. "You granted me the power I needed. It is only because of you that I emerged victorious."

"Is that so?" said Velixar.

"It is."

"And yet Karak was here, with me, the entire time. That being the case, how is what you say possible?"

"I don't know, High Prophet. All I know is that I prayed for the strength to end Avila's chaos, and Darkfall alighted in purple flame."

"Hmm."

Velixar lowered the sword and approached the kneeling man. Ever since their first meeting at the door to the Tower Keep, Captain Gregorian had greatly interested him. He was truly devoted to their god, that much was obvious, yet Velixar sensed an irresponsible and frenzied streak in him, a trait the captain tried to conceal beneath layer after layer of ritual, routine, and convention. Still, he had always been loyal, obeying Karak's edicts without question. It would be a shame if the man were lying, and his clash with Avila involved some personal issue. He sighed, wishing again that his ability to detect truth from lie had not fled him when he turned his back on Ashhur.

Though in the end, it didn't matter.

Velixar reached down and ran his fingers over the scar that marred the left side of the captain's face, where the Final Judges had made their everlasting mark.

"I believe you," he told the man.

The captain bowed even lower. "Thank you, High Prophet."

"I deserve no thanks, Captain, for though I find you to be truthful, the fact remains that you convinced your men to slaughter two hundred converts who had sworn their lives to Karak. And despite your good intentions, you still took the life of the Lord Commander, named so by our god. The proper channels were not followed; none were told. You acted on your own. This army is about order, Captain, and you catered to chaos."

"It is true," Gregorian whispered. "I knew it was true the moment I lifted my sword against my leader." He held his arms straight out before him, threw his chin back, and squeezed his good eye shut. Disturbingly, the milky one remained wide open. "My life is my god's to do with as he wishes. Take it from me, purge the turmoil from my veins, for I have sinned, and there is no mercy for agents of chaos."

Velixar raised his eyebrows. "You would give your life away so freely?"

"My life is not mine to give."

"Enough," said Karak. He strode toward them across the open space.

"Yes, my Lord," said Velixar. He backed away from the captain, bowing.

Karak stepped up to the kneeling man and placed a massive hand atop his head.

"You are indeed my humble servant, Captain. Your actions prove it more than your words. Now stand up, my child, and have a physician mend that arm."

"Yes, my Lord," the captain replied. When he looked at the god, tears flowed in twin streams from his good eye. "Forever for you, my Lord."

Gregorian rose to his feet and kissed Karak's hand. The god smiled down on him, then reached behind him and grabbed Darkfall off its slab. He handed it to the captain.

"The instrument of your faith," he said, his voice soothing. "And the instrument of the Lord Commander, as well."

The captain's eye bulged and his lips quivered, but he said nothing.

"Now go, Malcolm, and uphold my word as you always have."

"Yes, my Lord."

"One last thing," Velixar chimed in before the man could leave. Gregorian halted and pivoted toward him, stiff as a good soldier should be, even while his injured limb dangled uselessly.

"What is it, High Prophet?"

"Some of the men reported that the Lord Commander's fall came about because of a young girl. Is that true?"

The captain nodded.

"And where is this girl now?"

"No one knows, High Prophet. She seems to have disappeared."

"Interesting," Velixar replied. "That is all, Lord Commander Gregorian. You may go now."

"Thank you, High Prophet."

When Gregorian left the pavilion, Velixar examined Karak's expression. The god looked pensive, perhaps even whimsical. It was an odd way for a deity to look—dangerous, even—but Velixar decided it best not to question him. Given his own failures over the last few days, the last thing he needed was to give his god a reason to strike him down.

"He is a devoted man," Karak said finally.

"It would appear so," Velixar said. "And his story is true?"

"Of course. Gregorian has proven that he believes my teachings completely. I do not think any human alive loathes chaos as much as he does."

"But what of his slaughter of those of Ashhur's children who bended their knees? Should he not suffer punishment for that?"

"He ended those lives out of love for order, not because he was a curious man intent on meddling with powers he does not understand."

Velixar winced at the slight. He hesitated before speaking again, but in the end he decided that if he was to be the High Prophet, he should not fear questioning his deity's decisions.

"However, I must point out, my Lord, that he did end the life of the Lord Commander. Should that sort of insubordination be rewarded? What if every underling who wishes to be rid of a pesky superior does the same to achieve a higher station?"

Karak stared at him in disappointment. "You should know better than to ask that question, Velixar. None will rise up that way, for I reward my children with titles as I please. If I were to take the lowest delinquent in the dungeons of Veldaren and place on *him* the mantle of Lord Commander, the men would treat him with just as much respect as they do you. Do you understand why?"

"Because you were the one who named him," he said, lowering his head.

"Correct. As a god, my title was neither earned nor given to me. It was a station I was *created* to hold, and none can strip it from me." His eyes blazed. "I, on the other hand, can strip any man of his title, deed, and even life if I so desire."

Mine as well, Velixar thought, but kept it to himself.

Karak continued: "While the death of Lord Commander Crestwell is indeed unfortunate, Gregorian believed, with all his heart, that she had turned her back on me." He pointed to her face. "You made mention of her different appearance earlier, and you were correct. Look closely at her eyes and mouth, Prophet, and you will see it: the lines of age, the withering of skin on bones. She was no longer ageless."

"Is aging a sin, my Lord? Only a select few have been blessed with agelessness, and even those who denied that gift were not cast aside. Vulfram was mortal, and you never once expressed distrust in him…at least until the end."

"They were different people, with different ways of thinking. Vulfram was a man who balanced the love of his family and his dedication to me. He was objective. Avila was not. Her beliefs were strident, singular. If she grew to love that girl more than me, as she visibly did, it would only have been a matter of time before she deserted me."

"I see. That does, however, beg one question, my Lord."

"Which is?"

Velixar wandered toward the bodies again, poking his finger inside Avila's gaping chest.

"This wound," he said. "I have seen none like it, burned the way it is."

Karak joined him, peering down into the scorched cavity.

"Faith and power are interchangeable, Prophet," the deity said, lowering his voice to a soothing whisper. "And occasionally faith can manifest itself as power in times of great need, leading to greatness. I have observed it time and again throughout the journeys my brother and I have embarked on, though this is the first instance I have seen the phenomenon here on Dezrel. It makes perfect sense that Gregorian, the only man to survive my Judges, would perform such a miracle."

Velixar frowned, mulling it over.

"So his belief in you gave him strength and power beyond himself?" he asked.

Karak shook his head. "How disappointing that you do not see the truth even now. The universe is fickle, and that which is given always requires payment. Gregorian's faith was a *conduit* for power…*my* power. He was in a dire moment of need, with order hanging in the balance, and his belief reached through the ether, borrowing a small piece of the fire that burns within me."

"The same as with my own abilities? All of your followers' power must come from you?"

"Correct."

"So without you, we would merely be human."

"Without me, none of you would exist."

Good point, Velixar thought. "Did you feel it when it occurred?"

The god laughed. "The energy he borrowed was tiny, like a single blade of grass in a field hundreds of miles wide. I felt nothing."

"How much power do you have at your disposal?"

Karak glanced away, raising an eyebrow.

"It is finite," he said. "For now, that is the only answer I can give."

Excitement hummed through Velixar's veins, and on reflex, he searched for writing implements. The space was empty but for the two slabs and the bodies that rested on them. With a pang, he remembered what had been stolen from him, and he curled his hands into fists, breathing heavily. A disgusted grunt left his mouth.

"You are fretting about the book," Karak said.

"It is not just any book, my Lord. All of the knowledge I have gleaned since you and Ashhur created me is written within it. There are passages of great power in there, ones that may be used against us if your brother recognizes the journal's worth, which he most certainly will. Should that occur, any advantage we have may be lost."

"The journal may not be on its way to Ashhur," Karak said. "Your certainty in Patrick DuTaureau's thievery is unwarranted."

"Who else might have taken it?" Velixar asked. "The book vanished that very night, while I was away from my tent. I can think of no other reason for the mutant's presence in our camp. Besides, Ashhur knows of the journal, as do many others in this godsforsaken land. It would not surprise me in the slightest if your brother were the one who sent Patrick after it. And if he knows of my plan with the demon…"

Karak looked at him sidelong, a glance Velixar returned.

"Darakken, my Lord. I have studied his memories, and within the elven tombs I found many secrets, some showed to me by Errdroth Plentos, some of which he would have preferred I never discovered. The spells to banish the beast are complicated and cannot be remembered, but I did find them in writing. Over the past months, I've worked to reverse the spell, to resummon—"

Karak shook his head, interrupting him, and he seemed strangely undisturbed.

"Once again, Prophet, you forget your place. Why would I, a part of the deity who originally created the beast, require a book written by you to make it whole again?"

"You know the spell?"

Karak laughed. "There is no spell, Prophet. What these hands created, these hands can bring back once more."

Velixar stepped back, clenching and unclenching his fists.

"Ashhur lied," he whispered.

"My brother is incapable of lying, Prophet."

"He told me resurrection is impossible. He would not bring Brienna back to…would not bring the elf girl back for Jacob."

"The elf was not his creation."

"But if I were to perish, he could have brought me back? You could do the same?"

The god pursed his lips and squinted. After a few moments of silence, he replied, "It depends."

"On what?"

"Think on it, Prophet. The demons were cast away from this dimension by Celestia, their bodies destroyed while their essences were trapped in nothingness. Yet there *was* one demon who perished in the great war with the elves, was there not?"

"Yes. Sluggoth."

"You brought back the other two. Why not him?"

Velixar closed his eyes, thinking back to the moment when his entire life had been obliterated into something new.

"I couldn't," he said. "I reached for it, but it just wasn't…there."

"It was killed, not banished," Karak said. "And as time passes, the essence continues on to its final resting place. It populates the abyss below Afram, a ghost among ghosts. The longer it is there, undisturbed, the greater the difficulty. To bring it back to mortality? A soul can be separated from a body, but it must immediately be trapped or placed within another. The moment the soul transcends the barriers between this world and Afram, bringing it back becomes near impossible. Perhaps Ashhur could have brought back this Brienna, but it would have only been a shadowed form of her, disjointed and in a body doomed to rot and break. Either that, or she could have been brought back as a ghost, barely able to hear or understand the sight and sound of you. I am surprised that you did not realize this in all your wisdom."

"I am sorry to have disappointed you," Velixar said, dropping to one knee. Again, he'd been shown that he was lesser than he thought himself to be, yet instead of letting it frustrate him, he let it remind him why he had sworn his life to Karak. Better to think on that than to relent to thoughts of Brienna.

The god dismissed his apology with a wave. "Enough. Stand up."

With that, Karak stepped up to the two corpses and placed his hands on them. Both burst into layers of raging black flames. Their dead flesh charred and melted off their bones, and then their bones caught fire as well, succumbing to the flames' hunger until the slabs contained nothing but two human-shaped outlines in ash. Velixar drew back from the scene, remembering a similar one that had taken place many months before, when the lifeless form of that beautiful elf had been handed the same fate by Ashhur.

Velixar cringed, his heart sinking once more.

"Do not be dismayed," the god told him, misreading his expression. "Fret not about Darakken, Prophet. If what I plan comes to pass, we will have no more need for the creature. But I need *you*, Velixar, the swallower of demons. No matter what your failings, you are still my greatest disciple. I handed you the medallion and named you High Prophet for a reason."

Velixar bowed, taken aback by the uncommon espousal, but the taint of his failure was still like a festering boil on his soul. No matter what his god told him, no matter how strongly the pendant pulsed on his chest, he could not let it go. He wanted to discuss these matters with someone other than his deity, wanted to talk with someone like Roland, a receptive ear with a desire to learn, only one who would not turn away from him.

That man exists, he reminded himself. *I will seek him out tomorrow, and perhaps I will ride with him all the way to Mordeina.*

"Now go get your rest, High Prophet," Karak said. "Tomorrow we march, and victory will not be very far behind."

Come high noon the following day, after fifteen thousand men packed up their belongings, donned their armor and weapons, and joined their formations, the new Lord Commander gave the order to advance. Line by line they marched over the bridge, armor clattering, horses plodding, banners floating limply in the stifling summer air.

Velixar remained at the side, watching man after man clomp onto the Wooden Bridge. Nearly six hours had passed by the time the wagons that took up the rear, including the one that had housed Lanike Crestwell, bounded onto the bridge's sturdy slats. Velixar sat tall on his charger, fingers tapping Lionsbane's hilt, his lips tightening into a thin white line of concern, before he finally shook his horse's reins and guided the beast to follow the rest.

He had spent the morning searching for Boris Marchant, questioning the young soldier's superiors and even those who served in his platoon. None of them knew Boris's whereabouts, so Velixar had resigned himself to carefully examining every soldier who crossed the bridge. Still, he had never once seen Boris's face. He concluded that the young man must have fallen prey to one of the wolf-men's claws. He shook his head, feeling foolish for his sorrow. There were other capable students here, young men who would serve him just as well. When all was said and done, he would find another.

CHAPTER

36

The dark became a living thing, pressing in on Laurel, wrapping her in its ethereal arms, suffocating her. In the blackness she had no concept of the passage of time: she might have been down in the dungeons for a day, a week, or perhaps even a lifetime.

With no outside stimulus, her mind retreated inward. Whenever she rubbed her eyes, the bright flashes that lit her vision became faceless loved ones calling out to her from a distance. She saw her mother and father, her sisters and dead brothers—even Mite and Giant, their wrappings glimmering with the phosphorescent light of inner space. The stinking corpse beside her became a dozen different monsters and hateful people, and she cowered in the corner, as far away from it as possible.

Formless voices stalked her in the darkness, growing ever closer with each passing moment. *You are as worthless as a whore.... You have turned your back on your god.... You deserve your fate.... There is no more hope.* She screamed in protest against them, but they did not stop their assault. Day and night, through the indistinguishable margin between sleep and awareness, their accusations stabbed at her, driving her further from sanity.

She almost wished for the Final Judges, the new rulers of Veldaren, to come for her and end her suffering. Almost.

It was Guster, her father figure in Veldaren, who helped her hold onto the final threads of sanity. As she lay suffering, the old man's calming words, imagined though they were, echoed throughout her skull, pleading with her to uphold her end of the bargain. *I put my faith in you,* his voice said. *You are the key—you who were not a slave to blind belief...you who learned the errors of your ways...you who love Karak despite the Divinity's obvious lack of love for you...*

Laurel began laughing.

"I am mighty!" she shouted, sobs wracking her every other word. "I am strong!"

The blackness closed in on her yet again, and she felt the ground shift beneath her. Creaking noises pierced her ears, as well as the scrape of stone ground against stone. It wasn't only the darkness that was alive, but the dungeon itself. She sat up, pressed the heels of her palms against her ears, and rocked back and forth. She pictured her god in the months after the creation of man, long before her birth. In her mind's eye, she saw him pounding the earth with his fists, digging deep into the land, and shaping the walls of this very dungeon. He lifted his glowing eyes, smiling wickedly at his children as they gathered around the rim of the crater he had created, Laurel among them. *If you turn away from me,* his voice said in her mind as his stare burned through her, *you have turned against the light of order. Let the shadows of chaos embrace you hereafter.*

"I will not," she whispered, defiant. "I am Laurel Lawrence, and I am strong."

"Yes, you are, my lady."

Laurel ceased her rocking and glanced up. All had gone silent; even the rats seemed to have stopped skittering. She drew a breath into her lungs and held it, in the grips of an even greater terror.

She then heard the sound of breathing—not her own, but someone else's—and the soothing male voice spoke again.

"Laurel, I am here for you."

"Karak?" she murmured.

A soft, kind chuckle was her answer.

"Not Karak, my lady. Not even close."

Her world suddenly assaulted by an explosion of brightness, Laurel kicked herself backward, screaming. It was as if she had been hurled into the sun, its flames roasting her flesh and melting her eyeballs in their sockets. She flopped over and cried, arms held over her head, waiting for the rest of her to be set aflame until even her ashes were scorched to nothingness.

The gate to her cell creaked open, and a new sound hit her ears—footfalls sloshing over wet stone. Her body was not on fire. Laurel swallowed her tears and glanced up.

Two figures stood over her, a man and a woman, lit from behind by flickering torchlight. She focused on the man, a handsome, slender sort with a dark complexion, kind hazel eyes, and a head of curly black hair. Her eyes traced the strong outline of his jaw and curly locks that bounced above his shoulders. She knew him, even though he was wearing a buttoned-up cloak rather than the armor of the Palace Guard.

"Ca–Captain Jenatt?" she said.

The man squatted down, holding out his hand. "Pulo," he told her. "There are no titles needed. None exist any longer."

Laurel hesitantly grabbed his hand, and Pulo Jenatt, former captain of the Palace Guard, helped her to her feet. Beside him stood Mite, crouching low, her covered head swiveling. Laurel hovered unsteadily, her knees shaking, and then looked down at herself. The elegant dress that Lady Connington had given her was a torn and sloppy mess, covered in a slimy black substance so thick that none of the original turquoise could be seen. Most of the gems that had been stitched to it had broken free. Strangely, the fabric seemed to be moving. She glanced to her left and caught sight of the rotten corpse, the trail of maggots that had wound its way into her corner.

"Get them off me!" she screamed, pushing herself away from Pulo while desperately tearing at her dress. It came off in clumps, as if its threads were as decayed as the corpse. She felt the maggots writhe against her and came close to vomiting.

"My lady, it's all right, Let us help."

Feminine hands were on her in an instant, shoving her against the wall. Laurel braced her hands against it, leaning forward and wheezing as her clothing was torn from her body. The drenched material slopped against the stone floor, leaving her naked as the day she was born, but she didn't care. A damp towel was then run over her from head to toe, cleaning away the filth. She began to gag. Something was pressed into her hand. Laurel looked down and saw a small burlap sack in her palm.

"Place it over your nose and mouth," said a youthful female voice. "To help with the smell."

Laurel did as she was told, and the nauseating stench of decay and feces was muted by the fresh smells of hyacinth and lilac. She took a deep breath, her nerves stilling with a final shudder.

"Thank you," she said through the sack.

Mite nodded and backed away from her, joining Pulo. The realization struck her that Mite had broken her vow, and Laurel's mouth gaped beneath the sweet-smelling bag.

"Come now, Miss Lawrence," Pulo said. "We haven't much time."

Her wits slowly returned to her. She lowered the sack and asked, "What is happening?"

"Not now. I'll explain on the way."

She looked down again, feeling suddenly modest. She crossed her arms over her bare breasts, even though Pulo seemed not the slightest bit interested in her nakedness.

"I'm sorry, Miss Lawrence," he said, seeing her reaction. "We will find you something to cover yourself with once you are safe."

Mite grabbed her hand and gestured to the opened gate with those soft blue eyes of hers. For the first time, Lauren noticed something oddly familiar about them, but she had no time to question it. Before she could even get her bearings, the diminutive Sister was yanking her into the corridor. Pulo had snatched the lighted torch from the wall and was holding it out in front of him as he ran forward, leading the way. Laurel's feet ached as they slapped against the hard stone floor, and the air burned in her lungs. She pleaded with her saviors to slow down, but Mite's grip was firm, her drive unstoppable. They passed cell after cell, the stench of decaying bodies overwhelming. Laurel brought the sack she had been given to her nose once more.

They stopped at the stairwell that led into the lower hall of Tower Justice. Pulo snuffed out the torch, and in the darkness Laurel heard him shove it into the metal ring embedded in the wall. She was yanked up another staircase in darkness, and then they passed through another doorway, turned a corner, and raced up yet another stairwell. Finally they reached the top, and when Pulo threw the door opened, she was once more bathed in light.

There was only one person in the hall, a tall Sister who lingered by the main entrance, a dagger clutched tightly in her hand. Laurel could tell right away, from the way she held her shoulders back as if in a constant state of insolence, that it was Giant. She dropped the small sack of hyacinth and lilac and smiled. Her girls hadn't abandoned her after all.

"We should be safe for now," said Pulo as he unbuttoned his cloak. "The lions remain in Tower Honor during the day. They only hunt at night."

"What time of day is it?" Laurel asked.

He kept his eyes averted from her nakedness.

"Sunrise was only an hour ago. We watched from the roof of the closed brothel on South Road until the coast was clear to rescue you."

"How did you know I was here? And how in Karak's name did you get past the Sisters?" Mite and Giant both peered at her. "The *other* Sisters, I mean."

"Your two protectors told us of your...situation," said Pulo, nodding toward Mite and Giant. "I don't know how they knew where you were, but be thankful that they did. As for getting into the castle...to be honest, it was quite easy." He cast aside his cloak, letting it flutter to the ground. He was wrapped from head to toe in the bindings of the Sisters of the Cloth, all the way to his neck. The wrappings were skin-tight, and Laurel gasped at the effectiveness of the illusion. Pulo's bulge was nowhere to be found, and he even had a pair of modest lumps on his chest.

"Trickery," he said with a slight frown. "But not a costume I wish to wear for long. It is rather binding in all the wrong places, and certain...er...painful tucking is required." He turned to Giant. "We should begin now."

Giant kicked the sack beside her across the floor, and Mite stopped it with her foot. After gesturing to Pulo, Giant raced across the room, slipping through the dungeon door and closing it softly behind her.

"Where is she going?" asked Laurel.

"She is using the underground tunnels that connect the towers," Pulo answered. "She will leave from Tower Honor this afternoon, when the castle is at its busiest, while we will leave from here."

"Why?"

"Three Sisters were seen entering this structure, my lady. It would seem odd if four were to leave."

Mite opened the sack and began to pull out yard after yard of off-white fabric. Laurel couldn't help but laugh at the absurdity of it. The order she despised, the one that helped the men who ruled the kingdom suppress women, was to be her mode of salvation. If only she'd had a true bath beforehand to wash away the lingering scent of decay from the dungeon below....

Pulo turned away, and Laurel held her arms out to her sides as Mite began the agonizingly slow business of swathing her every square inch with thin strips of material. She worked up one leg, then the other, and Laurel was amazed at how constricting the garb actually was. It felt like her lower half was being squeezed in one of her father's lemon juicers.

"Captain Jenatt…Pulo," she said, trying to keep herself together despite her ordeal. *Cornwall Lawrence would do the same.* "Please, tell me what is happening in our city."

Mite continued to work, now busily wrapping her midsection. Pulo took a deep breath and stared directly into her eyes. She was impressed with his self-control.

"It happened suddenly," he said, his gaze still locked with hers. "Soon after the mumbling priest began to set the lions loose at night, the Sisters arrived. They entered the throne room as a huge mass. The king was confused, as were we all, since they'd arrived with Joben, not their merchant owners. The priest then told the king that he knew of his plan to overthrow Karak's law and cast all of Neldar into chaos in the god's absence, and he was guilty of blasphemy. King Eldrich was beside himself. He demanded that we remove Joben from the throne room, but before we could take hold of him, the fighting began. The Sisters attacked the Palace Guard, killing many men before they could raise their weapons in defense. Then the two damned lions came bolting through the doors, ready for blood. In a blink of an eye, they slaughtered six more of my men."

Laurel shuddered, expecting worse to come given what she had just experienced.

"The king's bodyguard—you know him, Karl Dogon—snatched up the screaming king and pulled him into the Council chambers behind the throne. My fellow guards and I followed, holding off the Judges and Sisters as best we could. Once inside, we barred the door and ushered the king into his quarters, where we led him to the secret exit behind his bed. Twenty of us left the castle while our pursuers broke the door down below us. From there we fled into the city. Luckily, none followed."

Pulo paused.

"What then?" a breathless Laurel asked as Mite began the process of binding her breasts beneath the cloth.

"We headed north, toward the slums. It was there we hid, only coming out at night. We called the rest of the Watch, who were themselves being hunted, to join us. This was all two weeks ago."

Two weeks ago. That must have been just after Mite, Giant, and the Crimson Sword saved her from the Judges. *So much horror in so little time.* Her shivering began to subside, and a sort of numbness took over.

"What have you done since?"

"We have called others to our cause. Thieves, miscreants, rapists—we embrace any we find who are fleeing the Judges' wrath. We remained hidden until the day our lookout spotted you entering the city. King Eldrich demanded that we protect you from certain death—he is very fond of you, Miss Lawrence—and so we assaulted the gates. We lost thirty men before we retreated. The king fell into a deep depression, for he was certain you were dead. It wasn't until your servants sought us out that we learned you were being held captive."

She looked at Mite. "But they are Sisters. How did you know to trust them?"

Pulo shook his head, obviously more at ease now that her womanly features were concealed.

"They did not come to us as Sisters, Miss Lawrence. They were not wrapped. And seeing who they were...who one of them was... well, we felt inclined to trust the story they told."

"What do you mean?" she asked, feeling baffled.

He pointed at Mite, but said nothing.

Mite was busy tying up Laurel's hair with a piece of twine when Laurel grabbed the Sister by the wrist, stopping her.

"Please, Sister," she said. "In the dungeon, you spoke. Would you do so again?"

The diminutive Sister dropped her head. "I will, if you command it," she replied.

"There is no commanding here." She placed a kind hand on Mite's shoulder and smiled, the numb feeling slowly growing stronger. "Please, I don't wish for you to wrap my head. I would like to do that myself. Will you show me how?"

"I…I suppose."

"It would be most appreciated."

Those deep blue eyes stared at her with uncertainty before her hands finally got to working, undoing a knot in her own wrappings and slowly uncoiling the fabric from the top down. The Sister's hair was revealed first, a dark shade of brown and hacked short. Next were her feminine brow, her exotic nose, her full lips and slender jaw. It was a young girl who stood before her, no older than sixteen and dainty, her pale cheeks flushed red. Laurel traced the girl's jaw with her fingers. There was something so very familiar about her, but she did not know what.

"Did you see, Mistress?" Mite asked.

"Did I see what?"

"How the wrappings are applied?"

She shook her head. "I apologize, I wasn't paying attention. But forget that for now. Tell me your name, please."

Mite bowed slightly. "Mistress, I am called Sister," she said.

"I am not your mistress," Laurel said kindly. "Call me Laurel, or Miss Lawrence if that pleases you. And the name I want is your *true* name, the one given to you before you were forced into the Order."

The girl backed away from her slightly, her lips twitching. She glanced all around her, as if to speak such an atrocity would summon a bolt of lightning from the heavens to strike her dead.

"My name was taken from me," she whispered. "By Karak's law."

"Karak's law is shit," said Pulo from behind her. "Just answer the question, girl."

She took a deep breath, straightened up, and met Laurel's eyes.

"My name was Lyana. Lyana Mori," she said finally.

Laurel fell speechless. She took a deep breath, her numbness replaced by a burning anger that rose up in her gullet. Deep inside, she channeled her father, the strongest and most righteous man she had ever known, who hated the Sisters of the Cloth as much as she.

"You were once Lyana Mori, and now you are Lyana Mori again. As your rightful owner, I free you from your bonds, from any servitude to me."

Lyana's eyes widened. "But if I serve neither you nor Karak, whom *do* I serve?"

Laurel thought of those corpses, of Soleh and Ibis and Vulfram, the girl's father. She thought of what her own father might have said under the same circumstances.

"You serve vengeance," Laurel said. "Now show me again how to put these wrappings on. I want out of this damn tower."

CHAPTER

37

The weary travelers circled a bend in the road, and suddenly Mordeina loomed before them. Patrick's jaw dropped the moment he saw the wall surrounding his place of birth. It was at least sixty feet high and stretched out in either direction for what looked like miles.

"By gods!" he said.

"Impressive," said Preston.

"Never seen a wall like that," added Tristan.

"Eh? The one around Port Lancaster's just as high," Ryann said.

Big Flick punched the smaller man in the arm. "You never even *been* to Port Lancaster."

"I have so," whined Ryann.

"Have not."

"Enough!" shouted Preston, and all went silent. "I swear, if you didn't look like men, I'd mistake you for babes who still suckled at your mother's tit."

"I'd suckle on *your* mother's tit," Patrick heard someone say. When he glanced behind him, he noticed that Preston's two sons were smirking. A chuckle escaped his throat. *That* was humor he could appreciate.

Preston, apparently deaf to the jibe, rode up beside him.

"You grew up here," he said, "yet you seem shocked. Why?"

"Because that wall wasn't here when I left," Patrick said. "There were fields and forests and rolling hills for as far as the eye could see."

"It's been a long while since you've been home, eh?"

"It has. At least a year, give or take a month."

Preston grabbed his arm.

"You've only been gone a year?"

Patrick nodded.

"And now there's a huge wall around the city?"

"That's no city. It's not even as advanced as Haven was. I would say it's more like a…huge collection of well-built tents."

"Not really the point I was making," said Preston. "It would not be humanly possible to raise a wall that large that quickly. By Karak's stinking nutsack, when my sons and I built the wall around our field in Felwood, it took three months to finish…and was only three feet high, circling a single field!"

Patrick shrugged. "That was you and your sons. Trust me when I say that Mordeina is home to more than three people."

"I don't care. Even ten thousand people slaving away day and night could not have raised this structure in such a short time." He shook his head adamantly. "It's not possible."

"Argue all you want, but it wasn't there before, and it is now, plain as day. Let's just thank the stars it's there instead of bickering about how it was built, eh?"

"I'll give you that one," Preston said with a nod.

"Good. Now can I please have my arm back? Hard to ride with one hand, especially for one as top-heavy as me."

"Sorry."

The closer they drew to the wall, the more impressive it became. Patrick realized that it was not a single wall, but two, the one in front shorter and gray, with a slightly taller one behind it that was reddish-tan in color. This realization brought on yet another series of admonishments from Preston, which made him shake his head and sigh.

A branch of road from the east led toward the walled settlement, and all eight horses turned onto it. A massive gate loomed before them, its bars made of ominous black iron. Patrick's face scrunched in confusion, as there was, of course, no mining for steel in Paradise, so far as he knew.

When they reached the gate, Patrick dismounted and walked up to it. He peered through the bars, only to see the secondary wall staring back at him. He had to crane his neck to see the porthole cut into that second wall, itself barred, off to the left.

"Hello?" he shouted. "Anybody there?"

No one replied, but he could clearly hear the clamor of voices and other noises that indicated there were plenty of people inside. He took a step back and looked up. There was nothing to see but the ridged top of the outer wall.

"What's wrong?" asked Edward.

"No one's answering," he said.

Ragnar cleared his throat. "Can we open the gate ourselves?"

"What do you think?" Patrick shot back. "We're in front of a wall that was obviously built to keep out an army. Do you really think it would be so simple to storm our way in?"

"You never know until you try," said Joffrey with a shrug.

"The boy has a point," added Preston.

Patrick rolled his eyes. "Fine," he said. "But you really think one man could lift this on his own?"

The Flicks, Ragnar, and Edward joined him at the gate, and the youths wrapped their hands around two of the bars. "How's that?" Big said with a grin.

"Whatever," Patrick mumbled.

The five of them stooped and shoved upward, and surely enough, the twenty-foot-high gate lifted off the ground, and the sound of pulleys spinning echoed from inside.

"Looks like they were right," he heard Preston say.

Patrick felt his ears grow hot. He grunted, dug in, and helped the rest shove the gate up as high as they could. He then snatched his mare's reins in frustration and led the beast through. The horse had to duck in order to avoid impaling its head on the spiked ends of the bars, and the rest followed suit.

The space between the first wall and second was slim, barely ten feet. Simply being in the gap made Patrick feel claustrophobic, with two unscalable walls on either side of him and no way out but through one of those two gates. The effectiveness of such a constricted killing field left him more than a little impressed.

He turned to the left and walked the fifty or so paces leading to the second gate. When he looked through the bars—iron as well, he noticed—he was shocked to discover he could not see the expanse of Mordeina stretching out before him. There were strange rock formations lining the other side of the entrance, blocking his peripheral view, and a mass of people was gathered in between them. The only thing he could see was Manse DuTaureau, looming over everything from its spot on the distant hill.

He tried to lift the second gate, but it didn't budge. *At least this one is locked.* "Hey!" he shouted through the bars. "Anyone feel like letting in a tired group of travelers?"

One from the throng between the stone barriers turned his way. It was an older man, someone he recognized but couldn't place. The dumb smile on the man's face faltered as he neared the bars, his head cocked to one side.

"Patrick?" he asked finally. "Patrick DuTaureau?"

Patrick stepped away from the gate and gestured to his body. "Anyone else look like this?" he asked.

The man spun around and jogged past the gathering of clueless chatterers, disappearing into the crowd beyond. Patrick could hear his voice shouting out to someone, but there was too much clamor on the other side for him to distinguish his words clearly. The itch of panic made him shuffle his feet. He hadn't known what to expect in Mordeina, and he wasn't sure what to make of these new developments.

"What's going on?" asked Tristan.

"Shush," Patrick said. "Be patient."

"Fine," the youth grumbled.

Patrick rolled his eyes and clenched his fists. Someone had better arrive to let them in soon. Otherwise, he just might smash someone's head in.

A few minutes later, an imposingly tall figure emerged. He leaned over the group on the other side, saying something inaudible, and the gathering dispersed quickly, as if there were lions on their heels. Patrick grinned as the Warden turned their way and approached the gate. Patrick knew him quite well, and he actually remembered his name.

"Judarius," he said, nodding to him, "I heard you were here. Pampering a king, as it's said."

Judarius's expression was stony. "How did you get through the gate?" he asked.

"Someone forgot to lock it," he replied, flexing his fingers. "Pretty easy to open an unlocked gate."

"Damn," Judarius grumbled to himself, then turned around and glanced over the stone barriers as if searching for someone. A moment passed before he returned his attention to Patrick. "You are late," he said, and then he leaned forward, staring at Patrick's companions. His round eyes widened. "And who are they?"

"Friends of mine."

"They bear the mark of the lion."

"That they do," Patrick said with a nod. "Deserters."

"Deserters?"

Preston stepped up to the bars. "We come here seeking Ashhur's forgiveness. We wish to offer our services in defense of his people to repay our debt to him."

"And what kind of debt do you owe?"

Patrick stopped the old soldier before he could answer.

"That doesn't matter, Judarius. All that *does* matter is that I can vouch for them. These are good men. They will help us."

"I am not sure if your word is good enough."

"Is Ashhur here?"

"Yes. In fact, he was worried you would not make it."

"Well, I did. Ask *him* to let us in if you won't."

Judarius scrunched up his mouth.

"There is no need for that," he said, disappearing to the side of the gate. There was a loud grinding sound as the bars slowly lifted off the ground. Once it was all the way up, Patrick led his new friends into his old home.

Looking to the side, he saw Judarius emerge from a nook between the wall and the stone barrier, where a wooden wheel resided, a heavy hemp rope wound around it and attached to the top of the gate. The Warden walked past him and leaned over the stone barricade.

"Mordecai, find Sheldon Miner and Mattrice DuReiner," he said to someone on the other side. "They left the outer gate unbarred. Teach them that they cannot do that again."

"Yes, Judarius," the unseen Mordecai replied.

Judarius turned to look at them again, running a slender hand through his silky black hair. "I apologize for being less than cordial," he said. "I have to be careful."

"Seems you're the only one who feels that way," Patrick said. To prove his point, he jabbed his thumb toward the opposite barricade, where the sounds of raucous laughter could be heard.

"Yes," said Judarius. "The people have much to learn."

"A little late for that."

"It is never too late to learn," Judarius replied.

"It is if you're dead," Patrick muttered under his breath as he followed the Warden into the city.

The barricade was taller than Patrick, almost six feet high, and it stretched farther than he'd initially assumed. The man-made tunnel was at least two hundred feet long, and then the whole of Mordeina opened up before him. He gasped as he spun in a circle, his eight travel companions doing the same. The two walls did indeed circle the entire city, rising above the trees in either direction like a pale horizon line. Even more shocking to him was the sheer number of people he saw. The throng of humanity before him made those who had traveled with him and Ashhur look insignificant by comparison. They were everywhere, forming tightly packed groups whose crude shelters and piles of belongings took up nearly every inch of grass on every hill and valley he could see. He did not know how many souls had resided in Mordeina when he left, but there had to be at least four times that many now. Many sets of eyes turned in their direction, and whispers were passed back and forth. Patrick was momentarily confused before he remembered what his cohorts were wearing…and the fact that each of them carried swords, which was not exactly a common sight in Mordeina.

"They are from all over Paradise," said Judarius, as if reading his thoughts. "Every village, alcove, and settlement from here to Ashhur's Bridge, and some from as far north as Durham."

"So many," said Patrick.

"There are. Warden Leviticus estimates that there are more than two hundred thousand humans in Mordeina. And Leviticus is rarely wrong about these things. He has a nose for mathematics."

Patrick whistled. "Is the whole enclosure as packed as this?"

"No," replied Judarius, shaking his head. "Most have chosen to make their homes in the eastern quarter, close to the granaries. The forested areas are still vacant, and only a few thousand chose to settle on the other side of the hill." He looked down at Patrick. "In fact, that is where some of those who arrived with Ashhur now reside."

"Huh. Why there and not close to the others?"

"You will have to ask them, I think," the Warden said.

Preston shoved his way forward, still dragging his steed along behind him. "Tell me, Warden, how were these walls built? Patrick told us they didn't exist a year ago, but now there is not one wall but two, encircling miles of land. How did you accomplish this?"

Judarius chuckled, though there was very little humor in the sound.

"Teams of men and women, sweating from sunup to sundown, along with four spellcasters from the north."

"Ah, my brother-in-law's students. They have talent, I take it?" asked Patrick.

The Warden nodded. "Indeed. Escheton taught them well. With their assistance, we were able to raise three quarters of the outer wall in only eight months."

"Three quarters? But what of the rest? And what of the inner wall?" Preston asked.

"For that, we required godly assistance," Judarius replied. "When Ashhur arrived, he not only completed the outer wall but decided it was not enough and raised the second wall as well." Again, the Warden chuckled. "What took us months to complete took him only three days."

Patrick grinned. "I bet you wished you hadn't worked so hard."

Judarius didn't reply to that, but he had no need. The look on his face said it all. Instead, he turned to Preston and his gang of youths and said, "Patrick has assured me that you mean to help us, and I will trust his word." He lifted his hand and snapped, summoning five other Wardens from a nearby group of people. "However, whatever help you have to offer will need to wait. You all look exhausted, filthy, and injured. I ask you all to follow Corrineth to the bathhouse we have built in the valley where the granaries reside. Our healers will help you mend. My only regret is that with so many mouths to feed, we are a bit short on food at the moment.

The most we can offer is rutabaga and beet soup and a few scraps of bacon."

"I don't care *what* we eat," muttered Little Flick. "We've had nothing but roots and leaves for weeks."

"Very well." A human approached then, a young lad still in his teens, his hair as flaming red as Patrick's and his face covered with freckles. A team of similar-looking youths gathered behind him. "Paddy and his brothers here will care for your horses," Judarius said. "Please understand, however, that we will have to strip them of their decorations, as well as those adorning your armor. For obvious reasons."

"We understand," said Preston, with a bow, as the gang of youths began to lead their horses away.

"No need to bow."

"My apologies."

Patrick punched Preston in the arm, then worked his way down the line, roughhousing the rest of his new friends. "Get going," he said. "Get tended, and get washed. You all smell like shit."

"Well, at least we don't *look* like shit," he heard Ryann say.

Patrick gave the young man a swift boot in the rear. "Get out of here before I do worse."

The Wardens led the eight deserters away, leaving Patrick alone with Judarius...or at least however alone anyone could be in the midst of two hundred thousand people.

"You are not leaving with them?" the Warden asked.

Patrick shook his head. "I can't. I need to speak with Ashhur."

"I apologize, but that is impossible," Judarius said with a frown.

"Why?"

"Our Lord is resting now. Has been since he raised the wall. It weakened him far more than I might have expected. Ashhur requested that he not be disturbed while he revitalizes. He wishes to have as much strength as he can when Karak arrives at our gates."

Judarius gave Patrick a queer look. "The eastern god *is* coming, is he not?"

"He is. In fact, he was mighty close behind us. Had to fight a few of them to get across the bridge. Given how many soldiers there were, I imagine it will take them quite some time to get here. Five days, perhaps six."

"So you had a confrontation with the God of Order. That explains your…condition."

"Oh, you mean the fact that we're all splattered with blood? Yes, we had a run-in…but not with Karak. I don't think we'd be here otherwise."

"Very true."

Patrick gnawed on the inside of his lip. "Listen, Judarius," he finally said, feeling nervous even to ask, "I need you to tell me something."

"Of course."

"Is Nessa here?"

"Nessa, your sister?"

"Yes."

The Warden shook his head. "Last I knew, she was with you, and your mother has not mentioned her name once in all the time I have been here. Perhaps you might ask her?"

Patrick shook his head, his heart sinking in his chest.

"Trust me, Judarius, my mother knows nothing. If she did, everyone else would as well. She was with the son of Clovis Crestwell when she fled into Paradise. If they were here, the great Isabel DuTaureau would *not* keep it secret."

The Warden's green-gold eyes brightened.

"In that case, perhaps she did and is hidden among the crowds? There have been massive clusters arriving nearly every day. She might have slipped in with them."

Patrick felt a glimmer of hope. That sounded *exactly* like something Nessa would do.

"I'll do some searching, then. See what I can find."

"Very well, Patrick, and I wish you luck. If there is anything I can do to help you, please feel free to ask."

"I will. In the meantime, I think you need a bath yourself. You smell like a grayhorn shit you out."

The Warden shook his head. "Good day, Patrick, and good luck." He turned, walking back toward the blockaded path that led to the gate.

"Wait, Judarius," he said.

"What is it?" the Warden asked, turning slightly.

"My mother…my father…please don't tell them I've returned. I'd rather do that myself, in my own time."

Judarius bowed and continued on his way. Patrick hoped the Warden would remain true to his word as he always had in the past. He had absolutely no desire to speak with his parents yet.

He made his way through the throng of people. For the first time in a very long while, he actually felt the weight of his armor, of Winterbone as it bounced on his back. He realized then that he was wincing and scowling, which could have been why many of the people he saw cringed and ducked away from him. Not that he wished otherwise. He found himself feeling irritated by the carefree smiles that painted most every face he laid eyes on, the dismissiveness the people seemed to feel about the danger they would soon be facing. He felt completely alone in the throng.

You are a different animal now, he reasoned. *But you are not alone. Your god will always be with you.*

"Damned inner reason," he muttered.

Swallowing his anger, he put on the best pleasant face he could muster and dove into the crowds. He searched from one family camp to the next, asking questions as he kept an eye out for Nessa's bright red shock of hair. None he spoke to admitted to having seen her, and many gaped at him as if he were some idiot for even asking. "Why would your sister be *here*?" one of them asked, hands up in confusion. "She has a room in the manse. Only a simpleton would think she'd sleep anywhere else."

It took every last ounce of his restraint to clench his fists and turn away.

Afternoon passed into early evening, and still his search was fruitless. He went from the new arrivals to the longtime residents, knocking on cabin doors and peeling aside yurt flaps. Still, there was no sign of her. He was feeling hopeless when an innocent voice called out his name, and he heard the patter of bare feet running up behind him.

"Nessa?" he said excitedly, spinning around.

A small form collided with him, arms wrapping around his neck. The head pulled back, revealing a nest of sandy blond hair and a slender, pretty face devoid of freckles. Patrick's heart dropped. The girl kissed his cheek and released his neck, stepping back. The demure smile she wore fell away when he simply stared at her in response.

"You…don't remember me?"

Patrick cocked his head, then closed his eyes. He saw the girl writhing atop him while her pelvis ground into his.

"Of course. Bethany. How could I have forgotten?"

"Brittany."

"Right. Sorry."

The girl bit her lip. "You don't seem happy to see me," she said.

"Why should I be? The last time we were together, you said you were only with me in the hopes of having a child, and then you left."

His words brought back memories of Rachida. He wondered where the splendid woman was now, if she were safe, and if the child he *had* planted in her had been born without complications…

"That was before," Brittany said, breaking him free of his recollection. "It's said you're a hero now, that you battled Karak and beat him back."

"Don't believe every story you hear," he said with a grumble.

She stepped forward and threw her arms around him once more. It aroused him a bit, but only a bit, to realize that she did not seem to mind the grime and dried blood that covered him. However, when he looked in her eyes and saw his reflection, he cringed and pushed her away.

"Not now," he said. "Not ever again."

As he walked away from her, that familiar feeling of loneliness swept over him. *You should have just gone with her,* his inner self chastised. *She was willing and eager, and you haven't been with a woman for months. You need it.*

There were tears in his eyes when he said, to nobody in particular, "But that's not what matters now. Karak's Army is what matters. Helping Ashhur is what matters. Finding Nessa"—he choked up, which drew odd looks from passersby—"is what matters."

Deciding he'd had enough of crowds, he maneuvered toward the outskirts, staying as far away from the many groups of people as he could. He made sure to keep space between himself and Manse DuTaureau, fearing that at any moment his mother might emerge from inside, spot him, and flag him down. But she didn't. Although a great many individuals strolled in and out of the sprawling building his family called home, he saw none of his relatives.

His unrest grew the longer he walked. He saw folks laughing and chatting, tending to the meager garden plots in front of their tents, caring for children, or simply lazing about, eyes to the sky as if they had not a care in the world. The lines heading down the side street to the granaries were long, and the people who emerged from them were carrying huge baskets filled with goods. He saw no evidence of rationing, as had been done in Haven when Karak's Army was approaching, and no one was being schooled on how to defend themselves. In short, the people acted as if nothing were wrong in the slightest, as if the gargantuan walls that surrounded them were novelties and nothing more. He made a fist, digging his fingernails into his palms. For a moment he was tempted to head for the manse so that he could chastise his mother and the new king for their ineptitude.

Alas, he did not. Instead he kept walking, circling the great hill until the crowds thinned. At the edge of the column of old birch trees where he used to play run-and-chase with his sisters as a boy, he spotted a new collection of ramshackle tents. There were perhaps a thousand, sprawling from one end of the miniature forest to the other, but those who had gathered around the cookfires here had the air of those who had experienced hardship. Chatter was sparse, and he actually spied sparks flying as a few folks ran stones over steel blades. These were *his* people. Most of them had journeyed through the lands east of the Wooden Bridge with Ashhur, though where they'd found actual weapons was beyond on him. He thought perhaps their god had forged them.

Eyes lifted as he approached. Expressions brightened and bodies rose from the ground, approaching slowly, moving like people who had endured a long and arduous journey—which of course they had.

Recognizing face after face, he called out to those whose names he remembered and offered warm hugs to those he didn't. An endless stream of gratitude was offered to him, spoken in hushed and weary tones.

"We never thought you would return."

"We thought you had died....Thank Ashhur, you haven't."

"You were missed, my friend."

"Good to have you back."

"Thank the gods you were returned to us safely."

On and on it went, the greetings stretching on for nearly an hour, until finally Patrick was approached by a teen boy with a somber face. The boy said nothing, simply wrapped his arms around Patrick's thick shoulders and held him tightly.

"Missed you too, Barclay," he said.

The boy squeezed him tighter, so tight that the ridge of his breastplate began to dig into his side.

"Whoa there, boy. That actually hurts."

"Sorry."

When Barclay pulled back, tears were dribbling down his dirty cheeks.

"It was not the same when you left," the boy said, wiping snot from his nose with the back of his hand.

"I apologize for that, but there was something that needed doing."

"Will you leave again?"

"Not until it's all over."

The boy smiled a little at that. "After we kick Karak in the nuts, right?"

"Right," Patrick replied with a chuckle. "A swipe here, a lunge there, and we'll have him."

Barclay's face lit up suddenly. "Oh, I need to show you something," he said with excitement. He grabbed Patrick's hand and yanked him through the crowd. Patrick was amazed at how strong the boy's grip was.

Moments later, they emerged in front of a hastily constructed shanty made from a few felled tree limbs and topped with a bed of leaves. Barclay's father, Noonan, sat in front of a clay pot filled with boiling liquid atop a fire, surrounded by his wife and many children. The man offered Patrick an appreciative nod but did not stand to greet him. It was understandable, given that his children kept pestering him about how much their tummies hurt.

Barclay stopped on the other side of the firepit, where a dull gray sword rested against the rocks. The boy grabbed the handle and lifted it. The blade was a decent size, two and a half feet long, and Barclay needed both hands to keep it steady. He turned to Patrick, doing his best to mimic the stance his hero had demonstrated to the many visitors who had decided to remain in their homes even after Ashhur warned them of what was coming.

"Your back foot is in the wrong position," Patrick said, "and your back is too hunched. Otherwise, nice form."

Barclay corrected what was wrong, standing even taller now. "See? I was listening," he said.

"You were," Patrick said with a nod. "Though I must ask where you came by that sword."

The boy lowered the blade, staring at it as he did so. Though the metal was old and faded and not entirely sharp, it was solidly made. Patrick could tell as much from the grip, which did not wobble when the boy tilted it from one side to the other.

"A Warden gave it to me."

"A Warden? Which one?"

"Don't know his name. Short black hair, bright green eyes, short for a Warden. He and a bunch of other folks came upon us while we were still on the Gods' Road. He was really hurt, and Father helped heal him."

"Where did they come from?" he asked, though he already knew the answer.

Barclay's face twisted up in concentration; then he nodded and said, "Lerder. They said they came from Lerder."

"Azariah."

"Uh-huh. That's his name. How did you know?"

"Long story." Patrick looked about him, rising up on his toes to try to see over the crowd. There were few Wardens present, and none of them matched the description of Judarius's brother. "And where is he now, Barclay?"

"Where is who?"

"The Warden. Azariah."

"Oh. He's in the woods with a girl. Saying good-bye to a friend. They've been there for a couple days now."

Patrick turned toward the birch forest. "In there?" he asked.

"Yes."

He reached out and ruffled Barclay's hair. "Thank you, boy. We'll chat soon."

"You're leaving? But I wanted you to show me some new stances!"

"When I come back," said Patrick, and turned away from him.

The birch forest felt smaller and more cramped to him than it once had, and the trees were packed so tightly together he had to turn his armored body sideways to slip between them. The sound of light sobbing guided his steps.

Soon he reached the clearing where he had spent many afternoons alone as a child. His feet got tangled up in a thick nest of vines, and he literally fell out of the woods, landing on his knees. Someone gasped. Glancing up, he saw a very pretty young woman with hair just as black as that of the Warden who stood beside her, only hers was curly. She stared in his direction, a look of surprise on her face, signaling Azariah to do the same.

"Who are you?" asked the young woman.

"That would be Patrick DuTaureau," said Azariah.

"DuTaureau…of the First Family DuTaureau?"

"That's the one," Patrick said, picking himself up off the ground and brushing dirt off his clothes.

"I heard you were dead," Azariah said.

"No such luck, old friend. Still very much alive."

"I see. Well, that is good."

Patrick cocked his head, staring at the Warden in confusion. Azariah and Judarius had been two of his mother's favorite Wardens, the personal teachers to him and his sisters. He had always felt a strong connection with Azariah, in particular, and an appreciation for the Warden's offbeat humor and sense of adventure. However, neither trait was in evidence at the moment.

"Az, what is wrong with you…?"

He required no answer, for when he shifted his eyes to the right he spotted a stack of stripped kindling. Atop the pile of wood was a strange lump surrounded by flowers. Patrick shuffled forward, peered down at the wood pile, and saw the lump for what it was.

A body.

"Oh shit."

He turned to the young woman, whose eyes had exploded with fresh tears. She leaned into Azariah, sobbing against his chest, while the Warden stroked her coiled black hair.

"That's Roland," Patrick said softly.

Azariah nodded.

He had known Roland Norsman for only a short time, having met the strapping young man in the aftermath of Ashhur and Karak's confrontation in Haven. Though their time together had been brief—barely two months had passed on the road before Roland had chosen to stay in Lerder with Azariah—he had made quite an impression on Patrick as a strong-willed, intelligent lad who was completely dedicated to their god. He had been Jacob Eveningstar's steward before the First Man's betrayal of Ashhur, and Patrick had sensed that he'd held onto the pain of that betrayal, growing from it.

And now, just like so many others in the delta and Paradise, he was gone.

"How did it happen?" he asked.

The girl sobbed harder.

"We were about to cross the Wooden Bridge," said Azariah, his eyes locked on the body, "when Jacob descended on us with twenty men."

"So the First Man is taking an active role in Karak's war."

The Warden nodded. "And he would have killed us all had I not sensed a strange presence in the forest. These creatures bore Ashhur's touch, and when I prayed for assistance, they barreled out from the trees—wolves turned men. They attacked the soldiers, allowing those who fled Lerder to escape across the bridge. Roland and I were the last to cross, and we were halfway to freedom, riding fast atop my horse, when an arrow pierced his back."

Patrick shook his head.

"Even with the pain," continued Azariah, "even with Roland screaming, I kept on riding. He fell silent after only a few short minutes, and I felt him slump against me. Finally I came upon the rest of our party and collapsed. It was too late to save Roland. The arrow had punctured his heart, and he was already dead."

"How long ago was this?"

"Seven days."

Patrick started, then leaned over the woodpile. *Seven days... in this heat?* On closer inspection, he saw that Roland's body was in a late stage of putrefaction. His skin had gone black in spots, as had his fingernails. And his gums were retreating, exposing the crowns of his yellowish teeth. Had it not been for the flowers stacked around the corpse, the scent would probably have been dreadful.

"And you haven't burned the body yet? Why in the name of Ashhur not?"

The young woman gaped at him, eyes blank.

Patrick pointed to the girl, raising his eyebrows at Azariah.

"Her name is Kaya," the Warden said, embracing her once more. "She and Roland were...close."

She gazed at Patrick, her eyes red, her lips quivering, her knees trembling. Despite the horrific circumstances, he almost envied her. He stepped up to her, twining one of her black curls around his finger. She recoiled slightly, but judging from the way she was look-ing at him, it had nothing to do with his appearance.

"You were lucky, Kaya," he said, not unkindly. "You knew true love, and though he is gone, no one can take that away from you."

"I don't c-c-care," she sobbed. "He is n-n-never coming back."

"No, he's not. And no amount of wailing is going to make a difference."

"Patrick, silence," Azariah growled. "Do not be cruel."

"No, Az. I'm *not* being cruel. I am simply telling her the truth."

Kaya buried her face in the Warden's chest once more. Patrick groaned, then turned his gaze back to the corpse. He noticed the flies this time, just a few, buzzing over the flowers. *There will be more soon,* he thought. *After whatever treatment Azariah placed on the body wears off, they will come in droves.*

Sighing, he reached beneath his breastplate and removed the satchel that held his flint. He knelt before the woodpile as if he were about to offer his respects, and then, his wide back concealing his actions, he struck the flint together. It only took two strikes for a small flame to flicker to life, catching at the edge of the pile, gradually working its way over the dry timber. The clearing began to glow an eerie shade of red.

"No!" he heard Kaya shout.

Patrick turned, still on his knees. His hump made it hurt to lift his head to see Azariah's face, but he withstood the pain so he could stare coldly at the Warden who had taught him to read as a child.

"What have you done?" Azariah shouted.

"What you should have done long ago," he answered. He grunted as he rose to his feet, the fire building strength behind him, buffeting his backside in heat. Crackles and snaps filled the air as Roland's corpse was swallowed in flames.

"You had no right…"

"Of *course* I did!" snapped Patrick. He stormed toward Azariah and stopped a few feet short of the Warden, pointing an accusatory finger in his face.

"You have lost someone, but so have many," he said, his voice a menacing growl. "I feel for you both, I do, but don't you *dare* linger in sadness. There is no time for that. Not now, not when Karak is nearly at our door."

"And what would you have us do?" Azariah asked stubbornly.

"I would have you *fight!*" he exclaimed. "I would have everyone in this godsforsaken place wake up and *do something!* And if I am the one who must force them to do so, then so be it."

He spun around and began storming away.

"Where are you going?" Azariah called out after him.

"I am going to pay a visit to our god," he shouted over his shoulder. "It's about time *he* woke up as well."

CHAPTER

38

T he giant looked greatly discouraged, even angry. He sat on the rocks beneath the cliff, his fist firmly planted on his chin, his gaze locked on the hole in the earth and the dark treasure hiding within it.

Aully looked at Kindren, her nerves bubbling over. When he squeezed her hand, she gave him a small smile, then turned her gaze toward her mother. Audrianna Meln was a picture of beauty, her long golden hair blown by the intense breeze off the ocean. Her sadness over Brienna had lessened with the prospect of returning home, and no more did the name *Carskel* pass her lips. It was good to see her this way—stately, strong, dignified, as she was intended to be. Those who stood alongside her, the thirty-one other elves who had made their home in this village by the sea for many long months, bowed to her in reverence. The Lady of Stonewood's station seemed to have returned along with her strength, which made her daughter proud.

"How long have you known of this?" Bardiya asked in his deep voice.

"A few weeks," Audrianna replied, motioning to Aully and Kindren. "My daughter and future son-in-law informed me of the existence of this cache the very morning they discovered it."

"Why did you wait so long to tell me?"

"We had our reasons. We are not captives here, nor are we beholden to you, as you have been adamant in saying."

"I offered you shelter," grumbled Bardiya, his tone disapproving. "I provided you with food and water when you were lost and hungry. I saved the boy's life when he was near death. I deserve to know of all that is discovered within our borders, especially in times like these. You *owe* me that."

"Bardiya, calm yourself," said the tall, slender, dark-skinned man beside him. "There is no need for anger."

"Speak for yourself, Ki-Nan," he shot back, swatting his friend's hand away. Aully took a step backward. It was unsettling to see Bardiya so upset.

Lady Audrianna approached the giant, dropping to one knee before him. He did not respond, not even when she grabbed his massive right hand.

"Bardiya, we are eternally grateful for what you have done for us. We are. The only reason we did not tell you about the discovery was because we were unsure what it meant."

"How so?"

She returned to standing and gestured toward the sea. "Anyone could have placed the crates here, be it our people, Karak's, or even your own—"

"That isn't possible."

"Be that as it may, we could not move forward until we knew more about the situation." Audrianna pointed to the handsome elf beside her. "My daughter led Aaromar here the very next day to take inventory. He counted two hundred and ninety-four swords of various lengths, ninety-nine daggers, twenty battle-axes, and fifteen mauls, and that is only what was inside the crate that split when my daughter attempted to open it. One sword in particular caught his eye, which was our reason for not coming to you sooner. Aaromar, bring it out."

The elf dropped down into the hollow where the large wooden crates had been stacked, and when he reemerged, he dragged behind him a length of sharpened steel nearly as long as himself. Aully gaped at the sight of the sword, which could only be wielded by a giant. She watched as Ki-Nan's jaw fell open as well.

Aaromar dropped the blade in front of Bardiya, the clang as it struck the rocks echoing around them like a bell. Bardiya narrowed his eyes, staring first at the sword, then at Audrianna.

"This gave you pause? Why?"

"Because it seems to have been made for you, Bardiya. Of all the beings in Dezrel, there are only three for whom such a blade would make sense. And I do not think Ashhur and Karak, being gods, would have need of a man-made sword."

The giant leaned forward, ran his finger over the cutting edge, then abruptly drew his hand back and shivered. He drummed his shaved scalp, which glistened with sweat and mist.

"Of course, I did not believe you were lying to us," said Lady Audrianna, "but you must understand my hesitancy."

Amazingly, Bardiya seemed to be in agreement.

"What changed your mind?" he asked.

"For a week I had the crates watched from the top of the cliff. Not once did anyone pass by this place. The tide came in, concealing the hollow, and then rolled out, exposing it once more. The only thing that seemed to care for the hidden treasure was the seaweed." She smiled. "But your reaction not a minute ago is what truly proved it to me. The revulsion you displayed on touching the sword could not be feigned."

Bardiya nodded to her, then glanced again at the giant sword.

"If you would please remove this…thing…from my sight, it would be greatly appreciated."

"Of course."

Aully watched Aaromar retrieve the massive blade, straining as he lugged it behind him before dumping it into the hollow. With the sword gone from sight, Bardiya seemed to relax. He leaned back on the slippery rock, grimacing each time his joints audibly popped. His friend Ki-Nan wandered over to the hole, dropped down on his hands and knees, peered inside, and whistled.

Bardiya shook his head, turning his attention to Lady Audrianna.

"I apologize for my outburst," he said. "As I have told you many times, my people have decried violence, just as Ashhur has taught. The sight of such things as these within our borders is worrisome. Do you have any idea how they came to arrive here?"

"I think the Prince of Dezerea has theory on that," she said.

Kindren winced, squeezed Aully's hand once more, and stepped forward.

"I think they were a gift," he said.

"A gift?" asked Bardiya. "From whom?"

"From Celestia," Aully said, refusing to shrink away when all eyes turned to her.

Bardiya chuckled. "Why would the goddess give me that which I do not want?" he asked.

"Because Celestia is the goddess of balance," Audrianna said before her daughter could answer. "There has always been equality between our people and the Quellan, an equality that no longer exists. The same can be said for Paradise and Neldar. So the goddess sent these gifts to allow us to fight for ourselves, to retake what we have lost, to even the scales."

"Why would the goddess not do so openly?" asked Ki-Nan, lifting his head from within the hollow.

"Because that is not Celestia's way," said another voice. From the rear of the group of elves, an ancient female approached. She hobbled on unsteady legs, her cane shaking as the tip sought gaps in the wet stone. "You know this, son of Gorgoros, for you have studied her as well as Ashhur."

"Noni, be careful!" Aully shouted. She ran up to her nursemaid and wrapped her arm around Noni's slender waist, helping the ancient elf draw close to Bardiya. The giant slipped off his perch and dropped to one knee, hunching over so that his gaze was level with hers. Aully studied his face, the twitch of his lips, the furrowing of his brow. It seemed to take extraordinary effort for him to complete such a seemingly simple task.

"Nonallee Clanshaw," he said, and Noni bobbed her head in greeting. It was the first time Aully ever remembered hearing her nursemaid's full name come from lips other than her own.

Noni placed a withered hand on the giant's cheek. "You have always been a fine lad, Bardiya. I was there on the day of your birth and helped bring you into the world alongside your Wardens."

"Mother told me as much," Bardiya answered. He seemed to melt beneath the compassion of her touch.

"And I was the first one to speak with you about Celestia's glory when you were but a tot. Do you remember that as well?"

He nodded. "I was six. The stories you told…they implanted me with wonder, taught me that *all* gods were to be respected, not just my creator."

"Then you know the way the goddess works." Noni tilted her head, the side of her mouth lifting into a smile. "You know she would only interfere with our lives as a last resort, when the signs show that the balance she created might shatter."

"And that is now?"

She nodded. "That is now."

"So you are saying Celestia put these weapons here to force us into a war?"

"Not at all, Bardiya," Noni said with a sigh. "She would never *force* anyone to do anything. Rather, she wished for you to have the *choice.* To have the opportunity to defend your life and land should the renegade god attempt to conquer all."

Aully turned at the sound of a chuckle and noticed that Ki-Nan was standing behind the rest, laughing softly into his fist as he shook his head. She couldn't decide if he thought her nursemaid's reasoning absurd or if this was a nervous tic of his in unfamiliar situations. She liked Bardiya's friend; he had been very kind to her and her people. So she chose to believe that latter.

Bardiya's voice returned her attention to him. "I take it you will be accepting her gift," the giant said, gazing at each of the elves in turn. "You wish to return to your home."

Noni nodded.

"We do," said Lady Audrianna.

"I cannot help you if you go," Bardiya said, "and I cannot accept this gift from your goddess, if that is indeed what it is. Do you understand?"

"Of course," Noni said. She then leaned in to place a kiss on the tip of the giant's broad nose. Aully rushed back to her side to help her waddle away.

"We respect your sovereignty," Lady Audrianna said. "We would never ask you to go against your own code of ethics. It is not our place. We simply wished to let you know you have…options."

Aully passed Noni off to one of her father's old assistants and then wheeled around. "We also did not want to disappear in the night without telling you."

He bowed his head. "I am grateful for that."

"And we are grateful for all you've done for us," said Kindren. He draped an arm around Aully, kissing her on the top of one pointed ear. She squeezed him in return, grateful for the millionth time that he was by her side. "*I* am grateful. I will forever be in your debt, and when this is all over, should we both come out breathing, I will do all I can to close the rift between our peoples. That is my promise to you."

The giant smiled warmly, looked first at Aully, then at Lady Audrianna.

"You have chosen a fine husband," he said, "and an even finer heir. Young prince, I look forward to that day, should it ever come to pass."

"As do I."

"But how do you plan on retaking your home?" asked Ki-Nan. The giant's friend had circled back and was standing beside the giant once more. "You cannot hope to recapture the forest with only thirty of you."

"Oh, but we do," said Audrianna. "There have been no disturbances for months, not since the death of Bardiya's parents. I have known Detrick for a very, very long time. He is a much gentler soul than even his brother, my husband. He would never have agreed to such egregious horrors as have been committed in his name. The Meln family name runs deep in Stonewood. At worst, there is a rebel element that is making Detrick's life…difficult. It has been quiet for far too long for us to consider any other possibility. We owe it to our people to return home, with a young prince and princess whose command of magic grows each day, and assist them in their fight for freedom."

"And if you are wrong?"

"Then we shall meet our error head on rather than in hiding," said Kindren.

"We miss our home," added Aully. Her insides clenched. "*I* miss *my* home. We don't belong here, Bardiya."

The giant smiled at her, held out his hand. She went to him and accepted his embrace. His body swallowed hers like she was a mouse, but rather than being scared, she actually found it comforting. She suddenly wished Bardiya would cast aside his beliefs and join them. Should their assumptions prove wrong, it would be advantageous to have a giant on their side…even if that giant seemed to ache every time he moved.

"When will you be departing?" she heard him ask from above her.

"In two days," her mother's voice answered. "We will string our own bows and take what weapons we require from the cache, and then we will be gone."

"I will miss you," said Bardiya.

Aully leaned back. "Not too much, though," she said, grinning. "We'll be sure to come visit often after we retake the forest."

"You do that," the giant replied.

From the look on his face, she could tell he didn't believe a word of it.

✦

Bardiya watched as the Stonewood Dezren walked back to their camp. The sun was descending in the sky, casting a glow around the elves as they moved steadily away from him. It made them look like celestial beings descended from on high to walk among them, a thought that made him shudder.

He stole a glance at Ki-Nan, who shielded his eyes with one hand as he waved with the other. His friend was smiling, but he had known Ki-Nan for long enough to know that his expression was less than sincere. He had been much more terse than usual since his return, with occasional dark moods.

"What bothers you?" he asked finally.

Ki-Nan turned to him. "Nothing, Brother. Why?"

"You cannot lie to me. I know you too well. Tell me."

"You already know," Ki-Nan said with a sigh. "I won't go over this again."

Bardiya grunted. He and Ki-Nan had taken to debating the virtues of peace and nonviolence almost nightly since his friend had emerged grievously wounded from his skiff. Only recently had those arguments come to an end, and not because the two had reached an agreement— it was simply easier for them to ignore the issue. But there was no ignoring it now, not when his friend's gaze constantly returned to the buried crates and the sharpened steel that resided within.

"I only ask you to trust my judgment," Bardiya insisted. "These tools of destruction are evil. They're not welcome in Ker, nor will they ever be."

"We already fashion our own spears and arrows," Ki-Nan said. "Is a sword really so different? Seems to me they serve the same basic purpose—slicing flesh, bringing blood. One is simply more efficient than the other. That does not make them evil."

"Evil does not lie in the practicality of the tool, but in the *intention*. You know this as well as I. We use arrows and spears to feed our families. When we end an animal's life, we put it to good use. Its meat fills our bellies, and its hide creates our clothing. We use it for survival. The sword, on the other hand, is used only to main and kill. There is no practicality, no pure intention."

"Is destroying those who might destroy us not necessary for survival?"

"You know how I feel."

"Very well, Brother. Have it your way."

Bardiya sighed. "I wish you understood my words."

"I do. I simply don't agree."

"Do you trust me?"

"Of course I do."

"Then trust me on this."

He shook his head. "I've tried, Brother, but I cannot."

"You wish to hold on to these weapons, don't you?"

He nodded.

Bardiya squeezed his eyes shut. "Please know that I will not give you the chance," he said. "Once the Dezren have taken what they need, I will cast the crates back into the ocean. I will not stand by as you rally my people to violence."

"*Your* people?" Ki-Nan said with a laugh. "Last I knew, they were *our* people, Brother. People brought up to live free in a land of peace. They can make their own choices, just as we can." He shook his head. "It is the same tired argument, over and over. Do as you must to convince our people to put out their necks. I will do what I can to convince them to fight."

"You will lose," Bardiya whispered.

"We will see," his friend said. He then turned to Bardiya and offered an exaggerated bow. "Until then, I will bother you no more, *your Grace*," he said mockingly.

With those words, he walked away, following the path the Dezren forged back toward Ang. Unlike the elves, his body was not wreathed in light. Instead, darkness surrounded him, as if all the brightness had been swallowed the closer it got to his dark flesh. Bardiya leaned forward, cradling his head in his hands.

"You will see, my friend," he told the air around him. "I will make you understand."

Two days later, the Dezren departed for their home, taking with them twenty-five swords, twelve daggers, and three battle-axes.

Three days later, when Bardiya returned to cast the boxes of terror into the sea, he found that the crates, and Ki-Nan, had disappeared.

CHAPTER

39

For days without end, Ceredon blinked in and out of consciousness, the potions the Quellan healers had given him to ease his pain leaving him in a state of delirium. At times he cursed his foolishness for demanding that Thane be so brutal.

He rolled over in bed, a spike of pain stabbing through him. His left arm had been broken, along with five ribs, his right foot, and his nose. His body was covered with lacerations and deep gouges which the healers had treated with boiling wine to ward off infection. Biden, sworn healer to the Neyvar, had told him he was lucky to have survived. Ceredon had chuckled at that, knowing as he did that luck had nothing to do with it.

Ceredon had been found on the path to the hills by the retreating Ekreissar, who were fleeing from the rebel's supposed hideaway. Sixteen had been killed by booby traps—swinging spiked logs, deep covered holes, and bolts fired by tripwire. After stumbling on Ceredon's unmoving body, they'd scooped him up and carried him back to Palace Thyne. Ever since, he had resided in the room down the hall from his father's.

The human Clovis Crestwell had come to question him more than once, asking him why he and Aeson had been separated from the rangers, a question to which Ceredon always shrugged in response. He claimed he couldn't remember, which wasn't a complete lie. His brain had been jarred by Thane's beating, leaving him with only spotty memories of that night.

At least he was spared questions regarding Aeson's whereabouts, as pieces of the Neyvar's cousin had been found scattered throughout the forest in the days following the attack. Iolas had broken the sad news to him, the old bastard nearly in tears as he sat on the edge of the younger elf's sickbed. Ceredon found it quite humorous that Iolas trusted him enough to show weakness, considering the fact that the last living member of the Triad was the final one on his hit list.

Thoughts of Iolas brought him to wakefulness. He sat up groggily, glancing about his shimmering emerald room, then through the window at the night sky twinkling with stars. He wore no clothes, and the wounds covering his body still stung beneath their wrappings. His mouth felt parched, so he reached over and snatched a cup of water from atop the table next to his bed. After he downed the liquid in one gulp, his senses began to return to him, which was when he smelled the lingering odor of the half-full chamber pot on the floor beside him. He doubled over, gagging, then reached for the wooden jug that sat on the table for more water. It was empty.

Groaning, he swung his feet over the side of the featherbed, making sure he gave the chamber pot a wide berth. When his bare toes touched the cool crystal of the floor, a shiver rocked his spine, bringing on a new spasm of pain. He accepted the torment, flattening his feet against the ground until the feeling subsided. He flexed his broken right foot, which was expertly wrapped. The bones had been set and were healing nicely, or so Biden had told him. Still, he'd been assured that he would feel echoes of this injury for a long while, possibly even decades.

Once again, Ceredon cursed Thane's effectiveness.

There was a long walking rod propped against the wall, and Ceredon grabbed it before standing up. He wedged the padded top of the rod into his right armpit and rose to his feet. Using the rod to put as little weight as possible on his broken foot, he hopped toward the door, the empty pitcher dangling from his other hand.

He knew he could shout for help, but the hour was late, and most in the palace were likely asleep. Besides, he couldn't stand to be alone in his room any longer. He felt completely in the dark, limited by the knowledge that Iolas and Clovis were willing to share. He knew nothing about the status of the rebellion or how his father felt about the whole situation. The Neyvar hadn't once come to see him, and that fact alone led Ceredon to wonder if he had completely misread his father from the beginning. He hoped not.

The hall was empty when he exited his room, just as he'd expected. He hobbled down the stairs, taking care to hop down a step at a time, and each time he landed, new agony shook his battered body. He paused and glanced down. His room was on the seventh story. That meant he had a hundred steps and six turns to go until he reached the ground level. He groaned, sucked in a deep breath, and hopped down yet another step.

It took him nearly a full hour to reach the bottom, and by the time he got there, he was in so much misery that he had to lean against the wall to wait for the worst of the pangs to ebb. When they did, he got moving once more, working his way slowly through the vestibule, heading for the Chamber of Assembly, where a fountain of water bubbled up from a spring far below the palace.

He paused at the sound of someone's approach. A shadow appeared at the end of the long hallway that led to the chamber where Clovis was residing during his stay in the emerald city. The shadow grew longer, taller, and the sound of metal clinking on crystal echoed all around the approaching figure. Ceredon froze in place, a feeling of dread coming over him. In his pain-wracked mind he saw the spirits of those he had helped slay, from Teradon to Conall, to Aeson, coming for him. He wished he had brought a weapon with him—a dagger, a length of rope, anything. He then realized that he'd be in no shape to defend himself in any case.

The shadows were eventually cast aside by the flickering torches, revealing the figure to be neither a ghost nor Clovis, but a young soldier. He was handsome in a human way, wearing his armor adorned with the roaring lion as if it were a second skin. His eyes were kind, and he possessed a head of wavy dark hair that seemed to have a mind of its own. Ceredon teetered to the side and lost his balance. Taking in the sight of him, the young man squinted and picked up his pace.

"By Karak, you look like shit," the soldier said, hastily throwing his arms around Ceredon to keep him from falling. "Whoa there, I have you."

Ceredon leaned into the man, thankful for his strong arms and quick actions. When he took a closer look at the soldier, he saw that he had an odd, diamond-shaped scar on his left cheek.

"Thank you," Ceredon said in the common tongue. "I do not believe we've met."

The soldier paused, then said, "You can call me Boris Morneau. And there's a good reason we haven't met. I only arrived a few hours ago."

"What is the nature of your business?"

"Information," Boris said proudly. "I had an urgent message for Master Clovis."

"Oh. And what was that message?"

Boris looked at him sidelong. "I'm sorry, my message was for Master Crestwell's ears only," he said. "And besides, you haven't told me *your* name yet."

"My apologies," Ceredon said with a chuckle. "Ceredon Sinistel, at your...actually, *in* your service."

"Ceredon? As in son of the Neyvar?"

"The one and only."

"Well, what do you know? I just arrived in Dezerea, and I've already met a prince." His head cocked to the other side. "Granted, a very *injured* prince, but still. What in the world happened to you?"

"Short, uninteresting story. However, do you think you could do me the favor of helping me to the big room down the hall?" He lifted the wooden pitcher, an action that hurt like hell with his broken arm. "I was not thinking and attempted to retrieve some water for myself despite my...condition. If you were to lend me your shoulder, I promise you this prince will never forget it."

"Of course. Consider me at your service."

With Boris's help, it took no time at all to reach the Chamber of Assembly. The young soldier even went so far as to fill the pitcher for him, then fetched a cup for him to drink from. It was while he was mid-gulp that a shrill scream pierced the night air.

"What was that?" he asked Boris.

The soldier shook his head. "I told you. I came with a message for Master Crestwell. I never said it was a *good* message."

"I see."

Boris steered him out of the chamber and back down the hall, heading for the stairwell. It was then that Biden came tearing around the corner, eyes wide with fright. When the healer spotted Ceredon, he stopped short.

"My lord, what are you doing down here?" Biden exclaimed in elvish.

"I needed water," Ceredon said, as if the agonizing trip down to the lowest floor had been nothing.

"You should have told someone," the healer said, panting. "You frightened me half to death. If you had been taken..."

"Why would I have been taken? By whom?"

"Why, by the rebellion." Biden looked at him as if he'd sprouted a third eye. "Did you not hear?"

"Hear what?"

"There was an attempt on Councilor Iolas's life tonight. One of the insurgents snuck into his room and attempted to put a dagger through his heart. If the guard on duty had not gone in to check on him, he would have perished."

Ceredon's heart rose into his throat. "Oh," was all he could say.

Biden walked up to him, looking him over. "At least you seem to be healing, my lord. How does your foot feel?"

"Like it's the size of a watermelon."

"But at least you can feel it. This young man assisted you down the stairs?"

He thought of telling the truth, but instead said, "He did."

"Thank goodness for him." Biden looked at Boris. "And what is the human's name?"

Boris stared at him, dumbfounded.

Biden chuckled and switched to the common tongue. "Many apologies. I am simply wondering the name of the human who assisted my prince in his time of need."

"Boris," he replied. He looked as if he were about to speak his last name as well, but he tripped over the word and fell silent.

Ceredon grabbed the healer by the sleeve of his robe. "Biden," he said, switching back to his native tongue, "enough of this, I feel fine. Tell me what happened to Iolas. You said he was attacked, but was he injured? If so, was it serious?"

The healer shook his head. "The guard put an arrow through the rebel's heart before he had a chance to do him any harm. However..."

"Go on, Biden. Tell me."

The healer looked around, then said, "Iolas does not feel safe here any longer. As the last of the Triad, he is returning to Quellassar to name two new members of the sacred trinity. It is an obligation he has been putting off for weeks."

"And the attack gave him reason," Ceredon muttered.

"Indeed," said Biden.

"When does he leave? Has he decided?"

"Three days." The healer cocked his head, staring closely at Ceredon's face. "My prince, do you wish for my help in returning to your room? You have grown pale."

Ceredon shook his head. "I am sure my friend Boris can manage. You must have things to do."

"Are you certain?"

"I am."

"Very well," Biden said. "I must check on your father. But I will be back to look in on you as well. Try to remain in your bed from now on. I will send two guards to keep watch over you until morning."

Ceredon nodded to the healer, who then ambled away, heading for the main entrance to the palace. He shook his head, feeling his insides tense. Iolas could not be allowed to perish by any hand other than his, but he could not be allowed to return to Quellassar either. Ceredon would need to take care of him in the next two days...which, given his condition, would be a near impossible task.

"What was that about?" Boris asked.

Ceredon looked at the young soldier and shook his head. "You weren't the only one delivering bad news this night," he said, leaving it at that.

"Oh. I see. What will you do about this 'bad news'?"

"Honestly, my new friend? I have not a clue."

Two days later, Ceredon set his plan in motion. Lord and Lady Thyne had visited him briefly, and before they left, Orden had dropped a scrap of paper into Ceredon's hand. Scrawled on it were five words:

Two days—light a fire.

Ceredon hoped he was strong enough to pull it off and that he understood what it meant. Luckily, Biden had come to him with a new concoction of wickroot, ground coffee, and ground poplar seeds to help ease his agony. The potion was strong, and the pain wracking his body subsided less than an hour after the bitter fluid had slipped down his gullet. In fact, it was as if his flesh had been made numb. Even the ache of his mending bones was reduced to a dull throb. That, combined with the jug of strong brandy he had requested earlier in the day, made him feel better than he had in ages.

He waited for the song of the whippoorwills to begin, the irksome whooping that signaled the witching hour, before slipping out of bed, a box of tindersticks clenched between his teeth. Dragging the jug of brandy behind him, he crawled across the floor. Once he reached the window, he rose up on his knees, ripped a piece of cloth from his nightshirt, and stuffed it inside the mouth of the bottle. When it was firmly in place, he struck one of the tindersticks against the flint, setting it alight. He held the flame to the cloth, and it caught quickly. It took a few moments for the fire to gain force, and then he threw the jug from the open window as hard as he could. He watched it soar through the air, unseen by the Ekreissar who paced below, until it struck the ground. The jug shattered, the fire igniting the brandy inside. Spigots of flame shot in all directions, and the guards began to shout. Then came the *whoosh* of arrow and the battle cry of the insurgents. Steel clashed and rangers bellowed out orders. Ceredon ducked from the window before any could see him, then crawled to the door.

He rose unsteadily and opened it.

The guards turned to him quizzically. "Prince Ceredon?" one said.

"Do you not hear that?"

The walls of the palace were thick and almost soundproof.

"No," one of the guards said.

"The insurgency is attacking! Your brothers need you."

"Huh?"

Ceredon hobbled to the side, opening the door wider. "Go, see for yourself," he said.

The two guards rushed into the room and peered out the window, from which emanated a red glow and the unmistakable sounds of conflict. They turned to him and nodded, then rushed into the hall.

"The rebels are attacking!" they shouted to the other guards. A dozen booted feet thudded against the crystal floor as the Ekreissar raced down the stairwell and disappeared from view. Only one remained behind in Ceredon's room.

"Should you not join them?" he asked.

"My duty is to watch over you, my prince," the ranger replied. "You are injured. Should any insurgent climb the walls, you would be an easy target."

The guard turned toward the door, readying his khandar. Ceredon had expected this turn of events, though he was surprised that only one of them had stayed.

With the guard's back to him, Ceredon stealthily grabbed his walking rod and raised it above his head. He took a few hobbling steps forward and, just as the ranger began to swivel in his direction, brought it down as hard as he could. The wood thumped against the side of the guard's head, and Ceredon heard a *snap* as the fragile bones of the elf's temple broke. His eyes rolled into the back of his head as he collapsed backward, thudding on the crystal floor.

Ceredon stood over the felled ranger, giving him another two violent whacks to make sure he stayed dead. The elf's face was a bloodied mess when Ceredon painfully bent over and slipped the dagger from his belt. When the body was found, it would be plainly obvious what had happened, but Ceredon did nothing to cover his tracks. He no longer cared to hide his involvement, even though he knew what that might mean for him. Killing Iolas was all that mattered.

He took a deep breath and tucked the weapon into the rope around his waist, before hopping on one foot into the hallway and then dropping to his hands and knees. Luck seemed to be smiling down on him. Not only had Iolas moved to the seventh floor of the palace from the sixth—"to consolidate our protection," he had said—but every other part of his cobbled together plan had come together perfectly. He just hoped the rebels could hold on for a little while longer.

The door to Iolas's chambers swung open, and Ceredon flopped to the side in a panic. He groaned and held his side, hoping that the old elf hadn't seen him crawling down the hall. Iolas was beside him a moment later, holding up his head with hands twisted from the weight of nearly five hundred years on Dezrel.

"Ceredon, my prince, what are you doing out of bed?" he asked. Ceredon glanced up at him, saw the way his eyes were flicking from one corner of the hall to the other. "What is that noise outside? Where are the guards?" Iolas asked, panic creeping into his voice. "There were supposed to be guards!"

"Insurgents…attacking…" Ceredon said, feigning injury. "Fires spreading…outside."

Iolas's face went even whiter than it normally was.

"Come, young prince," he said, grabbing tight to Ceredon's nightshirt and pulling him along the crystal floor. "Come into my room, and we will be safe there together."

One of us will be, Ceredon thought.

Iolas might be old, but his strength was impressive. In no time at all, he had dragged Ceredon the thirty feet or so into his quarters and slammed the door shut. After barring it from the inside, he bolted for the opposite side of the room, cracking open the blinds to peer down at the courtyard. From his position on the floor, Ceredon could hear the guards still running and shouting below them and the *clang* of steel, but the sounds were less urgent than before. He didn't have much time, though he allowed himself a moment to pray that Tantric hadn't lost too many men.

"It seems quiet out there now," said Iolas. He glanced at Ceredon and offered a nervous smile. "Perhaps the rebels have moved on."

"Perhaps."

Grinding his teeth, Ceredon dug his knuckles into the hard floor and pushed himself upright. This time pain did come, and he grunted against it. Iolas turned to him as Ceredon forced his body to stand.

"Stay on the ground," the older elf said. "You will be safer that way."

Iolas turned his back, and Ceredon sat up, pulling the dagger from within his breeches. The blade reflected the light bouncing off the emerald walls, which he had not expected. Iolas caught sight of the glimmer and spun around.

"My prince, what are you doing?"

Ceredon staggered to his feet, stalking the old elf with the dagger.

"I am correcting a wrong," he said, huffing. "Correcting a great many wrongs, as a matter of fact."

Iolas moved away from him, his back to the wall. He hopped up on the bed, then jumped down on the other side, and Ceredon mimicked his movements, like a desert cat playing with its prey.

"Stop this, Ceredon!" Iolas said, panic in his voice. "If you kill me, you are done for. Everyone will know."

"I don't care," Ceredon snapped back. "I tire of games, I tire of the quest for power, I tire of the gods and their useless pissing match. What I do now, I do for revenge. Conall, Aeson, and now you. You say death to traitors, Iolas? I agree completely."

The elder elf's mouth went slack. "My cousins…"

"Yes," Ceredon said, and then lunged with the dagger, forcing Iolas to scamper over the bed once more.

"But why?" Iolas pleaded. "We are your people…your *family*!"

"Family?" Ceredon barked, unable to suppress a laugh. "My family would not murder children. My family would not enslave an entire race. No, you're no family of mine."

He lunged again, and Iolas ran from the bed. Ceredon noticed him eyeing the door, and he silently hoped the old elf would try for it. If he did, his struggles with the bar would give Ceredon time to fall upon him. As things were, this was taking far too long.

"This has been your plan…all along…," Iolas said, backing toward the opposite side of the room.

Ceredon lurched after him, not saying a word.

"The delegation from Stonewood escaping…skirmishes with the rebels…the constant traps and ambushes. Those were you, as well?"

Ceredon dug his broken foot into the floor, pushing himself onward, getting ever closer.

"Answer me, Ceredon," Iolas said. He had reached the far wall and was trapped beside the closet door. "I deserve that much."

"Yes," Ceredon growled. "All me."

He lunged, dagger leading, its killing edge aimed for Iolas's throat. Iolas screamed and threw his hands up to block the blow. The blade sank into his forearm, causing him to shriek all the louder. Blood spurted when Ceredon ripped the dagger free, splashing against his cheeks, dripping off his chin.

"Now, damn you!" Iolas bellowed in the common tongue. "He has confessed! Do it now!"

Before Ceredon could react, the closet door burst open, striking his left arm as it swung violently outward. New rivers of agony flooded him, and he collapsed to the floor, howling. He lost his grip on the dagger, which skittered across the floor. From the closet emerged three armored humans bearing the sigil of Karak who descended on him, showering him with fists, thrusting the back of his head against the crystal floor again and again. The whole while, Iolas shrieked.

Then came a loud cracking sound, and the room was bathed in light.

"Stop!" a familiar, terrible voice shouted. Those who had beaten him backed away, allowing him to rise on his elbows. Blood dripped from his lips, and his entire body was awash with torment.

"You hit…like human girls," the newcomer spat.

Black boots entered his vision, the right foot tapping. Ceredon could hold himself up no longer. He collapsed onto his side and craned his neck to see the face of Clovis Crestwell staring down at him. The human's features appeared larger than normal, and his eyes glowed a brilliant crimson. It looked as if something alive were squirming beneath his scalp. Ceredon began to laugh at the absurdity of it, clutching at his newly cracked ribs with each painful guffaw.

"Please…a healer…help me…," he heard Iolas whine.

Clovis's twin voice spoke again, only this time the gruffer layer, the one that sounded much less than human, took precedence.

"Get the sniveling fool out of here. And you had best silence yourself before I decide you look too tempting not to have a taste, old elf."

Ceredon stopped his laughing and watched as two soldiers dragged Iolas from the room. The wicked gash in his arm left a trail of blood on the floor behind him, and Clovis ogled it like a starving man eyeing a roasting chicken. The red-eyed human then returned his attention to Ceredon. He smiled, revealing a mouth that was too wide, filled with too many teeth.

"You know not whom you deal with," the man said, only to call him a man would be sacrilege. His cheeks shifted, his ears bulged, and his forehead retreated. His every feature was in a constant state of flux, and his voice now seemed to hold no human qualities whatsoever. Ceredon squeezed his eyes shut, certain the potion he had taken was giving him illusions.

"You will learn," that bestial voice spoke into his ear. "I will keep you alive, and you will watch them suffer for what you've done."

A sharp blow landed in the center of Ceredon's face, bringing stars to his vision. A moment later, his world went black.

CHAPTER

40

housands of women packed the streets of Rat Harbor. They formed a stinking horde on either side of the road as they craned their necks to watch the armor-clad soldiers march past.

Matthew waited for the soldiers in front of the same theater where he'd met with the Conningtons months before. The location was symbolic as well as strategic; if they were to accuse him of treason, which was his fear, it seemed appropriate for it to happen in front of the very place where that treason had been hatched, while keeping Karak's representatives off-guard by meeting in a place of filth rather than the relative luxury of his estate.

Catherine squeezed his hand, and he passed her a worried glance.

"All will be fine," she said, winking.

"How can you be so confident?" he asked.

"Because you are powerful and strong, and a worthy leader for this city."

"Ha! A city of women and children. What a bounty."

She smiled. "Remember who you're speaking to, darling. And chin up. Here they come."

Matthew turned toward the approaching soldiers, and the three billowing red cloaks who led the charge. He took a deep breath and shook his head to ease his nerves. An elbow jabbed into his left shoulder.

"Stop fidgeting," Bren said. "You look too damn nervous. Might as well hang a sign above your head that says, 'I done bad things.'"

"Easy for you to say. You're not the one set to lose his head if this goes wrong."

"Shush, both of you," said Catherine.

I don't know you at all, thought Matthew, a thought that had rarely left his mind since Catherine's confession. Though she had returned to being the demure and doting wife he had always known, he could now see the layer of strength hidden just beneath her frilly garments and rouge-painted cheeks. He wondered if that strength had been there all along, and he had simply been blind to it.

The cloaked figures drew closer, and now Matthew could see their faces clearly. They were the same ones who had arrived months before to secure use of his river barges, their red robes bearing the roaring lion of Karak. They walked with their heads down and their hands clasped. The soldiers followed behind dutifully, more than two hundred of them. Matthew's grip on his wife's hand tightened. He peered at his remaining eighty-six sellswords, who formed a line on either side of the street in front of the gathered women, then at those standing beside him, which included his maids Penetta and Lori, and finally back to the soldiers. Moira was nowhere to be found, and his men were outnumbered more than two to one. If talks went sour, they were in trouble.

The three acolytes stopped before him, as did the soldiers, leaving ample room between them and their holy leaders. The middle acolyte lowered his hood and lifted his eyes, while his two compatriots kept theirs downcast. The one in charge was no older than sixteen, though he carried himself with poise far beyond his years.

"Master Brennan," the acolyte said with a slight bow. "May Karak bless you on this fine day."

Matthew nodded in return. "Yes, Noel, you are well met," he said, hoping he remembered the name correctly.

"It is Noyle," the acolyte said, his frown deepening. "Though I must ask you why we have gathered here in the slums rather than at your home. If I were a distrustful man, I would think you were attempting to hide something from us."

You are no man, thought Matthew, but his lips recited the words Catherine had told him to say.

"We have nothing to hide. Holding our business here is symbolic. We are all beggars in the shadow of Karak, and I wished to demonstrate that humility to his most trusted servants."

He bent his knee then, as did Catherine and Bren.

"Stand up, Master Brennan," Noyle said. "Your respect is noted."

Matthew stood once more, his knees popping in the process. Noyle stared at him, his doubt obvious in the rise of his eyebrows and the twitch of his youthful nose. In the silence that followed, it seemed the murmuring of the crowd of women climbed tenfold.

Noyle blinked first.

"You received our letter," he said. "Have you brought all we requested with you?"

"We have," Matthew replied. "I present to you the last eighty-six of my men, those who have guarded my estate diligently. They are yours to do with as you wish."

"Good." Noyle turned to address the two lines of sellswords. "You have been given a great honor, chosen to serve in the army of our Divinity and protect the ideals of the almighty Karak."

The sellswords grumbled and shook their heads.

Noyle looked back at Matthew. "These men are to be sent up the Rigon, to join the force that has gathered in the elven city of Dezerea."

"How will they get there?" he asked. "You conscripted our barges during your last visit."

"At this moment, one of your barges awaits at the mouth of the Rigon. Our own representatives will escort them on their way. Now, onto the matter of our other requests…"

Matthew pointed down the crowded street. "There are fifteen wagons waiting in front of the postern gate. They contain a third of our wheat, vegetables, and salted meats, to be used in whatever way Karak requires."

"A third is not enough. We require half of your stores."

Matthew's insides twisted, the dire warning of the Conningtons manifesting itself before his eyes. The part of him that wasn't afraid, small as it was, silently applauded his decision to help them.

Catherine nudged him, and he shook himself out of his stupor.

"If half is what you require, half is what you will get," he said.

"And what of the weapons?" asked Noyle, one eyebrow lifting.

"Weapons?" asked Matthew, a hitch in his voice.

"Yes, the weapons I requested in the letter. It is on record in Veldaren that you purchased a large cache of steel from the Connington family two years ago. We require those weapons to fight the brother god's scourge of Paradise. The production of the northern armories has declined precipitously since most of the workers have been called into service to our Lord. Where are they?"

"We—"

"We don't have them any longer," said Catherine, cutting him off.

Noyle eyed her, seeming aghast that she'd had the nerve to speak.

"Where are they?" he demanded.

"They should be with our god already," she said, sounding entirely at ease. "Just after your last visit, when you drafted our ships, my husband mulled over your dire words for a solid week. He decided to get the weapons to Karak without delay. The cache was loaded onto our last remaining galley and sent along the coast to enter the Rigon and join our barges before they traversed the shallower parts of the river."

"Is this true?" asked Noyle, staring Matthew down. "We have received no word from our Divinity about these weapons."

"It is possible the galley never made it to the river," Catherine said before Matthew could reply. "The sea storms were quite harsh at the time. It is common for a ship bearing a heavy load not to survive the waves."

"Does your wife always speak for you?" Noyle asked Matthew.

"Not always," he mumbled in reply.

Noyle turned and walked away. The other two acolytes stepped forward to meet him, and they huddled together, speaking in hushed tones. The sellswords shuffled about uneasily, as did Bren, Penetta, and Lori. Matthew felt for them. It amazed him how unmoved Catherine appeared. She simply stared straight forward, chin lifted, eyes bright and alive.

Finally, Noyle approached him once more.

"If what you say is true, your god thanks you for your sacrifice. Rest assured, however, that this matter will be further explored." He gestured behind him. "Kipling, my fellow acolyte, will remain behind to review your records. If there is any evidence of treachery, you will answer to our god. Is that understood, Master Brennan?"

"It is," Matthew said, a lump in his throat.

"Unfortunately, since you do not have the weapons to give, there is something else we require in their stead. An army of fighting men has needs other than weaponry, after all."

Matthew felt proud of how well he hid his cringe.

"What might that be?" he asked.

Noyle stepped back and gestured to the crowd of women.

"The soldiers in our Lord's army have basic needs that have gone unmet for some time. All we ask is that you hand over three hundred of your young ladies to serve in that regard. All those who are given this honor will be greatly rewarded, both while performing their duties and when the war is finished."

"Wait…what?" said Matthew. He couldn't believe what he was hearing. Bren chuckled beside him.

"You heard me, Master Brennan," said the acolyte.

"You…you would make *prostitutes* out of them?"

Noyle laughed. "I am sure many of them already were, Master Brennan. Are you that naïve to think otherwise? Now their womanly virtues will simply be serving a higher purpose."

Matthew grabbed the young acolyte by the front of his robe, pulled him close. The soldiers in front drew their swords, looking ready to charge, but the other two acolytes held them back.

"According to Karak's law, these women are free," Matthew growled, spittle striking Noyle's cheek. "What you ask is to *enslave* them."

Noyle never even flinched.

"It could be worse," he said. "We could place them on the battlefield to be slaughtered. This way, the men get to stoke their inner fire, and the women who receive their gifts might be rewarded with a child."

"That isn't right, you sick fuck. How can you—"

"Matthew, release him."

He shifted his eyes to meet Catherine's gaze as she stood there, hands on hips, glowering at him.

"Do you think it right that—"

"I said release him, Matthew."

He opened his fists and allowed Noyle to take a step backward. Matthew stormed toward his wife. Bren took a step closer to Catherine, as if to protect her.

"You will let our people be turned into concubines?" he asked, seething.

She leaned closer to him. "Remember, Matthew. Whatever they ask for, you give them. It is the only way."

"But—"

"But nothing, darling. Do it. Now."

He blew out a disgusted breath and turned around. Noyle had straightened out his robe, and a pair of soldiers were at his sides, swords raised.

"Consider your demand met," Matthew said with a disgusted wave. "If you want women, you can have them."

Shocked cries rang out from the crowd.

"Good. And since laying your hands on a representative of Karak cannot go without punishment, we will require a hundred more, your house servants among them."

Matthew winced and peered over his shoulder, where Catherine was nodding. "Very well. You want them, you have them."

The clamor of the immense gathering of women ratcheted up. Now there were shouts and weeping from the throng. Noyle turned around in a circle, addressing them.

"You heard the words of Master Brennan!" he shouted. "If any wish to volunteer their services, step forward now. Should our required count not be met, we will begin choosing those of our liking from among the rest."

The volume of the protest climbed, but none stepped forward. Matthew crept back to Catherine's side and clutched her hand once more. She was smiling. On the other side of him, Bren began breathing quickly, almost expectantly.

"Why are you smiling?" Matthew asked his wife.

Catherine jutted her chin out, urging Matthew to look. When he did, he saw the crowd part and a lithe, dark-haired woman wearing a simple smock emerged. His jaw dropped open.

"We have our first volunteer!" announced Noyle. He left the protection of the two soldiers as Moira Elren kneeled before him, hands on her knees. "Do you welcome this chance to serve our beloved god as we defeat the enemies of our lord?"

"I am but a servant," she said, smiling up at him. The man paused, his expression confused.

"Do I know you?" he asked. "Your face—it is familiar."

"It should be," she said. "I'm the woman who killed you."

In a single, swooping motion, Moira reached beneath her smock, pulled out a curved dagger, and jammed the blade beneath Noyle's ribcage. The young acolyte's face grew white with shock and pain, his eyes bulging from their sockets as she gave the weapon a vicious twist. The other two acolytes stared, mouths agape, as she lowered their leader to the ground.

"I am no one's whore!" she screamed at the throng of women. "And neither are any of you!"

The two soldiers who had been standing with Noyle leapt forward, swords leading. Matthew cried out a warning, but it was unnecessary. Moira yanked her dagger from Noyle's chest and cartwheeled to the side, dodging their attack. When she landed back on her feet, she hurled the dagger. It flew through the air, flinging Noyle's blood as it spun, until it plunged into the neck of the first soldier. The man fell to his knees, clutching at the hilt as blood poured from between his fingers.

"Now!" Moira shouted as she leaped back into the crowd.

The two hundred soldiers who had arrived with the acolytes were just beginning to draw their weapons as a volley of arrows rained down on them. Matthew glanced up, saw women with bows standing on the rooftops of the shanty buildings lining Rat Harbor's main street. The soldiers, caught unaware, were pelted with the bolts of sharp steel. A few fell to arrows in the neck or face; still others doubled over as arrows found purchase in the gaps in their mail and plate.

Matthew's sellswords were on the startled soldiers a moment later, swords drawn. Then the crowd of women surged forward, armed with kitchen utensils—knives, iron pots, wooden spoons sharpened to shanks. Their sheer numbers swallowed the soldiers, who disappeared beneath a sea of long hair and ratty clothing. Matthew couldn't believe his eyes.

A strong hand gripped his arm, yanking him backward. He looked Bren in the eye, and there was a strange aura of melancholy about him.

"Alright, boss, show's over," he said, shoving Matthew into the open door of the theater. "You too, Miss Brennan. It ain't safe out here for you."

The chaos and raucous noise of the conflict died away somewhat after Bren slammed the theater door shut behind them. Matthew, his wife, and her two maids stood in the middle of the open space, looking at the tables where Connington's men had once sat, staring at the now empty shelf of liquor. The clang of steel and the shrieks of dying men and women pierced the building's walls.

"I could use a drink," he heard Catherine say. "Lori, Penetta, please go to the cellar and find some wine. I'm sure there's a reserve here somewhere."

Two pairs of feet shuffled away, and Matthew slowly brought his eyes to his wife. Catherine seemed to be relishing the moment. Her dress, a stately violet number edged with yellow gems, wasn't rumpled in the slightest.

"This…this was your doing," he said. It wasn't a question.

"Of course."

"You knew what would happen."

She nodded. "A message came from Riverrun two weeks ago. The Conningtons were given similar demands, and they handed over half their guard and a large number of their Sisters, just as the Garlands and Mudrakers had already done." She shrugged. "I had Moira prepare as many women as she could. Had you not been busy murdering those poor people who delivered the Gemcroft woman's child, you would have known."

"But you…you *hid the message from me*!" he exclaimed. "You should have told me, Catherine. This is *my* business! Do you know what you just did? We will be considered blasphemers, enemies of the kingdom! When Karak returns, he will have all our heads! And should any more soldiers arrive at our gates…"

"Matthew, my dear, I thought you took measures so that Karak would *not* return. And besides, there are no more soldiers in Neldar. These were the last. The rest are all…occupied elsewhere." Her grin turned into a sly smile.

"How can you be so smug? How can you be so *sure?*"

"I've learned from the best," she answered.

The door swung open then, admitting the deafening clamor of the battle. Bren entered, lugging a groaning soldier behind him. The man's arm had been severed just below the elbow, the jagged stump spurting blood.

"What are you *doing?*" Matthew shouted. "Get that man out of here, or at least put him out of his misery."

"Can't," said Bren.

"Why in the name of the gods not?"

"Because this is the murderer," said Catherine.

"Murderer of who?"

Bren answered without words, driving the soldier's sword into Matthew's gut. Pain exploded throughout his body, followed by a strange weakening sensation as blood began to flow out of the mortal wound. Bren released the sword's handle and Matthew fell backward, landing on his rump. The tip of the sword, which had exited his lower back, clanked on the slatted wooden floor.

He gawked at the handle, at all the blood, and then back up at Bren.

"Why?" he was able to croak out. His throat felt as if something were lodged into it.

Bren cast his eyes aside and turned away from him. By the rise and fall of his shoulders, it looked like he was crying. That was when Catherine approached, kneeling down before him and placing a velvety hand on his cheek. Her skin was hot to the touch, almost burning. The expression on her face was an odd mixture of resolve and sorrow.

"My poor Matthew," Catherine whispered. "Does it hurt?"

He groaned.

"The pain will end soon, darling. Worry not."

His head grew faint, and he felt his body begin to tip over. Catherine guided him to the floor, resting his head atop the hard wood. He coughed, and a spray of red left his mouth, forming tiny dots on Catherine's elegant dress. His chest hitched, and he began to sob despite the pain.

His voice was nothing more than a sigh when he asked, "Why?" once more.

Catherine shook her head. "I do love you, you know. I always have, ever since I was a girl. But love fades, love *changes*, and when that happens, the only thing you can do is change along with it."

Matthew's head lolled. Catherine grabbed him by the hair, making sure their eyes met.

"I know you love me in your own way, Matthew," she continued. "And I never lied to you. I have long since forgiven your trysts and your long absences from our home. That is not why I must do this."

The pain became too much to bear, and his eyes rolled into the back of his head, but then a heavy hand struck him across the cheek, returning him to wakefulness.

"Stay with me, Matthew. I have not made this decision out of spite, but out of *survival*. You are a powerful man, and yet you are weak, so weak. Your fortune, though vast, pales in comparison to what it *should* have been. When this war began, you freely gave of your own ships, of your own purse, of your own *people*, when Karak came calling. It was not until Romeo and Cleo invited you to their secret meeting that you showed any backbone. Though even that should not have happened. You should have perished on your way to that meeting."

Matthew's eyes widened. "You…" he moaned.

"Yes, me. One of your guards told me of your summit with the brothers, so I brought hired men into the city through your own secret whore tunnel. Unfortunately, the men I hired were simple brigands, not skilled enough to deal with Moira and the lug. I learned my lesson."

Matthew's eyes flicked to Bren as his vision began to waver.

Catherine glanced at the bodyguard, who still had his back to them.

"Ah, yes, your protector. A week after the failed attempt on your life, I offered him half the coin I had stowed away, along with the deed to the lands we hold north of the river. He almost leapt at the offer." She *tsk'd* at him. "You have always been a silly man, Matthew. You cannot get much sillier than blindly trusting a man whose love of gold outweighs his love of you."

"Sorry, boss," Bren's cracking voice said.

Catherine frowned. "Don't you see, my love? I do this for our children. For our girls, for little Ryan. You would have ruined us by giving Karak all we had and then letting the Conningtons swoop in to take what remained. There needed to be someone smarter in charge of the family fortune, someone with the stomach to make tough decisions. That someone is *me*, dear husband. It always has been, though you were too proud to see it. Perhaps now you do."

She let go of his hair, and his cheek slammed against the floor. His thoughts were awash with his wife's betrayal, of the life that was rapidly leaving him. Images of his children flashed in front of his eyes as tears poured down his face. He would never see Mary get married, never watch Christina ride a horse for the first time, never teach Ryan how to sail along the rough ocean waters.

"I'm...sorry...," he whispered to their memory.

"You are indeed," said Catherine in reply.

Matthew closed his eyes, and his body lost all feeling. He was brought back to better times, when he and Catherine had been but two teenagers in love, happily frolicking through the reeds, drinking wine while sitting on a blanket in front of the ocean, making love beneath the full moon. Somewhere in the back of his mind, he knew that he was being dragged along the floor, and he heard Catherine shrieking in horror. Then the heat of the sun was on his face for the final time, and the world seemed to stop spinning as the dying sounds of battle filled the air.

The last thing he heard was Catherine's voice, shouting above the din.

"My husband! They murdered my husband!"

They sure did, he thought, and then everything went black.

CHAPTER

41

Ahaesarus didn't like this. Not one bit.

He and Turock Escheton stood in a secluded room in the rear of Blood Tower, staring at the man tied to the pole opposite him. The man was dressed in one of Abigail's nightshirts, which was torn and spotted with blood. There was still more blood on his chin, coating his brow, dripping from his missing left ear.

Oddly, the prisoner was grinning.

Turock grunted, twirling a switch in his hand. "You have something to say?" he asked the bound man. He pointed to the map hanging on the wall, the same one they had taken from the man's tent in the Tinderlands. "What do those red marks mean? Are there other factions?"

The man spit a bloody wad of phlegm onto the floor and said nothing.

"This is unnecessary," Ahaesarus said. "This is *wrong*."

"Spare me your sermons, Warden," said Turock.

"I will not. You requested my help, and my council comes with it."

"Bollocks. I asked for your muscle, and your ability to see truth, not your brain."

Turock stepped up to the prisoner, reared his hand back, and lashed out with the switch. It whistled as it flew through the air, striking the bound man across the cheek. A new gash opened up, another scar to join the others that marred the left side of his face. Still he remained silent. Turock wiped the bloody switch on his robe, which had been lime green before they'd started but was now crisscrossed with red lines.

"Tell me," he said, his voice a low growl. "Is the camp where my men captured you the only one? If not, where they are on the map?"

Ahaesarus bristled from the knowledge that he was being included as one of Turock's *men*. He might be one of humanity's Wardens, beholden only to Ashhur, yet he had gone into the Tinderlands at the cranky spellcaster's bidding, and then he'd hastily summoned him as soon as they returned with their quarry. He had stood silently by with his brethren as the humans mocked and ridiculed the captive after draping the womanly garb over his head. *You say you aren't a soldier,* he thought. *Yet this is how you act?*

"How large is your force?" continued Turock. "What are Karak's plans? When does the real attack begin? Where?"

All of these questions went unanswered, the grin still pasted on the captive's bleeding face. The spellcaster huffed in frustration, lashed him with the switch again, and then stormed away.

Ahaesarus was like Turock's shadow as he paced.

"This is a hard man, wholly devoted to his god," he said. "Look at him, actually *look* at him. He has endured trials in his life that far outdo any torment you might bring him. There must be—"

"Is that so?" Turock snapped, wheeling on him, a mad gleam in his eye. "You think I couldn't give him worse? Let us see, shall we?"

"Turock, no."

The spellcaster brushed aside Ahaesarus's hand and stomped toward the prisoner. He began murmuring, the tips of his fingers developing a glow. The bound man stared at him, his grin faltering for the first time in four hours. Ahaesarus, his own anger steadily rising, reached out to stop him, but he retreated when Turock shot him a look. Turock was volatile, and there was no telling what he might do if Ahaesarus tried to be forceful. His words would have to do the job for him.

"You are a good man, Turock," he said, somehow managing to keep his voice steady. "Ashhur has often sung your praises, as have others in Mordeina. Your people trust you. Do not ruin that praise, that trust, by torturing this man. You are better than that. Do not become a monster."

"A monster?" asked Turock without turning around. He raised his hand, the glow of his fingertips intensifying to bright flames. "Murderers of children, assassins in the night, a man who lets those he loves suffer and die...*those* are monsters, Warden. This bastard you see before you...he fits two of those categories. I refuse to become the third."

He tore open the nightshirt's frilly bodice and pressed his fingers into the man's chest. Fire crackled across the prisoner's flesh, not on the surface but *beneath*, spreading outward in a pattern like cracks in a sheet of ice. One of the glowing veins split the skin, and a thin spiral of black smoke rose into the air. Sweat beaded on the man's brow, his neck pulled taut, and his smirk abandoned him, but he remained admirably silent nonetheless.

That silence only drove Turock to try harder.

He pressed his other glowing hand to the prisoner's temple.

"You say I'm a good man," he said. "That might have been true at one point." The gray hair on the bound man's right temple burst into flame. "But we have lived in turmoil for a year, Warden. A *year*!"

He snuffed out the flames, took a step back, and then offered a few more words of magic. From the cracks in the stone floor rose tiny vines, which danced before the prisoner's feet, then plunged their pointed tips beneath his toenails. The man squirmed, grinding his teeth in obvious pain as they drove deeper and deeper into the quick, drawing blood.

"Men, women, and children perish while helping to forge the weapons we need to defend ourselves. I have been kept awake at night in expectation of the next assault. Nature was once full of wonder, but now every bird's caw, every bat's tweet, every insect's chirp might be a signal to rain fiery death down on all I created."

The vines withdrew, retreating into the cracks that had sprouted them. The prisoner huffed for breath.

"I understand how you feel," Ahaesarus said. "You forget where my kind came from."

"Yes, you brave Wardens who hid like children in your cages while winged demons slaughtered your loved ones. Forgive me if I don't have that kind of restraint."

"That is unfair. We were not given a choice."

"You're right," said Turock. "But we have been."

With a snap of his fingers, needlelike shards of ice formed in the air around the prisoner. Turock waggled his hands, and at once the shards drove into the bound man's flesh. He struggled in his restraints, a human cactus prickled from head to toe with crystalline barbs. He uttered the first sound Ahaesarus had heard from his mouth since his capture: he moaned.

"I am a father," Turock said as he slowly went about grinding his palm against the ice shards, one by one. "I have not seen my three youngest sons for so long, I have forgotten their faces. They were only supposed to be in Mordeina for a month, to tutor under Howard Baedan and spend time with their grandmother. Byron is a man now, eighteen and full of vigor, with Jarak not far behind. And Pendet...our baby...do you know what a year means to a seven-year-old? It is everything. I fear I may never see them again, and even if I do, Pendet might look at me as a stranger."

"Yet you still have your children here, children who love and need you just as much as they."

Turock cackled. "Ha! Lauria is married, Cethlynn soon to be, and Dorek is as much my apprentice now as he is my son. I need *them*, and their partners, more than they need me."

"Does that not count for something?"

Turock finally turned around, and spittle flew from his lips when he spoke. "Something? *Something?* I want *everything*, Warden. I want my children, my wife, my *people* to be safe!"

"Make it so, then," Ahaesarus said, a hard edge entering his tone. "If you think your soul is an acceptable price, then so be it. But I will not be an accomplice to this torment. You have turned your back on Ashhur's mercy."

"What, you wish me to bake him a cake? Or perhaps draw him a bath and dangle grapes over his mouth?" Turock pointed an accusing finger at the prisoner. "This man would kill us in a heartbeat should we give him the chance, and you wish for me to give him *mercy?*"

Ahaesarus folded his arms over his chest. "Should he or any of Karak's children attempt to take the life of myself or any of my Wards, I would strike him down without a second thought. But I would *strike him down*, Turock, not prolong his suffering. *That* is the mercy I speak of."

Turock shook his head. "We need to know.... We have been trapped here for so long...."

"If you are trapped, it is of your own doing," laughed the prisoner.

Ahaesarus and Turock both wheeled around. The man was upright in his binds, head cocked, staring at them. The ice shards had melted, leaving him soaked and covered with tiny, leaking red wounds. He winced, flexed his jaw, and then seemed to shake off the pain.

"Your isolation ended when Uther Crestwell died," the prisoner continued, and he chuckled even as a bit of blood ran down his lips.

Ahaesarus was too shocked to answer. The same could not be said for Turock.

"So those are your first words to us? We'll see how much you laugh when your balls are gone."

The spellcaster stepped back and cupped his hand. The blue glow around it intensified, and the prisoner doubled over, finally screaming. Ahaesarus forcibly grabbed Turock by the arm, spinning him around, and the spell died in a cascade of slaps and curses.

"Out!" Turock screamed at him. "Leave my tower now! Leave my fucking lands as well!"

"I will not, Escheton," the Warden shouted. "The man is telling the truth!"

Turock stared at him, but at last there was a hint of comprehension in his eyes.

"What?" he asked.

"You wanted me to tell you if he spoke a lie or not. He is speaking the truth now. Allow me to question him."

Turock rolled his eyes. "Fine. You think you can get more of a response than me, then be my guest."

Ahaesarus approached the prisoner. "What is your name?" he asked "What is your purpose?"

The man closed his lips and shook his head.

Ahaesarus sighed and leaned in close, whispering in his ear.

"I can end this quickly if you cooperate," he said. "There will be no more torment. Your death will be painless."

The prisoner's eyes lifted to him, and for the first time there was no hardness in them.

"My living torment might cease," he said, "but my soul will burn in the abyss for all eternity should I betray him. My god is noble and mighty. All I have, all I have become, I owe to the one who created me. I would rather hurl myself into the flames than turn on Karak."

"You want to burn?" Turock asked, stepping closer, fire on his fingertips, Ahaesarus struck him with the back of his hand. The spellcaster stumbled away, holding the side of his face and cursing. The Warden picked up the sword he had laid on the ground, grabbed Turock by the loose collar of his cloak, and pressed the tip of the blade to his throat. The spellcaster's eyes grew wide.

"No more," growled Ahaesarus. His menacing tone scared even himself. "This ends now. Leave this tower. Leave the prisoner to me. If he cooperates, you will know all you wish to know. If he does not, he will not see the sunrise. Am I understood?"

Turock nodded, though his entire body looked ready to explode.

"Good," Ahaesarus said. "Now leave."

He spun the dazed, red-haired man around and guided him to the door. Opening it, he pushed Turock out to where his son-in-law Uulon stood guard, blond hair matted and eyelids at half-mast. The young man was shocked to attention by their sudden appearance. Ahaesarus gave Turock a shove and shut the door quickly behind him. With that done he leaned against the wood, breathing heavily. What he'd done was rash, dangerous. Turock had proven himself to be powerful in the ways of magic. Had he not been taken off guard by Ahaesarus's sudden aggression, the Warden might have found himself set ablaze, transformed into a mudskipper, or worse. Breathing out a sigh, he barred the door and returned to the prisoner, who stared at him, an odd look of gratitude on his battle-scarred face. With a twinge of sadness, the Warden remembered something Eveningstar had told him one evening, after Ahaesarus had expressed frustration about his progress with Geris. The boy had been drifting in his studies, but each time Ahaesarus lashed out at him, the child would draw inward and stop speaking.

"Sometimes saying nothing is better than saying the wrong thing," the great betrayer of Ashhur had said. "There is only so much silence a man can take."

It was time to put those words into practice.

Ahaesarus pulled up a chair and sat across from the bound man. He asked no questions and expected no answers. All he did was sit, his gaze never leaving the prisoner's face. For a while the man was admirable in his fortitude, standing tall in his restraints, his blood-splattered chin held high. But after what felt like an eternity, when the sounds of the first stirrings in camp came seeping through the thick walls, he began to crack.

"Wallace," he muttered, his voice raspy.

"Say again?"

"Wallace. My name is Wallace."

"Thank you, Wallace." He stood, retrieved a pitcher of water from the table in the corner, and poured liquid over Wallace's parched lips.

There was silence again for a few moments, until Wallace, some of his many wounds still seeping blood, sighed deeply and closed his eyes.

"Karak forgive me," he said.

"For what?" asked Ahaesarus.

He took a deep breath.

"I will give you two questions. You are a Warden, so you will know that what I say is truthful. After that I will say nothing more, and I ask that you end my life quickly. I do not wish to endure more of the angry man in the funny cloak."

"Very well," Ahaesarus said, inclining his head. The aura seeping out of this Wallace told him he was a man of his word. No matter what he or Turock did to him after those two questions were asked, they would get no more answers. The amount of discipline he showed was breathtaking. *If this is the type of dedication Ashhur must face...*

He retook his chair and threw one leg over the other, his mind racing. Wallace leaned his head back against the post, closed his eyes, and waited.

Settling on his first question, Ahaesarus asked, "How long have you been in the northern deadlands?"

"Too long," the prisoner replied. His eyes opened sleepily. "Though in truth, it must be eighteen months, give or take. I was the trusted council of Uther Crestwell, whose authority I supplanted after his death."

It was the truth. Ahaesarus almost asked how many were in his force, which should have been the first question, but he snapped his mouth shut. Wallace was laying a trap for him, one he could ill afford to fall into. *Two questions.* He cursed his stupidity.

He nodded instead.

"Anything else?" asked Wallace again.

"One moment."

He mulled it over, trying to craft the one question that would give him the most information. There was simply too much he needed to know. He could ask for Karak's plan, but Wallace was an underling, a man in command of a force stationed far from those assaulting from the east. It was unlikely he would know anything but his own group's role. Ahaesarus closed his eyes and prayed to the god who had saved him, asking for guidance. The right question came to him almost at once, and his eyes sprang open.

"How will you rejoin Karak?" he asked.

Wallace sighed, a tired smile coming across his dry lips.

"We won't," he said. "My duty ends here, on the banks of the Gihon."

Again, it was the truth. Ahaesarus gaped at him. "What does that mean?"

"Two questions, no more. You have your answers. Now fulfill your promise."

Ahaesarus stood once more, his thoughts whirling in his skull. He hovered in the empty space between the prisoner and the door, unsure of what to do. Had he doomed those he had been sent here to protect? He buried his face in his hands, praying again for guidance.

"Your promise, Warden," said Wallace.

Ahaesarus ignored him. "Please, Ashhur, I am your humble servant. Give me your wisdom."

He took a deep breath, leaned his head back, and stared at the ceiling. He felt a presence then, as if another entity were looking through his eyes and weighing his options, with him. As the presence retreated, a vision entered his mind, and a hornlike bleating sounded, so deep and loud that it shook the stone walls surrounding them. He looked over at Wallace, whose eyes were wide with bewilderment.

"What was that?" the prisoner asked.

A second, then a third, then a fourth bleat joined the first, until the air was rocked by a relentless concussive assault. The barred door shook on its hinges, and voices shouted from outside, demanding entry. The Master Warden heard a voice in his ear, a command to travel south, and his body flooded with relief.

"What *was that?*" repeated Wallace, sounding desperate.

Ahaesarus offered a prayer of thanks to his distant god, then turned to the prisoner.

"No questions," he said. "Your reward is waiting."

He placed his huge hands on either side of Wallace's head and jerked it violently to the side. The man's neck snapped, severing his spinal column. His eyes bulged from their sockets, his final breaths bursting forth raggedly. Ahaesarus released him, let his head dangle on his fractured neck as bloody spittle dripped from his mouth. He felt sick at the sight of the body, the very first life ended by his hands, but he did his best to shove aside his feelings of guilt. *Ashhur forgive me for this horror.* He rushed to the door, threw aside the bar, and opened it to find Turock, Uulon, Judah, and Grendel standing there panting. Meanwhile, the bellowing hornlike sounds continued to blare.

Turock was enraged when he spotted Wallace's dangling corpse.

"You killed our prisoner!" he shouted.

Ahaesarus shoved him aside.

"I gave him mercy," he answered, approaching his two fellow Wardens. "And he told us all we needed to know."

"And the sound?" asked Judah. "What is it?"

"The battle cry of the grayhorns," Ahaesarus said with a nod, thinking of what Ashhur had shown him in his vision. "Grendel, get the others. We are leaving this place."

"You can't do that!" protested Turock, following on their heels as they strode down the corridor.

"You told me you wished for me to leave."

"I changed my mind!"

Ahaesarus didn't answer him. They walked out of the tower and into a morning that was nearly blinding in its brightness. The people of the camp all seemed to be awake, glancing around in confusion as the grayhorns' bleating continued to sound. Only after Grendel ran off to gather up the other Wardens did Ahaesarus turn to face the spellcaster. He continued to follow the path alongside the mountain as he looked at Turock, heading toward the rise that hid the camp from view. The greyhorns were much louder here, almost swallowing all other sounds.

"We are done here," he said. "Our duty lies to the south, in Mordeina. That is where we are needed most, as are your spellcasters."

Turock shook his head.

"But what of those across the river? What happens when they attack? You came here to assist us! Are you saying you wish us to abandon our *homes*?"

"I came to assist Ashhur," he shot back. "To protect Paradise from destruction." He waved his arm back toward the river. "This is merely a diversion. The force gathered in the Tinderlands is a distraction, nothing more. Karak or Jacob or *someone* decided the best way to weaken Ashhur's defenses was to thin out his resources." He looked down at the strange man, whose bloodstained robe billowed around him as he struggled to match the Warden's much longer strides. "They consider those you have trained to be the biggest threat to their victory, so they will continue to torment you and keep you guessing. Those across the river are willing to give their own lives to keep you out of the way. They know they cannot win against those you have trained, but they do not care."

The man grabbed his arm, halting him in place. "Wait. Are you saying...?"

"Yes. It is a ruse, Turock. A grand ruse to keep you and your students out of the way. You have been played on all sides."

"The prisoner told you this?"

Ahaesarus smiled. "He did not need to."

He scaled the hill before them and gazed out across the grayhorns' grazing fields. Turock seemed calmer now, displaying a dutiful sort of pride. *It takes acknowledgment of your talents for you to listen?* Ahaesarus felt pity for the man.

"Your home will not go undefended," the Warden said. "You will stay behind with half your apprentices and whatever townsfolk choose not to leave. The others will join me and my fellow Wardens...and *them*...on the trek to Mordeina."

Turock's gaze shifted to the field.

"Oh my," he said, jaw slack. "Where are they going?"

Ahaesarus watched the massive wrinkled hides of more than a thousand grayhorns as they marched south, disappearing into the distance, their bleating fading away.

"They are going to the same place as us," he said. "The capital of Paradise. Ashhur is forming his army."

CHAPTER

42

The dungeons below Palace Thyne used to be the only place in Dezerea devoid of color. When Ceredon joined forces with Kindren Thyne to free Aullienna Meln and her people, there had been nothing down there but walls of lime rock and granite and thick steel bars. It had been drab and lonely, a truly hopeless setting for those without hope.

That had changed, for now the dungeons were speckled everywhere with shades of red.

A despondent Lord Orden had once told him the dungeons had not been used since the emerald city's creation nearly a century before. All that had changed when the Quellan arrived and conquered their cousins. Afterward, not a day passed when Ceredon didn't see a member of the Ekreissar march a beaten and bloodied Dezren down the stairwell behind the palace. As he looked around now, locked in the very cell that had once held Aully, he saw evidence of what had happened to those poor souls. Their bones were stacked up in the nearby cells, ribcages on pelvic bones, on femurs, on skulls, large and small, adult and child. The walls were painted with their dried blood, a sickening brown and black, while patches of writhing white marked where thick chunks of flesh and innards had been cast aside. Flies buzzed around it all.

It was the most awful thing Ceredon had ever experienced, the macabre answer to his questions about what Clovis Crestwell did during his long hours locked away in the dungeon.

Ceredon was weak and starving, forced to sleep in the lone corner of the cell he had managed to clear of elven remains. Time dragged on, day and night indistinguishable, while he stared with ever-growing acceptance at the ruin that surrounded him. The torches on the corridor's rough granite walls always burned brightly despite the fact none came to change them.

Even though his situation was hopeless, Ceredon did not give up, did not give in. He was the prince of the Quellan, the future Neyvar of his people. He would be strong for them. He had no choice. At least that was what he told himself.

His stomach rumbled, and he reclined in his corner and closed his eyes. *At least the smell doesn't bother me anymore,* he thought. The rancid stench of decay had made his head spin at first. Now that sensation had passed, the reek becoming as normal to him as the scent of the flowering dogwoods that lingered in the air from spring until fall in Quellassar.

Thoughts of home brought back his concerns for his father. When he had first awoken in this terrible place, he'd expected the Neyvar to free him at any moment. In between bouts of nausea he would sit idly, hands wrapped around his knees, and watch the distant door to the outside world. But that door never opened. His conscience constantly chided him: *He is ashamed of my failure and has disowned his only son.* There were many moments in which Ceredon, who had never so much as shed a tear for as long as he could remember, felt close to crying.

"Did I do you wrong, Father?" he pleaded at the ceiling. "Did I not do as you wished? Please, tell me!"

You did not disappoint him, my child. He could not be prouder.

It was a woman's voice, as soft and comforting as a velvet pillow, which seemed to come from everywhere and nowhere at once. Ceredon's eyes snapped open, darting this way and that, but he saw nothing but the desiccated corpses of a hundred Dezren. He winced in pain when he brought his hands up to his ears and shook his head. An odd sort of calm overcame him.

"Is this my punishment?" he asked. "For not acting in time? For allowing so many innocents to perish?"

You did what you could, my child, the voice said again. *You have acted as a true hero should, with honor and dedication, with love for your goddess in your heart. No single elf can right all the wrongs in the world, but it takes a true hero to try.*

"Celestia?" he whispered. This time the tears did flow.

I am here for you, my love, my greatest of creations, my righter of wrongs, but I do not wish for you to join my side just yet. You are my agent in the flesh, and you must go on.

His body grew numb as the fractured bones beneath his skin began to heal, the cuts and bruises disappearing from his body. He laughed then, the sound bouncing off the walls of the dungeon and coming back to him distorted, as if it had issued from the mouth of a demon from the abyss. It should have frightened him, but it did not.

You are loved, you are complete, the disembodied voice of the goddess said, answering his doubts.

Ceredon shook his head and wiped the tears from his cheeks.

"What would you have me do? Please, tell me."

You must remain strong, my child. You must not give up hope, no matter how unbearable your existence might become. There is balance in all things, and the great pain you experience now will be rewarded tenfold in the many centuries to come.

"Will you not free me?" he asked. "Please, release me so I may confront those who have done evil in your name."

That, I cannot do, she answered. *You must find your own way, or your existence will mean nothing. But remember this—you are my children, never forgotten, never unloved. Trust me, Ceredon. Trust your goddess.*

Ceredon stood and wrapped his hands around the bars to his cell, gazing into the flickering hall as if he might see Celestia in the lurking shadows.

"But what of the brother gods? Their war will consume and destroy us! If one of them finds victory over the other, what will become of us?"

There was a long pause in reply to his question, and for a moment he thought he had offended his goddess, that she had abandoned him. But soon the ethereal feeling of comfort washed over him again and she said three simple words: *They are wrong.*

Another sound reached his ears—a hard, clunking noise, like a sack of potatoes being dragged across uneven ground. The handle of the door leading into the dungeon began to jiggle.

You must remember, the goddess said, *that no matter what you see, no matter what is taken from you, you still have your life. That is what matters. Do not bend, my child. Do not break. Become like the mountain I love so dearly. Unyielding. Unmoving. Forever.*

With that, she was gone, her essence leaving the dungeon just as the door flew open and struck the wall with a thud. As pounding footsteps approached, Ceredon held onto the words of his goddess. He stood tall in his cell and walked toward the bars.

It was Clovis Crestwell who approached his cell, though to call him a human any longer would have been akin to sacrilege. He wore no clothes, and Ceredon could see, for the first time, that there was not a strand of hair on his body. His flesh was stretched taut over musculature that seemed to shift from one moment to the next—first bulging, then retracting, then broadening again. His face was rippling as well, the jaw elongating, the brow distending, until all would suddenly snap back into place. It was if the human's flesh was a prison that his insides could not wait to escape.

Clovis dragged two sacks behind him, one large and one small. He stopped when he reached Ceredon's cell, his meaty fingers releasing the scrunched end of the larger bag. The smaller one he placed almost gingerly on the ground, propping it against the wall. That was when Clovis finally glanced at him, his eyes glowing a red so intense that looking at them would be enough to sap most mortals' inner strength.

Ceredon did not turn away from whatever this man had become. He remained standing, the words of his goddess infusing his heart with power.

With a chuckle, Clovis turned away and bent over the larger sack, removing four long iron stakes from within. One after another he drove the stakes with his bare hands into the solid bedrock that formed the dungeon floor. Ceredon watched his show of strength with awe. Then, once all four stakes had been set, the beast of a man reached into the bag once more, creating a wet sloshing sound.

Clovis worked with his back to Ceredon, a back that had grown so wide that the elf could not see what he pulled from his bag. He watched the rippling shoulders tense as the arms came down, heard the *thwump* of something soggy being wedged atop the stake. Three more times Clovis repeated the task, until finally he sighed, cracked his neck, and stepped aside.

It took every ounce of faith in Ceredon to keep from screaming.

A head was propped atop each stake, eyes bulging in horror, mouths hanging open, lifeless tongues lolling. Ceredon took them in one by one, refusing to look away, etching the memory of their last expressions in his mind's eye. There was Orden Thyne and Lady Phyrra, their flesh battered and bruised; Tantric Thane, his nose cut from his face, a wicked gash running from the right side of his lip to his stunted right ear, exposing broken teeth and blackening gums; and finally, and most horrifically, was Ruven Sinistel. The most grave of insults had been reserved for the Neyvar of the Quellan. His eyes had been plucked from his skull and now rested on his tongue, a pair of dead orbs staring from the center of his gaping mouth.

Unyielding. Unmoving. Forever.

"I thought you might like some company," the man said, only it was not Clovis Crestwell who spoke. The dual voices were now singular—throaty, like the grunt of a wild boar.

Ceredon stared back at him with a façade of indifference. Inside, he was reeling.

Clovis breathed in deep, his chest expanding all the more. He stepped up to Ceredon's cell, wrapped his fingers around the bars. The atrocity was mere feet from him, and Ceredon could smell the rankness of its breath.

"What are you?" he asked. Amazingly, his voice did not crack.

"I am the teeth in the dark, the shadow that descends over all, the devourer of races, the fire that burns all. I am the one after which the abyss was named."

It was a stanza from a popular children's story, told with a personalized touch. The story had been taught to nearly every elf child in all of Dezrel. *It cannot be.* He narrowed his eyes and stepped closer to the bars, determined to show no fear. The reek of the thing's breath assaulted him anew.

"You know what I am," Darakken said. It almost sounded like it was laughing.

Ceredon nodded, and the demon smiled, revealing row upon row of sharp teeth within that human mouth. Ceredon took another step closer, now near enough to grab the bars, positioning his hands just below the beast's. The sharp-toothed smile faltered ever so slightly.

"You do not fear me?" the beast asked. Strangely, even with its deep, inhuman baritone, it sounded almost childlike.

"I do not," Ceredon lied. "What is there to fear? All I once had has been stripped from me." Though it nearly brought him to tears again, he pointed through the bars to the Neyvar's head. "I do not have a father any longer, or a kingdom, or my freedom. There is nothing else of value you could take from me."

"I could take your life."

Ceredon threw his head back and laughed. It took a great amount of effort to do so.

"A life without freedom is no life at all," he said. "There are a great many things worse than death."

"And I am one of them," the beast snarled.

"So I have heard."

The demon in the Clovis suit plunged its hand through the bars, fingers wrapping tightly around Ceredon's tunic. The beast yanked him so hard that his forehead smacked against the iron, bringing stars to his vision. Still, he refused to show his terror.

"You *will* fear Darakken," the beast said.

"I will not."

It glanced down at itself. "This body is not menacing enough?" it said.

"That is part of it."

The meaty fingers released him, and Ceredon dropped back down onto the balls of his feet, rubbing the lump that was rapidly growing above his left eye. It was a wholly casual action, and Darakken's head tilted to the side, those glowing red eyes studying him as if he were some puzzle to be solved. The thing whirled around suddenly and snatched the smaller satchel off the floor. It tore apart the twine binding it, yanked a large tome from within, and held it up for Ceredon's inspection. It was a large book, nearly a foot and a half tall and a foot wide. Strangely, its leather cover was adorned with the three stars symbolizing the cooperation of the three gods of Dezrel.

"This vessel," Darakken said, "is a prison."

"The body of the human Crestwell?"

The beast nodded. "A weak vessel." The thing laughed, revealing those sharp teeth once more. "It might have been forged by the hands of the gods themselves, but it was still a slave to human needs and despair. And just like all mortal beings, when its soul was wrapped in that despair, it ebbed away, leaving this body to Darakken and Darakken alone."

"What brought about this despair?"

"News from afar," the beast said. "An unexpected gift from Darakken's creator."

Ceredon drew back, squinting. He recalled the young human Boris Morneau, the newcomer to Dezerea who had assisted him on his quest for water.

"The soldier," he whispered. "The one with the scar beneath his eye."

"Yes. A useful mortal, that one."

"What did he bring you?"

"News of the death of the vessel's wife. News that Karak, a fraction of the mighty Kaurthulos, changed his mind. And this." Darakken lifted the book even higher.

"What is it?"

"The journal of the one who swallowed my brother."

He leaned forward, staring at the book, but the beast yanked it away quickly, as if Ceredon might try to reach through the bars and snatch the book from it.

"It is mostly useless, save for a few wondrous pages. But those pages hold the key to my rebirth."

"Rebirth?" asked Ceredon, dreading what it might mean.

The beast inclined its head, staring at him from beneath its brow.

"The means to rebuild my true form."

Ceredon pursed his lips and fell back a step. It was an involuntary motion, but one that did not go unnoticed. The beast chuckled then, issuing coughlike fits of laughter that flung pink spittle from its almost human maw.

"So you *do* fear me," the demon said.

Ceredon gathered himself, shook his head, and defiantly stepped toward it once more. "I do not, and I do not fear death. Come and cut me down. End this game."

The beast seemed uncertain, its fingers flexing. For a moment, Ceredon thought it looked as if Darakken were afraid of *him*.

"No," the demon finally said in a growl. "You must live, elf. You must watch as Darakken leads your people into war, as their life-blood is spilled, and you must look on in horror as I use that blood to bring the order of Karak to this land. You must watch"—the glow of its eyes intensified, appearing more hopeful than confident—"and you must understand."

"And if I do not?"

The beast tucked the journal beneath its arm and slammed a fist into the bars. Anger washed away the beast's doubt. "You elves are not timeless, but your lives are long. I will have plenty of time to teach you the glory of dread. Until then, make peace with your father…or what is left of him." The beast licked its fingers and grinned wickedly. "The rest of him…was delicious."

The creature pivoted on its heels and lurched away. The heavy door to the dungeon slammed a few moments later. Ceredon closed his eyes, said another prayer to Celestia, and then sat down, cross-legged, on the floor. When he opened his eyes he stared directly at the four heads, focusing on his father's in particular. A chill worked its way up his spine.

"Orden Thyne, Phyrra Thyne, Tantric Thane, Ruven Sinistel," he whispered in reverence. "For you, and with Celestia in my heart, I will show no fear, no matter what may come.…"

CHAPTER

43

T he raft system that led over the relatively calm waters of the Corinth River was intact. Aully stood on the bank and looked around nervously. There had been no signs of danger in their journey to the edge of Stonewood: no warnings, no traps, no eyes spying on them from the treetops. In fact, to Aully it seemed suspicious *because* of its normalcy, for the most dangerous monsters lurked in the quiet.

The Corinth was a relatively slender river, only three hundred feet across at its widest. The raft system had been built where it was a mere sixty feet across. Three lengths of thick rope were secured to the trees on either side of the river, one running the length of the span, five feet off the water, the other two fastened to either side of the rickety raft. All one had to do was stand on that raft and use the upper rope to guide it across. Not that the system was necessary under normal circumstances: the Corinth possessed a gentle current that lent itself to swimming. Aully herself had crossed the river many times that way. Yet when she glanced at her people, all of whom were carrying weapons from the cache found along the coast of Ang, she was grateful for the alternate mode of transportation.

"If we aren't ready now, we never will be," Lady Audrianna said after Aaromor used the pulley system to lug the raft from the other side of the river. The Lady of Stonewood stepped onto it without another word.

It took ten trips to convey all thirty-two of them to the other side, as the raft could only transport three at once. Aully and Kindren went last with Noni. "For protection," Aaromar told them. Should an ambush await on the other side, the two youngsters would have the opportunity to flee back into the giant's land. "Our future lives and dies with you."

It was a responsibility Aully wasn't sure she wanted.

When they stepped off the wobbling raft and onto dry land once more, Aully turned to look behind her. The desert and grass-lands of Ker were but memories now, the sight of them blocked by the massive trees of Stonewood Forest. She offered a silent prayer to her goddess, and was answered by the hypnotic tweeting of song-birds, a morose sound that did not fill her heart with hope.

Lady Audrianna guided her people through the woods, weaving an indirect path toward their home. The prince and princess were placed in the middle of the party for protection, their cohorts creat-ing a wall of flesh around them. Aully found it more than a little irritating, as her short stature meant that her view was blocked on all sides. The only thing she could see clearly was Kindren, who held her hand as they walked. She kept her eyes on him, drinking in the wonder of his beauty. His devotion to her shone in his eyes whenever he gazed down at her, and she allowed his love to wrap her in a warm bubble.

They walked for an hour without running into any elves. The sun was bright in the sky, sending shafts of illumination through the dense canopy; the birds sang; the forest critters scurried through the underbrush, the larger predators trampling after them. Still, there was not a single familiar face to be seen.

"Where is everyone?" asked Aully.

"I don't know," Kindren replied.

"It's not late. Should there not at least be some children out and about?"

"I don't know. I have never been here before, remember?"

"Hush," scolded Aaromar, his gray-green eyes squinting. "I think I hear something."

The rest of the group halted in their tracks as Aaromar strode away from them, head cocked, ears twitching. Then came the sound of snapping branches, followed by thudding footsteps, and Aully's breath caught in her throat. These were the sounds of men, not elves. Suddenly, she wondered if they had made the right choice after all. Using Kindren's shoulder for support, she rose up on her tiptoes so she could get a better view.

Aaromar drew his sword and hunched down, preparing for whatever might come. When finally someone stepped into plain sight from the thick copse of trees, Aully let herself relax. They were elves after all—two girls and one boy, youngsters like her. She knew them well, and a smile stretched across her lips.

"Mella? Lolly? Hadrik?" she said, wedging her way through the wall of flesh. Hands reached out to grab her, but she slithered away. Once free she ran toward her three friends, tears in her eyes.

Her friends' eyes opened wide and their mouths went agape, like they had just seen a phantom. Narrowly avoided Aaromar's swiping hand, Aully ran headlong into Hadrik. Fourteen, yet already as tall as Aully's father had been, the elf careened back on impact.

"Aullienna?" he said as she embraced him. "Aully?"

She drew back from him, and then looked to the left and right, where Mella and Lolly were waiting. There were tears in their eyes, and they leaned into her at once, the four of them becoming a tangle of arms and legs.

"We never thought we'd see you again," said Lolly.

"They said you were dead," said Mella.

"Who said she was dead?" asked the voice of Lady Audrianna, and the four young elves detached from one another.

Aully looked up at her mother. Her heart continued to soar until she spotted Kindren's dejected expression. She tried to beckon him forward without speaking, but he averted his eyes.

The three youths bowed before Lady Audrianna without replying.

"I asked a question," she said.

Still they were silent. Aullienna stared at their faces, and she realized that her excitement at seeing them had completely blinded her to their expressions.

"They're scared," she said, looking to her mother. Audrianna took a step closer to them, still looking regal as ever.

"Speak to me, young ones. What is it that frightens you?"

Hadrik lifted his tear-filled eyes. Aully did not like the look on her friend's face one bit. She wished Kindren were holding her, especially when Hadrik began glancing this way and that around the clearing.

"Them," he said.

Silent as an ant crawling across the dirt, countless forms popped up from the dense foliage, some dropping on vines from the treetops. There were at least fifty, Dezren all, pale skinned and slender. They were older elves whom Aully had known her whole life, but a few had their bowstrings drawn, arrows aimed at Lady Audrianna, and the rest kept their hands close to the hilts of their khandars. She recognized Enton, Liliquick, Agnon, and Frellum, among others, all of whom had served her father well over the years. These were the elves who had been chosen to keep watch over the forest in the absence of the lord and lady. Not a single one appeared friendly.

The new arrivals formed a circle around the thirty-two survivors who had fled Dezerea. They then parted, and a single elf approached, his jaw rigid, his blue eyes brimming with arrogance. Aully knew him immediately—Ethir Ayers, the elf Bardiya had accused of murdering his parents. Panic filled her. She dropped her hands to her side, curled her fingers into claws, and began whispering words of magic as the elf drew closer to her mother. Slowly she raised her arms, ready to do to Ethir what she had done to the sandcat on the day Kindren had almost died.

But before energy could leap from her palms, her arms were forced to her side and a hand was pressed over her mouth. She struggled against the grip, but it was too strong.

"Leave her be!" she heard Kindren shout, and when she glanced to the side, she saw her love charging toward her, his sword held high. He never reached her, though, for an arrow pierced his shoulder not a moment later, dropping him to the ground. She tried to call out to him, but the fingers that bound her would not loosen their grip. The rest of those who had made the journey, including Aaromar, dropped their weapons and huddled close together.

Aully was hauled to her mother's side, the hand of her unseen assailant still pressed firmly over her lips. Lady Audrianna did not flinch, not even when Ethir stopped mere inches from her and leaned in so close their noses were almost touching. Aully's eyes widened, and she kicked all the harder, torn between concern for what might happen to her mother and what had already happened to Kindren.

Ethir glanced at Hadrik, Mella, and Lolly. He jutted his chin at them, and they took off running, disappearing into the trees. He then stepped back and scowled as another elf dragged Kindren toward the rest of the group.

"Mordrik, release her," Ethir said.

The hands holding Aully finally fell away, and she ran to her love's side, gaping at the arrow that still protruded from his flesh.

"What is the meaning of this?" her mother asked, voice icy.

"You are no longer wanted here, Audrianna," Ethir said. "You should have remained dead."

"You haven't the right."

"We have *every* right."

"We shall see about that. I demand to see Detrick right this moment. If he truly believes that he can—"

Ethir's fist struck Lady Audrianna's face with such force that her nose shattered on impact. The *crack* was loud as a thunderclap to Aully's ears. Audrianna teetered to the side and then collapsed, landing hard on the ground beside Kindren. Aully was thrown into a panic as the surrounding elves descended on her fragile group. She remembered the day the Quellan had turned against them, the day she'd watched her father's head fall from his body. She sobbed and sobbed, certain it was happening again. The last thing she saw was Kindren's hand squeezing hers tight, and then a bag was flung over her head, covering the world in darkness. She was hauled off the ground and carried, unable to fight her captor. Her body bounced up and down, up and down. Her senses were muffled by the sack, and she could only hear indecipherable sounds.

Suddenly something hard whacked her in the head, then in the legs, and she began to sway. It was a weightless feeling, and she began to feel sick. She clamped her mouth shut, closed her eyes, and prayed for the goddess to keep her safe.

We made the wrong choice, Celestia, she thought. *I am sorry.*

Eventually the sick feeling passed. After a while, she heard muted voices, and the creak of hinges, and then her ankles, the only part of her not covered by the sack, were brushed with cool air. The sounds that assailed her were much louder now. She could make out distinctive voices, the tramping of feet, the *thud* of spears being jabbed against a wooden floor.

She was carelessly tossed to the ground, landing hard on her side and jarring her elbow. The sack was then lifted from her, and she was blinded by brightness. Covering her eyes with one hand, she curled into a ball, ready for whatever horrors awaited her.

For a long moment, no sound reached her ears but breathing. Feeling eyes upon her, she swallowed her fear and dropped her hands from her face. To her astonishment, she was in a place she knew well—the courtroom of the Lord of Stonewood. She was sprawled out in the middle of the floor, with elves standing guard to her left and right. In front of her, sitting in the Lord's Chair that had once been her father's, was her Uncle Detrick. He was dressed in a simple robe and his long russet hair was tied in a knot atop his head.

Detrick looked down at her, eyelids raised. "Aully?" he said, his voice as surprised as Hadrik's had been earlier. He looked at those standing guard. "Why was I not told that my niece had returned? What was I not told that she was *alive*?"

"Because we just now discovered her, Detrick." Ethir appeared from behind Aully, wiping blood from his knuckles. "Along with Audrianna and thirty others. Oh, and I believe the prince of Dezerea was with them as well."

"You shot him with an arrow," Aully growled. She reached out toward him, words of magic on her lips once more. Ethir grunted and ground her hand into the floor with his heel. She shrieked.

"Stop that!" shouted Detrick. "You did *what*? Ethir, what is going on here?"

"The prince is alive, Detrick," the hard elf replied. "He is being cared for as we speak." He lifted his foot and Aully withdrew her hand, clutching it tightly to her chest.

"And Audrianna? Where is she?"

Ethir smirked. "Resting. She had a…rough go of it."

"And the rest?"

"They were taken to the bathhouse for cleaning," he replied with a chuckle.

"They are not to be harmed, are they?" asked Detrick.

To Aully, it sounded like an actual question, and she was thrown into confusion once more. Though her uncle sat in the Lord's Chair, he was not acting like a Lord.

"That is not for us to decide," said Ethir.

Detrick frowned, looking from Ethir to Aully. "Please, leave us," he told the guards. "I wish to speak with my niece alone."

The elves saluted and exited the chamber single file. Only Ethir lingered.

"You too," Detrick commanded. "Alone means *alone*."

"I cannot do that, my Lord," the militant elf replied. "You know very well…"

"Go, Ethir," said a new voice, one Aully had never heard before. "I think we can handle a young girl on our own."

"Yes, my Lord," said Ethir. He bowed in reverence and backed away. The door clicked shut behind him a moment later.

Aully slowly rose to her feet, gazing to the left, in the direction of the chamber's darkened washroom. Her eyes grew wide as she watched an elf who looked very much like her father stride proudly from the shadows. He was tall and slender, his hair smooth like satin, his eyes dark like the river at night. When he reached Aully, he knelt down before her, then took her injured hand in his and kissed it. His smile lit the room.

"I don't think we have ever met, have we?" the elf said, and the mirage was broken. His smile was too forced; the way he carried himself was all wrong; and his hands were too rough when he touched her. There were lines on his face that weren't quite right either, and his eyes had a sprinkle of gold in them.

"Who…who are you?" she asked.

"I am your long-lost brother," he said, as if it were simple, obvious. "Carskel Meln, come home at last."

Aully was in a daze as she hefted her body off the floor. The weight of the world seemed to press down on her shoulders, and her thoughts were jumbled. She had heard her mother whisper that name while in mourning for Brienna….

"You were exiled," she said. "Sent away by our parents."

She heard Detrick snort, which was answered with a nasty look from Carskel. When he turned back toward her, his calm had been restored.

"I was in love once," Carskel said, almost wistfully. "In love with the most beautiful elf in all of Stonewood. Alas, she loved another, a *human* no less. That, I could not allow. I was determined to make her love *me*, so I snuck into her room one evening, and we made love then and there. It was beautiful."

Aully's face twisted in confusion. "What?"

"Your own *sister*!" Detrick shouted. He rose from the chair once more, this time storming across the floor toward them. "You attacked Brienna while she slept, you rotten bastard."

"Silence, Uncle."

"No! I will not let the same evil happen twice." He gazed at Aully, his eyes panicked, his tone desperate. "He forced himself on your sister after the First Man defeated him in a duel. He took her, beat her, and left her bloodied. She would have been ruined for life had Cleotis not ordered his best mage to dull her memory!" Turning, he pointed an accusatory finger at Carskel. "Your brother was not exiled. He *fled*. The coward ran before Cleotis could get his hands on him, or else his head—"

Carskel grabbed Detrick by the font of his surcoat and yanked him close.

"Keep your mouth shut," he said. "Or I will end you."

"You won't," her uncle said, his quavering voice revealing his fear. "You *need me*."

"For now," Carskel said. "For now. However, *you* do not need that finger."

Carskel's movements were so quick that Aully could barely track them. He swung his leg behind Detrick, dropping him to the floor with a thud. He tackled him and reached into his belt, yanking out a dagger with one hand while pinning Detrick's wrist to the floor with the other. In one swift motion he plunged the tip of the dagger into the cherrywood floor, pressing down on the handle the way one would when slicing a carrot. Aully watched in horror as her uncle's index finger was severed. Blood sprayed from the stump as Detrick shrieked helplessly.

Carskel turned to her, grinning, hands wet with their uncle's blood.

"*I* have ruled this kingdom since our dear parents left for your betrothal," he said. "*I* ordered the execution of the giant and his parents. Our uncle is only acting as Lord until our people learn to love me once more…which they will."

"They will fear you, as indeed, they already do…but never love you," wheezed Detrick.

"Oh, they will. Once they learn what we have been promised, they will love me very, very much."

"You are…a pathetic and needy child…and you always have been…no matter how long you have lived."

Carskel stood, wiped the blood off his hands with a cloth, and tossed the soiled fabric at Detrick, who wrapped it around the still squirting stump of his finger. The exiled brother then looked down at Aully, his calm demeanor returning once more. A sly smile crossed his lips, and he dropped down to one knee before her.

"Our beloved uncle is correct in one regard," he said softly. "I am needy. Very, very needy. I need to be adored—it is what makes me strong. The Quellan are not the most tender of races. I have not known family—*true* family—for a long, long time. I want it back."

Aully cringed inwardly. "Brienna is dead," she said.

"I know, Sister." He reached out and brushed a stray hair from her eyes. "But Bree was not alone in her beauty. You are very similar to her. You have her hair, her eyes, her temperament. Given that our uncle is intent on insulting me, you are the only family I require."

"You bastard," said Detrick.

"I will never love you," said Aully, slowly backing away. "You are no brother of mine."

"Even if I promise not to hurt you?" asked Carskel with a frown.

"You will not lay a finger on her in that way!" her uncle shouted.

The slender elf stood swiftly and stormed across the room, planting a fist firmly in Detrick's face. Her uncle fell flat on his back and moaned.

"Do you think me a monster?" Carskel asked, sarcasm leaking into his tone. He turned back to Aully. "A hundred years spent roaming this land with no true home has changed me, Uncle. I have no desire at all to soil my only sibling, nor injure her in any way. All I wish is for my people to reclaim what is rightfully theirs, as Father should have done long ago."

"But what do you want from *me*?" Aully asked.

He grinned. "You are well loved here. You will trumpet my return, shouting it from the treetops, and you will make the people love me as they love you."

"I won't," she said, shaking her head vehemently.

"Oh, you will, sister of mine. Or I will slaughter everyone you love, starting with that little shit to whom you're betrothed. And I will make you watch every agonizing moment, until each of them stops breathing. But not you." He grinned, showing his teeth. "As I said, I have no desire to harm my new favorite sister."

Aully broke down. She crumpled to the floor and rocked back and forth, sobbing. Carskel looked down at her, and something that resembled real concern washed over his features. Turning on his heels, he strode elegantly to the chamber door.

"Think it over," her long-lost brother said. "But not too much. Events are moving quickly, and if we are to present our reunited family to all of Stonewood, we must do so soon. I will send Ethir to gather up you and our uncle in an hour."

With that, he swept out of the room. Aully glanced at her unconscious uncle, then stared at the plain wood of the door, her fists clenching, her mind reeling. She wished she had the power to knock that door down with her mind, to burn her bastard brother to a crisp with flames from her fingers, but she knew she was not strong enough.

She felt, in a word, helpless.

CHAPTER

Having grown up in the northwest of Paradise, Patrick recognized the sonorous bleating immediately. The only place in all of Dezrel where the great grayhorns roamed was a hundred miles or so to the north, in the area between the Craghills and the Gihon. His elder sister, Abigail, had loved the North Country, and in his youth he had often been guilted into joining her on her expeditions there. During those trips he had spent many a night lying under heavy blankets, with his hands over his ears, trying to block out the colossal tusked beasts' constant bellows. If there were one noise he hated more than a woman's counterfeit moaning, that was it.

Now he was hearing them during his morning walk in Mordeina for some odd reason, while he was fighting off a nasty hangover to boot. Strangely, the way the sound was muted made it even worse, like the constant hum between one's ears after a solid thump on the head. He climbed atop a nearby rock and scanned the area. All he could see from his location, halfway up the high hill that was crowned with Manse DuTaureau, was a never ending sea of people and Ashhur, perched atop the wall, gazing east. *Of course you wouldn't see them, you dolt,* he thought, shaking his head. Even if a pack of grayhorns had wandered south of their grazing area, they would never be able to make it inside the new double walls. The gate simply wasn't big enough for them.

He sighed and hopped off the boulder, wincing when his feet hit the ground, the headache that tormented him doubling with the impact. Rubbing the heel of his hand on his temples, he promised himself he would make sure to snatch up one of the more talented Wardens before speaking with his mother.

Speaking with Mother. He cringed at the thought of it. He had been home for five days, and it had taken her that long to come calling. He did not cherish the thought of her disapproving looks or the inevitable roll of her eyes when he told her what he had been doing in the interim.

That's not why you delayed and you know it....

"Shut up," he muttered.

He put his head down and continued up the hill once more. The crowds seemed larger than usual on this day, but still there was a feeling of good humor in the air that bothered him to no end. In fact, only in the somber camp on the other side of the hill, where he had spent much of his time since returning, did any of the people seem prepared for the coming attack. The corner of his lip rose slightly as he thought of the previous day, when he'd trained a group of young men and women as Corton had trained him, teaching parries, thrusts, and defensive stances. It almost felt like he was in Haven again, among friends, among people who actually *cared.*

The land flattened out, and he had almost reached the congested walkway leading into the manse when someone tapped on his shoulder.

"Patrick?" a tentative voice asked. He sighed and turned to see a skinny, sandy-haired youth standing there, nervously fidgeting with his hands. For a moment Patrick didn't recognize the young man, for he had no dirt on his face and was wearing smallclothes in the place of armor.

"Tristan," he said with a nod. "You look...well."

"You look like shit," the youth replied.

"Thanks. Never heard that before."

"No, I mean you're pale," Tristan said, his voice cracking with nerves. "And you got big bags under your eyes. You sick?"

"Yes. No. I'm just...forget it."

"I'm sorry."

Patrick sighed. "It's fine."

Tristan stayed silent, but would not stop staring at him. Finally, Patrick couldn't take it anymore.

"Tristan, did you stop me to gaze lovingly into my eyes, or do you have a purpose?"

"I'm sorry."

"You said that already."

The youth swallowed hard. "I know. But...listen, this is hard for me."

"What is?"

"Well...you see...I have something to tell you."

"Very well. So tell me."

"I...well...um...it's like this...."

Patrick jabbed his thumb over his shoulder toward the manse. "I have business to attend to now. How about you tell me when I get back?"

"No, this is important."

"Then spit it out."

"All right, all right...we were given a place to pitch out tents, down by the wall, with the Wardens," Tristan said timidly. "Preston's been teaching them about swordplay, and a few regular folk too."

"Yes..."

"Wait, I'm getting to the point. A man with black hair wearing a bed sheet came to watch us work, and he started asking us a bunch of questions. Seemed nice enough, though now that I think about it, I don't remember him smiling."

"That would probably be mother's steward, Howard Baedan," said Patrick. "Don't worry, he doesn't smile."

"Oh. Okay. So anyhow, when Preston asked him where you were, and he said you were off looking for your sister—well, I couldn't take it anymore. I just...I just..."

He stopped there, his gaze dropping to his feet.

Patrick's heart began racing.

"Tristan, what does this have to do with anything?"

"I'm sorry we haven't told you," the youth said in a low voice.

"Haven't told me *what*, Tristan?" Patrick's heart picked up its pace some more. "Why are you being so cryptic?"

Tristan opened his mouth, then shut it just quickly. He wouldn't look Patrick in the eye, which was maddening. Patrick's edginess won out. He grabbed Tristan by his shoulders and shook him. Hard.

"Out with it, boy!" he yelled, drawing the attention of a group chatting nearby.

"I...I don't know if I can," he whined.

Patrick shook him harder. "Just fucking tell me!"

"Nessa's dead!" the youth blurted out.

Patrick froze in place, his fists still squeezing the youth's shoulders. The entirety of his being went numb, and his powerful hands opened, slipping off the youth who stumbled backward. He stared at Tristan, entranced by the tears rolling down the young man's cheeks.

"I was born in Veldaren," Tristan said softly, as if in a dream. "Father served as a squire for Joseph Crestwell when he was a boy, and I was to follow in his footsteps. My brother Leonard squired for Crian. My father's dead now, and I...I don't know where my brother is...." He cleared his throat, looked at the sky, and continued. "One night, a couple months after Karak returned from his absence, Leonard called on me. 'Something exciting going on,' he said. 'You must come to the fountain.' So Father and I went with him, and we watched as this little redheaded girl was baptized by the Divinity himself. Crian was there too, and the looks they gave each other..."

Tristan wiped the tears from his eyes.

"Go on," said Patrick. His voice sounded alien to his ears.

"Two days later Leonard called on me again, distraught. He said he'd heard that Crian and Nessa had been murdered, and by Lord Commander Vulfram, of all people. He said it was a lie, that the Lord Commander wouldn't have done that. I thought he was joking, because he never mentioned it again, not even when he was sent back to Omnmount. I almost forgot about it...until Karak returned from his assault on Haven. Three days later, there were corpses hanging from the walls of the castle in Veldaren. For some reason Nessa was too. The only way I could tell was her curly red hair, because the rest of her—"

Patrick raised his hand. "Enough," he said. "I don't want to hear any more." He gulped down bile, feeling dizzy. "Did all of you know about this?"

"We did," Tristan said with a hesitant nod. "*Everyone* did. The story became a legend throughout all of Karak's Army. Please believe me, Patrick, we never wanted to hurt you. I wanted to tell you when I first learned your name, but Preston said no. He told us in private that if you truly loved your sister, you might lose control; you might kill us just because we're from Neldar. Even if you didn't, he said if we wanted to live, we needed you focused, that having you brood over your sister would make us all dead men."

Patrick found it difficult to form words.

Tristan swallowed hard. "We are your friends, Patrick. We all love you. And it isn't a lie. I wish I could take it all away, make her okay again, just so you wouldn't hurt. Preston does too. Please don't be mad at us."

"I know. I'm not," he replied, and it was true. Though every part of him railed against the story, he *felt something* during the telling that confirmed its validity. In some ways, a part of him had known it all along. "Thank you for telling me, Tristan. I know that must have been hard."

Tristan nodded, sniveling. "I'm sorry. Is there anything…?"

Patrick patted him on the shoulder. "There isn't. Go join your friends. I have something to do."

The youth turned tail and disappeared into the crowd, leaving Patrick to stew over what he'd just learned. He closed his eyes and took a deep breath, trying to steady his nerves, but in the darkness behind his eyelids he saw Nessa's face, blackened with rot, empty eye sockets staring blankly ahead while crows pecked at her flesh. His breath began to come in ragged bursts as a lethal combination of rage and sadness built up inside him. He squeezed his hand into a fist and clouted himself in the head once, twice, three times, bringing red flashes into his vision. Through the percussive sound of his heartbeat, he heard a few people shriek. This made him all the angrier. He threw his head back, screamed at the blue morning sky.

In the back of his mind, the inappropriate part of him thought, *At least the headache is gone.*

His oversized arms swinging wildly, he stormed the rest of the way up the walk and entered Manse DuTaureau. All who saw him gave him a wide berth, and he stared down everyone he passed. A few he even pretended to charge, just to watch them shrink in fear. He felt like the monster he had long been accused of resembling, the Ogre of Haven made flesh.

Howard Baedan was turning the people in the hall away, telling them that King Benjamin was busy at the moment. He did not try to stop Patrick, though; in fact, he left his post when he saw him approaching. Patrick continued down the now empty hall until he reached the central junction. He then veered north, toward the old dining hall, which his mother had reportedly turned into their new king's throne room. His mind already in a dark place, he scoffed at the notion. A king of Paradise! What a fucking laugh that was.

With the way things were going, that king would soon rule a heap of bones.

Without any focus for his rage, his anger turned to a sorrow so sweeping that it was as if the entirety of his being was sinking into a pit of oil. Feeling sick with grief, he ducked into the nearest empty room, slamming the door behind him. There he wept, his bulk quivering uncontrollably. He pictured Nessa as she had been, as she would have become; the youthful vigor in her eyes, the way her every movement seemed to be part of some secret dance, her childlike wonder, her caring and loyalty and capacity for *love*. It began to sink in that he would never see her again, and he spiraled even deeper.

Pull yourself together. You must tell Mother.

Patrick dug his uneven teeth into his lip hard enough to make it bleed, then stood up as straight as he could. He looked down at himself, at the plain breeches and drab brown tunic he was wearing, and wished he had put on his armor instead. He felt naked without it, vulnerable.

After taking a deep breath, he pulled the door open and stepped back into the hall. There was still no one about, though he could hear voices. He placed one foot in front of the other, making his way toward the dining hall, and then *he* appeared: the one whose presence Patrick desired even less than Karak's.

His father.

Richard DuTaureau skulked along the wall, his face twisted into a scowl, his hands clasped before him. His shock of red hair was oiled and brushed straight, bobbing just above his shoulders. He was short and willowy, just like his wife and their daughters, though he carried himself with an air of superiority. His face, a close reflection of Isabel's, had no lines or creases, no blemishes save the freckles sprinkling his cheeks. He did not look up as his son approached.

In an instant Patrick was transported back to Haven, to the moments before Karak's Army marched over the bridge and a fireball fell from the sky. He heard Deacon Coldmine's voice in his head as the would-be Lord of Haven told him the story of Patrick's own birth, of how his father had poisoned him while he was still in his mother's womb, cursing him with the deformities that would shape his life. At the time he had said he didn't care.

Only now he did.

Just before they passed each other, Patrick charged his father, his meaty fingers gripping Richard's gem-encrusted surcoat as he slammed the smaller man against the wall. A surprised yelp left his father's throat, and the man's eyes nearly bulged from their sockets. Patrick braced his legs and drove his shoulder into his father's breast. Richard DuTaureau offered a pathetic whine in protest, spit flying from his lips. His cheeks reddened, his nose flared, and he stared at Patrick with surprise and disgust.

"You made me like this," Patrick growled. "Did you ever once feel regret for it?"

Richard sneered and opened his mouth as if to offer a biting retort, but Patrick didn't allow him the chance. In one swift motion he drove his fist into the side of his father's head. Time seemed to slow down for a moment as he watched his knuckles connect with Richard's cheek, his father's flesh rippling outward from the impact of the blow. He heard a pop as the man's neck shot to the side and his head collided with the stone wall. His father stood there a moment, tottering, his cold eyes vacant, until he collapsed backward, landing on the carpet with a *thump*.

Patrick loomed over him, breathing heavily, fists clenched at his sides. He watched his father's chest rise and fall, rise and fall, and then turned away, sorrow threatening to overtake him once again. He had dreamed of laying his father out like that even before Coldmine told him the sordid truth. So why did he not feel any better?

When he reached the dining hall, he grasped both handles and threw the double doors open with such strength, they bounced against the solid walls. He expected a surprised reaction from all inside, but the only one who looked his way was a plump young boy who wore an odd looking wooden ring around his head. *King Benjamin, I presume,* he thought. He had known the Maryls, who were from Conch, most of his life, and seeing Benjamin with that silly wooden crown on his head made him want to laugh. The boy was all the way on the other side of the room, yet his eyes still widened at the sight of Patrick. He rose slightly from a high-backed wicker and ivory chair that was just as odd a choice as his headgear. The boy king seemed to think better of it, however, for he sat back down, staring with equal parts fear and awe at the huffing creature before him. He turned his head to the right, where a pair of individuals were locked in a heated debate.

Patrick followed the boy's gaze and there she was—Isabel DuTaureau, his mother and the second of Ashhur's first children. She and Ahaesarus, the Master Warden of Paradise, were the ones talking. It had been almost a year since Patrick had seen her, yet the sight of that lithe yet powerful figure still disarmed him. His shoulders slumped, and he retreated inward as if no time had passed at all.

As for Ahaesarus, Patrick had not laid eyes on him in nearly twenty years, not since the days when he used to visit Safeway with Bardiya. Just like Patrick, the Master Warden looked exactly the same now as he used to then. That he was in Mordeina was strange, since rumor had it he was supposed to be up in Drake assisting Turock's sister. Then again, if the grayhorns had wandered south…

Just get it over with.

"Mother, a word," he said, loudly but respectfully.

Ahaesarus glanced in his direction, but Isabel didn't even turn her head. She continued laying into the Master Warden, calling Ahaesarus a traitor for freeing some child whom she saw was "a danger to us all," telling him he would be punished severely for his crime. Ahaesarus shot back that he did not care. Isabel never once registered Patrick's presence.

"MOTHER!" he screamed.

Isabel wheeled around, rage burning in her green eyes. Patrick was glad for it. At least her anger made her human.

"Can you not see I am *speaking here?*" she shrieked.

He scowled, disobedience rising to the top of his mixed emotions.

"It is good to see you too, Mother," he said calmly, "and it brightens my heart to receive such a warm reception."

"Why are you here?" she asked.

"You summoned me, didn't you?"

She nodded, still seething.

"Did you receive my letters?"

"I received them."

"That's all? You *received them?* You aren't worried about your daughter, your youngest, the jewel of the family?"

Isabel shrugged. "No. Nessa went off with you to the delta without my permission. She is *your* responsibility, not mine. I do not know why you expect me to help find her."

His anger churned. "Oh, Mother, there is no need. I have already found her."

"Is that so?" Isabel shook her head. "Bring her here, then, so I might discipline her."

"I would if I could, Mother, but that would entail marching through the enemy's army, crossing a few bridges, and traveling deep into Karak's land. And even if I did all that, I don't think there is much you could teach a corpse." Those last words were choked with tears.

Isabel opened her mouth, shut it again, and then backed up a step.

"What are you saying?"

"I'm saying your daughter's dead, O great Lady Isabel," he said, his voice low and cracking. "I'm saying she was murdered in Neldar and now hangs from the walls of the castle there."

"You...you lie."

"He speaks no falsehood," said Ahaesarus in an undertone.

Tears rolled down Patrick's cheeks. "Yes, Mother, your daughter is dead. My *sister* is dead. Is that lesson enough for you?"

Isabel's legs wobbled, then folded under her, and she sat clumsily on the floor.

Patrick sobbed and laughed at the same time. "I want you to remember that, Mother. I want you to remember how little you cared until it was too late. And then I want...I want...I want you to look at the rest of the people inside these walls and wonder what it would be like if they *all* perished. Just like *Nessa*."

Knowing he would be unable to say anything more without breaking down completely, Patrick wheeled around and stormed toward the door. From the corner of his tear-blurred vision, he caught sight of the boy king, who looked so young, feeble, and powerless in his chair. He paused by the door, gathered his nerve, and then made a final statement before leaving the makeshift throne room.

"You'd best find someone to care for Father," he called out over his shoulder, without turning around. "He seems to have thumped his head quite badly."

With that he walked away as fast as he could, listening to a sound he had never before heard in his life, one that filled him with despair and joy and fright and loathing, all at once.

Isabel DuTaureau was crying.

With those howls of despair fresh in his memory, he hurried out of the manse and into the open air once more. Incessant chatter and the bleating of the grayhorns greeted him. He headed forcefully down the hill, ignoring the faces of those he passed. The crowd parted for him, giving him ample space as he headed east, toward the staircase that led to the wide rampart atop the inner wall. He ignored any and all who called out to him. Only one entity in all of Dezrel could cure his pain, and that entity happened to be standing sixty feet overhead.

It was nearly a half mile from the manse to the wall through terrain packed with people, and by the time he reached the staircase,

656 ■ ■ David Dalglish · Robert J. Duperre

he felt drained beyond belief. Still, he climbed those wide, steep stairs, placing one foot dutifully over the other, his uneven legs sending shooting pain through his rump and up his back with each step. Though it tormented him, it was still a feeling he appreciated. As long as he focused on the physical pain, he could forget, if only for a moment, the pain that seared his soul.

It was seventy steps to the top of the wall, and by the time he reached the rampart, he felt close to passing out. He stopped there, hands on knees, and panted, listening still to the obnoxious trumpeting of the grayhorns.

When he finally felt strong enough to move, he straightened up. Ashhur was just a few hundred feet away from him, sitting cross-legged on the wide walk, gazing up at the sky. Patrick didn't need to be told what his god was looking at, and he closed his eyes and took a deep breath before spanning the distance between them. The walls lining the wide walk were low. On one side, he could see the broad expanse outside Mordeina, all rolling, hilly grasslands and thick forests, and on the other, the whole of the enclosed settlement. The vastness of both sights made him feel dizzy.

Ashhur did not look at him when he approached. Patrick stopped a few feet away, keeping silent, watching Ashhur's godly mouth move up in down in a silent plea to the heavens. That was when Patrick noticed how unwell his deity appeared. Ashhur's flesh had lost its luster, and there were deep bags under his eyes. He had never seen him this way before, even when he had awoken him from his slumber the day of his arrival in Mordeina. It was even more frightening than seeing his mother cry.

Patrick cleared his throat. "My Grace," he said, dropping to one knee.

"Yes, my child?" the god replied. He sounded as tired as he looked.

"Did she respond this time?"

Ashhur closed his glowing golden eyes. "She did."

"And what did she say?"

"That she loves me."

"That's all?"

"That is all."

"Oh."

The god turned, looking him over with compassion. "Something troubles you."

He nodded.

"What is it?"

Patrick fell into his creator's ample lap and started blubbering. "Nessa…she's dead. I know…I know about my father. I hit him… might have hurt him terribly. I miss her, Ashhur, and I hate my mother, I hate this place…I think I'm becoming a monster.…"

Ashhur stroked his hair with his massive hand, tracing the lumps on his distended brow. Warmth began to spread through Patrick's body.

"You are no monster," Ashhur said. "You are the most perfect of my children."

Patrick sniveled and clutched tight to his deity's robe.

"No one else in Paradise has been given so many obstacles as you, my child. And yet you have embraced each one, turning it into a source of strength. You are all I could have ever asked for, and more."

"But I have killed," Patrick said, staring up at that tired yet smiling face. "Many, in fact. And I think I…enjoyed it. I think that might be why Nessa died. It was a punishment. My punishment."

Ashhur shook his head. "Nonsense. It was in no way your punishment. I can see into you, my child. You enjoy killing no more than you enjoy poking yourself with a needle."

"How can you know that?"

"Because I feel your guilt. It consumes you. One who revels in the destruction of others does not feel remorse after the fact. Do not confuse the rush of battle with pleasure in violence. One is a survival instinct all humans possess; the other is the seed of evil."

"And what of a man who poisons his own child while he is still in the womb? Is *that* a seed of evil?"

"It can be," said Ashhur with a sigh. "In the case of your father… it was not. Your father's failing is one of pride and ignorance. He is a cowardly, jealous creature…though that is no excuse for what he attempted to do to you."

"Yet you forgave him."

"I did."

"Why?"

"Because he was sorry. Truly sorry." The god shook his head. "And he longs for my approval just as much as anyone. If Paradise survives the coming onslaught, he may come to be my biggest failure."

Patrick chuckled as he wiped away his tears. "Wouldn't that be my *mother's* failure? She was the one who made him, after all."

At those words, Ashhur grimaced.

"I feel your mother has had other, far greater failures."

"What would those be?"

"Not now, my child. I will explain after I do what must be done."

"Which is?"

The deity gently lifted Patrick off his lap, placing him down on his feet beside him. Ashhur then rose to his full height and leaned over the low partition. Patrick did the same, and when he saw a gathering of massive grayhorns foraging on the grasses beyond the lower outer wall, his heart nearly stopped in surprise. There had to be at least a thousand of them down there, perhaps the entire population in Dezrel. It was then he realized that their hornlike calls had ceased.

"So many…they're silent," he said. "Why?"

"They are connected with the land. They know what is to come."

"Which is?"

Ashhur offered him a sad smile, then knelt down and held his hands out before him, hovering over the wall. He closed his eyes, though Patrick could see their glow intensify beneath the lids.

"From the flesh you gain sustenance," whispered Ashhur, "and like the plants, from the soil you grow."

Patrick had heard these lines before, and he made a dash for the walkway that connected the two walls, stumbling on his uneven legs until he crashed into the outer parapet. Wedging his shoulders into one of the notches, he wiggled until he could look down. It had started by then.

He looked on in awe as the grass field outside the walls shriveled and died, watched as the leaves and needles fell from the trees in the nearby forest, the trunks shriveling into brown clumps. The giant bodies of at least a thousand grayhorns shifted as their stumpy rear legs grew, fingers sprouted from their three-toed front legs, their necks extended, their snouts widened, the horns on their noses extended, and the tusks wrapping around the front of their elongated snouts drew back, allowing them to open their mouths wide and scream, which they all did, seemingly at once.

By the time the transformation was finished, a wasteland as dead as the Tinderlands stretched a good mile in every direction. The newly altered grayhorns stood on their powerful two legs, rising upright to a height of twenty feet each. They formed a living wall in front of the one made of stone, standing still, their eyes locked on the horizon.

"By Karak's hairy ballsack," Patrick mumbled, his troubles momentarily scuttled to the back of his mind. He moved away from the outer wall, and when he turned, he noticed that Ashhur was slumped over the inner wall's low barricade. "My Grace!" he shouted, running back up the walkway.

Ashhur groaned and collapsed when Patrick reached him.

"My Grace, why?" he asked. The deity's skin was now so white it was nearly translucent, and it seemed to take him a great amount of effort to lift his arm and gather Patrick near.

"It was…necessary…" Ashhur said. "Protection, for my people."

"No, it wasn't. We need to train the people, wake them up! There are two hundred thousand people within these walls. More than enough to mount a defense of this land."

Ashhur grabbed him by the front of his tunic, pulling him close and cutting off his words.

"No time," the god said. He pointed over the short wall with his free hand. "They are here."

The deity released Patrick, who whirled around and gazed over the now dead valley. To his horror, a black shadow was spreading over the distant hills, swallowing the land like a disease. Ashhur joined him, kneeling now, a bit of color returning to his cheeks.

"Oh shit," Patrick said.

"Go," his deity told him. "Ready my children. The hour of dying is upon us."

CHAPTER

45

After so much time, so much marching, so much fighting, so many successes and a few setbacks and failures, they had finally arrived.

The army approached from the southeast, spreading out in waves from the Gods' Road. Karak took the lead, guiding his forces through the wide expanse of grassland nestled between tree-covered hills. Velixar trotted beside his Lord, with Lord Commander Gregorian and the large Quellan, Captain Shen, on their flanks. Behind the foursome, the rest of the army spread out in a wall of steel, leather, and flesh that seemed to stretch for a mile.

They crested the hill, the sound of thousands of marching feet swallowing all else, and Mordeina finally came into view. Velixar gawked at the sight before him. A massive wall encircled what had once been a sprawling landscape of tents, crude huts, and the manse on the hill. A collective gasp rose from the soldiers, though when he turned his head to glance at Gregorian and Shen, he saw no awe in their eyes. It took an individual of might and faith not to look on that wall with fear or uncertainty—even wonder. In all of Dezrel, even Velixar had only seen one walled city: Port Lancaster, in the far south of Neldar. While that wall had taken many years to construct, this one seemed to have popped up overnight.

"Ashhur has been busy," Velixar said.

"As I told you he would be," his god replied.

"I never doubted your wisdom, my Lord. But there is a difference between being told something and seeing it with one's own eyes."

"You seem impressed."

"I am. It is an impressive wall."

Gregorian chuckled humorlessly. "It is still but a wall, and any wall can be brought down."

Karak held up his hand, and the massive force came to an abrupt halt, almost in unison. The deity then looked down at Velixar and nodded, before striding toward the walled enclosure. Velixar signaled for Shen and Gregorian to stay put, then urged his horse onward, keeping stride with his god.

When they had put a good five hundred feet between themselves and the waiting force, Karak drew to a stop. They were three-quarters of a mile away from the settlement, yet the wall was still large enough to fill their peripheral vision. It was strange. The grass was brittle and dead beneath his horse's hooves, and the forests on either side of the valley were filled with leafless trees, their empty branches jutting out like dried bones, snapping with the slightest breeze. Velixar looked toward the wall again and saw a tall figure standing atop it, facing them. Even from such a great distance he could see the twin glow of Ashhur's yellow eyes, the fluttering of his white robe in the wind. Velixar's gaze then wandered down, and he noticed giant forms standing before the wall, their color a gray so deep that they almost blended in with the stone.

"My brother greets me," said Karak.

"Yes, it seems he does. And he has also brought pets. What *are* those things in front of the wall? Why is the land dead?"

"Those are grayhorns, altered in the same way Ashhur altered the wolves that fell upon our camp. The earth looks the way it does because of the way the universe is balanced. One cannot improve on one creation without draining life from another."

"I see." Velixar began to feel edgy as he finally saw the giant beasts for what they were—horned monstrosities standing twenty feet tall on two legs. Any one of them could easily wipe out ten or more soldiers without injury, and there looked to be at least a thousand of them. He took a deep breath and clenched his fists. Closing his eyes, he pictured Karak filling him with strength, and the demon's magic inside him expanded tenfold. He suddenly did not feel so afraid.

"Why are they not attacking?" he muttered.

The deity did not need to respond.

"Karak!" called out a booming voice that rattled Velixar's bones. "Turn away now. Return to your lands across the river! There has been enough bloodshed, enough meaningless loss of life."

Karak stood there, silent, looking smugly at Ashhur as the distant god stared down at them.

"We do not have to destroy each other!" continued Ashhur. "We were brought here to live in peace. Turn your soldiers around and return to Neldar! All will be forgotten."

Still, Karak remained unmoved.

"Will you answer him?" Velixar asked.

The deity shook his head.

"The time for speaking is done," he said, "and the time for bringing your plan to fruition is upon us."

"But what are we to do? Charge the wall? Bring a fireball from the sky as you did to the temple in Haven?" Again, the fear of his lost journal resurfaced. "How are you to destroy your brother without assistance?"

"I do not want my brother destroyed," Karak replied. "I want him shamed. That is why I preserved my power over this long journey. I will show my strength, and then his children will bow before me. They will acknowledge my superiority while he still breathes. It will defeat him more surely than death ever could."

"Why bring an army with you if you plan to use your power?"

Karak stared at him disapprovingly. "My children *are* my power, High Prophet. Do you not understand that yet? When the wall tumbles, when our soldiers rush inside, when the blood flows... *then* the citizens of Paradise will understand my *true* might. Then, my brother will bow."

"And what of the wall?" Velixar asked. "How will we topple it?"

Eyes fixed on the wall, Karak said, "I brought fire from the sky to destroy a temple that blasphemed my name. This wall is an even greater insult, and it will burn in a greater fire."

With that, Karak raised his hand, pointing two fingers at the sky while chanting long-lost words of magic that not even Velixar recognized. His chanting grew louder and more intense, until his voice overrode all other noise. Velixar looked at the wall, at Ashhur still standing atop it, and somewhere beneath his god's chanting he heard thousands of voices screaming at once, from both ahead and behind.

The sky lit up as a ball of flame at least three times as large as the one that had impacted the Temple of the Flesh appeared overhead, screaming down as if from the hidden stars. Velixar felt his skin grow hot, felt the hairs on his arms smolder as it careened toward the massive wall.

When it struck, just like in Haven, there was a moment when all sound disappeared. A blinding light came next, spreading out from the wall like a living cloud, followed by an explosion so powerful that Velixar was almost knocked from his horse. He braced against the force of the blast, squeezing his eyes shut and wrapping his arms around his horse's neck as it whinnied and bucked. The noise rocked his head, threatening to deafen him, and then suddenly there was silence. A hot wind blew the hair back from his face, seeming to last forever.

Velixar opened his eyes. For a moment he thought he was blind, but then the giant white spot blotting out his vision dissipated. He sat up and righted his bucking horse, his head pounding from the deafening din of the blast, and looked to the rear, where the untold thousands of Karak's Army were picking themselves up off the ground, shaking their heads, holding their ears. To a man they appeared rattled, more like a massive throng of children dressed up as soldiers than an army. Even the elves were shaken. Of them all, only Gregorian appeared to be no worse for the wear. The new Lord Commander straightened himself in his saddle, his good eye narrowed in concentration, his hand on the hilt of his sword.

Swiveling his head around, Velixar examined the wall. A great plume of smoke rose from it, and fire spread across the dead grasses in the foreground. There was a hole in the wall itself, a jagged aperture of crumbling stone that looked to be hundreds of feet wide. He then peered to the sides, where a smattering of the altered grayhorns stumbled about, looking confused. At least half of them took off toward the dead forest.

Mordeina was ripe for the taking.

"It begins now!" Karak bellowed, addressing his army. "Lord Commander, gather the captains and have them lead the first vanguard through the gap! We will be unrelenting! There will be no mercy until the false god of Paradise concedes defeat!"

His injured left arm in a sling, Gregorian organized the first vanguard, gathering his soldiers into a tightly packed group. The three captains—young, hard men wearing full platemail—circled around the throng. Karak then leaned down and whispered into Velixar's ear.

"Do you feel my power flowing through you, High Prophet?"

Velixar closed his eyes, his every nerve dancing on end.

"I do, my Lord."

"There are still many beasts remaining. Use the Ekreissar to destroy them. Pave the way for my soldiers to enter the walls unscathed."

"Yes, my Lord."

Shouting voices followed as Lord Commander Gregorian whipped the vanguard, two hundred of his most eager men, into a frenzy. Velixar gazed straight ahead, the glow from his eyes casting a red haze over his vision. The grayhorn-men trumpeted their strange call, then made their charge from a half mile away, their multiple tusks leading the way as they galloped on all fours.

Velixar turned to Chief Shen. "The beasts! Slay the beasts!" he shouted. Shen drew his two black swords from his back and clanged them together. The elven rangers roared their approval. Velixar then drove his knees into the sides of his horse and took off to greet the beasts head-on. Shadows and purple fire rose from his body, and his vision narrowed to the grayhorn-men's twisted, horned faces. The pounding of the rangers' horses followed fast behind him, creating a dull thud like a second heartbeat inside his head.

He released the reins with his right hand, raising that arm into the air. The pendant bouncing against his chest throbbed, and energy crackled at his fingertips, siphoned from Karak's well of otherworldly power. Pressing down on the stirrups and holding tight to the reins with his left hand, he rose from his saddle, feeling mighty, feeling invincible. At least a hundred of the grayhorn-men had not fled, each a ton of flesh and bone, and they were a thousand feet away and closing fast.

"Ignite!"

The word flew from his lips with the force of a hurricane, awakening the ancient knowledge of the demon he'd swallowed. From his raised hand came a spiraling tentacle of shadow, spurting upward and outward, an extension of himself. The tentacle raced over the dead earth, fast as a bolt of lightning, and then descended on the first of the grayhorns. The beast was thrown backward as if walloped by a boulder, the shadows pouring into its eyes, its snout, its ears. Velixar grinned as the creature's taut flesh became bloated, and smoke rose from its every orifice. The grayhorn-man then exploded, destroyed by fire from within. The air was filled with flaming blood and bits of meat, and the nearest of the creature's brethren were impaled by jagged bone fragments. Those few fell screeching to the ground, their great bodies slumping, their elongated snouts trumpeting in pain as their newly created hands tried to rip the shards from their hides. The other grayhorns raced past, casting only cursory glances at their fallen comrades, their eyes alight with rage.

The beasts were close now, too close for Velixar to perform the same trick twice without endangering himself and the elves. Pulling up on the reins and halting his horse mid-stride, he allowed Shen and the Ekreissar to pass him. Shen shouted commands, and half the rangers splayed out wide, lifting their bows with practiced ease, calmly nocking arrows. Their discipline was awe inspiring, and Velixar promised himself that he would help teach the human army to display the same control. The elves released their bowstrings, and shafts flew through the air, the elves' aim just as impressive as their discipline. Each arrow found its mark, embedding in the thick hides of the charging beasts. Three grayhorns died immediately after being impaled through the eye, and their bodies tumbled down. The dead earth was torn up by their graceless descent, and a few of their brethren fell after colliding with them. Still others clumsily maneuvered around the piles of flesh, the ground shaking beneath their cumbersome weight. Velixar shouted more words of magic, his hands performing a dance before him, and two more of the beasts were cut down, their bones snapping, their innards liquefying, their gray, hard flesh splitting at the seams and pouring out blood.

Shen charged, the dexterity of the huge elf a sight to behold as he held his wicked-looking black swords out wide and raced his horse toward a pair of grayhorns. The muscles in the beasts' shoulders rippled with each lumbering stride as they raced for the Ekreissar chief, deadly tusks and horns pointed forward. Shen pulled his right foot from the stirrup, planted it firmly on his horse's back, and at the last moment launched himself into the air, tucking into a roll.

His horse ducked its head, and the creatures' tusks passed over it, slicing through the empty space where Shen had just been moments before. The two beasts roared in pain when Shen fell from the sky, his swords held out like daggers, and buried both blades into their backs. The elf's downward momentum added force to his attack as he dragged his swords along the creatures' hides. Flesh sliced open in a wide arc, spilling the grayhorns' guts in a macabre red rain. Shen landed and rolled away as the two dying beasts collided with each other and collapsed, their blood and entrails soaking the dead ground. He was on his feet a moment later, leaping back atop his horse and charging the next grayhorn. His fingers never lost traction on his two swords. The whole while, arrows launched by his underlings rained down around him, yet he never seemed in danger of being struck by one.

A breathtaking spectacle, indeed.

Inspired, Velixar ripped Lionsbane from its sheath and urged his steed forward. Nearly half the remaining grayhorns had fallen, and the Ekreissar, who continued to pummel the beasts with their arrows, were encircling the others. One of the creatures stampeded the circling elves and managed to gore a ranger through the midsection. The elf shrieked as he was lifted high into the air on the grayhorn's tusks, and then impaled by the horn on the beast's snout. The elf fell limp as the grayhorn roared, thrashing this way and that, blinded by the flopping dead thing attached to it.

Velixar raced behind the creature and hacked at it with Lionsbane. Its hide was tough, but his blade sliced, severing the tendons on the back of the thing's tree-trunk legs. It collapsed to its knees, while a blast of panicked air left its elongated snout, filling the air with its trumpetlike bleating.

It was silenced by a wave of Velixar's hand, which turned both creature and impaled elf inside out. The tide of the battle seemed to be turning, with the grayhorns pushing the Ekreissar back now. Two more elves were killed, their bodies trampled and broken in the dry brown grass, and while Shen and the rangers continued their assault, the grayhorns seemed to be learning. When the twang of bowstrings sounded they dropped their heads, allowing the shafts to enter their thick hides while protecting their more sensitive areas. They also formed defensive positions, grouping shoulder to shoulder with one another, their flailing horns and tusks keeping the elves' khandars at bay. For mere animals, their survival instinct was remarkable. In many ways, Velixar began to admire them.

Just not enough to let them live.

Bringing his horse to a halt behind the eviscerated grayhorn and its victim, Velixar sheathed Lionsbane and accessed the deeper recesses of the demon's knowledge. As he twined his hands together, he felt Karak's strength surge through him, and his eyes rolled into the back of his head. Arcane words left his mouth, and a liquid feeling of *connection* permeated his being. His vision returned to him, and he saw the blood and bone of the elf and grayhorn he had eviscerated circling in the air, a funnel of ruin that twisted with the force of gods, ever widening, ever spiraling. The funnel lashed across the ground, guided by Velixar's own hand, collecting the ruin of the dead that were strewn about until it was nearly as wide as Tower Honor itself. As if sensing the potency of the spell, the grayhorns packed tighter into their defensive circle. The elves, who had ceased with their rain of arrows, backed their horses away. It seemed all eyes were on him, including his divinity's. Now was the time for him to prove, once and for all, that Karak's faith in him was not misplaced.

He leaned forward and then thrust his interlocked hands toward the huddled beasts. The death funnel surged into motion, ripping up chunks of dirt and grass as it spiraled toward the beasts. The base of the funnel grew as it went, the bone fragments within becoming sharper and more deadly with each revolution.

The grayhorns turned to flee, their primal gazes filled with fear. Their giant rumps rose and fell with each leaping stride, the creatures deceptively fast given their size.

They weren't fast enough.

The death funnel swallowed the slowest grayhorn, ripping the beast off its feet and into the massive spiral of blood, tissue, and bone. Its shrieks were deafening, and Velixar could see the shadow of its form whipping back and forth inside the cyclone. When it was ejected, flesh and muscle flayed from its bones, it landed on the dead ground in a steaming lump.

The funnel's density grew with each beast it devoured, until it became so large that it seemed to swirl nearly a thousand feet wide. The fleeing grayhorn-men were annihilated, one by one, until a scant few remained. Velixar watched from a distance as they disappeared into the skeletal forest, their massive bodies colliding with the dead trees in their horrified flight. He snapped his fingers and the death funnel abruptly ceased to spin. Each bone fragment, each strip of blackened flesh, each drop of blood hung in the air for a precious few seconds before falling to the ground in a deafening rain of gore.

Shen glanced over at him, his wide-set eyes alive with fear. The Ekreissar chief then dismounted, crossed his black swords over his chest, and fell to one knee. The rest of the rangers followed their chief's lead, showing subservience to the swallower of demons.

Velixar's belly filled with pride as the pendant against his chest pulsed with heat. He spun his horse around to look for Karak and saw that the deity was staring at him, eyes aglow, arms crossed. The god nodded in approval while the thousands of soldiers behind him gaped in awe. Velixar then caught Lord Commander Gregorian's eye, raised his right hand to the sky, and pointed two fingers toward the smoking hole in the wall around Mordeina.

The Lord Commander needed no further invitation. The man yanked his horse's reins with his good arm, urging it to the side.

"March forth!" he shouted. "Slay the worshippers of the false god!" The entirety of the first vanguard hollered their approval. The riotous thudding of clanging armor and stomping feet sounded as the soldiers began to charge across the dead field covered with the remains of the grayhorns. The second vanguard stepped up, preparing to follow.

Velixar sat and watched as the soldiers rushed past him, weapons raised, spittle flying from their lips. They would do their god proud, just as he had.

The assault on Mordeina had begun.

CHAPTER

46

T he demons were upon them, swooping from the heavens, snatching women and children, slaughtering any who opposed. As Ahaesarus listened to them scream, his vision blacked out, his body searing with pain. He sensed people leaping over him as he lay on his back.

A foot connected with his side, rolling him over. He remained where he was, elbow pressing into the soft earth, while his sight slowly returned. Muffled voices shouted warnings. Something slumped to the ground beside him, and he lifted his head, not wanting to see Malodia take her final breath, but bound by honor and love to do just that.

The world came clear to him, and he saw that the body alongside him was not his dead wife's, but rather that of a young man with curly red-blond hair. His dead eyes stared at Ahaesarus until they were covered in blood from the ugly wound on the side of his head. The Warden reached over, his every muscle aching, and felt the man's chest. His heart was still.

The screaming and clamor of the stampede continued as Ahaesarus sat up. There were bodies everywhere, some writhing in pain, most stilled, all covered with gashes and bruises and surrounded by large chunks of heavy, jagged stone. The Warden looked up at the twin walls Ashhur had helped raise, at the wide crevasse that had been solid stone moments before. Someone crashed into him from behind, knocking him forward, and he bent painfully at the waist, his chin almost kissing his knees.

He rolled, got up on all fours, and surveyed the pandemonium all around him. The people were rushing about in a mad panic, an endless mob of them, their roughspun stained with grime, ash, and blood. His fellow Wardens tried to usher them along in an organized manner toward the manse on the hill, but the mob's panic was too great. He watched as one of his brethren was trampled by a swarm of terrified men and women, disappearing from view. The last Ahaesarus saw of him was his hand rising above the bobbing heads in a feeble attempt to make them stop.

With the crowds moving steadily away from him, he took a moment to grab hold of his ears and rock back and forth. There was a persistent buzzing in his head that muffled all other sound, almost as if he were underwater. Confusion abounded as he tried to remember what had happened, why everything had gone so insane so quickly.

Then it came to him. He had been in Manse DuTaureau, arguing with Isabel about what his punishment should be for releasing Geris Felhorn from his prison, when her son Patrick barged in with his incendiary revelation. After that he had left Isabel to her tears and walked down the path to the gate to rejoin his regiment of Wardens and a few of Turock Escheton's pupils. Almost as soon as he'd arrived, he was temporarily blinded and blown backward by a massive explosion. He remembered seeing Ashhur atop that wall moments before his world became a complete whiteout, and he flung his head from side to side, searching in a panic. It did not take him long to spot the western deity, sprawled out on the ground a few hundred feet away, surrounded by a congress of Wardens.

Judarius was among them, a wound between his green and gold-flecked eyes leaking blood. His fellow Lordship mentor shouted out orders. Ashhur's arms were grabbed, and the Wardens proceeded to lug him across the debris-littered ground.

A horn sounded, drawing Ahaesarus's attention back to the gaping fissure in Mordeina's wall. The gap was wide enough for twenty grayhorns to stride through abreast of one another. He peered through the smoke and flames, watching as a considerable number of black shapes moved ever closer to the enclosed settlement. He stood on shaky legs, stumbling over corpses and chunks of wall. It was hard to see clearly through the smoke, but he swore there was a strange sort of lightning striking the ground on the other side. What followed were inhuman howls, and the repetitious *clomp-clomp-clomp* of charging horses' hooves.

Not a moment later, three men came charging through the smoking breach atop majestic black chargers. They wore full plate armor, painted black, and great helms covering their faces. Each helm was adorned with a pair of horns, like a bull's, and the soldiers' breastplates bore the roaring lion of Karak. The three stopped once they reached open ground, spinning about on their chargers. The one in the center lifted his helm, exposing the youthful face of a young man no older than twenty, and then brought a horn to his lips and blew it in the direction of the aperture. That done, he returned the horn to his saddlebag and drew his sword, waving it in circles above his head. Before his helm was pulled back over his face, Ahaesarus caught a glimpse of his eyes. His gaze was hard and intense for a youth, much like Wallace's when faced with Turock's interrogation.

The roar of a mob followed, riotous like a legion of drunkards after a night of inebriation, and a stream of armor-clad men came screaming through the breach. They ran with their weapons held out before them, madness in their eyes. Any stragglers were cut down instantly, their blood filling the air. The people shrieked, fleeing as fast as they could, only to be slaughtered by the three who had rode on horseback.

"We must fight!" he heard someone yell, and Ahaesarus spun around to see Judarius leading a cluster of Wardens toward the invading soldiers. Mennon was with him, as were Ludwig and Florio and Judah and thirty others. The soldiers kept coming, their numbers too great to count, their movements too frantic for Ahaesarus to follow.

Steel met steel with a violent *clang*.

He then remembered what he had told Isabel before Lady DuTaureau had sent him to Drake: *"If any were to lash out at Ashhur's children, I would strike them down or perish trying. And when Karak arrives on our doorstep, he will discover just how much I mean those words."*

It was time for that pronouncement to become a reality.

Ahaesarus swallowed his fear and charged into the melee with a roar. His fist flew, connected with the head of a helmless soldier. The young man's head snapped to the side and he crumpled to the ground. Ahaesarus dodged the thrust of yet another soldier, slid to the ground, and lifted the sword of the man he had struck. He was not skilled with it, but what he lacked in skill he made up for with determination. He wielded the sword like he would wield his sickle back in Algrahar when it came time to trim his fields, swiping it wildly back and forth, keeping his motions low. He hacked off feet and clanged the weapon against thighs enclosed in chainmail. A blade pierced his side, but he barely felt it. Instead he looped around, catching the one who'd stabbed him with an elbow to the chin. The man fell to the side, howling, only to be replaced by another. Ahaesarus kept fighting, even though he was rapidly tiring as he became drenched in blood.

Something hard caught him underneath the chin. The force of the blow was enough to snap his head back and make him bite his tongue. Ahaesarus stumbled, barely keeping hold of his sword, and collapsed to his knees. Hands were on him in an instant, yanking him backward by the arms.

"No!" he shouted, struggling against his captors.

"Stop fighting!" shouted a familiar voice.

When Ahaesarus craned his neck, he saw that Mennon and Grendel were the ones lugging him away from the battle. He heard screams and looked down again. More and more soldiers poured through the hole in the wall like ants from a mound, at least three hundred of them. Any who stood in their way, Warden and human alike, were slaughtered. And in the midst of it all Judarius stood tall, swinging a massive club of stone, pummeling those unlucky enough to stand within reach.

"We mustn't stop fighting!" screamed Ahaesarus. He jerked his arm free of Mennon's grasp and then tried to shove Grendel away as well. "It is our duty to protect our wards!"

"We cannot do that if we are dead," Grendel snapped back at him. "We must reach higher ground and make our stand there. There is no other—"

His words were cut short by a burst of bright flashes that soared overhead. Fireballs and the crackle of lightning connected with the oncoming horde, charring a few soldiers, felling others, *forcing them back*. He glanced behind him and saw Turock's apprentices, both those who had helped build the wall and those who had returned with him from Drake, approaching in a line. They continued to hurl magic at the enemy, looks of determination on their faces.

The pounding of hooves came next, and Ahaesarus spun around. At the base of the hill leading to Manse DuTaureau, the mindlessly fleeing citizens of Mordeina suddenly parted, creating a wide path. Down that path galloped a great many men on horses, led by a snarling demon with red hair. It took him a moment to recognize him as Patrick DuTaureau, decked out in ill-fitting armor and wielding a gigantic sword. One of those who followed him was Judarius's brother, Azariah. A small group of others bore blackened armor similar to the soldiers who were invading their sanctuary.

"Who are *they*?" he heard Grendel ask.

"The survivors from Lerder, and some of those who traveled with Ashhur," Mennon answered. "The ones who made camp on the other side of the hill. It appears to be…all of them. And the newcomers. The Karak deserters."

"What do you say we rejoin the fight, my brother?" Ahaesarus asked. The fireballs and lightning from the spellcasters continued to flash overhead as he put his body in motion, charging back toward the conflict without waiting for an answer.

✛

There were so many of them, flooding through the wall like some acidic liquid.

Patrick rode at the head of his own personal phalanx—two hundred and seventy-three brave men and women who had made the journey down the Gods' Road and through the forests of Paradise, losing all they ever had to reach the safety of Mordeina. Only now that safety was badly threatened. The Wardens were outnumbered, and Patrick's friends and neighbors were ill prepared to fight for their lives. And now there was a breach in the wall, and the soldiers were coming.

It was Haven all over again, and Patrick knew deep down that this was the end for him. He had seen the staggering numbers Karak had brought with him from Neldar. Fifteen thousand trained soldiers against barely four hundred courageous yet unskilled defenders. *Not the best odds,* he thought with a scowl.

"Come, with me!" he shouted, Winterbone held high above his head as his mare hurtled toward the gap in the wall. The thousands who were fleeing barely gave him a second look, focusing instead on finding whatever shelter they could in a land of elongated flatlands and sparse forests. "Do not be cowards! Fight for your lives!"

It seemed none were listening, but then he saw flashes of light to his left. Swiveling around, he caught sight of a gaggle of bearded men he had never seen before, who were marching down the hill toward the conflict, their hands raised as if performing some strange dance. Fire and lightning leapt from their fingers, bombarding the attacking soldiers. Magic. Spellcasters. *Turock.*

At least someone else was willing to listen.

His excitement growing, Patrick leaned forward in his saddle and drove his mare at a faster clip. He held Winterbone out to the side now, facing forward like a lance. The three captains on horseback were charging toward him, detonations sounding behind them.

"Azariah!" he shouted.

The Warden's white steed galloped alongside him, and Azariah's green eyes met his. Patrick could tell that the shortest Warden was terrified.

"Lead the others onto the hill with the magic users!" he screamed, spittle flying from his lips. "Their soldiers are on foot, which gives you the advantage."

"And what of you?" asked the Warden, though it was hard to hear him over the pounding of hooves and the roar of fire.

He jutted his chin ahead. "I'll take out their leaders."

Azariah nodded and then veered off to the left, climbing the hill that bordered the manse. Patrick heard the Warden shout, and then watched as his poorly trained crew followed him. The last one to look his way was young Tristan, once again dressed in the armor he had worn for most of their acquaintance. The youngster blew him a kiss before riding off, following closely behind Preston and his six brothers-in-arms. *Good-bye, brave warrior. Let us die well.*

Patrick took a deep breath, leaned forward once again, and focused on the three captains. They were so close now that he could see the whites of their eyes through the great helms they wore.

When the three captains were mere feet away, the closest two widened the gap between them, raising their swords to chop at him from either side. Instead of trying to engage them, Patrick took a chance; he grabbed Winterbone with both hands, uttered a profanity-laced prayer to Ashhur, and rolled out of the saddle to the right, toward two of the captains. He held his sword's hilt tight to his midsection, the blade extending from him like it grew from his belly, and maneuvered his body in midair. A pair of blades passed over his head, and then his sword found purchase in the abdomen of the closest captain's horse. Flesh tore open, and blood and a mound of intestines fell on Patrick's face. Momentarily blinded, he struck the ground on his left side, losing the air in his lungs, but he rotated swiftly, trying to avoid the dying horse's hooves while blindly slashing Winterbone at the second beast. He felt another strong jarring pull, and then the sword ripped free of its quarry. He whipped off his gore-splattered half helm to see that he'd clipped the back of the second horse's leg. The animal careened to the ground and rolled, crushing its rider beneath it.

Patrick got to his feet as quick as he could and thrust the tip of his sword through the eye slit of the first rider, whose leg was wedged beneath his now dead horse. He then wheeled around at the sound of charging hooves, ducking as another sword sailed over his head. The blade glanced off his hump, which was thankfully layered with chainmail, though the impact struck fresh agony down his spine.

Once more he swiveled, watching as the last remaining captain circled him. He stood his ground, elbow cocked by his ear, holding Winterbone at a slight downward angle as Corton had taught him. He did not move until the captain swung his blade. Then he dipped and drove upward, allowing his enemy's sword to skim past his ear while the tip of his own blade found a gap in the soldier's platemail. Once the man was impaled on his sword, he shifted his weight and flung the captain from his saddle. Winterbone's bloody tip slid out of the man's armor, sending him hurtling through the air. He landed on his face with a sickening crunch as his body flopped in the other direction. The body offered a couple of final shudders, and then fell still.

Patrick looked around for his mare, but could not see it. There were horses everywhere now, running around him on all sides. Riding them were extremely frightened looking men and women wearing roughspun and holding sticks and gardening tools as bludgeons. *They finally understand.* Patrick grinned ear to ear, admiring the courage these people were showing, and then spun around and began running toward the raging battle.

The Wardens, many of the survivors of the journey to Mordeina from the other side of the Corinth, and Preston's crew had all descended the hill and were locked in a losing struggle. Karak's soldiers still poured through the walls, shoving back the defenders. With everyone fighting in such close proximity, the spellcasters were forced to aim their magic deeper into Karak's ranks, slowing their forward flow.

Blood and bodies were strewn everywhere, the victims from Paradise and Neldar alike. The conflict was chaotic, an undulating mass of struggling bodies that surged forward and back, forward and back. Patrick remained on the outskirts, hacking down those he could, trying to order his fellow defenders into forming a wall, but none could hear him. So he kept on attacking, shouting obscenities with each thrust, each parry, each arcing blow, even as his body began to tire and pain shot up his uneven legs. Despite all the blood he was spilling, it seemed hopeless, especially when a sword pieced his lower back, where his chainmail was thinnest, running him through. He shrieked and spun around, burying Winterbone in the shoulder of the young soldier who had injured him. He almost halved the man with the blow, and his sword became lodged in the soldier's chest. Patrick collapsed to his knees, clutching the spot where the enemy's blade had exited his stomach, trying to stop the blood flow. He remembered the moment he had gutted Joseph Crestwell on the battlefield in Haven. He did not feel like he was dying, but perhaps he was being paid back in kind.

"In any case, this is a good death," he whispered with a laugh.

The soldiers rushed around him, pressing ever inward. This was it. He tore Winterbone from the soldier's cadaver and lifted it, his body leaking from its many wounds, and battled them back. He fought with such intensity that the ground seemed to shake beneath his feet, rumbling and creaking, affecting all around him. The ground then shook so hard that he was knocked to his knees, and he remained there, panting, trying to regain his equilibrium.

What the fuck? Patrick wondered.

The roar of thunder came next, followed by what sounded like a mountain crumbling to the ground. Then came the screams, and Patrick rose once more, looking on in awe as the earth beneath the hole in the wall split open. Pointed spires emerged from within the chasm, impaling soldiers who had yet to cross through the breach as they rose upward. It was an immense tree, and it grew up and up, higher and taller, its base widening, stretching across the length of the hole. The soldiers skewered on its many branches struggled and thrashed, until the limbs grew in width and their bodies were torn asunder, raining gore onto the ground below. Leaves sprouted, a fiery burst of yellow and red bathing the city in its shaded aura.

The rumbling stopped, and so did the battle. All eyes turned to the newly formed tree, whose surface was a spiraling pattern of thick veins and tough bark. It looked to be the hugest and strongest tree in the world, and it plugged the hole that had been blown into the walls without a gap.

Patrick began to chuckle, which evolved into light laughter and finally an all-out guffaw.

"She did it, my Grace," he managed to choke out. "Celestia… loves…you!" He could feel eyes upon him as he laughed, but didn't care.

The only thing that stopped his bout of madness was the sound of Preston's voice, loud and authoritative, rising above the din of whispers and the shrieks of the dying.

"It is not over!" the man said. "The enemy is within your gates! The children of Karak who have killed your brothers, your sisters, your Wardens! They are trapped here! Take them down!"

The bestial cry of a thousand voices rose up, and Patrick lent his voice to the fray. He felt lightheaded and weak, but he moved to charge anyway, hefting Winterbone in the air. Powerful hands grabbed him, halting his progress and dropping him flat on his back.

"Let me go, you son of a whore!" he screamed.

The bloodied face of Master Warden Ahaesarus loomed above him.

"Quiet," the Warden told him. "You are badly injured."

"But I need to help them!" he protested, thrashing wildly. "Let me *help them!*"

"There is no need," said another voice, and then Azariah's face appeared as well. "The children of Ashhur can care for themselves."

The dark-haired Warden shifted to the side to grant him a view of the proceedings, and Patrick rose up on his elbows. He looked on as Preston and Judarius led their charges, a blend of men and women trained by Patrick, Wardens, spellcasters, and countless everyday citizens of Paradise rushing against Karak's now fleeing soldiers. The enemy's men ran headlong into the tree blocking their exit, trying to scale it, but their fingers could find no purchase in its bark. All of the soldiers, both those attempting to flee and those attempting to fight, were overrun by the massive swarm of angry people defending their home. Screams filled the air anew, and though it was a horrid sound, Patrick thought there was a sweet ring to it.

"We did it," he said softly. "We lived."

"For now," replied Ahaesarus. "And only with the goddess's help."

"Thank the stars for her," muttered Azariah.

"Does Ashhur know what happened?" asked Patrick. "Where is he?"

The two Wardens shared a look but said nothing.

"You know what? I don't care," said Patrick. "Just heal me already."

He reclined on his back and felt the warmth of the Wardens' hands as they chanted above him. He allowed that feeling, and the screams of the dying, to wash over him as he fell into an uneasy sleep.

✛

Velixar looked on, stupefied, as a giant tree sprouted from the ground, filling the gap in the wall created by Karak's firestorm. Those who had been standing nearby when it emerged from the earth had been knocked backward by its rapid ascension, while still others were impaled on its branches. The two stone walls groaned, rivulets of cracks spreading as the tree pushed its boundaries against their limits, sealing out even the slightest gaps. The soldiers of the third and fourth vanguards backed away from the tree, appearing uncertain. Lord Commander Gregorian rode his horse along the wall, inspecting the new obstacle, craning his neck to see the top, before turning his horse around and trotting back to join his charges.

Karak watched in silence, the glow of his eyes intensified a hundredfold.

"What happened, my Lord?" Velixar asked. The deity glanced over at him and then approached the massive new growth, veering around the liquefied bodies of the grayhorns. Karak stopped before the tree and rammed a fist into it. It was solid as stone. Not even a piece of bark crumbled beneath his blow.

Screams erupted from the other side of the wall, and Velixar knew what that meant. The soldiers who had been abandoned were being slaughtered.

"Was it Ashhur?" asked Velixar once his god returned to him. Karak shook his head.

"That tree is thicker than steel. My brother doesn't have enough power to create that. It seems as though Celestia has showed her hand."

A lump formed in Velixar's throat, but he did not say a word.

Karak's glowing eyes lifted skyward. "You have shown your true colors," he shouted to the heavens. "Let us see how far you wish to go." He stepped back and lifted his hand as he had before, uttering words of magic.

"No, my Lord!" he yelled. "Not with so many so close!"

The deity continued with his spell. Velixar quickly spun his horse away from the wall, hurrying in the opposite direction. "Run, all of you!" he shouted at the other soldiers who still stood in formation, a few hundred feet away.

A second fireball formed, illuminating the dead earth in glowing reds and yellows. The air hissed around it as it soared through the sky. Velixar allowed himself a single upward glance as his horse raced away from the walls, and he noticed that this fireball was smaller than the first. He ducked his head and drove his horse to a faster pace.

His flight proved unnecessary, for a sound like someone striking an enormous drum came next, deafening him for a moment until all sound disappeared. After a brief flash of brightness, the ground beneath him went dark once more.

Velixar pulled back on his horse's reins and turned in his saddle, looked on as Karak stared at the sky. He was about to say something, but thought better of it. The god's shoulders slumped, and he appeared exhausted.

He swiveled his horse around and cantered back to his deity. Karak glanced over at him, a tired smile on his face. "Celestia is protecting him," he said. "She swatted aside my magic."

"Do you wish to try again?" asked Velixar.

Karak shook his head as he stared at his hands. "It would do no good. I am weakened, and the goddess's magic is stronger than my own. We will have to do this another way."

With that, Karak pivoted on his heels and began to march back toward the bulk of his force, which remained a half mile away.

"Lord Commander!" he shouted.

Velixar kept pace with Karak, while Malcolm, who had been organizing the troops who were closest to the wall when the second fireball came, rode out to greet them. Finally he reached the god's side, and Karak addressed them both.

"Velixar, find a courier to send to Dezerea. I want Darakken here as quickly as possible. As for you, Malcolm, fit the men with axes. Fell as many trees as you can, as quickly as you can. And have those who are not swinging axes begin to build the camp."

"What is the plan now, my Divinity?" asked Malcolm, bowing respectfully before his god.

"We build armaments. And ladders. And catapults. I will show you how."

"Why, my Lord?" Velixar asked.

Karak grinned. There was anger in the expression, yes, but he swore he saw excitement as well.

"We begin the siege. We show no mercy. We will kill every last one of them, my brother and his harlot included."

EPILOGUE

The courtyard of Palace Thyne was filled to near capacity. The Quellan Ekreissar were situated to the right, heads held high and fists pressed firmly over their hearts. The elves glared across the courtyard at the human soldiers, who stood tall and proud as well, their polished armor gleaming under the late afternoon sun.

There was obvious dislike between the two groups, and Ceredon couldn't help but think that was foolish, seeing as they were the same beings wearing different skins. Both sides followed the orders of their superiors, seemingly without question; both sides would take an innocent life if it were demanded of them. All of which made the disdain they showed one another laughable.

"A soldier is noble," he whispered through his gag. "A soldier protects those who cannot protect themselves."

Those had been the words of Cleotis Meln, the dearly departed Lord of Stonewood. Ceredon had heard him say that to his father, the Neyvar, during the Tournament of Betrothal so many months ago. He knew not the topic of their discussion or why such a subject would even be broached. All he knew was that there was noble wisdom in the simple statement, the type that seemed to have been banished from Dezrel.

Cleotis was dead, so was the Neyvar, so were the Thynes, so was Tantric and the rebellion. All those who had sought to end suffering and fight for goodness, had themselves been ended. *Celestia,* he thought, *you wished me to be your champion, but champion of what?*

His forearm itched, and he instinctively attempted to scratch it, but the effort was futile. His hands and feet were strapped to a pair of crisscrossing beams, which were themselves strapped to a tall pole that was displayed high above the congregation. He sighed and worked his arm up and down, but he only succeeded in worsening the sensation. Sucking in his lip, he let his body fall forward, feeling his hips and shoulders stretch as gravity pulled at him. He wondered how long it would take before his joints were strained to their limits and popped.

Down below, the soldiers from either side ignored him, but that did not mean he went unseen. Many of the Dezren, gathered in a massive throng between the ranks of elf and human warriors, looked in his direction. He could not see their expressions, but he knew they must be terrified. He tried to smile even as pain wracked his body. *If I can only give them hope....*

A door slammed, and the engorged form of Clovis Crestwell exited Palace Thyne. The demon in human clothing paced along the dais, with a limping Iolas on one side and the young soldier Boris Morneau on the other. Of the three, only Boris, the human with the odd scar, looked up at Ceredon, wincing when their eyes met. He quickly turned away.

Clovis—Darakken—stopped pacing, moved to the edge of the dais, and held its arms out wide to the thousands gathered there.

"Today," he shouted, his inhuman voice bounding throughout the valley, "a great bond is being forged. Today, not only do the Quellan, the Dezren, and humans set aside their differences, but all three races unite under the banner of a single cause."

He paused as if waiting for the crowd to react. The humans and the Ekreissar remained stoic; the Dezren murmured among themselves. The man-creature stepped back, lowered its head, and appeared to argue with itself. Only a moment passed before it was on the edge of the platform once more. This time, it faced the human soldiers.

"Soldiers of the Divinity!" it roared. "Who is it you fight for?"

"KARAK!" they shouted in unison.

"Who is the only true god of this land?"

"KARAK!"

"Who is the order in the chaos whose word is law?"

"KARAK!"

The demon turned to the Quellan. "Do you hear that?" it said. "Your brothers in arms have spoken! Will you not raise your voices along with theirs, proclaiming your loyalties to the heavens?"

Silence.

Iolas touched the massive half-human thing on the arm, wincing when its head snapped around. He moved in front of Darakken to address the crowd.

"Ekreissar, our leader is no more. The Neyvar died a traitor, and his son will die the same. Celestia has abandoned us in our time of need. We are alone in this world, but we need not be! Karak is willing to accept us into his arms, if only we will join his cause. Although he might not be able to restore all that we have lost, he will give us land aplenty, *fertile* land where our crops will grow, *expansive* lands where our children can grow up happy, *living* lands where there is rich game! It is Karak who has promised this to you, not Celestia, not the fickle goddess who ripped our homes from us!"

Ceredon struggled in his restraints, biting down on his gag. He could not believe what he was hearing, could not believe the muttering that washed through the ranks of the Ekreissar. *They would never,* he thought. *We may be a cynical race, but we would never turn our backs on the one who created us....*

"All you must do," said Darakken, "is bend your knee and pledge your loyalty to the Divinity! All you must do is submit, and not only will you receive the lands you desired, but *all* of Paradise, to live on as you choose! No longer will you be subservient to any god. You will be *conquerors!*"

A voice rose up, but not from the Ekreissar. Ceredon strained his eyes and peered into the throng of Dezren.

"Karak, Karak, Karak," it began, a low murmur and nothing more. "Karak, Karak, Karak." From his vantage point above it all, Ceredon could see what was really happening. A pair of young Dezren males was making the cries at knifepoint, threatened by humans dressed in the simple greens and browns of the elves. They raised their voices louder. *"Karak, Karak, Karak!"*

Darakken turned to face the downtrodden citizens.

"The nation of Ker must burn!" he shouted. "Unleash your vengeance on those who have surrounded your lands, pushing you deeper into your forests, hunting your game, betraying your lawful boundaries. By the sword, by the spear, and by the bow, slaughter my enemies and take these lands for your own. Join your brothers in praise. Your bonds will be lifted, and your emerald city will be set free if you pledge your love to Karak!"

"Karak, Karak, Karak!" echoed all the louder.

The demon leapt off the dais and stormed toward the Ekreissar. Now the chants were virtually deafening as the soldiers joined their voices with the desperate Dezren. Darakken tilted its head slightly, its eyes glowing faintly in the blinding sun, and winked at Ceredon. "Glory will be yours!" it shouted, turning around once more. "Prosperity will be yours! Paradise will be yours! *Ker must burn!*"

Then it began. The rangers in front holding staffs began to beat them into the ground, creating a cadenced beat, followed by thousands of voices. *"KARAK, KARAK, KARAK!"* shouted the crowd. Iolas fell to his knees, shouting the name of the deity along with the rest. Soon everyone in the courtyard was on their knees save Darakken, all with the same name on their lips.

The voices filled Ceredon's head, squeezing his brain inside his skull. The demon then turned to face him again, holding its almost-human arms out wide in victory, baring its pointed teeth as the refrain was chanted over and over again.

"*KARAK!*"

"*KARAK!*"

"*KARAK!*"

-THE END-

A F T E R W O R D

David

I'd like to think this collaboration between Rob and me is something professional and consistent, but that's hardly the case. Each of these books is by far the largest I've been involved in, with massive story lines, yet some of them get changed for the simplest and most selfish of reasons. For example: Rob's the one who has this story line down, knows its ins and outs, and he's the one who comes up with the initial plot line that we follow. Well, when he finished the outline of book two, I read through it, and a lot of it was awesome, but there was one problem, and I called up Rob to discuss that. Our conversation went pretty much like this:

Me: "Uh, Rob, where the heck are the lions?"

Rob: "I was worried you'd ask that. They aren't in this book."

Me: "No, Rob, they *are* in this book. We will get yelled at if they are not in this book. *I* will yell at *you* if they are not in this book."

Rob: "All right, I know a spot I can put them in, give them at least one scene. Will that make you happy?"

Me: "Yes. Yes it will."

So we reworked a chapter, all to include Kayne and Lilah, because you know what? Kayne and Lilah are awesome and I wanted more of them. But now Rob had something to prove, so when I read Chapter 12, where they make their appearance and talk for the first time, I was grinning like an idiot. *There we go,* I was thinking. *There's at least one solid appearance of the lions prior to book three* (where their role gets increased). I was thrilled, and I told Rob as much.

He, of course, did not mention to me his plans for Chapter 31. You'd think we wouldn't keep such secrets from each other, but yeah, this is the stuff we do to keep sane during a project like this. So yes, I knew Laurel was going to go in, get captured and thrown into a dungeon. What I did *not* know was that the lions would be sitting there like kings on freaking thrones, with piles of gore all over the place like they just had a dang Sunday afternoon buffet. Nearly brought tears to my eyes, I was so happy. Horrified too, but you've got to be a little demented to do what Rob and I do, so happy as well. There were my lions, and I could only imagine the grin on Rob's face as he wrote that chapter. I hope he muttered a few curses to me as he did it.

"Lions? He wants lions? Fine, I'll give him lions...."

Hopefully, he thinks it's worth it, because for me, this has been phenomenal. I love throwing in references to my various books when I write, and *The Breaking World* is just overloaded with character names, places, the lions from the Paladins, Velixar from the Half-Orcs, the beginnings of the Trifect from the Shadowdance Series. With Rob's help, my silly little world feels that much less silly, the corners of the world filled in, breathing, fully alive. You longtime readers should be catching glimpses of even more, the early hints of the Faceless or the glow on certain weapons, signifying the coming creation of the paladin orders. I hope they put a smile on your face, because they put one on mine.

The story's entering the final stretch, and this is when Rob and I get to go nuts. Whatever limits we've been putting on ourselves, they're gone now. This is the Gods' War, and it's full speed ahead.

Real quick, I want to thank Rob for suffering through all my rants and demands, with the patience of a saint; Sam, for not minding when we spend way too much time chatting on the phone, figuring this stuff out; Angela, for going through our story twice in herculean efforts to trim the word count down and get everything to make sense; and last, Michael, for landing us this opportunity in the first place. You all are amazing.

And, of course, thank you, dear reader, for sticking with us for nearly four hundred thousand words. I hope the time was well spent in our world, and come the next book, I pray you fall right back in as if you never left.

Robert

This one was fun.

I said in my note in *Dawn of Swords* that I'd never had a more pleasurable experience writing a book. Well, that pretty much doubled, if not tripled, with this tome you now hold in your hands. With the groundwork set, Dave and I were free to go many different places, explore tons of different avenues, to bring his world of Dezrel to an even greater sense of *realness*.

As Dave said above, although we do plot out these books and know where they're going and the specifics involved, the intricacies bring a breadth of color to the story and are free flowing. They change, they warp…sometimes becoming bits of humor, sometimes going down that deep well where my past as a horror lover sometimes wallows. Rather than being a point of weakness, this is, in fact, an area of strength. It allows us to play to each of our strong points and bring you something that, quite frankly, I think is awesome. This free-flowing process led to Avila's wonderfully bloody downfall; to Matthew's unfortunate end; and, of course, to the macabre beauty of Kayne and Lilah. And also, because I am mostly responsible for writing the rough draft of each manuscript before Dave hacks it to pieces, I like putting little surprises in there for Dave to discover and then call me saying, "No kidding, you did *that*? I should do something similar in my Warhammer 40K session. Awesome!"

(At least, that's how I imagine him talking most of the time. I tend to zone out when he brings up his favorite hobbies....)

So again, thank you, Dave, for giving me the chance to do this, as it has been a freaking blast working with you. And also thanks to Jess and my kids, who are absolutely everything to me. In truth, they are as much a part of the writing process as Dave is. Thanks also to Angela, the best damn editor in the world, and Michael Carr, the greatest agent. Heck, the whole 47North team is included in this! Yeah, everybody rocks!

But most of all, to reiterate Mr. Dalglish's words, thank you to the readers. Without you, there would be no us, and frankly, I like us a lot. I hope you've enjoyed this book, and we'll see you soon for *Blood of Gods*, which—and I can guarantee you this—will be one heck of a ride.

David Dalglish and Robert Duperre
September 21, 2013

ABOUT THE
AUTHORS

David Dalglish currently lives in rural Missouri with his wife, Samantha, and daughters Morgan and Katherine. He graduated from Missouri Southern State University in 2006 with a degree in Mathematics and currently spends his free time playing not nearly enough Warhammer 40K.

Born on Cape Cod and raised in northern Connecticut, Robert Duperre is a writer whose main ambition is to create works that defy genre. He lives with his wife, the artist Jessica Torrant, his three wonderful children, and Leonardo, the super one-eyed Labrador.

Gregory Duffey